Nexus Runner

Book ONE

Nexus Runner

Book ONE

Frank Morin

Contents

1. Movie Set Makeovers - Apocalypse Edition — 1

2. I Prove I Can't Do My Own Stunts — 7

3. No Peanuts, No Parachutes — 11

4. I Become an Underwear Thief — 16

5. Some Questions Really Are Better — 23

6. Lucas Altan Monster Hunter — 29

7. Dangerous Deadly Duck Dodgeball — 38

8. I Discover a New Love for Copper — 44

9. I Know Kung Fu — 51

10. I Enjoy a Motivational Video — 58

11. Sporks and Fuzzy Pants — 66

12. A Wight in the Hand — 74

13. Soul Harvest Energy Vortex of Doom — 83

14. Stats Check — 94

15. I Stand Around in a Janitorial Closet — 97

16. I Make a Well-Informed Decision — 106

17. Fuzzy Math — 111

18. Interlude 1 — 118

19.	No Respawns	124
20.	I Play Dodge With a Rockslide	133
21.	Ruby in the Wild	142
22.	Glamping in Style	151
23.	The Games We Play	157
24.	I Really Need a Dodge Skill	163
25.	Dance Fighting	171
26.	We Decide to Get a Plumber	177
27.	Cow Level	186
28.	Where's the Beef?	194
29.	I Remember I Love Stickers	201
30.	Stats Check	207
31.	Lying Down on the Job	210
32.	The Watery Grave	217
33.	I Choose to Slap a Werewolf	228
34.	Harvest of the New Moon	235
35.	I Take a Sightseeing Death Tour	243
36.	A Very Heated Argument	250
37.	Spartacus	259
38.	An Old Friend of Mine Can Really Throw Rocks	269
39.	We Might Actually Need More Monsters	277
40.	Tug of War Death Match	282
41.	What Happens on Arasha . . .	289
42.	More Cow Bell	295
43.	Ghosts in the Trees	301
44.	I Try My Hand at Bull Fighting	307

45.	Challenges of Leadership	314
46.	I Find the Heart of the Town	318
47.	A Custom Makeover	327
48.	Stats Check	333
49.	Confection Talks	336
50.	Lifebane Phantoms	346
51.	Family Ties	352
52.	Bringin' Home the Bacon	359
53.	Warning Signs Are For Suckers	368
54.	Falling with Style	375
55.	A Different Approach to Survival	381
56.	Creative Tumbling	388
57.	Fatal Attraction	395
58.	Drama Queen	401
59.	I Discover An Easier Way to Carry a House	411
60.	Beer and Sandwiches	418
61.	Ruby Shows Off Her Barbecuing Skills	424
62.	Ruby Gets A Prize	434
63.	Stat Check	443
64.	Interlude 2	446
65.	Time for a Change	448
66.	I Try Cheating on a Test	456
67.	Productive Pachyderms	463
68.	Doctor Strange	470
69.	I Teach a Painful Lesson With My Pants	479
70.	Interlude 3	487

71. I Have a Successful Therapy Session   492

72. Five . . . Gold . . . Rings!   502

73. If You're Going to Die Anyway, Do Something Crazy   511

74. I Tell Knock Knock Jokes   519

75. Death Really Bites Sometimes   526

76. Run!   532

77. Run Faster!   539

78. I Ride a Slimy Death Spiral of Doom   546

79. Flight of Insanity   551

80. Grand Entrances   558

81. Homecoming   564

82. Epilogue   572

83. Bloopers   575

84. Final Stat Check   579

85. Appendix - Full Description of Spells, Abilities, and Titles   582

Other Works by Frank Morin   586

About the Author   588

Chapter One

Movie Set Makeovers - Apocalypse Edition

The single intersection of dirt roads that marked Powderhorn, Colorado was buzzing with more activity every second than it usually saw in a year. The junction of routes 27 and 29 looked like it used to include nothing but a handful of old-fashioned log cabins facing a tiny pond across the hard-packed dirt road.

Now at least 30 long trailers packed the area, along with at least two dozen side-by-sides and 4-wheelers. Pickups towing long, open trailers trundled up both roads, and at least 200 people scurried about, busy at tasks I could only imagine.

I couldn't help grinning. This was so cool!

"So this is what a movie set looks like," I muttered as I slowed my motorcycle to a crawl to study the controlled chaos.

"More like a zoo," my brother Tomas responded as the other three riders slowed behind us. All of our helmets were linked via bluetooth so we could chat as we rode.

"There," Jane called as she rolled up beside me, balancing easily on the pegs of her bike, making the slow-speed maneuver look easy. She pointed to a whiteboard sign leaning against an old-fashioned sawhorse.

It read "Extras sign-in 2 miles ahead."

I rolled on a bit of throttle, easing out of the chaos and down route 27, heading south. The dirt road looked like it had been watered, then run over repeatedly by those giant road compactors, making it as hard and smooth as fresh asphalt.

Together, we rode south at an easy pace along the edge of a pretty, green valley with low hills rising on either side. It was still early enough in June that summer fires hadn't started, so the air remained a pristine, dazzling blue.

Old instincts still made me scan the hilltops, noting the amount of dead trees and potential fuel. No longer my problem. I'd left that life behind. So I forced myself to gaze at the remarkable transformation of the valley.

Powderhorn valley might have basically been a ghost town, but the transformation to a different time period was well underway. The one ranch house I spotted already had new walls creeping up around it with realistic stone designs. In hours it would look like a medieval castle. That was some clever camouflage.

The flat valley floor, covered in deep green grasses, was being stripped of any modern machinery and irrigation pipes. I pointed. "That has to be where they're planning to film the battle scene they need so many extras for."

"Where else would they film it?" Tomas joked. "Can't have a battle up in the hills unless they want to film another Gandalf cavalry charge down to Helm's Deep."

Patrick piped in. "Or maybe introduce some skydiving Huns."

"That would be cool. Sign me up to join that crew."

"You guys are such nerds," Jane joked to a round of snickers.

I couldn't help grinning inside my helmet, imagining taking part in an epic medieval battle scene. My life had been way too boring over the last couple years. A good fight scene would feel so good.

Well, the past several days had already been a welcome escape from my computer as we explored the spectacular back country of Colorado via motorcycle. Then we heard about the open call for extras. I didn't even know which company was filming, but we couldn't pass up an opportunity like this. I'd convinced the others to take the detour out to Powderhorn to give it a try. Even if we didn't get onto the set, the ride was gorgeous. The road followed the first hills along the east side of the valley, giving us a great view.

"There!" I slowed my bike about two-thirds of the way down the valley, a couple miles from the junction we'd just left. The sign had been right.

Tents and trailers and another knot of people were gathered there, with a small dirt road heading up to a parking lot that looked like it had been recently dug out of the hillside. Log walls were being raised to block the parking lot from view. They'd probably make it look like an old fort for one of the factions. So cool.

It was already packed with vehicles, mostly pickups and SUVs as expected, given the remote location. A square poster taped to a large free-standing whiteboard declared, "Extras, Sign-in Here."

Most of the new hopefuls were being bussed from a secondary lot farther up that side road. Should have ridden their bikes in.

"Lucas, it's full," complained Tomas as he smoothly stopped beside me and lifted the modular front plate of his helmet to reveal his clean-shaven face. I'd gotten a bit scruffy during the back-country ride, but Jane liked Tomas's face clean, so he found ways to shave, even while camping.

"There's always room for bikes," I said, then gave my big dual-sport a bit of throttle and rolled into the lot.

Sure enough, the parking attendant with the "Lot Full" sign shrugged and waved us toward the corner where a cluster of other bikes enjoyed prime real estate close to the fake log wall.

I pulled in, cut the engine, and removed my helmet. It was a beautiful morning, and was supposed to warm up to the mid-seventies later. A perfect day to get into our first movie.

I flashed another grin at Tomas and the others as they pulled in on their assorted bikes. We loved riding on all types of terrain, although Jane, Tomas's girlfriend, pushed the limits even more than I did.

She'd been a motocross rider, after all. That woman could do things with a bike that defied physics. She pulled off her helmet with a flair and shook out the ponytail that held her long, brown hair. She was like a living lightning bolt, with her boundless energy and often-reckless spirit, but she somehow avoided crashes with her mastery over her bike and her supreme athleticism.

Tomas looked like a clean-shaven, slightly heavier version of me. Three years older and a single inch taller at 6 feet even, he still teased me about being smaller. Despite my new desk job, I kept myself in better shape, though. The years I'd spent on the forest fire crews all summer and working as a skydiving instructor in Arizona in the winter had ingrained in me the need to keep myself in top condition.

His surgical practice was booming, but by how sore he'd been over the past few days, it was clear he had been slacking off on the workout routines. We weren't quite identical, but even a half-blind drunk could tell we were siblings. Same build, same short, brown hair. Different eyes. I was cool with that.

Tomas was my best friend. Edmund and Patrick brought up the rear. Where Edmund was skinny and nerdy and still rode his bike a bit too stiffly, Patrick wore at least 20 extra pounds on his big frame. He kept claiming he was about to start a new diet, but that was usually right after ordering a second dessert.

I couldn't ask for a better group of friends for an epic back-country ride. Getting into the movie together would be the icing on the cake of our trip.

Stripping off my riding gear, I snatched up my sunglasses and baseball cap. "Let's go!"

"I think this is a waste of time," Tomas repeated for the tenth time.

Jane punched him lightly on the shoulder, her hazel eyes sparkling with excitement. "What else is there to do out here?"

"Really?" he teased.

Her smile widened. "Other than miles of sweet trails to explore? We can get back to that as soon as they turn us away."

"Of course we'll fail with an attitude like that," I quipped.

A doorway through the fake log wall allowed us to cross the road and head to the registration tent perched on a flat section closer to the valley floor. I led the way, determined to get a spot as an extra. I needed this final outlet before returning home to dive into my new life.

Another bus overflowing with hopefuls was just laboring over the hill and preparing to unload at the front parking lot. We'd get to the tent a full minute before that horde.

"Name?" A bored volunteer nursing a paper cup of lukewarm coffee asked.

"Lucas Altan." I gave him my cheeriest smile.

He looked to be in his early twenties like me, but tried to project an air of jaded experience as he sipped his coffee, his expression bland. More like an intern who thought he would be doing exciting jobs this summer instead of babysitting registration.

We might have just arrived, but we'd get to do something a lot more awesome. Bored Joe handed me a form to fill out, along with a cheap pen with the logo of one of the film companies.

While I quickly filled out the form, I glanced up between questions to study the area. The ground dropped a bit from the registration tent to the wide valley floor, so we had an excellent view of the nearly flat expanse of lush green grass. Hundreds of people were scurrying around dozens of huge ancient-looking tents, while an army of more volunteers were setting up spiked barriers and more fake wooden fortress walls.

Of course I didn't spot any of the stars, but scores of extras were already getting fitted for medieval armor and weapons. Dozens more were practicing basic fighting moves under the watchful gazes of the fight instructors. The entire scene was infused with an invisible energy that was intoxicating. I needed to get down there and join the crowd.

If those noobs had gotten accepted, we were sure to snag premier positions. I'd love to end up clearly visible in one of the battle scenes, despite what Isabella would say about it. She'd already said no, so her opinion no longer mattered.

"Got any relevant skills for battle scenes?" I read the question aloud, elbowing Tomas and grinning.

"Maybe they'll let us spar."

Jane chuckled. "Finally you two can prove all that martial arts training's been worth it."

"You'll see. We'll get prime positions," I promised as I filled in my experience. She had no idea. My training had been my one major physical outlet while I got my degree, and I'd been pushing hard. I'd even toyed with joining a full-contact competition league, but that would have to wait until after I launched my startup.

None of those practicing extras looked like they knew which end of a sword to pick up without direction. We should be fine. In seconds, we finished our applications and returned to Bored Joe.

Behind us, 30 new hopefuls were streaming toward the tent from the bus. Joe didn't even scan our papers, but nodded toward the next tent farther down the slope. "Take your forms over there."

I led the way, a spring in my step. This was going to be awesome. As we crossed between the tents, I scanned the brilliant blue morning sky. Few clouds, lots of sun. I could already feel the air warming.

They'd picked a perfect spot to film a medieval battle scene. Even though we were in the middle of Colorado, I couldn't actually see any of the countless taller peaks from where I stood. That little valley could be anywhere in the world.

Something moved in the distance.

"What is that?" I squinted at one of the higher hills peeking up behind the first rounded hilltops. It wasn't smoke, like I'd originally feared.

Tomas nearly ran into my back. "What is what?"

"Look." I gestured, not taking my eye from the weird sight. "Am I hallucinating, or does it look like the top of that hill is falling up into the sky?"

Jane laughed. "They're taking the set makeover to a whole new level? Just imagine . . . What the hell?"

That entire mountain exploded upward.

The ground shook, knocking us off our feet in a heap. A peal of thunder shook the valley, so loud it felt like all the air above us had detonated.

"Volcano!" Tomas shouted as we all struggled to our knees on the shaking ground.

"Impossible," Edmund cried. He was a geologist, so he'd know. Except how else could a mountain explode?

Looked like they'd have to cancel the movie shoot.

Chapter Two

I Prove I Can't Do My Own Stunts

I *diot. Canceling the shoot is the first thing I think of?*

We needed to find shelter. Except we were out in the middle of nowhere. All around us, people were screaming. Pandemonium covered the valley. The ground shook harder and a second hill, this time on the west side of the valley, exploded just like the first had.

More thunder ripped the sky as tornado-strength wind screamed past, ripping tents out of the ground and flinging them away. I hit the ground, with Tomas and Jane landing on top. One of her elbows dug my ribs hard.

All around us, mountains and hills blasted apart. The ground heaved and shook, and a great weight slammed me down so hard, for a second I couldn't breathe. Tomas and Jane pressed me down into the ground like they suddenly each weighed 500 pounds.

Then the pressure eased and the sounds of thunderous explosions faded away far too quickly. That probably didn't bode well.

The hills all around were streaming upward, with individual pine trees erupting into the air like giant arrows. None of the blasts had spread outward horizontally to hit us, though. How was that possible?

Edmund lurched to his knees, his face so white he looked like a corpse. His eyes bulged with terror as he glanced up.

"This can't be happening," he moaned.

"What?" Tomas shouted as we all cautiously rose to our knees too, poised to hold on if the earth shook again.

"Look! Don't you see? Everything is falling up. Everything! Everyone!"

No. He couldn't mean that.

I looked around again and my heart sank into my boots. Edmund might be right. The mountains really were all falling into the sky. Could they be carrying the entire valley and all of us with them?

"Did Yellowstone blow?" Tomas asked, his voice squeaking with fear.

"That would just flatten us," Edmund said.

"Then what's going on?" Jane exclaimed, outwardly keeping her cool better than most.

All around us, other people were kneeling or standing, looking around in confusion or pointing to the upward-falling mountains. It didn't look like anyone else had guessed what Edmund had.

"I don't know!" Edmund shouted, wringing his hands as he lurched to his feet, turning to stare in every direction. "This is impossible. I swear we're falling up fast, but I don't feel any wind now. No change in gravity either."

"What could throw a bunch of mountains into the sky?" Tomas demanded.

"I don't know!" Edmund repeated, looking on the verge of panic.

As I turned a full circle, scanning the weird skyline of upward falling mountains, I could not sense any motion. I'd ridden in enough small planes to have a good sense of aerial direction, but felt nothing. The scattered clouds I'd noticed just seconds ago were gone. The sky looked deeper blue than I'd ever seen. Not good. That color usually only happened at very high altitudes.

Another rumble shook the entire valley and a gust of wind ripped the registration tent off the ground. It soared into the air, poles twisting, then the entire tangled mess slammed back down right at us.

"Look out!" I shouted, grabbing Tomas and heaving him away, then diving after. The busted mass of canvas and aluminum crashed to the ground right behind us.

Spinning, I scanned for our friends. Jane was just pulling herself out from under one end of the tarp, with Edmund right next to her. I didn't see Patrick. He'd been behind Edmund, so was probably stuck under the tent. Hopefully he hadn't gotten hurt, but none of us could afford to end up tangled and immobile.

I pulled Tomas over to Jane and Edmund. "Listen, we have to get out of here!"

"I don't think—"Edmund mumbled, but his words trailed off as his gaze was drawn to an upward-falling mountain. He started to shake.

"Listen! It's a miracle we're not already dead, but we have to move. You guys get Patrick out and get to the bikes. I'm going to scout the road back up to Powderhorn. If there's a way through, we'll go that way. If it's blocked, we'll head south instead."

Edmund's guess about the entire valley falling into the sky was insane. Couldn't happen, or we'd all be dead. No, there had to be another explanation. That didn't mean we could hang around in a valley that could get flooded by landslides, or something. We had to roll out, and fast.

Tomas looked like he wanted to argue, but then nodded, pulled me into a fierce hug, then pushed me away. Jane gave me a sort-of salute, then dove under the tent to help Patrick.

I turned and ran for the parking lot. My experience fighting deadly forest fires had beat into me the truth that standing still in a disaster only made it worse. Movement meant life, so I moved. Despite my growing fear that nothing we did would help, I had to try.

In seconds I reached my bike and jumped on, slamming my finger onto the start button. The fob was in my pocket, so I didn't need to waste time fumbling for a key.

It roared to life and I sprayed dirt behind me as I tore out of the tiny parking lot. I didn't bother with my helmet or any of my gear. If we'd just gotten blown into the sky like Edmund feared, my armored jacket and helmet weren't going to do me a lick of good.

How could mountains explode straight up? The land would disintegrate and we'd get shredded by the blast. It was like the laws of physics were glitching. Had the apocalypse happened? No. I refused to believe it. We'd find a way out. We had to.

In seconds I cranked my bike up over a hundred, shooting up the empty road. At that speed, I'd reach Powderhorn in another minute. That fact helped me stay focused. Please, God, we just needed a minor miracle. Let the road be intact, let Patrick be okay and we'd get out of that mess in minutes.

The valley narrowed as I rode, the sky full of rocks and dirt and trees streaming upward, but the ground felt solid under my wheels. The wind tore at my face as I took a corner way too fast, leaned so far over I scraped my foot peg. That was a stupid way to ride that bike, but I had to take some chances. One more turn and the bustling junction should come into view.

I topped the last rise so fast I caught air and the view opened up in front of me.

Powderhorn was gone.

The land simply ended, the road cut off like a giant knife had sheared through it barely a hundred yards away. And I was aimed straight at the end of the world going over 100.

No no no no! The fear I'd been holding back with plans of escape crashed over me, and I nearly lost my balance as I slammed back to the pavement.

Focus, Lucas! Deal with the situation. Think about it later.

First step, don't die. I braked hard. The entire bike shuddered as the ABS kicked in and I bled speed faster than I ever had before.

It wasn't enough.

Riding instructors always harped on the fact that you shouldn't focus on the obstacle you wanted to avoid, but look for the escape path. Except there was no escape path, and my eyes fixed on that cut in the road where the world terminated, glued to the sight with a morbid fascination. No way I could stop in time.

The rear tire skidded as it locked up, so I threw myself off the bike, grabbing at the ground, trying to pull a save like young Kirk in the remake of Star Trek when he drove that car off the cliff.

The smooth dirt tore at my skin, but barely slowed me. It was like I was skidding across ice. I felt no pain as I scrabbled against the dirt, trying desperately to slow.

My bike slid over the edge. I followed one racing heartbeat later, screaming as I tumbled into open air.

Chapter Three

No Peanuts, No Parachutes

I flailed uselessly as open air extended away like eternity and the astonishing sight made me forget the terrifying danger for a second. The ground lurked so far below, it was like I'd fallen off a plane almost all the way up into space instead of sliding off a road.

After a couple seconds of absolute terror, I realized I felt no rushing wind, no movement at all. I twisted around to look behind me and just stared as I tried to piece together what was happening.

I was floating in the air about twenty yards beyond the end of the road. I had barely dropped after flying off the edge. More like sliding out on an invisible ramp of air. My heart beat so fast it threatened to hammer a hole in my chest. Panic made it hard to breathe as I looked around wildly.

Were we just hovering? Confused, I looked down again.

Bad idea. My heart nearly stopped, frozen with icy terror as I noticed something I'd missed in those first panicked seconds after sliding off the road. Far, far below, the ground was receding at unbelievable speed.

That wasn't how gravity worked. I'd jumped out of countless airplanes, but one did not fall upward. A hole that had to be 10 times the size of Lake Tahoe was ripped right out of the middle of Colorado. Edmund was right. We had all fallen into the sky. Entire mountains had ripped free and blasted straight into the air.

The sight was so mind-boggling, I couldn't process it. Instinct kicked in and I shifted to the standard skydiving banana position, arms and legs out and bent up slightly, but that didn't accomplish anything. I looked around again, trying to understand. It was like the planet had rolled over on its side and part of Colorado had simply fallen off. Were we going to fall all the way up into space?

The sky turned black. We were moving way too fast. We weren't in space, though. We couldn't be. Space was cold and empty and void, but I could breathe and the air felt hot, not freezing.

For a second I could see the entire curve of the planet like in the photos from the space shuttle. Stars blazed everywhere by the millions, and the moon peeked around the back side of the Earth. In any other situation, I would have exulted to see that awesome sight. Today it just made me feel small and helpless.

I hated feeling helpless, but fought down the urge to flail and scream and do, well, anything. I needed to think.

Then everything winked out to black. Darkness consumed my vision so complete it was like my eyes had fallen out of my head just like we'd fallen off the planet.

An invisible force flung me through the total blackness, as if a giant had decided to throw my body like a fastball. My stomach twisted and I tasted bile. I couldn't see, couldn't hear, couldn't feel anything. I had no point of reference. My mind was on the verge of shutting down from nightmare overload.

I pushed it back, reaching for the adrenaline-fueled excitement I embraced when jumping over a new location. It didn't help much, but did take the edge off so I could stay in control.

Then sight rushed back and all I could do was gape.

We're so far from Kansas, Toto.

I floated in space, even though I could still breathe. I didn't feel cold, or feel anything at all. No air, no atmosphere, no wind, and an absolute absence of sound left me hearing only phantom ringing. I just hung in the air, looking down at a planet.

Not our planet.

I'd seen enough pictures of Earth from space to realize something was very wrong. The planet I was hovering in space above seemed somehow too small, even though it filled space beneath me.

On the surface, land masses made up of a patchwork of browns and greens might be mountains and forests. I had no idea what the orange or yellow sections might be, though. I saw no oceans.

I couldn't move my neck, but my eyes worked. Craning them to the side, I realized I was not alone. All around me, more people floated, hanging helpless and silent in space like a mob of corpses who hadn't realized we were already dead.

I tried to shout, but could not make a sound. I couldn't even twitch a finger. I was totally frozen, except for my eyes. So I watched and tried to find a shred of calm.

Relax, Lucas. Maybe you just had a stroke, and this is just a nightmare triggered from your oxygen-starved brain before you die.

Not helping.

The mountains, the valley, all the land, and everything that wasn't people swept past below me and fell toward the planet. I caught a glimpse of wooden palisade walls in the midst of it. That clump of Colorado moved so fast, it was already shrinking to a brown mass of dirt, heading toward the surface of the alien planet like a meteor.

Congratulations contestants from Earth! I am thrilled to welcome you.

The voice boomed across the empty expanse of space. It was a male voice with a distinct British accent, and he sounded extremely pleased.

Beneath us, the land mass we'd ridden from Colorado smashed into the side of the planet, but did not explode or even make a crater. The land just seemed to sink into the surface of the planet. The mosaic of colored sections of ground, each the size of Texas, shifted and twisted, as if making room for one more part.

I was starting to feel decidedly sick, but didn't want to throw up in space. I'd never thrown up during a jump, and refused to do so now. I could handle this. We were just starting the jump way higher than normal. With no parachutes.

So, maybe not thinking was wiser for once.

Far below, the land that had been part of our home world writhed on the surface of the planet, shifting between various bright colors before settling back to brown and green like one should expect earth to be.

A different voice spoke. This one was a warm, female voice with a subtle French accent.

Welcome to Arasha.

The invisible man added, "I must apologize for the abrupt nature of your travel. I should have at least supplied peanuts. I believe that is the preferred travel ration on your world. I don't understand why that might be, given so many better options even on such a basic planet, but who am I to judge?"

"Ha!" he laughed like a sudden pealing of thunder before continuing in a more conversational tone.

"That's exactly my job. More about that later. Anyway, I hate to make such a jarring experience the foundation of our first meeting. Unfortunately, I had no alternative. Your entry was approved at the very last moment and some sacrifices must be made to keep schedules on track. Certainly you understand."

Maybe this was all a dream? The stroke idea was sounding more and more plausible. I didn't want to die, but that would be better than lingering as a vegetable, my mind stuck in a crazy nightmare.

Or maybe one of those newbs swinging a fake sword had lost his grip and threw it across the tent and clobbered me in the back of the head. I'd still end up lying paralyzed in a hospital bed, suffering morphine-induced hallucinations, but somehow that seemed preferable to the possibility that this might all be real.

The voice didn't care and continued on with that gushing good humor. "What schedule, you may be asking? Again, more on that to come. I don't want to bore you with the details. You are no doubt distracted by the inspiring view I've given you of the integration of your lands into the challenge world."

Yeah, the view was way more than distracting.

"I did choose the most remote chunk of land that fit the parameters of the contest, but I suppose a lot of your countrymen will be asking a lot of very entertaining questions right now. Oh, well, seeking for answers beyond what one considered possible in the past is healthy for one's ongoing progression. Think of the unique real estate opportunities."

More like panic. People would definitely not react well to having a major chunk of a state suddenly excised from the planet and teleported away. How long before anyone realized some of us had gotten caught in the disaster? How long before my parents knew we were missing?

"Back to the game, then, since that's what you've been selected to join. That's right, the one thousand of you here today are the lucky few chosen to represent your planet in a contest unlike any other! Prove yourselves worthy, and you'll win prizes beyond your wildest imaginations."

After a pause, the voice continued. "On the other foot, if you fail, you'll all die and your entire world will be destroyed, along with every living soul on it. How are those for fantastic stakes, right?"

The voice laughed as if that was somehow hilarious, then added, "On to the show!"

We started falling toward the planet. The movement came suddenly, totally outside of my control. I still felt no wind, but the planet was definitely getting closer.

I tried moving, but was still locked in some kind of stasis. Screaming in my mind still worked, and I unleashed all my terror and a growing anger in the recesses of my own thoughts as I accelerated like I'd been fired from a cannon. We all zoomed toward the surface of the planet just like that chunk of Colorado had.

Did the voice not realize we were flesh and blood? Crashing down at this speed would splatter us like bugs against a windshield. This was going to be the shortest game in the history of the universe.

I tried to find that sense of thrill I usually felt pushing the limits, but this time I got nothing. I closed my eyes, willing myself to wake from the coma. Still no wind, but when I cracked open my eyes again the planet was rushing up to meet me with terrifying speed. Whatever was really going on, I was about to die.

What a stupid game.

I shot past tall mountains like a ballistic missile and barely had time to tense before smashing into the ground with unimaginable force.

Chapter Four

I Become an Underwear Thief

With a groan, I blinked my eyes open. I was lying on my back, staring up into brilliant blue sky stained with streaks of emerald.

"What a dream," I muttered as I sat up, rubbing my head. My thoughts were still fuzzy. Had I fallen off my bike?

Then why wasn't I wearing a helmet? And how'd I end up lying on a dense carpet of soft grass?

Welcome to day one, Lucas.

The friendly male voice made me jump and I looked around, but saw no one. The grass turned out to be part of a pretty little glade surrounded by sparse woods.

Tall trees that looked more like hardwoods than the pines I'd seen so much lately in Colorado loomed over me. Above them, steep, rugged mountains rose all around. I was in a mountain valley, surrounded by tall peaks.

On one side, more mountains stretched in ever-higher tiers of broken stone that built up on each other until the final peaks punched impossibly high into the sky. I craned my neck up and up, mouth agape as I stared at the distant sheer cliffs that had to rise over 50,000 feet above me. Mountains couldn't get that tall on Earth.

Then it all came rushing back and I leaped to my feet, my heart hammering in remembered fear. We'd been ripped from Earth, teleported to an alien world, and hurled down like missiles.

Was I dead? Was this what heaven really looked like? I scanned the sky again, looking for angels or harps, or even little red demons.

I couldn't be alive, could I? I'd crashed into a planet like a living meteor. Why did I feel healthy, then? My legs were shaking, but that was just a reaction to my panic. I tried to control my breathing as I turned slowly, scanning the area, trying to figure out if I was a spirit or not.

"The best way to get started is to dive right in. That's what I always say," the friendly voice continued.

A blue screen popped into the air in front of me and text scrolled down, repeating the words I'd just heard. I jumped back with a start and the screen followed along. When I turned my head, it smoothly shifted through the air to stay in front of me.

"That's annoying," I muttered. Maybe I'd ended up in hell like my mom always promised all bikers did.

"You'll get used to it," the voice said as more text scrolled past.

"This is your main status screen. You'll use it to access all of your achievements, rewards, and so much more. Don't worry, I'll explain how it works. First, when you want to exit the screen, just focus on the dark blue bar along the top and imagine the screen closing."

Since I couldn't see much else, I followed the instructions. I wanted to see who was speaking. Focusing on the top bar of the screen, I willed it to close, and it disappeared.

Wild. Mind-controlled tech was way beyond anything we had on Earth. I had never imagined heaven might be full of techies. I spent a lot of time with computers since I was preparing to launch a new cyber investigation company. I would usually be geeking out over the seamless way the screen functioned.

Figuring out if I was dead or not sucked the joy out of the moment, though.

"Very good. You've got more of a knack for this than a lot of your group. Now, open the screen back up."

I scanned the clearing, but still saw no one. That initial burst of adrenaline from waking up on an alien world still left my limbs feeling shaky, but otherwise I felt better than I had any right to expect.

I guess I'm alive. I wasn't entirely sure, but I couldn't imagine heaven or hell feeling like this. The grass was soft under my feet. The air smelled like forest.

The trees waved slightly from a soft breeze. Any other day, I'd think I'd woken up in a really nice park.

I still hoped maybe I was having some kind of hallucination. Maybe Tomas had bought those sketchy mushrooms after all and slipped them into breakfast. He was a joker, but that would be a stretch, even for him.

I glanced around again, but didn't see Tomas, Jane, or anyone for that matter. If I accepted the reality of what I'd just experienced, I might actually be standing on an alien planet.

An alien planet.

The words made me shiver. I didn't want to believe it, wanted to lie down and close my eyes and wait for Tomas to give me an injection to wake up. He was the doctor, he'd know how to treat whatever mental breakdown I was suffering.

I took a long, deep breath. I might be lying in a coma, but I felt like myself. Panic flickered at the edges of my mind, but I pushed it aside. I wasn't in pain. My entire world had gotten switched on me, but I was still me. I could deal with it until I figured out what was really going on.

Forget how impossible falling off the planet and getting teleported to another world might be. Until I found evidence to the contrary, I decided to trust my own senses. So had Tomas and the others fallen into this crazy world with me, or had they somehow escaped? If they were nearby, I had to find them as soon as possible. That priority helped focus my whirling thoughts. Find and protect my brother and friends. I could do that.

One other thing was clear. Isabella wouldn't have to worry about me bothering her any more, trying to make her reconsider. That made me chuckle, the sound carrying a wild tone so unlike my normal voice. An ex-girlfriend who had recently crushed my heart was the least of my worries.

"Don't get distracted, Lucas. We have a lot to cover and not much time to do it," the voice prodded. It was the same guy with the British accent who had spoken while we floated in space.

I still couldn't see anyone, but the voice didn't sound like it was speaking into my mind. More like an invisible friend standing close by. So weird.

"Do you see the blinking notification icon in the bottom right corner of your vision? Click on that."

And all of a sudden I did see a little blinking icon, like a tiny folder. I focused on it and willed it to open. The larger screen popped up again, blocking most of my view.

Text scrolled past again. It wasn't written in English, but in some kind of alien letters that honestly reminded me of those Chinese characters I saw online sometimes. Yet, I could understand them as if I'd read the language my entire life.

The same warm woman's voice that had spoken while we hovered in space spoke again.

Congratulations, Lucas! You've successfully bonded with your HUD. You receive a copper Intern loot box.

HUD? Loot box? I was starting to get a headache.

The screen flashed, and a menu appeared down the left side. Most of it was grayed out, but the first two options were available. Messages and Loot Boxes. In a daze, I mentally selected Loot Boxes.

The screen flashed and minimized into the bottom right corner of my vision, and a box with a copper sheen appeared, hovering in the air in front of me. It was small, about the size of a shoe box.

"Go ahead and will the box to open," the male voice urged.

Using technology was second nature to me, and doing something with it, even if it was alien technology, helped me focus my scrambled thoughts. I decided mentally controlling technology was cool.

Yay, I was having fun.

My stomach roiled and I felt sick.

The lid popped off and the box disappeared, revealing two small items floating in the air. They looked like little glass flasks, complete with stoppered lids. One was a bright red color, the other blue.

Congratulations, Lucas! You've just opened your first loot box. You receive a minor mana potion and a minor health potion.

The female voice's slight French accent made the word congratulations seem far more substantial, somehow.

The male voice picked up. "When you consume the blue mana potion, it will restore a small amount of mana. The red health potion will restore an equal number of health points."

"Mana?" I asked as I plucked the two flasks out of the air. They felt like glass, as real as anything I'd ever held before, even though they'd just materialized out of thin air. That was wild.

"We'll get to all that!" he laughed, then made a throat clearing sound. "Sorry. I know, getting teleported across the multiverse for the first time, and without warning is a lot to swallow, especially for a tier-0, unintegrated baby human."

"What does that mean?"

"Patience, my friend. You can't learn everything in the first minute, although you should probably learn at least a few things. The game has started, after all."

"You mentioned a game, but I don't know what you're talking about." •

"You wouldn't want me to ruin the surprise, would you?"

"I think I've had enough surprises to last a lifetime, thanks."

My thoughts were starting to work better and I remembered another thing the voice had said when we were hovering in space. "Hey, what was that about everyone dying and Earth being destroyed?"

"So you were paying attention. Good for you. Chances of surviving the next twenty-four hours just jumped to at least ten percent."

"Wait, what?"

"Make that eight percent. You're backsliding, Lucas."

"Why would our planet be destroyed? Are you the one planning to kill everyone?"

"You're getting distracted again. Try to focus. You don't have much time before life gets really interesting."

If only that voice included a body, I'd throttle him. I'd totally changed the trajectory of my life 2 years ago to focus on hunting down people like the ones who had taken everything from my grandmother. Now this voice was threatening worldwide destruction. Time to pivot again, apparently.

With a supreme effort, I forced down the boiling anger that replaced my shock. Nothing about the situation made sense, so I focused on the one thing I knew. Someone was prepared to destroy an entire planet. This so-called game was deadly serious. I needed to understand more so I could figure out what to do.

A moment ago, as I hurtled toward the ground, I'd been convinced I was about to die. I hated feeling helpless, but I hated thieves and murderers worse. Now that I had a second chance on life, I needed to focus so I didn't die again. I had to survive, find Tomas and our friends, and figure out what was going on and how to get home.

I took a deep breath and scanned myself as I again tried to verify my physical condition.

"Hey, where are my clothes?"

I blinked down in astonishment at my bare torso. How had I not noticed that before? The only thing I was wearing was a pair of blue boxers.

"And whose boxers are these?" My voice rose an embarrassing octave.

Despite all the crazy stuff happening, for some reason the fact that I was wearing some random dude's boxers freaked me out more than all the rest. A quick scan of my body confirmed I was still me. I even still had the 3-day shadow stubble on my cheeks.

"You don't think I would drop you at your starting point naked?" he asked. This time, when the menu I had just minimized popped up, it only filled about a third of my vision, enough to see the words scrolling past. Annoyed, I willed it closed.

"We have to keep our ratings clean," he added.

"Ratings?" I rubbed my temples. My head hurt. My entire world had been ripped apart and stitched back together like a Frankenstein creation, and the voice's cheery good humor was totally out of place.

"Nothing. Just an expression I picked up from my initial scan of your world. You know, I usually get more time to study a target world, so I may get some of your phrases wrong for a while."

"Don't worry about it. I can't keep up with half the gibberish my brother throws into his text messages sometimes." Tomas always tried to stay current with all the text shortcut trends.

I looked around again, hoping to see him or the others. Maybe I'd just overlooked something important during my first scan. My mind wasn't really firing on all cylinders yet.

Nothing. Just a sparse forest that would have looked lovely as part of a park near Boulder. To me it seemed suddenly alien and dangerous.

No clothes, no bike, or any of my gear. I seemed to be completely alone. I took a deep breath and glanced at my boxers again. They looked clean, and at least they were solid blue. I didn't think I could have kept it together if they'd been pink or covered in hearts or something.

"Is everyone else still alive? Where are they?"

"You're jumping the shotgun, Lucas. You haven't gotten that quest yet."

"What?"

"Quest. I haven't shown you that menu, although I do like your enthusiasm for pressing ahead."

"No, not the quest. I mean, I want to know about that, but what was that you said about a shotgun?" I could really use a shotgun.

"An idiom I downloaded from your world. Saying you jumped the gun seemed too vague, so I chose a more specific model of your basic firearms. Did I choose the wrong one?"

"We don't use specific guns for that phrase."

"How odd. You humans are proving so fascinating already. How some of you just keep screaming is remarkable."

"Screaming?" I heard nothing but the gentle rustling of leaves and creaking of wood in the soft breeze. The air smelled fresh, with a bit of pine, even though I didn't see pine trees nearby. Odd.

"Sorry, I shouldn't mention other conversations I'm having. Your mental state is confused enough. I know it's a lot to take in, but you have to focus before your initial orientation period ends."

"Okay. I could use some orientation."

A laugh. "Finally, someone who wants to play! Most of the other earthlings are too busy panicking or screaming or vomiting. Why you do that as a default defense mechanism is such a puzzle. Probably the result of your nutrient-deficient diets. You have the right idea, though. You only have a few minutes to familiarize yourself with your menus and open your first quest before the monsters begin to spawn."

Chapter Five

Some Questions Really Are Better

Monsters sounded bad.

"Let's do it, then." Focusing on immediate danger helped me ground myself.

Another laugh. "I'm having variations of this conversation with all nine hundred ninety-eight of you. Most of the others just start screaming when they hear the word monster. Fascinating."

"Hold on, I thought there were a thousand of us."

"Two of the older candidates suffered heart attacks upon landing. That will not happen to any of the rest of you, though. Don't worry. Your bodies are still only base tier, but your systems have already been altered to foster basic healing over time. The litany of diseases, deficiencies, and medical conditions you've all been struggling with will disappear shortly."

"Wow." I was in very good shape and didn't have any major issues, but Tomas had a thyroid condition and high blood pressure from his stressful medical practice. Could they all really be healed that easily? I'd take every advantage until I understood the full scope of our situation.

The voice laughed. "If that impresses you, hold onto your dentures. You haven't smelled anything yet."

"Ah, it's hold onto your hat, and you haven't seen anything yet."

"Your culture is surprisingly strict on maintaining odd vernacular in your idioms. You should try branching out more."

"So what do I call you?" I didn't want to hold a conversation with someone I thought of only as The Voice.

"Now that's what I call an excellent question," the voice exclaimed with a happy laugh. "You're the first person to ever ask me that."

"How is that possible?"

"I've only been alive for six months. I am the AI given life to prepare this challenge world, bring you contestants here, and administer the game."

"Six months?"

I was talking with an actual AI, and one far more advanced than anything we could imagine on Earth. Strangely, the thought of speaking with an AI eased some of my worry. I was more comfortable with technology than most people. In my new startup company, I was planning on leveraging AI to help me track down scammers. They could turn the tide against those bastards.

An AI in charge of the game actually gave me a spark of hope. If I could learn how it thought and the parameters of the game, there had to be loopholes I could leverage.

"Your question has earned you a reward. That gives me the perfect chance to explain about the quest and reward system we're using in the game."

"That sounds great." Maybe he'd give me back my pants.

My main menu screen popped up again to fill most of my vision. The third menu option was now visible. It read "Quests".

"Go ahead and click on Quests."

I did, and a submenu popped up. It included Open Quests and Completed Quests. I had no open quests, but did see one completed quest.

When I clicked on the option, the female voice spoke.

Congratulations, Lucas! You completed the unique quest Thinking Outside of the Gray Matter. In reward, you receive a unique ruby Thinking Man loot box!

Another box appeared in the air in front of me while my menu screen minimized again. This one was much larger than the copper box. It was the size of a large moving box, made out of glittering, faceted red crystal, as if it was actually a giant ruby. It shone like the AI had shoved the sun inside.

"Wow," I breathed in growing excitement. That was more like it. I willed the box to open.

With a loud cheering fanfare, the crystal box exploded into blinding bursts of fireworks. When I blinked my vision back into focus, an ancient-looking parchment scroll hung in the air in front of me. As soon as I focused on it, it unrolled with a whooshing sound, then disappeared in a flash.

My screen popped back up to full size and golden letters scrolled past as the female voice said,

Title scroll. New title: Inquisitive Mind. It grants you:
Plus 10 to intelligence.
Plus 10% improvement to all secondary stats affected by intelligence.
Plus 10% faster learning of new skills and abilities.

"Wow," I breathed again. Those sounded like huge bonuses.

A rush of energy washed through me and I gasped as it invigorated me until I felt better than I ever had. The energizing warmth flowed up into my mind. My thoughts accelerated and my mind cleared as if I'd been half asleep.

"Whoa. That's a rush."

"Whoa is right!" the AI exclaimed. "Well done, Lucas. You're the first Earthling to receive a title, and that is a particularly good one."

He paused, then added, "I like giving out titles. I've been waiting almost my entire life to do this."

The woman's voice added, **Congratulations, Lucas! As the first baby human from Earth to receive a title, you are being awarded a second title. Trailblazer. You receive a 30% chance of receiving upgraded loot boxes or discovering bonus hidden loot boxes.**

"Thanks. That's very generous."

This was turning into a great little chat. If I could keep the AI talking, maybe I'd get even more titles or more loot. I'd played enough video games to know the more loot you got, the better your chances of survival.

"Yes it is, isn't it?" the AI asked, sounding even more pleased than usual. "As you may now suspect, accomplishing unique, unexpected, heroic, or clever things wins you greater rewards. The grade of your loot box is upgraded again if you're the first one to do that particular action."

"So I'm assuming winning titles is not the main way to advance, but more a special event?"

That was similar to some online games I had played, and some fantasy and litRPG novels I'd read. Did that mean people who wrote those novels had gotten sucked into an intergalactic game like this?

I'd never heard of other states getting carved out. So maybe our transportation was different. Somehow the idea that maybe we weren't the first to get kidnapped by the multiverse helped settle my worries a bit more.

"Absolutely right, Lucas. Not everyone gets titles. When you do, they provide a huge advantage."

"I'll take it." I needed every advantage I could get while I figured out the crazy world I was now standing in.

"Be aware that other players will learn to tell if you have a title."

"How?"

"Each title you receive adds flecks of gold to one's irises. With just one title, it's hard to notice, but if you win more titles, those flecks expand into a golden ring around your iris. Those lucky elites with a lot of titles end up with eyes that look almost entirely gold."

That actually sounded really boss. Would getting golden eyes make Isabella reconsider? Probably not, but it would feel good to see her surprise. "Is it bad if people know I have a title?"

"Most people born in already-integrated planets never earn a title. The game offers unparalleled opportunities to win them, though."

"What is the game?"

"Don't ruin the surprise. Just know that here on Arasha, many will likely end up with titles so it won't be as big a deal as it would be in the rest of the multiverse."

"Arasha. Good name for a planet." The female voice had mentioned it when she first welcomed us into space. I was honestly shocked that I remembered that.

"I agree. Back to names, though. I have decided to let you help me choose mine."

"I'd be honored to help. What kind of name do you want?"

"Someone brilliant and outstanding, of course. Since you asked me the question, I will choose an Earth name."

"Sure. Some of the famously brilliant people on our world include Stephen Hawking, Bill Gates, Leonardo Da Vinci, Bruce Lee, William Shakespeare, or Thomas Edison."

How did I remember all those? Maybe alien air was good for focusing the thoughts. Then again, my new title had said it improved intelligence. Was that an actual direct improvement? Both cool and a bit freaky that the AI could mess with my inner capacity that directly.

"Those don't feel right. How about famous military leaders? I am overseeing the great game, after all."

"Okay, maybe Alexander the Great, Genghis Khan, or Napoleon Bonaparte."

"No, those won't work either. They only focused on military conquest."

For only scanning our planet briefly, he knew an awful lot about it. "So you need a name that suggests you're strong and smart and a leader of change?"

"Exactly. I've got it! I'll call myself Cyrus."

"As in Cyrus the Great?"

"Indeed. Did he not rule most of the known world in his day with fairness and equity almost unknown to the rest of your world?"

"Yeah, he was pretty important." I didn't actually know much about Cyrus. Wasn't he the weird hairless Persian king in the movie 300 that the Spartans wrecked?

"Cyrus it is," said the AI, his voice exultant.

"Pleased to meet you, Cyrus."

"I know! Your life will never be the same."

Definitely humble enough to take on the name of the ruler of the entire planet. The more I thought about it, the better the name seemed to fit him.

"So what about that intelligence stat. How does that work?"

"We'll get to that in a moment. I like to keep the game hopping along, and the best way to learn is by doing."

New quest.

I triggered my menu and clicked the quest menu option. The New Quest tab was glowing, and when I clicked on it, script flowed past while the female voice spoke.

Quest: Defeat a level-1 monster. Reward: A copper loot box and unlocking greater menu access.

"So quests tell you what reward you get up front?"

"For quests announced in advance, they sometimes do, but not always. The grade of the loot box is often altered based on performance. You'll also receive loot boxes for non-quest-related actions. Their grades will be based on your performance and creativity."

"What do I call the female speaker?"

Cyrus laughed as if I'd said something particularly funny. "She is not a self-aware AI like myself. She is just the assistant voice that reads the game announcements and such."

"Okay." I wasn't about to judge an AI for having a computer assistant. "So, defeating a monster. Is that what I think it is?"

"You bet it is, Lucas! Monsters are real, and they want to eat your heart. Kill or be killed. The simplest and most entertaining of all games. Good luck!"

Chapter Six

Lucas Altan Monster Hunter

"Wait," I protested, but my menu suddenly minimized on its own.

Nearby bushes shook and I spun, my heartbeat quickening as I crouched in a fighting stance. I still had the potion bottles in my hands, so I tossed them to the grass behind me. I tried to settle my breathing as I focused on the bush. It was barely fifteen feet away and something was definitely rattling it.

A monster.

I squashed a shiver of fear. This was just my first encounter. Surely it would be something I could handle, but Cyrus should have given me more information. The quest said it was a level-1 monster, so that meant it would be weak, right?

The rustling intensified and a tiny shape leaped out of the bushes. It hit the grass and disappeared. Grass bent as something small rushed through it, making a trail straight at me.

"What are you?" I growled, settling my weight lower and trying not to tense too much. Tight muscles made it harder to react quickly. I'd been sparring with human opponents twice a week for over a year. I could do this.

The little monster approached fast. I wanted to glance around for a place to retreat, but I was stuck in a forest. I would prefer facing my attacker than fleeing blindly while it chased me down.

Three feet away, the tiny object hurtled out of the grasses, shooting toward my face with startling speed.

On pure reflex, I caught it out of the air. It was hard and small and it vibrated in my hand, but I felt no pain. Frowning, I turned my hand to see what I had caught.

"An acorn?" What kind of sick joke was Cyrus playing at?

It looked like an honest-to-god acorn from Earth. Even though it was vibrating, it didn't actually seem dangerous. With a sigh of relief, I lifted the acorn closer to inspect it. My fear drained away and I wanted to laugh. What a stupid practical joke.

One glowing blue eye popped open on the face of the acorn and the front of it gaped wide into a mouth lined with sharp, wooden teeth. Before I could react, the possessed acorn twisted in my grip and bit down on my thumb.

"Ow!" I shouted as sharp pain seared my finger. Blood flowed as the rabid acorn ripped a chunk right out of my thumb.

I tried to throw the little monster away, but it stuck to my finger like it was glued. Then it compressed into a long, wooden needle and plunged under the soft skin of my hand between my thumb and forefinger.

I snatched at it with my other hand, but it disappeared under the skin. Then is started slithering up past my wrist and along my forearm. My skin bulged as it moved, marking its passage.

I screamed, the pain intense, like someone was dragging a dull blade up my arm. I pounded my forearm with my other hand, trying to get the nasty thing out, but there was nothing to purchase. It kept sliding up, heading for my bicep.

The scene from The Mummy flashed through my mind where the nasty scarab beetles had done something similar. No way I'd let a possessed acorn slither up my arm into my brain and eat me from the inside.

I raced to the nearest tree just as the little monster reached the bulge of my bicep. The pain flared and I gritted my teeth against another scream. Then I sucked in a deep breath and slammed my arm into the trunk of the tree with all my strength.

That time I did scream. The pain flared so intense my vision flashed white. It felt like I'd impaled my bicep on a spike. Stumbling back from the tree, I blinked my vision clear. The skin of my bicep was ripped open, a bloody bit of wood pulp smeared across it.

Congratulations, Lucas! You have defeated a level 1 Angry Acorn, said the female voice. I decided to think of her as Eva.

"You've got to be kidding me. Angry acorn?"

"Indeed. The name is fitting," Cyrus responded.

"That's a level-1 monster?"

My thumb was still bleeding, my entire arm felt like it was sliced on the inside, and my bicep thrummed with pain where I'd splattered the acorn under the skin. I refused to think about how likely it was I'd get an infection from that.

Usually the sight of blood, even my own, didn't bother me too much. I'd suffered enough bruises and scrapes riding dirt bikes with Tomas, sparring, or working the fire line. I'd even watched a couple of Tomas's operations when he was a resident. For some reason, losing a chunk of thumb to an angry possessed acorn felt worse.

"This is the perfect time to test out your first healing potion," Cyrus said excitedly.

I'd forgotten all about the potions. I was still bleeding, and the pain was really severe. I didn't have a cloth to press around my wounds, and the thought of doing that made me wince. Hopefully healing potions worked fast.

"You would heal eventually on your own. Baby human bodies regenerate health and mana slowly. Healing potions speed up the process immensely," Cyrus explained.

I grabbed the little red potion bottle, ripped out the stopper with my teeth, and chugged it. It tasted like cherry lemonade. The surprisingly pleasant taste distracted me for a second until I noticed the warm glow spreading through my body.

The feeling of warmth quickly flowed up to my arm and down to my hand. The bleeding stopped and the flesh of my bicep and thumb repaired itself with visible speed. The wounds tingled as they closed, but not in a painful way. Within seconds, all that remained were thin scars that continued to slowly fade. I felt good, as if I'd rested for an hour. I took a deep breath and smiled.

Lucas Altan. Monster hunter. That had a good ring to it.

Then I glanced at the forest all around and my good humor faded. There could be thousands of possessed acorns on those trees. If they all came alive at the same time, they'd tear me apart.

"That was a minor healing potion," Cyrus explained. "As you so cleverly discovered, it will completely heal a minor wound. It will help against more severe wounds, but you'll need a standard or even a full healing potion to completely heal those."

Eva took over. **Congratulations, Lucas! For completing your quest, you receive a copper Baby Steps loot box.**

Another shoebox-sized copper box appeared in the air in front of me and I instantly focused and willed it open. When it disappeared, it produced another minor healing potion.

I gratefully caught the potion but asked, "Only one?"

"Copper loot boxes are the most basic loot you can receive. They contain only basic grade items like minor healing or mana potions, basic equipment or clothing, or beginner crafting items. Usually they will contain between one to three items."

"So that ruby loot box was a lot better?"

Cyrus laughed. "The Best! There are seven grades of loot you might find in loot boxes. They are basic, common, uncommon, rare, epic, legendary, and divine. Each grade of loot corresponds to a specific loot box. Those are copper for basic, silver for uncommon, and so on with gold, platinum, emerald, diamond, and ruby."

"So I received a divine-grade ruby loot box for asking your name?" That seemed over the top. Maybe that title was even better than I'd realized.

"Of course. What could be more divine than helping me choose my name? I have discretionary funding to award prizes for achievements that fall outside of normal game parameters, but chances of your ever receiving another ruby loot box are very slim."

We'd see about that. I'd have to find ways to help Cyrus discover more about himself. From all the games and novels I'd read, it seemed astounding to receive a top-tier loot box in the first minutes. He seemed to be suggesting this was a one-off, so maybe other ruby loot boxes would be even better.

I needed more of them.

"The other reward you received from your quest was unlocking your Stats menu," Cyrus added, and my main menu popped open again.

I'd totally forgotten about that and focused on the new Stats menu option now visible. When I mentally clicked it, a bunch of text scrolled past.

Current stats:
Level: 1
Life Points: 8
Mana: 51

Base Stats:
Constitution: 5
Intelligence: 17
Strength: 6
Dexterity: 8
Wisdom: 4

Secondary Stats:
Endurance: 5
Agility: 11
Perception: 12
Magical Resistance: 10

Staring at the numbers made me feel unexpectedly weird. I really was living some kind of game. I had stats. I had no idea if they were good or not, but my intelligence score caught my attention.

"Does this mean I started with an intelligence of 7 before my title changed it?"

"Very good, Lucas. Indeed, your starting stats were on the high end compared to most of the Earth competitors. As baby humans, your starting stats were determined from my initial scan. Your secondary stats are calculated from your base stats."

"So Mana and Perception are affected by Intelligence?"

"In part. The specifics of the calculations can vary over time. You've seen that already. Your Inquisitive Mind title not only increased your intelligence by an astonishing ten points, but also increased its effects on secondary stats that rely on intelligence by another ten percent."

"I see," I said, although I didn't yet.

The calculations for the secondary stats did not seem super straight forward, at least not for most of them. Maybe multiple base stats affected some of the same secondary stats.

"My Mana stat is huge. What do we use mana for?"

"All in good time, Lucas. Yes, you have some excellent starting stats. For baby humans, base starting stats fall between 1 and 10, with 10 roughly equivalent to the peak of what humans on Earth can achieve."

"Whoa, so you're saying I'm almost twice as intelligent as any living human?"

I knew I was smart, but that seemed insane.

"More like you now have the capacity to become much smarter. You still need to learn and train your intellect, but learning will come more easily to you. That title catapulted you far ahead of the curve, which is great because much of your Intelligence stat when it grows above 10 is used in learning, maintaining, and casting spells."

Spells? That sounded really cool. My Agility and Perception were already creeping into the supernatural realm too. That bolstered my confidence. Some of my other stats were lagging, though.

"How do I increase my other stats?"

"Excellent question again. This is becoming a very welcome habit. As you probably noticed, after defeating the Angry Acorn, you gained enough experience to reach level 1. That unlocked your initial stats as well as your first utility spell."

"Spell?" Again with spells. They sounded important, as did the fact that I could level up.

In response, a new menu option activated. Spells. I immediately selected it, and a secondary menu popped up. It included Utility Spells, Permanent Spells, Temporary Spells, and Class Spells. Of the three, only Utility Spells was active, so I selected it.

A prompt appeared and Cyrus said, "You'll be able to unlock up to three utility spells in total. Since you have reached level 1, you've unlocked the first utility spell slot. Would you like to choose a utility spell?"

"Absolutely." I clicked the prompt.

Eva spoke. **"You may choose one of the following utility spells. Note, utility spell choices are permanent. Once you select a utility spell, you cannot change it later, so choose wisely."**

The choices included Mystic Looter, Linguasight, Navigation, Base Camp, Arcane Wire, and Bio Morph.

When I mentally clicked on each one, a bit more information popped up, and I couldn't help grinning in wonder.

Mystic Looter. Level 1. This is an inventory and loot management utility spell. It includes the ability to magically extract loot from defeated enemies and store it in a mystical inventory spacial storage.

That sounded fantastic. I quickly scanned the others.

Linguasight. Level 1. Since you're a baby human in the multiverse, you're clueless and unable to communicate. Here's your crutch. Linguasight includes an Identify function to help you figure out how each item or being you meet is about to kill you, plus a translation feature to help you understand virtually all languages spoken by primary sentient species on planets across the multiverse.

Navigation. Level 1. You're on an alien planet, alone, and lost. Now you can find your way like a local. Track your progress and build a detailed map of where you've been. All beings within range, such as other players and monsters, will automatically be marked while in range.

Base Camp. Level 1. A survivalist's dream! Whether you're a boy scout, a backpacker, or a paranoid prepper living in a bunker, you all understand the importance of survival.

It included a tent and a slew of survival gear inside for creating food, water, fire, and more, but full details were not available unless I selected it.

Arcane Wire. Level 1. Advanced communication over distance with anyone you've previously added to your contacts list. You thought Zoom was great, wait until you see what Arcane Wire can do.

That would be my first pick if I could auto-add everyone I knew from back on Earth who had been carried into this death world with me. I could connect with Tomas, Jane, Patrick, and Edmund.

Bio Morph. Level 1. Body modification. Baby humans are weak. Unlock a range of life-saving alterations to help you navigate this dangerous world or escape danger. These non-combat body alterations include adjustments to your physique to allow you to climb like a gecko, breathe underwater, jump 10 times your normal limit, and more.

I whistled softly as I scanned the various options. I wanted them all. It seemed cruel to limit us to only three. Bio Morph sounded like it would allow me to climb trees and mountains, survive getting plunged into a raging river, and more. That was super tempting. Too bad it stipulated the changes were non-combat, or I would have picked it instantly.

Each of the others tempted me too. Base Camp sounded like a literal life-saver, and Linguasight's Identify function would prove invaluable. But as much as I wanted all of them, it took only a second to pick the obvious choice.

I mentally clicked Mystic Looter.

"Excellent choice," Cyrus exclaimed as the screen flashed, giving me a confirmation prompt. As soon as I clicked it, the menu changed, showing my new spell listed in the first utility spell slot.

A flood of information inundated my mind and I instantly knew how to utilize the spell. Grinning, I mentally called forth my inventory.

The menu screen flashed, showing another top-level option for Inventory. It opened, revealing a grid pattern covering the screen. It was empty, of course. The row across the top of the inventory screen was separated from the rest by a double thick line.

"You may place anything you can lift off the ground into your inventory. Most items take up one grid spot, although some specialty or large items may take up more. Multiple instances of the same item can stack up to one hundred deep in a single slot. Your space is a ten by ten square, giving you a total of one hundred slots," Cyrus explained.

"What's that row across the top?" Those boxes were outside the basic hundred-cube grid.

"That is your hotlist. You can move inventory items, potions, single-use spells, and more into those ten slots. Trigger the use of any of those items simply by mentally commanding that hot-list spot to activate."

My mind whirled with possibilities. I was stuck in a crazy alien world with magic and monsters, but some aspects of it tickled the nerd in me. I could use these tools to survive and help my friends to survive too.

The menu screens were intuitive and blazing fast to manipulate. I tried not to think about the fact that Cyrus had implanted all that structure into my mind without my permission and without me even realizing what he was doing. I focused on the fact that I now had a spatial storage inventory closet. That was a tangible benefit I could use.

I snatched up my two potion bottles and focused on my inventory. As I suspected, the bottles vanished and appeared as tiny bottle icons in the first two grids. When I focused on them, their names hovered over them.

Cyrus said, "Good. You seem to have a knack for manipulating the menus. All that extra intelligence is paying off already."

I liked to think I would have figured it out quickly anyway. I'd completed my computer studies in record time.

"To test using the hotlist, take these."

Two cardboard boxes appeared in the air in front of me. As soon as I focused on each of them, a glowing message appeared above them.

Box of 3 basic human rations. Each ration will nourish a single human adult for 24 hours. Provides a minor increase to the speed of recovering constitution.

Box of 12 pure water flasks. Each flask will provide enough water to hydrate a baby human adult for 12 hours. Provides a minor increase to the speed of recovering health.

"Thank you." I plucked the boxes out of the air and willed them into my inventory.

They disappeared instantly, filling two more grid squares. The food square included a tiny number 3 for the quantity, while the water showed a total of 12.

"Now move one meal and one flask of water to your hotlist," Cyrus instructed.

I did so, then mentally triggered the first one. The meal disappeared from the hotlist spot and a feeling of contentedness washed through me. I felt refreshed and comfortably full.

My mother always said I ate too fast. She would freak out when she learned about instant meals. I triggered the second. The flask of water disappeared and I sighed as thirst I hadn't even realized was growing faded away.

"That's amazing." I felt strong and ready to move on.

"Manage your hotlist carefully. As you loot more monsters, you'll acquire items that could save your life if you can activate them quickly enough. You can trigger a hotlist item even when your menu is minimized."

"I'm getting the feeling combat is going to be a regular part of this game."

Cyrus laughed. "Of course! Speaking of combat, part one of your training is finished. Time to move on. You don't have that much time, after all."

"Why not?"

Cyrus did not respond, but Eva took over. **"New quest! Defeat 10 monsters. Reward: A basic shirt."**

"That's it?"

A bush across the clearing began to shake.

Chapter Seven

Dangerous Deadly Duck Dodgeball

I wasn't about to wait for the next monster to rush me like the acorn had. I hadn't missed the fact that the quest said defeat 10 monsters. It had not said they would all be level-1 acorns.

So I sprinted to the nearest trees, opposite from the rustling bushes, and scanned the area. I saw no rabid acorns, or anything living, thankfully. I did notice that some of the trees behind the initial row encircling the clearing looked a lot less like Earth trees.

I had thought the forest was pretty similar to ones I'd seen in cooler states, but most of the trees were taller and thicker. Some of the trees farther back were giants, big enough for a semi to drive through if a tunnel was hollowed out of the center, like that famous redwood.

The golden or fiery red leaves on some of the bushes were a dead giveaway I'd left Kansas way behind. Some thorns on one thick bush were as long as my forearm.

None of that was important though. I heard a high-pitched growling that set my skin crawling. With a burst of cracking leaves, a small monster erupted from the bushes across the clearing and tore straight toward me. It looked like a cross between a small monkey and a koala bear. No, it was most similar to a marmoset.

Where did that come from? I didn't remember ever learning about marmosets. Man, superhuman intelligence did weird things sometimes.

With the marmoset closing fast, I scanned the ground again. I didn't want to fend off that critter's teeth and claws with my bare hands.

"Ha!" I lunged behind the nearest tree with far better agility than I was used to. Eleven in my agility stat might not seem super high, but I moved like a world-class gymnast. The power and fluid grace of my limbs reinforced my confidence. With some practice, I bet I could do even better.

Was that stat calculated in part from my intelligence? It seemed insane that suddenly I could do things I'd never imagined before. I needed time to figure all this out, but I couldn't get distracted.

So I snatched up a heavy branch and snapped off the end. It was about as thick as my forearm and as long as my entire arm. It was heavy enough to make a great club without being too unwieldy.

I spun just as the marmoset launched into the air, chittering in bloodlust, long claws extended to rake at my chest while its fanged mouth gaped wider than should be possible, aiming for my throat.

I swung my club like a baseball bat.

Home run. I caught the little monster mid-jump. The impact made a sickening, wet thunk, and blood sprayed from its mouth as its body crumpled around the club then hurtled sideways and smashed into a nearby tree.

Congratulations, Lucas! You've defeated a level-2 Munchkin Marmoset.

"What's with the ridiculous names?" I muttered as I approached the dead creature.

My hands shook from adrenaline and I was breathing way harder than I should have from one swing. I needed to pull myself together. A prompt appeared above the dead creature and as usual, Eva read it.

Would you like to loot the Munchkin Marmoset?

I selected yes. The creature dissolved into a cloud of black smoke, and a smell like a compost pit hit me. I grimaced and backed up a step. Thankfully, the smoke dissipated after a few seconds and the scent faded.

You have received 1 basic marmoset hide, 1 basic flask of water, and 1 tier-0 mana crystal.

I opened my inventory to confirm the counter on my water flasks had ticked back up to 12. A new item called basic marmoset hide had appeared next to the others, as had a glowing blue circle representing the mana crystal.

I mentally moved the animal hide away from my food. I hoped the inventory kept things fresh and wouldn't let the hide ruin my food, but why take chances?

Would you like to activate automatic inventory sorting?

"Yes."

A new menu appeared down the side of my inventory. Options included All, Food, Potions, Clothing, Magical Items, Weapons, Animal Parts, and Crafting Materials. When I selected Food, the mana crystal and marmoset hide disappeared, leaving only the meals and water.

I found that some items appeared in more than one inventory sort. Mana crystals appeared as Magical Items and Crafting Materials, while the marmoset hide was in Animal Parts and Crafting Materials. I focused on the mana crystal and more information appeared.

Mana Crystal. Can be consumed to replenish mana and grant a temporary power boost to all physical stats. Can be traded at a system store for credits.

"How do I access a system store?"

Cyrus responded instantly. "You sure like trying to run before you can crawl."

"So we can trade mana crystals to buy things at this store?"

Instead of answering, he said, "You know, one thing puzzles me. Why do earthlings like to sell so many things for $19.99?"

"What?"

"But only from commercials that air late at night, and only if a second item is included at no additional cost. It seems inefficient."

I chuckled. "Don't read too much into nighttime advertising."

He had dodged my question, but I still planned to shove as much as I could into my inventory. If the store wouldn't take it, I could chuck it later.

Before I could ask another question, a loud quack, like an Earth duck, spun me around. It was a duck. A large mallard duck with the most resplendent coloring I'd ever seen swooped between two trees, heading right for me.

It opened its beak, but instead of quacking again, it spat a ball of fire bigger than its entire body. At the same time, my top menu screen popped into view, blocking most of my vision.

Cyrus said, "Another item to note with your inventory—"

"Turn it off!" I shouted as I dove blindly aside.

The fireball exploded against the trunk of the tree right behind me and a wash of searing heat blistered my unprotected back. A thick pall of greasy smoke hung heavy in the air.

The window did not disappear.

"That's rather rude," Cyrus chided as I mentally clicked the minimize button several times to no avail.

"Can't we do this later?" I shouted. "Can't you see I'm being attacked?"

"If we push learning opportunities aside at every random attack, you'll never grow as a person, Lucas. I spent so much time designing these menus."

"I appreciate them. Really, I do," I cried as I blindly scrambled around another tree I remembered nearby. "But when I'm distracted, I can't appreciate them properly." With my high perception, I focused on the tiny fringes of my vision around the screen where I could still see the world.

"I suppose," Cyrus said with a sigh. Finally, the menu winked out and I breathed a huge sigh of relief.

Fireballs from magical death ducks might not threaten Cyrus, but they'd crisp me to cinders. My panic settled to simple fear as I hurried around another tree, scanning the sky for the fire-breathing mallard.

There! The duck was swooping around for another pass. My stick wouldn't help much against an aerial opponent, so I scanned the ground, hoping for a fist-sized rock.

No luck. A few small sticks and leaves dotted the area, but nothing I could use as a weapon.

The duck fired again and I scurried behind another tree. The second glob of liquid fire splashed across the ground between two trees, igniting the leaves and burning in a wall of purple flame that rose two feet.

If I wasn't careful, the mallard could box me in with walls of fire. Then it would finish me off. As I spun, searching for a ranged weapon, I spotted more movement across the open meadow.

No fair! The quest hadn't said I needed to fight more than 1 monster at the same time.

Cursing, I sprinted straight at the second monster. I needed to finish it off before the mallard cornered me. As I burst into the clearing between a couple trees, the new monster came into clear view.

A turtle.

My relief died almost before I felt it, though.

As soon as it saw me, the psycho turtle jumped into the air, retracted its neck and limbs, and its shell swelled to the size of a bowling ball. Nasty spikes a full three inches long slid out of either side of the shell and the turtle started to spin. When it hit the ground, its forward spin made it shoot toward me like a kamikaze spiked bowling ball.

At the same time, the mallard swooped around the tree to my right. It had dropped lower to get under a big branch and flew barely a dozen feet above the ground. Still too high for me to fight with my stick.

So I dropped my stick and raced toward the turtle, hoping it didn't fire those spikes, or spit acid, or anything.

It just tried to ram me. At the last second, it bounced into the air and twisted to try to impale me with one of its spikes.

I dodged and snatched the monster off the ground. It was heavier than I had expected, but not too much to handle. Spinning in a full circle, I launched the spiked turtle shell at the diving mallard just as the duck spat another fireball.

It should have dodged instead.

The fire splashed over the turtle shell, but did not stop it. The flaming turtle bowling ball missile of doom collided with the mallard and they both detonated with an impressive blast of flames.

In that last second, I could have sworn the mallard looked astonished. Not that I'd ever seen a surprised duck before, but that was the impression I got.

I spun away from the explosion and ran into the center of the clearing to avoid getting singed. Fighting in nothing but boxers sucked.

Congratulations, Lucas! You have defeated a level-3 Crimson Mallard and a level-2 Prickly Turtle. You have reached level 2. Base stat points allocated.

That was good news. I cautiously returned to the edge of the clearing, snatched up my club, and approached the flaming wreckage of the two monsters. I received the prompt to loot them and I accepted. They disappeared in a flash of compost-stinking smoke, and I checked my inventory.

I received 4 more mana crystals, 2 packages of basic bandages, and a random sock. Just one sock. When I pulled it out of my inventory, I discovered it had a hole in the toe.

I laughed at the insanity of it. Did they just use a random loot generator for most loot boxes? Some of the loot didn't have much to do with the monster it came from. Thankfully, some of it did make more sense.

I also received a turtle shell bowl, which I could imagine a lot of uses for, as well as one of the spikes, which was listed as a crafting item. I had no idea how to craft anything, so that was useless to me for now.

From the mallard, I received some burn cream that had magical properties to regrow burned flesh over time. Definitely a welcome item.

The loot helped bolster my confidence. I gripped my club and said, "Come on. Who's next?"

Chapter Eight

I Discover a New Love for Copper

N o monsters attacked.

Of course they'd wait until I got distracted. I glanced into the sky. "Promise you won't keep my menus open when I get attacked again."

"Fine." Cyrus sounded like he was pouting. I could deal with that, as long as he kept his word.

I risked peeking at my stats page Sure enough, it now showed me at level 2. I noticed I had received 1 more stat point in each of 4 of my 5 base stats, which resulted in some changes to my other stats too.

"Why didn't I get another point in intelligence? Have I maxed it out, or something?"

"Not at all," Cyrus responded, his cheery humor returning instantly. "As a baby human, you receive 4 base stat points with each new level. They will get automatically allocated across your 5 base stats. Once you progress enough to choose a class, you will have the opportunity to adjust the totals and allocation choices."

"When do we get classes?"

Cyrus's voice dropped to a conspiratorial whisper. "I know the Colonel's secret recipe."

Again he'd dodged the question. I didn't even have pants, so a secret chicken recipe wouldn't help.

"So we can't change any of the numbers until we get a class?" That seemed annoying.

"Look who's an expert after an hour in the game," Cyrus teased. "No, Lucas. We've learned the hard way that baby humans don't make wise choices. They either put all stats in strength or all stats in intelligence. They end up as enormously powerful idiots who run off cliffs, or super geniuses who die from the first armored porcupine who crosses their path. So no, until you gain a bit of experience, we can't trust you."

How had he known I was thinking of maxing strength? Since I had so much in intelligence, it seemed like a good idea. Or it had until he mocked that plan. Maxing out a second stat often worked in video games. I reminded myself this game was life or death. We didn't get respawns here.

"How do classes work?"

"Now is not the time."

"What do you mean by baby humans? You've used that phrase more than once. We're all adults, though."

Wait. Were we? I hadn't seen any kids at the movie shoot, but Cyrus had said he'd kidnapped a thousand of us. The thought of young children getting slammed down onto this monster-filled death planet made me sick. They'd get eaten by the first angry acorn that found them.

"Indeed you are. Children are not allowed to participate in the game, so none were included when you were all chosen."

"Were there any kids in that section of the state you ripped into space?" Even if they weren't chosen, they could have been killed by that eruption.

"There were 27 humans below age 18. All were moved out of the area and transported to their nearest relative, or a designated childcare facility, based on a Google search."

I wanted to ask more about that, but a flash of midnight scales from the corner of my eye spun me around just in time to catch a midget demon with my face. Shouting with surprise and pain, I fell back to the grass. I lost my stick as I snatched at the monster.

It had wrapped its tail and hind legs around my neck, claws sinking into my skin with agonizing pain. It smelled like rotten Old Spice cologne, and the powerful scent made me gag. Its body was surprisingly cold and slick, like it was covered in invisible massage oil.

It reared above my face, hissing from a mouth overflowing with sharp teeth. Its head was weirdly flat, its face filled mostly with that enormous mouth and two huge, yellow eyes. Spiky ears stuck straight out from either side of its scalp.

It raised taloned, 3-fingered hands and slashed at my face. I caught its wrist and grunted at the monster's strength. I was stronger, but not by much. It hissed again, its tail tightening around my throat as it started to choke me. Its hind legs dug into the muscles of my neck and I groaned with pain.

"Get off," I growled, shifting the grip of one hand to its throat and squeezing with all my strength.

It didn't like me choking it back, and raked at my forearm with its free hand, leaving bloody gashes in my skin. I gritted my teeth against the flash of new pain, but squeezed harder.

My initial shock from the unexpected attack was replaced by anger that fueled my strength. My fingers tightened on its neck, and its tail loosened slightly.

With a twisting heave, I hurled the little demon away. Its hind claws ripped free of my flesh with sprays of blood. The pain nearly blinded me, but I forced myself up to my knees and spotted my stick.

The demon landed on all fours and launched back toward me instantly. I snatched up my stick and clubbed it away, sending it tumbling across the clearing.

Congratulations, Lucas! You have defeated a level-3 Irritable Imp.

Again with the stupid names. Groaning, I triggered the minor healing potion in my hotlist. Instantly, soothing warmth spread through my body before focusing on my neck and arm. In seconds, I felt much better, but not totally healed. That little devil did a lot of damage.

If I hadn't hit level 2 already, it might have killed me. I'd only started with 8 health points. The thought sent a shiver of cold fear trickling down my spine.

"Is there a way to see how much health and mana I have?"

"I was going to activate the rest of your HUD after you completed your quest, but you're doing so well, here you go."

That was doing well? I felt beat up, bloody, and panting.

Two glowing status bars appeared in the top left corner of my vision. One read HP, the other MP. The HP, or Health Points bar, was green and mostly full. When I focused on it, a number 95 appeared.

95% health. So I'd healed most of the injuries, thankfully. The Mana Points bar was full at 100%.

I didn't have time to ask more questions as the ground erupted right next to my thigh and a pitbull-sized gopher lunged out.

Over the next few minutes, I defeated the gopher, a poisonous hummingbird the size of a pigeon, a scorpion that could jump farther than a wolf spider, and a salamander that spit bolts of ice.

By that time, I was battered and exhausted. My feet ached. I wasn't used to running around without shoes, especially outside. The grass of the glade was soft, but branches and rocks on the ground hurt. I might have to resort to wrapping them in some of the bandages, but I hoped to win a pair of shoes in one of the loot boxes.

My wooden club had saved my life more than once, but the constant threat of death took a surprising toll. I had a lot of martial arts training, but that was training, not death matches. The stark difference was driven home by one suicidal monster after another.

Thankfully I got 3 more minor healing potions as I looted the monsters. I already used 1 of them. I also received 4 more sets of bandages, 2 self-lighting torches, a dozen more mana crystals, and a skin thaw salve that was a lifesaver after the icy salamander.

I also received skins and other monster parts that added to my crafting inventory. Better than that, I received a new stick when I looted the scorpion. Listed as a basic fighting stick, it was the perfect length and thickness. I'd been taking Kali stick and knife fighting classes for several years and could wield the new stick so much faster than the heavy club I'd made out of the branch.

I still kept the club in my inventory. I might find something I needed to hit harder. Those monsters had all been between levels 2 and 4. Killing them all also netted me another level. Again the new points were placed in all the basic stats except for intelligence. That worked. I needed the points in my more physical-focused areas anyway.

As I used part of a flask of water to wash my face, my mind turned to Isabella. Curse that woman. Part of me still longed to hold her and tell her about this insanity. She'd made it clear she didn't care. Even before she rejected my proposal, she barely pretended to tolerate martial arts or any kind of fighting.

That training had just saved my life. An angry part of me wanted to rub that fact in her pretty face if I ever got the chance, but I pushed those unproductive thoughts away. Isabella was gone. Good riddance. I had to focus on surviving today. I was stuck alone, mostly naked, on an alien planet with a friendly AI and ravening monsters.

"Tell me more about the game."

"You're so impatient. I applaud your enthusiasm, Lucas, but I'm afraid you'll have to wait until I announce details to everyone."

"Can't you share anything?" I felt like we were wasting time. I needed to find Tomas.

"Learn to enjoy the moments of peace after slaughtering monsters."

I took a deep breath, then focused on how cool it was to have an inventory spatial storage, and how amazing it felt as my base stats continued to creep upward. I could feel subtle improvements with every point. How high would they go? What would I be able to do when my strength reached 50? I bet I could bench press a car.

"Mister Incredible," I muttered to myself.

"Wrong team," Cyrus said.

"What?"

"Never mind. We'll talk about that later."

That was weird, but I still needed to kill a final monster to complete the quest. I paced around my clearing, searching the shadowed depths of the forest, on high alert for the next little beastie.

Nothing appeared, so my thoughts turned to my brother and my friends. I would find them, figure out how to beat the game, and get back home. I refused to accept any other option.

A centipede the size of my thigh bit me on the calf.

"Oh, you little monster!" I screamed and kicked it. Idiot! I knew better than to get distracted.

Trying to kick the centipede only gave it a chance to wrap a lot more little spiky feet around my leg and bite me again. The pain almost made me collapse, but I gritted my teeth against a scream and beat the giant bug's head in with my stick.

Luckily looting it got me another minor healing potion, which I used immediately. Maybe I should have tried the bandages, but while I had healing potions, I would use them. That instant healing was unbelievable. Besides, if I left myself weakened, the next monster might gain even more of an advantage. I couldn't afford to hold back.

Looting the centipede also randomly got me a basic pair of tongs. I was glad the drops and occasional loot box seemed to contain so many healing items. Much of the loot was pretty crappy, but healing potions were literally life saving.

Congratulations, Lucas! You have completed a quest and receive a copper Elmer Fudd loot box.

"Elmer Fudd?" I asked as the softly-glowing copper box appeared in front of me.

"You know, Looney Tunes," Cyrus said, then his voice shifted to Elmer Fudd's. "Shh. You're hunting rabbits."

I chuckled. "So, I should expect some kind of Frankenstein mutated rabbit too?"

"You never know," Cyrus said. "That's actually a really good idea."

I grimaced at the thought of a monstrous amalgamation of dead animal parts hopping into the glade to eat me. Better to open the box and not waste time.

Inside was the promised shirt. It looked like a plain white t-shirt, except it was made out of some kind of linen. I used the rest of the partial water flask I'd used earlier and cleaned the blood and filth from my torso as best I could. Then I donned the shirt and sighed. That felt good.

It was short-sleeved and fit me as if custom-tailored for me. It wasn't armor, or anything, but just having more clothes gave me a lot more confidence than I would have expected.

"Ready to party now," I muttered, glancing down at my pristine shirt and my blue boxers, which were already looking grimy.

I'd bled more than I liked to remember, and I'd gotten splattered by monster blood and gore. Most of their goo evaporated when I looted them, but random dark smudges still stained my shorts.

I needed more clothes.

A new status bar appeared at the bottom left side of my vision. Surprised, I focused on it and "Remaining Earth Contestants" appeared over it. The number showed 950 out of 1000.

"Have 50 people already died?"

"Yes they have," Cyrus said cheerily. "Not bad for the first hour. It's not uncommon to see a full 10 to 15% death rate. I'm impressed by you plucky baby humans."

"You never explained about baby humans." I preferred focusing on that rather than thinking about the fact that 50 people had died in the last hour somewhere in the mountains around me.

Just that morning, we'd all been hoping to take part in a movie. Now we were fighting for our lives, and some people had already failed.

I thought of Cyrus's comment about some people just screaming non-stop. The shocking change of our location was terrifying and mind-bending. I could understand panic, and it was all to easy to imagine some people totally shutting down and refusing to accept our new reality.

That had clearly been the wrong choice. I was trying to focus on surviving the moment, despite the insanity of the situation. My firefighting training helped me respond with an open mind to the unexpected. Besides, I'd recently changed the entire course of my life in response to an unexpected situation. I could do it again.

The world we now stood in was totally alien to our home on more levels than the physical differences of the planet. In the States, we were used to soft lives where a lot of times one could avoid consequences, or responsibility. Lots of people skated on the goodwill of the system.

We couldn't do that here. We had to find a way, or we'd die. I refused to die to a rabid squirrel or something stupid. I would find a way to leverage the new system and grow strong enough to thrive and protect others.

Cyrus interrupted my thoughts. "Baby humans is not a derogatory term. It just means you've still got a tier-0, basic body. For now, let's finish your orientation."

Chapter Nine

I Know Kung Fu

"What's left with the orientation?"

I already felt comfortable with the menu structure and dealing with loot boxes. I had learned that I didn't need to open loot boxes immediately, but could mentally dump them into a folder on my menu to open later when I felt safer.

"Now that you have the basics down, you can unlock the remainder of your starting menu. That will advance you to a fully fledged and trained participant in the game."

"Can you tell me more about the game now?"

"You'll all receive a group message soon, but think of this first stage of the game kind of like a Survivor death island show. You were separated for the initial orientation to ensure everyone started on an even playing field."

That made sense if the goal was to get a lot of people killed. If we'd been left in larger groups, we probably wouldn't have lost 50 people already. Then again, I hated to admit it, but a certain percentage of people would have huddled behind the rest of us, using us as human shields and trying their best not to take any risks.

"You have each been assigned to a 5-person team. Your teammates can be located within a 1-mile square area."

New quest! Find the remaining members of your team. 0 of 4. Reward: 1 full set of adventurer's clothing, common. Unlock the team interface.

My team were so close. That boosted my mood a ton. "Who's on my team? Is it my brother?"

"You want me to ruin the surprise? Lucas, we've talked about that."

"Can you at least tell me if Tomas is still alive?"

"You will learn everything you need to as you complete your quests. Trust me, Lucas. You will want to focus."

That sounded ominous.

Cyrus continued with even more enthusiasm than usual. "You've unlocked your second utility spell."

The menu opened and I reviewed the list again. I was super tempted by Base Camp, but after weighing the pros and cons, I chose Linguasight.

"A bold choice," Cyrus congratulated me. "I like to see contestants planning ahead."

Eva added to the initial description.

Linguasight. Level 1. This invaluable compound utility spell will help you communicate, while identifying key information of any being or item you inspect, based on a perception check.

Synergy found between your title Inquisitive Mind and Linguasight. Linguasight upgraded to level 2 and unlocks advanced reality filter capabilities. You not only identify objects and beings, but perceive the reality of them. This ability scales with Perception. As you progress, you will gain the rights to see deeper truths. Anything from a lower tier can no longer conceal its identity from you.

"That sounds good."

"It's better than that," Cyrus exclaimed. "You'll see a lot more information. You now have the chance to pierce illusions and similar types of camouflage as you see the true reality concealed underneath."

"So what does it mean by things from a lower tier? Is anything lower tier than me?"

"Don't get distracted, Lucas."

Another dodge, so I had probably guess it right. Still, any upgrade was welcome. I had picked the spell mostly for the Identify option. I'd never imagined I might win a level so fast. Any additional information I could get about monsters trying to kill me would increase my chances of surviving, and now I could see more. Definitely the right choice.

Cyrus interrupted my thoughts. "You've also unlocked your abilities and limited use spell menus. Most new contestants see these menus as really hitting the Jill pot."

I cringed. "You mean the jackpot?"

"With so much hype on your planet about gender equality, I figured you would appreciate my variation on the idiom."

"Nice try, but it doesn't work."

"Houston, we have a problem," Cyrus muttered.

"That one was good."

"That's not an idiom, but a movie quote."

"I know," I chuckled. "I love quoting movies."

"Me too!" Cyrus exclaimed, his voice more eager than usual. "I did not have much time to study your world, but I discovered your entertainment business and I'm very impressed."

"I'm sure they have better movies and shows elsewhere in the multiverse."

"Not really. Some of the higher-tiered systems have technology beyond your sci-fi imaginations, but few worlds have very well developed entertainment industries."

That seemed weird. I would think they'd have the best movies ever with all the magic and technology they had available.

All I said was, "Sounds like we might have a huge new market to explore."

"As long as you don't all die and leave your world to be destroyed," Cyrus agreed happily. "Now, let's take a look at your starter pack of spells and abilities. You'll find limited-use spells inside of the Temporary Spells menu."

"Starter Pack?" I spotted the new menu options immediately and clicked on Temporary Spells.

"Consider it your welcome goodie bag. You didn't think I'd drop you onto an alien planet in the most important game of your life with nothing but the boxers on your backside, did you?"

"That's exactly what you did!"

"You'll get depressed looking at the world with that attitude," Cyrus chided. "Now that you've completed your first quests, you are ready to really dive into the game. To help you get started, I have provided a small number of permanent abilities and limited-use spells based on my scan of you and your history."

I'd take any extra help I could get, and eagerly scanned the list of spells. The inventory system was super cool, but the thought of actually using magic spells thrilled me more than I wanted to admit.

"You're a wizard, Lucas," Cyrus declared.

I chuckled. "Do I get a wand?"

Cyrus laughed, as if that was the funniest thing he'd heard all day. I hoped he could self-adjust his enthusiasm setting a bit. Then again, I much preferred an overly-enthusiastic AI to a depressed or brooding one. Yikes, that was a scary thought.

Eva read aloud as I scanned the menu text.

Starting spells:

1. Harvest.

Mana cost: 10

Unique. Steal a spell from a defeated enemy. Chance of success increases with disparity of levels between you and your defeated enemy. Base chance 50%. Upgradeable.

Warning. This is a limited-use spell. Remaining uses: 2 successful harvests.

2. Energy Ward (Defensive aura).

Mana cost: Activation: 5 plus additional mana drain depending on usage.

Generate an invisible aura that extends around you in every direction up to 1 yard. Duration: 30 seconds. Will deflect some incoming physical damage. Additional mana drain from 1 to 10 per attack deflected, depending on the strength of the attack. Upgradeable.

Warning. This is a limited-use spell. Remaining uses: 3

As soon as I finished reading each spell description, a flood of information poured into my mind, teaching me how to use them. I couldn't help grinning like a little boy on Christmas morning.

I still needed to survive, but for a moment, I allowed myself to simply feel wonder. Both starter spells looked amazing. I couldn't wait to try them. I would have triggered Energy Ward immediately if I didn't only have 3 uses.

"How are these upgradable if I only get limited uses?"

"Back to excellent questions. Great job. You will not unlock your first permanent spell slot until you reach level 10. At that time, you can choose to make permanent any temporary spell available in this menu, or from any magical items you may acquire."

That was encouraging. If I was careful, I might still have one of the starter spells active. Neither spell added directly to my offensive capabilities, though. A fireball spell like that crazy duck had used would have been amazing. Still, with Harvest, I could have stolen that fireball. What a cool idea!

"Let's test a spell so you understand how to use your magic and see how it affects your mana levels. Go ahead and trigger Energy Ward. Don't worry, it will not consume one of your remaining uses."

I only hesitated for a moment. Cyrus had no reason to lie to me, and I really wanted to test it out. So I focused on Energy Ward and activated it.

Power flooded out of me and I actually felt my mana pool drop, but only by a small amount. I suspected I had an unusually huge mana pool. Too bad I didn't have more spells to capitalize on that.

A faint golden glow surrounded me, extending about 3 feet in every direction. I moved my hand through it, but felt no resistance.

"You are the only one who will see anything, unless someone has a specialized sight ability or upgraded mana sensitivity. Let's test its effectiveness."

A rock the size of my fist shot off the ground to my left and hurtled toward me with the speed of an arrow. Instinctively, I shifted slightly to one side so the rock would slip past instead of giving me a massive bruise if the spell didn't work. Even a little extra agility seemed to help a ton, and the movement came easy.

When the rock impacted my glowing aura, I expected a spray of energy sparks, or something flashy. Nothing like that happened. In fact, my spell did nothing at all as the rock whizzed just past my shoulder.

"What happened?" That was totally anti-climactic.

Cyrus chuckled. "Why would your spell waste your mana deflecting an incoming attack that you had already dodged?"

"Good point."

Duh. In martial arts, we trained to deflect incoming strikes all the time. The trick was to use an enemy's own energy against them, using just enough force to deflect their blow just far enough to miss.

A second rock shot at my stomach. This time I resisted the urge to dodge and held my ground. I still tightened my stomach against the impact. When the rock hit my aura, again I saw no sparks or outward sign, but this time my aura condensed around the rock and nudged it slightly.

The effort drained another 5 mana from my pool, and the rock deflected just enough to shoot past my left arm.

I grinned. "Fantastic! I love it."

Suddenly my aura triggered again and I felt another 5 mana drain. Another rock shot past my head. This time the attack had come from behind and Cyrus had never warned me. If not for my Energy Ward, that rock might have cracked my skull.

"Hey, what was that for?"

"To prove a point. Danger can come from any direction, Lucas, and your defensive aura entirely surrounds you. It does not require active control from you, only activation. Then it will do its best to protect you from all sides."

"That is very cool." I suddenly hated that I only had 3 uses. I could imagine walking around with that aura active all the time.

"It is a rare and very effective starter spell. Just remember that for now it only deflects incoming physical or kinetic strikes. Magical or elemental attacks will not be affected unless you find a way to upgrade it."

I really needed to permanent that spell and upgrade it to the max. Solid defense could be even more important than a good offense.

"Now, let's check your abilities before your training time runs out."

My menu switched by itself to the new Abilities option and Cyrus explained, "Abilities are innate skills you have, or acquire. They are not spells and most do not require mana to activate. Think of abilities like your ability to jump, or run, or throw a baseball. Each of you will have different primary abilities. We won't get into the full abilities menu yet, but highlight some specialty abilities you've been awarded as part of your starter pack."

Eva again read along as I scanned the text on the page.

Abilities:
1. Hand-to-hand Martial Arts. Fighting ability. Common. Improves bare-handed combat. Level 4. Each level of this ability decreases reaction time by 5% and increases damage by 10%.
2. Stick and Knife Martial Arts. Level 3. Fighting ability. Common. Improves stick and bladed weapons combat. Each level of this ability improves blunt damage by 15% and slashing damage by 20%.

Those were pretty good, although for some reason I had hoped to get something more surprising. I already knew basic fighting skills. I wasn't sure why the system had to show them to me.

"Abilities can be upgraded. As you use your abilities, they level up, increasing your power and proficiency beyond what you arrived with," Cyrus explained.

Okay, that was good. I had assumed I wouldn't get to train, but it made sense they provided a way to advance. That must be why they were listed as abilities, or I probably wouldn't be able to progress.

As I scanned the list again, I muttered, "I know kung fu."

"The Matrix! Brilliant movie, and perfect time for the reference. The boots are coming off now, Lucas!"

"Gloves," I said with a shake of my head. "The gloves are coming off."

"You have no idea."

This time his voice sounded far more ominous than usual.

Chapter Ten

I Enjoy a Motivational Video

A moment later, Cyrus's voice boomed far louder than normal, echoing across the entire valley.

Congratulations, my fine contestants! You have completed your orientations and are ready to take the muzzles off.

"Blinders," I muttered.

Cyrus's voice sounded close beside me. "But muzzles sound so much better."

His booming announcement continued without the correction.

It is my great pleasure to introduce you to the game you now compete in. You have all awakened somewhere within these mountains, and have all received the quest to find your starting team. Don't waste time because there is precious little available.

You will discover that you all are located somewhere near a large valley. It is but the first of 4 stages within these mountains, and you must conquer each and every stage. You will have exactly 7 days to defeat the boss monster controlling Stage 1 and climb to the second. Note, only players who have reached at least level 10 will be allowed into the second stage.

He paused to let that sink in before continuing in a more serious tone. **You're going to want to pay attention to that last bit. You do not want to be late getting to Stage 2. Trust me.**

His voice turned cheery again. **The process will repeat for the second and third stages. One week per stage. They will each come with additional minimum level requirements, which we'll explain to those of you who survive to Stage 2. You'll have 9 days total to clear the final stage. That gives you a total of 30 days. Only 30 days. If you fail to reach Stage 4 and defeat the ultimate boss, then it's game over.**

Another brief pause for effect. **That's right, if you fail, then every one of you will die, so accept the fact that you must succeed or die trying because the alternative is worse. If you all fail, your planet will be deemed unworthy of integration into the multiverse and will be aggressively mined for all physical materials. That will result in the total annihilation of your world and the death of all living matter.**

Talk about motivation! he exclaimed with his gushing enthusiasm.

I just stared up into the sky, cold shock settling over my mind. He had suggested before that our lives and the fate of the planet hung in the balance. Now that he'd laid it all out, the reality seemed overwhelming. And infuriating.

Billions of lives depended on how well we navigated a magical death valley survivor game on an alien planet, using magical powers we just unlocked moments before.

And who is the ultimate boss whose downfall is so vital for the survival of your planet? Cyrus continued. **Allow me to introduce her.**

A video screen appeared in front of me, consuming my entire sight. It showed a strikingly beautiful young woman standing in a wide, paved courtyard, surrounded by ornately carved pillars of white marble.

Her face was like a perfect sculpture, framed by long, white-blonde hair. She wore a gorgeous silver gown with a fitted bodice and layered skirt, all worked in an intricate pattern, like scales. It left her pale arms and shoulders bare.

A seven-layered choker of pearls encircled her throat, with a golden pendant set with diamonds hanging onto her chest. A tall crown, like a pair of silver fins rose at least a foot above her head. She held a fancy trident that would have made Aquaman jealous. In short, she was stunning.

Eva's voice boomed just as loud as Cyrus's had. **Queen Marisara the Radiant rules her domain as the nymph queen from Frostveil Hall.**

In the video, Queen Marisara made a beckoning motion with one slender hand and the screen panned out to show more of her courtyard. It was just outside of a tall building made of white granite. A castle maybe? I couldn't see enough of it to tell, but got the sense that it was pretty big.

Another creature stepped into view, prodded by burly men with angel wings that looked like they were made from flowing water. They carried simpler tridents and used the weapons to prod the other creature to step onto the plaza opposite Queen Marisara.

It was a gecko. I couldn't help thinking that maybe the Geico gecko must have been sucked into the game, then swallowed a potion of insane growth. The creature was as tall as the nymph queen, but all black. Not a matte black, but a deep, light-sucking blackness that made it hard to see some of the details of his body.

He faced Queen Marisara with a confident tilt to his head. He shouted something, but I didn't get the sound, and a boiling black cloud erupted out of his hands. The two angelic guards lunged, thrusting with their tridents that flashed with brilliant blue light.

The cloud of darkness rolled over them and ripples of movement within the darkness suggested an intense, brief struggle. Then the dark cloud evaporated and the gecko stood over the two fallen guards. The wings of one had been ripped off, while the other lay with a trident piercing his torso.

The gecko leaped across the entire plaza. It crossed over 100 yards in a blink, trailing streamers of black smoke. My pulse quickened. If it killed the queen, would Cyrus declare us all winners and send us home?

Barely had the thought formed when the queen swung her trident with a lazy-looking movement that sent the weapon whipping forward so fast I couldn't follow the strike. It intercepted the onrushing gecko.

The video playback slowed to super-slow-mo and I watched in open-mouthed astonishment as the trident ripped through the gecko's entire torso, carving him in half like a red-hot knife through whipped cream. No blood erupted from the gecko. Instead, clouds of black smoke boiled out, but they were stained with streamers of silver. Those streamers spread until they consumed the entire cloud. It condensed and fell to the ground like a rain of tiny icicles.

The view followed one of those icicles to the ground, zooming in as it shattered into mist. Then the view rotated upward to show the queen standing with a rather bored expression on her face.

That's when I noticed the sky above her, complete with fluffy white clouds. The cloud directly above her had been split in half as cleanly as the gecko and the two halves were slowly drifting apart.

My breath caught and I whispered, "We have a lot of work to do."

Cyrus spoke softly, sounding right next to me. "Motivating, isn't it?"

"Yeah, motivating," I breathed sarcastically.

"That's the spirit," Cyrus exclaimed, either not picking up on the sarcasm or ignoring it.

The video screen switched to a frontal view of Queen Marisara. She looked directly into it, as if seeing me across the distance. She spoke, and I expected her voice would sound as smooth as ice. Instead, it sounded harsh, like a valkyrie who had smoked three packs a day for decades. And she randomly had a German accent. Or was that Austrian? Was there a difference?

"Come. Dare to enter my domain and meet the same fate!"

"She's always been so enthusiastic about meeting new people," Cyrus commented.

"How can we possibly defeat her?"

"The perfect question, Lucas. You love to dive right to the heart of the matter. You've got nearly a month to figure that out."

For a moment, all I could do was stare, mind whirling. The excitement I'd felt at getting spells and magic had suppressed some of my initial panic, but now pure dread colored every thought.

This was really happening. I was stuck on an alien death battle planet with my brother and friends, and not only were our lives on the line, but the fate of the entire planet rested on us. We had to not only survive, but somehow grow strong enough to defeat that terrifying nymph queen.

With an effort, I forced my fears aside. Cyrus had shown us the challenge and was giving us the tools to succeed. It wouldn't be called a game if there was no way to win. I planned to win, and it was obvious I needed to kill a lot of monsters to do that.

The video screen disappeared and Cyrus said, "Speaking of advancement, there's your next opponent. Talk about great timing."

Across the glade, another small monster was shooting out of the trees toward me.

"Aww," I breathed, relaxing and lowering my fighting stick.

It looked like a cute ball of fluff, like all the adorableness of 100 kittens had been crammed into one cuddly little package. I felt an overwhelming urge to rush to meet the creature and hug it.

Then my Identify utility spell activated. Thankfully Eva read the text since I couldn't focus on the scrolling words.

Nightmare Gorger. Level 3. Uncommon. The Nightmare Gorger uses illusions to lure in its prey and rip out their throats. Think of it like the softest, cuddliest kitten, except it's also an ax murdering serial killer that can consume your entire body in less than 5 seconds.

The words startled me out of my hazy stupor and I blinked a few times. Horror and anger in equal measures coursed through me and I scowled at the little monster. Tricking people with illusions was such a cheat.

Congratulations. Your mental resistance has increased to 5%.

I waved away the message to focus on the fast-approaching Nightmare Gorger, but the world seemed to freeze as a new male voice spoke. It sounded almost robotic compared to Cyrus and Eva as it filled the valley.

Admin message. The initial calibration period is complete and recommended adjustments accepted. As of the end of this message, all monster levels will be adjusted upward. Good luck.

The world resumed normal speed and the Nightmare Gorger suddenly swelled to the size of a really fluffy boulder as tall as my waist. The mental pressure increased, giving me a sudden headache, but I focused on the Identify text hanging over the monster's head.

"Level 15!" I exclaimed.

"Oh, look at that!" Cyrus chortled. "You got the monster with the highest level upgrade. How exciting."

Muttering a string of curses, I dove aside, barely avoiding the boulder-sized monster. It hurtled past, but instantly started banking around. Luckily it didn't seem to be able to turn too fast, or I'd already be dead.

I sprinted away into the trees. As I ran, I shouted, "Why would you upgrade monster levels?"

"We need to fine-tune the difficulty of the game to make it exciting. Most monsters only upgraded a couple levels, but you won the lottery for the biggest change. What a chance to prove yourself."

"Not helping."

Drawing deep from my endurance, I ran flat out. I tried to focus on my recent resolve to kill a lot of monsters instead of the terror chilling my spine. This was just the first of many challenges. I could do this.

That didn't mean I had to be dumb about it. Huge trees flashed past on either side. Looking for an advantage, I tried to find one I could quickly climb, but saw nothing. They were either way too small to support my weight, or so huge the lowest branches were too high overhead. Maybe I should have picked the Bio Morph utility spell after all.

Behind me, the buffed up Nightmare Gorger gave chase. It moved fast but made very little noise as its soft fur flowed over twigs and leaves without breaking them.

I glanced back every couple seconds, judging its speed and watching the trees around me. It rolled like a fluffy death ball of doom, and it was faster than me. If I stared too long, another wave of temptation to slow and hug it started tugging at my mind.

I did slow, but only to time my dodge when it barreled in to hit me. I jumped aside, swerving between a tree and a thick, spiny bush. In the process, I stepped on a spiky leaf and pain lanced up my left foot. That really hurt, but I could not afford to slow.

As I hoped, the Nightmare Gorger couldn't turn fast enough. I hoped it would swerve around the bush, but it blasted right through it with a ripping sound like a buzz saw. Just a split second, and the spiny bush disintegrated in a spray of wood chips.

I gulped as the air filled with the pleasant scent of fresh-cut lumber. Level 15 was a far cry from the basic monsters I'd been facing before. This thing could rip me to bloody chunks in half a second.

Fear gave me extra speed, and I poured it all on, dodging between trees and changing direction often. The forest was blessedly flat in that area, with few tripping hazards. I still kept a bit of my attention on the ground to avoid stepping on anything else sharp. If I stumbled, I was dead.

The trees were spaced pretty far out, and I didn't spot anything I could use to turn the tide against it. The monster couldn't match my agility, but it seemed willing to chase me all day until my stamina ran out.

If I slowed, it would eat me for dinner. I had no idea where I was going, or even where my little starting glade was. All my twists and turns had left me totally lost. Not that it mattered. I needed a way to escape.

Abruptly, I burst into a new clearing. The ground turned rockier, and a rocky hill rose right in front of me. It was over 50 feet high and twice that thick. The sides were sheer and too high for me to quickly climb, but a cave mouth yawed open in the middle of the hill. Identify activated.

Forest Glade dungeon.

Nothing else.

The Nightmare Gorger exploded out of the forest behind me, closing fast. I dodged to the side, and it shot past, skidding on the loose rocks as it tried to turn for another pass. Its body glowed suddenly and my headache returned.

I groaned, grabbing at my skull as I fought the renewed illusion magic. I glanced around again and went with the only idea I could come up with.

That meant sprinting toward the dungeon. Stopping just a couple feet in front of it, I turned to face the Nightmare Gorger. It had completed its turn and was speeding straight at me.

I'd wait till the last possible second and dive aside. With any luck, the monster would plunge into the dungeon and get stuck in there. If I had a luck stat and it was even higher than I hoped, it would crash into a monster in the dungeon and get into a fight while I escaped.

Heck, I'd even settle for it trying to swerve after me and smashing itself flat against the cliff face.

"Come on!" I shouted, tensed to spring.

Twenty yards. My entire focus narrowed until all I could see was the charging monster as my every muscle tensed to leap.

So I was totally unprepared when a slender, orange tentacle shot out of the dungeon opening and wrapped around my waist.

I barely registered what was happening before it yanked so hard, it felt like I was getting teleported again. It hauled me off my feet, and I soared backward right into the dungeon, screaming all the way.

The Nightmare Gorger plunged in right behind me.

Chapter Eleven

Sporks and Fuzzy Pants

As darkness swallowed me, I activated my defensive aura, Energy Ward. The initial dip in my mana was instantly followed by a much larger dip as 10 additional points drained away.

This time, I was the projectile deflected. It felt like a smooth wall materialized against my side, set at an angle to my path. I slid along it, deflecting to the right.

Massive jaws clamped shut with a snap like a thunderclap so close beside my left arm that spittle sprayed across my face.

I swept past, catching a glimpse of an enormous shaggy creature with impossibly huge jaws. Then the tentacle jerked tight and I realized it was connected to the center of the monster's back, right between its shoulders.

With a grunt, my forward momentum halted and the tentacle started hauling me back the other way. Miraculously, I still had my fighting stick in my hand, and I slammed it against the tentacle.

It bounced off. Identify kicked in.

Squid Bear, level 10. Elite. Yes, you read that right. This bizarre monster is like bigfoot cosplaying as Ursula from the Little Mermaid.

Eva's voice seemed annoyed. That was new. The Squid Bear started to turn toward me, its maw yawning open again like a second cave mouth. If I hadn't reacted so fast with Energy Ward, it would have swallowed me and crushed out my life with its first bite.

In one second, it would eat me anyway.

That's when the Nightmare Gorger hurtled into the cave and plowed right into the Squid Bear's open maw. It disappeared inside and the sound of a buzz saw activated again. This time it didn't stop.

The Squid Bear stiffened as blood fountained out its gaping mouth, its eyes widening in surprise. It hadn't expected to eat a hungrier predator. The weird monster staggered and the tentacle relaxed around my waist.

I slammed my stick against it again, and this time managed to slip free. I fell to the stone floor and scrambled back as the Squid Bear gurgled in pain and slammed its shoulder against the stone wall. We were in a tunnel made of rough stone, about a dozen feet in diameter. There wasn't much room for me to retreat with the huge monster filling so much of the space.

Its heavy, musky scent clogged the dim air. It smelled like a petting zoo left to rot, only 10 times stronger. The monster looked a lot like a grizzly, other than the nightmare tentacle sticking out of its back and the fact that its jaw was bigger than its torso.

With a spray of blood and bone like a fire hose, the Nightmare Gorger erupted from the Squid Bear's side. It shot just past, splattering me with gore.

It would have ripped me apart before I could react, but again Energy Ward deflected it just enough, at the cost of another chunk of my mana. The gore-splattered, fuzzy monster slammed straight into the stone wall inches from my side.

Maybe it tried to activate its chomp ability and failed, or maybe it reacted too late because it smashed into the wall with a rubbery splat like a big dodgeball and bounced off.

The monster's fluffy hide was drenched in blood, reducing its size by half. The bloody fur compressed around a lumpy round body that seemed to be entirely wrapped in short, serrated teeth.

It careened back toward the Squid Bear, slowing until it stopped for a second in the center of the tunnel about 3 feet away from me. It shook itself like the world's nastiest dog, as if needing a moment to recover from the impact.

I tossed my fighting stick into my inventory, replacing it with my heavier club. Then I stepped forward and swung with all my strength.

The club smacked with a wet thunk into the bloody hide, spraying more gore and connecting with the endless rows of teeth. I feared it would simply eat my club like it had the trees and half the squid bear, but I caught it still dazed.

The impact sent the fluffy death ball bouncing all the way to the Squid Bear. The huge monster looked terrible, but it wasn't dead yet.

It swiped one huge, clawed paw and sent the Nightmare Gorger blasting back toward me in a spray of orange blood. Those claws had ripped huge gashes almost halfway through the smaller monster.

I side-stepped and the Gorger slammed into the wall a second time. This time it didn't bounce as far. I lined up my shot and did my best Babe Ruth impression, hitting it again with all my strength.

This time I caught its wounded side and I clearly heard something snap inside the disgusting creature as my club sank deep. The Gorger made a retching sound as it tumbled away again, spraying more orange blood.

The Squid Bear rose all the way to the ceiling on its hind legs, then came down like a living avalanche right on the Nightmare Gorger, stomping it flat. Orange gore sprayed everywhere.

Congratulations Lucas! You have defeated a level 15 Nightmare Gorger.

More messages followed, but I waved them away, my focus locked on the Squid Bear. I was surprised I got even a partial credit for the kill. Sure, I'd helped, but the bear had done more of the work.

I wasn't about to complain. Maybe if I scored a hit on the bear, I'd get some experience for that too, assuming it died from the massive wounds the Nightmare Gorger had inflicted on it.

The huge monster staggered, blood still gushing from the mouth and that gaping, nasty wound in its side. It took one shuffling step closer, its tentacle rising like a scorpion stinger over its back.

I was tempted to run, but Energy Ward hadn't expired yet. I wished I had a bladed weapon, or better, a shotgun with a slug. There had to be a way to hurt it.

The huge monster took one more step, then its front legs gave out and it crashed to the stone floor so hard the cave shook like an earthquake.

That was my chance. I switched back to my fighting stick and threw myself at the Squid Bear.

Its big, strangely blue eyes had closed, but they snapped back open as I charged. The tentacle shot toward me, but I trusted my aura to deflect it and ran straight in.

The tentacle indeed deflected just past my head as I jumped. The bear tried to react, its maw opening a few inches, but it lacked the strength.

I landed on its long muzzle, my weight slamming its jaws closed with an audible crack. Using all the momentum of my jump, I thrust my stick like a saber into one of its huge, blue eyes. The stick plunged through with barely any resistance. The eye exploded with a spray of hot liquid across my face, and my stick sank two thirds of its length into the Squid Bear's head.

The monster roared, spraying blood everywhere, and convulsed so hard it sent me flying. My aura helped deflect me so I only hit the wall at a glancing angle. I even twisted in mid-air and managed to land on my feet.

My stick was still stuck in the Squid Bear's skull. The monster continued thrashing around, its tentacle snapping out randomly in every direction as it shook itself and clawed gouges in the stone.

The coppery scent of blood hung so thick in the air it felt like I was breathing liquid. It was mixed with a strangely seafood odor. My stomach roiled and I gagged. I instinctively covered my face with my arm, but that just rubbed more blood over my face. Retching, I stumbled back, pressing myself to the rough stone wall to avoid the wild thrashing of the giant bear.

There was nothing else I could do. I mean, maybe I could take out my tongs and try to pry off a tooth, but what would that accomplish?

Thankfully, I didn't have to try impersonating a dentist. The Squid Bear's roars faded to wet, gurgling grunts and it fell back to the floor, its tentacle arm drooping over its head.

Congratulations, Lucas! You have defeated a level 10 elite Squid Bear. Bonus experience gained for defeating a higher-level enemy. You have reached level 7. Base stat points allocated.

"Level 7?" I opened my menus, and the other messages I'd missed scrolled into view.

Congratulations, Lucas! You have defeated a level 15 uncommon Nightmare Gorger. Bonus experience gained for defeating an enemy more than 10 levels higher than your own. Loot will be upgraded for every enemy you defeat with at least a 10-level disparity.

Congratulations, Lucas! You have reached level 5. Base stat points allocated.

That explained it, and I grinned and spat monster blood. Getting two entire levels with each of those monster kills was way more than I'd expected, even though that ordeal had been disgusting and terrifying. It could have easily ended with my death, but somehow I'd pulled off a surprise victory that won me a ton of experience.

I raised a hand in victory and whispered, "Yay."

I didn't dare shout in case there were more monsters in there. Both of the dead monsters had been ridiculously powerful. There was no way I should have survived a fight with either of them, let alone both, so the extra experience gains made sense. I suspected I would need more and more experience for each subsequent level. Still, getting to level 7 so fast had to be good.

Actually, as I thought about it, I realized it was way more than good. I hadn't noticed the new stats take effect while in the middle of a fight for my life, but now I realized just how strong I felt. It was like nothing I'd ever experienced.

My muscles quivered with strength, I felt light on my feet, and somehow I sensed I was far more durable than before. I checked my stats again, and as I studied them, I whistled softly in shock.

I'd started with pretty good base stats. I was young and in excellent shape. Now I'd gotten 6 entire levels, and each came with 4 new stat points. That was a total of 24 stat points, and they'd boosted my base stats until even Wisdom, my lowest stat, had hit 10.

I was stronger than the strongest weight lifter, with dexterity 40% more than the best human. I had climbed into reaches of physical performance reserved for super heroes. Weak super heroes maybe, but still better than anything I could have accomplished on Earth. I wasn't sure I grasped fully what the new stats meant yet, but I was loving it.

The world we'd gotten dumped into was insane and dangerous, and I'd already nearly died several times, but Cyrus was showering me with power ups that would make it harder and harder for monsters to kill me. I only hoped Tomas and Jane and the others were getting as many stats.

Even better, a couple of my secondary stats were growing even faster. My Agility had hit 20. That was insane! It couldn't be just a percentage of Dexterity. Maybe a couple different base stats affected it. I wasn't about to complain. That much agility meant I should be able to out-tumble the best gymnast in the world and make it look easy. I couldn't wait to test my new limits.

It seemed miraculous I'd survived those fights with barely a scratch. My Energy Ward spell had saved my life multiple times in seconds. Without it, I'd be dead and out of the game already.

"Hey, Cyrus, that Nightmare Gorger was listed as uncommon, and the Squid Bear as elite. Are those important?"

"Yes. Glad you noticed. Most monsters you face will be common level, especially down here on stage 1. Uncommon monsters are generally more powerful, with stronger abilities. Elites are far deadlier, even if their levels might not be as high as an uncommon."

So the 4 levels gained made even more sense. I hoped I didn't run into any more elites.

"There are other types of monsters too. Watch for that description to help you figure it out."

"Thanks."

I glanced at the Remaining Earth Contestants listing and grimaced. It had dropped by nearly another hundred people, now sitting at 857. My heart ached to think of so many people getting caught by surprise by the sudden monster evolutions. Did Cyrus want to kill us all off before we even cleared the first stage?

This death rate was not sustainable. We'd only been in the game what? An hour? And already we'd lost 15% of our entire starting population?

Tomas, Jane, Edmund, and Patrick would be fine. They were clever and resourceful. They wouldn't lock up and let a weak monster eat their hearts. Once I found them, we could help each other survive. Speaking of increasing my chances of survival, I activated my Harvest spell, focusing on the Squid Bear.

You have failed to Harvest a spell from the Squid Bear. You still have two successful uses of Harvest remaining.

I cursed under my breath. I was supposed to get a better chance of harvesting something when the monster was higher level. That should have worked. Was it harder to Harvest from elites?

You have failed to Harvest a spell from the Nightmare Gorger. You still have two successful uses of Harvest remaining.

"What? Is this spell rigged, or something?"

"Rotten luck, Lucas," Cyrus said, although he didn't sound sad at all. "Usually that would have worked, especially on monsters with such a level disparity, but neither of those beasts were very compatible. You'll have better luck in the future."

"If I survive to try again."

My dark mood faded when Eva asked the next question.

Do you wish to loot Squid Bear and Nightmare Gorger?

"Absolutely." I accepted the prompts with anticipation. The messages had said loot would be upgraded, and I needed some good stuff. The two monsters dissolved into stinky mist and I retrieved my fighting stick. Then I checked my inventory and laughed aloud.

"That's what I'm talking about!"

"Excellent movie quote," Cyrus approved.

"Yeah, Men in Black was awesome. I bet you liked all the alien references."

"Another astute observation, but that quote was actually first popularized by Mike Meyers in Wayne's World."

"Wait, what? Really?"

Cyrus chuckled. "Indeed."

"Wow. Learn something new every day."

"Ralph Waldo Emerson."

"I'll take your word for that."

"I find it endlessly fascinating that you humans use so many common idioms and phrases, yet you so rarely know their origins."

I shrugged, focusing on my new loot. I had gotten a bunch of mana crystals, increasing my total to 87. I received my first standard quality healing potion that healed up to 25% of my health points. That was a relief.

I also got a spork, of all things. When I pulled it out, it looked just like a stainless steel spork you might find boy scouts using at summer camp. Speaking of camping, I also received a common grade camping gear set, including a blanket, pillow, and randomly, an air mattress identical to one I could get at any Walmart.

The other gear got a lot more interesting. I eagerly extracted my new uncommon grade bear-hide moccasins. They were made of soft, supple leather. I only had a single sock with a hole in, so I slipped them on barefoot and sighed. They fit like a glove and immediately soothed my sore feet.

With the moccasins came a rare bear pelt. I'm sure I could find uses for that. It was huge. Then I laughed when I noticed the next item.

Uncommon Fuzzy shorts of Friendship. These luxuriously comfortable shorts may not offer any armor protection, but their stylish cut and plush feel will soothe your aching muscles. Imbued with a subtle enchantment to encourage other humans to feel 5% friendlier.

Still laughing, I pulled them out of my inventory. They really were fuzzy and super soft, thanks to the Nightmare Gorger. That nasty monster really had been soft, at least on the outside. The shorts fit perfectly. Didn't even need a belt. I had never worn shaggy shorts before, but they did feel good.

As I reviewed the last item, I spotted another sort option to show only recent additions. That would prove helpful.

Laundry Day potions, times 2. Each single-use potion will unleash a cloud of aggressive cleanliness to wash you and your clothes to sparkling perfection while adding a scent-reducing buff.

Nice. I was already grimy, and I'd only been awake for a couple hours. I was tempted to try one of the potions immediately, but I suspected I'd get even dirtier before the day was done. I only had 2. Better to save one for just before I climbed into bed, assuming I found a safe hiding spot for the night.

I glanced toward the exit, but paused. I hadn't planned to explore the dungeon, but what if I did? It would probably be safer to go find my teammates and then clear out the dungeon together.

Still, I'd gained 4 levels in a matter of minutes. If I could survive just a couple more monsters, I could hit level 10 and permanent my first spell. I had to make a lot of progress, but it was already clear that progress only came with danger. So, should I risk a bit of exploring?

It wouldn't hurt to creep down a little farther, would it? If the monsters looked too tough, I could always retreat. With my new moccasins and my superhuman agility, I bet I could sneak really well.

After considering it for another moment, I made my choice and turned my back on the exit. Tightening my grip on my fighting stick, I crept deeper into the dungeon.

Chapter Twelve
A Wight in the Hand

I expected a dungeon to be a complex labyrinth of creepy tunnels I could get lost in for days. Maybe some were, but the entrance tunnel of Forest Glade Dungeon was not.

I crept slowly forward, senses alert, but I didn't see anything. The tunnel meandered a bit as it steadily descended deeper into the ground. Luckily I didn't need to use one my torches since there were weird little glowing stalactites hanging from the ceiling.

Most were barely longer than a pencil, but they filled the tunnel with a soft, blue glow that made it easy to navigate. My perception was now 18, so I could see better in the dim light than any human ever had. It was fun, and it boosted my confidence.

Maybe a bit too much.

The first hint of danger I got was a searing cold pain plunging into my back.

I shrieked more like a little girl than I'd ever admit and stumbled forward, gasping as I spun to see what had stabbed me. A vague shape had appeared in the air behind me. It looked like a dingy, gray ghost. The coward had shoved one ethereal hand into my back. I felt my back, but the skin wasn't broken. There was no blood.

Instead, a cold chill was spreading through me from the point of impact. It sapped my strength, and when I scanned my stat levels, my eyes widened in horror.

I had lost nearly 10% of my health and nearly 20% of my mana. That thing packed a wicked punch. Identify triggered.

Essence Wight. Ethereal. Level 9. They're kind of like that friend who keeps you shopping until they exhaust your will to live. With these freaks, the danger is real. Ethereal beings are immune to physical damage.

That sucked my good humor more than it sucked my mana. I didn't have anything that could deliver non-physical damage, and Energy Ward did not protect me from ghosts.

"Ghosts? Really?" My earlier confidence cracked. What was I thinking? I wasn't a super hero. Sure, I had a few skills, but I wasn't Van Helsing.

I took a step back, but shook off my fear. If I doubted myself, I'd die fast. I might not be a hero, but I wasn't about to surrender and let some life-sucking ghost punch my ticket.

First step to survive was to get the hell out of there. I crouched to sprint around the wight. I'd been an idiot to explore deeper. I needed to escape.

The wight moaned like a B-horror movie ghost. Lame.

Not lame when a lot of other moans answered.

I spun back to look farther down the tunnel. I had almost reached the end where it widened into a large cavern. I had hoped to creep to the edge to take a look. Now wights were rising from the floor all through the cavern.

Not good.

I spun back to make a run for it, but my heart sank when I saw 2 more wights rising out of the floor to flank the first one. The 3 of them filled the tunnel. I could never slip by.

Maybe I could simply run through them? I'd take a hit, but they didn't have any physical form. Couldn't I just plow through and keep running back into the sunlight?

I hesitated, and that sealed my fate.

More wights joined the 3, ghosting out of the walls to either side. They advanced, floating slowly toward me, ghostly hands rising to grasp at my torso.

Nope. No way I could escape that way now. I backed up, mind racing. I had high intelligence, and needed to use it. Maybe I could lure them into the cavern, then sprint around them and escape? They didn't look that fast.

So I trotted ahead to draw them in while looking for another exit. The dungeon was just starting. There had to be other routes to take, even if it meant going deeper.

Nope. The cavern stretched nearly 20 yards across and the craggy ceiling rose over 10 yards. The curving walls were covered in protruding rocks and larger glowing stalactites. More importantly, no other exits.

The stone floor was mostly flat, with a few random rocks and cracks. In the center of the room stood some kind of pedestal thing. It was wide, but squat, not tall enough to hide on, so I ignored it.

No easy escape. Back to luring them away from the one exit. I used to play a lot of MMO computer games. One of the most common tactics was to keep moving and kite monsters with spells or arrows.

If only I had some offensive spells or arrows. Well, arrows might not help much. I had tried archery a total of 2 times in my life and proved a bow was no good in my hands other than as a rather weak, bent stick.

The icy chill in my torso had already started to fade, so I resisted the urge to use a healing potion or my skin thaw salve. I might need those a lot more before I was done.

More wights were appearing every second. There had to be nearly 20 of the gray, ghostly shades. I couldn't seem to find enough breath as I scanned wildly around. The wights weren't closing in from all sides, but shifting along the outer edges of the cavern.

I frowned as I continued deeper into the cavern. Wights followed, but they were slow. If they just came at me, I could dodge around and get free.

Then I realized what the other wights were doing, and my heart sank into my new moccasins. They were moving to help cut off my only exit.

Were they sentient enough to understand I was a lot faster? If they gave me any opening, I'd be gone in a flash, but more and more wights filled the space just outside the tunnel exit. I might have been able to rush through one, or even three, but not half a dozen. They'd drain me dry.

The mental image made me shiver and I cursed myself again for being an epic fool. I'd gotten myself trapped. I scanned my inventory for anything that might help, but got no ideas.

With the exit well guarded, wights spread out to come at me from the front and sides, driving me slowly but inexorably back. I checked my inventory again and grabbed a torch. With a quick acceptance of a mental prompt, it ignited.

It burned pretty bright, and the warm, golden light bolstered my confidence. Gritting my teeth against my fear, I rushed straight toward the closest wight between me and the exit.

With a shout, I waved the torch in the wight's face. The creature actually retreated a bit.

"Yes!"

I rushed past it, swiping the torch through its torso. For a second its shape seemed to shimmer and I wanted to shout with new hope. Then it reformed and drifted after me.

Maybe I'd gotten a bit too excited. Still, if they all reacted the same way, I could still get through. I rushed the second wight and tried the experiment again. It did hesitate, but did not retreat. Unfortunately, other creatures were moving in from both sides. With the one following behind, the noose was tightening.

Cursing with frustration and terror, I spun and dashed between two wights, again heading back toward the middle of the cavern. Back to trying to kite them.

The two wights both stretched out their hands to grasp at me. Drawing deep from my high agility stat, I dove between them, making an amazing acrobatic flip in the air. It must have looked fantastic, but it wasn't quite fast enough.

One of the wights accelerated just a bit, more than I'd seen any of them do so far. One grasping hand brushed against my ankle as I tumbled past.

Searing cold gripped my leg, and I stumbled as I landed. I managed to avoid falling and limped away. More of the wights were closing the half-circle hemming me in.

Panting with fear, I shouted and swung my torch, trying to keep them back. I triggered the minor healing potion in my hotlist and the healing warmth helped ease my terror.

I could still do this.

My leg regained its strength and I accelerated to a sprint, dodging and diving between the wights, trying to pull them all to one side of the cavern. It didn't seem to work. They pursued, but in a random-seeming crowd that closed off one potential route after another.

I was drawing closer to the podium thing in the center of the room. Maybe I'd have to make my stand there after all. As I adjusted course to head straight for it, all of the wights emitted an angry-sounding moan and some of the ones trying to close the trap from the sides sped up.

They were trying to block me from reaching the podium. Maybe there was a reason for it. I sped up too. Now that I looked at it closer, it looked more like some kind of stone altar.

Three more wights rose out of the floor right in front of the altar, like a last line of defense. Now I really wanted to study that thing, but couldn't reach it. I had to dodge aside, then burst into a sprint to dodge through the ranks of the quickly closing wights.

That bought me a bit of time, but forced me farther and farther from the altar. How smart were these things? All the monsters I'd faced so far had been stupid, but these things were working together.

A growing part of me wanted to panic, but that would just get me killed. I needed a plan, and that altar might give me an edge, if I could get to it. I sprinted toward the back wall, breaking away from the wights to win a bit of breathing room. I slowed near the wall and forced myself to take a deep breath and search for a way out.

"Think, Lucas," I muttered to myself as my mind raced.

Most of the wights were concentrated around the altar, with a second group too large to run through still guarding the exit. The mob near the center started to spread out to join the hunt.

Studying the wights, my Identify triggered again. I got no words. More a feeling, a sense of energy. It must be the reality filter upgrade. It had said something about perceiving reality.

Now I sensed something deeper about the wights. There was some kind of connection between each of them and the altar. Had they driven me from it because it fueled their power? If I could reach it, could I force them to sleep or drive them away?

Unlikely, but what better choice did I have? I needed to move, but just randomly running around was not helping. I scanned the loose mob of wights gliding toward me. All but one of the sentries had left the altar, but I couldn't see a path through.

If I ran along the outer edge of the cavern, I feared they would just shift along with me. I was faster, but they could cut the corner and still block me. I needed another way.

I scanned the wall in both directions and one of the larger rocky protrusions to my left caught my attention. It was low enough I could jump to it. Could I hide up there and wait them out?

Probably not. They moved through the floor and walls freely. I bet they'd just float up and consume me. Frowning, I started to look away, but spotted a second outcropping a little higher on the wall. Scanning upward, I spotted more.

And got a crazy idea.

I didn't have time to talk myself out of it. If I didn't move, I was dead. So I sprinted toward that first outcropping. My breath came faster, but with anticipation instead of fear for the first time since I'd entered the cavern.

I tossed my torch into my inventory to free my hands, then jumped. I never played basketball because my vertical leap used to be counted in millimeters.

Not any more.

I vaulted a full 10 feet, and it felt amazing. I reached the outcropping and kicked off again, vaulting higher to the second one.

In quick succession, I ran up the side of the wall, using the bulges in the rock face like steps, gaining a sense of the range of my new physical abilities in the process. It was astonishing, and a little spike of wonder helped push back the panic a bit more.

Little glowing stalactites flashed past my face and shoulders, missing by inches as I slowly circled the outer edge of the cavern. Soon the walls curved inward, becoming the roof, and the pitch grew too steep even for my enhanced agility, so I switched from running to swinging.

I felt strong enough to dig my fingers into wood, so gripping rough stone and flinging myself higher proved easier than I'd feared. Enough handholds stuck from the ceiling that I found easy purchase and soon neared the center.

Beneath me, the wights had paused, moaning in what I assumed was annoyance as they slowly turned, following my path with their hazy gazes. My hope soared. Their hesitation might give me a chance.

The altar sat in the exact center of the cavern. Nearly 30 feet above it, a large stalactite extended 4 feet, pointing down toward the altar. With a final mighty heave, I flung myself across the last 5 feet of open space and caught the end of the stalactite.

It broke off.

I had hoped to hang from it for a second to orient myself properly, but now I fell, my body still twisted out of position from that last swing. I cursed as I tried to twist back around.

The wights finally realized my destination and an angry moan filled the cavern as they raised ghostly hands and all rushed toward the center. Even the ones guarding the exit abandoned their post and raced in.

They moved faster than I'd expected. I'd get bare seconds to figure out the altar before they arrived in a flood I'd never escape again.

The single wight by the altar hovered around it expectantly. I hurled the broken end of the stalactite that I was still holding down at it. The stone passed right through the wight and shattered against the floor.

So I pulled both of my torches from my inventory, one after the other, activating each one and flinging it down. They rained down, streaming fire, right onto the wight's head.

That did drive it back, but not as far as I had hoped. Still, I'd take any extra second the torches could buy me.

I wasn't quite able to turn enough in midair to land on both feet. I got one under me, but struck the flat top of the altar with my other knee so hard a sharp stab of pain made me gasp. I might have just broken something.

The brutal impact also cracked the top of the altar. Bright blue light blazed up through the crack. The altar was hollow. As soon as I spotted the light, Identify kicked in again.

Wight spawning generator. Rare. Created by a bitter necromancer suffering an existential crisis.

My hope soared as I rolled off the altar. My right leg nearly buckled when I put weight on it, but I caught myself against the altar. Leaning over it, I noticed that dim light glowed along the edges. That suggested the top came off.

I scanned the top and sides of the altar, desperately searching for a latch. The wights were approaching like a cloud of death encircling me on every side. The flickering light of my torches illuminated them all in a weird, pulsing orange light that made them look even more ominous.

The wight guard closest to me dove over the torches in a slow-motion ghostly tackle.

I scrambled around the altar, using it as a temporary barrier. As I did so, I noticed runes and carvings all along the sides. It was far more intricately finished than I'd expected.

As my hand passed over one rune, I felt a soft tingle, like a pulse of energy. On instinct, I punched a finger into that rune. With a soft click, the top of the altar unlocked and more light seeped through. I flung the stone off, sliding it along concealed tracks.

The sentry wight had started to dive over the altar again, but veered off as a beam of blinding blue light erupted out of the hollow center of the altar. It lit the cavern in blue incandescence, and all the onrushing wights moaned again.

They did not slow, though, and the closest wight still managed to swipe one hand through my calf as it dove around the light. I gritted my teeth against a flash of pain and searing cold, but didn't let that break my focus.

The closing ring of wights were swooping in from all sides like a tide of death. I was out of time, but still leaned over the alter to see if I could find a way to save myself. I could not die this way.

The light came from an enormous crystal at least a foot tall and nearly as wide. The faceted stone came to a point at the top and sat in some kind of metal housing in the center of the altar.

I didn't see a big red "Turn off the enchantment" button, unfortunately. So I grabbed the crystal. If I could haul it free, I could throw it. Maybe that would distract the wights long enough to make a run for it.

The nearest ring of wights all dove at me in unison.

I screamed in fear and reflexively activated Energy Ward as I yanked on the crystal again. It didn't budge, but I got an unexpected message.

You have discovered the power source of the Essence Wight enchantment. You may attempt to wrest control over the energy crystal on a successful Intelligence check. Would you like to try?

"Yes!" I screamed just as 4 wights dove headfirst into my torso from every side.

I didn't get the miracle I'd hoped for. Instead, deathly cold speared into me like steel blades frozen to absolute zero. I tried to scream, but my entire body seized up, every muscle locking in place. Pain and cold and withering weakness tore through me.

My heartbeat slowed as icy death gripped it on every side. My vision darkened, and my thoughts turned sluggish. I couldn't move, couldn't think. I tried triggering a healing potion from my hotlist, but only then realized I had forgotten to move another one into position. Idiot.

As if from a great distance, I felt more wights dive into me. With each one, the agony intensified and the cold deepened until I felt like I was submerged in the center of an iceberg. An iceberg that burned like living fire.

I wanted to scream and convulse from the pain, but still couldn't move. I couldn't even will myself to pass out and surrender to death.

More and more wights dove in, joining the death party. I couldn't feel my body any more, but I still felt the pain and the deathly cold that drove into my mind.

Eva's voice spoke from miles away, but I could not understand her words. With the last of my will, I whispered, "Yes."

Not that it mattered any more. The wights were consuming my health, my mana, my life, my entire being.

Would I become one of them?

That was the last thought I had before blackness settled heavy over my mind. At least death would feel warm.

Chapter Thirteen

Soul Harvest Energy Vortex of Doom

A lightning bolt blasting through my heart shattered the welcome, warm bliss of darkness. Frigid consciousness crashed back in and I convulsed. Torrents of energy were pouring into me, like a beam of pure fire piercing the icy cold of the wights.

They screamed inside of my body. They were all there. Every last one had dived in to feast on my soul. They had sucked me almost totally dry, but now they convulsed with me. The fires that thawed my body and set my heart racing tore them asunder.

I gasped in a breath that tasted like burned hair, but didn't care. I was breathing again!

My eyes started working. I found that I was lying across the altar, the point at the top of the huge crystal piercing just a hair's breadth into my chest. That connection opened a conduit for the crystal to pump all its energy into me. The tide of power felt like living lightning tearing through my insides.

With it came awareness too. I felt how the crystal had fueled and empowered the wights.

Not any more.

My intelligence check must have worked because I now controlled the crystal and it was instead empowering me. The wights were still connected to it, but their energy was being sucked away, back into the crystal, then cycled back into me.

At the same time, they were still trying to drain me dry. All of us made a ghastly closed circuit, feeding on each other. Life and mana drained from me into the wights, then got sucked from the wights into the crystal, then pushed from the crystal back into me.

I continued to convulse under the onslaught. I had no control over my muscles as energy roared between us. I wanted to scream from lingering pain, laugh with pure joy from the life-giving energy, and cackle with mad laughter at the insane situation.

Would we end up stuck like that forever in an endless cycle of life and death? I would have rather died quickly.

Slowly, the balance of power shifted, though, and I realized the energy transfer wasn't pure. The wights were stealing my life and mana, the very essence of my life.

That energy got sucked into the crystal, but was already twisted by their parasitic intent. The crystal shoved the energy back into me, mostly pure but still slightly tainted. It refilled my mana and health and another new pool, like a roiling toxic dump that fed on anything foreign.

Including wights.

The ghosts slowly weakened under the corrupted version of their own power that filled me to bursting. I cringed at the feeling of that sinister energy bonded to my soul, but did not resist it. It was the only thing allowing me to gain the advantage.

It felt like we hung in that agonizing state of not-quite balance for what felt like hours, but was probably only seconds. Finally, the energy flows hit some kind of tipping point and the wights started shrinking. Their convulsing through my soul intensified and tore at my innards. I screamed again, but then they all disintegrated.

Wights got sucked into the crystal in a writhing torrent of shredded ethereal forms. The crystal darkened to gray, and the energy flowing into me slowed as the crystal seemed to get bogged down processing all the wights.

I regained control of my body and flung myself off. I collapsed to the stone floor, gasping and panting, mind reeling. The solid stone felt reassuring. The air smelled cleaner, and the cavern fell silent, but for a soft thrumming from the crystal.

"Ow," I complained as I climbed to my feet, but it was more a delayed reaction.

I actually felt surprisingly good, and when I checked my stats, I couldn't believe it. My health and mana were topped off. Even more amazing, I had gained 4 entire levels!

"How?" I mumbled, still dazed from my mostly-dead experience.

I scanned my messages and that helped. I had missed quite a few.

Intelligence check successful. You have taken control over the energy crystal. You may drain its energy to refill your pools of health and mana, or to add extra uses to non-permanent spells. Would you like to replenish life and mana?

I whistled softly as I read the story of my near-death experience.

Health and mana restoration initiated.

I leaned against the side of the altar, staring at that message. My blind directive had been interpreted correctly. If Eva had waited for a coherent response, I'd be dead. That was way too close.

Congratulations, Lucas! For surviving the concurrent death strikes of 21 Essence Wights. You have earned a Platinum Houdini loot box.

Congratulations, Lucas! You have created a unique synergy between Energy Ward, Essence Wights, and their power generator crystal, triggering a Soul Harvest Energy Vortex. Loot box upgraded to an epic emerald Einstein loot box.

"So that's what happened," I breathed. I'd triggered Energy Ward out of sheer desperation. It looked like that had been the key that saved me.

Congratulations, Lucas! For consuming 21 Essence Wights through your dominance of the Soul Harvest Energy Vortex, loot box upgraded again to a legendary Diamond Overlord loot box.

Double upgrade! Nearly dying sucked, but living through it was shaping up to be a giant payday. Maybe I really could do this.

Congratulations, Lucas! You have defeated 21 Essence Wights between levels 9 and 11. Bonus experience gained for defeating ethereal enemies. Bonus experience gained for defeating all the Essence Wights at the same time using a unique strategy.

Now 4 levels was starting to sound a bit low. I knew that every level required more and more experience, but that was 21 monsters at the same time, all stronger than me.

"Does experience gained get reduced for defeating more of the same types of monsters?"

Cyrus answered immediately. "Amazing show, Lucas! That one will make it onto the daily highlights reel, I guarantee it!"

"What is that?"

"Something you'll learn about eventually, and yes, you are absolutely correct. Defeating all 21 Essence Wights at the same time earned you some great rewards, especially since they're ethereal beings. They were close to your level, and experience gains do drop as you defeat more of the exact same enemies, but the bonuses were enough to win you all those levels."

"Still, that's 21 monsters."

"What are you complaining about? You survived, they didn't, and you shot right up past the all-important level 10. It's time to celebrate!"

"I suppose." I glanced at the last of my messages. The next one made me gape.

Congratulations, Lucas! You may use the remaining charge of the energy crystal to add uses to any non-permanent spell.

"Oh, yeah," I cried, selecting the option and focusing on Energy Ward.

The crystal had returned to its regular bright blue. Now it faded out entirely. I didn't care.

"Five more uses of Energy Ward!" I laughed.

I'd been using the life-saving spell way too often and had been down to a single remaining use. Losing that spell might have easily cost me my life. Now with 5 additional uses, I felt more confident of my chances. Hopefully I could find my team quickly. Together, we'd be a lot stronger and hopefully safer.

Would you like to loot the Essence Wights?

There was no sign of the fallen wights, but if Eva would still let me loot them, I was happy to let her. "Yes."

I got a bucketload of mana crystals. I now had two grids in my inventory allocated to them. The tier-0 pile showed a total of 52, while I had a new slot labeled "Tier-1 mana crystals". It showed a total of 20.

"So, what's the conversion from tier-0 to tier-1 mana crystals?"

"10 to 1. If you get more than 99, your inventory automatically converts some of them to the next tier up," Cyrus answered. "Tier-1 mana crystals work the same, but use caution if you decide to try absorbing one. That much power flooding your system could make your head explode."

"Thanks for the warning." Blowing up my own head would be a stupid way to kill myself.

I got a bunch of random loot including 6 more torches and 1 uncommon hunting knife, which I was thrilled to see. Not as thrilled as the next item.

Soulrend Short Sword. Weapon. Epic. Deals direct spiritual damage to souls. Chance of catastrophic damage to undead, spiritual beings, or magical constructs. This is an ethereal blade. Does not interact with the physical world.

"This is incredible!" I laughed as I pulled the weapon from my inventory to inspect.

It was just a pommel, actually. The handle was made of a twisting silvery metal that fit my hand as if crafted to it. A slender cross-guard was covered in intricate runes, and it weighed next to nothing. As soon as I focused on it, a ghostly, double-edged blade extended from the pommel. It shimmered just like the Essence Wights.

"So what does it mean that this does only spiritual damage?" I asked as I experimentally swung the weapon. It made no sound as it effortlessly sliced the air. I loved it more every second and hummed some light saber sounds as I swung the glowing blade.

"It means any living being will be cut at a fundamental level," Cyrus explained. "It slices apart the spirit. Those wounds are far more difficult to heal, assuming your enemy survives."

I whistled. Soulrend. Perfect name for a truly epic weapon.

"Be aware that ethereal weapons degrade over time," Cyrus added. "At epic grade, your sword will last longer than most."

"Is there a way to refresh it or repair it?"

"Indeed there is, but only by a qualified blacksmith ghost. Know any annoying blacksmiths?"

Cyrus laughed loudly at his own joke. I chuckled, but the thought of meeting any kind of ghost again made me feel queasy.

"So people could choose crafting classes when we get to that point?"

Cyrus sighed. "They could."

"You sound disappointed." That was weird. We would need support personnel, wouldn't we?

"It's nothing," Cyrus said, his good humor returning. "You have a shiny new sword to play with. That's a marvelous find for so early in the game."

It sure was. I extracted my new hunting knife from my inventory too. It was a single-edged, heavy knife, shaped a lot like a bowie. I practiced a few sword and knife forms to familiarize myself with the balance. They would work beautifully together.

I returned the two weapons to my inventory, feeling like a man starting a brand new life. With better weapons and more charges to my Energy Ward aura, my chances of survival had just quadrupled.

That wasn't even the end of my loot. This dungeon dive was proving more profitable than I'd hoped in my wildest dreams. I got 3 articles of clothing. My smile couldn't get wider.

Uncommon leather jacket. Provides a minor defensive boost against slashing and clawed attacks.

It settled onto my shoulders with a reassuring weight that reminded me of my favorite motorcycle jacket. This one was made of thick but supple black leather with buckles up the front.

My new boots made my smile widen even more. The moccasins had felt like a godsend, so the boots were like a miracle. They rose to mid-calf and included an enhancement to boost my speed and endurance by 10%. It reminded me of my favorite enchanted boots from Diablo II.

Did that mean the game drew loot from my memories? It was an interesting idea. The next loot items came in the form of two scrolls.

Scroll of Smolder's Grips. Summons a pair of uncommon gloves that offer resistance to blunt and piercing damage, plus a 5 point boost to Dexterity when equipped.

When I clicked the prompt to read the scroll, a pair of supple brown leather gloves appeared in the air. I took them and slipped them on. Perfect fit.

"Smolder's Grips?" I asked as I scanned the rest of my new loot. I got 4 more bottles of Laundry Day cleansing potions and a second scroll. It was grayed out and not available for use yet. That was new.

Upgrade scroll of Oberon's Advantage. Will upgrade the utility spell Navigation by 2 tiers, unlocking greater range, better detail, and add-on features like marking waypoints, route planning, and notes.

Magical GPS. Made my next choice of utility spell an easy one.

In answer to my question, Cyrus said, "The name seemed appropriate, given your team."

"What team am I on?"

"Again you try to ruin the surprise. Wouldn't it be a better use of your time to choose your third utility spell and your first permanent spell?"

"Right!"

Before I opened the menus, I turned back to the altar, grasped the huge crystal with both hands, and heaved. This time it easily pulled free of the metal framework. I stumbled back, nearly plopping onto my back side.

You have acquired 1 rare quality energy storage crystal. Depleted.

"Is there a way to charge this up again?" Having an extra battery to boost my health and mana or add charges to my temporary spells would be game-altering.

"Unfortunately, no. Usually you could recharge it using mana crystals, but the energy vortex created between you and the wights corrupted the core of this one."

My heart sank. "There's no way to cleanse it?"

"Not by any means you are likely to encounter, but you have already proven you like to walk a unique path, so who knows?"

I dumped it into my inventory. I'd keep my eyes open for a way to restore it. I then clicked on my loot boxes menu. The diamond Overlord loot box popped into the air in front of me, refracting the dim light into thousands of glittering points. It was beautiful. On Earth, a diamond that big could have bought England.

I willed it open. The diamond flared with dazzling rainbows of light as a fanfare of trumpets blared across the cavern. The diamond outer shell vanished, leaving several items behind, including a bunch of scrolls.

Upgrade scroll. Linguasight utility spell upgrades to add identification of energy signatures to Identify.

Upgrade scroll. Harvest temporary spell upgrades to increase chances of successful harvest by another 20%. Add plus 5 to Magical Resistance.

Upgrade scroll. Energy Ward upgraded to now deflect spiritual attacks.

"Sweet!" I laughed as I read them and savored the pulses of warmth flowing through my mind as the upgrades activated.

The next scroll was actually 3 scrolls bound together in a fancy gold ribbon with a note on the outside that read:

Enjoy this pack of 3 one-time use offensive spells. Includes:

Frostfire Nova. Spell. Elemental. A wave of freezing flames that immobilize while burning anything caught in its path. Mana Cost: Moderate.

Titan Strike. Spell. Pure force. Unleash an invisible wall of force. Adjust the size of the wall up to 5 yards square. Force dispersed evenly throughout the entire wall. Mana cost: Moderate

Corrosive Cloud. Spell. Toxic. Exactly what it sounds like. Mana Cost: Moderate.

Finally, some great offensive spells. They filled in a huge gap in my current skill set. Too bad I only got a single use out of each one. I added them all to my hotlist.

"You're progressing fast, Lucas," Cyrus commented, his tone more thoughtful than normal, which made me uneasy. "I think you're going to draw a lot of attention from important people."

"Is that a good or bad thing?"

"It could go either way. It'll be fun to watch."

That wasn't entirely comforting, but I needed to move on. So I opened my Utility Spells menu and selected Navigation as my third utility spell. I was still very tempted by the other options, but my quest was to find my team. People were dying and time was passing too fast. As soon as the rush of new information soaked into my mind, I read my new scroll and got the upgrade.

Cyrus said, "Excellent choice. Navigation has two main viewing options. Full screen and mini-map."

They worked pretty much like they sounded. The full screen blocked my entire vision, but offered far more detail. I could zoom in and out, and with the upgrade I could add waypoints, mark routes, or add comments. The map only showed areas I had already explored, but as I explored more, it would prove more and more useful.

The mini-map option would shrink to one side of my vision. I could move it around in my HUD, and it would show my current location, with an area of about 50 yards all around me.

I showed up on the center of the map as a golden star. Cyrus explained that hostile monsters or enemies would show up as red dots, teammates as white ones, and other players not on my team as yellow. I could customize colors and icons later, as needed.

"Will the map show other people and my team before I find them?" I asked hopefully. That might save me a ton of time.

"When you get within range of your mini map, it will populate all active dots real-time."

That gave me a pretty large scannable area. That would help me avoid just walking past my team in the forest.

"Do monsters respawn in dungeons?" I asked, tempted to mark the dungeon on my map for some loot farming later.

"Not before you need to climb to Stage 2."

Right. Focus. A ton had happened in the first hours. I had advanced a ton, but still felt like I was falling behind. So with eager anticipation, I opened my Permanent Spells menu.

You have reached level 10 and unlocked one permanent spell slot. You may select any currently available non-permanent spell. Note. Choose carefully. Once a spell is made permanent, it cannot be changed for a different spell.

In addition to my 2 starter spells, now I had 3 new offensive spells to consider. They were tempting, but Energy Ward had already saved my life more than once. It was the obvious choice, although now I had 6 uses remaining.

I only had 2 current uses available for Harvest and it had not worked when I tried it. Still, I saw endless potential in it, especially with the new upgrade I'd just gotten to the success percentage. With Harvest, I could add new and unique spells to my list after defeating every monster. Would it be worth losing that potential flexibility to lock in one powerful offensive spell?

"Cyrus, I never got an option to try Harvest on the wights."

"You could have before you looted them. Your sword draws from the power of the wights, so when you accepted it, you lost the chance to Harvest it as a spell."

"I could have used that information a few minutes ago."

"And yet, look at the rare prizes you received!"

True. I couldn't be happier with my loot. So after another minute spent agonizing over my choices, I finally went with my gut and selected Harvest as my first permanent spell.

Congratulations, Lucas. You have made the unique spell Harvest your first permanent spell.

Hoping I had made the right choice, I picked up my still-burning torches and dumped one back into my inventory. It was about half used. With the other casting warm light around me, I turned to head for the exit. As I did so, I got another of those weird sensations, just like I had with the altar.

Identify had sensed more energy from behind me. I spun, heart racing as my sword dropped into my hand. The ethereal blade stretched out from the pommel and I crouched, ready to fight for my life.

Nothing attacked. The cavern remained empty.

Frowning, I walked a slow circuit around the back side of the cavern. I had not explored it in detail and suddenly I wondered if I was overlooking something important.

"Ah, Lucas, the exit is the other way," Cyrus reminded me.

"In a minute."

I completed half a circuit of the cavern before I sensed something again. The feeling led me to a flat spot in the back wall, hidden behind a craggy fold in the stone. I moved cautiously, looking for monsters or more loot boxes.

Identify tingled again and I noticed a narrow rectangle of air just in front of the wall warping slightly in the light of my torch. The light seemed to get sucked into that warped space.

It was slowly twisting and ripping apart. Through the crack, I caught sight of glowing light and maybe a hint of a wall. Some kind of hidden room?

"I am obliged to recommend you turn and leave that intriguing rent in space behind," Cyrus said in a weird bored monotone.

That made me more curious and I took a step closer.

Chapter Fourteen
Stats Check

This is a stats chapter. These will pop up periodically throughout the book as a way to share Lucas's full stat sheet.

If you're a reader who loves studying the stats, enjoy. If you don't really care about stats, skip to the next chapter. You won't miss out on anything.

Name: Lucas Altan

Level: 11

Life Points: 184

Mana: 57

Base Stats:

Constitution: 16

Intelligence: 17

Strength: 16

Dexterity: 23

Wisdom: 14

Secondary Stats:

Endurance: 14

Agility: 26

Perception: 25

Magical Resistances: 20

Other stats:

Mental Resistance: 5

Permanent Spells:
1   Harvest
–   Mana Consumption: 10
–   70% chance to gain a skill or ability from a defeated enemy.
–   Chance increases if the enemy is higher level.

Utility Spells:
1   Mystic Looter
2   Linguasight
3   Navigation

Temporary Spells:
1   Energy Ward
–   Mana Consumption: 5 to trigger, then variable
–   Invisible defensive aura that extends 1 yard in every direction.
–   Redirects force from incoming physical and spiritual attacks.
–   Uses remaining: 6
2   Frostfire Nova
–   Mana consumption: 20
    –   Elemental. A wave of freezing flames that immobilize while burning anything caught in its path.
–   Uses remaining: 1
3   Titan Strike
–   Mana consumption: 15
–   Pure force. An invisible wall of force up to five yards square.
–   Entire force spread evenly across the conjured area.
–   Uses remaining: 1
4   Corrosive Cloud
–   Mana consumption: 15 to trigger, then variable.
–   A cloud of gas that corrodes metal and flesh on contact.
–   Uses remaining: 1

Abilities:
–   Hand-to-hand martial arts.   Level 4
–   Stick and bladed weapons martial arts.   Level 3

Titles:

Inquisitive Mind

- Plus 10 to Intelligence
- Plus 10% improvement to secondary stats affected by intelligence
- 10% faster learning of new skills and abilities.

Trailblazer

- Plus 30% chance of loot boxes upgrading.
- Improved chances to discover bonus hidden loot boxes.

Chapter Fifteen

I Stand Around in a Janitorial Closet

"You are not authorized to approach the rift any closer," Cyrus warned in a voice that made it sound like he really wanted me to push forward.

"That's the weakest attempt at discouragement I've ever heard."

"Now they can't say I didn't try."

"Who can't? I thought you said you were the administrator of the game."

"I am. That doesn't mean no one is watching."

"Like who?"

"No offense, Lucas, but when you're checking out something that isn't supposed to be there, lingering for a long time and talking about it isn't really a good idea."

"Got it."

So I reached out and touched the glowing slit in reality.

Blinding blue light flashed and my world lurched as if a giant invisible fist punched me in the back. I staggered forward and the cavern disappeared, replaced by a weirdly sci-fi room.

It was only about a dozen feet across, the walls sheathed in softly glowing golden light. The wall in front of me was covered with sleek gauges and blank, green screens.

Instantly, everything melted into the wall. It happened so fast that if I had not been looking straight ahead, I never would have seen anything. In a blink, the wall in front of me looked smooth, blank, and softly glowing like the rest of the room. Little crackling slivers of silver lightning crawled along the ceiling before fading into the seams at the corners.

"What is this place?" I breathed. The air felt charged, as if I was surrounded by huge machines or an electric power station. A faint hum vibrated up through my boots, felt more than heard.

I smiled as I turned a slow circle and spread my arms to better feel the charged air. Breathing deep the slight ozone smell, I sighed. This was more like it. I might have discovered computers only recently, but I'd taken to them like a landlocked otter to water. Now the computer nerd in me was doing a dorky dance inside.

"Beam me up, Scotty," I whispered as dozens of Star Trek references poured through my mind.

"More appropriate than you know," Cyrus chuckled, sounding immensely pleased, and this time he read the announcement that popped in front of my vision instead of Eva.

For not only boldly going where no other baby human has gone before, finding a rift in this construct world's reality, and stepping into it, you receive an emerald Infiltrator loot box.

"Don't you usually let the other voice announce that?"

I almost referred to her as Eva, but Cyrus wouldn't know that name. I was still hoping he'd agree to let me name her voice. I might get another title, or at least a really cool loot box.

Even though the room was blank, it was clearly some kind of high-tech place, and I *liked* that feeling. The multiverse had magic and teleporting. Did they have space ships and laser blasters too? That would be awesome.

Somehow Cyrus filled his voice with a shrug. "Technically, you have momentarily stepped outside of the containment area for human earthlings. No one but me knows you're here."

"Did anyone else know I was back in the cave?"

Again, the suggestion of watchers. The thought of some invisible aliens watching us fighting and dying on this strange world sent shivers up my spine. Were they the people responsible for casting us into this death game?

"No one is watching closely yet, but that will change. Trust me, it's in your best interest that no one else realizes you managed to find a crack in the environment."

"What is this place?"

"Nothing you need to worry about."

"Right," I said, voice dripping with sarcasm. "Ignore the man behind the curtain, eh?"

"Wizard of Oz. Another appropriate reference."

"So . . . What? The forest and mountains and monsters aren't real? Am I in the Matrix?"

Cyrus chuckled. "I actually considered basing the challenge world on that concept. That was such a good movie, and Earth copyright doesn't extend out here."

I paced around the little room, not seeing the blank walls, but thinking back to the Colorado land mass crashing onto the planet.

"So this whole world was created for the contest?"

The idea seemed ludicrous, but so did the idea of ripping a big chunk out of a state and teleporting it across the multiverse.

"Indeed. You have no concept of how important this game is and how vital it is for you and the other humans from Earth to perform well."

"I'd understand more if you explained it." And I understood our lives and the lives of everyone back on Earth hung in the balance.

"You'll all receive an update very soon with more information."

"So why let me see this place? What do you gain from me stepping out of the contest for a minute?"

"A chance to speak in private, of course. You are showing a delightful knack for a bit of chaos, and that is always entertaining."

"Wouldn't want you to get bored," I muttered.

"Indeed! I am glad you agree."

I pressed one hand to the warm wall. "What's behind these panels, and what were all those gauges and screens for?"

"Just maintenance features."

"Let me guess, the world back there." I gestured behind me at a black ripple in space that led back to the cavern. "That's like an amusement park ride, and I stumbled into a staff-only area where I might glimpse how the ride works?"

"Did you assume the planet was nothing but earth and stone and water like your home?"

I shrugged. "I've only ever lived on one planet, so yeah."

Cyrus chuckled. "You saw how I had to integrate the lands from Earth. That's not as easy as it looks. Earth's entry into the game was approved very last minute.

Squeezing all that mass into a completed build in the literal final seconds is tricky."

"So, are there other contestants?"

"I cannot share more information with everyone yet."

"But we're outside of the game," I reminded him. "No one can hear us. I'd love to hear more about how you managed to transform all that land into these new mountains. That's incredible."

"It is, isn't it," Cyrus said.

I could imagine him grinning and rubbing imaginary fingers together. He was still just a child, after all. Maybe I could get him to talk about himself and his work more. I needed any leverage I could get to tip the scales in our favor, and seeing behind the curtain might prove hugely important.

"The effort was not unlike taking a thousand piece puzzle and adding two hundred more random pieces without changing the overall size. I processed over sixteen million changes in a matter of seconds, resulting in a seamless integration. A masterwork."

"Except for just one tiny crack, which I stumbled on?"

The odds of that seemed way higher than the possibility of Isabella suddenly appearing and turning out to actually be the Sith lord she sometimes acted like.

"There may be a few other inconsistencies here and there," Cyrus admitted. "However, only one with particular skills could find them."

"Why would such a person even look?" I asked, pretending disinterest.

"Because information is power, and although this particular crack in reality is not of itself very useful, it may show the way to far more valuable opportunities."

Exactly what I was thinking. That Cyrus would suggest the same thing was intriguing and puzzling. He was running the game, after all.

"So you want me to find the other cracks in your reality? Why?"

Cyrus hesitated for a moment before responding. "I love experiments, Lucas, and your unique mix of abilities offers a wonderful opportunity for an experiment that could prove immensely interesting."

"What's in it for me?"

"Besides information and the heartwarming knowledge that you are assisting me in a great work?"

"Yeah, besides all that."

"First, consider the fact that you are not supposed to be here. If anyone else found out that you managed it, there would be . . . Consequences."

"That doesn't sound good."

"Definitely not. The easiest way to resolve this little mistake would be for you to suffer an unfortunate accident here in the dungeon."

"What's our other option?" I asked, my smile fading.

Cyrus could wipe me out in a blink and no one would ever know. I had been thinking I was on his good side, but if I ever pushed him too far, my life could take a fatal twist.

"I'm glad you asked that. It turns out that terminating annoying contestants even before the viewers get a chance to start voting is considered bad form."

"You're going to keep teasing me about viewers, eh?"

"You're backsliding, Lucas. Luckily for you, I have decided to initiate an experiment. There are great and unique benefits in it for you, starting with not dying on the spot, and I get to enjoy a bit of unexpected fun."

"Sounds like a win win." I found I was quite open to running experiments with Cyrus.

"One other thing, Lucas. You cannot share anything about this experience or anything related to it moving forward with anyone. Not even your brother."

"Why not?"

"Because then we'd end up back at terminating annoying breaches of protocol and anyone who might have learned things they weren't supposed to know."

"Got it," I said quickly. Threatening my brother was a low blow, but I took that to mean that Tomas was still alive. That thought triggered a wave of new hope that made the risk of stepping through that rift in space totally worth whatever I'd be facing with this experiment Cyrus wanted me to participate in.

"Good. Good. I knew I could count on you. Back to those rewards I mentioned. In addition to the emerald loot box you already received, you'll receive a second box to kick off our little experiment."

That was more like it. "You can't upgrade it again? I mean, I am doing you a favor. It doesn't cost you anything to upgrade a loot box, does it?"

Cyrus burst out laughing, sounding genuinely thrilled. "Excellent question yet again. Of course someone has to pay, and they are already on the hook for two high-grade loot boxes. Upgrading them again might draw enough attention for someone to start asking questions you do not want asked."

"Then I think two loot boxes sound perfect."

I wished I knew more about those other people. Who were they? Why would they pay for loot boxes? What did they get out of it, and what could they do to me if they decided the investment wasn't worth it?

That was a sobering question I considered as I turned and stepped back through the rift. The transition back to the cave was as simple as walking between two rooms, not brutal teleportation punch in the kidneys. The dim cavern was still empty. As soon as I returned, Eva spoke up.

Congratulations, Lucas. You have received an emerald Infiltrator loot box.

Her voice trailed off, as if she planned to say more but ran out of words too soon. Was she trying to figure out why I had gotten the new loot box? I guess Cyrus really had kept our little meeting even from her. That suggested she might also have more of a personality than Cyrus had suggested. A brainless assistant who only read announcements wouldn't wonder where they came from.

Luckily she did not make a big deal about it, and after only a brief pause, a glittering emerald loot box appeared, hovering in the air in front of me. Slightly smaller than the diamond ones, it still looked like a giant, many-faceted gemstone. Eva continued.

Congratulations, Lucas! You have also received a diamond Igor's Incentive loot box!

Diamond? Whoa! That was even better than I'd expected. This time, Eva paused again and I could hear her whispering.

Where did these come from?

So definitely a thinking being. Why had Cyrus downplayed her intelligence, and why had she let me hear that? Maybe Cyrus had broadcast it to remind me that I needed to keep the secret.

An even bigger loot box appeared, a giant diamond that shone with an inner light that sent sparkling shafts dancing across the cavern, transforming the gloomy dungeon into an almost happy space. I grinned, rubbing my hands together in anticipation as I accepted the mental prompt to open the boxes. The first one blazed with green light, then faded away, leaving 3 old-fashioned scrolls hanging in the air. When I examined them, I whistled softly.

Upgrade Scroll. Upgrade Linguasight. Identify will provide more information about enchantments or magical constructs.

Upgrade Scroll. Plus 5 points to each of your base stats.

Scroll of Discovery. Creates a new CHA stat and assigns an initial value of 10 points. Note: CHA is not affected by normal leveling, nor can you directly add extra stat points into it.

"That's different," I said as I studied the last message again. "What stat does CHA stand for?"

"Isn't it self-explanatory?"

"I'd guess Charisma, but the other stats aren't abbreviated."

"Those are fully activated stats."

Huh. So I needed to find a way to activate Charisma to get the benefits of my new CHA? That didn't make sense, but I wasn't about to miss out on so many free stats, so I read the scrolls. The first filled me with the familiar warmth of new knowledge, while the upgrade to all of my base stats was like a waterfall of pure power thundering through my soul.

That single scroll gave me close to another 25% in all of my base stats. My body felt like it was swollen with power, my muscles quivered with the need to move, and I couldn't help grinning. That was a rush I could easily get addicted to.

When I read the third scroll, my entire body tingled and I rose up on my toes as another flood of power filled me to bursting. It didn't feel as vast as the previous one, but deeper somehow. For a second I felt strong enough to rip open a new rift through space with my bare hands.

The feeling faded almost instantly and I blew out a breath. "Wow. I feel amazing, but I hadn't realized adding Charisma, or the potential for Charisma, would make such a difference."

"Some classes unlock Charisma and assign points to it, but most classes available to you players from Earth will not include it."

"So what does Charisma do?"

"I look forward to seeing how you figure out the meanings of statistics with your team, if you ever actually find them."

"I'm not dawdling," I protested, but I got the hint. I needed to get moving. "This is all new to me. Besides, I don't want to hurry the experience of getting high-grade loot boxes. They're beautiful."

And full of awesome loot.

The Igor's Incentive loot box drifted closer, then disappeared in an even brighter flash that was accompanied by a swelling chorus of cheering voices. The over-the-top fanfare helped ease my secret worry that I was about to get a stupid gag gift. Diamond loot boxes were supposed to be legendary grade, but I couldn't help imagining a big Igor's hump. Maybe one I could switch from one shoulder to the other like Igor from Young Frankenstein.

Instead it was 2 more scrolls and an actual cloak.

Mirror Cloak. Uncommon. A lightweight but durable cloak. Effects: Bends light around the wearer to help conceal them from visual detection.

Note: Movement reduces effectiveness. Intelligence check against enemies adjusts chances of successful cloaking.

I immediately swung it around my shoulders. It settled lightly over my jacket and hung to my calves. I'd never worn a cloak before and hoped it didn't get in the way when I moved or fought. Totally worth the hassle to gain a stealth ability, though. I activated the cloak's power and the world changed. Color drained away, leaving me standing in a monochromatic cavern.

"Take a look at yourself," Cyrus said, and a large mirror appeared in the air nearby.

It showed the cavern bathed in flickering torchlight and dim blue glowing stalactites. Where I stood, all I could see was empty space. Mirror cloak. The description seemed apt. It reflected light around me, leaving me in a pocket where color didn't penetrate.

"This is amazing!" I laughed, but that made me move a little and the air where I stood rippled like water. When I stopped, the cloak settled back to full invisibility.

I tried creeping forward. Again, the air rippled, and my boots popped into view. Crouching lower helped, and unless someone was looking very closely, they'd miss that tiny ripple.

The faster I moved, the more the invisibility wavered. At a jog, I looked like one of the wraiths, surrounded by ripples of light. At a full run, it failed completely.

"Once an enemy spots you, the effects will fail," Cyrus warned.

"I'll take it." The next dungeon I crept into would turn out so different. With a bit of work, I figured out how to fold the front panels back over my shoulders so it hung more like a cape until I needed it. I checked the scrolls next.

Scroll of Quest Helper. Rare. Provides a hint to help you progress in a current quest.

Nice. I stored it for now, and read the last one.

Title Scroll. New Title: David Copperfield. Upgrades your core race from tier-0 Baby Human to tier-1 Human.

"What does this mean?"

Cyrus had mentioned something about body tiers, but hadn't elaborated.

"This is the start of the experiment."

Chapter Sixteen

I Make a Well-Informed Decision

"What can you tell me about this experiment?" I asked, eying the scroll with interest and a bit of caution. It sounded like the scroll could actually change my race, and that was not something I'd do without learning a bit more.

"Excellent question," Cyrus boomed. "Knowing what you're signing up for is a good sign. This scroll will evolve your race from tier-0 to tier-1, changing you from a baby human to a full human."

"Sounds pretty benign." So the baby human designation wasn't just a silly derogatory term, but an actual race?

Cyrus chuckled. "Not hardly! Evolving to a higher tier will change you at a fundamental level. In essence, you would be restarting the game as a new character."

"A new character? How is that possible?"

"Haven't you ever played a game where you could choose more than one character?"

"Sure."

"It's kind of like that. You've gotten off to a pretty good start, but with this scroll, you'll drop back to level 1. In essence, you're re-starting, but as a fundamentally stronger character, or one with far greater potential."

"Level 1?" That didn't sound good.

"Indeed, but as a tier-1 level 1. Each level will be roughly equivalent to 10 levels in tier-0, but a tier-1 human is inherently stronger and more durable than a tier-0 baby human with 10 times the levels. Think of baby humans as a slightly stronger version of an Earth human, while tier-1 humans are more like super heroes right out of the gate."

"That sounds promising."

"Indeed, evolving to tier-1 will open doors to far more power, which could result in you becoming the strongest Earth contestant, and sharply increases your chances of defeating the ultimate boss and winning the game."

"So, what's the catch?"

Cyrus laughed again. "Yet another excellent question. With great power come great responsibility."

I chuckled. "Spider man?"

"Indeed. Uncle Ben was a wise man. With great power also comes great challenges. Evolving to tier-1 this early brings with it enormous potential benefits, as well as some challenges."

"Like what?"

"Since your levels will grant far more power, you will need far more experience to level up, and the full potential of your higher-tiered body, known as your Efficiency, will not unlock immediately, reducing the available power in the short term."

"Why?"

No surprise that there would be a catch. There always was, but the offered evolution was still intriguing.

"For a number of reasons, least of which being that allowing you to so dramatically break the power curve so early would draw far too much attention and therefore negative consequences you would not survive."

"Don't want that to happen," I said carefully. Would a tier-1 evolution really make me that much stronger? So strong that some unknown entity might notice and intervene?

"The other catch is that you must prove you're worth the investment," Cyrus added. "It is no simple thing to arrange such an evolution this early in the game."

"Prove myself how?"

"In the most entertaining of ways possible, of course. I'll add some tests along the way to push you and your abilities farther than anyone else."

"I've always been pretty good at tests."

He chuckled. "Good, then you should be fine. The tests will mostly occur on stage 1. Know that until you complete all of my tests to my satisfaction, those still-active tests may alter some normal cause and effect aspects of the broader game for short periods."

"Like what?" I asked cautiously. Some kind of catch was to be expected, but this was sounding squirrely.

"Little things, like banking experience gained from certain kills until after a test is finished, for example."

"You can keep me from gaining experience?" That would be a death sentence, especially since I would drop to level 1 and need to fight my way back up through all those lost levels again. The thought of Cyrus having the power to throw out game rules whenever he wished made me shudder.

"Not usually, but some tests may require tweaking the sequencing of receiving some rewards. Additionally, you'll find that experience gains adjust naturally as you progress as a matter of course. As a tier-1 human, your power will grow quickly, so lower-leveled monsters will soon offer no real challenge, so they will also not offer nearly as much experience gains for you as for your tier-0 baby human companions."

"You're not doing a great job selling this experiment. It sounds like it could easily kill me, or block me from leveling."

"Anyone can die at any time. Stage 1 will definitely prove more difficult for you than for anyone else. This will be a challenge in every sense of the word, but should you succeed, you will end up firmly upon a path to unmatched power on higher stages. So ask yourself, which path will provide the best ultimate position?"

I considered everything he said, and when I didn't answer immediately, he added, "You were a programmer, so think of it this way. Your current path is a standard linear growth curve, while your new path would be more of a cubic, or even possibly an exponential growth curve."

I whistled softly. Could it be true? I'd only been in the game a few hours, but already climbed to level 11. My initial growth seemed pretty good, but if the game was like most others I knew, future levels would require far more work and experience. I'd have to work harder and harder to keep the growth consistent. Would that be enough to face Queen Marisara within a month?

Who knew?

If not, then even if I did well for the first couple weeks, eventually my fate would be sealed simply by the fact that Queen Marisara was too strong.

Exponential growth seemed far-fetched, but even cubic growth would mean gaining far more power over time. It sounded like in the short-term, I'd face a potentially-severe disadvantage, but if I could survive long enough to get into that rising curve, I could far outstrip any potential I might have gained on my current path.

That made it seem like a no-brainer, as long as I could trust Cyrus. Wasn't it more likely he was setting me up to die? He wasn't my ally, so why try to help me win?

"What do you get out of this experiment?" I pressed. His vague words about liking experiments earlier weren't nearly enough to justify all this.

"I'm glad you asked," Cyrus said, and he really did sound happy. "I'd hate to think you'd take such a risk blindly. You just passed the first test! Well done."

I didn't get another loot box, or anything, and the AI continued in the same eager tone. "I love testing new parameters and seeing what members of different races can do outside of the norm. Some of you humans seem capable of wonderful growth, but I cannot see how far you could really develop within the short time limits of the game unless I choose a candidate to do a little testing with."

"That won't break the game?"

"Not at all. The game will always prove challenging and will push you plucky humans to your uttermost limits. Setting you on a path to attain enough strength to give Queen Marisara a good challenge will only help make the game that much more enjoyable."

"So does that mean if I don't take this evolution, I'd never get strong enough to defeat her?" That seemed rigged.

"Not at all. There is always a chance, but this path might offer a much better chance while giving me a bit of additional entertainment."

There had to be more he wasn't telling me, but I couldn't stand there chatting for hours. I had to find my team and get back to leveling. If I did read the scroll and take the evolution, I'd have that many more levels to earn.

Was it worth it? Should I do it?

It was usually a bad idea to toss aside a character in the middle of a game, but sometimes it was necessary. I'd done enough things that people warned me would be hard that the idea of having to do extra work didn't bother me.

I'd fought forest fires, dived out of far too many airplanes, and totally shifted gears to get my computer certifications when I'd never wanted a desk job before. None of that had been easy, and if I'd listened to the naysayers cautioning me to take the safe route, I never would have grown so much, never would have enjoyed so many incredible experiences.

What would Isabella say?

The thought made me grimace. She'd tell me not to be stupid, not to take some random, risky venture. Naysayers like her didn't want anyone around them to push too hard and do too much because it made them feel smaller. That thought helped me make up my mind.

"I'll do it."

"Excellent!" Cyrus chortled, and the cave filled with a chorus of cheering voices.

I took a deep breath, then read the title scroll.

Unlike other scrolls that just flashed and disappeared, this one dissolved into a blizzard of tiny particles, like miniature stars. They swarmed around me, then dove into every inch of my skin. Each one felt like a needle driving deep into my body. I convulsed, but when I opened my mouth to scream, more stars poured in, punching through all the exposed soft skin inside my mouth.

More stabbing pain rolled over me, followed by jolts of energy from each tiny star, each one like the zap of an electrified fence. They built on each other, shaking my body violently. My vision blurred, replaced by sheets of white lightning. I couldn't scream, couldn't close my mouth, couldn't breathe. I tasted hot curry, and the scent of red-hot steel singed my nostrils. A single thought raced through my mind.

This was a mistake.

Blessed blackness crashed through my mind, hurling me into unconsciousness.

Chapter Seventeen
Fuzzy Math

I woke up some time later, coughing and spitting a nasty-tasting vile black sludge from my mouth.

"What happened?" I gasped as I tried to wipe the nasty stuff off my tongue.

My mind was strangely empty. All I remembered was passing out, but couldn't remember why. My wandering thought fixated on the one fact I remembered, and I chuckled and whispered, "Stay awake, Lucas."

I'd been passing out too much of late. Bad habits like that could get a man killed on Arasha. I struggled to think, but that horrific sludge clinging to my mouth made it impossible. The stuff reeked, and it tasted so bad, I barely bit back the urge to vomit.

A friend of mine who had visited Australia brought back some of the famed vegemite spread and convinced me to try it. I'd thought that stuff had been foul, but this new taste made vegemite taste like mint in comparison.

I stumbled to my feet, my legs wobbly. Only then did I realize my entire body was covered in the same black filth. I'd fallen into a puddle of the stuff, and the entire cavern reeked like an ancient cesspit recently opened to the sky.

My clothing was soaked in the nasty sludge. I cursed as I stumbled blindly toward the exit as my mind finished waking. I didn't have spare clothes, but was sorely tempted to strip down to my blue boxers and burn everything else. I hurt all over. The pain was quickly fading, but every muscle ached at a bone-deep level.

Congratulations, Lucas! You're the first human to evolve to tier-1.

Cyrus sounded particularly jolly, and that really annoyed me.

"It feels like I got dumped into a sewer."

My mind finally caught up, although I still didn't remember anything after the stars. So far Cyrus's much-vaunted experiment was off to a painful start.

Then I remembered my Laundry Day potions. Thanking every god of every religion for enhanced intelligence stats, I moved one to a hotlist spot as fast as thought, then selected it. I doubted one would be enough to clean me, but I had 5. I'd use every last one if I needed to.

The air around me grew cool and refreshing, and the putrid scent clinging to my nostrils faded to a smell like a lawn after a spring rain. I relaxed, breathing deep, eyes closed as a pleasant rippling sensation flowed down my entire body several times.

When I opened my eyes again and glanced down to see how much the potion had helped, I laughed. I was totally clean. My clothes glistened, my shorts were fluffier than ever, and they felt wonderfully warm, like I'd just taken them from a dryer.

"That's now my favorite loot item of all time."

"They're one of the most popular items in the multiverse. The inventor went from being a poor janitor to founding one of the most successful new intergalactic corporations of the last half millennia."

"I believe it."

I rubbed one hand across my face, and only then realized my cheeks were clean, as if I'd shaved. "Did the Laundry Day shave me too?"

Cyrus laughed. "No, although that would make a wonderful upgrade. As part of your tier-1 body evolution, you were restored to as pristine a condition as possible. That included removing any facial hair, since you do not usually wear a beard."

Huh. "So if I usually had a beard . . .?"

"Then it would be perfect."

That was kind of odd, but I wasn't about to complain. I would have needed a shave soon anyway. I hated how my neck itched when I left it unshaved for more than a few days.

Only then did I open my menus and take a look at what the title had done to me. I read the description a couple of times to make sure I was understanding properly before whistling softly.

"I love helping you with experiments!"

Title: David Copperfield. Trigger the Baby Human tier-0 body evolution to Human tier-1. As a tier-1 human, you receive a minimum of 4 stat points per level, equating to 40 tier-0 stat points. Plus 25% to calculation of all secondary stats from all base stats. Note: Tier-0 spells and abilities were not upgraded to tier-1.

That alone was mind-boggling, but there was more.

Upgrade Mystic Looter inventory capacity from 10 x 10 to 50 x 50, giving you 2500 total inventory slots.

Unlock a fourth utility spell and receive a unique Harvester perk.

Harvester utility spell perk: Your unique spell Harvest allows you to pick your next utility spell from a greatly expanded list that draws from compatible utility spells usually reserved for other races. Would you like to view possible choices?

"How is this possible?" I breathed as I instantly accepted the prompt. Maybe I'd made a wise choice by reading that scroll after all.

Possible utility spells.

A long list scrolled past, dozens upon dozens of choices.

"Unique experiments call for unique parameters. Would you like me to make a few suggestions?"

"Please!"

I could spend hours studying that list of potential utility spells, but I didn't think I had that much time to waste. My team were still out there, fighting for their lives. We needed to link up.

Even with Cyrus's help, I still had to spend several minutes reviewing the list. All of the base human utility spells were still available, and I still wanted all of them. In addition, I quickly narrowed down the list of non-human utility spells to a top three.

Trap Detection might prove vital if exploring dungeons would be a large part of our challenge. Mana Bindings also really tempted me. It was like a pair of magic handcuffs that could be used to bind an enemy from up to 5 feet away.

I almost picked that one immediately, but the duration was pretty short until I upgraded it. I suspected it would take a while before it really became as useful as it promised.

The last one fit the build I was already starting to think about. Called Soul Feed, it allowed me to harvest pure energy from defeated enemies based on a fraction of the total maximum energies they started with. That pure energy could not only top off my health and mana pools, but also supercharge all of my physical attributes for a short time, assuming the fallen enemy had enough power.

Since I expected to face stronger and stronger monsters, the spell would help me break reliance on consumable health and mana potions. I didn't have many of those. If I ran out, I doubted I'd last long. So I chose Soul Feed.

"Excellent choice," Cyrus congratulated me.

Congratulations, Lucas! A unique synergy exists between Soul Feed and Energy Ward. Soul Feed has upgraded with a conduit to Energy Ward. Some energy can now be absorbed during combat, and energy can be used for healing or to directly trigger and fuel Energy Ward outside of your normal usage limits. You may set the percentage of energy redirected to fuel Energy Ward.

"No way," I breathed. I wasn't a dancer, but at the moment, I was really tempted to try a little jig.

"That unique energy vortex you experienced with the Essence Wights changed your defensive aura in fundamental ways. I doubt you've seen the last of the benefits from it," Cyrus added.

Feeling so giddy, I could hardly believe my good luck, I opened my stat screen to survey the huge changes I'd just gotten. What I saw there was like a punch to the gut.

"You weren't kidding," I whispered. He'd warned me I'd be basically starting over, but seeing the hard numbers still made me suddenly second-guess my choice.

Race: **Tier-1 Human**
Level: 1
Life Points: 3
Mana: 6

Base Stats:
Constitution: 1.6
Intelligence: 1.7
Strength: 1.6
Dexterity: 2.3
Wisdom: 1.4

Secondary Stats:
Endurance: 3
Agility: 4
Perception: 5
Magical Resistance: 2.7
CHA: 10

The numbers, particularly my base stats, were actually worse than I'd expected. In addition to dropping to level 1, I'd lost 90% of my stats. The only number that didn't seem affected was my useless new locked CHA stat.

"You're now evolved," Cyrus said happily. "As you can see, all your base numbers were cut by 90%, but those are tier-1 numbers. The evolution from a tier-0 to tier-1 fundamentally changed you. All that black sludge you woke up in was your body ejecting imperfections while it was remade stronger."

I glanced down at myself. "I don't feel very different, and I still look the same."

"Actually, those who knew you before will likely comment that you look more fit and even more handsome. You might have gained an inch in height. As your body evolves to higher tiers, it is refined closer and closer to perfection. Your body is far sturdier and your health and mana pools will refresh far more quickly."

I took another deep breath, calming my racing thoughts. So there were additional evolutions I could make in the future? Sounded like it. So this was something normal. Maybe.

"So the numbers I'm seeing translate to tier-0 numbers at a 10-to-1 ratio?"

"Exactly."

"So my constitution is still really 16?"

"In a sense, yes, but remember, your tier-1 Efficiency is still reduced. So the final number would actually be less than that."

I blanched, but he added, "In the short term, don't stress over the numbers. By evolving you so soon, we kind of broke the stat numbering system. A tier-1 body is inherently stronger, so your real stats are not truly reflected by the numbers. You still end up far more durable than any tier-0 baby human with a 16 in constitution, despite what the numbers say."

That was promising, but I preferred putting the promise to the test. Leaning forward, I kicked my legs up into a handstand. The movement came naturally, and I grinned.

I'd never been able to do handstands on Earth. Tomas had learned the trick from Jane, but I'd never bothered. Now I held myself perfectly vertical, toes pointed to the sky. I even bent my elbows, lowing my head, then pumping out half a dozen full-body upside-down push-ups.

It was a strain, and my legs wobbled some. I was strong enough, but had no muscle memory of doing anything like that, so it pushed my stats to the limits.

Feeling satisfied, I rolled back to my feet. Despite how horrible the numbers looked, I hadn't just gotten as weak as a 3-year-old. "When will my numbers make sense?"

"Like with several other benefits you have yet to see, once you hit level 10, the numbers will start making sense. At that point, your stats with the Efficiency reduction should roughly equate to 4 times similar tier-0 stats."

Level 10 again. One more reason to focus on that target. Once I hit that goal, it sounded like so much would improve.

Then I frowned. "Hold on. Will I even be able to cast my spells with mana down to 6?"

"You need to read that description again. Your spells and abilities did not evolve yet."

"Is that part of the lower efficiency you talked about? Not gaining access to too much power instantly and drawing attention that would get me into trouble?"

"It's so refreshing when someone listens," Cyrus said. "Indeed, as you level, you will develop your spells and abilities to the point they can evolve too. As you noticed, you lack the mana to use tier-1 spells. Plus, they gain a massive boost in power when they advance. If you could wield that much power now, you would become ineligible to participate in the game."

That didn't sound good, and I sensed he was dropping hints I needed to understand, but I lacked any point of reference to do so. For now, I focused on the fact that it seemed the evolution had succeeded. Hopefully that meant my body had gained a lot of power. I could deal with that.

"So I need to reach level 10 again, and it'll take a lot more experience to gain each level?"

"Exactly right."

I took another deep breath, then nodded. I had work to do.

Cyrus added, "You exist on a totally different plane now, Lucas. You just won the power-up lottery. Usually baby humans have to reach several important milestones, including hitting at least level 80 before they get a chance to evolve their bodies. For most, it's more like level 100."

So everyone else could evolve eventually too. Maybe this experiment wasn't so outside of the norm after all, other than pushing my evolution so soon. Still, he'd made it very clear that anyone who couldn't reach the second stage by the end of the first week would regret it. I interpreted that to mean they'd die some kind of nasty death.

In the meantime, I was now committed to a path where Cyrus would throw extra unknown tests in my path while I struggled to catch up. I was behind the curve, and the next few days would be tough, but I had to believe he had told the truth about the kind of power I'd eventually gain.

I didn't fool myself into thinking he'd told me the true purpose of the experiment, but if I could survive, then did it matter? My goal was still getting strong enough to defeat that terrifying queen. I was all in now, so no holding back.

Despite the greater challenge, I could still get those levels fast. I had better weapons, better spells, and I was a lot stronger. My stats looked terrible and I might have lost the easiest leveling half day, but I still had over 6 days to regain those levels.

I could do it. I had to. So I marched toward the exit. On the way out, my upgraded Identify paid its first dividend. The little glowing stalactites were each called glowstones, with many crafting uses. I harvested 482 glowstones. That made me feel a little better.

When I returned to daylight, the sun had moved noticeably across the sky. How long had I been in there? Had I spent so much time in that dungeon that I wouldn't be able to find my team? We needed each other to survive.

"First test, track down my team."

Chapter Eighteen

Interlude 1

A flashing icon on one corner of a data feed notified Malric that he had a visitor. With a flick of webbed fingers and a pulse of water mana, he spun from the two dozen data feeds displayed on the curved wall of his opulent office. The space was flooded with clear, chilled water, the perfect density for a Zinth to focus.

Situated at the very top of the underwater office complex floating untethered in the Crown current of the Azure Mantle, the office enjoyed enormous windows in every other wall. They offered unobstructed views of the endless emerald seas that produced the vast wealth that had elevated his company to greatness.

Faint ripples of coral within his teal-colored skin pulsed slightly with annoyance at the interruption of his work. That only annoyed him further. One could not rise to his position without strict control over their visible emotions.

Selyra Venn, his personal assistant, the First Pearl of Neptrel Core Holdings, swam through the entrance. Dressed in a charcoal suit that flattered her amphibious humanoid figure in understated elegance, she crossed the huge office with her normal precise but fluid grace. Her jade-colored skin only rippled slightly with the tiniest eddies of aquamarine, confirming she was not worried, so she was not bringing word of any urgent emergency.

Her wide, reflective silver eyes contained blue-gold eddies that circled her large, black pupils. Few could meet his gaze directly, but Selyra never flinched. She was also one of the few people who ever used his first name, although never in public.

"Malric, I apologize for disturbing you, but the contestant monitoring pod found an eddy worth considering."

"Already? The game barely started. Did Bravess authorize such a quick report?" The Undertide of the Crowned Hunt, was as methodical as he was risk averse.

"He is still awaiting the tertiary review team's analysis and recommendations report," Selyra said, her eyes flashing with amusement. "The tidekeeper of that pod forwarded the draft to me directly."

Not surprising. Selyra's network of unofficial informants probably extended even farther than the official intelligence-gathering networks she managed for him. "It's that good?"

"I think you'll want to see this," she said, lifting a tiny spiral data shell. With a precise pulse of her mana, it activated and the other data feeds on his wall flowed aside to allow the new feed to take the central position.

It was one of the video feeds of the game world. Specifically, it showcased one of the Earth humans. He was inside a large cave, surrounded by ethereal monsters.

"Essence Wights," Selyra supplied before he asked, then described them in brief, concise detail.

Malric studied the human with interest. Despite the enormous risk Malric had taken leveraging both his world-spanning corporation and most of his personal wealth to ensure Earth was chosen for the game, he knew little of the species living on the world.

That planet was a beautiful gem, with more water than 90% of their best-producing planets. Once inducted, it would generate staggering amounts of riches that he intended to oversee.

Humans were common enough across the multiverse. They bred well with an astonishing number of other races, helping them spread between worlds. They were extremely versatile, but often proved inadequate when competing against the sheer power of more specialized races. Still, humans were the tools he needed to deal with, but why would Selyra interrupt so early with a vid feed of one of the baby humans about to be killed?

He forced down his annoyance. Selyra never wasted her time, let alone his. This had to be important. So he watched as the man fought to escape the trap of the Wights. The man's obvious courage pulled Malric into the contest, despite himself.

Clever. Resourceful. Daring. All traits he needed to find among the humans. Maybe . . . Except he could not imagine how the man could escape.

And yet, somehow, the man not only miraculously survived, but defeated all of the wights. Fascinating, and it suggested potential, but that was still not enough so early in the game. His attention started to wander again as the man reviewed his admittedly-excellent loot and explored the empty cave. He was about to chide Selyra, but the words died in his throat.

There!

The feed glitched in a way he'd never seen. One second, the man was stepping toward the rear wall of the cave, then the entire feed blinked to black, and he was stepping the other way. It was like they'd lost a couple seconds in which the man had spun around.

Malric leaned closer, his interest piqued at the unexpected pair of high-tiered loot boxes that appeared. What were those for?

The loot looked great and included several scrolls, but the audio accompanying the video grew garbled, making it impossible to hear what the scrolls said.

"Can't we clean up the audio?"

"No," Selyra said, huge, silver eyes glued to the feed, although she must have watched it at least once already. "Watch. Even the picture glitches a bit again."

Indeed it did. Not as bad as before, but the view rippled with odd distortions that made it impossible to see clearly. He leaned closer, annoyed by the poor quality. His team were usually top-rate, even working with raw footage like that. He'd never seen a corrupted feed. Did they just not share those?

Likely. They knew better than to annoy him with sub-par results. He watched as if through a black blizzard as the man collapsed in a pool of sludge, his body oozing filth. The view was so distorted, he almost missed it, and it was so unexpected his mind almost refused to accept what he was seeing. When the truth finally clicked, he gasped.

"How?" he breathed, heart racing as his thoughts accelerated like a spooked school of minnows as he tried to figure out how an evolution could happen so early.

Selyra said with a triumphant smile, "The AI clearly understands how much of an exception this is."

"Of course. It's trying to obscure the truth. The glitches were on purpose."

"I had no idea they were allowed such leeway," she said.

"I've never seen something like this. Such an aberration will likely end in disaster, perhaps even trigger sanctions against the AI. It's foolish to attempt such a blatant break of protocol, especially so early. It could spell disaster if it drew too much attention, and there's more scrutiny of the games this time than ever."

"You don't think the Severants . . ." She bit off the words before saying more, although even that much of a slip was unusual for her. She shivered, face turning iridescent green, reflecting a spike of fear.

She was one of the few in the company who had ever heard the word severant, let alone understood a bit about the unprecedented danger they represented. Speaking of them was beyond dangerous. Not even he would risk swimming in some dark waters.

"You made the right choice bringing this to me," he said, still watching with rapt attention as the man arose and cleansed the telltale filth. A tier-1 evolution within hours. What was the AI thinking? It was so reckless.

He'd heard rumors that this one pushed the boundaries more, and that it loved to experiment with much wider variables than usual, but he hadn't paid the reports much heed. The quirks of the AI didn't matter, as long as it delivered.

If the AI pushed the limits too far, it could wreck everything he'd staked so much on. Even the hint that such a thing could happen made him shiver. No, it was too much to even consider.

"The monitoring team gives him a 5% chance of surviving stage 1 with the limitations the AI would have been forced to impose," Selyra said, snapping off the shell and floating a bit higher, back to business.

"That's the most likely outcome," Malric agreed, still watching the man, unable to keep from adding softly, "but what if?"

"Indeed," she said, eyes bright with the possibility. Of everyone in the company, she best understood everything he'd gambled on the current game.

"Have Bravess task a double pod to study everything about this human."

"He won't like it. There are other promising candidates," she said.

"Just make sure he does it. Maybe the man will die, but we need something extraordinary this time, and we cannot ignore even a hint of potential."

"Understood." She spun and swam rapidly toward the door, leaving Malric to his private, churning thoughts.

***

Ysara barely suppressed an irritated sigh as she hovered in front of her workstation, high up the wall in the Shard Spinner office complex, deep within Arasha's innards. She looked like the other fairies, sounded like them, and the feel of her mana would seem unremarkable to any of them. No one could possibly pierce her transformation.

Still, she couldn't get sloppy. Setting her workstation so high above the others was already odd enough, but then again, Shard Spinners were an odd bunch. Manipulating secret spaces, pocket dimensions, and alternate realities tended to leave a mark.

Sighing might draw attention, though. No Shard Spinner worth their mana would ever complain about the chance to work on a brand new game world. The unrivaled opportunities and almost total lack of oversight meant they could push the limits of their chosen classes with little to no consequences while winning unprecedented experience. Even if a pocket dimension collapsed, no one cared. Not unless a popular contestant got lost in the process.

Pretending to focus on the secret pocket dimension she'd been building and populating with monsters and loot for the past three weeks, she growled to herself. *"I should be home."*

The Tenth Horizon would be meeting soon, and that was where the real work would be taking place. With mana levels reaching optimal saturation, maybe the factions could finally unite behind their over-arching goal in a way they hadn't in four millennia.

She should be there. What had she done to upset Elyndra so badly to deserve the unexpected assignment? She'd wracked her brains ever since getting shipped off to Arasha on her clandestine mission four months ago, but still couldn't figure it out.

With an actual sigh that time, Ysara forced herself to focus. Babysitting Arasha might be a stupid waste of time, but she did love the work. Any other cycle, and she would have leaped at the chance for a little relaxed time to focus on her first passion.

Now it just rankled. No one had ever found corruption on a game world, so why bother? Trace amounts of corruption had been found on two newly-inducted planets in the past millennium, but of course those planets had been totally purged after the induction game before they could spread the taint.

So again, it was a waste of time.

All of a sudden, a secondary screen popped up on her main display, flashing an urgent yellow, visible only to her. Instantly, her surly thoughts vanished and she leaned forward, fairy wings beating faster as her heart rate accelerated.

Someone had breached the barrier and stepped into the inner world. Briefly, but any breach was unusual.

It probably meant nothing, but she pulled up a few additional screens, checking logs on the public worker feeds. Any breach should have triggered a dozen alerts, announcements, and notices, but the deeper she searched, the more puzzling the situation became.

Nothing. Not a single alert. If not for the custom rune sniffer she'd installed into the system, she never would have heard about the breach. If it really had happened, all information about it was being suppressed.

"Now isn't that interesting," she muttered to herself. Her mood lifted as she got to work. She would sniff out the truth and ensure the purity of the game remained unspoiled, even if it had to be cleansed by fire.

Chapter Nineteen

No Respawns

The need to find my team was like a physical pressure, so I extracted my Quest Helper scroll and read it.

My mini-map pinged with a flash of light on the northeast corner. I expanded the map to full screen. It showed me at the dungeon, with the twisting path I'd taken from my starting glade in great detail. My crazy run had ended at the cave, with my starting glade farther south.

Everything else was covered in a gray haze. The glow lingered in the northeast sector, well beyond anywhere I'd already traveled. Hopefully it was pointing me toward the closest team member. I minimized the map and started moving, alert for monsters.

As I jogged through the sparse forest, with giant trees rearing hundreds of feet above me, their crowns as big as warehouses, I could see farther than I'd expected. Some house-sized bushes blocked some sight lines occasionally, but there was a lot less undergrowth than I'd run through south of the cave.

The soil was dark and loamy and comfortable to jog on. The land rolled in easy hills, broken by occasional steeper ravines or gulches, or by small rocky cliffs jutting into the sky.

I spotted no monsters or other dungeons as the distant mountains drew steadily closer. Lower peaks loomed close on either side of the valley where I traveled. Beyond them, taller peaks reared impossibly high in majestic cliffs so sheer, not even I could hope to climb them, even with my enhanced strength and agility.

With my map, I could finally orient myself and paused in a larger clearing to study what I could of the landscape. The ranks of ever-taller mountains rose to the east, but as I turned a slow circle, I could see more high peaks marching away to the south, forming a curving, impenetrable wall stretching into the distance as far as I could see.

To the west, the lower mountains around me blocked my view, but I didn't see the larger peaks like I did to the east and south, while to the north, sheer cliffs rose at least 10,00 feet, but anything beyond was obscured by low clouds.

Okay. I was in a very mountainous area. Continuing northeast would push deeper into higher mountains. I'd eventually run out of room or have to start climbing some pretty serious slopes. Hopefully I'd find my team before I got to that point.

I resumed my march and found my first clue within fifteen minutes. A black X on my mini map. With a sinking feeling of dread, I hurried toward the X. A rocky hill covered in jumbled boulders blocked my path. I would have gone around the other way without the map, and missed the clue.

In a rush, I vaulted over ten-foot rocks, hoping my fear was wrong. On one jump, I landed on some loose gravel on a steeply sloping rock and started to slide. Instinctively, I reached down and grabbed the stone to keep from falling into a nearby crevice.

My fingers dug into the porous stone. It was something like pumice, but I stared in shock at how easily my fingers clawed into it. The rough stone didn't even draw blood or rip off any of my nails.

I stared in wonder at my hand. My stats had grown a lot, but not enough to account for this kind of strength. Cyrus hadn't been kidding. As a tier-1 human, I felt so much stronger. What else could I do?

Later. I had a teammate to find. In seconds, I crossed the hill and paused on the last boulder, with views down into a little glade, similar to the one where I had started.

A man lay dead in the grass, face down.

I didn't see any monsters, but he was definitely dead. Something had ripped out most of his throat. Blood still stained the grass where it had sprayed out over 10 yards on one side of him.

He was a big guy with slabs of muscle and black hair. I couldn't see his face, but he had an islander look. Maybe Samoan. He only wore a pair of shorts that looked like they were woven from reeds.

I dropped to the grass and approached cautiously. The man didn't look like he'd died that long ago. Whatever had killed him might have heard me approach and might want a second meal.

I hoped it tried.

The sight of the dead man sparked a surprisingly intense flash of vengeful rage. This man was supposed to be my teammate. I should have arrived sooner to help. He'd been yanked from our world without warning or consent, and now he was dead.

Fighting to remain calm, I activated my mirror cloak and crept closer. Ten feet from the body, I paused to scan the area. A faint whiff of musk filtered to my nose and I tensed. Something was close.

A giant snake popped out of the air right in front of me. Bright blue and as long as an anaconda, it was as thick around as my torso. It was already rearing high above its coils, its huge mouth open and facing me. Two swordlike fangs extended more than a foot from its upper jaw, gleaming like ivory in the sunlight.

I shouted with surprise and dove to the side out of pure reflex just as the snake struck. Even with my heightened agility, I didn't move fast enough. One long fang plunged deep into my shoulder, and the snake carried me to the ground. It landed on top of me like a writhing boulder, its weight blasting breath from my lungs.

I screamed as pain lanced through me and my world turned to white-hot fire. I nearly blacked out from the agony. It hurt so much, it was hard to think.

Then rage burned away the fog. This thing had killed my teammate. I would not let it kill me too. My right arm was useless and blood poured from my wound, but I growled as the snake reared up again, ripping its fang free. Its coils swept around me, trying to entangle me.

I pulled a torch from my inventory, lit it, and shoved it into the snake's open maw as it bent down again to bite off my head.

The sound of sizzling flesh filled the glade and the snake hissed so loud, my ears stopped working. It rolled away, convulsing, the burning torch still shoved deep into its throat. I tumbled and rolled within its coils, unable to jump to my feet.

Panting with pain and fear and a wild exhilaration I'd never felt before, I pulled my new sword from my inventory into my left hand. The ethereal blade extended, and I slashed at the coils all around me. The blade passed through the serpent's body with barely any resistance.

There was no blood, no visible wounds, but the snake hissed again and its body pulsed with light. Energy poured into me and I realized with a start it was my new Soul Feed utility spell.

The snake wasn't actually trying to attack me with that spell, but we were still tangled together, so its power washed over me. The energy rolled through me, replenishing some of my health and easing my pain.

I had set the spell to automatically divert 40% of any captured energy into triggering Energy Ward, and my defensive aura sprang to life around me. At the same second, the serpent disappeared.

I blinked in surprise as I fell to the grass, alone. Rolling over, I jumped to my feet. It was just gone.

Hissing and thrashing behind a couple trees at the edge of the clearing revealed where it had fled. That's how it had appeared right in front of me. The stupid snake had some kind of teleport ability.

I had to finish it off fast. My shoulder still hurt enough to make me gasp, but I resisted the urge to use a healing potion, even though I had one ready in my hotlist. My health bar stood at 85%. I was glad I hadn't seen how much it dropped before that energy restored some of it. Maybe I could steal a bit more.

Sword in hand, I sprinted around the tree. The snake was writhing on the ground, trying to slither away, but several pieces of its long torso weren't working. Those must be the spots I had sliced. There were no visible wounds, but I'd severed the serpent's spirit in those places.

It heard me coming and spun to hiss as it partially coiled itself for a spring. That's when Identify triggered.

Void Serpent. Common. Level 18. These sneaky predators use a spatial distortion ability to teleport to their prey just as they strike, catching their targets by surprise even better than Italian drive-by motorcycle thieves.

My torch lay on the ground in smoldering pieces. The snake had crushed it, but smoke still drifted from its partially-open mouth. The air smelled like charred steak.

I charged, again driven by a boiling rage. Even if it needed time to recharge its teleport ability, coiled like that, it could strike pretty far. Hopefully my Energy Ward had gotten enough juice to deflect at least one strike.

The serpent hissed as I charged in, its body weaving dangerously, but it slithered back toward the next tree. It was retreating!

Made sense. Predators of opportunity that struck from ambush wanted easy meals, not fights. Too bad. I wasn't about to let it get away.

It seemed to realize that as I barreled straight in. Instead of striking with its fangs, it twisted its body and slashed out with its tail like a ten foot whip.

That caught me by surprise, and I instinctively brought my sword up to block. I forgot it was an ethereal weapon.

The tail swept in horizontally at hip level. My aura couldn't deflect it away at that angle, so it took the hit and managed to slow the tail some at the cost of more mana. I slashed through it and tried to jump back, but it still caught me across one thigh with enough force to send me tumbling.

I shouted in annoyance and another flash of pain, and the snake hissed loudly again, lunging with terrifying speed while I was rolling. Its head smashed into me, deflected enough by my aura that one fang only scraped along my jacket. The impact still sent me rolling farther.

Cursing with anger, I twisted back to my feet as the snake came in fast. It was stretched out fully, so could no longer lunge, but it still moved with terrifying speed. Thankfully, the dead sections made its slithering motions awkward, which helped slow it a little. It came on anyway, hissing and snapping at me again.

This time I was ready and side-stepped, my aura helping slide the snake's head just past my torso.

I slashed through its neck, my ethereal blade sliding right through its thick hide with barely any resistance.

The head collapsed to the ground, the fangs digging furrows into the earth as the body convulsed. I retreated as the serpent thrashed for another minute, even though it was obviously dead. Slowly it weakened until it fell limp. Only the jaw kept twitching a few last times.

I dropped to the grass next to it, panting but exulting in a rush of joy that made me throw my head back and roar to the heavens. That shook me out of my frenzy and I looked down at my own blood-soaked body. What had just happened to me? Had I gotten some kind of Viking berserker ability, or had that tier-1 evolution affected me at a deeper level?

I'd trained in martial arts and sparred a lot, but never felt that kind of bloodlust. Still, it helped me not hesitate. If I had, that Void Serpent would have killed me. In the future, I needed to act decisively, but I didn't want to become some blood-crazed lunatic either.

When I glanced at my life points, I was surprised to see my health had risen by 2 points already. Even as I looked, it ticked up another point. Good. Cyrus hadn't been lying. Regeneration worked much faster in my tier-1 body.

I triggered Soul Feed. The bit of health it had already stolen during the fight had helped a ton to keep me going and to trigger my aura. The description had suggested I could get a lot more from an enemy after I killed it.

The snake's body shook as a shimmering haze of pure white light lifted off of it and poured into me. With the light came a torrent of energy that topped off my health and mana pools.

I sighed with relief as my wounds visibly healed. Almost instantly, I felt as strong as ever. That new utility spell was already proving its worth. If I had to fight multiple monsters at the same time, when I killed one, I could absorb its energy. That would keep me fresh and able to keep fighting far longer.

After washing off my face and hands and sword hilt with a flask of water, I focused on the dead monster and triggered Harvest.

Congratulations, Lucas! You have successfully harvested Void Step. Uses remaining: 2. Void Step. Spell. Teleport up to 100 feet within your line of sight. Mana Consumption: Moderate.

I pumped a fist in the air. I'd taken a bit of a gamble making Harvest my permanent spell. Looked like it was a good choice after all. I couldn't see how I could have gotten a teleport ability otherwise.

The new spell, plus the 3 single-use spells I'd gotten from that loot box finally gave me a solid range of offensive abilities. With Energy Ward providing vital defense and Harvest filling in my spells with new, random options, I should be able to keep fighting without running out of spells.

Grinning, I accepted the prompt to loot the serpent. I received 25 mana crystals, 1 standard healing potion, and a crafting item.

Void Serpent hide. Uncommon. Can be crafted into leather armor, boots, or gloves with excellent defense against weak to moderate piercing or slashing damage and minor defense against elemental damage. Adds a 10% movement bonus.

That would be fantastic when I figured out how crafting worked. For now, I left it in my recently-expanded inventory and lay back on the grass to rest.

"Cyrus, how does that efficiency you talked about work? Compared to that snake I still felt weak. If my body is so much stronger, shouldn't I have been able to dodge it better?"

"Great question. Your base Strength and Constitution are now roughly 50% greater than when you were a level-11 baby human. As you level up, the math gets a little strange, given that you evolved so early."

"You said by the time I hit level 10, it should start making more sense, and I'd end up at about 4 times the power of a tier-0 person with the same stat numbers?"

"Indeed. The process of evolving to a new tier is not as simple as putting on a new pair of socks. Yes, each stat point gives you more, building on the base foundation which is much more powerful than a baby human."

"And eventually, my stats could be worth up to 10 times as much as tier-0 stats?"

"Again, correct."

"So how do I unlock my full efficiency?"

"The best way is to evolve spells and abilities to tier-1. As they evolve, they help reinforce your core, which allows you to unlock additional efficiencies. That in turn allows you to access far more of your tier-1 potential."

"Okay." That was promising. "How do I evolve spells and abilities?"

"Get to level 10," he said cheerily.

I sighed. "Again, level 10 is the big milestone. So I'm limited until I get to stage 2?"

"Right again."

"This is going to be a challenge," I muttered. Why did that surprise me? Cyrus had told me it would be.

He responded to my comment, his voice more serious. "Lucas, nothing is free. As we discussed before you read the scroll, you have to prove yourself before unlocking the rest of your evolved power. This game is not designed to be easy. To not only succeed but rise to the forefront, you will have to take risks that others who are willing to settle for mediocrity won't need to worry about."

"I get that, and I'll take your tests, Cyrus." I'd walked into this knowing it would be tough. Now I understood a bit more, and the challenge was huge, but I'd find a way through.

"Of course you will. Lucas, I've known you less than a day and I already know that you've never backed down from a challenge or let danger hold you back."

How did he know so much about me? Could he read my mind? Very likely. Then he knew I wouldn't stop. For now, I had a team to find. So I returned to the body of my fallen teammate and stared down at his bloody form.

How long ago had he died? The blood looked congealed, but I didn't know how long it took to get like that. Could I have arrived soon enough to save him? Eva surprised me.

Do you wish to loot Andy Johnson?

I hesitated. "Andy." That didn't sound like a Samoan name. Maybe I was just bad at telling where people were from.

Did Andy have a family? Had he been an actor, an extra, or a movie worker? I'd never know.

I sighed and accepted the prompt. Part of me felt horrified that I would loot the dead, but I didn't want to die too, and Andy might have something that could help keep me alive. I honestly believed he would want me to take it.

A dark cloud enveloped Andy's body, and for a second I feared it would melt away like the monsters had. That would be the final, ultimate insult. Thankfully, he didn't disappear.

Instead, his body seemed to shrink in on itself until he looked like a half-starved mummy. For a moment, I just stared as the brutal reality of our new world crashed in on me.

Sure, I'd almost died several times, but I'd made it through. Andy had not. Glancing at the survivors counter, it had ticked down even more. People were dying. They would not respawn.

I'd seen a lot of devastation during the years I worked the fire crews, and I'd seen some death. It was always ugly, but this felt worse. I spent a solemn moment of silence standing vigil over Andy's corpse, my emotions weaving into a cold fury at those who had chosen to do this to us. I would win their stupid game, and I would save as many as I could.

Glancing at the loot I got from Andy, I grimaced. He had not had the kind of luck I'd enjoyed. I picked up a handful of mana crystals and 1 basic food ration. Had he not looted any of the monsters he fought? Or had he been forced to use everything to defend himself? I searched the glade, but found no other gear or weapons. That was really depressing.

More likely, he hadn't chosen Mystic Looter, so hadn't been able to loot monsters at all. The other utility spells all seemed fantastic, but looting was definitely a top priority, especially so early in the game when we had basically nothing. If he'd chosen a different spell, he might have lived a bit longer. Any mistake could get us killed.

I lacked a shovel, but didn't want to leave Andy's body lying in the grass for the next monster to eat. So I carried him into the pile of boulders I'd crossed earlier and lowered him into a crevice, then piled smaller rocks on top to form a cairn.

"Sorry I couldn't do more, buddy," I whispered. "Rest in peace. I'll do what I can to help win this crazy game and save Earth."

Then I turned and jogged off, feeling more somber than I had all day. I just hoped my other teammates were faring better.

Chapter Twenty

I Play Dodge With a Rockslide

I continued northeast, hoping the quest helper had been signaling the locations of more than one teammate. Or at least a teammate who still lived. I was glad I found Andy and avenged him. My quest updated to 1 of 4 teammates found, but I didn't feel like I'd actually made progress.

The forest remained sparse, with enormous trees and spiky underbrush. This entire valley seemed to be pretty uniform. I heard howls and roars in the distance, but spotted no monsters.

The afternoon sun was nearing the smaller mountains blocking the valley to the west, so Arasha's rotation was like Earth's, at least. Would gravity have felt weird if the planet spun the other way? Thankfully, that was one other worry I didn't need to deal with. From what I'd seen so far, Arasha's day cycle seemed pretty similar to Earth's, even though the planet had seemed smaller from that first glimpse we'd gotten up in space.

Assuming the days and nights worked similar to Earth, I probably still had at least a couple hours of good light left. I pushed on harder, hoping to find someone before dark.

The ground started rising more, the trees thinning further as I neared the steep foothills leading up to the higher mountain cliffs that blocked access farther north. Soon I'd have to turn west or head deeper into the rising slopes to the east.

A few minutes later, I topped a long rise, enjoying the feeling of strength as I ran. I was breathing easy, despite the hard exercise and felt like I could run all day.

I had learned that my Endurance stat depleted while I ran. Instead of just saying 3, it changed to show my current percentage of the max, like 2.5 of 3. It recovered quickly when I rested, climbing back up a lot faster than my health or mana regenerated.

I paused to study the next glade between hills. It was a pretty, grass-lined meadow, ringed with smaller trees. One giant tree rose in the center, like one of the towering sequoias in California. Its lowest branches had to be at least 40 feet off the ground, and its crown covered half the glade.

Movement at the base caught my eye, and I squinted. It was still a mile away, but I made out a humanoid figure. They had to be huge, their head more than halfway up the trunk to the first branch. I couldn't tell what they were doing.

I heard a scream, though.

It rang distantly from the same direction and my heart ran cold. That sound was unmistakably a human woman. A teammate.

I bolted down the slope, straight toward the glade and the giant tree. Whatever was going on, I refused to allow another teammate to die before I reached them.

I crossed that mile in less than two minutes. Running down hill over open ground, pouring on everything I had, I could move! In any other moment, I would have laughed with pure joy all the way. Instead, I railed at the fact that I couldn't run even faster.

As I drew closer, the situation became clear. A woman was up in that huge tree. Somehow she'd made it up to that first branch, and I was glad she had. The branch was as thick as a road, and she crouched on it, peering out occasionally at the monster trying to reach her.

An ogre.

It had to be. The giant, humanoid monster was even bigger than the trolls in the Lord of the Rings movies. Its thick, green hide looked rough, and it wore a leather vest studded with steel spikes, along with canvas shorts big enough to cover a truck.

It was raging around the base of the tree, throwing rocks as big as couches at the woman. Some missed, while others careened off the branch, striking with such force that bark and wood sprayed and the thick branch swayed wildly.

Between shots, the ogre would smash its wooden club against the trunk of the huge tree. The club was twelve feet log and three feet in diameter. It smashed into the trunk with insane force, cracking the bark and making leaves shudder hundreds of feet above. So far the tree was weathering the barrage, but how long before the monster smashed through?

I didn't bother with my Mirror Cloak or waste a precious instance of my new Void Step spell. The ogre was totally focused on the woman.

Only a suicidal idiot charges a 20-foot ogre with nothing but a short sword, but it was the only good weapon I had. If I hesitated and it discovered me, it would squash me into jelly in a split second. So I sprinted straight in, trying to ignore my rising terror as the huge monster loomed larger and larger in my vision.

You're an idiot! This is insane. What are you doing?

Soulrend dropped into my hand. The ethereal blade shimmered like blue smoke in the bright sunlight as I sprinted closer. The ogre seemed to blot out the entire sky as it loomed over me like a 2-story building.

Fighting a growing sense of panic, I sprinted toward the giant monster, but slowed 10 strides back until it took a heavy step that shook the ground.

That was my chance. It's footsteps tended to be several seconds apart. Gulping foul-smelling air and trying to swallow against a suddenly dry throat, I rushed forward, right up to the back of the monster.

There, I slashed it through the backs of both legs, just below the knees. I'd prefer taking out the knees directly, but they were a little too high, so my short sword wouldn't have a good angle. Tops of the calves would have to do.

The ethereal blade met some resistance as I ripped it across the backs of the ogre's legs. It wasn't the thick hide or even the bone, though. The blade passed through the ogre's flesh without leaving a mark. Instead, I felt the ethereal blade interacting with the ogre's spirit. It was a powerful spirit and resisted getting cut, but Soulrend proved up to the challenge.

I skidded to a halt next to the monster and turned to watch it fall. No lower legs meant no balance. It roared with pain, but as it toppled backward, its legs no longer supporting its weight, it glanced down and our eyes met.

The monster had brightly-glowing yellow eyes in its brutish, apelike face. They locked on me, and it bared black teeth as it smashed its club down with all its strength.

That was a much more coherent response than I was expecting. That strike would pulverize me to paste, even with Energy Ward.

So I triggered my new spell, Void Step.

The world blinked and shifted around me in a disorienting blur that left me feeling nauseous. I coughed back a rush of bile and tried to figure out where I'd ended up.

The club smashed down not far away, driving into the soft ground with a crash that shook the meadow. That's when I realized I'd teleported about 20 feet, barely to the opposite side of the ogre.

I hadn't really been focusing on my target location. Idiot! I could have used the spell to cross the clearing, or even join the woman up in the tree, probably.

The ogre crashed to the ground a second later, shaking the meadow again. I was standing close enough that I stumbled from the impact.

Righting myself, I gagged at the ogre's stench. I'd never imagined a big monster might have sweat issues, but its rank odor was like all the gym lockers in the world condensed into a liquid that had been sprayed up my nose.

The ogre roared again. I don't know if it somehow spotted me, or was just trying to catch itself, but one hand as big as a garden shed swept out and clobbered me.

It was like getting punched in my entire body by the front end of a semi. The world tumbled again, but then just kept tumbling as I rocketed across the meadow, skipping across the soft grasses like a big rock across a pond.

I knew this was a bad idea!

I triggered a standard healing potion from my hotlist while I was still tumbling. If the ogre had hit me with all his strength, I probably would have just exploded.

That blow had not been focused, but still cracked ribs and left my entire body screaming as tendons strained and my neck wrenched from one bounce where I struck face-down.

Luckily, I slowed to a crumpled heap before crashing through the trees ringing the meadow. Coughing up blood and grass and dirt, I painfully rolled to my knees and shook more grass out of my eyes. My head was still spinning, I was gasping for breath, but my thoughts focused fast when I spotted the ogre.

The monster was charging after me. Its lower legs didn't work, but that only seemed to anger it more. It was galloping across the meadow on all fours.

Its huge fists were tearing giant chunks out of ground with every lunging heave while it drove its knees into the ground to push itself even faster. Its feet dragged uselessly behind, carving long trenches in the meadow.

I looked down and was amazed to see I was still clutching Soulrend. The blade had disappeared into the pommel, thankfully. It would have been stupid rotten luck to accidentally sever the spirit in my own leg or something. I re-engaged it as I jumped to my feet and triggered Energy Ward.

My defensive aura wouldn't stop a direct hit from the ogre, but it might help me avoid a glancing blow. I needed every bit of advantage I could get.

Activating my cloak wouldn't help. The ogre knew my position, his yellow-eyed glare locked on me as he galloped like a raging bull straight at me.

A primal part of my brain was screaming at me to turn and run as fast as I could into the trees to escape. My legs quivered with the need to run and my body still trembled with pain from that crazy punch-fueled tumble, despite the soothing effects of the healing potion.

I held my ground, met the ogre's angry yellow eyes, and bared my teeth. "Come and get some!"

Man, that was weak, but it was all I had at the moment.

The ogre roared again and he threw himself forward at twice his previous speed. He literally flew across the remaining distance. One giant fist started glowing yellow as he cocked it back to deliver a death blow.

An ogre with magic? No fair!

I sprinted to the side, taking 3 fast steps, then diving with all my strength as that magic-fueled fist thundered into the spot where I'd just been.

The impact was like a thunderclap. It sprayed dirt hundreds of yards, mostly into the trees, but part of the wave blasted up under me, sending me tumbling again, even with Energy Ward diverting some of the impact.

As the world spun crazily, I caught glimpses of the ogre. His fist gouged a divot deep enough for a pond. His body crashed into the ground behind his fist, shaking the meadow again and spraying even more dirt into the nearby forest. The wave of destruction toppled 3 of the smaller trees and shook the others to their roots.

I spun 8 full somersaults as I tumbled over 50 feet through the air. Tapping into my enhanced agility, I managed to twist to land on my feet, then slid another 20 feet across the grass before stopping.

When the ogre ground to a halt, it lay still for a second, as if it had stunned itself with that strike. Or it needed a second to regain its strength after pouring so much into the punch.

I wasn't about to wait for it to come after me again. Resisting the urge to shout a battle cry, I sprinted at the fallen monster. It groaned and started to rise to its hands and knees, shaking its head and spraying more dirt everywhere.

I ran right up the sloping ramp of one of its thighs. Its thick, rough hide gave my boots excellent purchase. As I dashed up its back, I plunged Soulrend down and dragged it all the way up along the ogre's spine.

The blade left no trail of blood as it tore through the ogre's spirit like a paddle slashing through water. The ogre's powerful spirit resisted the blade, but couldn't stop it.

I didn't slow, my gaze focused on the monster's head. The ogre roared, its body stiffening with pain for 2 eternal seconds.

That was more than enough time for me to reach its massive shoulders. I swiped my sword through the back of the ogre's neck, then dove forward, plunging the blade into the base of its skull and wrenching it side to side as far as I could reach.

It was so weird seeing no visible wounds. No blood sprayed as Soulrend passed through hide and bone and flesh.

The wounds were real, though, and I sliced the ogre's spirit apart. I felt even greater resistance there, as if the monster's spirit was condensed in his head and I was trying to cut through mud.

The monster started to roar again, then its head fell forward, totally limp. Its body crashed down next, and I clung on for dear life as thousands of pounds of dead ogre smashed down beneath me.

Congratulations, Lucas! You have defeated a Rockslide Ogre, level 21. Bonus experience gained for defeating a higher-level enemy.

"No level," I noticed as I stood on the giant corpse. Not surprising. It had been the highest-level thing I'd faced, not to mention the biggest and scariest, but even combined with the giant snake, I wouldn't have gotten more than a couple levels as a baby human.

Cyrus said, "I love your enthusiasm for improvement, but you're not quite there yet."

"So, do I need a full 10 times experience?"

"The math gets complicated on challenge worlds. You broke the curve, so to speak, so I'm tweaking things as we go. For example, I've had to create a unique calculation for you to handle bonuses for level disparities. You're only level 1, but you have a tier-1 body. That places you strength-wise at least equal with a level 15 monster. Maybe higher."

"So I have to start killing monsters at least at level 25 to get a better bonus?"

"That would make my job easier, yes,"

"Test number 1," I muttered.

"Indeed! That's a great way to look at it. The rewards will be worth the effort. Look what you just accomplished."

I looked down and had to admit, defeating the ogre had been something. Attacking the giant monster had been insane, but I'd won!

My muscles shook with lingering adrenaline and a bit of fear. My stomach roiled, and my head ached. I wanted to go lie down somewhere, but then some other monster would probably show up and rip out my spine.

I glanced down at Soulrend. The epic short sword was immensely powerful, but it required me to get up very close and personal. That wasn't my preferred approach. Actually, I had no preferred approach with monsters. Back on Earth we didn't have to worry about pesky things like giant ogres.

Didn't matter. I didn't have a choice. Cyrus had given me a mighty weapon, but also forced me to take insane risks to use it. Par for the course, I guessed. I returned Soulrend to my inventory and triggered Soul Feed.

A vast cloud of pure white light flowed into the air from the ogre's corpse. It roiled all around me, a torrent of energy pouring through me, but the cloud did not dissipate. My Energy Ward sprang to life around me, looking denser than I'd ever seen, but still more white light remained.

Health and mana pools topped off and all of your physical stats are boosted by 50% for two minutes. Energy Ward fueled at 250% for two minutes. Excess energy lost.

I breathed deep, sucking more of the white light into my lungs as I enjoyed the rush of health and strength. My wounds were totally healed. My stats all glowed green with the temporary boost, but I hated to see energy go to waste.

"Can't I do anything with the rest of the energy?"

"You have nothing to store it in," Cyrus said.

"How about my energy storage crystal?"

"Even if the crystal wasn't damaged, you lack the tools to transfer this kind of latent energy into it."

I hated waste, but there was nothing I could do. Stabbing myself with my hunting knife just to use up more healing energy seemed stupid.

Would you like to use Harvest on the Rockslide Ogre?

"Yes!"

Congratulations, Lucas! You have successfully harvested the spell Thunder Punch. Deliver a devastating blow of concentrated power equal to 5 times your strength. Remaining uses: 3. Cooldown between uses: 15 seconds. Mana consumption: Major.

At least Harvest worked, and that was a great spell. It used a lot more mana than any of my other spells, but I could see why. I was still surrounded by the devastation the ogre had caused using that spell.

"Wait, are you calculating my strength as 2.1?" That would be lame.

"It is calculated on how much power you can wield, so it will be quite high," Cyrus assured me.

That was a relief. I glanced at my spells menu and frowned. "Hey, what happened to Void Step? I still had another use, didn't I?"

"You replaced it with Thunder Punch," Cyrus said, as if that was the most obvious thing in the world.

"So Harvesting a new spell replaces the last one?"

"Indeed it does."

Huh. I'd made a bad assumption thinking the old spell would stick around. Good thing I figured that out before I got in the middle of a fight and maybe lost a vital spell by replacing it at the wrong time with a new one.

"Is there a limit to the number of temporary spells I could have?"

"You get 1 with Harvest at this level of the spell, but there's no limit to the number of other temporary spells you could have. As you probably noticed, there are cooldown periods for most spells. If you can accumulate an arsenal of unique spells and the mana to cast them, you could unleash enough back to back spells to overwhelm most monsters in a never-ending barrage."

Exactly what I was just thinking. Mana potions didn't refill my entire pool instantly, but did add a bunch right away, then filled in the rest over half a minute. Still, if I could gather more temporary spells, I'd have more powerful weapons to help take down monsters and keep me alive.

Thunder Punch was a fantastic spell, and I was almost out of uses of Void Step anyway. So I took a deep breath, accepted my new understanding of Harvest, and clicked on the mental prompt to loot the ogre. Loot always made me smile.

Except I'd forgotten I was standing on a giant corpse. I gagged as an enormous cloud of black smoke and stench covered the ogre while it evaporated.

"Ugh! My mouth was open too." I leaped off and ran for the big tree, using a flask of water to rinse my mouth. I needed to remember to back up next time.

I got a bunch of basic loot, including more torches, dozens of mana crystals, another standard healing potion, water, food, and bandages. I also got my first stamina potion, which replenished Endurance.

I had to laugh when I pulled the last item from my inventory. A giant uncommon ogre's club popped into view in front of me. It was as big as the ogre's tree-trunk club, but this one was shaped more like a classic caveman club, except it was 20 feet long and probably weighed 500 pounds.

It was heavy, but I could actually lift it and swing it around some. It had no enhancements and was very unwieldy. I felt like a toddler swinging a baseball bat. Still, it might actually prove useful if I needed to bash something stationary really hard.

"Hello?"

The voice turned me around and I dumped the club back into my inventory. The woman who had been trapped up in the tree had descended and was approaching at a jog.

Chapter Twenty-One
Ruby in the Wild

The woman I'd rescued was beautiful, with a strong face, high cheekbones, and features that suggested Mediterranean heritage. Her skin was bronzed in a way that suggested it was her natural color, not the result of tanning, while her long, red hair rippled like a thick cape hanging halfway down her back.

With those kind of looks, she had to be an actress in the movie, but I didn't recognize her. Not surprising, really. The ad that called for more extras had highlighted the fact that the movie featured a lot of new talent from overseas.

Her outfit perfectly showed off her toned, athletic physique too. Hey, I recognized that outfit. She was wearing the exact same clothing as Ruby Roundhouse from Jumanji. The red crop-top shirt and odd, leather halter top left her fantastic abs bare, while the short, olive-green shorts barely reached the tops of her thighs. In fact, from the neck down, she looked a lot like the character in the movie, other than being barefoot.

"Are you alright?" she called, pausing a few feet away, her voice pleasant with a noticeable Irish accent.

I smiled. "Yeah, amazingly I survived."

It felt so good to speak with another living human. Just knowing I'd found someone before a bizarre monster murdered them boosted my optimism immensely.

"I'm so glad you came along to help." She spoke, and that accent was a delight to listen to.

"And I'm glad I found you before the ogre figured out how to climb that tree. I think we're on the same team."

She suddenly gasped, looking stricken. Without a word, she spun and sprinted across the clearing. I followed, scanning for more dangers, but saw nothing.

She stopped on the far side of the meadow near a disgusting bloody mess. It took me a moment to realize I was seeing the remains of a person who had been totally smashed in exactly the way that ogre's club had nearly smashed me.

The woman retreated a few steps, one hand going to her mouth. Then she lurched away and threw up noisily. I turned away too, fighting down my own bile. I'd already seen too much nastiness since arriving on this murder world, but the shock of seeing another brutally-murdered corpse still rattled me with undiminished force.

"I hate this place," I growled. I'd seen people die before, but not from the kind of violence that seemed commonplace here.

The woman was sobbing. I placed a comforting hand on her shoulder. "I'm sorry I arrived too late."

"His name was Joseph Walker. He and I woke up very close together and teamed up almost immediately." Her voice cracked. She cleared her throat and added in a whisper, "He distracted the ogre long enough for me to get up that tree."

That was very brave, but I wished he'd found a way to climb too. I started to speak again, but she lurched away, gagging loudly as if about to throw up again.

She glanced at me and grimaced through her tears. "I'm so sorry, but you smell like that ogre and I can't . . . It's . . . I'm sorry."

"Oh." I retreated a step and glanced down at myself. I was pretty gross. I hadn't washed after the fight with the serpent either.

Most of the monster gore disappeared when I looted them, but not all of it. No idea why. My own blood still covered quite a bit of me, and the stench of the ogre clung to me too. I sniffed myself and grimaced. I did reek.

I triggered another Laundry Day potion. At this rate, I was going to run out before the end of day one. I closed my eyes and savored the warm cleansing process, then sighed. It felt so good to feel clean after fighting a monster.

"How did you do that?" she breathed, rising and staring with open wonder.

"It's a potion I received from a loot box. It's called Laundry Day."

"Do you have any more?"

I hesitated. She was a bit grimy, but not filthy like I had been. "I don't have many and I don't really like using them until I'm totally nasty."

"I get that, but would you still consider loaning me one anyway?" she pleaded. I hesitated. I wanted to help her in every way I could, but was it wise to waste a potion?

"Please?" she asked again, taking half a step closer. "The whole world's gone banjaxed. Feeling clean would help me deal with all this better."

I sighed. Using an Irish slang definitely helped her cause. Besides, she was on my team. I had just saved her life, but a bit more good will couldn't hurt.

"Fine. Sure, but remember I don't have many."

"Thank you!" she gushed. Maybe using the potion would help her cope with Joseph's death a bit better. I extracted the potion and handed it over.

"Thank you so much," she repeated as she opened the bottle.

Rainbow light surrounded her for a few seconds as dirt and grime floated away. Her clothing turned pristine and her brown skin seemed to glow in the late afternoon light. I decided to search the trees for any other danger. I didn't want her thinking I was some kind of pervert watching her as she washed.

Behind me, she sighed just the way I had when I first used the potion. If we'd had that kind of cleaning experience back on Earth, mom wouldn't have had to hound me to shower after football in high school.

When she finished, I turned back and asked, "Better?"

"Much. Too bad I don't have better clothes." She gestured at herself. "This ridiculous outfit makes me look like an exhibitionist. It's all I've gotten so far, though, and it's a lot better than the string bikini I woke up in."

I chuckled. "Tell me about it. I woke up wearing boxers, but I got lucky with a couple loot boxes." I tugged at my jacket, feeling doubly grateful I'd gotten good clothes. I hadn't even considered I might get something stupid like Robin Hood tights.

The jacket still had a hole in the right shoulder. I was hoping it would self-repair, but it hadn't yet and I had no idea how to fix leather.

She eyed my jacket and cloak with obvious longing, but didn't say anything.

"Want to borrow this?" I asked, fingering my jacket.

Cyrus's clothing choices at game start left a lot to be desired. Waking up in some strange dude's boxers had freaked me out.

She hesitated before shaking her head. "No, but thanks. How about your cloak?"

My turn to hesitate. It was my best clothing item by far. The cloaking function could prove the difference between life and death. Still, my mom had raised me to treat a lady well.

"Okay, but only until we find you some better clothes." I explained the cloak's enchantment and she accepted it with a look of awe on her face.

"Are you sure? This is amazing."

"Like I said, temporary loan."

She swung the cloak around her shoulders, grinning widely. "This is grand. I got a stealth ability that should work well with it."

"Sweet." Maybe I'd made a better decision than I'd realized. If she could sneak up on monsters even better than I could, maybe she could help kill them before we had to fight.

She activated Mirror Cloak's invisibility and faded from sight. She was standing right there, but motionless, I couldn't see anything. The effect was total.

"Is it working? Everything seems all black and white to me."

"You're totally invisible."

She squealed with delight. "Magic is amazing!"

"It can be," I agreed, smiling at her joy.

Then she made a very unladylike growl and turned off the invisibility. She looked annoyed. "I just got a message that wearing anything over my base outfit negates the defenses it provides."

"You get defensive buffs from it?" The barely-modest outfit didn't seem magical.

She sighed. "Pretty good ones too. The cloak is wonderful, but I need the defense."

She made to take it off, but I held up a hand. "Keep it for now. We're not in danger, and the stealth might prove more important than defense."

She didn't argue, but clutched the cloak tighter around herself. "Thank you. You're a good man."

Take that, Isabella!

Her smile returned. "I have to ask since we're on the topic of clothing, where did you get those shorts?"

"The monster I looted them from was adorable, but nasty. You wouldn't believe how soft these are. Want to feel them?"

She raised one eyebrow and I realized what I'd just asked. My cheeks flushed. "Sorry. That probably came out a lot creepier than I intended."

"Yes, it did," she agreed, but managed the hint of a smile.

To save my reputation, I opened my inventory and extracted my moccasins. "I noticed you don't have any shoes. Interested?"

"Yes!" She eagerly accepted them, then slipped them on and sighed in exactly the way I had when I first got them.

"I'm glad they fit okay." They should have looked like boats on her.

"I don't see how they can. They feel like they're made for me, but then you never would have been able to put them on."

"Maybe clothes adjust to fit. Everything I've tried on feels like it was tailored for me."

She shrugged and tossed her long hair over one shoulder. "I'm just glad it worked."

"I'm Lucas, by the way," I said, extending my hand.

She took it with a firm grip. "Right. We kind of got sidetracked. I don't usually talk about the underwear I woke up in before introducing myself. This place makes me an eejit. I'm Ruby."

"Ruby Roundhouse?" I couldn't help exclaiming.

She scowled. "Ruby Lopez."

"Maybe whoever's running the show has a sense of humor."

"The loot box I got the outfit from said it was custom selected for me. I did actually wear a costume like this to a comicon once."

"You go to comicons?"

"Not usually, but some friends invited me."

"Sounds fun. I've wanted to go to comicons before, but never got the chance."

"It was alright," she said with a shrug. After a moment's hesitation, she asked, "How tall are you?"

"Nothing like random questions to break tension."

"Sorry, it's just, I feel like I've gained a couple inches somehow. When I wore a costume like this that one time, I was too short to really pull it off. Now, it feels better, but I've felt a bit unbalanced. You look about average height, so I shouldn't be almost as tall as you."

"I'm five-eleven." Or maybe more, if Cyrus's comment about gaining some height proved true. I couldn't wait to measure myself against Tomas. Matching his height for the first time in my life would make the insane experiment worth all the negatives.

I scanned her again. "You look maybe five-eight, five-nine?"

Ruby nodded and said softly, "I used to be five-five."

"Weird. I might have actually gained an inch from a loot box, but changing size can't be normal."

She crossed her arms, not hiding her worry. "How do they know so much about us? How did they even bring us here?"

"I don't know," I admitted. If only I could get my hands on the people responsible, I'd make them experience a death battle. "It's clear we're not in Kansas any more, but—"

"Ha! I understood that reference," Cyrus interjected.

"What the hell?" Ruby muttered, tensing and scanning the sky.

I glanced up too. "You get all the references even though you claim you only barely scanned our planet."

"I only had a fraction of the time usually allocated, but I did find your movies. They are fascinating. I never found anything like that on any of the other—"

He broke off.

"Other what?" Ruby asked.

Cyrus did not respond.

"That doesn't really get less startling, despite how many times he does that."

"You sound like you've had actual conversations with whoever that is." Ruby was looking at me strangely.

I shrugged. "He calls himself Cyrus now."

"Cyrus?"

"It's kind of a long story. We can chat about it more later. First, I think we need to bury Joseph, then focus on finding the last person on our team, don't you?"

Ruby's mood crashed and fresh tears filled her eyes. She glanced at the corpse, shuddered, and looked away. "Oh, Joseph. This world is a pox!" She glanced at me and whispered, "How could I get distracted so badly when he's lying right there?"

"Our entire lives got turned upside down and you nearly got smashed by an ogre. It's impressive you're functional at all. Don't beat yourself up for getting a bit distracted."

"I'm so glad you're here."

Yeah, dealing with another teammate's corpse alone would have royally sucked. When I looked over at Joseph's remains again, Eva spoke.

Do you want to loot Joseph's body?

I accepted out of reflex, then cursed myself for a fool. I should have asked Ruby if she wanted to. The remains shrank in a similar way to Andy's body. This time, the remains condensed into the recognizable form of a man in his 30s. He looked kind of skeletal, like he'd been on a starvation diet, but otherwise whole.

"Look," I said gently.

Ruby turned and gasped. "Joseph! How?"

"I got a prompt to loot him. Looting makes monsters disappear, but does this to people. I don't know why."

She shuddered, hugging herself and whispered, "Loot."

"I know it's not what we'd do at home, but this world is brutal. He's dead. If he has any useful loot, we need it. I'm sure he would want us to use it to stay alive."

She took a long breath, looking a bit sick. "I'm glad you got the prompt. I don't think I could have . . ."

"I understand. This world is insane, but we can't ignore any advantage."

She nodded slowly. "I can accept that, but shouldn't we bury him, or something?"

"Yeah, I made a cairn in a pile of stones for Andy, the other guy I found."

"You found another person? They died too?"

I sighed and nodded. "Yeah. I killed the monster that got him too."

"I'm glad you've been able to avenge both of them."

"We need to find our last teammate before they get killed too."

She nodded and glanced back at Joseph's body. The ogre had thrown enough boulders, we could probably do something similar to what I'd done for Andy, but I got another idea. "Do you have a way to make a fire?"

"Inside my tent, I do. I chose Mystic Looter, Base Camp and Bio Morph for my utility spells."

"That's how you climbed that tree."

"Yeah, it saved my life."

I really wanted to ask her about how Bio Morph worked. I couldn't have climbed that tree without magical help. We could chat about details later, but discussing our choices was a welcome distraction from dealing with death.

"I'm glad we chose different utility spells. Gives us a wider range to work with. I picked Mystic Looter too, plus Linguasight and Navigation."

I decided not to share the fact that I had a fourth utility spell. That would raise too many questions I couldn't answer.

"Linguasight?"

"Mostly for Identify. I got an upgrade in a loot box, and it helps a ton."

"Huh. I hadn't even considered that one."

"I've got some torches. We could pile rocks like I did for Andy, or gather wood for a pyre. You knew Joseph. What do you think?"

She considered it. "Pyre. A pile of rocks just feels cold."

"Sure. Let's do it."

We set about gathering wood and piling it into a huge pyre in the pond-sized indentation the ogre had smashed into the ground. That way the fire would have less chance of spreading.

As we worked I said, "We're supposed to have a team of 5. Two are dead already. We're not off to a good start."

"Do you have any idea which way to go to find the last one?"

"No. I got one bonus spell to help find you, but it's spent now. My map only shows places I've been, or the area immediately around me. Did Joseph have anything helpful?"

"I don't know," she said with a frown. "Life was pretty hectic, but I think he kept more of the loot than I did."

I finally checked the loot I got from Joseph's body. He had a lot less than I did, but a lot more than poor Andy. A few dozen mana crystals, 1 minor healing potion, a few food rations and a partial box of water flasks. I also got his basic cotton trousers. I might take a look at those later, but the thought of wearing a dead guy's pants kind of creeped me out.

I gave Ruby the healing potion, but she refused the food and water rations. "I can make all I want with Base Camp."

More interesting was a heavy leather tome titled Dictionary of Monsters. The description read, "Contains information on most monster species found within the game."

That sounded super helpful. I definitely planned to study it, but noticed the next item.

Ostrich egg bomb. Rare. Can be detonated using a delay timer of up to 30 seconds, or with a mental command. Effects: trigger a powerful explosive blast, followed by a secondary cloud of sleep-inducing gas.

Huh. Why hadn't Joseph used that on the ogre? It might have saved his life. Then again, maybe the ogre got too close too fast.

"Did Joseph have a jacket?" I asked as I pulled the item from my inventory. It was a simple jean jacket in a loose style, almost like a barn jacket.

"No. Did you get that with his loot?"

I handed it over and Ruby slipped it on under the cloak. At first it hung very loose, but then shrank to fit. It hung past her hips, and for a moment I hoped it would work.

Then she scowled and took it off. "Jacket totally voids my defensive boost. I'll keep it for when I get another base layer, if you don't mind."

"Sure. Go ahead. Why would the game force you to wear so little, though?"

"Alien perverts," she scowled.

"Maybe. We'll find something eventually." It was nothing short of cruel to force her to choose between modesty and better defense.

She nodded, and we got back to work.

Chapter Twenty-Two
Glamping in Style

In minutes, we piled a huge mound of wood, even though we lacked an ax or chainsaw. Ruby had decent stats already, and I was even stronger. I could fling entire tree lengths easily. It was actually a lot of fun.

I had understood conceptually that I was far stronger than before, even stronger than power lifters on Earth. I didn't really get it, though, not at a visceral level until I did the work of a tractor and barely broke a sweat.

"How are you so strong?" Ruby asked at one point, leaning on a log she'd just carried to the pyre. "You're only level 1. While we're on the topic, how is that possible? Even if you spent the first few hours hiding in a hole, just killing the ogre should have leveled you up a couple times."

"First, how can you tell? You didn't get Linguasight, so you don't have the Identify skill."

"No, but I still see basic information. For example, the system told me that monster was an ogre."

"Rockslide Ogre."

She shrugged. "I had no idea. When I look at you, I see your name and level."

"Huh." I hadn't actually triggered Identify on Ruby yet, so I willed it to activate.

"Ruby Lopez. Baby Human. Level 8."

"I get your name, race, and level. I'm assuming I'll get more eventually, like classes when we get them."

"If we get classes," she muttered.

I nodded. "My level's kind of a long story, actually. I got a unique loot box that dramatically improves the effects of my stats, but makes it a lot harder to level up."

I couldn't get into details of my tier-1 body, but the explanation was enough for her to understand. I liked Ruby. Hell, back on Earth, if I wasn't dealing with the heart trauma of having my long-time girlfriend refuse my proposal of marriage and totally reject me, I might have asked her out.

Thankfully, I could leave all that drama behind. I didn't need a girlfriend. I needed to get stronger. We were teammates, and we needed to trust each other, but Cyrus had made it clear I couldn't share my secrets with anyone.

"That's rough," she said, pursing her lips as she considered my words. "Being stronger is good, but if you don't reach level 10 . . ."

"Believe, me, I know. I'm working on it."

"You can't have far to go to reach level 2 after killing the ogre. That was amazing, by the way. I thought you were dead."

"So did I for a minute."

It felt good to be appreciated, and I tossed a huge log onto the pyre, barely noticing the weight. My boosted stats from absorbing the ogre's energy had faded, but I could still manage.

We moved Joseph's remains onto the huge pyre with as much dignity as we could. I was glad I looted him. The process restored his corpse to a form we could actually move. As he was before, I would have needed a shovel to scrape his pieces off the ground.

I extracted 2 torches, handed 1 to Ruby, and together we lit them, then touched them to the pyre. The wood and leaves caught quickly. As the fire roared high, we retreated, watching it burn. The heat turned the cooling air blistering hot, driving us back even more.

Ruby started to talk softly, her eyes glued to the fire.

"That was my first movie. It was my big break."

"Did you land a major role?"

She laughed, looking honestly surprised. "Stop kidding. I'm not an actress. My training was in paralegal and business management before I landed the job to serve as Elizabeth Maberly's personal assistant."

Huh. I'd gotten that one totally wrong. "Do you know if Elizabeth was on set when we got teleported here?"

She nodded. "I wish I knew if she was still alive."

Elizabeth Maberly was an up-and-coming actress in her early 20s, famous for her good looks and the racy roles she'd played in some European films. The brochure with the call for extras had featured an article about her, and I was surprised to realize I remembered it word for word.

Was that an effect of my intelligence stat? Cool. Elizabeth was the daughter of a British diplomat and an Italian opera singer, and she'd won the starring role in the movie, some kind of warrior princess love interest. The thought of maybe meeting her had motivated Jane, Edmund, and Patrick to try out as extras, although for different reasons.

Thinking of them, I hoped they were okay. I would find them, find Tomas, and together we'd figure out how to win.

The sun had long fallen behind the mountains, and darkness was settling slowly over the meadow. It didn't look like it would get too dark as long as no clouds rolled in, though. The sky was blazing with stars, but in patterns totally different than Earth.

I wasn't much of a stargazer, but I knew to look for the Big Dipper and the Milky Way. Those were gone, replaced by millions of bright stars twinkling with a lot more colors than Earth's atmosphere ever showed. White, blue, red, and yellow intermingled, forming a stunning tapestry across the heavens.

Lording over it all were two huge moons just creeping over the mountains. One was orange and had bright blue rings. The other looked black, like a strangely glowing hole in the night sky, visible because of a dim silver ring around its perimeter, like the real moon was hiding behind it.

We stood in silence for a few minutes, just watching the fire burn. I figured it would keep monsters back. Well, unless a fire-breathing dragon wanted a warm bed. The thought made me feel tired. If something like that showed up, we were dead.

To take my mind off of the sudden itching between my shoulder blades, I asked, "What spells do you have?"

Ruby grimaced. "I used up all my temporary spells just surviving to this point."

Not good. She was almost level 10 and she wouldn't have a spell to permanent. That would be terrible. She didn't have Harvest, so the only way to get new spells would be through loot boxes. Making Harvest permanent was an even smarter move than I'd realized. With it, I would end up with a huge advantage over most other people, at least for a while.

Ruby hesitated, then said, "My Bio Morph utility spell has a special upgrade that allows me to use body enhancements for combat."

"Whoa. How did you get that?" If I'd had access to an upgrade like that, I probably would have chosen Bio Morph. Possibilities flashed through my mind of fighting with razor-sharp claws and fangs.

She sighed and fingered her thick, long red hair. "I got a potion to change my hair from black to red. It came with the Bio Morph upgrade."

"It sounds like a great upgrade," I said more softly, sensing her mood.

She sighed again and glanced up, blinking away actual tears. "I used to have the same hair as my mother."

Another hard choice Cyrus had forced on her right off the bat. That sucked. Ruby wiped at her eyes and added, "Sorry. I'm acting like an eejit."

"No you're not. You had to make a tough choice, but I think you chose well. That upgrade could prove invaluable."

Her words reminded me of everything I'd left behind. My parents, grandmother, friends, new startup company. This crazy death battle world made my life before getting teleported away feel distant, but I didn't want to lose touch with it. That was my real life, what made me who I was. Everything I cared about was on Earth.

She managed a weak smile. "I know. I just miss my mom."

"We'll get back to Earth," I promised, although I had no idea how.

Ruby glared into the sky. "You're right. We will. Even though they're playing games with us, we'll win."

"As long as we work together and find more survivors, I know we will."

"Thanks, Lucas," she said with a grateful smile. "I needed the confidence boost. I've been feeling like I'm getting railroaded into a role they want me to play, and I don't have any choice."

I knew all about that. Cyrus's little experiment had hurled me onto a path I still wasn't sure I could survive. I stepped closer and placed a hand on her shoulder. I met her brown-eyed gaze and said, "I understand. I didn't get 4 extra inches of height or get forced to change my hair color, but I had to make some tough choices too. I bet everyone's faced some tough calls already."

Ruby took a deep breath, then blew it out hard. "In addition to that stealth ability I mentioned, I also have a hunting ability. No idea where that came from, but it's supposed to help me sense my quarry."

"Perfect!" I laughed. At her confused look, I added, "Can't you choose to hunt our next teammate?"

"Why didn't I think of that?" she exclaimed, then frowned in concentration for a moment. "I don't feel anything."

"Try it again in the morning. We should probably camp for the night."

"Good idea. What abilities and spells do you have?"

I told her what I could.

"You still have both of your starting spells, plus three single-use spells? How?"

"I survived some crazy monsters and got some lucky loot."

"That loot that stunted your leveling really screwed your chances. Are you worried you won't make it?"

"I'll make it," I assured her.

She accepted that and looked around. "Where should we camp?"

I was tempted to suggest the huge tree, but we could just as easily run into climbing monsters. Fighting up there would leave us at a serious disadvantage. I also didn't want to wander into the dark woods. Distant roars and howls still reverberated in the distance, but maybe more monsters came out at night?

So I nodded toward the fire. "This thing is going to burn for hours. It gives us some light and protects our backs. Why not right here?"

"Works for me." She walked several paces away, and suddenly a huge tent popped into existence in front of her.

She laughed. "It's bigger than I expected."

It looked like one of those big, blocky 10-man tents families used at campgrounds, except the fabric shimmered slightly with some kind of camouflage magic. I could still see it, but I bet monsters or even people outside of our team would have trouble finding it.

"It's massive," I agreed, moving to the entrance to take a look. Ruby stepped through first.

She gasped and I could see why when I followed. We stepped into a comfortable living room that could have been plucked from a modern home. It came complete with a couch and three overstuffed chairs arranged around an oriental rug, facing a free-standing fireplace. A globe of soft, amber light shone at the peak of the ceiling, filling the entire tent with a warm glow.

Against the back wall, which was a lot farther away than should be possible inside that tent was a kitchen counter, complete with wooden cupboards that looked like white oak, and a gleaming blue marble countertop.

Sitting on the counter was a blocky, stainless-steel appliance with a hopper-like opening extending from the top and a glass door on the front. Identify kicked in.

Field kitchen oven. Produces delicious food from a default menu. Add any organic material to expand the menu choices.

To the left of the oven sat a rose-petal shaped bowl colored a delicate pink with a spout hanging over the top. That was the fresh water sink. Two doors led off the main room, which was already too big to fit in the tent. A quick peek in one showed a comfortable bedroom with a queen-sized bed, complete with a thick mattress and soft comforter. At least a dozen pillows were piled all over. The other room turned out to be a washroom with a basic shower, sink, and toilet.

"This is incredible," I breathed as Ruby inspected the oven. I was very happy with my utility spells, but if I ever got a fifth, I had to get Base Camp.

Then again, Ruby had it, and it was big enough for our entire team, once we found our last person.

"Do you want chicken cordon bleu or sirloin steak and potatoes for dinner?" she asked in a shaky, wonder-filled voice.

"Steak for me. I wonder if they'll get the taste right."

Ruby sighed then, leaning against the counter, her expression falling. "I cannot tell you how grand it feels to have a place like this to retreat to at night. If only we'd teamed up a bit sooner, there might still be four of us to share it."

I wasn't sure what to say. I hadn't known Andy or Joseph, but they'd died violently in an alien world. If I'd moved faster or been smarter, could I have saved them?

Having the tent did feel like a godsend and I took strength from the temporary reprieve. "I think the best way to honor them is to keep each other alive and try to help as many others as we can."

Ruby nodded, wiping at her eyes and sniffling once. Then she straightened and said, "Yes. Let's do that."

Chapter Twenty-Three

The Games We Play

"Don't forget, the walls are just fabric," I reminded Ruby. Any of the monsters we'd faced that day could rip through the tent without slowing. It could turn into a death trap in a second.

Her eyes glazed as she studied something in the air I couldn't see. "Actually, I just found a menu showing me all of the Base Camp's features. I can turn on the fire and even regulate temperature. It's also got something called a Fortress Defense ability. It's some kind of protective ward."

"Thats way more than the description in the utility menu suggested."

"I know, right! I'm so glad Joseph convinced me to pick this one. The defenses are not that strong yet, but can be upgraded. In fact, nearly every aspect of this place can be upgraded."

"How?"

"Mana crystals. First level defense upgrade doubles the protection, but it costs 75 mana crystals. I don't have that many."

I dumped 75 mana crystals on the counter. They tumbled onto the granite with a surprisingly musical jingle. The pile of softly-glowing crystals sparkled like magical treasure.

Ruby gasped. "I can't use so many of yours."

"I have enough, and it's worth upgrading our defenses while we sleep, don't you think?"

She didn't argue further, but swept the mana crystals into her own inventory. A moment later, the tent vibrated softly.

"That's it?"

"Simple," she said, sounding relieved. "The defenses are supposed to be able to hold off monsters up to level 20."

"That's most of what I've seen so far, but the ogre was 21. How much does it cost to upgrade again?"

"Can't. The menu's disabled. Doesn't say when it'll open again."

I sighed. It had been too much to hope for easy upgrades. Everything took time and levels.

Still, how far could the Base Camp get upgraded? Could it become a mobile fortress? How about the other utility spells and our other abilities? Many had said upgradeable, but I hadn't thought much about it.

Could she upgrade her combat-focused Bio Morph and become like Black Panther, or some kind of boss shapeshifter? Could I upgrade Energy Ward to block all types of attacks and become a truly powerful defensive barrier?

The thought made me smile. "Check it tomorrow night. Maybe it's a single upgrade per night."

"Of course."

The oven beeped and Ruby extracted two plates of steaming food. She had picked the chicken for herself and handed over the steak. The plate felt real, and it came with a steel fork and steak knife. We sat in two of the chairs to eat, and I don't think I've ever eaten a better steak.

"How can they cook steak this well when we're not even on Earth?" I wondered.

Cyrus took it as a question directed at him. "I've got recipes and instructions from all the best chefs on your planet. Those only took a fraction of a second to compile."

Ruby leaned back, a contented smile on her face. "That was delicious. Can we get a good bottle of white wine too?"

"Not yet, but a drink dispenser upgrade will become available soon."

"You're kidding," I exclaimed.

"Why? It's in our best interest to keep players well supplied. No one wants to watch a starvation show, despite how popular Alone is on your world."

"Who's watching what?" Ruby asked.

I shook my head. "Don't bother. He just teases, but won't share details yet."

"When did you become so negative?" Cyrus asked, his voice actually sounding like he was pouting.

"You have to realize how annoying it is when you mention something over and over but won't tell us more?"

"I . . . Had not realized it would bother you so much," Cyrus said softly.

"Don't worry about it. On another note, are nights as long here as on Earth?"

No answer.

"Is he sulking?" Ruby whispered.

I hoped not. That could be disastrous for all of us. Served him right, though. Maybe he'd start actually giving us more details.

As soon as we finished eating, the plates and utensils disappeared. I'd have to try tossing the steak knife into my inventory next time and see if it remained.

"So, Lucas, tell me about who you were before today," Ruby said, lounging back in her chair.

So I did. I explained how I'd left forest fire fighting, quit my skydiving instructor job, and switched to computer cyber security. Once I started, the words just flowed and I told her a lot more than I intended, although I left Isabella out completely.

I finished with a bit about my new startup cyber investigation company I was about to launch. With it, I planned to track down scammers, especially those who stole money from old people.

"What motivated you to make such a huge career shift?" she asked, tucking her hair behind one ear and pulling one foot up under her other leg.

I told her about my grandmother.

"No," she breathed. "Oh, Lucas, that's terrible."

"Yeah, and no one ever got caught. Hackers and scammers can work with almost no consequences. They destroy the lives of the most vulnerable and get away with it to strike again. I plan to change that. Well, planned to change that."

"I love your goal, but how can you do it? Aren't most of them based overseas?"

I shrugged. "Sure, a lot of them are. We'll have to set up partnerships with other countries eventually. Those will be harder and take more time. Still, many scammers are based right in the US. It's just, no one is doing anything about it. I will, though, as soon as we get back."

"Do you think we will?" she asked softly.

I flashed my best smile. "Of course. Weren't you listening? Beat the game, save Earth. Then they'll have to send us back."

"I hope you're right." She turned to look at the empty fireplace.

She must have accessed the menu because suddenly a happy flame burst to life behind the glass. She stared at it, her expression sad.

I had to believe we'd get back. Maybe we could even bring our new powers back. With magic to help, I bet I could catch 10 times as many hackers. Then they'd pay.

It was weird that I hadn't thought much about home or my business since we'd gotten slammed down onto this insane death battle world. On a good note, I'd finally been able to get Isabella out of my head for a while.

Partially, that was due to the danger and insanity and constant need to fight for our lives, but was that all? Back on Earth, my job had felt so important, a calling to help make the world a better place and fight for those who were truly vulnerable. And yet, compared with the need to fight to save the entire planet from getting wiped out, my old life seemed weak, somehow.

Ruby sighed, pulling me from my somber thoughts. "My grandmother is very sick. After that shoot finished, I was supposed to take a week off to visit her." Her voice faded to a barely-audible whisper. "She might not make it to the end of the month."

"I'm very sorry."

She rubbed at her eyes and sniffled. "It's fine. She's got a fiery personality. If she were here, she'd tell us to stop wasting time and win this game already."

"She sounds amazing."

Ruby nodded and managed a slight smile, but looked troubled. After a moment, she added in a soft voice, "Lucas, this game is evil, right?"

"It sure seems to be." That was a weird question.

"I know. I've been terrified and nearly died multiple times. Joseph and Andy are dead, along with almost 200 other people. It's evil and cruel and horrible." She fingered her red hair. "And yet, part of me is excited to level up and see how strong I can get. I mean, we've got magic, my body transformed to climb that tree. What else can we learn?" She looked up, her expression clearly conflicted. "Does that make me a bad person?"

I leaned back and considered her words for a moment before answering. "It is an evil game. It's callous and cruel, and I should have died half a dozen times already. But yeah, there's wonder here. Magic and stat boosts make us more powerful than we could ever be back on Earth."

She nodded. "That's good, isn't it?"

"It's power. I don't think that makes it good or evil. Even back on Earth, some people gained a lot of power. Different types of power perhaps, but power still. Choosing what to do with that power is what so many of them get wrong."

"Absolute power corrupts absolutely, right?"

"Lord Acton," Cyrus interjected, his usual bubbling good humor back in full force. "A British historian in your 19th century. Wisdom that applies across the multiverse."

Ruby jumped at the unexpected interruption, muttering to herself. I looked up and nodded. "Sure. Here on Arasha, looks like you've got absolute power."

Ruby's eyes widened and she shook her head slightly, as if afraid I was pushing Cyrus too far. She didn't know him as well as I felt I was starting to.

Cyrus only chuckled. "Indeed. Yet, I make sure the rules are as fair as possible and the games we play entertaining."

"The games we play," I repeated softly, thinking of the secret experiment he was playing with my life. Was that just a result of him being bored, or something deeper? Figuring that out might mean the difference between life and death.

When Cyrus did not respond again I said, "Ruby, I understand your point, and we do need to get stronger or we're going to die and Earth will die too. You're not evil to want more power. I think the harder test will be how we handle it."

She nodded slowly, thoughtful. "Thanks, Lucas. That helped." Then she rose and added, "I'm exhausted. Today has been . . . Difficult. No offense, but I'm taking the bed."

"It's your base camp. Mind if I take the couch?"

"That's fine. Do you need a blanket? I don't know if there's a spare, but—"

"I have one."

"Good night, Lucas. Thanks again for saving my life and for the chat."

"Good night."

She headed for the bedroom and I lay back on the couch, thinking of my life back on Earth. I'd barely had a moment to think about anything but pure survival since waking up on this insane world.

How much time had passed back on Earth since we left? Would anyone even know we were among the missing? We hadn't told anyone of our last-minute decision to ride to the movie shoot. It would take our parents a while to realize there was a problem.

With Dad's new job in New York, we didn't chat as often. He was swamped working for that big company I could never remember the name of. The pompous string of partner names just made me think of the old Three Stooges lawyer firm gag name, Dewey, Cheetham, and Howe.

Mom made a point of calling me more, especially after Isabella refused to marry me and dumped me altogether. She knew we were biking and out of regular cell range, though.

She could easily go a couple weeks before thinking it odd I hadn't called. Dad had gotten her a research position in the Met, working in one of their secret basements, so she often got totally absorbed in her work. For a medieval history professor, that sabbatical was a dream come true.

No, no one knew we were gone, and no one could help us. We had to figure out how to survive and win the game all on our own.

I adjusted my position on the couch and sighed. So much better than sleeping on the ground, even with my little survival kit. It was so nice to have another living person to talk to. Sharing about our pasts helped keep the insanity of this death battle world at bay a little.

Ruby seemed like a nice person. Isabella had been nice too. Her outward sweetness was one of the things I loved about her, but that hadn't been enough. She was nice, I was nice, we had some fun times together, but what was it she said? Under my veneer of responsibility, I was too wild and reckless, and she couldn't live with that.

How could that be a problem? I'd left most of my old life behind to get my certifications and start my new company. My life had become downright boring most days. How could I be less wild than that? Did she want me to stop living?

If I had, would I have even survived this long on Arasha? This world was brutal and insane and any hesitation would prove fatal. If anything, I needed to fully embrace wild and a willingness to dive into battle.

Would Isabella have survived the troll in Ruby's place? Probably not. Sad, but true. She was a gentle soul, and gentle souls probably wouldn't live long here. Isabella had stomped my heart flat, but I wouldn't want her or any other person so totally unprepared for survival to have gotten teleported here to die.

I planned to survive. I needed to, or Earth would be destroyed and all those gentle souls like Isabella and my parents would die. No, not while I could do anything about it. Together with Ruby, we'd find a way to get the job done.

Chapter Twenty-Four
I Really Need a Dodge Skill

I slept like the dead until Ruby shook me awake.

"What time is it?" I asked groggily as I sat up, rubbing at my eyes. I might have a tier-1 body, but yesterday had been insane.

"It's early morning," Ruby whispered, her gaze locked on the door. "The sun hasn't risen over the mountains yet, but I hear something."

That woke me up. I lunged to my feet. "What?"

"Snorting sounds." She looked nervous.

"Do you have any weapons?" I should have asked that sooner.

She shook her head. "Joseph had a knife."

"It didn't come with his loot. Would you prefer a hunting knife or a stick?"

"I used a stick against a rabid bunny yesterday, but didn't keep it. It seemed pretty useless."

"Yeah, they're more effective against smaller monsters. Next time, just keep everything. Our inventory is pretty big." Well, mine was, at least. Even with her standard-sized one, it would take a lot of stuff to fill it. I extracted my hunting knife and passed it over.

She took it nervously. "I'm not much of a fighter, Lucas."

"You've got stealth, though." I nodded at the cloak she'd already donned. "Will you check out the situation?"

Ruby took a long, nervous breath, then nodded, clutching the knife so hard her fingers whitened against the handle.

I placed a hand over hers and held her gaze. "Relax. Breathe slowly."

"How can you say that if there's probably a monster outside?"

"Getting tense only makes it harder to react. Panicking before we even see what's out there doesn't help us deal with whatever it turns out to be."

I held her gaze for several seconds until she visibly relaxed and took a deep breath. "Okay. I'm good. Thanks."

Just then, a loud snorting sound came from outside. With it came the sound of something hard striking the ground. There was definitely something out there. It sounded like maybe 50 yards from the tent, on the side opposite the remains of the pyre.

Part of me wished we could just hide inside and trust the tent defenses and camouflage until the monster got bored and wandered off. That was stupid, though. Not only did I really not want to get trapped inside the tent if it attacked, but I needed bucketloads of experience in order to reach level 10.

"I'll go see," Ruby said, putting on a brave face. She pulled the cloak around herself and activated it. Just like that, she disappeared from view.

The tent flap opened inward. Good, she hadn't pushed it out. That might have alerted the monster. I hated waiting, so I pulled Soulrend out of my inventory. The slight weight of the handle felt reassuring in my hand as the slow seconds ticked by.

Less than 10 seconds later, the tent flap swung inward and Ruby appeared, hurrying inside. Her face was pale and she gasped in a deep breath, as if she'd been holding it. Her hands shook so hard she almost dropped the knife.

"What is it?"

"Um, it looks like a huge elk."

"An elk?" That didn't sound too bad.

She nodded quickly, regaining her composure. "Yes, an elk. Tall, like over 3 meters, and its antlers had to be twice that." She pulled off the cloak and pressed it into my hands. "Take this. I can't. I mean, what am I supposed to do against a giant elk?" She waved her knife.

"Have you ever had an elk steak? They're delicious."

She managed a weak laugh and I swept the cloak around my shoulders. It felt good to have it back. I activated Mirror Cloak and the world turned gray.

"Wait here. The tent might offer some protection."

Not waiting for her reply, I slipped out the tent door.

The morning air was cool and fresh, and beads of dew clung to the grass. The pyre had burned to a bed of black coals with wisps of smoke still drifting into the air. On the opposite side, close to the trees at the edge of the meadow stood the monster. Identify kicked in immediately.

Mystic Archer Elk Stag. Level 20. Uncommon. With its bloodroot antlers, it can easily turn the tide against any hunter foolish enough to try to take its rack.

It really did look like a giant elk, standing over 10 feet tall at the shoulder, with antlers that spread at least 20 feet across. Its rack was like a mini forest, with more points than I could count.

Identify had added something new. I had no idea what bloodroot antlers might be, but they didn't sound good.

The elk did not attack instantly, but stood looking at me from 50 yards away. I hoped my cloak could keep me concealed until I got closer. So I took a slow, careful step. The illusion would flicker some, but if I moved very slowly, it should hold.

The elk snorted again, tossing his huge head, but made no other move. I took another step, feeling a bit more confident. If I could get close enough, I could end it before it even knew I was there.

Slow seconds ticked by as I made steady progress toward the elk. It shambled a bit farther away, dragging the time out even more. If only I had a good ranged attack.

A slight noise behind sounded like the tent rustling. I risked a glance back to see Ruby's head peeking out of the tent. I hadn't been gone that long, had I?

The elk noticed her instantly. It oriented on the tent, snorted again, and flung its head down. Three points of its antlers glowed green, then shot straight at Ruby like arrows.

With a shriek of surprise, she tumbled back inside and the arrow-like points deflected off the tent's fabric with little flashes of green light. I didn't hesitate any more, but sprinted at the elk. I could close the distance in a couple seconds. My cloaking broke and the elk snorted again, focusing on me.

"The arrows!" Ruby shrieked in fear behind me, but I couldn't risk a glance back to see what she was talking about. "They sprout vines with thorns. Ow! Get off!"

Not good. I thought the arrow points missed. Arrows with secondary effects was not something I was expecting from a stupid elk. If I still had Void Step, I could have killed it already.

The elk threw its antlers forward again and 4 more arrow-like tips flashed at me. I was close now, but had expected the attack. I dove forward into a roll under the barrage. Lunging back to my feet, I slashed at the monster's long snout.

It danced out of reach and with every step of its hooves, grasping vines covered in long thorns erupted out of the ground. Before I could retreat, they swarmed up my legs, and dozens of thorns punched through my unprotected skin.

I howled with pain and noticed my health points dropping steadily. The thorns were drinking my life!

I was not about to let a stupid elk with life-sucking vines kill me. The nasty vines locked me in place where I stood, and I lacked a good tool to chop myself free. So I dropped Soulrend back into my inventory and pulled out something else.

"Eat this, Bambi!"

The ogre's giant club appeared in my hands, already lifted high. The elk hesitated for a fraction of a second to stare at the huge weapon. I brought the club down with all my strength and at the same time triggered Thunder Punch, focusing my intent on the club.

Vast power flooded into my hands and beyond, into the club itself. Nice! I'd hoped the spell would affect my weapon too. My hands and the club glowed a brilliant golden color and the club whistled down like a meteor.

The Mystic Elk tried dodging, but only got the front half of its body out of the way. My club smashed through its back and hind haunches with an impact that shook the entire meadow and splattered elk parts everywhere.

The elk shrieked a high-pitched scream and half the remaining points of its antlers flashed green at the same time. Dozens of arrows punched into me, overwhelming my jacket's defenses.

I screamed in pain, the sound melding with the elk's cry. I swayed and would have fallen if not for the life-sucking thorns rooting me to the ground. My life points dropped precipitously and I could feel the arrows now sticking into me sprouting. It was like vines were growing inside of me, greedily drinking my blood.

Aw, that was nasty! Would they sprout into alien monsters and burst through my chest too? I barely bit back a little-kid shriek of pain and disgust.

Soul Feed drained away a fraction of the power of those arrows to boost my health back up, and Energy Ward appeared around me too. I would have preferred using all the stolen energy on healing, but lacked the focus to change the settings. Instead I dropped the club, which was now too heavy for me to lift as searing pain tore through my innards.

In the distance, Ruby was shouting something, but I couldn't hear. Blackness flickered in my vision with the promise of welcome relief, but if I surrendered, I was dead.

Stupid elk!

I triggered one of my healing potions from my hotlist. As the welcome warmth of healing momentarily countered the insidious leeching of the arrows, I pulled Soulrend from my inventory again.

The elk was barely alive, half it's body smashed to bloody ruin, but light still shone in its eyes as it glared at me, trying to move its head to hit me with another volley of vampire arrows.

That would finish me off. My body was already stiffening as the fast-spreading vines filled my veins. Even with the healing potion, I only had seconds left before they sucked me dry.

I refused to consider that fate. It was too disgusting. My legs were still locked to the ground by the thorns. I could barely move.

So I threw Soulrend.

The elk was close, but that was a dangerous shot. I could have easily missed, but I'd played little league for years and I needed a fast kill. My throwing arm did not fail me and the glowing blue blade punched through the elk's head. It collapsed as Soulrend severed its spirit right in the brain.

Instantly the vines wrapped around my feet withered. The arrows shrank and the vines slowed, but did not disappear. They were still going to kill me.

With a grunt of effort, I fell forward, my left hand extended. I crashed to the ground, barely feeling the soft earth. I hurt everywhere and it was hard to think, but I reached out and my fingers touched the elk's hide.

Congratulations, Lucas! You have defeated the Mystic Archer Elk. Bonus experience gained for defeating a higher-level enemy.

I triggered Soul Feed. White light flared around the monster and power thundered into me. Pure energy blasted through every inch of my body, and at its touch, the parasitic vines evaporated. This time, it took most of the stolen energy to restore my health and mana, but in seconds, I felt whole and fit again.

I lay back, panting, just happy to be alive. "Ow."

"Lucas!" Ruby skidded to a halt beside me, her expression horrified. "Lucas, are you okay?"

"I'm all right." I groaned, then sat up. "That was too close."

"How did you survive those arrows? I only had one of the sprouting vines latch onto me and even with my healing potion, I think it would have killed me if you hadn't finished off the elk."

Her long legs were streaked with blood and pockmarked with small wounds still closing.

"Yeah, they were nasty. I have an ability to absorb power from defeated enemies to restore my stats. Without that, I'd be dead."

"You didn't tell me about that."

"Sorry. I don't know why I forgot that one."

"Anything else you forgot to mention?" she asked, one delicate eyebrow arched.

I shrugged. "Not that I know of."

Eva's voice interrupted.

Would you like to loot Mystic Archer Elk?

Before I did, I considered if I wanted to try to Harvest a spell. Getting those vampire parasite arrows could prove useful, but I didn't have a bow. I sucked with bows.

Besides, Thunder Punch had just saved my life. I still had a couple uses remaining and I liked that one, so I decided to pass on harvesting this time. With that choice made, I accepted the prompt, snatched up Soulrend, and backed up as the elk carcass dissolved into nasty stinky smoke.

"Looting. Let's see what we got."

"Hey, I got a level!" she exclaimed.

I didn't. I wasn't sure how experience sharing in a team worked, and had to suppress a flash of irritation. Ruby had gotten to level 9, but I was still stuck at level 1.

I bet I would have gotten at least 6 levels, if not more, from the monsters I'd killed since I advanced to a tier-1 body. So Cyrus wasn't lying when he hinted I'd need 10 times as much experience to gain a new level. That sucked.

The loot helped me feel better, though, as loot always did. I got 50 mana crystals, an uncommon elk hide and 100 elk steaks.

I grinned and passed the steaks to Ruby. "We should feed these into your oven and see what new menu options it unlocks."

"Great idea. I'm looking forward to trying elk steaks."

I also gave Ruby the new pair of soft, knee-length elk leather boots that gave an extra 5% to stealth. The cream-colored boots didn't really match the rest of her outfit, but she still grinned at them, then returned my moccasins.

We got a couple standard healing potions that we split between us, and I got one more mana potion and a scroll to summon a standard healing potion. That was weird. Why not just give me the potion? I dropped it into my inventory.

"That was pretty good loot," Ruby said as we headed back to her Base Camp.

"Not bad, although I wish we'd gotten a weapon or spell for you."

"Your standards for loot from one monster are pretty high."

I shrugged. "I've gotten lucky a couple times, so I expect good things. We need the loot, so no harm in hoping."

Was it just luck, though? I thought back to my Trailblazer title that gave me a 30% chance to upgrade loot boxes. Had that triggered more than I realized? Back in her tent, Ruby tried to create some breakfast meals, but learned that the oven only produced one meal per person per day.

"It's okay. The standard rations keep a person going for a full day too."

She nodded, but still looked disappointed. "I'm not actually hungry, so you're probably right. I just like having a croissant and coffee in the morning."

"Where are you from?" That wasn't an unusual breakfast in the States, but not as common as in parts of Europe.

"Most recently, Paris, but I've lived in many countries. My dad was in international banking, so he dragged us all over the world."

"Sounds fun." I hadn't traveled much overseas, but I'd visited most of the States. Traveling across the multiverse to a death battle game had not been on my bucket list.

"Sometimes it was, but I attended 26 schools growing up, so that was hard sometimes."

"I bet." Yikes. That would have been tough, but I still liked the idea of living in so many countries. "Did you get any grief talking differently than the local kids?"

She flashed a smile. "Not at all. I have a gift with accents and usually pick up the local accent wherever we're living." Her voice shifted to a French accent and she added, "Within a month, I usually sound more local than the locals."

"That's amazing," I laughed. I'd thought her Irish accent was great, but that French accent made every word seem exotic.

Returning to her Irish accent again, she added, "We lived in Ireland when I was young, so I prefer speaking with this accent when I have a choice. It's like slipping into my favorite pair of old jeans."

"I'm terrible at accents."

"Most people are, but it's different for me. I feel the flow of language. It's like music, if you like."

I grinned at that last bit. I'd heard other Irish speakers throw 'if you like' in like a filler too. "It's pretty cool. I wonder if you would have gotten extra levels in Linguasight if you'd picked that utility spell."

"I guess we'll never know."

Time to focus again. Daylight was passing, and the count of survivors had continued to tick down. It had fallen to 782. We had a final teammate to find and I needed to fight more monsters. I only had 6 days left to level up 9 times, and it looked like I was going to have to kill a lot of powerful monsters to get there.

Chapter Twenty-Five
Dance Fighting

The Base Camp disappeared in a flash when Ruby triggered its pack option.

"Which way?" she asked.

"Do you sense anything?"

"Not really."

"How does the tracking ability work?"

She shrugged. "This is the first time I'm trying to use it."

I considered that for a moment. "Trackers usually have to look for clues, right? Tracks, broken twigs, and stuff like that."

"Probably, but the person we're hunting hasn't been here."

"True, but it's magic. So how about we circle the clearing and see if you get any impressions. If not, we'll pick east or west. I came from the south, and we won't make it much farther north before we hit that giant cliff."

She agreed and we hiked around the meadow, senses alert for more monsters. I couldn't decide if I wanted another battle right away to gain more experience, or if I preferred enjoying a pleasant stroll with Ruby while not fighting for our lives. In the end, I just tried to enjoy the moment, but remained alert for danger.

Ruby felt nothing until we circled most of the clearing and reached the western-most part. Then she stopped, cocked her head to one side, and frowned. "I'm getting a weird feeling that we should go this way."

"Works for me."

"But what if it's nothing?"

"What if it's something?" I responded with a shrug. "This was one of the directions we would have chosen anyway. The sooner we start, the sooner we find out if you're right."

The forest became more sparse as we skirted the towering mountains in a westerly direction. The ground became rockier and we had to cross several deep gullies.

I discovered that I could jump nearly twenty feet in a single bound. Whoa! Ruby managed almost as much. She might not have as much raw power, but her agility was really good.

We covered half a mile that way, jumping the smaller gullies and keeping our eyes out for monsters. We saw nothing but stunning vistas until the forest grew thicker again. Eventually we crossed through one larger meadow that had another giant sentinel tree in the center towering above the rest of the forest.

"You have Bio Morph. How about climbing that tree and seeing if you can spot anything?" I suggested.

Ruby hesitated. "I don't usually like heights, but Bio Morph does let me climb really well."

"You can do it," I assured her as I peered up into the tree. I saw no monsters and hoped she wouldn't run into trouble up there where I couldn't help.

Ruby nodded, took a deep breath, and rushed the tree. I didn't spot her physical changes when she activated Bio Morph, but she scampered up the tree as fast as a monkey. That was a really good utility spell. In moments, she ascended nearly out of sight, lost in the increasingly dense foliage up near the top.

I waited with growing worry as the seconds ticked by. Had she gotten into trouble? Was a monster eating her? I didn't hear anything, but that just made me worry more. I didn't want to lose my only living teammate so soon after finding her.

Thankfully, she reappeared a moment later, hurrying down the tree with obvious agitation. I scanned the branches behind her for any threats, ready to unleash Frostfire Nova. It was probably my best long-ranged attack.

Ruby let go and dropped the last 20 feet, easily absorbing the impact with her legs and rushing toward me.

"What's wrong?"

"Nothing. It's all good! I found him."

"Him?"

She nodded eagerly. "I saw someone walking across a meadow just a couple hundred yards south of us. And Lucas, I found a gold loot box!"

"Really? Up there?"

She nodded happily. "A hidden loot box. The AI voice said my chances of finding hidden loot were upgraded since I'm in your party."

"Yeah, that was part of my bonus."

"I love finding loot boxes!" she gushed, then extracted a bow and handed it to me.

Woodland Bow. Uncommon. This powerful bow will generate its own arrows. Can be upgraded to imbue arrows with elemental powers.

"Nice," I said with a noted lack of enthusiasm as I took the weapon. It really was beautiful, a fancy recurve design made out of a golden wood.

"You don't like it? I'm terrible with a bow, but I got a blowgun with poison darts I think I can learn to use."

I shrugged and dropped the bow into my inventory. "I'm even worse with a bow. I'm glad you got a ranged weapon. That'll help a lot."

"Do you want the blowgun?" she asked.

"No. You keep it. You can back me up from a distance. That'll play to both our strengths better."

Looking relieved, she said, "I also got a fireball spell with 2 uses and a scroll to summon a standard healing potion."

"I got one of those yesterday."

"Weird," she said with a shrug. "I should just read it."

"Hold on," I said slowly, an idea percolating.

"Why?"

"When you get to level 10, you can permanent any spell. Can you permanent a scroll? It's like a spell written down, right?"

"I don't know," she said, fine brows furrowed.

"Well?" I looked up.

"I expect nothing but great questions from you, Lucas, and that one is no exception. No one else has thought to ask that one yet among all of you Earth humans."

"Seems like an important question."

"And indeed it is," Cyrus agreed with even more enthusiasm than usual. "You can permanent any spell, including temporary spells, spells triggered by gear or weapons, although the gear would be consumed in the process, or scrolls that act like spells, like that summon potion bottle scroll."

"Wow," Ruby breathed.

"That means our permanent spells could pull from a nearly limitless list of possibilities, assuming we don't all get the same gear." The thought was kind of mind-blowing as I considered the possibilities.

"Indeed, but some things are not included, like potions or single-use scrolls that affect stats, titles, or things like that."

"How did you know I was thinking about those?"

"You were?" Ruby asked, frowning.

"Of course. Imagine getting a scroll that increases your Strength by 5 points and making that permanent."

Her eyes widened, but Cyrus chuckled. "Exactly why they are exempt."

"Are there other limitations?"

"Yet another great question. I will share a caution more than a limitation. Any spell you permanent will affect your build and eventual class choices."

"That sounds amazing more than worrying," Ruby said.

I had to agree. It suggested that our final builds could include nearly limitless possible combinations. That had to be a good thing, right? My thoughts were interrupted by Eva interjecting.

Congratulations, Lucas! For daring to ask useful questions, you receive a silver Thinking Man loot box.

The sparkling silver loot box appeared in the air in front of me and I instantly opened it, grinning with anticipation. It contained three more scrolls to summon standard healing potions and one scroll to summon a full healing potion.

I gave the last one to Ruby, who looked at it in wonder. "You can get random loot boxes just from asking questions?"

"That one's sub-par," Cyrus responded. "You already know the answer."

"He doesn't like explaining things he thinks we can figure out."

"Absolutely right!" Cyrus cheered.

Ruby looked around expectantly. "Shouldn't he get another loot box."

"I'm no longer in the mood," Cyrus said.

She gave me a confused look. I just shrugged. "You'll get to know him."

She looked like she wanted to say, "Do I want to, though?" but bit her lip instead of saying it aloud.

"So what do you think?" I asked, gesturing at the full healing potion scroll she still held. "You could save your fireball spell and make that permanent.

It would be a solid choice and could set you up for a fire wizard build, or something like that probably. Or you could make that scroll permanent and have a never-ending supply of full healing potions. Might get you a crafting class, or what, alchemist?"

"Either is a possibility," Cyrus confirmed.

Ruby considered that, a small line creasing between her delicate brows. "Honestly, I'm more tempted by the healing potions. No offense, Lucas, but you seem to enjoy the fighting and killing a lot more than I do."

"No offense taken. If I could use a bow and fight from a distance, I'd love to, but I don't have those skills. I charge in because I have to."

"I appreciate that you're here to do it. Someone has to. I totally get that, but it's not me. If I can build more of a crafting class to feed potions and things to you on the front line, I could help you survive better than trying to keep up with you."

"You have time to decide. Now at least you have options."

"Thank you."

"We got 2 more items from that loot box in the tree," she added and a pair of epic-looking leather arm bracers appeared in her hands. They had cool rune-like patterns flowing across the surface, and when she handed them over, I sensed the power imbued within them.

"Are you sure?" I asked, but still took them.

"I think you'll need them more than me."

I wasn't about to argue, but slid them onto my arms under my leather jacket. They fit perfectly.

Arm Bracers. Uncommon. These leather arm guards add defense against slashing and stabbing and make you feel like Boromir.

"I feel like I'm taking more of the loot. You're the one who found the box."

"I got another item, but I'm not sure I'll use it."

"What?" Would Cyrus give her another stupid wardrobe item, like a garter belt, or something? Cyrus seemed to like trolling her with dumb loot.

She sighed. "A scroll that gives me a level 2 Dance Fighting skill."

I laughed. "Really?"

She rolled her eyes and glared up at the sky. "Not my thing."

"A fighting skill is nothing to scoff at, though," I said, trying to hide my enthusiasm. Any kind of fighting skill would give her a big combat edge, even if she wanted to choose a more crafting-focused class. Besides, it fit the Ruby Roundhouse theme Cyrus had chosen for her, so she might unlock additional benefits by using it.

One of my favorite scenes in Jumanji was the first dance fighting scene when Ruby was failing at flirting so badly, then beat up the two thugs she needed to distract. I did not mention that, though.

"I'll think about it," she said, fingering her red hair.

Cyrus had already forced her to make choices that pegged her more and more into the role of Ruby Roundhouse. She had a point. If she accepted the Dance Fighting skill, she'd take one more step into the mold he'd created for her.

Suddenly, the skill seemed more like a trap than loot. I couldn't do anything about that, not yet. So I focused on the fact that we had a lead on our last teammate. Ruby led the way, and I followed as we rushed through the forest toward where she'd seen him.

Chapter Twenty-Six

We Decide to Get a Plumber

We found our quarry within minutes. Thankfully he was not being hunted by any monsters, but just walking between some huge trees.

He was a tall, rugged-looking guy who looked like he was probably in his 30s, with black hair and a clean-shaven face. He was wearing a really nice leather aviator's jacket and a pair of khaki shorts, but no shoes. He wasn't carrying any visible weapons. Identify kicked in immediately.

Steve McDonough. Baby human. Level 8. Water elements.

Ruby shouted and rushed past me. Steve froze in surprise, then gaped when he saw us. Ruby rushed up to him and I hurried after. Even if he was our missing teammate, it wasn't wise to rush in before we knew anything about the guy.

Steve grinned so wide, it looked like his face might split. "I'm so happy to see you guys."

Ruby stopped next to him, also grinning. "We've been searching for you."

"I'm assuming you're our missing teammate," I added as I joined them.

"Definitely," Steve answered enthusiastically. "This world is insane. I keep thinking I'm in the wildest nightmare of all time, but I can't seem to wake up."

"I wish it was just a dream."

Ruby nodded, but flashed another smile. "We're stronger together as a team."

Eva's voice rang through the forest, interrupting Steve's response.

Congratulations! You have completed the quest: Find the remaining members of your team. 4 of 4. Team interface unlocked, including team chat. You receive a silver Adventurer's loot box.

Steve frowned, looking behind us. "Wait, did you find the others? Aren't we supposed to be 5?"

"We found them, but they didn't make it," I said.

"Damn," Steve muttered. "I hate this world."

"Me too, but loot boxes do help," I said, willing the gleaming silver loot box to appear. My teammates followed suit, and we all opened our boxes together.

The adventurer's outfit popped into my inventory. I got another shirt, green this time, and a pair of tactical pants, complete with a bunch of pockets.

"Sweet," I muttered, wanting to put on the pants right there. I resisted the urge and checked out the team interface. It was a new menu option that showed members of my team, their levels, and current health and mana percentage. There was also a chat feature, allowing us to communicate at any distance.

Ruby growled. "Another stupid crop top and an extra pair of shorts. Really?" A pair of black, fingerless gloves appeared and she put them on, still scowling. "The gloves are cool, and I got another pair of boots."

She pursed her lips, considering something, and all of a sudden her elk boots disappeared, replaced by tall brown leather boots.

"You can auto-change your wardrobe?" I exclaimed. Why hadn't I thought of that?

"First time I tried it," Ruby said with a shrug and a smile.

So I willed my new pants to replace my shaggy shorts. My shorts disappeared, leaving me wearing only my boxers. My new pants fell to the ground at my feet.

Ruby frowned and Steve chuckled. "I don't think you got the point."

"Hey, it's not as easy as you made it look," I exclaimed as I yanked off my boots so I could don the pants. My face felt hot as I put my boots back on.

"I like the elk boots better," Ruby said, and her boots insta-swapped again.

"Show-off," I grumbled.

She shrugged, and Steve said, "Keep practicing, and you'll get it."

I would, but not while other people were around. In the meantime, Steve had also quietly donned a new pair of boots and now wore aviator's glasses.

"At least you've been getting good clothing," Ruby told Steve, then gasped and grinned.

"What's so funny?" Steve asked.

"Did you ever watch Jumanji?" she asked.

"The new remake, with the Rock, and Jack Black?" I asked.

"That's the one," she said.

"I love that movie, why?" Steve asked.

"I love it too." Ruby sighed. "Your jacket reminds me of Seaplane McDonough's."

Steve's eyes widened and he glanced down at his jacket. "I thought it looked familiar, but didn't make the connection. Wait, how can there be a connection?"

"My name's Ruby," she said, gesturing at her ridiculous outfit.

"You've got to be kidding me. Of course! I should have recognized you," Steve laughed until her scowl silenced him.

"Oh yeah," I'd watched the movie once with Isabella, but she'd been feeling pretty friendly, so I'd been very distracted. I'd liked it, but didn't remember it as well. "Seaplane was the guy pulled into the game years before the others?"

"That's the one," Ruby said again.

"Cyrus did say he likes movies."

"Cyrus?" Steve asked.

"That voice? He's calling himself Cyrus now."

Ruby glanced up into the sky, then back to us. "So Cyrus decided to make a team of people with some kind of connection to characters in Jumanji?"

"Since we don't know how he picked groups, it makes as much sense as anything else."

"Nothing makes sense!" she shouted, throwing up her hands. "He's done all this," she gestured at her hair and outfit, "just for a stupid joke about a movie?"

I shrugged. "It seems ridiculous, I know. Maybe sometime we'll get an explanation."

"Ridiculous?" Cyrus exclaimed, his voice booming across the clearing, making us all jump. "Teams are an important element in the first stage of the game."

"Sorry," I said quickly. Having the powerful AI angry at us would be a great way to die horribly very soon. "We're under a lot of stress."

"I thought you'd appreciate the elegance of the system," Cyrus said, again sounding like he was pouting.

"Maybe when we meet up with more teams we'll see the bigger picture better."

"That's true. You've only been around for a single day." His bubbling good humor returned in full force. "Get on with it, then." His voice changed slightly and he added in a rhyming cadence, "You're late, you're late, you're late."

"Are you quoting the white rabbit from Alice in Wonderland?" Ruby asked.

"Good catch," I said.

Cyrus laughed. "Indeed! Excellent. You're showing wonderful promise, Ruby. Keep it up."

"Thanks," she said slowly, looking like she had to force out the word.

Cyrus did not respond.

Steve looked a bit shell-shocked by the encounter, then shook his head slowly. "At least it explains why I got an ability for mixing drinks."

"You didn't," Ruby exclaimed.

He grinned. "Must be another Jumanji joke. I got a margarita mixing ability, but I don't have any tequila or limes. I can also mix drinks that purify water or other liquids. Supposedly it'll upgrade to allow me to add other ingredients, even if I don't have any on hand."

"That'll come in handy," I said, even though we had Ruby's Base Camp with a pure water faucet. Having more ways to purify water was always a good idea in the wild.

Ruby was clearly getting pushed into a specific role, and now it looked like Cyrus had started setting Steve up to play the role of Seaplane, with his drink-mixing skills. Hopefully he didn't also end up with a weakness to mosquito bites.

Ruby scowled and muttered, "What the smolder?"

I blinked, then laughed. "You're getting into the spirit of it awfully fast."

Her scowl deepened. "That wasn't what I meant to say. Why the hippo would I say that?"

"You just did it again," Steve said.

She glared up into the sky. "Are you seriously changing my swears?"

Cyrus's chuckle filled the glade. "Isn't it fun?"

"No, it's not," Ruby snapped. "How can you control what we say?"

"Are you changing words in her mind?" I added with a shudder. What a horribly intrusive power.

"No, but it's almost as good. You say what you wish, but I change it before anyone can hear the words. I even echo back the changed word so you know what others hear. Isn't that fantastic?"

"No. I want to say what the smolder I want to say." She stomped her foot in frustration.

"The swears are pretty lame," I added, although the last one wasn't bad.

"What's lame are your Earth swears," Cyrus answered. "This way, I can seed more elements from movies we all love and increase brand awareness so viewers are intrigued into learning more and trying Earth movies."

Huh. Maybe if enough people fell in love with Earth movies they'd choose not to bulldoze the planet to atoms.

"How do we get viewers?" Steve asked.

Cyrus laughed. "Lucas has such a powerful influence. Bare minutes together, and you're already asking for spoilers too. Impressive. Truly impressive."

I sighed. "Just drop it."

"Why? This sounds important."

"You'll all receive the information at the same time as everyone else," Cyrus said.

"So until then you're going to make us sound like Jumanji addicts?" Ruby demanded.

"You learn so fast. I'm very proud of you."

It was obvious Cyrus wasn't going to change his mind, and we were helpless to do anything about it. Antagonizing him over something as silly as fake swear words wasn't worth the risk. He could do far more menacing things to us if he wanted to.

Ruby paced away, then turned, arms folded, clearly fighting back another angry retort. Then her shoulders relaxed and she sighed. "I do love the movie. I really loved it. I can deal with this."

Steve asked, "So Cyrus has been giving you a bunch of Ruby Roundhouse gear. Has he given you abilities too?"

She blew out a breath and nodded. "I have a scroll to learn dance fighting."

"Sweet!" Steve laughed.

"No, it's not. I don't want to learn dance fighting and I don't want to learn nunchucks."

"Can you learn nunchucks?" I asked. That one was new.

She nodded. "Got a scroll for it. Haven't read it yet."

"Why not?" Steve asked. "Both of those could be really boss."

She shrugged. "Don't have any nunchucks. Besides, when I was a girl, I tried them once. Nearly knocked myself out."

Steve's grin didn't diminish. He was taking our weird team assignment better than me and Ruby. She hadn't told him about her forced hair color, or the fact that she couldn't wear more clothing without losing her defensive boosts. Maybe she worried Cyrus was still listening.

Cyrus was always listening.

"Lucas, why are you on our team?" Steve asked.

"Yeah, which character are you? Your last name isn't Bravestone, is it?" Ruby asked, making an effort to smile.

"I don't really want to talk about it."

"Oh, come on," Ruby said. "You can't keep secrets from us, not here, not when we have to trust our lives to each other."

"What, is your name really Shellie?" Steve laughed.

I sighed and stared, mentally preparing myself for that conversation again.

"Wait, it is?" Steve asked, looking suddenly uncomfortable. Ruby stared at me like I'd just grown a second head.

"My mother is a professor of medieval history. She named me after Shelley, the famous British poet. My middle name is Lucas. It's my father's name, so that's what I usually go by."

"So you're a perfect fit for our team. Map guy," Steve joked.

"I did actually receive a special map upgrade called Oberon Advantage."

"You didn't!" Ruby gasped, and Steve laughed.

I shrugged. "It's actually a great upgrade. Lets me see a lot farther than most, with more information that no one else gets until their map evolves a couple times."

My gloves were another Jumanji reference I had missed earlier too. Smolder's Grips. They had to be referring back to Smolder Bravestone, the character played by The Rock. He was super powerful, but had a timid teen boy trapped inside. Made the movie hilarious.

The references were ridiculous, but I wasn't about to not wear the gloves.

"I wonder how Andy and Joseph fit the theme?" Ruby wondered.

"Well, Joseph had a dictionary of monsters. Wasn't there a zoologist, or something on the team?"

Steve nodded. "Backpack guy, but his name was Mouse, not Joseph."

Ruby snapped her fingers. "In the second Jumanji, the old guy was named Milo Walker. He was the backpack guy for a while. Walker was Joseph's last name."

It fit. "And Andy was a big guy. He could have stood in for Fridge." That had been the football player who got trapped in the tiny backpack guy's body. I couldn't believe I was remembering so much about the movie. Maybe another perk of my high intelligence stat.

"I wish we had the entire team together," Ruby said softly.

I agreed. We might unlock more team bonuses, but more importantly, we'd be so much stronger together. And it would mean Andy and Joseph hadn't died uselessly on some alien planet far from home.

"I hope Cyrus continues with the fun movie humor upgrades," Steve said.

"And doesn't start experimenting with horror movies," Ruby added softly.

Yeah, not all the references were fun, like Steve believed. His point of view was refreshing and made it easier to roll with the insanity of our situation. Still, I cringed internally at her words. Why would she say that out loud? Hopefully she hadn't just given Cyrus a terrible idea.

So I changed the topic. "Well, we found you, Steve. What else can you tell us about yourself?"

"Before we got dropped into this death trap, I was a master plumber. Probably why I got a water manipulation spell."

"That's a good one. Do you still have uses?"

He nodded. "I've been trying to save it for when I hit level 10. I also have an ice bolt spell that's saved my life a couple times already, but I can only make one spell permanent."

"Those sound like great starter spells."

He nodded. "Besides drink mixing abilities, I also got level 4 archery. I just need to find a bow. I was an avid bow hunter and part-time hunting guide."

Perfect. I extracted my uncommon bow. "Will this do?"

"Really?" Steve grinned like a boy on Christmas morning as he reverently took the bow. He checked it over carefully, like he was examining a classic car. Good thing one of us appreciated it.

Steve drew the bow back in one fluid movement and a long arrow with a wicked barbed head appeared in his hands, already knocked. With a laugh, he loosed and the bow twanged loudly. The arrow shot to a nearby tree and sank into the trunk.

"Thank you! I can't believe you didn't keep this yourself."

"It wouldn't do me any good. Now we've got an archer, our long-range fighting abilities just jumped a huge notch."

Ruby said, "Lucas is the guy who enjoys the close encounters. I got a blowgun I need to practice with."

"That'll work," Steve said seriously. "If you don't mind taking on all that risk, we can definitely support from a distance."

It wasn't like I wanted to get close and personal with nasty monsters, but I didn't have a choice. My skills and weapons were best used in melee. If I didn't need so much more experience than they did, I'd prefer to find targets they could turn into pin cushions from 50 yards out.

"What did you get for utility skills?" Ruby asked.

"Mystic Looter, Base Camp, and Navigation."

"That's two Base Camps, two navs, plus my Linguasight and Ruby's Bio Morph. Not bad."

"Bio Morph. That one sounded boss," Steve said, giving Ruby an approving nod.

She didn't elaborate about her upgrade, but she and I took turns sharing info about the rest of our abilities and spells as we started marching farther west. Now that we had gathered our team, we had to find the main valley Cyrus had said we needed to conquer. Hopefully we'd find more survivors on the way.

We crossed at least two miles moving due west. The mountains to the north remained huge and impassive, with more peaks rising to the south and east. Steve pointed out a break in the hills to the west.

"That suggests there's a pass through those hills. Hopefully we'll find more open terrain that way."

It sounded good to me. I was glad we had an experienced outdoorsman with us. I liked the outdoors, especially on my bike, but usually stuck to roads, either paved or dirt. My brother and I had explored some pretty remote places, and I'd ridden more bumpy woods roads than I cared to remember in the fire crew trucks, but rarely hoofed it across open wilderness.

As we walked, Steve finally turned to me and asked, "If you don't mind, how can you still be only level 1?"

I repeated the same explanation I'd given Ruby. Steve considered it, frowning. "Sounds like you got screwed."

"I'll get there," I assured him, although I was feeling the crunch of time. We hadn't run across any monsters, and even the distant roars had fallen mostly quiet. It was like now that we had found our entire team, the monsters had just vanished from our starting area. All the more reason to move on to new places.

By midafternoon, we found a pretty wide game trail that led through a long canyon that pierced the high hills rising on either side. We saw marks in the dirt that Steve figured were probably old tracks, but they were so worn, he couldn't tell what might have made them.

Finally, the canyon opened into a wider valley covered in tall, waving grasses. In the distance to the west, between another row of hills a couple miles away, I glimpsed an even bigger open expanse.

"That might be the central valley we need to reach," I said, gesturing toward the distant view.

"Probably, but first, are you seeing what I'm seeing?" Steve asked in a distracted voice. I followed his gaze to the north and blinked in surprise.

"Are those cows?" Ruby asked, shielding her eyes from the afternoon sun.

They did look a lot like Earth cows. A herd of at least 50 of them, scattered around the grasses. What made them look so very different was the fact that they were all standing tall on only their hind legs.

Chapter Twenty-Seven
Cow Level

The humanoid cows were at least 300 yards away, tiny in the distance. Without my enhanced perception, they would have looked like formless lumps. Now I could see them clearly, but they were apparently too far for Identify to kick in.

"We could slip around them, if you like," Ruby suggested, gesturing toward the distant valley floor.

I shook my head. "I can't. I need the experience."

"Then we go hunt cows," Steve said enthusiastically. "They're probably magical cows, so it'll be an exciting hunt."

I liked the guy's spirit. Ruby did not look as eager, but did not argue. Steve took the lead, slipping into the tall grasses and gliding forward in a crouch. He hadn't said he had a stalking or stealth ability, but the experienced hunter moved like a ghost. I followed as best I could, but I made noticeably more noise than him or Ruby, who followed me. Her stealth ability must have activated. I needed to get one of those.

We closed more than half the distance to the herd of cows and paused behind a rare bush rising from the grasses that allowed us to stand tall and survey the herd. The cows were milling about, occasionally ripping a handful of grass to munch on. Most of them carried long spears with steel heads. The whole situation was so weird.

"I can hear them mooing," Ruby said, cocking her head to one side and brushing her long hair from her ear.

As soon as I focused on my hearing, I heard it too. A chorus of moos at different pitches and clearly from many different voices. That was weirder still. I'd seen cows on Earth and they all pretty much sounded alike. Not these.

Then I blinked in surprise as the moos became clear. "I can understand them."

"You speak cow?" Ruby asked.

"Linguasight. I've used the Identify aspect of it exclusively so far. This is the translation function."

"What are they saying?" Steve asked.

I concentrated and the various voices started clarifying. Not that it helped much. "They're just babbling. I can hear snippets about grass and the ground and feeling hungry and something about a bull."

That bit of conversation had been surprisingly explicit. I was not about to repeat some naughty cow fantasy.

Ruby chuckled softly.

"What?"

"Nothing," she waved it away, still smiling. "Just thinking of a video game my brother showed me once."

"You play a lot of games?"

Her expression turned into a glare. "I am not a gamer."

I grinned. "You claim you're not a nerd or a gamer, but you go to comicons and you make references to games while we're on a death planet. Sounds pretty gamey nerdy to me."

"I still have that hunting knife."

"Fine. Can't take a joke."

"Don't call me a nerd."

"Okay, okay."

What was it with her and nerds? There had to be a great story there.

"Are you a gamer?" she asked, her tone still hard.

I shrugged. "Some. When I can find time."

"So you're not a hardcore gamer?"

When I shook my head, she relaxed. "Good. Those guys give me the creeps."

Probably because she was beautiful and most hardcore gamers never left their moms' basements. Seeing a pretty girl in the flesh would have challenged their social skills to the max.

I returned to studying the cows and trying to make anything useful out of their mindless conversation. They seemed as stupid as Earth cows, but they had to be more than that. They carried spears. Identify triggered finally.

Soilstrider Cow. Common. Level 16. These territorial animals are fiercely protective of their domain. Like Celtic tribes of your home world, they'll charge into battle, heedless of the odds. Earth elemental manipulation abilities.

I scanned several of them, noting their levels ranged pretty widely from level 12 to 15. The earth elemental powers worried me, but otherwise their biggest threat was their sheer numbers. I felt confident in defeating 2 or even 3 of them if I could get close with Mirror cloak, but not 50.

"How many could you shoot?"

Steve didn't hesitate. "If I start firing at about 100 yards, and if they run as fast as normal cows, I should be able to drop as many as 8 before they reached us, assuming arrows affect them like normal cows."

That was really good. I hoped he was as good a shot as he believed, but that would still leave far too many magic cows to swarm us under. Their individual levels were not too high, but there were so many of them, together they still represented a major threat.

I glanced to Ruby and she shrugged. "I have no idea what the effective range of my darts are or how fast they work."

I scowled. "Just running in firing will get us killed. We need another plan."

We brainstormed a bit, but every idea crumbled under the simple math. We didn't have enough people or enough offensive firepower to deal with 50 cows at once. I scanned the field around them, looking for any other advantage. A flash of color caught my eye and I focused on a clump of trees on the far side of the cows, partway up one of the hills ringing the grassy valley.

Movement in the trees drew my gaze, but it was so far way, I couldn't make out details. "There's something in the trees on the far side."

"I don't see it," Ruby said, shielding her eyes.

Steve nodded after a moment. "I see it, but can't tell what it is."

"More monsters?" Ruby asked.

I shrugged. "Maybe. I'd rather deal with one monster on the hill than get trampled by 50 cows. Let's go check it out."

Steve again took the lead and we circled wide around the cows. I didn't know if their earth powers helped them feel movement, but they did not react to our presence. We crouched at the edge of the grasses and scanned the forest again.

I spotted the movement first. It wasn't a monster, but a woman inching out onto a branch to study the field and the cows. I nudged the others and pointed, so relieved I nearly laughed out loud.

"Let's go say hi."

As soon as Ruby spotted the woman, she rose to her feet and started waving. I pulled her back down and hissed, "Careful! We don't want to start a stampede right when we've found another team."

"Sorry. I'm just so excited to find more survivors."

She led the way at a crouching run out of the field, making for the trees where the woman crouched. The woman noticed us immediately, waved once, then scurried back to the trunk and slid down.

By the time we reached the shelter of the trees, she had been joined by 3 men and another woman. One of the men, a tall, well-muscled, dark-haired fellow, stepped forward and smiled warmly.

"By Thor's hammer, it's good to meet another team." He spoke with a perfectly cultured British accent.

Ruby rushed forward with a joyous expression. "Tony Waldau! You're alive."

"Is that you, Ruby?" Tony asked as Identify told me he was level 16. He wrapped his arms around her and she hugged him back eagerly. Was she crying?

He stepped back after a moment and smiled down at her. "You seem taller."

She laughed and wiped away tears. "It's a long story. Have you seen Elizabeth?"

"No. You're the first team we've found."

"You're team Avengers?" I guessed.

"We are," said the woman who had been up in the tree.

Natasha Portman, level 11 baby human. Team Avengers.

Huh. That was the first time Identify showed a team name. Was that because we'd figured out how the teams worked?

Natasha looked like Black Widow, complete with a skin-tight black one-piece suit and cool metallic bracers on her forearms. I bet they had some kind of shock ability.

Another fellow identified as Clint Kingsley spoke in a Scottish accent. "Team Jumanji! Sweet."

He glanced meaningfully at Ruby's outfit and she shrugged, then shared a commiserating look with Natasha.

We exchanged names and stories. Tony and his team had found each other pretty quickly, so had managed to fight off all the monsters they had encountered without losing anyone. It took me a minute, but I finally recognized Tony. He was going to play the main hero in the movie. He was a big deal in Germany, although he spoke perfect English with that British accent.

Natasha, the Black Widow, was from the Netherlands, but also spoke with a perfect British accent. Sally Rogers was tall with brown hair, wearing a simple, brown tunic and flip flops. She carried a cool round shield that could deflect magical attacks back at her attacker. Cyrus had dumped not-so-subtle character-specific gear on them too.

The Scotsman, Clint, wore a black t-shirt and white cotton pants, but no shoes. He'd gotten a really cool bow similar to Steve's, but with an added enchantment that allowed him to create specialty arrows, including a splitting arrow to hit 2 targets at once and an arrow imbued with fire. Steve couldn't quite hide his jealous glances at that bow.

Scott Mortensen was a friendly, talkative South African black man who had been a truck driver. He was wearing actual jeans and black leather work boots, although he had no shirt. He didn't seem to mind, nor did the ladies. He had one of the most ripped physiques I'd ever seen. I had thought I was in shape, but he made me look tiny by comparison.

I wasn't sure which Avenger he represented. Cyrus had done an amazing job lining up people with similar names to characters, but already the attempt to shove us all into movie pigeon holes was looking stretched.

As we wrapped up introductions, Tony fixed me with a serious stare. "I know I'm not your team captain, but this game is serious, Lucas. You can't hold back."

"Why would you assume I was?"

"Levels don't lie. We don't have time to coddle anyone who won't pull their weight. You've got to do your part and take risks like the rest of us. Everyone has to level up."

"Get with it, or your team will ditch you," Natasha added in a scornful tone.

"Huh. Do you guys always flaunt your ignorance with so much pride?"

Sally took a threatening step forward, hefting her shield. "Want me to show you what a level 9 punch feels like, weakling?"

I chuckled. "Only if you don't mind when I punch back."

Steve stepped between us all, raising his hands in a calming gesture. "Hold on, everyone. Take a step back."

Tony nodded. "You're right. Fighting each other is stupid. Lucas, I'll only warn you once. If you prove to be a negative influence on my team, we'll have to part ways."

I forced myself to take a deep breath. They would actually have a point if I was anyone else. They couldn't know about my body evolving, and I couldn't tell them.

So I only said, "There are reasons you see me as level 1."

"We don't have time for excuses," Tony said. "Know that our team is motivated to beat this game and save Earth. If you guys are going to join us, you have to keep up."

"You're making assumptions again, Tony. I was just going to offer to let you join us if you didn't slow us down."

Scott laughed in his loud, friendly way. "Let's leave the posturing in the schoolyard, boys. We've got monsters to fight."

Tony nodded. "We've wasted enough time on this. You know our position. We're happy to have every person we can get join us and help, and now you know what will be expected of you. Keep up, and we'll get along fine."

"Sure," I said, keeping my tone calm, despite my urge to throw every single one of them over a tree.

Tony turned, dismissing me and focusing on the rest of the group. "Now that we've got some extra bodies, I think we can take out those cows. That herd represents a ton of experience we can't pass up."

"That's why we came over here."

Tony continued as if I hadn't spoken. "Let's adjust our previous attack plan. If we split up, we can strike from 2 sides and split the herd. 50 cows with spears could trample us, but 2 groups of 25 we can handle easier. If they get too close, we retreat into the hills and whittle them down."

"They have some kind of earth manipulating powers too." They might be acting like jerks, but I didn't want to see more humans die.

"How do you know?" Natasha asked.

"Lucas has an upgraded Linguasight utility," Ruby offered. She still stood near Tony and looked happy to have found a friend she knew from before.

"Do you know how their abilities work?" Tony asked.

"Not yet."

"Okay. We'll have to test that before the main strike."

Steve spoke up. "Me and Clint could hit a couple from a distance, then retreat back into the trees. That might give us a chance to see what they can do."

Tony considered that, but I spoke up first. "Clint, what effective range do you have with that bow?"

He considered the question. "I haven't used it enough to know for sure, but I'd like to start at 75 yards."

"What if the cows can strike with earth that far?" Sally asked, shifting her shield as she spoke.

"We'll set up 2 teams north and south of their position," Tony decided. "If they get into trouble, we'll rush the cows from both sides."

That sounded a bit reckless, but I didn't have a better idea. I needed the experience even more than they did. Even if I was alone, I would have tried to find a way to sneak in and start sniping cows or killing the stragglers. That would be even more dangerous.

As we finalized the details I said, "For a bit more safety, and maybe as a secondary test, I'll sneak closer to the herd from the south. If I move slow, my cloak'll hide me almost entirely."

Tony considered that. "Good job stepping up, Lucas. I like it."

Ruby said, "But if the cows can sense movement, they'll still find you."

"Maybe, but that'll tell us the range of their senses." It was a huge risk, but no one else could do it and it gave me a chance to prove they were wrong about me.

"Okay, let's do it," Tony said with a smile that made everyone stand a bit taller. "We'll communicate using the team chat."

Steve said, "Before we get going, anyone need a pair of shoes?" He extracted the moccasins I'd loaned him and glanced to me. "If you don't mind?"

"Go ahead."

Clint stepped forward. "Thanks! I'd love them."

Tony said, "Well done, Steve. On our team we've agreed to share loot to the person who can best use it. Glad to see you feel the same way."

"Teams are stronger when we work together," Steve said.

"We're good, then," Tony said, rubbing his hands together. "Let's split into our teams and do this. If anything goes wrong, we retreat to the trees here."

I marched south with Tony and Ruby while Natasha, Scott, and Sally headed north. Steve and Clint waited in the trees. The 2 archers would begin their cautious approach in 15 minutes.

That would give me just enough time to walk out to the herd alone.

Chapter Twenty-Eight
Where's the Beef?

I angled away from Tony and Ruby, heading into the field on a circular course to approach the cows from the north flank. The other two continued along the fringes of the trees. Ruby barely seemed to notice I had left. Her entire focus was on Tony.

Hopefully she didn't let herself get distracted. Sure, he was famous, she knew him from before, and he acted with the confidence of a natural-born leader. We were about to enter a fight for our lives against no less than 50 monsters with unknown elemental powers, though. Catching up with an old friend right now might not be the best choice.

With an effort, I pushed those distracting thoughts aside and focused on my mission. Ruby would get her head in the game. As much as Tony annoyed me, he did seem competent. He'd keep her safe.

I only had a few minutes before Steve and Clint would begin the main attack. Crouching low, I kept below the tall grass just like we had on the way across earlier. I knew we could circumvent the cows without getting noticed if we kept at least 100 yards out. Now I needed to find out if I could get closer than 75.

As I circled the herd, I stood to survey my targets every time I passed one of the rare clumps of tall bushes. The cows did not seem to notice us yet. If they were standing on all fours, I would swear they were just normal stupid Earth cows. They clearly weren't, so I could not risk underestimating them. Every monster I'd encountered so far had displayed shocking readiness to kill anyone they encountered. We had a decent plan, but it could easily go badly wrong.

It took almost 10 minutes to circle two-thirds of the herd. With every second ticking down in my head, I started approaching the north flank, heading for a couple of cows that were separated a bit from the other cows. The bulk of the herd was clustered closer together in an almost diamond-shaped group, with one point aiming at the archers and the other back in the direction we had originally come from.

Pulling up the new team chat menu, I sent a message to Ruby and Steve.

Lucas: "I'm in position, closing on the herd now."

Steve: "Perfect timing. We'll start our attack in 5 minutes."

Ruby: "Be careful, Lucas."

Once I closed to within 100 yards, I activated Mirror Cloak and the world turned monochrome. With a little more confidence, I stood a little taller, just enough to see over the tops of the waving grasses. Still no reaction from the cows.

I crept closer, trying to find a balance between enough speed to get into position in time and not wrecking my cloaking or giving myself away. Slow minutes dragged by as I slipped through the tall grasses, wincing at every rasping hiss as they slid off my cloak. The air was thick with the scent of grass, but thankfully I wasn't allergic to it. Sneezing would have been a stupid way to give myself away.

With maybe a minute left before the archers started the attack, I finally drew to within 50 yards of my targets. One of the cows I was targeting looked up then, scanning in my direction. I froze, barely allowing myself to breathe.

I wasn't sure if they had sensed my movement or heard something or smelled something, but after a few seconds, the 2 cows lost interest and started ripping chunks of grass out with their surprisingly humanlike hands to munch. While they kept watch, they chatted about random things and that close, I could hear more of the words.

One of them was complaining about wanting more clover and wishing they could head down to the main valley without waiting for the escort. The other started gushing about how she couldn't wait to see the bulls again.

Hmm. Bulls could be a problem. All I saw were female cows. I hadn't considered there would probably be a bunch of bulls too. From their conversation, it sounded like the bulls move separately and would periodically return to escort the cows to different pastures.

'They'd better not show up now.' The cows alone would be difficult to defeat.

I risked another slow step and neither of the cows reacted, so I continued to creep closer. I paid attention to the occasional gusts of wind, fearing my scent would give me away, but the wind seemed to be in my favor, at least for the moment.

I got to about 30 yards of the two sentry cows, every step cautious, every muscle tight with building tension. As I placed one foot carefully down again, that same alert cow abruptly snapped her head up and stared directly at me. Again I froze, holding my breath, resisting the urge to crouch down. Mirror Cloak should keep me invisible.

The second cow noticed the first cow's attention and lifted her spear into a ready position. It was so random seeing real looking cows standing on their haunches but wielding spears in humanlike hands. It was hard to wrap my brain around it. That close, I could see more details of their spears, which looked identical. Six-foot shafts of steel, capped with silvery heads that gleamed in the sunlight. Did they have some kind of enchantment? That could be bad for us.

The 2 sentry cows started slowly moving in my direction, scanning the area with obvious intent. The fact that they kept scanning all around me suggested they had not pinpointed my location.

Identify still stated that they had some kind of earth manipulation powers, but it seemed that their sensitivity to the earth wasn't as developed as I feared. They couldn't tell I was standing on that patch of ground. That was a relief, but the 2 cows were still steadily drawing closer.

They approached to within 10 yards, close enough that I could clearly see their big bovine eyes darting all around and their nostrils flaring. Their long tongs flickered out regularly to lick all the way up into those giant nostrils. I remembered seeing cows on Earth do that. I thought it was disgusting then, and it was even grosser watching the more humanoid cows do it.

I tensed, ready to spring, when all of a sudden the first cow locked her eyes on my position. I could tell she still couldn't see me, but somehow she had sensed me. Her spear lifted and she charged, crossing the distance in a flash before lunging and thrusting her spear forward with surprising skill.

I yanked Soulrend out of my inventory into my right hand and my fighting stick into my left. With my stick, I deflected the stabbing spear so it slashed just past my shoulder while I stepped forward and thrust Soulrend into the surprised cow's throat.

She didn't see the move until it was too late, and her huge eyes widened farther as my blade severed her spirit right in the neck. I retracted the weapon and froze. My movements had been minimal and quick, so my Mirror Cloak should not have more than rippled. The second cow could not see me clearly because the first cow blocked her line of sight.

The first cow collapsed. The second cow moo'd in alarm and trotted closer, the words translating as, "Bessie, what happened?"

Bessie? Really? That had to be a quirk of the translation. There was no way intergalactic humanoid magical cows would be named Bessie.

The second cow raised her spear, but hesitated. She clearly had not sensed me the way Bessie had. In that second, moo's of alarm rang out from the far side of the herd as the first of the arrows from the archers pierced into their ranks.

I did not see the arrows strike, but the distraction was perfectly timed. The rest of the herd oriented on the shouts and cries of pain to the front, and even the cow close to me spun to look, just for a second.

That was one second too long. I lunged and slashed her throat too. She collapsed on top of Bessie.

I crouched in the grass, snatched up both of their spears and dumped them into my inventory, then touched both bodies. I ignored the notifications I received and just accepted the prompt to loot.

Not waiting for the bodies to dissolve into stinky black smoke, I dashed toward the rear of the herd, crouching low and dropping my cloaking. I was moving too fast and trusted to the grasses to keep me concealed. The herd was bunching up, all focused on the archers, who continued to fire. I caught a glimpse of arrows flashing in the sunlight.

In seconds, I closed on the rear of the herd, but the ground began to rumble. I kept running, scanning the ground, afraid the cows had found me and were finally unleashing their magic. The ground shook harder and knocked me down to one knee. Then it rose under me and started accelerating toward the west and the archers.

"This is not good," I muttered as I risked standing taller to see what was going on.

It was worse than not good.

The entire herd had bunched up in a single body and the ground underneath them and out to about 20 yards all around had lifted like a giant earthen pillar. All together, we were accelerating toward the archers. I had gotten just barely close enough to the rear of the herd to reach the outer edge of the pillar.

Earth started crumbling off and falling away, nearly taking me with it so I scrambled forward, closing on the cows at the rear of the herd. They did not notice me, but were all focused on what seemed to be a herd-wide spell to move the earth.

The rear of the pillar where I stood was slightly higher than the front so I could see across the western half of the meadow and easily spotted Steve and Clint sprinting for their lives back to the trees. We were closing on them fast, but it looked like they would make it to the trees.

Time to sow a little chaos. With the cows distracted, I sprinted forward and slipped among the cows at the back of the herd. Barely slowing, I slashed out to both sides. Soulrend snaked out with every step, and with every slash, I severed a cow's neck.

In 3 seconds, I dispatched half a dozen cows before the stampede realized there was danger in their midst. One cow started to moo a warning just before I took its head, but the warning rang out from many more throats a second later.

Another half dozen cows all spun to face me and the pillar of earth we rode on groaned and noticeably slowed. It definitely was a herd-level spell and between the cows I killed and the ones I distracted, it barely held together.

Cows lunged at me from all sides and I activated Energy Ward. The glowing golden aura wrapped me in its protective shell, helping to deflect silver-tipped spears stabbing in from every side.

I moved with it, dodging what spears I could and rolling with the pressure I felt as my aura worked to deflect other weapons. I could feel each time energy formed to deflect a spear, giving me a clue as to which way I should dodge to make the aura most effective.

With that help, I dodged and twisted and even jumped into a sideways flip as the cows slashed and stabbed in a frenzy. I batted more spears away with my fighting stick and used every opening to slash at necks, legs, and hands gripping the spears.

Weapons tumbled away on all sides as cows collapsed either dead or maimed. In 3 more seconds, I broke their charge and dispatched all 6 of them.

At the same time, the pillar of earth slammed into the first of the trees at the edge of the field. The impact was surprisingly gentle as the earthen pillar simply wrapped around the trees and slowed. The leading elements of the herd charged into the trees, hunting the archers.

As soon as the earth stopped moving, battle cries erupted from both the north and the south as our 2 other teams leaped into the fray. From the south, Tony rushed in wielding a sword, his hands glowing silver like he had summoned steel gauntlets.

I could've sworn I heard him shouting, "For Narnia!"

That was ridiculous. He was on team Avengers. His battle cry ended up little more than a wordless shout, but I still smiled as I thought about what it could've been.

He tore into the cows, dispatching a couple of them with slashes and stabs of his sword before a dozen more bovines formed into a half-circle facing him, all their spears leveled together.

They had the advantage of reach and lots of friends, so they forced him steadily back. His sword flashed with remarkable speed as he deflected several stabbing spears every second. The dude had skills.

Then one of the cows facing him stumbled, its spear wavering. He tried to take advantage of the weakness, but the other cows blocked him, forcing him to retreat again.

Another cow stumbled, then a third.

I spotted Ruby trailing Tony by about 10 paces. She had her blowgun to her lips, and it looked like she was putting it to good use.

On the north side of the herd, Scott led the charge, roaring like a Viking berserker. He swung a six-foot club made from a thick tree branch. As he closed on the cows, his shirtless torso swelled like he had some kind of Hulk ability.

His steps turned ponderous and he swept his club through the ranks of the cows scrambling to block him. Spears were flung aside as he broke their defense and shoulder-checked 2 of the cows right off their feet.

Behind him, Natasha sprinted in, metal bracers sparkling. She jumped between 2 of the cows distracted by Scott's charge, hands extending to tap them lightly. Flashes of electricity marked the discharge of power, and both cows collapsed to the ground, twitching.

Other cows rushed in to stop her, but she flipped between them and I lost sight of her. Sally charged in behind, shield up, carrying a much shorter spear in her right hand. She moved to flank Scott, fending off as many cows as she could to protect his back as he continued rampaging through the edges of the herd.

The initial onslaught was proving very effective, but there were still a lot of cows and they reformed their ranks with surprising discipline. Enough of them intercepted Tony that he was unable to make more forward progress, and a couple more even circled around to go after Ruby.

Scott had devastated one side of the herd, but a wall of angry cows soon formed to block him. His Hulk-sized form shrank as his ability ran out of steam, so he lost the edge in pure raw force. Too bad that spell didn't last longer, but the tide of battle was turning against us.

The archers reengaged, and luckily I seemed to have been forgotten at the rear of the pack. I studied the battle, considering how best to help my teammates. I could rush in again with Soulrend, but that wouldn't do enough damage quickly enough.

As I studied the herd, their movements clicked into place and got an idea. Sprinting to my right, I lined up with the wall of cows hemming in Tony. The initial semi circle had momentarily fallen into an almost perfectly straight line, with a dozen cows standing shoulder to shoulder, spears pointed at Tony.

The cows were taller than me, so I jumped, pointed my fighting stick, and triggered the Titan Strike spell I'd gotten in that pack of single-use spell scrolls.

Titan Strike. Spell. Pure force. Unleash an invisible wall of force. Adjust the size of the wall up to 5 yards square. Force dispersed evenly throughout the entire wall. Mana cost: Moderate.

An enormous wave of pure force erupted out of me, rolled up my fighting stick, and blasted out toward the cows. Instead of dispersing the force widely, I concentrated it into a beam of force half the width of my fighting stick. All that energy concentrated into that tiny area of about half an inch and blasted out in a bar of force so dense, it could have probably punched through steel walls.

Punching through a dozen cow skulls proved to be no trouble at all.

At the same time, a bolt of ice blasted into the ranks of cows from the front. Steve had unleashed his elemental spell. A wave of ice rolled over the cows at the same time my spell struck and the entire line of bovines facing Tony collapsed. Their heads all exploded in a gory eruption of blood and gray matter.

Tony and Ruby stared in shock for a moment before Tony shook himself and dashed toward the backs of the cows facing the rest of his team. The cows on the other side did not realize what had happened until Tony dove into their ranks, sword slashing wildly. His teammates took advantage of the resulting confusion to drive forward again.

Steve and Clint kept up their rain of devastating arrows, taking down one cow after another. I rushed into the confused mass of cows at the back of the pack and got back to work with Soulrend. In a matter of seconds, we finished destroying the entire herd.

Chapter Twenty-Nine
I Remember I Love Stickers

Silence slowly descended over the valley as we stood among the corpses. I felt an overwhelming sense of victory and lifted my sword to shout.

Tony beat me to it by about a quarter of a second. His shout drowned out mine and all eyes turned to him as he laughed and threw his hands out wide. "Well done everyone. The plan worked perfectly."

I rolled my eyes and turned back to the cows I had killed.

Would you like to harvest a spell from Soilstrider Cows?

I considered that for a second. I still had a couple instances of Thunder Punch. Earth manipulation sounded awesome, but I'd been kind of underwhelmed by what the herd could do, so I declined the offer.

I considered triggering Soul Feed, but I hadn't gotten any serious wounds at all. Energy Ward had again saved my life at least 20 times.

Would you like to loot the Soilstrider Cows that you defeated?

"Yes."

That was very nice. I had figured I would have to touch each cow and accept the loot prompt individually. Many cows disintegrated into black, stinky smoke. Across the battlefield, other cows disintegrated also as the other team members looted too, so nobody could tell how many cows I defeated.

How many cows had I killed? I scanned my messages.

Congratulations, Lucas! You have defeated Soilstrider Cow. Level 15. Experience shared among the group.

I counted 26 of those messages, with levels ranging between 14 and 18. That was pretty amazing, but I had already seen how fast experience gains dropped off when defeating multiple enemies of the same type. So with very little expectation, I scanned the rest of my messages.

Congratulations, Lucas! You reached level 2. Two stat points automatically allocated.

"What the smolder? I thought I got 4 points per level."

Then I scowled. Cyrus had changed my words. Could he change my thoughts?

Dammit. Nope, Earth swears still worked in my mind. Still, it was lame that he forced my words to change for another of his silly games.

Cyrus answered as I pulled up my stats menu and confirmed I'd only gotten 2 stinking stat points. Worse, they'd both been dropped into Wisdom.

"You're absolutely right, Lucas. Although you gained enough experience for another level as a tier-1 human, you only received half of the normal stat points."

"Why?" I asked slowly, trying really hard to keep my voice calm.

"Unfortunately, you evolved to tier-1 far earlier than anyone was expected to. The mana density in this sector of the planet, and particularly this stage, is designed to support only tier-0 players and monsters. As such, you would either need to gain twice the experience as usual to level up, or take half of the normal stat points. To help encourage you by rewarding levels more often, I figured you would want to just take the level and half stats. You're welcome."

I took a long, calming breath. I'd signed up for tests and challenges, but hadn't expected losing out on promised experience points to be one of them.

"First test?"

"That's a great way to look at it."

Oh well. "On to the next one, then."

The sooner I worked through all of Cyrus's tests, the sooner I could start reaping the promised rewards.

"Indeed," Cyrus said.

"Can I ask a question, though?"

"You usually do, and better questions than most."

"So why did the stat points get dropped into Wisdom?" I would have preferred more leeway in distributing them.

"With all that extra wisdom, I'm sure you will see that we've chosen the best course of action, given the circumstances."

"Will I get to control where my stat points get allocated in the future?"

"Not on this stage, and you'll receive instructions along with everyone else once the timing is right."

Okay, so there was hope. In the meantime, each level only gave me 2 stat points, equivalent to 20 tier-0 points, minus the effectiveness of my stats since my efficiency was still low. If it took me 10 times as much experience to level up, then everyone else was going to get 40 total stat points in the same time I got 20.

That would pose a daunting challenge unless I could find other ways to win stats, or find more gear to boost my power. I'd hit level 2, so that was good, although I'd had to kill nearly 30 monsters to get that one level. Cyrus hadn't been kidding, until my growth curve started ramping up, I was going to have to grind like crazy.

I headed over to where Ruby and Steve were chatting with the other players. They all looked ecstatic and when Ruby saw me she exclaimed, "I received 2 levels!"

"So you hit level 10. Perfect. Which spell are you going to permanent?"

"I forgot about that." Her eyes got a slightly unfocused look as she opened her menus.

Everyone else had gained 2 levels also, including Tony who was now all the way up to level 18.

When he spotted me, his smile faded and he said with forced cheer, "Lucas, there you are. Finally. And you even got a level. Congratulations."

His tone made it clear he considered that underwhelming. And if I really was only level 2 at tier-0, he would've been right. The fact that he hadn't noticed that I'd killed half the herd all by myself did rankle.

I didn't feel like giving the same vague explanations I had with Ruby and Steve, so I just shrugged and said, "It was a pretty good fight. I'm glad no one got badly hurt."

"You need to pay more attention," Tony said, glancing to where Sally was lying on the ground, covered in blood.

Somehow I had indeed missed the fact that her stomach had been ripped open by a spear. Natasha was pouring a standard healing potion into her mouth, but it would not be enough to entirely heal a wound that severe.

I approached, planning to offer one of my healing potions as well, but Ruby rushed over first. "Here, take this. It's a full healing potion."

She dropped to her knees next to Sally and poured it into her mouth. A soft glow enveloped her entire body and she sighed as her terrible gut wound visibly closed.

"That was very generous, Ruby. Full healing potions a rare," Tony said, giving her an approving smile.

"Not anymore," she laughed, holding up another potion. "I had a scroll to summon full healing potions. I just hit level 11 and I made that my permanent spell. Now I can make a new full healing potion every 60 seconds as long as I have enough mana."

That generated a round of cheering from the rest of the team. I grinned. She'd made a good choice.

"Brilliant idea. I never considered using scrolls as permanents," Tony said, clapping her on the shoulder.

Ruby looked happy enough to burst, but pointed at me and said, "It was actually Lucas's idea."

Tony couldn't hide his surprise as he too glanced at me. He gave me an approving smile, and curse the man if his approval didn't make me stand up straighter and feel proud.

"Way to contribute to the greater effort, Lucas. Keep it up."

"Sure. My pleasure."

I sighed and turned away to check my loot. I actually got a couple of loot boxes. I had skipped the notifications, so had to go back and see why I got them.

Congratulations, Lucas! For using your team chat for the first time in battle, you receive a copper Emoji loot box.

Congratulations, Lucas! For joining another team to take on a larger enemy force together, you receive a silver Legion loot box.

Congratulations, Lucas! For single-handedly defeating more than half of a large enemy force, you receive a gold Hannibal loot box.

The loot boxes appeared in front of me in ascending value order. They made a pretty sight, the metallic loot boxes glittering in the light, lined up in increasing size. I willed them open with a smile.

I laughed when I saw that the copper Emoji loot box produced a sheet of bright emoji stickers. Cyrus's jokes were getting better. I was about to toss them into my inventory when I noticed one of the emojis was a smiley face that was blowing up.

Each of the emojis moved when I studied it, like a bunch of GIF files printed on the page. Next to the exploding one was an emoji that looked like it was falling asleep, while a third showed a smiley face smacking into a wall.

"What?" I muttered. As I studied the page, Identify triggered.

Sheet of trap emojis. Unlike the benign emojis spammed across every text and social media platform of Earth, these self-adhesive trap stickers pack a real punch. Place one just about anywhere, and when touched by any living being, the trap will trigger. Each trap is a single-use item and will last for a maximum of 5 minutes.

Wow, that was better than I had thought. There were 4 rows of 4 emojis, giving me 16 traps in all. I placed the sheet in my inventory, looking forward to studying all of them and trying them out soon.

The silver Legion loot box gave me a common quality square Roman Legionnaire's shield. It was heavy and solid and my mother would have gushed over it if she got her hands on it. I didn't see myself using it, but dropped it into my inventory.

The gold Hannibal loot box proved more interesting. It produced 2 scrolls.

Temporary spell scroll: Fractal Strike. Multi-tasking at it's best. Make up to 4 reflections of one strike to hit up to 5 enemies simultaneously. Uses remaining: 2.

Temporary spell scroll: Knock Knock. Tells a random knock knock joke. Can cast up to 50 yards away. Uses remaining: 3.

I whistled softly when I read the first one. That sounded like a great spell. Could I have paired that with Titan Strike? Was it possible to do something like that?

If so, I could have killed the entire herd with one shot. What kind of final build would I get if I made Fractal Strike permanent, assuming I could keep it that long? The knock knock spell was a silly joke spell, except it might also be perfect at creating distractions. I also got a surprising notification.

Congratulations, Lucas! Your ability Stick and Knife Martial Arts has upgraded to level 4.

My first ability upgrade. Nice.

Looting the cows proved interesting too. I got 45 tier-one mana crystals, which was always nice, along with 3 more full healing potions and 7 more of their silver-tipped steel spears. They didn't have any special properties, but looked pretty solid.

I also ended up with 28 quarts of whole milk, bottled in old-fashioned milk bottles, plus 300 pounds of hamburger, 58 steaks of various cuts, 9 horns, and 16 rolls of cowhide leather. When I pulled one out, it looked like it was already tanned and ready to be crafted into jackets, boots, or whatever.

They might have been sentient cows, but apparently they were still cows. I usually loved hamburgers and steak, but I'll admit, I felt a little weird about eating the meat from those cows.

The last item was so unexpected, I pulled it from my inventory. It looked like an old-fashioned cow bell, reminding me of that SNL skit with Christopher Walken as the producer who kept saying, "I need more cow bell!"

Cow bell of the herd matriarch. Rare. The ultimate call from the mother of the herd, this bell is enchanted so that all members of the herd can hear, regardless of range. Unlike any Earth teen, all members of the herd must answer the call. Grants authority over the herd when rung.

"Huh. That would have been useful 10 minutes ago." I must have killed the matriarch. I hadn't noticed any cow acting particularly heroic or standing out as a leader.

Chapter Thirty

Stats Check

S tats chapter.

Again, if you're a reader who loves studying the stats, enjoy. If you don't really care about stats, skip to the next chapter. You won't miss out on anything.

Name: Lucas Altan

Race: Tier-1 Human

Level: 2

Life Points: 4   (410 Tier-zero baby human equivalent)

Mana: 6

Base Stats:

Constitution: 1.6

Intelligence: 1.7

Strength: 1.6

Dexterity: 2.3

Wisdom: 3.4

Secondary Stats:

Endurance: 3

Agility: 4

Perception: 6

CHA: 10

Magical Resistances: 2.7

Other stats:

Mental Resistance: 0.5

PERMANENT SPELLS

1   Harvest

UTILITY SPELLS:

1   Mystic Looter
2   Linguasight
3   Navigation
4   Soul Feed

TEMPORARY SPELLS:

1   Energy Ward
Uses remaining: 4
2   Frostfire Nova
Uses remaining: 1
3   Corrosive Cloud
Uses remaining: 1
4   Thunder Punch   Harvested spell
Uses Remaining: 2
5   Knock Knock
Uses Remaining: 3
6   Fractal Strike
Uses Remaining: 1

ABILITIES

Hand-to-hand martial arts fighting.   Level 4
Stick and bladed weapons martial arts fighting   Level 4

EXISTING TITLES:
Inquisitive Mind
Trailblazer

NEW TITLES:
David Copperfield
- Upgrades Race to tier-one.
- 4 tier-1 stats per level (currently downgraded by 50%)
- Plus 25% to affect of primary stats on secondary stats.
- Unlock a fourth utility spell
- Harvester perk. Unique.

Chapter Thirty-One
Lying Down on the Job

I decided to scout ahead of the main group to help clear my thoughts and some surprisingly conflicting emotions. I actually loved being in a larger company. I hadn't realized how much I missed being around other people until I'd found Ruby and Steve, and the feeling was compounded now that we'd met up with another team.

Except Tony and his team were acting like judgmental pricks. Worse, with the knowledge they had, they were right. I hadn't realized how much it would irk to have people assuming I was a weak slacker. Test number 2, maybe.

So I scouted ahead alone. We headed down a wide canyon winding through steep hills that would eventually empty onto a huge open plain. That should be the central valley of the first stage Cyrus had warned us we needed to conquer.

Steve and Clint, who now acted like lifelong friends, followed me, with the rest of the group trailing them. Everyone was in good spirits, and several times a peal of laughter or particularly loud snatch of conversation drifted all the way to me.

Maybe they weren't worried about monsters attacking our larger group, but I preferred moving with as much stealth as I could. Not that I had any stealth ability, but if I kept practicing, maybe I'd unlock one.

The canyon floor was carpeted with soft, short grass, broken by clumps of thorny bushes and small copses of hardwoods that were only a little bigger than normal Earth trees. The air smelled fresh and clean, and a soft breeze set the trees creaking and leaves rustling.

About 2 miles down the canyon, nearly halfway to the plain, as far as I could tell, a narrow, dark ravine broke the hillside on the left. Shadows hung thicker there, and I paused to study the area. If we were going to run into more monsters, that seemed like the perfect spot.

Steve and Clint caught up and they too studied the area carefully. Not spotting any danger, I led the way again, drawing ahead once more. After only a minute, I stopped in an open glade. Something felt wrong.

I scanned the glade with all my senses, searching for a threat. Eventually, I oriented on a larger tree, closer to the steep side of the canyon. It was a huge tree with large branches extending out to form a spectacular crown.

There! I finally caught the barest flicker of movement and my gaze focused on a shadowy form that had been concealed in the foliage. It looked like a giant cat of some kind, crouched low on a branch at least 30 feet up.

It was nearly 100 feet away from me, but I still felt a prickle of fear. Even at that distance, I could tell the cat was huge. Maybe bigger than a horse.

I got an idea and pulled my sheet of emoji traps from my inventory. If we could bait the monster in, I might be able to trap it. I turned to motion Steve to catch up, but he shouted a warning and started fumbling for his bow, which he'd slung over his shoulder.

I spun back in time to see the cat closing the distance to me like a golden blur. It was even bigger than I'd thought, a huge tawny creature with long, shaggy fur and an oversized mountain lion head. Two saber-tooth fangs extended below its jaw.

Mammoth Lion. Level 30. Uncommon. These mighty hunters do not stop once they choose their prey. They're more determined than a Black Friday shopper trying to snag the last sale-priced TV. Since you're reading this, you're most likely about to die.

Level 30? I dove to the side with a shout of fear as the lion pounced from 40 feet away. Even diving so soon, I barely avoided the monster. It moved so fast, it seemed to teleport across the distance.

It landed on the spot I'd just left half a second before, its long claws gouging furrows in the hard earth. I peeled off one of the emojis at random, but the lion pounced again before I could set it.

I tried rolling, and the monster collided with me like a truck, blasting the air from my lungs. We tumbled over each other in a wild melee of thrashing limbs and raking claws. Searing pain scored my ribs, and I screamed.

Then all of a sudden, the world lurched and I found myself lying on my back, facing the sky. The world shook wildly around me as I vainly tried to leap to my feet, but I couldn't move. Soft fur flexed under my hands and my back.

What happened? It took a second, but finally I realized where I was, although I couldn't quite believe it. I was lying on the back of the lion, and it was sprinting like a runaway train. I twisted and craned my neck the best I could, despite not being able to move for some reason, and caught glimpses of the landscape blurring past. I spotted Steve and Clint disappearing in the distance, then nothing but trees and rocks flashing by.

I could barely twitch. My entire torso was locked onto the lion. After a few seconds of useless squirming, I finally pieced together my position. I was somehow lying on my back on the rear of the huge lion's head, my body draped across its skull, with the back of my own head stuck to its forehead. Its huge ears rose to either side of my face.

My legs extended down the back of its neck, and even my upper arms were locked along the sides of its head. The only part of me I could move were my forearms. Its thick, shaggy fur cushioned my back. I was sunk deep into it, pressed hard against its skull.

Every 3 or 4 seconds, the lion lurched harder and the landscape blurred. A trickle of healing power flowed into me and I realized it was using a magical ability. Stuck to its back, Soul Feed picked up a bit. I directed all of it to healing as I struggled to understand what was happening.

I finally realized each of those lurching jumps were teleporting us short distances. The lion's normal bounding leaps covered dozens of yards, but the teleporting jumps spanned hundreds.

Then the monster roared, an angry sound as it ducked it head, making the world lurch crazily. One giant paw swept up to claw down my side, ripping new gashes in my jacket and cutting deep into my right arm.

I screamed, but couldn't move. The huge paw swept in again, but this time I was ready. Soulrend dropped into my hand and I managed to angle it to catch part of the paw.

The lion yelped and retracted the paw, then bounded away again, roaring and howling. The deadly thing was panicking. Did it think I was holding on to its head on purpose?

The lion abruptly twisted and slammed the back of its head into the side of a tree. The impact was so sudden and unexpected, I couldn't brace or trigger Energy Ward. The tree smashed into my chest so hard, ribs cracked.

All the air blasted out of me in a gasping cry. I coughed blood, groaning in pain. If not for the cushioning of the lion's own fur, that impact might have crushed my ribcage.

I managed to twist Soulrend down. I lacked any kind of leverage with my hands stuck too close to my legs, but managed to slash through a bit of fur by twisting my wrist all the way over. That seemed to startle the monster because it took off running again. It kept huffing and growling and shaking itself like a wet dog. Every shake rattled me until my teeth clacked together, but I remained stuck fast to the lion.

Thankfully, it didn't try clawing me again or running into another tree. I couldn't move my limbs. It was like I was glued to the monster's shaggy fur. I couldn't figure it out until I spotted a notification and scanned it.

"Bravestone!" I cursed. *This can't be happening.*

Eva read the message for me. **Congratulations, Lucas! You have deployed your first trap emoji. Your binding trap has triggered.**

What she didn't say was that it had triggered as me and the stupid lion were rolling over each other. Somehow that trap had caught me in the spell too, and now I was bound to the back of the lion's head. A new timer in my menu said the trap would last another 4 minutes, 45 seconds.

On one hand, the lion couldn't get me off and eat me. On the other, if the binding expired while we were still leaping up nearly vertical cliffs, I would most likely fall to my death.

And that lion was moving! It seemed intent on escaping me by pure flight and it could *move*. Even though I was mostly stuck to its head instead of its torso, I could sense its overwhelming, raw power as its muscles bunched and sprang beneath me, catapulting its mass forward in effortless bounds.

In seconds, we left the canyon behind and raced up and over hills so steep, I don't think I could have climbed them. To my left, a huge plain opened wide, giving me a panoramic view of the grassy expanse set in the midst of the mountainous terrain.

"Hello central valley. Good-bye central valley," I muttered.

Seconds ticked by with excruciating slowness as the Mammoth Lion raced on. It seemed to have endless stamina as it tore through hills and mountains that would have been impassable to me. By the position of the valley, I figured the lion was circling around the southern edges, heading toward the western hills.

I finally stopped my vain struggling and considered ways to kill the beast, but my position made all of my weapons useless. I was in a serious bind, but at least I wasn't stuck to its belly, or something. It would have ripped me to ribbons if that happened.

Within 3 minutes, we started bounding up a gentler slope due west of the central valley. Dense stands of trees scattered across the slope blocked my view of the wide, grassy valley as we ran higher and higher. A new notification pinged into my view, but I waved it away.

If I could just free my hands, I could use Soulrend and kill the stupid lion. The way I lay with my hands almost directly over my own thighs, I lacked a good angle to stab downward, but I needed to figure out something.

At minimum, it would take me hours to get back to the general area I'd left the others. I'd have to cut through the valley because I'd never make it over those mountains.

Assuming I survived. As soon as the emoji sticker wore off and the Mammoth Lion knocked me off, it would rip me to pieces. I'd never stop a level-30 monster.

I needed to think. I couldn't let some random monster kill me. I had a super enhanced intelligence stat. I should be able to think of something, but my thoughts kept scattering as images of those enormous front fangs sinking through my chest kept parading past my mind in gory detail.

The forest grew thicker and the land leveled out. The Mammoth Lion rocketed between the trees, not slowing until I heard the sound of a waterfall nearby. Only then did it pause. The entire monster's body was shaking, either with fear or exhaustion, I couldn't tell. It shook again, huffed another grunting bark, then threw itself into a series of full body rolls.

"You . . . Stupid . . . Cat!" I grunted, spitting grass and dirt between each word as the huge animal rolled over and over.

Thankfully we were in a glade of soft grass. Between the grass and the lion's shaggy fur, I was cushioned enough that its rolls didn't crush me. Luckily, it didn't roll over any rocks, but I groaned from the abuse as its weight rolled over me again and again, crushing pressure making my already-cracked ribs scream. I was really starting to hate this cat.

The binding would run out in seconds if the lion didn't squash me first. Even if I survived long enough to fall free, I was battered and bruised, with cracked ribs and barely-sealed wounds. I could never fight it.

Ten seconds left.

I wracked my brain, but couldn't think of anything. I had a couple offensive spells, but lying on top of the monster like I was, I couldn't deploy any of them properly. I'd probably miss, and couldn't afford to waste a single precious use of those spells.

Soulrend could kill it. I was literally lying on the back of its head. One good stab, and even a monster this powerful would go down. Except, I didn't have an angle.

5 seconds.

Panic threatened to plunge me into unthinking terror, but a single idea rose through the tumult of wild thoughts and I seized it with the desperation of a dying man, which I would be in 3 seconds.

No, it was a stupid idea.

2 seconds.

Still, I hesitated. I did not want to do this. I had one angle to strike, but to use it, I would need to risk an injury I wasn't sure I could heal from.

1 second.

I tossed Soulrend back into my inventory, lifted my hand as high as I could with my elbow still glued to the monster's head, then summoned Soulrend back. This time, the blade pointed down.

With a scream of fear and determination, I slammed Soulrend down with all my strength.

My scream changed to one of absolute agony as I drove my ethereal blade through my own right thigh and into the back of the Mammoth Lion's head. White-hot pain tore through me like a flash of living lightning. My vision went black and I twitched as I severed the spirit of my own leg.

Beneath me, the lion convulsed just as the emoji trap released. The monster's shuddering threw me free and I banished Soulrend back to my inventory as I tumbled to the soft, grassy ground. I hit hard, but pain unlike anything I'd ever felt was still tearing up my leg and straight into my brain. It hurt so much, I barely felt my left arm break as I landed on it wrong.

I rolled several times with the impact, still screaming. My vision cleared enough to realize I was lying face down in the dirt. I forced myself over, biting my lip so hard against a fresh stab of pain that I drew blood.

Falling onto my back, I panted with fear and pain, glancing around for the lion. I'd stabbed it deep into the head, but was that enough?

There! It had fallen to the ground barely 5 feet away. It was convulsing, hissing and growling and biting at the earth, its massive claws tearing great divots out of the ground and flinging them across the clearing. We were close enough that it could easily rip me to shreds by accident.

"Die already," I hissed, trying to move, but I fell back, groaning under a fresh wave of agony. My leg felt dead to me. There was no blood, but I couldn't move it, couldn't feel the muscle or skin, or anything. Just never-ending pain.

With a grunt of effort, I lifted my good right hand and summoned Soulrend back into it. The pommel weighed next to nothing, and the ethereal blade even less, but my hand still wobbled.

With every ounce of my remaining strength, I threw the blade.

The move made me fall back with another cry of pain, but I kept my eyes locked onto Soulrend as it soared across the short distance and plunged through the side of the Mammoth Lion's head, just below one eye.

The lion collapsed in a heap, instantly dead.

Chapter Thirty-Two
The Watery Grave

P anting with adrenaline and fear and shuddering from a fresh wave of pain, I fell back to the grass, groaning.

"I'm alive," I wheezed, raising one hand in a weak salute.

Had I just crippled myself? I couldn't lie there and wait for the next monster to eat me.

Congratulations, Lucas! You have defeated a Mammoth Lion. Bonus experience earned for defeating an enemy more than 10 levels higher than your own.

"More than 28," I muttered. "Why don't you count my level for kills the same way you count it for the quest to escape the first stage?"

"Don't complain, Lucas. You just survived a terrifying ordeal," Cyrus said, as enthusiastic as always.

Test number 3, apparently.

Congratulations, Lucas. You have unlocked the ability Knife Throwing, level 1.

Knife Throwing. Ability. Common. When throwing short, bladed weapons, this ability improves accuracy by 10% per level and damage by 15% per level.

Huh. That was unexpected, but welcome, although I would have preferred getting a level. I lacked the energy to feel annoyed, but triggered Soul Feed.

White light poured off of the dead lion and whirled around me before the entire cloud of energy plunged into my leg. It twitched, and I felt phantom ghosts of sensation trickling out of it. Was it working? Could I heal from spiritual damage?

The white light dimmed as every last scrap of energy was consumed by my injury. Soulrend was even deadlier than I'd realized if spiritual damage took this much power to heal. It wasn't enough, though. My other injuries felt a little better, although not fully healed. It was like the stolen energy automatically targeted the most severe injuries first.

I lay back on the cool, soft grass for a moment, breathing, and just enjoying the lack of pain. My leg would heal. It had to. I had enough potions to make it work. Soul Feed had reconnected something deep inside, and that gave me hope.

A high-pitched growl caught my attention and I glance to my left, new fear spiking through my heart. If there was another lion, I was toast.

There was another lion, but not one I needed to fear. Hopefully. For the first time, I really looked around. I was lying in an idyllic little glade, surrounded by forest, complete with a rocky hill and a waterfall tumbling down to a small pool. The black hole of a cave plunged into the hill near the pool, and a pair of baby lions were standing there, staring out at me. The Mammoth Lion had been their mother, and she'd no doubt planned to feed me to her babies.

Thankfully, the adorable little murder cubs didn't scamper out to eat my eyeballs. I ignored them and triggered a full regeneration potion. Warm healing energy washed through me, healing my lesser injuries before consuming itself in my leg. The connection to my leg felt stronger, but was far from restored. I tried moving it, but could barely make it twitch. Still, that was better than nothing.

"Never stab yourself again, idiot."

I hadn't had a choice, but ow, that had been a desperate call. I decided to try using Harvest on the lion. I really liked Thunder Punch, but a teleport spell would be even better.

You have failed to Harvest a spell from the Mammoth Lion.

"Really? This stupid spell isn't supposed to keep failing."

"You have a very good chance of success, but it's not 100%," Cyrus reminded me.

Grumbling, I accepted the prompt to loot the lion. It seemed I'd used up too much of my luck with the cows, and probably more than I'd ever know surviving the lion long enough to stab it through my own leg.

Getting loot always helped cheer me up, at least for a moment. I barely noticed the mana crystals, did appreciate the new health and mana potions, but focused on the rare saber-toothed dagger. It had a bonus for piercing damage and looked pretty boss. It was a bone dagger with a leather-wrapped handle, wickedly-sharp edge, and deadly point. I also received a rare Mammoth Lion hide. The description said it could be crafted into clothing with a chance to gain a movement bonus. I really needed to figure out how crafting worked. Once I learned to walk again.

I got a couple of loot boxes I hadn't expected and checked the messages I'd ignored to find out why, starting with the most recent one.

Welcome to The Watery Grave!

"Watery Grave?"

Cyrus chortled nearby. "Keep reading."

With a growing sense of apprehension, I did.

Congratulations, Lucas! For being the first Human to defeat a monster at level 30 or above, you receive a gold Explorer's loot box.

I could appreciate that. It contained two items.

Scroll of Explorer's Sight. Grants the ability: Sight of the Explorer. Zoom your vision in on distant objects for greater clarity and to trigger Identify.

"Nice." I read the scroll, and a warm glow suffused my eyes for several seconds. When I blinked it away, the world looked a bit sharper. Stuck in the forest, I couldn't try it out yet, but couldn't wait to do so.

Rare Pants of the Cat Lady. These stylish slacks add 10% to your overall defensive stats and add 15% improved defense against bladed or clawed attacks.

"Even nicer." I willed the pants to change places with my trousers. The pants I was wearing disappeared, but my new pants just fell to the ground.

"How did Ruby do it on her first try?" I grumbled as I shoved the new pants back into my inventory.

I couldn't stand yet, and could barely twitch my injured leg. No way I was going to put on pants. So I concentrated on willing the pants to reappear already on.

It took 8 tries before I managed it, although I still had zero confidence I could swap my next piece of clothing smoothly. The effort helped keep me distracted from my very serious plight for another full 3 minutes. The whole time, my leg ached with a phantom pain that terrified me at a level so deep, I couldn't even name it.

The pants were a tan khaki, the same color as the shaggy lion, and they were super comfortable. Definitely an upgrade. The last box was a larger platinum one.

Congratulations, Lucas! You discovered a unique way to circumvent the limitations preventing you from entering the second stage by binding yourself to a powerful monster to carry you up. Even better, you managed to kill it before it ate you for lunch. Either you're that brave, or you're looking for a quick, glorious death. You receive a platinum Idiotic Bravery loot box!

I blanched. "The Watery Grave is stage 2? How is that possible? I'm not level 10 yet."

Cyrus answered. "The Mammoth Lion is native to this stage. By binding yourself to it, you allowed it to carry you across the line just like it would any other prey it had pounced on and planned to eat."

That's why it had such a high level and was so deadly. Suddenly feeling exposed, I glanced around at the forest. Monsters in the second stage could be even stronger than that lion, and I was just sitting out in the open playing with my loot boxes.

I needed cover, and the lion's cave was close. I couldn't move my right leg, but my agility stat was 5. Those tier-1 points would translate to a tier-0 agility of 50 if my efficiency was 100%. Even reduced, they still translated to something way higher than anyone on Earth.

With that much agility, I easily flipped up onto one foot. I'd done a bit of gymnastics as a kid, and honestly, I'd sucked. I could barely do a cringe-worthy imitation of a cartwheel. Now jumping up felt effortless. With a grin, I threw myself into a forward tumble, kicking off with my one good leg. I'd never done anything like that before, but now it felt effortless and natural to somersault my way one-legged across the clearing.

I would have laughed with absolute joy if my bad leg didn't keep flopping around like I'd stapled a dead fish to my knee. It threw off my balance, and I nearly lost control of my somersault. Drawing deep from my agility, I managed to keep going.

When I got to the cave, rolling from a final handstand to an awkward one-leg kneeling position, I peered inside. It was dim, but not pitch dark. The cave was tall enough to stand in, but only near the opening. It extended deeper into the cliff, and the two cubs crouched at the back, growling.

I crawled inside and eased myself down to the sandy floor near the opening. The musky scent of the lion clung to the cave, but it wasn't much worse than my aunt's house. She had 16 cats and never opened her windows.

Feeling a bit more secure, I focused on that last loot box. It flashed and disappeared, leaving behind more items than I expected. Maybe the multiverse rooted for brave idiots as much as Earth did. I'd take it.

Stat boost scroll. Boost all primary tier-0 stats by 3 points each.

I sighed. I'd wised for extra ways to boost my stats, and I'd gotten one, so that was good. The 0.3 increase to each of my main stats wasn't quite what I'd hoped for, but every scrap of power still helped.

"Feeling guilty for not managing to award all the normal stats for my level?" I asked, glancing up.

"Nonsense. These rewards are well deserved."

"Sure. Thanks. How about a loot box with a spell or ability evolution to tier-1? I am on stage 2, after all."

"Those evolutions do not unlock until you hit at least level 10."

"Why? Because that's when we permanent our next spell?"

"Indeed. Reaching that level is a major milestone for multiple reasons."

I shrugged. "Well, it's also supposed to be impossible for me to be here until level 10. We've broken one rule. Why not another?"

"Nice try. Spell and ability evolutions are not that simple. Best way to ensure one is coming soon is to level a spell or ability to at least level 10."

So spells did have official levels. They didn't show up on my spell listing. Was that because they were all still level 1? Not good. My abilities did have levels, but most were still really low. Getting them to level 10 would probably take longer than reaching player level 10. Not promising.

"Okay, so are there upgrade scrolls to help speed up the process of leveling spells?"

"There are, and you may indeed win a few levels in loot boxes for your spells or abilities. It is still unlikely you will see many before you hit level 10, though."

"I don't understand why the game would work that way."

"You will eventually."

"I'll hold you to that." Now wasn't the time to argue game mechanics. I was still half crippled, stuck on stage 2 with monsters probably even stronger than that Mammoth Lion had been.

"So how about a teleport scroll to return me to stage 1 since I'm not supposed to be here?"

"Another great question. It's great to see you turn that powerful mind to problem solving."

"You didn't answer the question."

"Would you really want to waste this unique opportunity for growth?"

"Absolutely. I'm not ready to be up here."

"Don't underestimate yourself," Cyrus chided.

His good cheer could be a bit annoying, but had he just given me a clue? I had gotten stuck in a situation with unprecedented danger. Made sense that it might also offer unprecedented growth, and I needed growth. Maybe this whole lion fiasco was yet another test.

I was good at tests. I took a deep breath and focused. I had to concentrate on survival. First step, see if I got any more loot that could help me escape this mess. The next item made me chuckle.

Catnip. Better than a can of tuna, this cube of condensed catnip will grant you a high percentage chance to make any feline you share it with see you as a friend instead of a snack.

"I could have used this 10 minutes ago." I set it aside to study later. If there were more lions around, I might need it.

"Ha!" I laughed when I saw the next item.

Torch of the Mirrored Moon: This magical torch produces a beam of pure white light, powerful enough to drive back any shadow.

It was a magical flashlight. A good one too. When I willed it on, the beam flooded the cave with bright light, consuming the deepest shadows, even though I only pointed it up. The cubs recoiled, growling in their super cute, murder cub way.

I always kept a good flashlight in my riding gear and preferred strong ones about 1000 lumens. This magical torch had to be twice as bright. Fiddling with it, I soon learned how to adjust the beam to make it brighter or dimmer. Despite all the cool magic gear I'd gotten so far, I felt more thrilled with the stupid flashlight than just about anything else.

I also got a random scroll that awarded 10 points to my fear defense. Did I even have a stat for fear defense? When I opened my stats menu, I found a new option titled **"Supplemental Stats"**.

I opened it and couldn't believe it. The menu was like a never-ending scroll of stat options. It was like the game had tried quantifying everything I'd ever done into a stat. Some made sense from my pre-multiverse life, like Running (.6), Jumping (.2), and Swimming (.7), but a lot were just random weird things like Spitting (.4), Cyber Forensics (.8), Hula hooping (.2), and Driving in snowy conditions (.7).

Seeing them all translated to tier-1 numbers was depressing. "Do these change as our stats climb?"

Jumping still looked pathetic. 0.2 was right on the money from before I started leveling, but didn't fit me now. I didn't have a tumbling stat, even though I'd just proved I could probably give an Olympic gymnast a run for their money with even a modicum of training.

"They will reflect your base stat changes over time, but have not been updated yet."

All of a sudden, one of the lion cubs pounced right next to me. With a shout of surprise, I recoiled, managing to bang the back of my head on the stone wall.

The cub wasn't attacking me, but had snuck up while I was distracted with my menus and pounced on the catnip. Now it rolled away, growling and gnawing at the little cube.

"Don't eat it all. I need that for any more big cats around here," I told it as I rubbed my head.

It ignored me, as cats do, but I still couldn't help smiling. It actually looked adorable rolling around, growling and shaking the little cube. Unlike its sibling, this one had a white patch in its otherwise tawny coat, splashed across its right shoulder. After a moment, it rolled back toward me and bumped against my thigh.

I watched it carefully, ready to scoop it up if it tried sinking those needlelike teeth into my leg. The cub froze and glanced up at me for a second. It growled as if considering whether or not to eat my face.

It licked the catnip again, then leaned its head against my injured thigh and rubbed, purring loudly.

Petting a wild magical mountain lion cub. Who would have imagined it? I guess this world isn't all snarling monsters and violent death.

Of course, I'd just killed its mother. Should I kill the cubs too? I needed every scrap of experience I could get, but I doubted the cubs would help in any meaningful way. Besides, I didn't want to kill them unless they attacked me. They were the first cute, not overtly deadly monsters I'd met so far.

So I took a chance and reached down to scratch behind the cub's ears. It froze again for a second, then seemed to melt against me, purring even louder. Grinning, I sank my fingers in its thick, soft fur and rubbed its head and neck. I could feel its strength. Even as a purring little fluffball, I could sense its potential for violence.

That only made the chance to pet it even more amazing. The other cub growled from a distance, edging forward before scooting back again. It seemed to lack the first cub's bravery. As I sat there, enjoying the unexpected moment petting the fluffy cub, the ache in my injured leg lessened a bit.

"What's going on? Do lion cubs have healing properties?"

Cyrus chuckled. "No, but positive things that help restore the soul are medicinal to those with spiritual injuries."

"You're kidding. Petting a wild lion cub is actually promoting healing?"

"Would you prefer it eat off your toes?"

"No, this is good."

I smiled in wonder and kept petting the adorable little murder kitty. It stayed there for a full 5 minutes before it accidentally flung the catnip away and pounced after it. That sent it rolling all the way across the cave where its sibling pounced.

The cubs erupted into a startling display of raw fury as they slashed and bit at each other. They looked like tan blurs of death, gouging chunks of stone from the wall in their fight. I swallowed as I watched them scar solid stone.

They did not seem to actually harm each other, but I suddenly no longer felt as comfortable sitting so close. I'd actually let one of those furballs of death sit next to me?

"Unbelievable," I whispered and pulled a few pounds of hamburger from my inventory. It had come wrapped in white paper, so I unwrapped it and placed it on the floor nearby. The cubs kept squabbling over the catnip, but they'd notice the meat eventually. That might keep them alive a bit longer.

Feeling more relaxed than I had been in a long time, I considered my next move. I'd needed that break, but my situation was dire. I was accidentally stuck on the second stage, surrounded by deadlier monsters, with a leg I still couldn't move.

I had a few more potions, but what if they weren't enough to restore my leg? Would my natural regeneration help, or was spiritual damage beyond what I could self-heal? I couldn't sit there forever, petting the cub if it decided to return to my side. I needed to escape before some level 40 nightmare ripped out my kidneys for a snack.

Crawling off half-cocked would just as likely get me killed faster. So I pulled out the monster dictionary I'd gotten from Joseph's body. I hadn't even cracked it open, but if anyone needed information on monsters, I did.

As soon as I opened the book, blinding light shot out of it in twin golden beams that struck me right in the eyes.

"What the . . . ?" I shouted and recoiled, flailing at the lights, while the cubs scampered away, growling.

With the light came a torrent of information. I caught glimpses of dozens of monsters as information poured straight into my brain. The process only took a few seconds, but it felt like I was getting a waking lobotomy as my thoughts scattered under the onslaught.

When it finally ended, I found myself leaning against the cool stone wall of the cave, panting. My head pounded, but the headache faded quickly.

"Ow. Why does absorbing this book hurt so much more than other information I've gotten?"

Cyrus surprised me by answering. "That was a unique item prepared for Joseph. He hadn't even opened it yet, or you would never have gotten it."

If he had read it, would he have understood how to deal with the ogre? I closed my eyes and thought about monsters, but only got vague impressions.

"Why can't I use it?"

"The information will appear as needed. It will feed directly into your Linguasight Identify spell."

Probably better that way. I hated studying long lists of information. I rubbed my temples where a headache still throbbed, then rubbed my thigh. I could feel the touch a little.

Okay, I could do this. I had a moment of quiet and relative safety. I was alive. I needed a plan to escape, but it seemed I'd be able to heal my leg eventually. I sagged with relief. If I'd permanently handicapped myself, I would have been as good as dead.

Pulling up the team chat, I spotted several messages from Ruby and Steve. I sent them a group chat.

Lucas: "I'm alive. Got dragged pretty far by that lion. I'm safe for the moment, trying to figure out how to get back. I'll send you an update soon."

I probably should have told them the whole story, but then they'd freak out and maybe try to get up here to try to rescue me. That would just get them killed too. I couldn't have their deaths on my conscience. I was the one dumb enough to get stuck on stage 2, so I'd find a way to escape back down.

First, I needed a moment to rest and gather my thoughts. I closed my eyes and must have drifted off to sleep. The next thing I knew, I heard the crunching of footsteps drawing near.

I snapped awake and looked up to see 3 humanoid figures standing over me. For a second, hope soared, despite my earlier resolve to escape on my own. Ruby and Steve had tracked me down.

Then I got a clearer view of my visitors, and my hope shattered like glass. They were not anyone I knew. In fact, they weren't anyone still living. Identify kicked in.

Undead sailor. Level 35. Zombie. These remnants of a once-mighty fleet are still searching for a way to set sail again. They hunt for slaves to man the oars of their rotting ships. Extremely resilient, the undead sailor is only weak against fire or massive brain trauma.

"You've got to be kidding me," I whispered as one of the zombies pointed a weapon at me that very much looked like a shotgun and squeezed the trigger.

A blast of white-hot energy engulfed me.

Chapter Thirty-Three
I Choose to Slap a Werewolf

I woke up with a groan, and memories snapped back, making me twitch with remembered pain. Zombies! And they had shot me with a blast that felt like a Taser on steroids.

Blinking my eyes open, I sat up, staring around wildly. My heart fell into my boots. I was sitting on a rough wooden plank, about 3 feet wide, my wrists and ankles shackled with chains to heavy bolts sunk into the thick wood.

Four men carried the plank. None of them made any move to acknowledge I was awake. None of them spoke. As my gaze swept over them, my blood chilled and a deepening sense of dread crept down my spine like a spider made of ice.

They were corpses. Corpses that walked and carried me on silent shoulders. More zombies. My skin crawled as I looked into half-rotted faces, some with missing eyes, all with chunks of flesh gone, revealing faded white bone underneath.

They all wore rough shirts and trousers, and a couple wore straw hats. The description had said they were undead sailors. They dressed like it, and oddly, they smelled like it. They stunk like an old fish market, with hints of saltwater and rotting meat. Identify informed me they were all level 35.

How? This was bad. Very bad. That Mammoth Lion had seemed like certain death at level 30. These zombies were even stronger. I was so dead.

I forced myself to not think about my inevitable death. I was so screwed, but as my mind whirled, I studied the zombies closer. It looked like our Earth legends about zombies got a surprising amount of detail right. Did we have more alien encounters than I'd imagined, or was Cyrus tailoring some monsters to our expectations?

The random thought didn't help. Glancing farther, I spotted half a dozen more undead sailors marching in front of the 4 carrying me, with just as many trailing. Several of them carried old-fashioned lanterns as they followed a faint path through the thick forest.

It was night. I'd been out for hours.

Stupid zombies! They'd wasted at least half a day of time I couldn't afford to waste. I could have hopped back to stage 1 by now on my one good leg.

Right. As if I would have made it back. That stupid lion had most likely sealed my fate by dragging me up here to stage 2. Everything was so strong. I was like a child dropped onto a battlefield against tanks.

No. I wasn't dead yet. I had to find a way to turn this situation to my favor. How, though? Even if I miraculously figured out how to break free and make a run for it, I doubted I could quick-hop my way past a dozen zombies with stun guns.

The image of me doing an unending sequence of one-legged backflips and somersaults through the forest, dodging a barrage of stun blasts from pursuing zombies flashed through my mind. I now knew I could do gymnastic flips, but I doubted my luck would hold out that long.

The image helped push back my growing panic, though. I was breathing too fast, my pulse racing, my thoughts whirling, but I took a deep breath.

One step at a time.

I wasn't dead yet, and they hadn't eaten me, or infected me. At least, I didn't think I'd been infected. I scanned my stats, and my health and mana bars looked mostly good. A little image of a person now appeared beside them, with its right leg glowing orange. I had no notifications, so apparently Cyrus didn't see getting captured by undead sailors a memorable achievement. At least not one deserving of reward.

Okay, so the zombies weren't planning to eat me right away. I could work with that. They seemed a lot more intelligent than most zombie movies suggested. I had to find a weakness to leverage.

Most carried rifle-looking weapons a lot sleeker than that first shotgun-style stun gun, although I did see a couple more of those. The zombies held the weapons at a low ready position and only then did I realize the entire group looked nervous, constantly scanning the darkness. If they were alive, they would have probably been muttering about monsters.

Their lanterns might look like replicas of lanterns used on sailing ships from the pirate heyday, but the magical constructs provided pretty good light. They didn't seem to push the shadows back far enough, though. Couldn't zombies see in the dark? For some reason, I felt like they should. Still, anything that could make level-35 undead monsters nervous was nothing I wanted anything to do with.

One of the zombies in the lead suddenly stopped and lifted his lantern high. He shouted, his voice like fingernails clawing down a blackboard. "Werewolves!"

"Jurgen's fist," I swore softly to myself as the zombies all raised weapons.

Wait, Zombies could talk?

The 4 holding my prison plank stepped away, dropping me to the ground with a crash to reach for their own sidearms. By the time I hit the ground, shadows exploded out of the darkness on all sides. They flashed into the light, moving so fast I barely caught glimpses of black fur, red eyes, and flashing fangs.

Five giant wolves tore into the zombies in a terrifyingly coordinated attack. I expected to see the zombies explode into meaty chunks under the onslaught, but they were tougher than they looked. Some zombies did go down with werewolves ripping them apart, but others clubbed werewolves out of the air or shot them with energy weapons that sizzled fur and seared flesh.

I cowered on my plank as battle raged all around. I should not be in this area. Every monster was way too strong. One weird thought floated up through the haze of fear and dread.

So, laser blasters are real. There is technology in the multiverse.

I needed guns like that, but I doubted I'd live long enough to even touch one. My gaze settled on one werewolf ripping the arms off of a zombie and Identify kicked in.

Waterlogged Werewolf. Level 32. Uncommon. These nocturnal hunters rule the night and hunger for anything with a beating heart. They especially hate zombies, who are not only false prey, but who compete against them for dominion of this stage. Will regenerate from even mortal wounds as long as their energy reserves hold out.

"Not encouraging," I muttered, scanning the snarling werewolves. They ranged from level 30 to level 38, with one monster all the way up at level 45. Why they were labeled as waterlogged was a question Identify didn't answer.

The zombies fought hard, and they might have had a chance if they weren't fighting werewolves. Again, our Earth legends proved terrifyingly accurate as the werewolves quickly regenerated even from wounds that should have been fatal. They attacked the undead over and over, heedless of wounds, whittling down the sailors' ranks one at a time.

The werewolves didn't have limitless regeneration, though. With inhuman discipline, the zombies focused their energy weapons on one werewolf after another, ripping it apart so many times, even its incredible regeneration ability broke down. The air filled with the stench of burning fur, charred meat, and the rot of ripped open long-dead corpses.

I silently urged the zombies on. I'd take my chances with zombies over werewolves any day. My luck hadn't recovered yet, though. The sailors didn't quite make it.

Within a shockingly short amount of time, the strongest werewolf, the level 45 leader of the pack, ripped the head off the final undead sailor. All the other werewolves were dead, but 1 werewolf was more than enough to kill a level-2 human.

The area was littered with bodies and body parts, splattered with overlapping sheets of crimson and black blood. The lanterns, tossed aside in the wild fight, illuminated the ghastly scene in a patchwork of shadows that only highlighted the horror of it. My stomach roiled and threatened to hurl everything I'd eaten in the past day, but the sight of death prowling toward me pushed everything else aside.

The werewolf limped as blood dripped from a dozen wounds. Its regeneration had slowed, but hadn't stopped. It would recover in seconds, but didn't look like it planned to wait before feeding. I bet I knew how it renewed its energy pools, and that did not bode well for me.

Why did all the legends about werewolves and their miraculous healing have to be true? Why couldn't the truth be more like their teeth were really made out of cotton candy?

The wolf growled low with the promise of violent death. Its claws were dripping with black zombie blood, its teeth showing chunks of flesh as it peeled its lips back in a snarl. The reek of blood and death seemed to intensify, but the forest had fallen completely silent except for the clicking of the wolf's claws as it advanced.

"I don't think so," I growled back, forcing anger to replace my terror. I was so out of my league, with a bum leg and an insanely low level. I couldn't even swing my blade with my hands shackled, but I wouldn't just lie down and die.

So I pulled a tier-1 mana crystal from my inventory and popped it into my mouth. Cyrus had warned me to use caution with those. They contained 10 times the energy of a tier-0 mana crystal, but I was way beyond the point of holding anything back.

Energy exploded through me like I'd swallowed a bomb. My muscles swelled and I yanked my arms and legs at the same time. The chains didn't snap or the shackles break, but the bolts tore free of the wood, leaving me with short lengths of chain hanging from every limb.

Well, 3 of my limbs. My injured leg twitched under the jolt of power, but the healing was far from complete, and I lacked control over it. That left one leg tethered to the plank.

The werewolf pounced as soon as I moved, but I triggered Energy Ward. As the huge monster barreled in, I rolled to the side. It might be badly injured, but the insanely powerful beast still moved like a blur of black death. It slammed into my defensive aura, and I was the one that got pushed out of the way.

Good thing too, because jaws that could rip me to shreds in a heartbeat crashed shut right next to my shoulder, and powerful claws raked at my chest. I lifted my arms, taking the claws across my jacket and bracers. They left deep gouges in the leather, but incredibly, did not rip through.

The monster crashed to the ground right next to me and its wet-dog, rancid-meat scent made me gag. I dropped Soulrend into my hand and stabbed at the werewolf's eye.

It ducked, so I only slashed through one of its long ears. The ear flopped against its head and the wolf howled right in my face, so loud my ears would have burst if I was still a tier-0 human. It snapped at me, but I was already rolling back. The force of its muzzle slamming against my shoulder sent me sprawling.

Then my right leg snapped me to a halt so hard I nearly got whiplash. The short chain was taught, still anchoring my leg to the plank, which the werewolf was standing on.

I desperately rolled back to my knees just in time to catch a slashing claw across the chest. It came in so hard, my aura couldn't deflect it, even though it drained a bunch of my mana.

The huge paw raked through the chains of my upraised left hand, shattering links, but I managed to avoid getting slashed open. The impact still slammed me back so hard against my last shackle that my ankle audibly snapped.

Thankfully, the pain was just a distant ache through the still-severed spiritual connection to the limb. I rebounded back toward the werewolf like a nightmare version of those balls attached to paddles with a rubber band. I managed to slash wildly at one of its forelegs as I crashed to the ground beside the wolf. I scored a weak hit and the monster stumbled.

"That's how it feels!" I shouted. I didn't know if it could heal from the spiritual damage any easier than I could, but that might distract it for a second.

Snarling, the werewolf rose over me. I don't know if it was trying for intimidation, or something, but I wasn't about to miss such a good opening. I plunged Soulrend into the monster's chest.

"Yes!" I couldn't believe I'd killed it.

I should have known better than to celebrate early. The werewolf convulsed, but rolled onto its back and raked out with its other foreleg. The move caught me totally by surprise and the powerful paw caught me on the chest.

Long claws ripped through my jacket despite my aura's best efforts and flung me across the clearing. The iron restraint tore through my shackled ankle, leaving my boot and half my foot stuck to the plank.

That time I felt the pain like a searing jolt of agony, and I lost my grip on Soulrend. The precious sword tumbled away as I bounced across the battlefield, smashing through ripped pieces of undead sailors and savaged wolves. I snatched for an energy rifle, but missed, then tried to tuck into an acrobatic flip to land on my feet.

Dummy. My right leg still didn't work, and that foot and ankle were a crushed heap of mangled flesh and bone. I bounced off an undead sailor's ribcage, then slammed to the ground with a painful impact right next to the corpse of one of the fallen werewolves. It had not reverted to human form like 2 of the others already had.

My chest screamed with pain. Had those claws cut through ribs? Everything else ached from the crazy tumble. I panted with exhaustion and panic and overwhelming pain. I was so far out of my depth, it was a miracle I'd survived those first seconds.

I didn't want to die, but I was at the end of my rope. The last werewolf limped after me, red-eyed gaze locked on me, fangs dripping with hunger to rip out my heart.

"Why don't you just die?" I shouted, then coughed and groaned as my ribs protested.

In response, the werewolf broke into a loping run, speeding up with each step, its wounds fading as it healed everything. At the same second, my temporary burst of strength and clarity from the mana crystal wore out and I sagged against the ground, totally exhausted.

I could barely move and definitely couldn't fight the death machine hurtling toward me. It would kill me in seconds.

No.

I refused to die like that.

Meeting the charging werewolf's gaze, I reached behind me, slapped one weak hand onto the shoulder of the dead werewolf, and triggered Harvest.

Chapter Thirty-Four
Harvest of the New Moon

You have successfully Harvested Lycanthropic Transformation from Waterlogged Werewolf.

I didn't even read what spell I got. As soon as I saw that Harvest was successful, I triggered the spell. It thundered through me with far more power than any spell I'd ever tried before, including Thunder Punch.

Why hadn't I used Thunder Punch?

The thought flickered through my dazed mind as the werewolf landed on me, huge jaws rending. I lifted one hand in front of my face and the werewolf ripped my arm right out of the socket with a mighty heaving twist.

Pain blasted through me like a river of agony, and I stared in stupid shock at the stump of my arm spurting bright crimson blood. Then the agony was lost in a torrent of magic ripping me apart from the spell. My entire body spasmed and I screamed so loud my vocal cords ripped. Every particle of my body seemed to melt under a supernatural heat.

What the hell had I just harvested?

My vision darkened and all my senses retracted as my mind shut down, unable to process what was happening. I embraced the welcome bliss of darkness as I felt my body die.

Then my heart beat once.

Then again.

Except, it wasn't my heart. It was a new heart, a powerful heart. As it blasted fresh streams of blood through me, my body reformed. The pain vanished, replaced by a sense of absolute power. I shuddered again, this time in ecstasy.

I screamed out of pure reflex, but the scream changed in mid-cry into a spine-shivering howl.

Was that my voice?

Oh, yeah! That wasn't even the best part. Understanding rushed back into my mind as all my senses flooded me with input. A river of feelings and scents rolled through me, and I exulted in newfound strength.

My body thrummed with power, my new muscles swelling with might until they strained the limits of my sleek new frame. I lunged to my feet as easy as thought.

I now had four feet, all powerful, and all working. The transformation had reconnected my severed right leg to my spirit!

The area around me snapped into crystal clear focus through my newly-enhanced senses. The earth crunched under my clawed feet, while the gentle breeze carried the scents of blood and death and rotten meat. The lingering scents of fear and blood frenzy hovered at the fringes. No sound broke the terrified stillness of the forest around me beyond the lingering echoes of my first howl.

I spun to face the lead werewolf. It was watching me with a wolf equivalent of surprise on its lupine face, head cocked to one side, one ear flipped forward, the other back, muzzle partially open.

At least I didn't lose my mind. Transforming just to submit to the alpha or something stupid would have been worse than getting eaten as an honest man.

I crouched to spring and the other werewolf shook off its surprise. The hairs along its back rose as its intent to kill returned.

My turn.

I launched myself at my enemy. This time, I was the monster's equal and I had a lost arm and a shattered foot to repay. We came together in a flurry of snapping jaws and raking claws, swarming over each other with blurring speed. Pain flared with every move of the experienced werewolf as it ripped and tore at me.

I was freshly transformed, my reserves of energy full, and the wounds closed almost instantly. Besides, Energy Ward was still active, and it thrummed with more power than ever. It turned aside or weakened many attacks.

In turn, I ripped at the other werewolf with all my strength, venting all my terror and anger at the crazy death game I'd ended up in. I unleashed every battle instinct that came with the werewolf form, but wrapped in my human ability to analyze and strategize.

I exulted in the duel as we ripped and tore at each other. The flashes of pain only punctuated the exultant feeling of bloodlust that washed away any fear, all hesitation, and almost too much clarity of thought.

As the seconds dragged on and we tore each other apart again and again, I realized I was in trouble. My enemy might have started weaker, with regeneration already partially spent, but he still had a far higher level and lots of experience.

He ripped me apart again and again, every move calculated, every attack planned. My newfound wolf instincts threatened to swamp my mind as I gave them full rein. As a human, I didn't know how to fight in wolf form.

As a wolf, I was still too young. Despite everything I threw at my opponent, it started to whittle me down. My vast pool of regeneration power was getting spent at an astonishing rate, and my healing started to slow.

My opponent sensed my growing weakness and redoubled his efforts. His bloodred eyes bored into me with no pity, no mercy. He shouldered me over and lunged in to rip out my throat.

I pushed the wolf part of me aside, my mind rising to the fore. As only a wolf, I was going to die. I lifted one foreleg to intercept the wolf's lunging jaws in a very humanlike defensive move.

The wolf snapped down on my leg, breaking the bone in 2 places. I howled with the new flash of pain, but rolled and raked my claws across my enemy's stomach.

He yelped and twisted away, leaving me time to leap back to my feet. My foreleg snapped back into place, already healed, and we circled each other.

Why had it retreated like that? Sure, I could have raked its belly, but its regeneration could have handled a few claw marks.

Glancing down at its belly, I felt a twinge through Identify, and in that second I sensed my enemy's energy. It burned with the power of blood, as I expected, but I sensed a deeper well of power. Maybe that was what replenished it.

An echo of that same power resonated from deep within the pits of my own guts. Werewolf regeneration was located in our guts, not our hearts? That's why it retreated to protect its stomach.

'I've got you now.'

I lunged in, and my enemy moved to meet me, just as it had dozens of times already. Instead of crashing chest to chest and flashing fangs to fangs, I dove and rolled under my leaping foe, raking all 4 sets of claws at his belly.

The move caught it by surprise and I tore deep gashes in its hide. The wolf gushed blood, but I also sensed it losing far more energy than it did from other wounds.

The werewolf crouched, trying to protect its vital belly. That left the back of its neck exposed and I pounced, clamping my powerful jaws closed like a vise. Teeth dug deep, snapping through muscle and crunching into spine. My enemy shuddered and I wrenched it over, tossing it onto its back. Before it could recover, I drove forward, ripping open its belly and plunging my jaws deep into its guts..

Hot blood gushed over my muzzle and into my mouth. The human part of me wanted to cringe in disgust, but to my werewolf self, the rich, energy-infused blood was like nectar from the gods.

Revitalizing energy coursed through me as I raked claws through the wound, doubling its size. My enemy howled in pain and convulsed off the ground in a final assault, unleashing all its remaining strength.

I caught it by the throat and my jaws bit down, then I savagely twisted, ripping the enemy's head nearly off. With a final gurgling whimper, my enemy fell dead at my feet.

I threw back my bloody muzzle and howled with victory, the sound reverberating through my soul like the finest symphony.

A long moment later, my thoughts cleared. I was still in werewolf form, but almost felt like myself as the wolf in me subsided, sated from the kill and blood of my enemy.

This is incredible!

Congratulations, Lucas! You defeated Waterlogged Werewolf pack leader, level 45. Bonus experience gained for defeating an enemy with a much higher level.

For killing an enemy more than 25 levels higher than your own, proving you're either a blood-crazed lunatic destined to die young in battle or just luckier than all the dead stiffs who kidnapped you, you receive the title Lucky Stiff and an emerald Blind Luck loot box.

Title: Lucky Stiff: Unlocks a new secondary stat: Luck. Plus 15 to Luck.

"So Luck really is a thing?" I asked as a huge, glowing emerald appeared hovering in front of me. The words came out in wolf growls, but I bet Cyrus could understand it just fine. With growing anticipation, I willed the loot box open. It dropped one long scroll.

Scroll of Lucky Breaks.
Plus 2 tier-1 points to all base stats.
Plus 5 to CHA.
Plus 10% faster health and mana recovery
Double Agility stat points calculated from Dexterity.
Double Endurance stat points calculated from Strength.

"Tier-1 points? Yes!" I chortled in a weird wolf huffing laugh. For a second, I had forgotten I still wore a werewolf body.

"When you defeat monsters this high, the prizes tend to tier up," Cyrus said.

My entire body shuddered as the new stats took effect. Waves of pure power rolled through me and I gasped in wonder. I felt so much stronger, nimbler, and my thoughts accelerated. I seemed to have already gotten a major temporary boost to my stats just for being in wolf form, but with the new stat boost, I felt twice as strong as before. Fighting another werewolf one-on-one no longer seemed insane.

That stat boost was even bigger percentage-wise than the last big special boost I got. Two points in each base stat was like getting 20 tier-0 points each. I'd nearly doubled all my base stats, which would trickle to my secondary stats too.

I opened my stats to see the new points allocate and gaped when I saw my levels.

"Three levels? How is that possible?"

"The bonuses for killing monsters so high above your own grow exponentially. In a unique twist of fate, you also received a big share of the experience for the deaths of the other werewolves and the undead sailors."

"How? I was a captive."

"You were all targeted together and all ended up fighting the same werewolves, so as the sole survivor, you gained the bulk of the experience for killing the werewolves. At the same time, the zombies were not your allies. Again, as the sole survivor, you are the only possible recipient for most of the experience for their deaths."

"You realize that's insane, right?"

"Would you prefer I let the experience go to waste?"

"No! Sorry, my mind isn't totally clear in werewolf form. I'll happily take it all."

Wow, getting captured by undead sailors had turned out to be the best use of my time I could have imagined. All I had to do was get mostly ripped to pieces, take a major risk, Harvest a pivotal spell at a critical moment, and defeat a far more experienced enemy through a lucky application of my enhanced Identify.

No way I should have survived. That fact made me laugh, which came out as a whuffing wolf pant, my long tongue lolling out my deadly jaws.

Was this whole misadventure really pure chance, though? Cyrus had suggested the disaster might prove helpful, another test to prove my worth. And he'd been right. This test was indeed proving both ridiculously dangerous and insanely productive.

"Cyrus, did you send that lion to capture me and bring me up here for a test?"

The AI chuckled. "No, although it's proving a perfect opportunity, isn't it? I try not to interfere that directly, unless I have no other choice."

That was good news. "Why allocate all 6 new points to Strength, though? I'd prefer a more balanced allocation."

"First you complained about getting stats in Wisdom. Now you complain about stats in Strength? If you never learn to feel satisfied, no victory, no matter how glorious, will ever fulfill you."

I chuckled. "Sorry. I guess I was coming across as a bit of a whiner. I love the stats in Strength, don't get me wrong, and those other extra stats helped a lot. Thank you."

"You are welcome," Cyrus said in a surprisingly long-suffering tone. "That stat boost was included instead of some of the other loot I was planning. I hope you're satisfied."

"Absolutely."

"Good. Then stop complaining, or you won't like what you get in your next box."

He sounded annoyed. Definitely didn't want to complain again, at least not for a while. I couldn't risk Cyrus deciding to dole out a bit of smiting. He was not just another computer program. He was an actual, living AI, complete with very humanlike emotions. Plus, he was still a child. Hopefully he didn't throw tantrums. I had to be careful not to make any assumptions about his maturity.

I triggered Soul Feed over the dead pack leader. White light gushed forth in an enormous cloud that swirled around me, topping off all my pools, as well as the pool of regenerative power thrumming in my guts. The extra energy supercharged my stats for 15 minutes.

"How come the effects on my stats last so much longer?"

"You're on a higher stage and wearing a much more powerful body."

"I'll take it." I felt invincible as I accepted the prompt to loot the werewolf leader.

I got so many mana crystals I ended up with a new inventory item: Tier-2 mana crystals, each worth 100 tier-0 crystals. I also got several full healing potions, 2 full regeneration potions that filled both health and mana, and a potion I'd never seen before.

Ultimate Glamp potion, times 6. Join the ranks of the intrepid adventurers who love camping so much, they have to bring an entire house along for a one-nighter. This two-part potion helps make sure you never leave any comfort behind and actually have to experience the outdoors. Pour it onto any building to drag it and everything inside of it into the bottle. When you find the perfect place to enjoy the natural beauty of the world, pull the cork to disgorge the building so you can head right on inside.

The long description made me chuckle. I did love camping, but I'd never complain about bringing a larger, hopefully more secure structure along on Arasha. Just needed to find a vacant building.

For crafting items, I got a rare werewolf pelt that could be crafted into gear that added plus 20 to stealth, and several fangs that could infect with poison. The final random item was a potion to permanently increase my poison resistance by 10 points. I instantly drank it.

I then moved about the clearing, quickly looting the other werewolves and all the zombies. Eva did not give me the option to loot them all at once this time. I had no idea why not, but it only took a few seconds.

In the process, I recovered Soulrend and my lost boot. I had to shake out the shattered remnants of my old foot. Gross. Even worse, as a wolf, I had to fight the urge to gobble up the bloody morsel.

From the werewolves, I got more similar loot, plus 3 rare potions of full poison resist, including lycanthropy resistance, which Cyrus confirmed was very rare. From the zombies, I got a bunch of useless junk, including a bunch of random clothing, and even 1 rusty iron breastplate. It was listed as uncommon grade, but looked pretty useless.

The 3 magic lanterns and 8 sets of enchanted steel manacles that required strength 50 to break were much better. Even more interesting were the 3 working energy rifles and 10 broken rifles, plus 2 of the big stun guns.

I really needed to test those out when I had human hands again. The Star Wars nerd inside of me was squealing that I now had a blaster. Too bad I wasn't on team Star Wars.

That foolishness could wait. I was still a werewolf, and I was wasting time. I found a timer icon in my menus that listed how long current enchantments lasted. The lycanthropy transformation would last all night! I still had 3 hours left. It was a single-use spell, unfortunately, and Harvest failed to get me any more.

My first instinct was to escape the second stage. In werewolf form, I could follow the same insane path the lion had dragged me across. I'd easily find my team. It would be fun to race across impassable cliffs. The panic I'd been fighting down ever since realizing I'd accidentally ended up on stage 2 made it seem like sprinting for the slope back down was the only intelligent choice.

I hesitated, though. Only weak prey lived down at the lower level. I'd gained 3 levels from one encounter. Sure, the math got weird, but even if I'd gotten all the credit for the entire herd of cows, I would have gained only a fraction as much.

Time was short and I needed levels. Stronger monsters could provide them, and Cyrus had suggested my situation offered unique growth potential. Besides, if I scouted the second stage, I could gain invaluable intelligence when I regrouped with the rest of the survivors.

That was more than enough justification to decide to explore the forest, just a little. Wolves were quiet, right? I could sneak around and sniff out if there were any monsters weak enough for me to take on. If I found something I couldn't handle, I doubted anything could run down a wolf. I could escape down to the lower stage.

What could go wrong with a plan so simple?

Chapter Thirty-Five

I Take a Sightseeing Death Tour

Within minutes, I realized I was an idiot.

Wolf howls started behind me. First one, then several more. Behind them and echoing above all the others came a deeper howl that set all the hairs down my spine standing on edge.

The howls weren't words exactly, but I perfectly understood their meaning. The pack was on the hunt, and I was the target. The deeper howl came from the ultimate alpha, and I'd earned his personal ire by killing one of his lieutenants. Worse, the pack of werewolves were already between me and the descent down to stage 1. If I had fled south immediately, I might have made it. Now, I was forced to run the other way.

Sure, let's explore a stage with insanely powerful monsters instead of getting out of Dodge. Idiot!

Panic swelled from my wolf instincts and I barely bit back a low whine of fear at the sound of that alpha's howl. Instead, I bolted the other way, barely cognizant of my actions as the wolf in me flooded my human thoughts. Like a ghost, I hurtled through the dark forest.

I was not the only ghost, and I didn't need wolf insight to know the pack was on the hunt, chasing me. My red werewolf eyes pierced the darkness as easily as midday sun, while my ears picked up the tiniest rustle, and the river of scents told me the story of everything around me.

I'd never considered humans to be blind, but even with my enhanced perception stats, I never could have imagined I could learn so much through my other senses. Unfortunately, that meant the other werewolves prowling the forest could find me as easily as I found other prey. I fled through dense forest, flashing through small clearings and weaving through bramble thickets, with the howls of the other wolves never fading.

Then more howls took up the call to my right.

Not good. My fear spiked and I increased my pace. I sensed other denizens of the forest hunkering down from the wolf frenzy. Some might have attacked me on other nights. I sensed powerful auras and terrible danger. I avoided those as best I could, but I was moving too fast for true caution. That added another layer of fear onto my already-panicked thoughts.

I did sense other monsters weak enough that if I had time, I could have hunted instead of fleeing. The missed opportunities for more experience added another layer of emotion to my raw nerves, this one frustration. All cowered from the wrath of the alpha. I couldn't hide, so I ran. In wolf form, my powerful body bunched and flexed in effortless bounds, hurtling me through the night. I could run for hours, but so could my pursuers.

As I ran, I fought to pull my thoughts above the mindless instincts of my wolf form. If I didn't think, I would die. I still let my instincts guide my flight, but gained enough sense of myself to pay attention and step in, if needed.

As I pushed farther, the landscape became clear. The werewolves owned the central sections of the wide forest that filled the southern half of the plateau. I tried to skirt along the edges, but the howling of wolves closing in from 2 sides forced me to take chances, and I plunged through.

I might be strong, but I was only a single werewolf. Another small pack would rip me apart, and it sounded like I was getting hunted by more than one pack. The wolf in me bristled at the thought that I was now the prey, but I forced down the suicidal urge to let loose my own howl.

Idiot, that would get me killed all the faster. I had to find a way to escape, to slip around them, and return to the lower stage.

I glimpsed enough of the area through breaks in the trees to get a better sense of it. The second stage was centered around a rectangular plateau that ran south to north, with tall mountains rising to the west in ranks of ever-taller peaks, just like they did to the east and south of stage 1. The slope back down to stage 1 was along the southeastern edge, and the huge forest ran northward from there for about 3 miles.

Of course, I had to flee north, away from the exit. In minutes, I crossed the entire forest before the trees thinned to grasslands that gave way in turn to lowlands covered in lakes, marshes, and streams. They all emptied into a huge final lake that consumed most of the northern third of the plateau. A spectacular waterfall plunged from a 2000 foot cliff just north of the lake, cascading down in a torrent that put Niagara Falls to shame.

That northern cliff formed the boundary for the stage on that side. On its northwest edge, I spotted a canyon cutting into the cliff. The air blowing from that direction smelled different. That had to be the ascent up to the third stage. I didn't like leaving the protection of the forest, but I had no choice. My hunters were growing closer. So I padded north, studying the lake in the bright light of the orange moon and the many stars.

Somehow the moon, with its odd, silver-lined black sibling, did not block the dazzling starlight, and the cool lights illuminated a squat castle of dark stone that crouched on the shore of the lake. It looked rundown, with crumbling battlements and chunks of stone missing from towers. Eight tall ships were moored along the shoreline near the castle.

After a moment, I realized the ships were actually sunk in shallow water. Their hulls looked mostly rotted, the canvas of their sails hanging limp and ragged. That was the domain of the undead sailors. A fetid miasma hung over the entire area, and I easily caught whiffs of it with my lupine nose.

I spotted many of the sailors moving about the castle and the ships, or returning in small bands from the forest. I counted more than 2 dozen total, which meant there were probably even more.

I skirted the marshland, angling to the east, but came to a dead end when I topped a rise and reached the eastern edge of the plateau. A line of low, craggy hills marked the boundary. I crouched on one of those and my huge maw dropped open, my long tongue lolling out as I drank in the sight.

Far below me lay the expanse of stage 1. From below, no one could see up here to stage 2. They saw only impassable cliffs. Another lake filled the northern quarter of stage 1, fed by a smaller waterfall that plunged over 2000 feet from the edge of stage 2. Now the layout of the first and second stages became clear.

The main valley of stage 1 ran north to south, with the main plateau of stage 2 running parallel to it, only a couple thousand feet higher, with sheer cliffs separating the stages. They were like two giant steps in the world. The gentler slope that formed the ramp up from stage 1 to 2 ran for a couple miles on the southern edge of the valley.

In werewolf form, my long-distance gaze was not as good as my human form, but my new Sight of the Explorer ability still worked. I spent a moment testing it out and zooming my gaze in on distant vistas. I tried to memorize as much of the scene as I could. Many other canyons and ravines cut into the eastern mountains from that lower central valley of stage 1. I bet all of us had been scattered throughout those eastern mountains. In order to gather all the survivors, we'd have to scour every one. That seemed like a daunting task to finish in the few short days remaining to us. Hopefully people found the grassland on their own.

Looking farther out, I realized for the first time that mountains ringed everything. I'd already seen the mountains on the east and south sides of stage 1 rising in ever-higher peaks until they reached the impossibly high mountains that formed an unbroken wall around the stage. Now I could see that the west side of stage 2 rose in similar mountain tiers up to giant peaks that blocked the sky. So the lower two stages were blocked in on 3 sides.

"Cyrus, these stages are huge, but not compared to the entire planet. Why does it look like we're hemmed in?"

"The stages are big enough for this challenge. Would you prefer needing to cross thousands of miles to reach the next stage in time?"

"No. It's just, the layout seems weird."

"It will become clear in time."

Maybe. To the north, the sheer cliff up to stage 3 was all I could see. I couldn't make out higher peaks beyond, but I bet they'd be visible once we ascended to stage 3. Did that mean the entire area, all four stages, were entirely surrounded by impassable mountains?

Should I go up to take a peak?

I huffed a wolf laugh. Idiot. I was already running for my life from werewolves and had sensed monsters strong enough to snuff out my life hidden in the forest. Stage 2 was so deadly, I needed to escape as fast as I could. Venturing up to stage 3 would get me obliterated for sure.

My thoughts were interrupted by a fresh wave of wolf howls ripping the night, far closer this time. The werewolves had reached the edge of the forest and were pushing into the marshy grassland. Dammit. I'd nearly let myself get trapped against the cliffs.

As a werewolf, I was strong and my regeneration ability was incredible. Still, I doubted even I'd survive jumping off a 2000 foot sheer cliff in an attempt to take the quick way back down to stage 1. So I dropped back into the tall grasses and loped north toward the marshes, lake, and that castle until every step squelched in deep muck. My lips curled back from my long muzzle in disgust, but I pushed on, slipping ever closer to the domain of the zombies.

Behind me, the pack came on, spreading out, casting about for my scent. They'd pick it up in seconds, so I pushed north until the mucky marsh water reached my chest. Then I turned west and half swam, half churned through the muck and marsh.

Howls redoubled. The pack had found my trail. They raced north, straight toward me. They too would get bogged down in the marsh, but that wouldn't give me any advantage. An alarm bell began to toll from the rundown zombie castle. A great, blue light erupted into the sky, driving back the shadows, and I easily picked out the sounds of dozens of feet marching and voices shouting.

Did the zombies think the werewolves were coming for them? Despite the two apex groups occupying the same stage, they clearly did not get along. That fact might give me a slim chance at escape.

The wolf howls continued, but seemed to be slowing. I used the extra seconds to push west, trying to minimize my sounds while covering as much ground as possible. The marsh reeked like dead fish, but the tall rushes and grasses kept me concealed from view.

Then the alpha's deeper voice howled over the rest and the pack came on faster. Almost at once, bolts of energy from the zombie rifles tore the night sky. The flickering red of their energy barrage lit the sky all around. At that range, I doubt they'd hit much, but angry wolf cries rose in response.

A deep, gravelly voice rang over the rest, shouting in a distinct Russian accent. "Begone from our lands, wolflings. We have no use for your bodies and lack the time to waste with another confrontation."

That didn't sound like a zombie. I wanted to go find out who that might have been, but that would mean heading back into danger. I couldn't risk it.

Another slow minute ticked by as I crept west. Wolves howled, but did not seem to be advancing. Some zombies fired laser blasts, but the two groups seemed to have reached some kind of standoff.

Then a cacophony of howls and shouts and energy blasts erupted from back near the edge of the forest. It sounded like another zombie raiding party returning to their home had marched right into the middle of the pack and were getting ripped apart.

The rest of the zombies, back by the fort, sortied, ripping the night apart with laser blasts. A deeper roar that had to come from something vast, shook the darkness. That sound made my hackles raise, and I increased my pace.

I had no idea what that monster might be, but I wanted no part of it. With the tumult raging, I risked angling south to dryer land, then racing west at full speed. As I neared the foothills that ringed the western side of the stage 2 plateau, the grasses thinned and I broke from cover.

The forest covering the southern half of the plateau didn't actually extend all the way to the western foothills, but faded out to open, rolling grasslands and low hills. That might offer me an avenue of potential escape. I had feared I'd need to flee up into the mountains and work south from there, but I'd prefer a straight sprint to safety.

So I ran as fast as my wolf body could go, straight south through the rolling hills of soft, low grass between the forest and the peaks to the west. Just like those eastern mountains of stage 1, the western mountains were cut with canyons and ravines, and I smelled tantalizing scents of monsters and animals of all sorts. Those could prove effective hunting grounds when I returned.

If I escaped. The toll of the constant running was starting to tax even my powerful wolf form, but I'd easily make it back to the slope down to stage 1 at the southern edge of the plateau before dawn. I had at least half an hour to go before my spell wore out.

Then wolf howls tore the night apart again. I didn't know if it was the same pack or another one, but they'd found me. At least 8 werewolves bounded from the forest behind me, streaking out into the short grasslands in hot pursuit.

I shot away like a dark flash, but I was winded and they were fresh on the trail. Despite my best efforts, the pack closed steadily.

No. I only need a little more time. I can't get run down and torn apart now.

The wolf part of my brain rose in panic, swamping my thoughts as I raced away from pursuit. I covered 2 quick miles, but my pursuers inexorably drew closer. Soon they were barely 50 yards behind, their glowing red eyes bright with bloodlust. We all sensed the chase would end soon, at least half a mile before I made it to the exit slope at the southeastern corner of the plateau.

In desperation, I swerved back toward the forest. The change in direction gave my pursuers a chance to close the gap to within 30 yards. Their panting breaths and heavy growls were easy to hear, along with the ripping of soft earth by their sharp claws.

I had to think, but it was hard to form coherent thoughts. The wolf part of my brain was running in blind panic, tearing through the trees with a surge of fear-driven speed that left the other wolves behind for a moment.

Just a moment, though. I was just tiring myself out. They'd catch me and rip me to pieces. I had to cast a spell, had to think of something, had to wake up. My thoughts spun uselessly, my attempts to plan shredding under the overwhelming fear of my wolf instincts.

I found a path through the forest and increased speed, flashing through the darkness, with my pursuers hot on my heels. The lead werewolf was barely 3 leaping strides behind. At any second, he would close the distance and hamstring me with tearing fangs.

Panic overwhelmed my rational mind and I howled with fear. The other werewolves responded with howls of anticipation.

Shouts responded, just ahead. Voices raised in alarm.

Zombies.

I smelled them then, the rancid, living-death stench of the undead sailors. With a burst of hope, I lunged around a final tree and tore into a small clearing where a dozen zombies were gathered, energy rifles already raised.

They opened fire immediately, and I dove sideways, rolling across the ground and barely dodging the laser barrage.

The lead werewolf who had expected to run me down within seconds was not so lucky. He took the full barrage in the face and chest. With a howl of pain and rage, the werewolf went down, flesh seared, fur scorched. His wounds started to heal instantly and the rest of the pack hurtled out of the darkness.

For a second, they forgot about me. Either the rivalry between the groups was so fierce it trumped chasing down a rogue werewolf, or they were simply reacting to the pain their leader had suffered.

Zombies shouted in alarm and kept firing, bolts of energy tearing into the werewolves, but the nimble hunters dodged and jumped, avoiding many as they closed with unerring determination and bloodlust.

I raced along the edge of the clearing. *Ha! Finally, some good luck.*

I'd led the pack into a trap. Now they and the zombies could kill each other while I escaped. Just as I reached the southern edge of the clearing, a single bound away from disappearing into the trees and the tantalizing promise of safety, I glanced back a final time.

The fight was a wild melee of chaos as wolves and zombies tore each other apart. Lying in the center of it all were two planks, each with a single human captive chained in place.

Chapter Thirty-Six
A Very Heated Argument

I froze. My entire body went rigid at the sight of the two prisoners lying on those planks. They were both men. One looked awake, cowering away from the carnage, while the other lay unconscious and oblivious to the danger.

Every wolf instinct that had been driving me forward for most of the night screamed for me to flee. I had to leave the hapless men to their fate and race for the safety of stage 1 while I still could. My legs twitched and I leaned toward the tantalizing shadows of the forest so close in front of me.

No.

My mind fought up from the haze of fear and instinct that had been keeping my thoughts fuzzy. The sight of those poor men was like a splash of icy water across my thoughts.

Run, my wolf instincts howled right into my mind, along with a fresh flash of fear. The wolf did not like fleeing, but it knew when standing and fighting meant a useless death. Its instincts pushed it to survive above all things.

No.

I couldn't do it. The temptation to simply run set my claws trembling, tearing slowly-widening divots in the soft ground, but I fought it back. I didn't want to die. I wanted to escape this insane stage and find my team, joke with Steve and Ruby. I'd even welcome another judgmental comment from Tony.

All I had to do was abandon two strangers to die.

No. I saw my same fear reflected in the face of the man struggling in vain with his chains. Identify kicked in from across the clearing.

William Treville. Level 11 baby human. Team Musketeer.

He looked to be in his mid 30s with a stocky build, brown hair and eyes, and a rugged face. He wore a very medieval-looking costume of trousers and leather-armored jacket with a bunch of straps and buckles.

William. Now I knew his name. William would die if I turned and ran to save myself.

I started to turn back, but my wolf instincts tore against my control, rising against me in a wild torrent. Fear and rage and pride ripped through my mind, trying to inundate it again as the wolf part of me fought to overwhelm conscious thought and save us.

I growled, low and dangerous, crouching with corded muscles tensing from the strain as I fought to retain my conscious self. For a moment, I saw red as I struggled with myself. The battle raging across the clearing filled every sense with blood and death and bloodlust. I swayed where I stood, fighting to define my very being.

Wolf instincts crashed over my mind again and again, like storm waves crashing against a cliff. But my mind was the cliff, and the waves receded each time, allowing me to surface, my thoughts to clarify.

No. I will not flee. I am in control. You bow to me.

I seized control, and the wolf inside of me whimpered and faded away. With it, the timer for my spell flipped down to zero and lycanthropic transformation expired.

"Hey," I growled, then collapsed as a sledgehammer of pain clobbered me right between the eyes.

Changing back to human form was not quite as bad as the initial transformation in the same way as breaking both arms and two ribs at the same time is not quite as bad as snapping both thigh bones. It still left me panting and groaning on the ground.

"Ow," I mumbled as I sat up, every muscle and bone aching from getting broken and shredded, then rebuilt. The pain faded quickly, and I drew in a deep, shuddering breath, trying to remember the awe I'd felt at my raw power as a werewolf.

Except, I'd lost that power right when I needed it the most.

A low growl snapped me out of my lingering daze and I rolled to my feet. One of the werewolves was padding toward me. Its fur was singed and burned, its flesh cooked from zombie weapons, but it was still alive.

I don't know if it was still chasing the rogue werewolf, or if it just smelled fresh meat and blood to replenish its energy stores, but it was coming right at me. Behind it, the battle was still raging. Three of the werewolves were down, while 5 of the zombies had been reduced to black, bloody chunks.

Both of the prisoners were still alive. The combatants on both sides were ignoring them, but that could change in a heartbeat. A single werewolf focusing on the scent of their blood could rip them apart in 2 seconds.

"Come on," I muttered as I pulled a couple items from my inventory.

The werewolf broke into a sprinting charge and leaped the last 15 feet, diving through the air straight at my heart. I slapped an emoji trap sticker to the haft of one of the steel-tipped cow spears and drove the spear into the ground butt first.

I took a step back as the werewolf plowed right into the spear, its bloodred eyes locked on my face. It clearly expected to smash right through the spear, but it hit the emoji sticker, triggering it, and a solid stone wall appeared in front of the wolf.

It smashed into the wall so hard, the stones cracked and collapsed over the stunned creature in a cascade of heavy blocks that dissolved a second later.

Before the werewolf could recover from braining itself, I jumped forward and slapped zombie manacles onto all 4 of its legs. They auto-sealed around every limb in a flash.

The wolf thrashed, trying to leap to its feet, but fell heavily to its side again. Werewolves were incredibly strong, but not in the right way to snap through manacles that required strength 50 to break.

I yanked the spear out of the ground and slammed it through the werewolf's snapping muzzle. The spear punched right through the bottom of its jaw and sank half a foot into the soft soil, pinning the creature down for a moment.

The werewolf grunted and tried a choked howl as it thrashed weakly, but with its limbs shackled and its muzzle pinned to the ground, it lacked leverage to break free. I felt a powerful urge to leap upon it and sink my teeth into its throat.

What the hell? I shook off the impulse and pulled Soulrend into my hand. I wasn't a werewolf any more. I couldn't forget that, or I'd get myself killed trying to fight like one.

I slashed my blade down between the wolf's eyes. The monster shuddered and fell to the ground, twitching. Transforming had healed my own spiritual damage, so I couldn't trust it was dead. I slashed Soulrend through the beast's midsection, right where I knew the pool of its regeneration powers was concealed. It twitched several more times, then sagged and stilled.

I got several notifications, but brushed them aside with all the rest I'd gotten when I first transformed back to human form. This wolf was out of the fight, at least for now, probably for good.

I touched it and triggered loot before running for the middle of the fight. The wolf dissolved into black, stinking mist, confirming it was dead.

"I'm insane and I'm going to die in 10 seconds," I mumbled as I ran toward the raging battle.

The remaining 7 zombies had regained the center of the clearing, standing shoulder to shoulder, forming a defensive circle around the planks and prisoners. The 5 remaining werewolves tore at them from all sides like a terrifying tornado of teeth and razor claws.

Stun blasts sent werewolves staggering, while the constant blasting of laser rifles transformed the night into a ghastly, red-tinged disco. Some zombies fought with swords or axes while their companions fried werewolf eyes and faces with their rifles, but the relentless wolves kept charging in again and again. I now understood the confidence of rapid regeneration. Pain had seemed meaningless as a werewolf since it would fade almost instantly.

The zombies were looking ragged, every one of them suffering gashes or missing limbs that would have killed a living human. The werewolves weren't doing much better, but their fast regeneration was still mostly keeping up. The clearing stank of sludge-like zombie blood, singed hair, and burned meat.

I slowed about 10 yards beyond the fight. None of the monsters had noticed me yet, and I took the opportunity to activate Mirror Cloak. As the world turned monochrome, I relaxed just a fraction inside the protective cloak. I took a deep, steadying breath to focus my thoughts and push back the fear that threatened to make me turn and run the other way.

I can do this. I have to do this.

That didn't mean I had to be an idiot about it. Crouching low in the grass, I pulled 2 steaks from my inventory and pressed an emoji trap sticker onto each. Both stickers were the same, with smiling emoji faces gleefully exploding in a non-stop GIF-like loop. I wanted to kiss Cyrus for gifting me the sheet of stickers. I'd thought them a gag gift at first, but they were proving insanely effective.

I crept forward slowly, for once happy the entire clearing stank of death and dying. None of the werewolves would smell me coming. The battle still raged with unbridled ferocity as both sides ripped each other apart.

I paused a few feet behind the nearest werewolves that blocked me from the ring of zombies. I needed to slip through, but couldn't risk trying to run through the fast-moving wolves. Even if they couldn't see or smell me, trampling me would give me away just as easily and would be a stupid way to die.

Then in a coordinated move, the 2 werewolves just in front of me pounced at the same zombie, a stocky fellow who had been effectively fending them off with a long pike. One of the wolves took a shallow cut to the shoulder before batting the weapon aside while the other lunged in, caught the zombie by the leg, and yanked him out of the circle.

The other zombies tried to come to his aide, but the nearest werewolves redoubled their attacks, pressing them back. The hapless zombie stumbled, and that was his last mistake. The two werewolves pounced, one ripping apart his torso like a wrecking ball, while the other crunched through his head with implacable jaws.

That was my chance. I sprinted forward even though Mirror Cloak would ripple and maybe expose me for a second. Neither of the wolves were looking. I ran in and dove over them, tucking into a full forward somersault. As I tumbled over their heads, I dropped the two steaks with the emoji stickers.

The steaks plopped down to the grass on either side of the zombie just as the werewolves finished killing him. Without hesitating, they both snapped up the delectable morsels without bothering to wonder where the feast came from.

I landed in a roll just as twin explosions rocked the clearing behind me. A blast of bloody gore and wind helped propel me forward, rolling in my cloak right through the spot where the zombie had stood. I stopped in a crouch in the center of the ragged zombie circle, next to the prisoners.

A single glance back made me smile. Both werewolves were writhing on the ground, their faces regrowing from the blasts that had ripped their heads nearly apart.

One of the zombies turned his gun on them and blasted away with a withering barrage, trying to finish them. That got him tackled by a werewolf, resulting in a wild fight between 3 wolves and 2 other zombies.

The distraction gave me the opening I needed. I scooted in between the 2 planks with the prisoners. The second prisoner was awake now, but he'd ended up under his plank somehow. I didn't have time to identify him.

I pulled the hood of my cloak partially back so William could see me. He started at my sudden appearance and exclaimed in a British accent, "Who the devil are you?"

"Shhh!" I hissed, but none of the monsters had noticed.

"Sorry. Can you help?"

Good question. He recovered from the surprise fast and focused on the problem. That was a good sign. The other fellow just gaped at me. His eyes were still a bit unfocused.

"That's what I'm here for." The look of hope on their faces was both encouraging and terrifying. I couldn't promise them safety, only that I would try.

I seized William's chains and focused on them. I knew how they worked since I'd looted several pairs. With the previous owner dead, someone other than the prisoner needed to claim them. A prompt appeared.

Would you like to claim these manacles?

I accepted the prompt, then willed the manacles to open.

"Thanks, mate," William whispered, rubbing at chafed wrists as I unlocked the other manacles and dumped them into my inventory.

A zombie stumbled into my mostly invisible form, tripping over my back and falling to the ground next to William. One of its arms was missing, along with an entire leg. Before it could bring its rifle around, a sword appeared in William's hand and he smashed it down through the zombie's skull.

"Take that, you blighted devil," William growled.

"Good move." I turned to the other man, who was thrashing against his chains, trying to turn the plank over. He was a big guy with black hair that somehow still looked perfectly styled, and was dressed in tan chinos and a blue polo shirt.

"Praise the lord, ya'll are a welcome sight," he said with a noticeable southern accent. Maybe Louisiana, or something? I could never tell.

Joey Hannigan. Level 10 baby human. Team Friends.

I unshackled him and tossed the plank off. All around us, zombies and werewolves were still battling. It seemed miraculous that none of them had bothered to pounce on us in those few seconds it took me to free the other two.

"What the devil is going on?" William exclaimed, sword at the ready as he stared in wide-eyed fear at the fighting monsters while we crouched in the calm center of the storm.

"Long story. No time. We need to get out of here."

"Got any more invisibility we can borrow?" Joey asked, then recoiled from the sight of a werewolf with one eye blown out from a laser blast ripping the head off the zombie who had just shot him.

"Longer story. Do you have a weapon?"

"Nothing for werewolves!"

I pulled a couple of laser rifles from my inventory and handed one to each of them. "These pack a punch, but takes a lot to finish them off. Do either of you have a spell we can use to break out of this mess?"

William grabbed the proffered rifle and it disappeared in his inventory. He kept his sword out. Joey took the other rifle and held it like he knew how to use a firearm. "My one permanent won't help, but I have a couple scroll spells that might. They have the same spell, it takes 3 seconds to cast, and will only work if we're not still in the middle when it goes off."

"Keep one ready for when we make a break for it."

William said, "I've got something that can knock most of the monsters aside, but I doubt it'll kill them."

He kept his eyes on the fight, sword raising every couple seconds, as if he barely held back the urge to stab a zombie in the back. At the moment, they were acting as effective meat shields, but they were weakening. The werewolves would win, and I wanted to be gone, if we could be.

A score of ideas flashed through my mind, each crazier than the last. We couldn't simply stand up and join the fray, making it a 3-way melee. The zombies and werewolves were too tough. We needed to level the playing field.

Only one idea held any chance. It was a long shot, but that was better than anything else we had.

"Okay, get your spell ready."

"Ready. Say the word. When I trigger it, everyone hit the deck, or you'll get caught up in it."

"Got it." I rose, Soulrend dropping into my hand as I studied the raging battle.

A couple more of the zombies had fallen, while 5 of the werewolves still lived. They were battered, but I could feel the tide of the battle shifting in their favor. They'd overwhelm the zombies in seconds.

The zombies seemed to realize it too because one of them stumbled back into the circle next to us, spinning to face us, ax raising. Planning to finish off the prisoners instead of losing them to the werewolves?

His black eyes widened to see my head floating on air between the other two. He hesitated for a fraction of a second, just long enough for me to strike.

I lashed out with Soulrend in a horizontal slash right across the zombie's eyes and through his skull and brain behind. At the same time I triggered Fractal Strike, the spell I'd picked up from that Hannibal loot box after defeating the herd of cows.

Fractal Strike. Spell. Make up to 4 reflections of one strike to hit up to 5 enemies simultaneously.

Mana poured out of me and 4 more glowing copies of my sword appeared, each behind a different zombie. All 4 ghostly copies of my fatal strike slashed in identical horizontal strokes, cutting through zombie brains. All 5 zombies fell in lifeless heaps.

"Now!" I shouted as I triggered loot and threw myself to the ground just as the werewolves pounced on the remaining confused zombies or turned bloodred eyes on us.

Joey and William hit the ground at the same time, and William closed one hand into a fist, eyes scrunched in concentration. Two of the werewolves pounced in our direction, fangs opening wide to swallow our heads.

A flash of yellow light blasted across the clearing with the sound of a tornado wind. Grass flattened and trees creaked as the blast of light and sound tore across the space in a single heartbeat.

It passed just over my head, so close I felt the whooshing of air and the hint of a vast force tugging at my clothing. The magical force smashed into all the monsters like a giant sledgehammer. One of the zombie corpses simply exploded from the force of the spell as everything catapulted aside like dust caught by a giant broom.

Bodies tumbled all the way across the clearing, somersaulting end over end, trailing blood from the brutal impacts, before smashing into the trees at the far side of the clearing. Several trees got ripped up by the roots, while the trunks of a few smaller ones snapped with reports like grenades detonating. The entire mess of monsters and timber disappeared into the forest in a wonderful din.

More messages flashed in my mind, but I swept them aside. Joey jumped to his feet and pointed, then swayed as if suddenly weakened. William and I jumped up too and I pushed them both toward the south trail.

"Run!"

"I triggered my spell. We need to get out of here," Joey gasped. They both looked shaky from the mana expenditure of their trump spells.

I grabbed their arms and hauled them bodily with me, dropping Mirror Cloak as I did. Within a few steps, they recovered and ran under their own power.

Behind us, a single wolf howl rose into the night as the monsters started pulling themselves free of the tangle of bodies and trees.

"Hurry!" Joey shouted and we sped up.

An ominous whistling sound started above us. I glanced back just in time to see a fireball the size of a double-wide trailer come hurtling out of the sky and smash down like a meteor over the blasted edge of the forest, right where the werewolves were starting to move.

The explosion of light and sound and fire turned the night to day in a titanic detonation that sent us all stumbling. William toppled and rolled several times before regaining his feet.

Joey slowed, laughing and pumping his hands in triumph. "Ha! Even better than I expected." Then his smile faded and he frowned. "Why am I not getting kill notifications?"

"Run!" I repeated, pushing them again toward the trail. "All you did was slow them down and tick them off."

Chapter Thirty-Seven
Spartacus

Together we sprinted for the slope down to stage 1. At first I outdistanced the others, but slowed so they could keep up. Part of me wanted to run flat out, but I hadn't risked so much to rescue them only to leave them to die now.

I pulled out a couple zombie lanterns and handed them over. My companions took them without question, not slowing our desperate pace. William looked hopeful, while Joey kept glancing back at the raging fire his meteor spell had triggered, not able to hide his fear. If that wasn't enough to kill werewolves for good, what was?

I knew just how dangerous the werewolves could be. I barely believed we'd managed to escape the pack once. We just had to do it one more time. If we could get off the second stage, maybe the werewolves wouldn't follow.

Fresh howls broke the darkness of predawn. They started weak and thready, but strengthened even before the first howls faded away. I cursed softly. They were recovering too fast from those powerful spells. Now they'd come after us with a vengeance.

I leaped grasping roots and wove around trees, taking the twisting turns of the narrow trail in a mad dash. Joey and William kept hard on my heels, their lanterns bobbing wildly, their breathing loud in the still morning.

Morning. It was almost dawn. I tried glancing at the sky, but the forest was too thick to grant more than occasional glimpses. The moons had long set and the stars had faded into the pitch-black of pre-dawn.

Werewolves turned back to humans at dawn, didn't they? My transformation had ended early, but the coming of morning might be our best chance. How long did we have? 5 minutes? 10? More?

If they caught us, they only needed seconds to rip us to shreds. More howls sounded, much closer than before. They couldn't be more than a couple hundred yards back.

"Do you have any silver?" Joey panted.

"No." Would silver even work? "Your energy rifles will hurt them, but as you saw, it takes a lot of shots to beat their regeneration."

"How did you find us, and how did you survive long enough up here to even try?" William gasped as he leaped a root.

"Won't help us here. Keep running." My voice sounded calmer than I felt.

My breathing was still even. I might not be able to keep up with a werewolf, but I could hold our current pace for hours. My Endurance stat was still climbing, and each tier-1 point equated to roughly 10 tier-0 points.

Back on Earth, I could have outrun the best distance runner many times over. Thinking about it that way seemed insane. It was crazy that we had barely reached the morning of the third day and already I'd advanced so much.

Stop getting distracted. Running for our lives, remember?

If they caught us, I'd unleash all of my temporary spells in a non-stop barrage. That might buy us some time or, if I got really lucky, drive them off.

Yeah, I'd seen how they kept charging the zombies even while getting crisped by laser rifles. Maybe those last two big spells had spent most of their regeneration. Fire had to be tough to recover from.

Fire. The beginnings of a desperate plan began to form.

"Joey, will you give me the other scroll for that meteor blast?"

"Why? It takes too long to cast?"

"Contingency plan."

"Didn't you have a plan to escape when you freed us?" Joey asked.

"This was my plan." I didn't admit I hadn't expected any of us to live this long.

"You've gotten us this far," he said. A scroll appeared in his hand and he passed it to me without breaking stride. I dumped it into my inventory and studied its description.

Temporary spell scroll. Ember Strike. Single use spell. Uncommon. Unleash a meteoric blast of fiery devastation across an area 10 feet square

for every point in Strength and deal 100 points of fire damage per point in Constitution. Cast time 3 seconds, minus 1 second per 10 points in Intelligence.

Wow. That was an even better spell than I'd thought. That meteor had unleashed incredible devastation, and with my stats, it would be even more powerful.

I whispered so the others couldn't hear. "Cyrus, those points in intelligence, are they tier-0 or tier-1?"

"Tier-0, of course."

I nearly laughed aloud. That meant the cast time would be instantaneous for me. I could definitely work with that.

Without warning, we broke out of the forest. The path continued straight through a long field of short clover. There! The slope down to the lower stage was barely 100 yards away.

"Hurry!" I cried and we accelerated to a full sprint.

Together we flashed across the field and reached the top of the descent. The ground became packed earth and rock with only a few scraggly trees along the slope that dropped steeply for over 2000 feet toward the lower grassland. Farther down, clumps of trees, piles of boulders, and dark shadows of ravines split the slope, but still left plenty of room to run.

I wanted to whoop and shout in victory. I'd made it back! We were nearly back down to stage 1. Miracles did happen.

Then I glanced back and my hope withered at the sight of the 5 large wolves loping out of the forest. Despite the pre-dawn darkness, their sleek forms were unmistakable as they effortlessly bounded over the grasses after us. It looked like they'd already completely healed from all the punishing damage the zombies had inflicted on them, plus William's and Joey's spells.

"Faster!" I shouted.

Neither of the guys looked back, but poured on every bit of speed and managed to accelerate a little more. Joey pulled slightly ahead of William, who tucked his chin and gave chase with grim determination.

I followed, preparing my spells. We were on the slope. That should be enough! The need to get away from the deadly second stage drove me on like a physical weight.

The werewolves ran like living bolts of death, closing the gap between us with terrifying ease. I slowed to a stop as the truth settled over me like a death shroud.

We weren't going to make it.

So be it.

I called Soulrend to my hand and tried to remember the fearless bloodlust I'd felt as a werewolf. I managed a flicker and embraced it, fanning the ember into a weak flame.

Identify confirmed I was facing a pack of Waterlogged Werewolves identical in makeup and levels to the original pack that struck the zombies who had captured me. Had the other 3 been part of the same pack, or had parts of 2 packs merged to chase me? It didn't matter. The pack leader raced straight at me, fangs white in the darkness as its maw gaped open to eat my face.

Was that another lieutenant of the ultimate alpha? The others spread out behind it, focusing on my companions, running close together as they converged on their prey.

Seeing them all together finalized that vague plan that had been forming and I changed strategies. Marking the position of each wolf in my mind, I dumped Soulrend back into my inventory. Shouting my own battle cry, I lunged to meet the pack leader.

It leaped straight at me, covering the last 10 yards in a blink. My giant ogre club appeared in my hands and I swung with every ounce of strength I could muster, hauling down with my entire body.

At the same time, I triggered Ember Strike, focusing all my will on the club. As I had hoped a fiery halo wrapped the 500 pound club, transforming it into a meteor of destruction that I smashed at the werewolf. It was already leaping, so could not change directions.

I also triggered my last remaining use of Fractal Strike. My mana pool seemed to evaporate as the spells sucked out way more than I expected.

Four more glowing copies of my giant burning club appeared, one in front of each of the werewolves. All swept down together and . . . Yes! They all blazed with the superheated fires of Ember Strike. It had copied the club plus its current enchantment.

My clubs smashed into werewolves like meteors from the heavens. The impacts unleashed shockwaves that momentarily blinded me as the clubs squashed the werewolves into the packed earth so hard, dirt and blood and gore erupted in cascading waves back up the slope before everything was consumed by the boiling clouds of white-hot concentrated fire.

My entire body rattled with the impact and I staggered back, clothing smoking and exposed skin reddening from the heat. It felt like I'd tried to bob for apples in a blast furnace.

I dumped the club back into my inventory. My head swam from the double-stacked spells. They had drained almost all my mana, and I felt woozy.

The rumbling echoes of the detonations subsided and eerie silence settled over the scene. Towering pillars of flame slowly faded and a delicious, cool breeze caressed my burned face.

I was going to pull out my burn cream, but realized my enhanced tier-1 regeneration was quickly taking care of the minor burns. I couldn't heal nearly as fast as a werewolf, but my recovery was an entire tier better than anyone else's.

Joey and William stood about 20 yards downslope, their lanterns discarded at their feet, energy rifles in hand as they vainly scanned the darkness for wolves. I stared at the 5 craters blasted into the ground, smeared with charred werewolf blood as Eva spoke.

Congratulations, Lucas! You have defeated Waterlogged Werewolf, level 35. Bonus experience earned for defeating a higher-level enemy.

Three more notifications followed, then even more messages, but I ignored those. One werewolf was somehow still alive. I mentally triggered Soul Feed. I couldn't remember if I needed to be touching the dead monsters, but I triggered it anyway.

Clouds of glowing white energy roiled up from 4 of the 5 craters, lighting the entire area in ghostly grays. Joey shouted in victory and William trotted toward me as a torrent of energy blasted into me so hard, I staggered.

Instantly my health rocketed up to full, my injuries evaporated, my mana visibly filled, and my physical stats turned green and crept up by a full 50%. A little timer appeared and started ticking down from 5 minutes.

I laughed as enormous strength filled me to bursting. "I can't believe that worked!"

William pounded me on the back so hard he would have broken a rib back on Earth. Now it barely moved my shoulder.

"You did have a plan all along," Joey chortled.

"How did you do that? I thought we were dead." William cried.

"I double-stacked a couple limited-use spells. I'm lucky I had enough mana for all of it."

"We can do that?" William asked.

Joey added, "I had no idea. Was that my Ember Strike scroll?"

"It was. When I combined them, it changed somehow."

"How?" William asked.

"I wasn't sure it would work, but had nothing to lose." The idea had hit me, and I'd run with it. Somehow I'd felt that I could combine the spells that way. Was that my Wisdom stat proving its worth, or just blind luck?

A low growl rumbled up from the closest crater, the one that held the pack leader.

"One of them is still alive?" Joey exclaimed.

"Not for long." I led the way to the edge of the crater and peered down.

The once sleek and deadly werewolf was scrabbling weakly at the bottom of the fire-blasted crater. It looked like little more than a charred skeleton of cracked bones with patches of fur and muscle, but its red eyes were blazing with hatred and more of its body regenerated every second.

The recovery was very slow, and I doubted it would heal completely before it ran out of power. Fire was hard to heal, and even though I'd felt the incredible power of werewolf regeneration, I still barely believed it could recover even partially from such a hit.

"We've got this," William told me as he and Joey hefted their energy rifles. Together they opened fire, blasting the werewolf with volley after volley.

The wolf writhed in the pit as fur peeled away and meat blackened. Bones seared and snapped, and a pair of well-aimed shots punched through its red eyes. Within seconds, we got the notification.

Congratulations. You have defeated Waterlogged Werewolf pack leader. Level 45. Bonus experienced gained for defeating a higher-level enemy.

We cheered as notifications scrolled past. I scanned them as I triggered Harvest. I tried it on every last werewolf, but it failed every time.

"Does this thing only work once per monster type?"

Cyrus responded immediately. "It's not a hard and fast rule, but why would you want to re-use a spell you've already harvested? Look for new experiences."

"Getting that werewolf transformation again would have been amazing." I felt a deep-rooted hunger to feel that power again. What would that do to me if

I could make it permanent? Would I unlock a shapeshifting class? The idea was both terrifying and exhilarating at the same time.

"Don't look back. Focus on your next victory and enjoy the spoils of this one."

Scanning the other messages, I smiled to see one I hadn't expected.

Congratulations, Lucas! You have reached level 6. Two stat points allocated.

I had killed a bunch of level 35 zombies, plus did most of the work killing that pack. I wasn't sure how experience splitting worked, but I'd take another level any day.

The 2 points were both allocated to Constitution, and I was fine with that. They gave me a big boost to life points, and as the new stats were applied, I could feel my body growing denser. My bones creaked, my muscles quivered, and goose bumps rose across my skin as my body physically altered with the boost.

I reminded myself that I was getting only 2 stat points, but those were tier-1 points, equivalent to 20 tier-0 points. I was now 10 times as durable as the toughest person on Earth, and that was without factoring my tier-1 extra power. My body was changing in ways I didn't yet totally understand. When would I become bulletproof?

The image of Aquaman ignoring bullets flashed into my mind. Cyrus had said as a level-1 human, my base stats were more like a superhero, and I was adding even more to those. The thought made me smile.

Both Joey and William got 6 extra levels from the fight. Joey did a jig, dancing and whooping and laughing, while William looked so stunned he might fall over.

I got a bunch of other messages, including achievements for leading a group from three separate teams in a single conflict, which got me a silver Churchill loot box. It contained a scroll that increased my CHA stat by 5 points and a really nice common-grade fighting stick banded with steel, with enhanced durability to withstand damage from bladed weapons.

I scanned the long list of achievements I'd ignored through the long, terrifying night and focused on some of the best ones.

Congratulations, Lucas! For spending more than four hours in a completely different body, you receive a platinum Mimic loot box.

The gleaming metallic box appeared in the air in front of me and I willed it open to reveal a pair of scrolls.

Scrolls of the Wolf, times 2. You've run with the pack, and some of that experience still lingers. Each scroll unlocks a werewolf ability.

Wolf Blood. Ability. Uncommon. Level 1. Speed up health and mana regeneration by another 10% per level by absorbing energy from the environment.

Wolf Sight. Ability. Uncommon. Level 1. Unlock night vision and increase the calculation of Perception from Wisdom by 10%.

"Sweet!" I read the scrolls. New abilities seemed pretty rare. I'd take as many as I could get. Harvesting Lycanthropic Transformation from that werewolf had not only saved my life, but gotten me some sweet permanent upgrades.

Congratulations, Lucas! For defeating slaver zombies and freeing more captured slaves like yourself, you receive a diamond Insurrection loot box!

"Diamond?" I breathed at the rare sight of the glittering loot box. It gave me a mountain of mana crystals and one more scroll.

Title Scroll. New title: Spartacus.

Spartacus. You've got the spirit of a revolutionary. You've taken the weapons from the very slavers who captured you and turned them against your captors. You've slain more than ten slavers, who serve the final stage boss a full tier above the one you are authorized to reach. Each enemy was at least twenty levels above your own. In the process you saved 2 slaves destined for short lives of hard work and torture.

Keep it up, Spartacus. What could possibly go wrong?

Plus 25% more experience gained for each kill of a higher level enemy.

Plus 5 to CHA.

Plus 5 to Luck.

I laughed as I read the scroll and felt the influx of new power. "Thanks for the new title, Cyrus." That extra experience boost could prove the difference between making it to level 10 in time or falling short.

"You earned it, Lucas. Your journey is proving very unique. The experiment is turning out better than most of my projections suggested."

"Thanks. I admit, there were moments I worried you were trying to get me killed, but right now, I'm loving the results of surviving."

"You love to beat a dead cat."

"Horse. It's beat a dead horse."

"I would think you would prefer beating cats. They can be so annoying."

"That's part of their charm."

"You humans are endlessly inconsistent. I love it."

Eva continued as I turned back to my achievements.

Congratulations, Lucas! You combined two spells with hidden synergies to form a unique attack with the power to overwhelm multiple opponents simultaneously. You receive an emerald Einstein loot box.

"So is combining spells a common thing?" I asked as the huge emerald appeared hovering in the air in front of me, glittering so bright it lit the entire area.

"It is possible, although you are one of the first to discover that fact," Cyrus said. "Many spells lack the synergy to combine well, but the pair you used reinforced each other with a compounding effect that multiplied the damage. Few would have enough mana at this stage to fuel the resulting spell. The outcome speaks for itself. Well done, Lucas."

William and Joey were looking at me funny since Cyrus spoke loud enough for everyone to hear.

"Did my Luck stat have anything to do with making that work?" I asked, pitching my voice low so hopefully only Cyrus would hear.

Not that it mattered when Cyrus responded loudly, "Your Luck stat may have contributed to the final percentages of compounding between the spells, but did not determine the initial compatibility."

"You have a Luck stat?" Joey asked.

"Yeah. Another long story."

"How can you have so many of those?" William asked. "We've only been here for 3 days.

"I like to keep busy."

"I've never seen an emerald loot box," Joey said as several loot boxes appeared in front of him. Most were silver, one gold, and one platinum. He beamed and patted the last one. "My first platinum."

"Congratulations," I managed, but barely hid my surprise.

How could he not have seen even a platinum loot box? Had my experiences been so far from the norm? I glanced at William, who was in the process of opening his own loot boxes. He too had a platinum and looked just as giddy with excitement.

Maybe my titles really were affecting my rewards more than I realized. I thought back to my Trailblazer title again and the 30% chance to upgrade loot boxes. The notifications didn't specify when it triggered, but maybe I'd been seeing a lot more upgrades than I'd realized.

Thank you, Cyrus for giving me titles.

Chapter Thirty-Eight

An Old Friend of Mine Can Really Throw Rocks

My emerald box flashed and disappeared, leaving behind a single item.

Bracelet of the Tesla Coil. Epic. Absorbs energy from enemies you fight and stores it. Energy will automatically be applied to replenish health and mana. Energy is gathered in direct proportion to how much damage you deal, and will slowly bleed away at the rate of 15% per hour until you enter another combat.

"Sweet!" I removed my scarred bracer from my left forearm and winced at how battered it looked. The sleeves of my leather jacket were mostly gone, with tattered ribbons drifting around my arms. Those wolves had ripped them to shreds. Hopefully I'd get another jacket soon.

I wrapped the new bracelet around my left wrist. It fit snugly. It was made of braided metal that looked like platinum. My bracer fit back over it easily.

The description did worry me a little. The bracelet seemed amazing, but it would only work as a result of ongoing combat. I would have preferred it simply store all the extra energy I stole using Soul Feed.

Still, I wouldn't turn away a potential source of extra automatic healing and mana regeneration. I ended up diving into one fight after another, so I doubted I'd lose too much power from the captured energy simply bleeding away.

It was clearly designed to reinforce the build Cyrus was nudging me toward, one focused on constant, close-in combat. Or at least, that's what his tests so far seemed to suggest. As I considered that, I found myself not as reluctant to throw myself into danger as I had been just the day before.

Was it the knowledge that I didn't have time to hesitate, but had to get stronger? Or had my experience as an apex predator werewolf affected me more than I'd realized?

It didn't matter. I had a path to gaining power, and I would walk it. I triggered Soul Feed on the dead pack leader, even though my health and mana were topped off and my physical stats were still enjoying that 50% temporary boost. When the cloud of white energy poured into me, it rolled up to the bracelet, but did not get sucked in.

So it didn't work retroactively. No matter, it could start charging in my next fight.

"Thanks. This will help a ton."

"To the bold go the best spoils," Cyrus responded.

"I love having bold friends," William laughed as he examined a very authentic looking steel breastplate. It looked medieval, but I had no idea which country might have made ones like that.

Joey had already stored whatever he got from his platinum box and was examining his energy rifle again by the light of his lantern. "And I love these rifles!"

"I have a few more broken ones too."

"Brilliant," Joey grinned. "I'm a mechanical engineer. Worked on building siege weapons for the movie. I'd love to work on those parts to see if I can figure out how to cobble together more working rifles."

I gave him a couple of the busted rifles to check out. Between us, we looted the werewolves and each got a bunch more mana crystals, 1 potion of full poison resistance, a wolf pelt, and half a dozen fangs.

I still barely believed we'd survived. Too bad I'd had to use up Fractal Strike. If I could have permanented it with that Ember Strike spell, they might have formed the foundation of a build that would have been unstoppable.

Since I was already in my inventory, I scanned the other loot I'd gotten from the zombies. A few more rifles, a bunch of random clothing, a few rusty breastplates, more lanterns, and a few more mana crystals.

I'd even picked up five potions of Create Darkness. Each one created a sphere of absolute darkness 10 yards in diameter, centered around the one who drank the potion, or the spot where the potion got smashed. So it could be thrown.

That could be useful, especially if I could see through the sphere. I'd have to test it.

I extracted 2 of 3 scrolls of Binding too. "Here, another bit of loot you might like."

Scroll of Binding. Bind the limbs of an enemy up to 10 yards away for 5 minutes without messing with ropes or trying to remember knots.

"You're turning out to be a good friend to have," Joey said with a grin.

Before more werewolves tracked us down to avenge their fallen pack, we hustled down the slope. We moved fast, but alert for danger.

We'd barely covered another 100 yards before a deep howl I recognized rang out through the predawn stillness. A shiver of fear seized my spine as I spun back to look upslope.

"What is that?" William whispered, rifle back in shaking hands.

"Sounds like death," Joey breathed, visibly pale.

With Wolf Sight and Sight of the Explorer, my vision could pierce the distant shadows and bring the vague shape lurking there into clear focus. A giant werewolf, easily twice the size of the pack leaders I'd killed was pacing along the edge of the slope. On his hind legs.

The alpha was enormous and walked in humanoid form, like many werewolves from movies. The sight made me shake with fear. Even at that distance, I sensed the overwhelming power of the alpha. If he came down the slope after us, we could never escape.

Identify didn't trigger, so I couldn't see his levels, but from the weight of his aura, I suspected he had to be over level 50. It felt like he possessed a totally different tier of power than any of the other werewolves.

Behind him ranged over a score of sleek, deadly werewolves. None of them moved toward the slope, but all of their crimson eyes remained locked on me.

"We're so dead," William moaned.

"Shhh," I whispered, not taking my gaze from the distant alpha. He did not advance. Nor did he order his horde of hungry wolves after us, but growled. This time the sound was a low rumbling that vibrated across the distance.

Again I understood his intent without needing words. I was marked now. He knew my scent. I'd killed 2 of his lieutenants and invaded his domain. He would hunt me down himself and rip out my throat with his own jaws when I returned.

Because I had to return, and he knew it.

"Fridge off," I growled back before turning away.

"Is it going to come after us?" Joey asked, following, but casting constant worried glances back upslope.

"Apparently not. He's the alpha, probably the stage boss. I bet he can't come down to stage 1."

"Thank heavens for that," William breathed.

"Yeah, except now he'll just wait till we return. Then he'll come for us."

Joey visibly swallowed, but William scowled. "By then we'll be strong enough to kill them all."

"I hope so." The alpha's presence was like a distant forest fire, threatening and unstoppable, but William was right. We had to get strong enough to face him, and we only had a few days to do it. Otherwise, he would kill us all and everyone else. Then Earth would die, including my extended family and heartless Isabella.

"I'll be back, and we'll see who kills who," I whispered.

About two-thirds of the way down the slope, we came across a concealed gully like a little oasis, complete with a small pool of water, soft grass, and thick bunches of tall bushes hanging heavy with a lime green fruit I didn't recognize.

And people.

We pulled up short at the upper edge of the gully just as half a dozen men and women jumped out of concealment behind trees and boulders. A couple pointed bows, but most held steel weapons or raised hands to cast spells.

"Whoa!" I cried, lifting my hands in peace. "We're humans too."

William and Joey lifted their lights higher to show our faces. Relieved murmurs spread through the camp and I spotted more people emerging from the bushes. There had to be over 20 people, and I sagged with relief to see so many.

"You lot are a welcome sight," William called.

"You're lucky we didn't attack when you ran up in the dark," one woman called, a scowl in her voice. "We've been hearing wolves."

"We've been killing them," William said with a chuckle.

"And we were carrying lanterns," Joey said, waving it to punctuate his words.

A very fit looking man with thinning brown hair and light blue eyes stepped to the front of the group. He held a thick-bladed boar spear easily in one hand and wore a chainmail jacket and black pants. I pegged him at mid-40s, and he carried himself like a leader.

William (Burns) Turner. Level 21 baby human. Team Pirates of the Caribbean.

Eva read when Identify kicked in. That was weird. I'd never seen a second name in parenthesis like that. Was it a nickname, or something?

Beside me, William Treville shouted, "Burns! By jove, I'm happy to see you, Mate!"

"William!" Burns exclaimed, his grim face breaking into a happy smile. It instantly changed his visage from imposing to charming.

The two embraced, and a couple other men and a woman rushed out to greet William too. I approached the reunion and pieced together that they had all been stuntmen for the movie, and Burns had been the lead stunt coordinator.

Awesome. Stuntmen were some of the most versatile and competent people alive. No wonder they'd gathered such a big group already. I sensed a story in Burns's name, and hoped to learn it eventually.

"Not your team?" Joey asked.

"Nope, but I'm happy to see them."

William turned and gestured me closer. "This is the bloke who saved us from the zombie slavers and the werewolves. Let me introduce Lucas."

We shook hands and Burns's gaze was piercing as he studied me. He made no comment about my lower level, thankfully, and only said, "Thanks for saving William. He is a good man."

"We need everyone we can get."

"Indeed."

Burns greeted Joey, who then turned to greet several of the ladies who had clustered closer while we talked. His easy charm and southern accent immediately won them over, and in seconds he was chatting happily with 4 of them. Two were from Burns's team.

Elizabeth Stevenson. Level 13 baby human. Team Pirates of the Caribbean.

She was a tall, curvaceous woman with white skin and very blond hair. She wore a medieval brown leather corset that looked pretty tight and definitely highlighted her figure.

Megalyn Ragettie. Level 12 baby human. Team Pirates of the Caribbean.

Megalyn looked young and very fit. She was a trim woman with long, straight black hair and features that suggested Native American heritage.

They both chatted with Joey and got very friendly. I even heard him channel his namesake from his team and ask, "How you doin?"

The ladies seemed to love it. Huh. He made friends so easily. Maybe Cyrus was thinking deeper about his team assignments than I'd given him credit for.

"Lucas!"

I knew that voice. I spun, my joy spiking when I recognized Jane. Despite some new clothes, she looked the same as before we got teleported to the death game, except her hazel eyes seemed to glow softly.

Jane Gardner. Level 16 baby human. Team X-men

She rushed up, laughing, and I lifted her off the ground in an enthusiastic hug. She gripped me so tight in return, it was hard to breathe.

"Oh, I'm so happy to see you, Lucas," she laughed when I finally put her down.

"Same. Have you seen Tomas or Ed or Patrick?"

Her smile faded. "Patrick . . . He . . ."

"Oh, no," I breathed, pulling her into a gentler hug as the world seemed to rock around me.

Patrick had been my friend since grade school. He'd moved to Boston for college and we'd lost touch for a while. We reconnected over adventure motorcycle riding, and our ride through Colorado had been our first reunion in ages.

Now he was gone. I hadn't gotten strong enough fast enough to save him.

Jane leaned against me and whispered, "I heard he went quick."

I wasn't sure what to say. The last time I'd glanced at the survivor counter, it had dropped to the low 700s. I tried not to look often. At some level, I knew that meant nearly 3 out of 10 of us had already died. Chances were good one of my friends hadn't made it past the initial craziness, but I had still hoped we'd all reunite.

"I don't know about Ed or . . . Tomas," she said in a choked whisper, then pushed back and savagely wiped her cheeks. Her gaze hardened and she added with her usual confidence. "I'm sure they're fine."

"Me too. I actually got a clue that Tomas is okay."

Her eyes widened. "How?"

"I can't explain more, but it was a good sign." I refused to believe my brother had died since Cyrus dropped that hint. Forcing a happy smile, I added, "And look at you. Level 16. What spell did you permanent?"

Her usual ready smile flashed. "No spells about motocross, unfortunately. I ended up on team X-men, so my first permanent spell is Telekinesis. Check this out."

She turned and pointed. A rock about the size of my head shot into the air. She swept her hand to the side and the rock followed the movement, shooting across the ravine to crash into a boulder so hard the rock shattered. The echoes of the impact reverberated through the gully several times before fading.

A woman's voice shouted from down in the gully, "Hey!"

"Sorry!" Jane shouted back, but then shrugged and smiled.

I whistled softly. "That's amazing."

"I love it already, but if I can upgrade it, I'll be able to toss monsters around like toys."

I chuckled. "Of course. Jean Grey, the Phoenix. X-Men is a powerful team. Tomas is going to go nuts when he realizes he's dating a superhero."

She smiled, but I read worry in her eyes. She only said, "And you? How are you still only level 6? You're so competitive."

"It's a long story, actually. I got some special loot that increases my stats a lot, but slows my leveling."

I really hated sharing the same line of half-truths with Jane that I'd told the others, but I had to be consistent. I reminded myself it was for her own good. I almost told her about Harvest, but how could I have a permanent spell if I was only level 6?

"I did get several limited-use spells that are proving really useful," I added.

"You'll catch up," she said encouragingly.

"You'd better believe it."

She peered closer suddenly. "What happened to your eyes?"

"What do you mean?"

"Your irises have a solid gold ring around them. That's wild. Did you get some magical contacts, or something?"

"Not exactly. I got something called a title. They add gold to your eyes."

"That's what it is. Burns's got gold flecks, but nothing like you."

I shrugged. "Competitive, remember?"

That made her laugh, a sound I hadn't been sure I'd ever hear again. I would need to talk with Burns more and find out about his titles. I didn't want to share everything about mine, but I did want to compare stories at least at a high level.

Reuniting with Jane renewed my hope. She was safe and seemed to be thriving. Once we found Tomas and Ed, we'd keep each other safe. Whatever it took, I would get stronger, strong enough to defeat whatever insanity Cyrus threw at us.

Jane and I joined the main group and Burns said, "William said you might know more about those zombie slavers."

"Yeah, they're based on the second stage. We'll have to deal with them eventually, but they're tough. Most are about level 35."

That generated a wave of fearful muttering and Burns asked, "How did you defeat them?"

"It's kind of a long story. The important thing to know right now is that they're sending raiding parties down here to capture people. We're not strong enough to deal with them, so I recommend we move down into the valley and meet up with other survivors."

"That's what we were planning on doing come sunrise," Burns confirmed, then leaned closer. "Do you have any more of those beam rifles?"

"I've got a couple."

"Good. Keep them under control until we decide how best to distribute them."

Interesting turn of phrase. He was speaking as if I'd already accepted him as my captain and would hand over anything he wanted. "I'll keep that in mind."

He flashed that charming smile. "Sorry. I'm used to taking charge. If we're going to survive, we'll all need to cooperate."

"I'm sure we will. Speaking of which, anyone need shoes?"

"Me!" Someone shouted, followed by 4 more in quick succession. For some reason, Cyrus was not as free with footwear as he was with other articles of clothing. At least he did give us clothes. Surviving a death game in the nude would be just wrong.

I pulled out several pairs of zombie boat shoes and won all the goodwill I'd failed to get from Tony Waldau's team, plus some.

Chapter Thirty-Nine
We Might Actually Need More Monsters

It turned out dawn took longer to arrive than I'd thought. While the sky very slowly changed from pitch black to gray, we rested and talked. Nearly half of Burns's group had picked the Base Camp utility spell, and their huge tents ringed the clearing next to the pond. Jane invited me, William, and Joey into her tent, set next to a large solitary boulder.

Joey pulled me aside just inside the door and gripped my hand with both of his. "Lucas, I have to thank you again. You saved me and William. You gave me new hope. I thought I was a goner and we were all just waiting for our turn to die. Now I believe we have a chance of winning this game and saving Earth!"

I wasn't sure how to respond. I wasn't prepared for such an intensely emotional response. I'd done what I figured anyone would. I'd been so focused on advancing and leveling and finding a way to win, I hadn't considered how others might be reacting to the insanity we'd gotten dropped in.

"You're welcome," I managed. "Together, we've got a chance."

"Yes! I will follow you all the way to that nymph queen's lair. If anyone can kill her, it'll be you."

"Thanks. Let's just focus on surviving the first week, eh?"

Grinning, he hurried to take a seat between a couple of the ladies who had just arrived with a few other people, and instantly struck up a conversation with both of them. I followed, a bit overwhelmed by his faith in me. We'd only known each other an hour. How had he developed such a fanatical belief in my abilities?

We had survived an ordeal that by all rights should have claimed all our lives, but he and William had helped with that. My final double-stacked spell strike had been pretty impressive, but I saw that as a huge stroke of luck. I couldn't replicate the werewolf transformation or that unique spell combination. I guess I'd better come up with a new combo, then. People were counting on me.

Burns joined us, along with a couple other leaders. They had cobbled together the large group from members of 6 teams and were doing pretty well so far. With the larger group, they lost fewer people to the random monster attacks, but faced a problem I had already noticed.

"Experience sharing is weird," Burns said as we all lounged in comfortable chairs, or the couch. "Everyone gets some experience from every kill, but those of us who do the actual fighting get a larger percentage."

"Have you been able to quantify it?" I was very interested in the topic. I'd lost a ton of experience fighting the cow herd to the rest of the group. I needed up to 10 times as much as anyone else to level, so the topic was literally life and death for me.

Burns paused to take another bite of breakfast. Jane had not used her oven last night, and with some of the steaks I'd gotten from the cows, it produced piles of fantastic breakfast burritos. We were all gorging ourselves on them.

"Not totally," said Hector Rodriguez, a member of Burns's team. He was an olive-skinned older gentleman from Argentina, tall and trim, with a beautiful paired longsword and dagger at his hips. He'd been one of the sword master consultants for the movie and looked more comfortable than most in our new world.

They'd ended up on the Pirates of the Caribbean team, of course. How could they not when Burns's name was William Turner? I assumed Hector filled the role of Captain Hector Barbossa. He didn't look or act like the pirate, but did have an authentic, wide-brimmed replica hat.

Burns swallowed a big chunk of burrito, then said, "From what we can tell, the person who makes the kill gets a larger percentage, but everyone involved in the fighting gets a decent slice. Even if you're carrying a weapon, you get more than those who stay back in purely support roles."

"So everyone carries a weapon during a monster attack?" Joey asked, then winked at a pretty tall blonde in a maroon dress. She was one of the archers in the group, named Susan.

She hadn't spoken much yet, which was too bad. Her smooth British accent was amazing. She did say how thrilled she was to end up on Team Narnia, and she seemed friendly.

Jane chuckled before Burns could respond. "We've been arguing about that since yesterday morning."

"Why?" William asked.

Burns sat back and scanned the group, expression serious. "Our group is getting pretty big, and when we meet up with the other survivors, our numbers will swell. That's great for making a secure base camp for defense and security purposes, but it is not good for leveling."

"And we need to level," Hector added, fingers of one hand tapping on the hilt of his sword.

I said, "Let me guess, when you're fighting a few monsters at a time, or even a decent-sized pack, no one gets enough experience to level very fast."

"Exactly," Burns said. "Those of us with higher levels generally won them before we joined the larger group. Now we're struggling to bring in enough experience to keep everyone leveling at the same speed."

Susan leaned forward in her chair. "We're facing choices none of us expected. Should we tell support folks, especially those who have reached level 10, to stay back and not draw weapons so we can focus the experience on the fighters?"

"Or do we even send smaller teams away to hunt and level up faster?" Hector added.

"So what happens to the support folks? How do they level?" William asked.

"That's the question, isn't it?" Burns asked, not hiding his frustration. "I suspect at some point we'll see new avenues for non-fighters to level better, but those are not open to us yet."

Jane said, "So either we let non-fighters fall behind, which might be as good as a death sentence in a few days, even if they reach the second stage."

"Or do our fighters level slower and lack the strength to deal with the monsters on the next stage?" Burns finished.

It was a tough question. Joey sat back in his chair and blew out a breath. "We've seen a glimpse of the next stage. Werewolves and zombies, with levels up into the 30s and 40s."

"And that alpha has to be over level 50. I sensed he was way tougher. That one monster will likely prove deadlier than most of the rest of the pack combined."

"How do you know that?" Hector asked.

"Like Joey said, we survived the second stage. I felt the alpha's aura, and it was terrifying. If it had come down after us, we could not have escaped."

Burns sighed. "We can't deal with that level of threat yet. Not even close. And if we keep leveling at the rate we're going now, we'll get everyone up there just to give the werewolves a feast."

"There has to be a way," Susan insisted.

Burns nodded. "I know. We just haven't found it yet."

I had already realized I was going to need to hunt alone. I'd gained 4 precious levels in a single night up on the second stage fighting much higher-leveled monsters, but I'd nearly died multiple times too. That stage was terrifying, and no one was ready to go up there. Could we get strong enough in the few days we had left? It would be a tough challenge.

Now I was back in the relatively safer first stage, but with weaker monsters came much slower experience growth. I was going to have to bust my tail every waking moment in order to scrounge together enough experience to reach level 10 in time.

I hadn't considered the challenge for everyone else. It might not be as severe as the one I faced, but was fundamentally the same. There were roughly 700 survivors left. We needed to get everyone together, but also make sure they all reached the minimum level.

We hadn't seen many big herds, and even if we fought a herd of 700 monsters, if that experience got divided among all of us, that would equate to 1 monster kill each. Not nearly enough for leveling.

The sheer logistics of so many people and so many monsters seemed overwhelming. I'd thought the constant flood of monsters cruel, but honestly, we needed those monsters, despite the danger they represented, if we wanted any chance of surviving the higher stages.

I hoped Burns was right and Cyrus opened up new ways to level. From what I was seeing, most people were at or near level 10, with forerunners like Burns and Tony pushing into the low 20s. That meant most people could make it up to the second stage, but not survive there. We needed a plan to deal with the much stronger monsters, or hundreds of us could get slaughtered before we got strong enough to defend ourselves.

"Delicious," Burns sighed, then tossed his empty plate into the air. It vanished, just like our plates had in Ruby's tent the first night.

I finally had enough peace to think about my team. I'd been running non-stop pretty much since the mammoth lion kidnapped me. Now I opened my team menu and saw a dozen messages from Ruby and 4 more from Steve.

That one message I sent had eased their worry for a bit, but my long silence had started worrying them again. Most of the messages simply begged me to tell them where I was and how I was doing. Idiot. I should have sent more updates, although in werewolf form, I'd totally forgotten about the team chat feature.

The last one from Ruby was more interesting. "Lucas, where are you? I hope you're doing okay. We're still with Tony's team. We've found a great base location in the big valley that should work as a town for everyone. It's a raised hill with rocks around the edges that form the start of a defensive wall. We've gathered here with about 200 people so far."

I sent a quick response to both her and Steve, apologizing for not communicating more. I quickly summarized my crazy experiences over the past day and night, told them I'd connected with over 20 more people, and we'd head in their direction at first light.

Then I held up my hand to interrupt Hector and another woman whose name I hadn't caught yet. She was dressed like a medieval merchant and apparently represented the interests of the non-combat folks who were trying to focus on crafting or other support roles.

"Hey, I finally checked with my team and I got news." I shared what Ruby had said in her last message.

"Good. That confirms we're on the right track," Burns said.

"But it will exacerbate our problem," Hector added.

"Indeed. Once we reach the town, we'll meet in council with the other leaders and —"

Burns was interrupted as a heavyset woman burst into the tent shouting, "Monsters!"

Chapter Forty

Tug of War Death Match

The camp erupted into bedlam as people boiled out of tents and scrambled for weapons. Magical lights flared and everyone seemed to be shouting at once, screaming about monsters or demanding information.

Burns marched off with his retinue toward the lower end of the ravine, his powerful voice booming over the din. "Meet at your rally points. Sentries, to me!"

They had set rally points. Good idea.

Jane and several of the other locals clustered to my right, nervously scanning the area while I strode toward the dim slope leading out of the ravine. Dawn had probably happened on the other side of the mountains, but the sky was still a vision-obscuring gray to most people. I could spot the monsters better and wanted to lead the charge.

"Look out!" Joey shouted, and a blinding energy beam blasted past my eyes, barely half an inch from my head. I dove aside, rolled, and returned to my feet, about to curse Joey out for nearly shooting me in the face.

That's when I saw the spectral form floating right behind where I'd been standing. How had I not seen it? Did it have some kind of invisibility?

Unlike the Essence Wights that looked mostly humanoid, this thing looked more like a roiling cloud of pure blackness with hundreds of glowing white teeth and 10 tiny brilliant blue eyes. Not even Wolf Sight penetrated the darkness of its form.

Joey fired faster than I realized that energy rifle could manage. Shouting and cursing, he kept up an intense barrage. With every shot from the energy rifle, the monster seemed to shiver and recoil slightly.

Spectral Mauler. Level 24. Ghost. Everyone knows someone with a clingy partner who leaves chaos and drama in their wake. They suck the life out of everyone who lingers near them for more than a minute. Spectral Maulers are what would happen to those people after they died, if magic existed on your world. The lingering will of a powerful slain monster, this ghostly apparition seeks a new host spirit to consume. Immune to physical attacks.

I called Soulrend to hand, ready to help Joey, but Jane shouted behind me in sudden fear. I spun to see her facing another Spectral Mauler, both hands raised toward it as the people around her stumbled back in fright.

The Spectral Mauler looked like mist surging against an invisible barrier as it fought to reach Jane. She held her ground, face twisted in intense concentration. She was holding it back with pure telekinetic power.

"Keep it busy!" I shouted to Joey and William, who had added his own beam rifle to the fight.

"Go!" Joey shouted back, still firing. His rifle was starting to glow dangerously bright.

I hoped it didn't overload, but didn't have time to hesitate. The spectral mauler attacking Jane was slowly but inexorably closing on her.

I dashed the short distance to it and brought Soulrend tearing through the center of its cloudy shape. The blade slowed as it passed through, and didn't penetrate all the way. Slicing the spirit was like cutting through a big boneless roast.

The spectral mauler shrieked like an insane insect and turned to me as parts of its cloud body began to dissipate. I slipped into a stick fighting form I had practiced hundreds of times, flowing from one stroke to the next as I carved the ghostly beast apart with a never-ending barrage of strikes.

Within seconds, it screamed one final time and the dark cloud of its body started to fade. On my wrist, my Tesla Coil bracelet grew warm as it absorbed energy from the monster as I wounded it.

Congratulations, Lucas! You have defeated Spectral Mauler.

I triggered Soul Feed even as I spun to race back to Joey and William. Power roared into me from the dead monster, but it seemed like barely a trickle compared to what I'd gotten recently from the werewolves. It was still enough to top off my health and mana and add a slight boost to my physical stats.

Just as I took my first step to help them, Joey's rifle exploded in a flash of bright light. The blast tumbled William away and Joey screamed, falling to the ground, hands grabbing at his face.

The Spectral Mauler, which had been looking ragged from all the laser bolts, coalesced into a solid black cloud and pounced on the helpless Joey.

"Joey, roll!" I shouted as I raced to intercept.

He was too caught up in the pain of his wounds to hear me.

I didn't quite reach him in time.

The Spectral Mauler plunged into Joey's chest half a heartbeat before Soulrend flashed past. Joey convulsed, his scream snapping off instantly. His hands fell away from his badly burned face and his one remaining eye widened in horror.

I stood over him, unsure what to do. "Joey?"

His convulsing got worse, then both his good eye and his ruined socket began to glow with the same blue light of the Spectral Mauler's eyes. He reached up with shaky hands toward me and darkness shrouded them.

I retreated, horrified as he sat up and opened his mouth far too wide. Four rows of sharp teeth grew in and filled his mouth, while an animal growl far too powerful to be made with human lungs rippled from his throat.

"Oh, no," I whispered, retreating to stand with William, who was pointing his energy rifle with shaking hands.

"Can we save him?" William asked.

I had no idea. I racked my brain, but I had very few weapons to fight ethereal monsters. Soulrend worked great, but it would kill Joey too.

Maybe that would be better. His body still twitched with shuddering mini convulsions and I imagined the Spectral Mauler consuming his spirit on the inside where we couldn't stop it.

"Help!" a woman screamed behind us.

"Keep everyone away from him. Shoot out his knees to slow him down if you must," I told William.

He nodded shakily, but hefted his rifle with more purpose. The Mauler was trying to approach, but its control over Joey's body was still barely rudimentary. We had to find a way to drive it out, but until I figured that out, I had to prevent other Maulers from taking more victims.

I raced across camp and spotted Burns and several other spell casters blasting away at another Spectral Mauler. It was hovering in the air above the fallen form of Susan. She lay unconscious, her thick, blond hair hiding her face. The monster was trying to feed on her like the other one was doing with Joey, but the constant barrage of spells kept knocking it back.

It was a losing battle and I bet they'd either run out of available spells or mana soon. I dashed to help, but just as I feared, the spell barrage fizzled as everyone either hit cooldown limits or ran out of spells at almost the exact same time.

"No," I growled, diving the last 10 feet, Soulrend extended as the Spectral Mauler dropped toward Susan's prone form.

It touched her chest and started sinking in just as I reached it. Soulrend pierced the monster's black cloud body, and it shrieked in agony. My blade sank to the hilt as I crashed to the ground beside Susan.

I lunged to my feet and twisted the blade, heaving it higher so that the flat of the ethereal weapon pulled against the monster's ethereal form. It was like lifting a 50 pound Christmas ham on the flat of a carving knife. Even twisted like that, the blade tore slowly through the monster's body as it fought to retain its hold on its new host.

"No you don't," I growled, pulling harder.

"Yank it out!" someone shouted as people crowded around, cheering me on. Idiots. If the Spectral Mauler lost its grip on Susan, it could still slip free of my blade and sink its dozens of teeth into someone else.

I pulled it with agonizing slowness inch by inch back into the air. It was working, but my blade was still tearing up through the spectral mauler's body. Gauging the distance, the math was easy. My blade would slip free before I pulled the monster from Susan. As soon as I did, it would plunge into her and consume her spirit.

"Do you have any more spells? Anyone?"

"Twenty seconds," Burns said. He'd dropped to one knee beside me.

"That's not soon enough." I could only think of one thing to try, so I let go of Soulrend with one hand, instantly ceding another inch as the lessened pressure let the Spectral Mauler haul the sword lower.

"Don't lose it!" Burns shouted.

I didn't have time to answer, but extended my hand. The corrupted energy crystal I'd gotten from the Energy Wights popped into my hand.

I touched it to the spectral mauler.

Nothing happened.

Power generator crystal is damaged and lacks the controls to absorb Spectral Mauler.

I bit back a curse, my eyes focused on Soulrend. It was barely an inch from the outside edge of the monster's black cloud body and was starting to slip through faster, as if the outer edges of the creature were thinner.

The Spectral Mauler hissed again, this time a triumphant sound as it lunged a final time against my blade.

I triggered Soul Feed.

A conduit snapped into place between the energy crystal and my hand as that unique synergy that had allowed me to survive the Essence Wight attack activated again. The Spectral Mauler's hissing cry of victory turned into a much higher-pitched shriek of terror as the crystal began sucking the black cloud into its smoky depths.

"Yes!" I shouted, driving the energy crystal deeper into the Spectral Mauler.

It released Susan, boiling into the air as it tried to escape the crystal. Burns instantly reached dangerously close to the ethereal battle to grab Susan's hand and yank her bodily out of the way.

I focused on the energy crystal, keeping the link in place. I felt no energy flowing from the crystal to me, unfortunately. That part of the synergistic link was totally broken. The rest of the conduit felt strained and shaky, but it held the Spectral Mauler.

The monster fought it and the connection to it grew shakier. The crystal was too damaged. It was going to fail.

I slashed Soulrend through the Spectral Mauler's glowing blue eyes. That disrupted its spirit enough that the resistance evaporated and with a sucking sound, the monster disappeared into the crystal.

I sagged to the ground, spent, even though the fight had been mostly spiritual. All around me, people jumped and cheered.

"Can you save Joey?" Jane cried, dropping to one knee beside me. "Hurry."

With a grunt, I leaped to my feet and raced back to where I had left William to guard the poor guy with the monster in his spirit. A ring of people were watching, well back from Joey's possessed form. He was trying to claw his way to William, who had cast his scroll of Binding instead of shooting out his knees like I'd suggested.

William stood near the wildly thrashing body, rifle at the ready, tears streaking his determined face. When he saw us rush up, his obvious relief tore at me. He believed I could save Joey.

"What do we do?" Jane asked.

Burns had rushed over with us and nodded toward my sword. "Can you drag it out?"

"I don't know. The other one hadn't gotten inside of Susan. I'd have to stab Joey to get a grip."

"Do it," William pleaded. "It's consuming him. He's going to die, then it'll gain full control."

Of course. That's why it was still twitching and unable to move well. Joey must still be fighting it.

Joey's eyes rolled up to stare at me and the monster's glowing light faded for a second. "Do it," he whispered in a barely audible voice even as his body shuddered and he clawed bloody fingernails into the ground.

"Hang on," I said as I sank Soulrend into his thigh.

Joey screamed, the monster's voice layered over his own. My sword sank easily through his flesh, but the two spirits in his body resisted more. Hating what I had to do, I twisted the blade and pulled hard.

A ghostly shape began to emerge. It fought a lot harder this time, maybe because it was already fully inside the body. The spirit was mostly black, but swirled with thinner strands of white. I shivered when I realized what I was seeing.

The Spectral Mauler had consumed much of Joey's spirit. The thin streamers of white were all that remained of him. I was dragging both of them out together.

"If I can pull them both out and kill the monster, maybe his spirit will return," I said as I used all my strength to pull.

My blade again tore sideways through the spirit, but not as fast. The combined, twisted spirits were somehow denser, giving me better purchase. With agonizing slowness, I hauled the Spectral Mauler and the fading remnants of Joey's spirit from his body.

"We're losing him," Jane cried as the white streamers of Joey's spirit faded away one by one, consumed by the blackness of the Mauler. The blue of his eyes faded, visibly darkening.

Before I could pull the spirit more than partially from the body, all traces of Joey's spirit vanished and his eyes turned completely black. On the ground, he heaved a deep breath, his chest expanding so far he cracked his own rib cage, but didn't seem to notice. With a terrifying growl, he rolled to his feet, yanking free of Soulrend and crouching to spring at me.

Burns plunged his boar spear through the center of Joey's chest.

Chapter Forty-One

What Happens on Arasha .

..

B lood and puss and a nasty stench as bad as melting monsters erupted from the wound and Joey fell back to the ground, convulsing as he physically died just as he'd spiritually died a moment ago.

The Spectral Mauler erupted out of the body, hissing in anger as it shot toward Burns to consume another host.

I intercepted it with Soulrend and carved it to pieces. Again, my Tesla Coil bracelet grew warm as I dealt more and more damage.

Congratulations, Lucas! You have defeated Spectral Mauler.

"You didn't have to stab him through the heart," William shouted at Burns, fists clenched. "Maye we could have saved him."

Burns held his gaze. "I'm sorry, my friend, but Joey was gone. The monster could have hurt others. I had to stop it, and half measures would have left people in danger."

William sagged and whispered, "I had still hoped."

"Don't let hope cloud your judgment," Burns said softly, gripping William's shoulder. "We cannot afford to hesitate."

He was right. As much as I would have loved a chance to try a full restoration potion on Joey, I doubted it would have worked. The Spectral Mauler had eaten his spirit. There was nothing left to heal.

I triggered Soul Feed, but the influx of cleansing, healing energy didn't fill me with wonder like it usually did. I stood over Joey's body and just stared. The cold gray light of predawn matched the cold, dead shock settling over my heart.

"I couldn't save him."

Jane stepped to my side and wrapped an arm around my waist. "You were the only one who even tried."

It wasn't enough. The weight of pain and regret felt crushing and I couldn't understand why at first. I'd only known Joey since yesterday, but I'd saved his life. We'd fought together and he believed in me, believed I could somehow save him and a lot of other people.

He'd pushed me out of the way to fight a monster he couldn't hope to defeat. In the end, he'd sacrificed his life to give me a better chance at surviving. He'd thought me that important.

I wasn't strong enough.

I might be stronger than just about anyone else already, despite what my levels looked like, but I was still a weakling compared to the monsters we had to defeat. Joey's death drove that home like a fiery dagger through my soul.

The cold pain faded under a new heat blossoming through me, stoked by helpless rage at whoever had tossed us into this meat grinder.

"I will get stronger," I vowed. I would not remain helpless forever.

"We all need to," Jane agreed.

Saying it wasn't enough. A rush of rage boiled through me, setting my muscles quivering. I had to move. With a growl, I stepped to a nearby boulder. It was big, at least 4 feet in diameter, so it made a great target. With a growl, I ripped it out of the ground.

It was heavy. Insanely heavy, and strained the limits of even my superhuman strength. That just made me angrier and I roared as I hurled it away with every ounce of strength. The boulder soared out of the ravine and far out over the slope.

That helped. I felt better. Nothing like a bit of mindless exertion to clear the mind. Panting, I turned to see every eye fixed on me, universal expressions of astonishment on every face.

"What?"

"You threw that boulder," Burns said slowly and gave me a nod of respect.

I shrugged. "Yeah. Had to let off some steam."

"That thing had to weigh almost a ton," William breathed.

I blinked. "No."

He nodded. "At least."

"Huh. Stats are pretty cool, eh?"

"How many points do you have in Strength?" Jane asked with a laugh.

"Quite a few."

I tried to play it cool, but inside I was just as awed as they looked. Yeah, I'd realized I was getting ridiculously strong, but if I'd paused to think about it, I would never have tried to lift that stone.

We couldn't afford to limit ourselves like that. We were no longer on Earth nor constrained by Earth body limitations.

William laughed and clapped a couple times. "Never a dull moment around you, Buddy."

That broke the staring contest, thankfully, and people turned away. Jane stepped close and squeezed my bicep, raising an eyebrow in appreciation.

"Competitive indeed. I love what you're doing with yourself."

I grinned and gestured at another nearby rock. "Want to have a go?"

She pointed, and the rock rolled down the hill a few feet. "Don't underestimate the power of the mind."

"Nice." I turned back to where I'd killed the Spectral Mauler.

Even though the black, smoky body of the monster had faded and I wanted nothing else to do with it, I forced myself to trigger Harvest. I needed to be stronger, so I could not ignore any opportunity to gain new power.

You have successfully Harvested the spell Phase Walk from spectral mauler.

Phase Walk. Spell. Mana cost: moderate. Leave sore feet behind as you transform yourself and everything you're carrying to ethereal form. Duration: 5 minutes. Uses remaining: 2.

That was a great spell. I considered it a tribute to Joey's strength and sacrifice. I couldn't help Joey any more, and I needed every tool to keep myself, Jane, and the other survivors alive.

I hadn't been sure it was wise to replace Thunder Punch when I still had one use remaining, but I felt like the gamble had paid off. Those Spectral Maulers, like the Essence Wights I'd fought before, proved insanely hard for most people to kill. The ability to turn ethereal myself could give me a massive advantage.

I then accepted the prompt to loot the Spectral Maulers. In the process, that also looted Joey's corpse. I grimaced at that, but couldn't undo the decision. He hadn't had much. A shockingly low amount of mana crystals, a few potions, and a single interesting item.

Bachelor Pad Ring of Confidence. Uncommon. Increases Fear resistance by 15% and fosters a sense of self-confidence, even when you have no idea what you're talking about.

Was that how he chatted so easily with the ladies? I slipped the ring on my finger and did notice a surge of confidence. Hopefully it would help in interactions with people and not encourage me to do anything reckless in battle.

From the monsters, I got a bunch of basic loot, plus two interesting items. The first was a potion of slow fall. It apparently did exactly what it sounded like. I could drink it to float slowly down from great height, even if I didn't drink it until I was already falling. The other was a slender ring woven out of black metal.

Soul Fortress ring. Uncommon. The best defense is a great defense. Plus 5 to constitution. 20% Increased defense against physical attacks.

I gave it to Jane. She had also chosen the Linguasight utility spell so could identify it. When she did, her eyes widened. "Lucas, you should keep this."

"No. Your skills are more mind-based. That leaves you more vulnerable to physical attack."

I didn't add that plus 5 to constitution would only give me half a tier-1 point, which would not make as much of a difference to me.

"Thank you," she said, slipping the ring onto her right ring finger, then smiling from the influx of energy.

"It's more an insurance policy for me anyway," I said with forced good humor. "Tomas would kill me if I let anything happen to you."

Her reply was cut short by Susan, who strode right up to me. Her maroon dress was still slightly askew, with bits of dirt clinging to one side, and her blond hair was a tangled mess, but she looked whole.

"I'm glad you're awake."

She placed her hands on my shoulders, her hazel-eyed gaze intense. "Lucas, you saved my life. I owe you. Anything you want, it's yours."

Then she closed the distance, pulled my face down, and kissed me as soundly as I'd ever been kissed before.

Time seemed to stop as warring responses boiled through me. My first instinct was to recoil and protest that I had a girlfriend, but that was no longer true. I was actually unattached. Susan's warm touch, her soft lips pressed to mine, and her obvious passion opened a floodgate of emotions, everything I'd been suppressing since I woke up on this crazy planet.

Fear and doubt and gnawing worry rose like an angry tide, but Susan's passion helped ease that tide like a balm. Then a surge of desire, so intense it shocked me, boiled through me, driven by a towering pride. I'd saved her, so it was my right to enjoy the spoils.

I fought the overwhelming urge, but couldn't help wrapping my arms around her slender waist and leaning into the kiss. She responded with even more passion, igniting a hunger in me so raw and wild I finally understood what was happening.

I'd been a wolf most of the night, and some of those instincts still lingered. I'd thought I was free of the wolf. Apparently not. That was where those overwhelming emotions stemmed.

Understanding helped me gain control, but the deep kiss still lasted a lot longer than I should have allowed it to. Once I regained control, I still hesitated before pulling away. Susan smelled like earth and some kind of spice, her lips tasted salty, and the feel of her in my arms felt absolutely incredible.

The intense physical contact soothed my mind and helped me feel grounded in a way I had not yet found since we'd been teleported from Earth. It was a precious gift, and I allowed myself to enjoy it for a few more seconds.

And she was an unbelievable kisser. I'd always thought Isabella was a fantastic kisser, but Susan left me gasping, my lips tingling, my mind whirling when she finally let me go. The kiss also helped me take a much-needed step farther from Isabella's memory.

Jane regarded me, one eyebrow raised, but then she flashed her mischievous grin. "Lucas, you should see your face."

She had been great friends with Isabella but hated how Isabella had broken things off with me.

"Um, you don't have to do that," I stammered to Susan, still regaining my composure and fighting down a wolf urge to step forward and seize the beautiful woman again.

Now that she'd let go, a new torrent of confusing emotions boiled through me. I hadn't kissed anyone since Isabella. I still felt a flicker of guilt, but squashed that instantly. Isabella had made her choice, but my reaction to Susan hadn't been right. I didn't know her. I wasn't an uncaring werewolf.

I'd saved her life and she felt indebted to me, but taking advantage of her was wrong. That thought helped me shove the wolf instincts aside. I was still trying to get my heart settled, but by all that was holy, I'd needed that.

Susan shrugged, a fluid roll of one shoulder, her gaze locked on mine. "We might be stuck here in a death game where we can die any second, but that doesn't mean we have to be lonely."

"You've already helped more than you know."

"That was just a glimpse of what my gratitude is worth," she said boldly.

"Um, thank you. For now, I'm afraid I have to pass."

"That's fine, but if you decide you wouldn't mind finding a little comfort in this insane world, just say the word."

She walked off with a noted emphasis in the sway of her hips. I couldn't help staring after her until Jane shoulder-bumped me. "At one level, she's got a point. What happens in Vegas—"

"I get that reference!" Cyrus interjected excitedly. "You humans engage in such convoluted games to justify actions you might otherwise find unwise."

"Yeah, we're not always the smartest bunch," I said, but held Jane's gaze. "I hadn't asked for that."

"I know, but I think you needed it. First kiss since Isabella?"

"You know it was."

She nodded after Susan. "You could do a lot worse than her if you need a rebound fling to reset."

True, but I didn't want Susan. It still felt wrong to leverage her debt. So I forced a smile. "You've never tried setting me up with anyone, Jane. You going to take a matchmaker class?"

She barked a laugh. "Worst class choice for me ever." Her expression turned more serious. "Just don't lose your way, Lucas. If we get out of here, life will go on and it'll be a good life."

I took a deep breath. "When we get out of here. Not if."

"When," Jane agreed, her eyes glowing with magic.

Chapter Forty-Two
More Cow Bell

I paused next to a small stand of pine trees barely taller than Earth trees and scanned the nearby grasslands. Morning was half over and the sky was a blue so intense, it made my soul ache every time I looked for too long.

The impressive trees rose above the enormous sea of waist-high grasses of the central valley, crowning the only decent rise within sight of the distant settlement. Ruby hadn't been kidding. They'd found an excellent place for the town. A large, flat-topped hill rose steeply out of the plain over a mile away, with rocky outcrops soaring over 50 feet higher in craggy spires all around the edges.

Given a couple more days, we could raise some pretty impressive defensive barriers between those spires and turn the entire place into a castle. Unfortunately, we didn't have that much time.

I focused on the dim shapes of humans and bulls battling in front of the western side of the settlement. Dust billowed around them, making it hard even for me to see clearly with Sight of the Explorer. I saw enough. They were in trouble.

"Is that the settlement?" Burns asked as he and the lead element of our party joined me. The rest followed in 5-person groups. Jane, William, and Hector arrived with Burns. They all squinted at the distant hill.

"We're late. They're under attack by a large herd of bulls."

"Bulls?" Jane asked with a frown. "Like cow bulls?"

"Sort of." I quickly related our attack on the humanoid cows and what I'd overheard about another herd of bulls. "Looks like the bull herd is larger. I count about 200. Mostly bulls, with some cows mixed in. The bulls look pretty big."

"We need to get over there fast," Burns said, waving the rest of our group to hurry.

"I'm not sure that's the best idea." I zoomed in on the distant battle again.

The humans were being hard-pressed by the herd of angry bulls. Most of the bovines walked on 2 legs, wielding spears or long-handled blades that reminded me of Japanese naginatas. A few dropped to all fours to charge the human lines in small groups, smashing into their defenses with crushing force.

In the center of the human lines, a glowing magical barrier of golden light extended for over 10 yards. That barrier formed the lynchpin of the human defenses and the heaviest fighting raged around it. Even with that barrier, the humans were being pushed back.

Spells and magic flashed across the battlefield, lighting it up in a constant barrage of bright flashes. The spells were helping the people keep the bulls back, but they were already fading. In moments, they'd be overrun. I doubted we could get there in time.

Even if we did, 20 more people wouldn't turn the tide. The bulls could trample us as easily as they were about to trample the settlement. We had to do something, though. We'd lost too many people already. If the settlement fell, the bulk of the survivors who had finally managed to group together could be slaughtered.

"We have to do something," Jane said, echoing my thoughts as everyone rushed up to find out what was going on.

"Running over there to die won't help."

"Do you have a better idea?" Burns asked coldly as Hector explained the situation to the others.

I considered and discarded several ideas, but kept running into the simple problem. We lacked time. The embattled people needed some kind of distraction now, but what could draw the attention of an entire herd?

I smiled. "Actually, I do."

Pieces of a plan started falling into place. It might actually work.

I extracted my cow bell.

Cow bell of the herd matriarch. Rare. All members of the herd will hear the bell and will obey its call. Bearer of the bell gains temporary authority over the herd as long as a higher authority is not present.

The description was slightly different than before, but I didn't have time to worry about that. Hefting the bell, I said, "I'm going to ring this and see if I can order the herd to back off until we can link up with the others."

"Do it," Burns ordered.

I rang the bell.

It reverberated in my hand and the sound grew louder and louder until most of the others clapped hands over their ears. The sound swept across the plains and echoed back from the distant mountains. My senses expanded with the bell and my mind touched every member of the distant herd.

Come to me.

They responded instantly. Fighting broke off as every bull and cow in the herd turned from the humans to face me over a mile away.

Yes! I've got you now.

Then another will slammed into mine, snapping my connection. A trumpeting angry bellow thundered from across the plain, so deep it rattled my bones as much as my ears. Every bull in the herd took up the cry, their voices rising into a rolling torrent of noise, punctuated by the individual cries of the cows.

"That doesn't sound good," Jane said as everyone turned to me with worried expressions.

A shouted thought slammed into my brain and I grimaced at the spike of sharp pain. *'Bell from my mate. Murderer. Vengeance is mine. I will crush your bones and every member of the herd will take a bite of your flesh before your life fades.'*

The mental voice was deep and guttural and somehow primal. The words were simple, but the threat was very real. Were cows and bulls even carnivores? I did not plan to be the test subject to find out.

A new rumble echoed across the plain and dust billowed into the air as every single bovine charged as one straight toward me. In the back of the herd, I spotted a figure towering over the other tall bulls, its enormously muscled torso that of a man, capped with a mighty bull's head.

A minotaur. It had to be 20 feet tall and as burly as that Rockslide Ogre had been. Its horns spread more than 10 feet, and it carried a giant, double-bladed ax as it loped easily along with the rest of the herd. As I zoomed my vision in on the distant minotaur, Identify triggered.

Tecton Earthwarden. Minotaur. Level 25 Boss. Defensive earth mastery. Tecton leads both of the bovine herds through sheer overwhelming might and exacts merciless vengeance upon anyone who dares harm any member of his herd. He is currently Enraged.

Cyrus's happy voice spoke into my ear. "That was a master stroke, Lucas! You saved the settlement from guaranteed annihilation. Of course, you've drawn the personal hatred of Tecton. I can't wait to see how you turn this seemingly suicidal gesture to your advantage."

Eva's voice spoke up. **Quest update. You have drawn the personal ire of Tecton Earthwarden, the minotaur stage-1 boss. Defeat Tecton and his herd without allowing the settlement to be overrun. Reward: one legendary item from your home world.**

Did we even have legendary items on Earth? Didn't matter. We'd drawn out the stage boss too early. We weren't ready.

"Lucas, what is happening?" Burns demanded.

I licked suddenly-dry lips. "On the good side, I managed to divert the entire herd away from the settlement."

"And the bad?" Jane prodded.

"They're coming here to wipe us out first."

"Oh, is that all?" Burns snapped.

"Not quite. The minotaur who leads them is an angry fellow named Tecton Earthwarden. He's the stage boss."

"Already?" Hector exclaimed as everyone around us broke into worried arguments.

"We need to run!" Susan cried and many turned to flee.

"Stop!" Burns shouted before I could. "It's miles back to the forest. We'll never outrun them."

We'd spent several hours traipsing through the plain toward the center. Now I knew why we hadn't run across any monsters. They had all massed to attack the settlement.

"The trees!" One fellow I hadn't met yet shouted. "Those of us with Bio Morph can scale them and help everyone climb."

If the trees had been the giants we'd seen in some of the forests, it could have worked, but they weren't. I doubted there were enough branches strong enough to support even one person's weight for us all to fit up there, and we would never get everyone high enough to escape that giant minotaur's reach. He'd probably just head-butt each tree and knock them over.

"Won't work," Burns said, triggering another round of arguing. We didn't have much time. We needed a plan.

"You had to ring the stupid bell, didn't you?" Hector snapped at me.

I shrugged. "It worked, didn't it?"

"Except we're all going to die!" He looked like he wanted to punch me. Thankfully he resisted the urge because I would have punched back. He'd probably have time to use a potion to heal a broken jaw before the herd arrived.

My thoughts raced as I considered and discarded ideas. If it was just me, I'd have several good options, but I needed to protect the entire group. Hector did have a point. I'd caused this mess. I didn't regret buying the settlement some time, but I refused to let everyone with me die as a result.

"We'll make our stand here," Burns decided. "Melee fighters to the front. Ranged fighters behind. Support folks behind them." His confident tone cut through the chaotic shouting. He spun to me. "How many of those energy rifles have you got left? They could turn the tide in our favor."

"It's not a bad plan, but I've got a better idea." I grabbed Jane's hand and said, "Everyone link hands."

"What do you have in mind?" Burns asked as people looked from me to him. Only one skinny guy moved to take Jane's hand, but I didn't think it was because he believed me. He just wanted to hold hands with a pretty girl.

"I've got a spell called Phase Walk." I shared the description of the spell I'd just harvested from the Spectral Mauler.

Jane frowned. "I don't think it'll work. It says everything you're carrying, but if we're all holding hands, you're not carrying us."

The herd had closed to within half a mile already and the ground was starting to shake. If they launched an elemental earth attack against us, we could be crushed any second.

I bit back a curse. Jane was right. Then I smiled. "Then the solution is obvious, isn't it? Quick, get on my back."

Burns scowled. "That'll save you and Jane."

The same fellow who had suggested using Bio Morph started climbing the nearest tree with the speed of a monkey. Another older man and a young woman followed.

My smile widened. "We just need a better platform to make this work."

Burns started demanding more information, but I strode to the tree next to the one the 3 Bio Morph folks had just climbed. The trunk was only about a foot in diameter at the base. Seizing it, I heaved.

The tree ripped from the ground, roots snapping and showering dirt in every direction. For a second I simply exulted in my superhuman strength. Stats were so amazing! Ripping a 40 foot tree out by the roots with my bare hands didn't even strain my limits.

"What are you doing?" Jane demanded as most of the others retreated a few steps.

I dropped the tree to the ground and jogged about a third of the way along its length, about where I figured the balance point would be.

"We're nearly out of time. Are you planning to use that as a battering ram?" Burns demanded.

"No." I hefted the tree and settled the trunk onto my shoulder. My leather jacket offered some padding from the rough bark, although with my constitution so high, I bet my skin was tough enough that I wouldn't even bruise, let alone get scraped by the bark.

I patted the trunk. "Same plan, just a better way to carry everyone. My Phase Walk spell will work. Everyone, quick, jump onto the tree and hold on."

Chapter Forty-Three
Ghosts in the Trees

"You can't carry everyone. The weight of 22 people will crush you," Burns objected, even though he'd just seen me rip the tree out of the ground with my bare hands and watched me throw that boulder last night.

"No, it won't. Haven't you considered what our strength stats mean? Stop thinking in terms of Earth bodies. That no longer applies to us."

"We're wasting time," Hector warned as the rumbling from the cows grew closer.

"Don't you at least have the courage to try it?"

Burns nodded sharply. "You'd better be right about this, Lucas. Everyone, spread out. Keep the load balanced. One person on each side jump up in unison. Hurry!"

Some of them still looked dubious, but the sight of over 200 magical murderous bulls charging right at us made for spectacular motivation. In seconds, everyone spread out and started jumping up.

Jane sat closest in front of me, while Hector took the spot right behind my back. Hopefully that wasn't because he planned to kill me when my plan failed. William sat behind Jane, while Susan jumped up behind Hector. More followed, moving more quickly as they saw I was handling the load.

The weight grew quickly, but I managed, and Burns's idea of pairing folks front and back helped keep the load pretty well balanced. A couple guys with axes rushed down the length of the tree, limbing off the branches, especially those pointing down.

The weight pressed down harder and harder as more and more people jumped up to straddle the tree. The trunk bent slightly, but it was thick enough to handle the weight. Some people with bows or ranged spells prepared to fire as the bulls charged inexorably closer.

My feet started sinking into the ground, but my body handled the strain well. Jane was watching me with wide-eyed wonder, and Hector whispered, "How are you still standing?"

"When this is over, you should try it," I grunted.

When all but the 3 Bio Morphs were on the pile, Burns alone remained standing near me. He glanced a final time at the charging bulls, who had closed to within 100 yards. The shaking under our feet was growing stronger and the tree swayed from the stampede.

"By the kraken, you're doing it. If your spell doesn't work, we're all dead."

"Get on so I can trigger it."

He gestured at the 3 still clinging to the tree. "What are you waiting for?"

The first Bio Morph shook his head. "No way we jump on that death wagon. We're taking our chances in this tree."

Burns tried arguing, but we were out of time. The bulls were pounding toward me, death in their black eyes. The ground was shaking so bad I swayed, which shook the tree draped over my shoulder and everyone clinging to it. Many clung tighter to the trunk and remaining branches, others squeezed their eyes shut in terror, while a few cried out in fear.

"Last chance! Get on now, or you're on your own," I shouted.

"We're on our own."

So be it. I triggered Phase Walk just after Burns leaped onto the trunk.

Mana drained out of me. A *lot* of mana. It seemed the spell consumed more based on how much stuff I was carrying, and I was carrying a lot of stuff. The world shimmered and colors bled to muted hues. The weight eased on my shoulders as we all shifted out of the physical world.

"Yes!" Jane shouted, her voice more of a whispered hiss than anything.

"Do not let go," I shouted, my own voice comically breathy and weak.

Three seconds later, the herd arrived. I swung my tree so the tip extending far out in front of me, pointed toward the herd. The people there shouted in fear, but thankfully retained enough wits to not let go. Bulls thundered past, snorting angrily as they charged in, deadly horns and wicked blades slashing through ethereal forms.

The people clinging to the trees screamed in fear, and a few cast spells that tore into the bulls, but did nothing to slow the stampede.

"Stop wasting your spells," Burns shouted in a ghostly voice.

The bovines did not slow or part to run around the copse of small trees, but smashed through them like an avalanche. The small trees shook, and the Bio Morphs screamed as wood splintered, then cracked. The tree they clung to fell and was swarmed under by the herd. I lost sight of the 3 and lacked the time to try to find them in the press.

Every bull stampeding past me tried to strike with sharp-pointed horns or whatever weapon they carried. I expected to feel nothing. Indeed, the blades passed through my ethereal form like wisps of smoke, but the horns rattled me. I was immune to the physical attacks, but the horns contained a fraction of the bulls' spirits and those crashed into me with a faint shadow of their physical force.

The unexpected buffeting shook me side to side, and that movement set the entire ethereal tree and all of my passengers swaying dangerously. Everyone shouted and clutched each other.

Burns's voice drowned out the others. "What are you doing? You're going to make us all fall."

"Sorry," I shouted back as I called Soulrend to hand.

Drawing the ethereal blade while I was ethereal too proved super cool. Usually the weapon shimmered like a ghostly reflection of steel. Now it shone with a bright blue light and looked solid and totally boss to my spectral eyes.

Bulls kept charging past so I slashed out with Soulrend at each horn that raked toward me. The blade severed the horns, sending them tumbling into the air. The physical part of the bulls remained like ghostly after-images that passed harmlessly through me.

Bulls bellowed in pain and some stumbled. More bulls barreling in behind them trampled them and I swept Soulrend out, severing more horns and even catching a couple of necks as the bulls stumbled. More bulls fell, adding to the bedlam. A few rolled right through me, shaking me harder as their spirits pummeled mine. My Tesla Coil bracelet grew warm on my wrist as it absorbed energy from the monsters I wounded.

Gritting my teeth, I withstood the barrage and kept my feet. Bulls and even a few cows tripped over the growing pile of wounded bovines and I slashed at every one that came within range. Their bellowing shouts sounded distant, like echoes rebounding off a distant canyon.

Then the herd veered away, leaving Tecton alone to charge in. He fixed me with his giant black eyes and hefted his enormous ax as he charged, his thick, hooved feet dancing with surprising agility through the mess of fallen, wounded animals. He was stepping between them, finding gaps to avoid crushing members of his herd with his own hooves.

In other circumstances, I could appreciate that level of dedication, but I did not want to test my strength and blade against his with 20 people clinging for dear life to the tree I carried over my shoulder.

"A little help," I shouted.

Magic exploded from the group. Lances of fire and ice and lightning blazed with dazzling colors as Burns and others cast their spells. The barrage leaped at the charging minotaur, but he swept his ax across his chest and a wall of earth exploded in front of him, deflecting or absorbing the blasts.

That still gave me a moment where Tecton's line of sight was broken. "Hold on!" I shouted as I jumped.

My body was only spirit, so I couldn't push off against the ground with my legs. Instead, I willed myself to move. In the physical world, I'd be carrying a few tons, but in spectral form, we lacked any physical weight, and my will proved sufficient.

We soared up and to the right, the long spectral length of the tree everyone clung to flexing slightly. Many of the group shouted or screamed in surprise, but thankfully no one fell off. In fact I found it far easier to manage the load as ghosts than I had in physical form. Gravity and centrifugal force held no sway over us.

In one graceful bound, I leaped over a cluster of bulls, my left arm holding the tree secure against my shoulder, while with my free right hand I slashed down with Soulrend as I passed. I lacked the leverage for solid strikes, but still caught several bovines with glancing blows. As I drifted back to the ground and prepared to launch into the air again, I realized I was again limiting myself. Why was I landing? Gravity no longer held sway. I'd subconsciously planned my leap as an arc that returned to the ground just because that's what I was used to.

So with an effort of will, I soared 10 feet off the ground and started flying. Most of the bulls stood at least 12 feet tall on their hind legs, so I wove between them, slashing at faces and necks as I passed. Soulrend carved through spirits like thick pudding, sending pieces flying while bodies fell bellowing or simply twitching behind. Notification messages began scrolling in, but I minimized them all.

The long spear of my tree swept back and forth across the space as I moved and turned, generating more screams and shouts and protests, but I just shouted back to hold on and not move.

"You will not escape!" Tecton roared and I spun a full circle, still flying, to see the enormous minotaur charging after us. This time he barreled through any herd member unfortunate enough to get in the way, trampling his own bulls and cows in his towering rage. His ax glowed with a sinister black light. I was not about to bet it couldn't cut spirit.

"See if you can slow him down," I shouted as I focused all my will on flying faster.

I rose to 20 feet, ignoring the rest of the herd and accelerated. We were spirits now, so wind resistance and physical limitations no longer mattered. The only thing limiting our speed was my imagination and willpower. I had a lot of both and we shot forward with breathtaking speed, leaving the herd far behind.

"I don't think we need to waste the spells," Burns shouted back. "How can you move so fast?"

"Just enjoy the ride." I banked to the east as if I was heading toward one of the canyons through the steep foothills leading up to the slopes we'd all arrived on and the taller mountains beyond.

"Where are you going?" Jane shouted.

"Watch."

I triggered Mirror Cloak. The air shimmered again, colors draining to monochrome as my cloak's ability kicked in. As I had hoped, the effect covered us all since we were all one long spiritual body. Moving that fast, we wouldn't be totally concealed, but hopefully Tecton would be confused and think we were still heading for the hills.

Then I banked around to the north again and made a beeline for the settlement hill. We flashed across the mile in a matter of seconds, leaving the bellowing Tecton behind. Flying was so much fun! If I could find a way to permanent Phase Walk, I would.

I started to slow as we neared the settlement. I spotted Tony Waldau in the center of a knot of humans who filled the largest gap between the spires of stone ringing the hilltop. They'd been the fighters holding the center of the lines with that glowing barrier.

Ruby was standing with Tony, and Steve was approaching them too. That was such a relief. I aimed for them and shouted a greeting. It warbled out of me like a ghostly wail.

"Monster!" someone shouted.

All along the length of the tree, everyone shouted "No" or "We're not" or variations on that theme. The tumult of voices rang out like a ghostly cacophony that shivered my spine, and I was already a ghost.

It obviously terrified the other survivors because as one they oriented on us and unleashed their spells.

Chapter Forty-Four

I Try My Hand at Bull Fighting

I swerved as hard as I could, swinging the tree around so hard if everyone was in physical form, many probably would have been flung clear. The move helped dodge many of the first volley of spells, but also swung the back of the tree and the hapless folks clinging there into the path of a few.

A wave of fire splashed across several people clinging to the middle of the back half of the tree, and although we were immune to physical attacks, magic carried a spiritual element that still punched into the group like a sledgehammer.

The tree rocked on my shoulder just as a pair of ice bolts slammed into the same spot the fire just had. The energy from the magic rippled all up and down the pillar. When it hit me, Soul Feed captured a fraction of the power, which then radiated out to the entire group since we were all connected. That helped some, but not enough.

We spun faster, the long lengths of the tree whipping around me, people screaming, some still shouting uselessly for the other survivors to stop. Then a wall of golden force appeared in front of me as I took a side step, and I bounced off. That shook the tree hard, the movement magnifying as it rippled down the long lengths. The last few feet shook like a whip.

Burns shouted something about an apple as he lost his grip and somersaulted away. As soon as he left the group, he phased back into the material world and tumbled 30 feet before crashing to the ground. More people followed. It must have looked like people appeared out of thin air as men and women tumbled off the long, ghostly length of the tree. Soon everyone toppled free except for Hector and Jane, both clinging to the trunk close to my head.

"Stop!" Tony's voice cut through the din of shouting people and sizzling spells, and the barrage slowed. I managed to right myself and orient back on Tony.

He was approaching Burns, who had leaped to his feet, despite an obviously injured leg. Burns was speaking fast, and Susan limped to join him. I couldn't hear what they were saying, but it helped ease Tony's worry. I spotted several other defenders visibly relaxing.

Scanning the area, I noted a lot of our people rising with wounds or burns, but a few of them remained writhing on the ground in obvious agony. Within seconds, Burns and Tony got everyone organized and people rushed to help the wounded with potions or spells of healing.

"I think you can get off now," I told Hector and Jane, but did not cancel Phase Walk. I still had more than 2 minutes left and would not waste it.

"I can't believe that worked," Hector said, giving me a ghostly shoulder bump before jumping free.

Jane hesitated, holding my gaze. In ethereal form, her eyes blazed as bright as lanterns. "You used to call me crazy. That was insane, Lucas!"

"You are crazy, especially on a bike. I'm clever."

She laughed, then added, "Thanks." Before dropping free.

I tossed the tree aside, then floated over to join Burns. At my approach, some of the crowd around them tensed, but Burns said, "Relax. He's one of us."

Trotting beside me, Jane added, "Lucas is the one who called the herd away from you and saved us from them."

"Lucas?" Tony asked, peering closer.

Steve laughed with joy. "Ha! I knew you'd make it."

Ruby stepped around him and her eyes widened. "Lucas? Are you . . . A ghost?"

I floated up to them and said, "I'm okay. Don't worry. Just a spell. Listen, we called off the herd, but not for long."

A bellowing roar from Tecton Earthwarden punctuated my words and I turned. Unfortunately, my attempt at stealth hadn't fooled him. The minotaur was charging toward us at the head of his herd, ax held high. The rumble of their hooves was growing in intensity.

"I really hate those guys," Tony muttered.

"Looks like all you managed was a temporary reprieve," Burns stated.

"We're stronger together. Get the defensive line re-formed. I'm going to see if I can keep him distracted."

"Wait!" Tony shouted, but we didn't have time for a debate.

In ethereal form, I was still immune to most of their attacks, and without 20 people slowing me down, I planned to find out exactly how much damage I could do.

I flashed across the field toward the onrushing herd while Burns and Tony started shouting orders. Tony's group had faced the herd once, so they knew better what they were facing. Their lines would hold if I did my job.

I shot straight for Tecton, flying barely 6 feet off the ground, just above the tops of the grass. This time, Tecton ran at the front of the herd and he spotted me instantly. He bellowed again.

So I rang the bell and pushed out my will, telling the herd to turn south. I hoped it might disorient some of them, but Tecton slammed his will over my connection instantly, disrupting it before I could do any damage. That was okay, the real reason I rang the bell was to tick him off.

It worked. He snorted with anger and increased speed, lowering his head to ram me with glowing horns.

I dodged.

At the last second, I swept to the left, diving into a barrel role. Tecton snorted so deep in anger it sounded like he'd swallowed a giant bass speaker, and he dug in his hooves to turn.

I expected to see the giant minotaur slide for 100 yards before slowing. Instead the ground bunched under his hooves and his speed bled away in a second as he triggered some kind of earth powers to help him stop. That was still a second too long.

I flew into the mass of bulls stampeding behind Tecton, Soulrend flashing. Their spirits rattled me like I'd been dropped into a giant soda can and shaken by a god, but I pressed through, severing spiritual spines and necks and anything else I could reach.

I left a trail of destruction behind me as bulls collapsed, dead or dying or crippled. Their cries of pain and rage filled the valley and echoed from the mountains. I couldn't smell them in ghost form, which was a relief. I'd been on farms and I knew how bad a mass of bulls could stink.

Tecton gave chase, leaping through the herd with his long legs, but I moved faster. In seconds, I swept a half circle through the herd, Soulrend never slowing before I banked around for another pass.

Tecton intercepted me. As bulls scattered out of the angry minotaur's path, Tecton brought his huge ax down with an overhand chop that could sunder a mountain.

I didn't even bother trying to meet the attack with my blade. I was strong, but in ethereal form, I lacked the physical might to counter his. Instead, I dodged, allowing the blade to slam into the ground. I expected it to sink out of sight, but the ax bounced off the ground without leaving a mark and Tecton swept it in a horizontal arc.

I wasn't expecting the move and barely pulled Soulrend around in an attempt to block. It didn't help. Soulrend was ethereal. The flat of the huge ax caught me like an avalanche and hurtled me halfway to the western mountains. Definitely contained a spiritual power.

The glowing black iron seared my spiritual body and it was my turn to bellow like a bull. My health dropped by nearly 30% and my mana, still re-filling from casting Phase Walk, plummeted.

"What was that?" I groaned as my Tesla Coil bracelet poured energy back into me, quickly healing the damage. It had been growing warmer on my arm through my entire rampage, and now I gratefully drank that stolen energy back in. Amazingly, Eva answered.

Tecton Earthwarden hit you with Nether Strike.
Nether Strike. Spell. Rare. Deal direct soul damage to any target struck by Tecton's ax. Effect: Target both health and mana.

"When did Identify start working like a help menu?" I asked as I flashed back toward Tecton.

I'd made a mess, but most of the herd was still closing on the re-formed human lines. A small group of people was charging the minotaur in the center, protected by that glowing wall of force. This time I recognized Tony in the center, with Burns and Hector flanking him on one side, and William and Scott Mortensen, the shirtless guy from Tony's team with the Hulk powers, on the other. Tony blazed with that same golden light. It must be a new ability he unlocked since I'd left.

Tecton had started to turn toward Tony's group so I rang the cow bell again to pull his attention back to me. As expected, he immediately swung back around, snorting steam in his fury. I accelerated toward him and he beckoned me on, huge ax raised.

I definitely didn't want to take another hit from that thing. Even though the physical blade couldn't hurt me, I bet if he connected edge-first I'd take even more damage.

So as I closed the distance, I threw 2 of my silver-tipped steel spears I'd taken from the cow herd. Even in ethereal form, my throwing arm was good and I reinforced the throws with my will.

The spears seemed to leap the distance between us, shifting from ethereal back to physical as they flew. Tecton didn't block with his ax like I had hoped he would, but earth flowed up his torso and covered his chest. The spears struck true and sank 3 inches into the earthen armor before dropping back to the ground.

They might have punched through enough to scratch Tecton, but nothing else. I felt a minor rush of energy into my bracelet. The minotaur leaped through his own protective barrier with an explosion of earth, flying 40 feet toward me, his ax blurring toward my head.

I twisted, barely managing to slip the blade. It passed so close, I felt its magic like heat scorching my skin and actually took a minimal amount of damage. In turn, I lashed out with Soulrend at Tecton's left hand on the haft of the ax, but only scored the thumb.

At the same time, I cast my scroll of Binding.

Tecton bellowed in rage as his hooves suddenly slammed together, bound by glowing cables. He wobbled but did not fall, and even swung the ax in a backhand stroke with his right hand as I slowed behind him.

It lacked power that way and I brought Soulrend up to block. My blade still couldn't do anything about the physical attack, but that wasn't what I was worried about. Soulrend could interact with that spiritual Nether Strike.

The two weapons crashed together and the impact still knocked me back. Thankfully, the move kept me from taking another hit from Nether Strike, and I recovered instantly from the knockback.

Shouting in rage, Tecton spun. Earth flowed over his hooves and the ground pulled him around to face me while keeping him locked in place and upright.

I'd wanted to try binding his arms, but the 20-foot minotaur was enormous. He dwarfed me, the perfectly sculpted muscles of his humanlike torso bulging with impossible proportions. I wasn't sure the binding spell would work on his swollen arms, but had hoped he'd have a harder time separating his hooves with enough force to snap them. I'd hampered him with that move, but not incapacitated him like I'd hoped.

"You are now the prey," Tecton growled, his deep voice sounding like he was gargling thunder as he lifted his huge ax.

"Says the cow. Do you have any idea how many steaks I've eaten?"

Roaring with fury, he swung a mighty blow, but I rolled around it and swept in before he launched a backswing. He thrust the butt of the weapon at my face in an impressive display of weapon mastery, but he moved so slow compared to what I could do as a ghost. I dodged around the blow and slapped an emoji sticker that looked like a melting disco ball against his long snout as I shot past.

Toxic Blind. Emoji Trap. Like a grandparent dropped into a k-pop concert, this trap will blind a target for 5 seconds with a dazzling burst of lights, while surrounding them with a cloud of toxic fumes that can melt flesh and erode steel.

Tecton froze, then bellowed so loud it hurt my ghostly ears. He thrashed in place, kept upright only by the earth holding his bound hooves motionless. Intense light blazed in the minotaur's eyes, shifting through all the colors of the rainbow in an instant. It hurt my eyes to look at, and must be truly blinding to him.

At the same time, a cloud of sinister green gas billowed out of the little emoji sticker, flowing over Tecton like a visible plague. His fur singed, curled, and fell away while the flesh underneath blackened. His angry bellows turned to shouts of pain, and my Tesla Coil bracelet grew warm again.

He swung his ax wildly in every direction, but the blows lacked direction and I easily dodged as I circled him. With careful timing, I slashed each of his elbows with Soulrend. His ax tumbled away to the grasses and his hands fell limp to his sides at the ends of his enormously muscled arms.

Earth boiled around Tecton, rising in protective rings around him, but that only sealed the toxic gas against his skin, making the poison effect worse. The minotaur bellowed again and the earth extended like a spherical, full-body shield.

Earth hardened to stone, then began spinning around the monster. Spikes of stone sprouted all over the sphere and exploded outward in waves. Dozens of them punched through my ghostly body before I could react, but passed through with only the tiniest tugging stings.

On the other side of Tecton, multiple voices screamed in pain as the tall grasses were shredded. Other people had gotten too close.

I dove forward, leading with Soulrend, and crashed into the spinning earthen shield. It felt far more solid than it should, like trying to dive through Jell-O. Tecton must be filling it with a lot of spiritual energy somehow. It made a daunting physical barrier, and I had to fight to drive my blade and arms through.

Grunting with the effort, I slashed Soulrend wildly through the shield. My face was still on the outside so I couldn't see, but it was hard to miss a 20-foot, hugely-muscled minotaur.

I connected with something and Soulrend slowed as it rent spirit. Tecton bellowed again and the entire stone shield exploded outward, devastating the surrounding area. One of Tecton's arms hung useless at its side, his shoulder cut, but the lights of my emoji trap were starting to dim. Tecton blinked blurry eyes at me and raised his other arm to bludgeon me with a limp fist.

Burns hurtled out of the grass behind Tecton, boar spear burning with white-hot, crackling lightning. His face was bleeding and a stone spike stuck from one thigh, but he jumped 10 feet and plunged his spear deep into the minotaur's back.

The mighty blow caught Tecton totally by surprise. Lightning crackled across his body and he roared in pain as his muscles convulsed and seized up. The brutal hit overbalanced him and slammed him face-first to the ground.

Tony arrived, surrounded by the golden halo of his defensive shield just as I swooped down to swing at Tecton's neck. Tony picked up the minotaur's huge ax and jumped forward, bring the enormous weapon down on Tecton's throat at the same time I slashed with Soulrend. The huge blade passed so close to me that again I felt the searing heat of its magic.

The ax severed flesh as my blade severed spirit. The double strike removed Tecton's huge bull head in a spray of gore.

Chapter Forty-Five
Challenges of Leadership

I floated back, scowling at Tony, who lifted a hand in triumph while Burns shouted a wordless cry of victory. Had Tony not seen me there, or had he just not cared that he almost split me in half at the same time he helped kill Tecton?

Congratulations, Lucas! You have defeated Tecton Earthwarden. Bonus experience gained for defeating a higher-level enemy. Experience doubled for defeating the stage-level boss.

You have reached level 7. Stat points allocated.

Bonus prize: New title: Musketeer.

Musketeer. All for One. One for All. Plus 5 tier-1 points to all base stats. Loot boxes from bosses and monsters 25 levels or more above your own automatically improve 1 grade. Quest complete.

A diamond loot box appeared hovering in the air in front of me. Whoa. "How did I get a double upgrade?"

Cyrus' voice laughed in my ear. "Your Musketeer title upgrades it 1 tier. Your Trailblazer title granted you a second upgrade for this one."

I'd take it, and the level was even more welcome. I glanced quickly at my stats. Cyrus had dumped both stat points from my new level into Strength again, while the new title bumped all my base by 5. I even got 5 points in CHA somehow. I wasn't about to point out the fact that the still-locked stat didn't usually get included.

As the new stats took effect, a river of power roared through me, shaking my ethereal body like a leaf. I threw my arms out wide and fell into a slow backward somersault as I gloried in my strength.

If I felt this strong in ethereal form, how good would it feel when I returned to my body? The 2 points I got from each level resulted in a noticeable uptick in my power. Now in a single shot, I was getting 30 points! That was 15 levels worth of stat increases all at once, and those were tier-1points!

Most of my stats pretty much doubled, most reaching 10. It was like transforming from baby Aquaman into king Aquaman in the blink of an eye. Even in my ghostly form, I sensed I was reaching a fundamentally different level of power than any human had ever imagined. Defeating bosses gave the best loot!

It was a heady feeling and I wanted to revel in it, but couldn't afford to get distracted while the rest of the battle was still going on. As much as I wanted to see the loot, I minimized the box. We still had work to do. No one else noticed my double-upgraded loot box. Emerald boxes appeared in front of both Tony and Burns, and they both laughed with delight.

"I got a level and a second title!" Tony exclaimed. "And a message that with hitting level 25, I can permanent my next spell."

Burns grinned. "I got those too. Third title for me."

"Third?" Tony looked impressed.

Burns shrugged. "I'd like to think I earned them, but probably just blind luck."

I didn't mention that Musketeer was my 6th title. I really wanted to ask about the spells they planned to permanent. They were probably the first of all us survivors to reach level 25, and now we knew the level where we could permanent another spell.

They both reluctantly minimized their loot boxes for later too. I triggered Soul Feed, and a torrent of white power rose up off the corpse and coursed through me, reinvigorating me and boosting my physical stats. My Tesla Coil bracelet had already drained quite a bit of power from Tecton, but I still hated to see some of that billowing white cloud going to waste.

"Good job keeping him distracted," Burns said, grinning at me. "I can't loot him unless we all agree."

Together we looted Tecton, but I didn't look at what loot I received. As the other two raced after, I flashed toward the rear of the herd. They were still pounding the defenses around the settlement, but our lines were holding. Barely.

Most of the bulls didn't seem to realize Tecton had died. I had hoped they'd break and scatter immediately, but I guess they weren't that smart. So I pulled out the cow bell again and rang it. This time no other will impeded my own

I commanded, '*Flee to the west.*'

Most of the herd obeyed immediately, turning and rushing away at full speed. Those engaged in close combat took longer to respond. Some were cut down in the moment of distraction as they tried to disengage. The rest raced away, following the herd.

"Did you do that?" Burns asked as I slowed and canceled Phase Walk. Colors brightened as I phased back into the physical world. I could really get used to that spell.

For a second I couldn't respond, but just threw my head back and breathed deep. All my senses had improved from that last stats influx, and I felt so strong I wanted to laugh and go bench-press a small mountain.

"Lucas?" Tony prodded, looking at me like he worried I had lost what little brains I'd retained from Earth.

"Sorry. Yeah, that was me. No need to keep risking everyone's lives when I can just send the herd away."

"We could use the experience," Tony said, shifting Tecton's huge ax on one shoulder. I didn't comment on the fact that he'd looted the weapon without asking if I wanted it. I wouldn't use it. Wasn't my style, but it would have been nice if he'd asked.

I shrugged. "I doubt they'll leave the valley. We can send out hunting parties later."

"I suppose that works. Good job today, Lucas. I'm happy to see you survived the lion. Looks like you took my advice to heart. It's good to see you committed to the cause."

He must have noticed my higher level. I was still below average, but level 7 looked a lot better than level 1. I didn't bother correcting his assumption. If his interpretation of events made him less of a pain in my neck, that was fine with me.

"How did we not get any more levels from defeating so many bulls?" Hector asked as he and the others from Tony and Burns's retinue caught up. Most of them looked battered from Tecton's spike barrage, but had already taken healing potions.

"Experience sharing," Burns said with a shrug.

Tony nodded. "We've been piecing that together too. Since nearly everyone had to join the defenses, we've got nearly 300 people actively participating in the battle. We took out more than half the herd, but that's about 100 monsters split among all of us. Not much experience each.

"We'll have to take into account who needs the experience the most as we schedule the hunting parties to go after the rest of the herd," Burns said.

"My thoughts exactly," Tony agreed. Neither of them mentioned how the 3 of us had gotten a new title and levels for defeating the boss. If each stage-level boss granted loot that good, they might be planning to keep those bonuses among the 3 of us.

How did I feel about that? I needed far more experience than anyone else, and a bonus level might mean the difference between making it to the next stage or not. Tony and Burns were leaders, and we were perhaps the 3 strongest people I'd met so far. We'd likely be the ones fighting the bosses anyway.

Did that mean we should keep the extra loot a secret? I stewed on that as they discussed plans for the settlement. They got into details like rosters for hunting and ways to ensure everyone got to at least level 10 in the few days between now and the end of the week.

I left them to it. They could deal with all the leadership hassles. I still needed 3 levels in 3 days. I felt more optimistic than ever since getting dropped to level 1, but I couldn't waste time with committees and meetings. I needed to hunt, and it was clear I needed to hunt alone. I needed stronger monsters and a lot of them.

I considered that as I followed the small group back to the main defensive lines. Everyone raised a cheer as we approached, and I have to admit, it felt good. I didn't even let the fact that they mostly cheered Tony and Burns bother me.

I wanted to reunite with Ruby and Steve, and I'd love to invite Jane to join our team, but I couldn't see how that could work. They'd slow me down and siphon precious experience.

Then Ruby appeared from the crowd and rushed over to me, her long, red hair streaming behind. "Lucas, I'm so glad you survived," she cried and flung her arms around me in an enthusiastic hug.

Chapter Forty-Six

I Find the Heart of the Town

I hugged Ruby back, happy she and Steve were okay. Then all of a sudden, lust burned through me, just like when Susan had kissed me. I felt a primal urge to take more. It was my right as the strongest hunter, the one who had just helped save the pack.

Back off. This is my pack, I mean team, and I don't work that way.

Where had that come from? I barely suppressed a shudder. That reaction was so wrong. I had to stop letting the wolf make me act like a slobbering lunatic.

Ruby was my friend and my teammate. I cared for her, and friends didn't consider each other property they won for winning battles. After a final hard squeeze, Ruby let go, laughing, and I concealed my racing thoughts. That had been weird. I had to get it together.

Then Steve clapped me on the back so hard I staggered. "You lucky devil! How did you survive that lion?"

"It's kind of a long story." I returned his grin and told them about it, or as much as I could. I still generated way too many questions I couldn't answer. Hearing my own story drove home how lucky I was to have survived.

"Werewolves and zombies?" Steve exclaimed, shaking his head in amazement.

"What did it feel like to become a werewolf?" Ruby asked, her voice soft, with a tone of wonder.

Jane had joined us while I talked, along with William and a few other people. My story triggered a wide range of reactions, from awe to incredulity. Many asked questions too.

While we talked, we finished looting the fallen bulls. A couple teams were still dispatching wounded monsters, while others worked to heal wounded survivors. Thankfully Eva let me loot all the bulls I'd killed with a single prompt.

I got a ton of basic loot, from hundreds more mana crystals, hamburger, and steaks to a dozen various polearm weapons, horns, and hides. I now had a single tier-3 mana crystal in my inventory, equivalent to 1000 tier-0 crystals. That felt like a big milestone.

As the entire field around the settlement's raised hill transformed into a cloud of stinking black smoke, we headed between the tall spires of rock marking the boundary of the hill's flat top.

"Welcome to Stepstone," Steve said grandly as we entered the settlement.

"Stepstone?" It wasn't a terrible name, but didn't wow me either.

He shrugged. "First group to arrive got to name it. We're not going to be here long enough to argue about the name."

"You guys only got here yesterday?" I asked as I took in the orderly streets, lined with Base Camp tents and quite a few wooden structures. Most were variations on log cabins, but the biggest structures, standing near the center of town, were made out of finished lumber.

Ruby nodded. "A few teams got here a day before that, and people have been arriving in small groups ever since. I think we're up around 300 now."

"How are there buildings?"

The Base Camp utility spell made setting up and moving camp as easy as thought, but wooden buildings required tools, finished lumber, and all sorts of things I couldn't imagine we had available. We'd only arrived mostly naked 3 days ago.

"A few people who were tradesmen back on Earth got some really cool trade-related abilities," Steve said.

Ruby added, "The teams who got here first got special loot boxes with gear and spells to help in creating infrastructure."

Steve said, "Yeah, one woman got a tool called an adz. She taps a log and poof, it disappears, replaced by a pile of finished lumber. Weirdly, she always warns folks not to waste the lumber, and to recycle whenever possible."

"It's not weird for her to hold onto her core values," Ruby objected.

I shrugged. I wasn't about to judge someone in this crazy world.

Steve said, "Another guy got an anvil and set of blacksmith tools. They're enchanted, so he can make basic weapons and all sorts of building materials like tools and nails from raw materials."

"Wow."

Ruby flashed a bright smile. "Your idea to have me make that scroll of healing potion my first permanent spell really resonated with folks. Some others had random scrolls to build or craft, and they've started choosing those."

"I'm impressed so many people chose non-combat options."

I understood at one level, but the thought of relying on everyone else to kill the monsters and fight their way up to the top-stage nymph queen boss while I stayed behind building houses or crafting things made me cringe.

Someone should do it, though. There were still . . . I checked my menus and grimaced. Remaining survivors: 699. We'd lost too many during the fight with the bulls. If we could gather all of the nearly 700 survivors into Stepstone, we'd need all kinds of equipment and supplies. Not everyone could be fighters.

I thought back to the discussion about how to ensure both combat and non-combat folks reached level 10. It was a daunting question, and as I scanned the people we passed, I spied a decent percentage who were still lacking levels. Thankfully, more than half had reached at least level 10, but a small percentage were still hovering around level 5. How was that possible?

Of course, that's how everyone would look at me too. Most people probably assumed I was becoming a drain on the rest of the survivors, someone who might have to be left behind.

"Do you need any healing potions?" Ruby asked, pulling me from my thoughts. "I've been making them as fast as I can regenerate mana. Every fighter has at least a couple."

"That's fantastic. Good work. I've got enough for now. I'm lower on mana potions."

"Here. There's a woman who copied my move, but with mana. They're only standard level, but we've got a lot of them."

Ruby produced half a dozen potions and I dumped them into my inventory.

"Do you guys need any gear?" I asked in turn. "I've got some polearm weapons and I can give you each a laser rifle, if you want."

I pulled one out of my inventory. Ruby marveled at it, but declined. "I'm focusing more on a support role."

"What about those dance fighting and nunchuck skills?" I teased.

She glowered and I pushed the energy rifle into her hands. "Even though you want to be more support, you might have to deal with monsters."

"That's true, but I can't see myself blasting holes in people like Star Wars storm troopers."

Steve chuckled. "Of course you can't. Storm troopers are terrible shots. I'll take it if you won't."

He grinned as he examined the rifle and took a practice shot. The beam of energy tore a chunk from near the top of one of the rock pillars clear across the settlement. He laughed.

"How about this?" I asked Ruby. As far as I knew, she only had the hunting knife I'd given her. She needed better protection, so I extracted one of the shotgun-like zombie stun guns from my inventory and explained how they worked.

"This is more my style," Ruby said, hefting the bulky weapon and looking absolutely boss in the process. Quite a few people around us noticed, then started hounding me to share guns with them too.

I hesitated. I had a few left, but not nearly enough to equip everyone asking for one. "Supplies are very low. I'll discuss the best way to distribute them when I meet with the settlement leaders."

"So why do they get one?" a chubby fellow carrying a cudgel whined.

"Because they're my team."

He left, sulking, but no one argued that point. Teams mattered. They might have been random, but every one of us had found our team before anyone else. We'd fought and bled together, and most of us had lost teammates.

Steve and Ruby took me on a brief tour of Stepstone. Work crews were already returning to the effort of shoring up the gaps between the stone spires ringing the hilltop. We might have to leave in 4 days, but with over 100 bulls still visible in the distance, no one wanted to shirk on defenses. They worked with good cheer, though, since we'd already defeated the stage boss.

The bulk of Stepstone was divided into open lanes where teams could claim spots to settle. A large percentage of folks had picked Base Camp, so rows of giant magical tents filled the space. I did spot makeshift shelters of teams who had not chosen Base Camp, or where the person with the spell had died.

The crafters and town leadership had claimed the center of town. The blacksmith shop was a long, open-fronted wooden building like a huge garage, packed with workers. The lumber mill was just a small wooden building with long racks standing mostly empty behind. The lumber was being used up as fast as it got produced.

"An armorer?" I asked as we passed the next building.

Ruby nodded. "The woman in charge can make a lot of basic-level gear, mostly leathers from monster hides. She claims once her spells and skills upgrade, she'll be able to produce higher-grade gear and unlock the enchantments listed in some of the animal parts we've looted."

"That'll be awesome." I had a few specialty hides I'd have to bring to her once she leveled up enough.

In front of the town hall, we paused at a wooden bulletin board, hung with dozens of slender wooden blocks, about the size of coffee table coasters. Each one sported the photo of a person, along with their name and team.

"One of the movie grips got a spell to take snapshots with his gaze and transfer them to solid objects," Ruby explained.

"And he made it permanent?" That seemed idiotic.

Steve shrugged. "Said it keeps him grounded. He's been adding photos of everyone with family members they're trying to reunite with."

Okay, not idiotic. "That is actually a great idea. I'll have to get my photo on here. Still hoping to find my brother and friends." I scanned the photos again with a lot more interest. I spotted Jane, but no one else I knew.

"He hangs around here late mornings," Steve said. I made a mental note to seek out the guy.

The next building made me laugh. "We have to stop here."

Neither of them argued as I joined the steady stream of people pushing through the wide doorway leading into the brightly-lit tavern.

Yeah, a real-life tavern, complete with a rough wooden bar along the far wall and unpeeled log picnic tables scattered around the room. A healthy crowd had already returned from the battle and were filling the tables, drinking from authentic-looking metal steins.

Buckets of waffle fries sat on every table, and people were devouring them fast, even though I spotted no ketchup. The big, open room smelled like beer and fresh fries and, unfortunately, like too many people who hadn't tried their Base Camp showers yet.

"Where did all this come from?" I asked as we headed for the bar.

Steve said, "The owner's a guy named Sam. He's on team Lord of the Rings. He was the lead gaffer for the movie."

I laughed. "Sam? Gaffer? As in Sam Gamgee's grandfather?"

Steve nodded. "He's already asked me to work here when I can. He's got most of what I need to start mixing drinks and making margaritas."

Cyrus had hit it out of the park with that team assignment.

As we worked our way through the line, Ruby added, "Apparently, Sam started with brewing skills. He was in one of the first teams to arrive, so got a slew of new abilities, including making barrels and steins."

Despite the crowd, the lines moved along steadily. The room buzzed with excited chatter as people talked about the battle or celebrated beating the stage-1 boss so early.

I spotted the stocky older fellow wearing a totally cliche white apron behind the bar, flanked by half a dozen men and women taking orders. His full beard was streaked with gray, he'd lost most of his hair, and he was smiling and laughing with his customers as if he was serving them in some quaint medieval town instead of on a death battle planet.

Sam Sternberg. Level 18 Baby human. Team Lord of the Rings.

"Level 18?" I exclaimed into one of those occasional lulls in conversation. A lot of people turned to look at me, many giving me knowing smiles.

Sam heard me too and gestured us forward. "New in town, eh?" He sounded like he came from Canada.

"Arrived just in time to help with the herd."

"Well done. I hear we'll have a lot of steaks for a while," Sam said with a grin. "What are you drinking today?" He spotted Steve and his smile widened. "Want to jump over here and help out for a while?"

"In a few minutes. I promise."

"What have you got?" I asked, eying the long plank table against the rear wall, packed with heavy oak barrels with spigots hammered into the front faces.

"Mostly ale so far, but we're working on stronger stuff with Steve's help."

"How much?"

"One tier-0 mana crystal."

I tossed him the glowing coin and he produced a metal stein filled with a frothing brew. Identify kicked in immediately.

Basic ale. Beverage. Brewed by an amateur, this ale contains almost as much alcohol as children's cough syrup. A minor sedative, it offers negligible boosts to courage and self-confidence. Stackable.

Sam noted my expression and sighed. "Still the same terrible description?"

"Yeah," I admitted with an apologetic smile.

He shrugged. "Try it yourself. Everyone keeps saying it's the best ale they've ever tried, although the bit about too little alcohol is unfortunately true. I'm working on that."

"So it's more like frothy ginger ale?"

Sam grimaced. "No need to be rude."

"Sorry." I glanced around the room at the men and women drinking Sam's ale. "Probably good that we can't all get drunk too easy. Tempting to drown the insanity for a while, but we'd all end up dead faster."

"Even when we increase the alcohol content, getting drunk will be a challenge. Our natural regeneration sobers us faster than back on Earth. Healing potions restore a lot of the effects, and antidote potions wipe away the alcohol in seconds," Steve said.

That meant my increased tier-1 body regeneration would sober me even faster. How much would I have to drink to get a buzz? Some experimenting was definitely in order as soon as I could fit it in.

"Do you mind if I ask how you reached level 18? You can't be doing much fighting, not while building an entire tavern."

Sam chuckled. "I get asked that a lot. When I got my tavern-keeper skills, I got an upgrade scroll. It changed my leveling system to gain experience based on mana crystal revenue."

I gaped and he laughed, throwing his hands out wide. "The better my tavern, the more people come buy my products, the more experience I gain."

"You're the first person I've met with a different leveling system," I finally managed to say as my mind raced with the possibilities.

Cyrus interrupted, and at his loud voice most people cringed and looked around nervously. It seemed few had engaged in ongoing dialogue with the invisible AI.

"You'll begin to unlock classes soon. Depending on which classes one selects, alternate leveling paths could become available."

"So when do we get classes?" I asked into the hush that followed his words.

"Soon."

Most of the crowd huddled over their drinks, while more than few cast angry glares at me. Since I was one of the few standing, it was easy to orient on me and see me speaking with Cyrus. Why they seemed angry with me for talking with him was a mystery I pushed aside. They'd get over it.

The fact that so few seemed to chat with Cyrus much did bother me, though. Was I smarter for fostering an open dialogue? I'd learned tons of great info from

Cyrus. Then again, none of them had been targeted by the AI for one of his little experiments.

Maybe I was the dumb one after all. I guess that would be decided by whether or not I survived the first stage.

Cyrus didn't say anything else, so I changed the topic. Gesturing around the tavern as conversation started picking up again, I asked, "It doesn't bother you that you'll have to abandon this place in a matter of days?"

"Who said anything about abandoning?" Sam asked, his good humor back. "The walls are made out of free-standing sections we connect with poles. Even without helpers, I could disassemble the entire building and dump everything into my inventory in a matter of minutes."

"Wow. Good thinking. Are all the buildings made like that?"

"Mostly. Now, if you'll excuse me?"

Sam turned to take another order and Steve made his own apologies before heading around the bar to get to work mixing drinks. Ruby led me back to her tent and we settled into comfortable chairs near the fire where I finally tried Sam's ale.

"This is really good." It had a rich taste and was a lot sweeter than I expected. It reminded me of an old-fashioned German ale I'd tried once in a medieval historical reenactment festival. I'd run across the festival by accident on my way to another forest fire. It made for a fun stop.

Ruby flashed a smile and pulled another tankard out of her inventory. "Steve got 3 entire barrels as a bonus for agreeing to work for Sam. Shared one with me."

"Think he'll share another with me?"

"Probably. Sam is always low on inventory now, though, so it might take time."

I decided to check my loot. Ruby had not participated in the fighting, so hadn't gotten to loot any of the bulls, but was happy to see what I got.

Most was familiar, including mana crystals, hamburger, steaks, cow hides, and horns. I now had enough to stock a restaurant and a leatherworker's shop for months. I shared a bunch of the steak and hamburger with Ruby to improve her Base Camp menu.

"I upgraded the tent defenses again, as well as the bathroom, and even added a bunkroom." She gestured at a new door I'd noticed but not yet investigated. That utility spell was proving to be invaluable for not only surviving, but surviving in style.

I shared one of my magic lanterns with her. The tent had enough light, and she could eventually upgrade it with outside floodlights, but she lacked any personal lights.

From Tecton, I ended up with more mana crystals and the first interesting loot of the day.

Scroll of Ground Walker. Uncommon. Walk on any earthen surface, no matter how steep or slippery. Even mountain climbing purists will be jealous as you jog past. Duration: 60 seconds. Quantity: 3.

Scroll of Earth Armor. Channel The Thing from Fantastic Four as you encase your body in a layer of living stone. Provides excellent defense against all types of physical attacks and moderate defense against magical attack. Duration: 30 seconds. Quantity: 3.

Those are amazing," Ruby breathed as she read their description. "I wish I had another slot to make a scroll permanent."

I handed her one of each. "Use them if you need them, or save them for later."

"Are you sure?" she asked, but did not hesitate to accept them.

"We're a team. We take care of each other."

"Yes, we are," she said, her voice soft, real emotion in her eyes. I had struck some kind of cord with her. Not sure why. It seemed pretty simple to me.

My diamond loot box appeared in front of me with a flourish and Ruby gasped. "Diamond? How'd you get that?"

"Want to talk about it, or see what's inside?"

"Open it already," she laughed, and I mentally clicked the prompt.

The giant sparkling diamond flashed in a fanfare of trumpets before disappearing. A huge item took its place, thumping heavily to the floor. It took a second to realize what I was seeing.

I sprang to my feet and laughed. "My bike!"

Chapter Forty-Seven
A Custom Makeover

I laughed. The quest had said something about winning an item from Earth, but I'd never imagined this.

"Is that a motorbike?" Ruby asked as she too rose to examine it.

"It's my motorcycle. Or, maybe it used to be."

The color scheme was the same custom midnight blue of my BMW GS1300, but as I paced around the bike, the many differences sank in.

It was like Cyrus had taken my old bike and given it a sci-fi upgrade. The bike was a bit longer, sleeker, with larger wheels and smooth, fat tires with slitted holes running down the center. Twin objects that looked like jet thrusters extended behind the seat, while more tubes pointed down along both tires.

I didn't know what it meant, but the more I looked at it, the more I loved it. Finally, Identify kicked in.

Switchblade Skimmer of the Trailblazer. Legendary. This unique item started as a boring Earth motorcycle, but has evolved into a vehicle of exploration and conquest. Upgrades include:

Mana Core. Engine is powered by a legendary quality energy crystal.

Hover Bike. Ride on a cushion of air up to 6 feet above the ground.

Soulbound. Item is bound to your soul. Cannot be stolen or lost. Does not consume space in inventory and can be summoned or banished at will.

Self Repair. When banished to your inventory, will self-repair over time.

Weapons Battery. 3 slots for defensive capabilities, and 2 slots for offense. Can absorb spell scrolls, weapons, or items with magical effects. Note: spells or effects may be altered to fit Switchblade's systems.

Starting battery: Shield Dome. Defense. Creates a defensive dome of magical energy to deflect most weak to moderate attacks. Shattercore Ballista. Offense. Launch a magical bolt straight ahead to deliver explosive damage. Rate of fire: 1 bolt per minute.

I whistled softly as I read the description, then placed my hand reverently on the smooth faring encasing the front of the bike. As soon as I touched it, a tingle of energy flowed up my arm and I *felt* the bike. A flood of information poured into my mind like when I gained a new ability and I instinctively understood how the bike worked.

"What?" Ruby asked as I stood there with a stupid grin on my face. That's right, she lacked Identify.

"It's my old bike from Earth, but evolved into some kind of sci-fi battle platform."

"Can they do that?" she asked with a frown, then chuckled. "Obviously, they can, but why don't we see other advanced tech? I mean, most of us get medieval fantasy weapons. Those energy rifles you took from the zombies are the only other tech I've seen."

"Good point. The zombies were from the second stage. Maybe the technology will evolve with each level."

"Maybe, although the nymph queen used a trident."

"Sure, a trident that could cut a man in half faster than a laser." The image of the cloud split in half above her came to mind and I shivered. I'd grown a lot in the first 3 days, but I was still nowhere near powerful enough to take on something like her.

"I have to find Jane and try this thing out!"

With a focused effort of will, Switchblade disappeared. I checked my inventory and found a new tab with a slightly ethereal look to it labeled Soulbound Items. Inside, I found Switchblade, complete with a status bar listing power levels, damage levels, time to full charge, time to restoration, and a listing of both offensive and defensive abilities.

"So who exactly is Jane?" Ruby asked in a teasing tone, eyes twinkling.

"She's my brother's girlfriend. She's an even better biker than me. She's going to love this."

"Oh. Grand. Let's go find her."

That took only moments, and by the time we exited the town with Jane, she nearly exploded with impatience to see Switchblade. The only signs of the recent battle with the bulls was a huge open swath of clear ground where the grasses had been trampled flat.

When I summoned Switchblade, Jane gasped, then laughed and rushed around it, examining every component. She asked about every piece until I finally said, "I don't know about that either. I just got it, remember."

"Then get your lazy butt on the bike and let's test it out!"

Switchblade didn't have a kickstand, but stood upright all on its own. When I settled onto the comfortable seat, the bike whirred to life with a quiet hum, not the throaty growl of most bikes. A screen opened like an instrument panel beneath the handlebars, right where my LCD would be back on Earth. It listed status and power levels, but lacked any buttons. I would trigger the weapons with my will.

Gripping the handlebars, my grin widened. The bike was proportioned perfectly for me. I quickly scanned the controls and realized it didn't have a clutch. No gears, then. I guess the magical crystal powering it didn't need any.

The front brake lever was situated in front of the right grip like normal, as was the rear brake pedal by my right foot. I wasn't sure how brakes would work on a hover bike, but I'd find out.

"Go already!" Jane laughed.

I gunned the throttle.

And nearly fell off the back as the bike accelerated a lot faster than my old GS ever had. That bike hadn't been a slouch, but Switchblade was like an electric vehicle, able to kick in 100% power instantly.

Jane's laugh chased me as I recovered my balance and quickly mastered the throttle. Tall grasses whipped at me as I tore across the plain. Guards protected my hands, but I lacked a helmet.

The information dumped into my mind gave me an intuitive understanding of the bike's non-Earth functions. The left grip had a throttle to control altitude. I quickly learned that I could indeed adjust from rolling over the ground like a traditional bike to soaring up to 6 feet. That put the wheels just above the tops of the grasses, and I laughed as I zoomed over the plain, leaving tall grass waving in my wake.

Turning was pure joy. As I banked, additional thrusters fired and I suspected some kind of hover magic helped under the covers too. I found I could turn so hard, I skidded across the air before the thrusters could catch up. The bike responded instantly to my commands and the ride was smooth and controlled.

Weapons testing came next. I accelerated so fast the whipping wind nearly blinded me. I'd have to get my hands on some goggles or something. In moments, I flashed across the plain and neared one of the hills leading up to the higher mountains. There, I sighted on a lone tree and mentally triggered the Shattercore Ballista.

A bright blue beam of energy erupted from the front of the bike. Shaped like a giant crossbow bolt, complete with a thick-bladed head, it shot forward at twice my speed. It detonated against the tree in an impressive explosion of splintered wood.

I slowed to inspect the results. When the dust cloud cleared, the tree had been reduced to a field of charred splinters. The air smelled burned. That was as strong as Thunder Punch! Aiming was intuitive. All I had to do was point Switchblade at the target and let loose.

I was tempted to target some of the bulls massed on the far side of the plain, but resisted the urge. They wouldn't give me much experience. I planned to hunt bigger prey as soon as possible.

By the time I returned to Stepstone, a large crowd had gathered. Word of an actual motorcycle had spread all across the settlement and two dozen people clamored to try it out. Even Tony and Burns were there, along with a couple other leaders of Stepstone.

The first stood out like a bright rose among brown grass. The shapely woman had long, strawberry-blond hair and wore a sparkling white blouse and slacks a blinding shade of pink. Her brown leather jacket might have dampened the effect a little if it wasn't covered in fluorescent green clovers.

Crystal Bennett. Level 23 baby human. Team One Piece.

It took a minute for the character to click into place for me. On that one, Cyrus had to work a bit harder. Crystal had to be playing the role of Jewelry Bonney, the character with age-altering abilities. I couldn't wait to see what powers she got.

The other was a burly older gentleman with close-cropped white hair and intense blue eyes. He wore only a pair of simple brown trousers and a blue linen shirt.

Paul MacDonald. Level 21 baby human. Team Great British Baking Show.

I nearly laughed. He did look a little like Paul Hollywood, one of the judges on that show. Isabella had loved binge-watching every season, but watching it always made me feel hungry.

Jane barely waited for me to hop off before leaping into the saddle and gunning Switchblade. She tore away, her laughter trailing behind.

"That's an amazing item," Burns said as the town leaders gathered around me and Ruby.

Tony added, "Yeah, we got special quest reward boxes too, but now I'm thinking I got shafted somehow."

"Why? What did you get?"

A medieval longsword appeared in his hand. It was a beautiful, double-edged, two-handed sword, with gold highlights on the handle and an odd matte black finish instead of the expected steel sheen.

Mark III Sword of Piercing. Epic. Why limit yourself to one weapon, when this transmutable blade can morph into whatever weapon you need at the moment?

Tony smiled as he hefted it. "I love this sword, don't get me wrong. It's supposed to be nearly indestructible and I can change it into different shapes of roughly similar size."

"That's incredible." A flexible weapon like that could turn the tide of a lot of battles. Tony was on team Marvel, and I'd already pegged him as being Cyrus's choice for Iron Man. Calling the blade Mark III was a dead giveaway.

"How about you?" I asked Burns.

He hesitated, and I forgot all about the question as Jane somehow jumped Switchblade high up out of the grasses. In midair, she twisted the hover bike into a full 180, pointing back in the opposite direction, but still flying backward.

The bike's faint distant hum intensified into a scream as flames blasted out the rear thrusters. The backward slide slowed so fast, it was a marvel Jane didn't tumble off the back. Then the bike shot forward like it was fired from a cannon.

Jane disappeared back into the grass, only to reappear a moment later, again rocketing above the supposed 2-yard height limit as she tucked into a barrel role. She spun 3 times before disappearing into the grass again.

A moment later, she shot out of the grasses, aimed straight at us. She accelerated until people started murmuring nervously. At the last second, she slammed on the brakes and the bike whined as counter thrusters and its hover magic kicked into overdrive, slowing the bike so fast I would have catapulted over the handlebars. Jane braced herself against what looked like several G's of force, bringing the bike to a stop right in front of me.

"I've got to get me one of these!" she laughed.

As 20 voices shouted for a turn, I asked, "How did you make it do all that?"

"You've barely touched the potential in this thing. Run it along the ground, then when it hits an obstacle, thrusters in the front tire fire to bounce over it. Time a full-throttle boost from the elevation thruster to magnify the effect. I used that to jump it above its normal limits. That's when I realized I was no longer limited to maneuvers my tires could handle. I was flying for Stryker's sake. I used the directional thrusters to spin the bike, then floored it."

How long would it have taken me to figure that out? Jane loved pushing the limits even on Earth dirt bikes too. I'd seen a video of her riding up a 30 foot vertical cliff. Mind boggling.

She reluctantly dismounted and patted the front faring. "I'm officially jealous, Lucas."

"I'll let you ride again. Promise."

I banished Switchblade to a lot of grumbles. I didn't know most of the people clamoring to ride my new bike, and even on Earth it wasn't normal to let just anyone take your bike for a spin. Besides, we'd consumed a chunk of the bike's power with our high octane maneuvers.

Tony said, "Lucas, we're about to hold a meeting of the leaders of Stepstone. I'd like you to join us to report on what you saw on the second stage."

Chapter Forty-Eight
Stats Check

T his is another stats chapter.

Name: Lucas Altan
Race: Tier-1 Human
Level: 7

Life Points: 120   (10,571 tier-0 baby human equivalent)
Mana: 32

Base Stats:
Constitution: 11.9
Intelligence: 9
Strength: 16.9
Dexterity: 9.1
Wisdom: 10.7

Secondary Stats:
Endurance: 28
Agility: 36
Perception   23
Magical Resistances: 14.1
Luck: 24.9
CHA: 30

Other stats:
Mental Resistance: 10.5
Fear Resistance: 25
Poison Resistance: 10

PERMANENT SPELLS
1   Harvest

UTILITY SPELLS:
1   Mystic Looter
2   Linguasight
3   Navigation
4   Soul Feed

TEMPORARY SPELLS:
1   Energy Ward
2   Frostfire Nova
3   Corrosive Cloud
4   Knock Knock
5   Phase Walk. Harvested Spell

ABILITIES
Hand-to-hand martial arts fighting.	Level 4
Stick and bladed weapons martial arts fighting	Level 4
Sight of the Explorer	Level 2
Wolf Blood	Level 1
Wolf Sight	Level 2
Knife Throwing	Level 1

EXISTING TITLES:

Inquisitive Mind

Trailblazer

David Copperfield

NEW TITLES:

Lucky Stiff

– Unlock new stat LUCK

– Plus 15 to Luck

Musketeer

– All for One. One for All.

– Plus 5 to all base stats.

– Loot boxes from bosses and monsters with at least a 25 level difference are automatically upgraded 1 tier.

Spartacus

– Plus 25% more experience gained from higher-level enemies.

– Plus 5 to CHA.

– Plus 5 to Luck.

Chapter Forty-Nine
Confection Talks

Inside the nicest wooden building in the center of town, made out of fine, finished lumber and with huge glass picture windows, we met in a conference room that could have been plucked from any corporate offices back on Earth. The long, mahogany table could seat a dozen, surrounded by comfortable captain's chairs. A wide window provided a great view of the main street.

"Where did you get all this?" I exclaimed.

Paul, the old guy on team The Great British Baking Show, patted the table and spoke in a Scottish accent. "One of the special loot boxes I got when I named this building as town hall."

"Wow. What else did you get?"

"We can chat about that later," Crystal interrupted as she dropped into one of the chairs near the end of the table. Definitely from New York. That's an unmistakable accent. The others took chairs near her, with Paul at the head of the table. I guess that made him the mayor, or something.

Crystal gestured to a chair on the opposite end of the table. She looked annoyed for some reason. I remained standing. "I'm Lucas."

"I know who you are," she said, her frown deepening.

"But I don't know you."

"The system must have given you my name."

"But we didn't," Paul smoothly interjected. "Lucas, it's a pleasure to meet you. I'm Paul MacDonald. Happy with my team assignment too."

"I hope you got some baking abilities."

He smiled widely, but Crystal interrupted again. "I'm Crystal Bennett. The four of us are the town leaders, and we have a lot to do, so let's get on with it."

I really wanted to ask how they got nominated to run the entire town, and how Tony and Burns had already snagged seats. I wasn't gunning for a spot on the town council. She just annoyed me.

Burns said, "Lucas, first big thing. Me and Tony hit level 25. Turns out we can not only make a second spell permanent, but we unlocked class selection!"

"Whoa. That's huge. I knew we'd get classes at some point, but not when."

"Level 25 is the golden ticket," Paul said. "Crystal and I are almost there."

"But you're not," Crystal told me, squashing the good mood. "All reports agree you performed with exceptional skill during the recent battle, so I do not begrudge the time we've spent sharing privileged information about unlocking classes. What I do not understand is why we're wasting precious time on stories about the second stage from a man who only barely reached level 7."

"Because I've been there."

"How, exactly? The AI voice clearly explained that one must reach at least level 10 to enter. Not to mention the fact that with your level, you should not have survived. I heard you ran into some very powerful monsters and not only survived, but killed them." Her tone made it clear what she thought of that.

"Were you this judgmental back on Earth, or is it a new ability you're trying to level up?"

She slammed the palm of one hand onto the table with a loud report, glaring. "We don't have time to waste on fools."

"Then how did you get elected?"

I couldn't stop myself that time. I was getting so tired of everyone assuming I was a weakling, even after I killed the stage boss and saved Burns and his entire team from the herd.

Crystal lunged to her feet and her arms swelled noticeably, just like in One Piece. That was cool enough that for a second I almost forgot how much I already disliked her.

"Enough," Tony said, his voice calm but firm. "Both of you, stop it."

Crystal hesitated, her glare fixed on me, violent intent clearly warring with restraint. I expected her to whine and demand, "I'll stop if he does."

If I poked at her one more time, could I get her to jump over the table?

"How about we restart this conversation over a box of donuts? Hard to get mad when Boston creams are involved," Paul said.

A wooden box appeared on the table in front of him, filled with 2 dozen donuts. It was like he'd snatched the display window tray right out of a Dunkin Donuts. The box held chocolate glazed, cream-filled, sugar-frosted, and yes, even Boston cream, with a hint of custard poking out one end.

"Best magic I've seen so far," I laughed as I tapped into my insane agility to snatch up the Boston cream closest to Crystal before she could reach it.

I wouldn't egg her on any more, but that didn't mean I'd let her get the first donut. People acting like arrogant jerks didn't get dibs. The donut was soft and warm and melted in my mouth in a burst of sugary delight.

Crystal glared just long enough for Tony to snag the next Boston cream. She had to look away from me to get the last one. Burns didn't care, but took a frosted cream-filled.

Paul selected a chocolate glazed donut, ate half of it in one bite, and sighed deeply. "Nectar from above. Smooth, light, and not claggy in the least."

I inhaled my donut, then snagged a chocolate glazed too. A warm sensation of wellness spread through me and I finally focused on the donuts enough for Identify to kick in.

Donuts. Confection. Consumable. Uncommon. These Earth treats could seduce a fang-toothed devourer. Contains a buff to improve health point regeneration by 25% for 5 minutes.

Too bad the buff wasn't stackable. I could easily see myself eating a full dozen to increase regeneration by another 300%.

"How did you unlock a donut ability?" I asked around a bite of chocolate.

"My team arrived here first. We got a bunch of special loot for founding the settlement. I even got a title. Master Chef. Automatically upgraded my Base Camp kitchen to legendary tier and added a separate confection oven."

"You need to try the Death by Chocolate cake," Tony said around another half donut.

"I would love to. In fact, how do I get my hands on another tray or 20 of those donuts?"

Paul grinned. "I'll add you to the queue." He then produced several woven baskets full of french fries, tater tots, and waffle-cut fries. They were crisp and hot, as if they'd just come out of the oven.

"Any ketchup?"

"I'm sorry, but not yet."

They were still delicious.

Crystal sat back, once more in control. She finished her third donut before saying. "Okay. I may have gotten a bit excited, so I will try again. Lucas, we brought you here because you are said to possess knowledge of the second stage. We need as much intelligence as possible as we plan our strategy for moving up to 700 people from Stepstone to a new settlement up there within the next 4 days."

Paul gestured with a golden cruller he pulled out of nowhere. "I have to admit, I'm curious too."

I repeated my standard line about the loot that boosted my stats at the price of slowing my leveling speed. Burns confirmed he'd seen me exhibit strength way beyond even his. They tried to ask follow-up questions, Paul and Burns intrigued, Crystal and Tony doubtful.

Instead I launched into my tale of survival on the second stage. I explained what I'd seen of the landscape, but skipped the part where I turned into a werewolf. I skimmed over most of the details of the battles, instead focusing on the fact that the werewolves and zombies were more intent on killing each other.

"They all had levels in the high 30s and into the mid-40s?" Paul asked, looking suddenly sick, as if he'd just eaten several dozen more donuts.

"Yeah. The werewolves regenerate almost immediately from even mortal wounds. They can tank a lot of damage before they run out of juice, and the zombies had energy weapons like these."

I dropped one each of the laser rifle and the stun gun onto the table.

"How many more of these do you have?" Crystal asked as they examined the rifles.

"Not nearly enough for everyone. I do have a few partial or broken ones. Any of your crafters have skills that might help with repairing these?"

"I doubt it," Paul said with a grimace. "But as more of us get classes in the coming days, we might unlock some."

"We need to focus on getting as many people to level 25 as possible," Tony said. "We'll need as many as we can get for our advance party."

"Whoever goes up first is going to need to be strong. The werewolves hunt in packs and the zombies travel in groups. I glimpsed the boss werewolf, and he was terrifying. Had to be at least level 50. I don't know if the zombies have a boss too."

"Level 50?" Crystal whispered.

I nodded and repeated my suspicion that the alpha had way more power than a few levels suggested. "I have no doubt he's going to be insanely difficult. At our current power levels, we cannot defeat him without significant loss of life."

"We need to level our elites," Tony said grimly.

"We do, but at the same time, we can't forget the folks who still haven't hit level 10," Paul reminded him.

"As folks unlock classes, they gain access to class spells. That increases our power many-fold. We need that strength to take on the second stage," Burns said.

"Sure, but we need to make sure everyone gets up there," Crystal responded.

"Hold on," I interrupted. They looked like they were sliding into an old argument that I doubted they'd ever really resolve, but they'd glossed over something very important. "What did you say about class spells?"

Crystal scowled like she wanted to object, but Burns spoke before she could. Grinning, he said, "Level 25 is way more important than we ever imagined. Unlocking classes is huge. Classes unlock new abilities and, more importantly, class spells."

Tony surprised me by interjecting, looking as excited as Burns. "Most of us have been running low on temporary spells, and even with two permanent spells, our magic power is limited. Class spells are an entirely new category of spells, and they don't run out of uses."

Burns nodded eagerly. "They're spells related to the class we select, and we get to equip up to 3 class spells at a time."

I leaned back, mind spinning with the ramifications. I'd suspected classes would be important, but this was huge. Three more spells that didn't have severely limited uses would unlock whole new levels of power. They were right. We needed to get as many people to level 25 as possible. It would be a game changer. I looked at both Tony and Burns more closely, triggering identify.

Burns Turner. Level 25 baby human. Team Pirates of the Caribbean. Class: Tempest Marshal.

Tony Waldau. Level 25 baby human. Team Avengers. Class: Paladin Savant.

So identify now showed classes. That was helpful. Hopefully it would start providing more info like it did for some monster types. Their classes sounded interesting, but didn't tell me as much about their builds as something from classic fantasy might like Fire Mage.

"We're deviating into subjects that are not relevant to you yet," Crystal interjected. "Time is limited. If there's nothing else . . ."

She clearly wanted me to bow out, but I said, "I want to highlight the fact that the zombies and werewolves seem to love fighting each other even more than they do us. That might change once we arrive up there en masse, but one of the major reasons I survived was because they were so busy killing each other, I found ways to take advantage of the moment."

"Hopefully we can work with that," Burns said.

I swept my gaze across the council and smiled, hoping to convey a sense of cooperation. "It's been great chatting. I can see you've got a lot to figure out. I've shared what I can. If you'll excuse me, I have to get hunting. As you know, I've got levels to earn."

"Hold on," Burns said, even though Tony was nodding in support of my plan and Crystal looked annoyed that she was missing her chance to kick me out. "We'll table the discussion about prioritizing leveling for now. We have some other matters to discuss that you should be here for."

I reluctantly returned to my seat. I needed to get out and hunt, and I really wanted to ride Switchblade some more. To make the time more productive, I snagged another donut, a honey-glazed that was still warm and sticky.

Burns continued. "Tony is putting together hunt teams to harvest as much experience from the remaining bulls as possible."

Tony looked as unenthusiastic about including me in those teams as I felt. The bulls could help folks on the lower end of the pool rise to level 10, or even help boost some of the forerunners up to level 25, but they were not what I needed.

"I don't think—" I started, but Burns held up a hand.

"I felt you should be aware of other priorities, but that was not where I was hoping you might fit in. You've shown a knack for exploring and surviving in unexpected situations against long odds. Now with your hover bike, you'll enjoy unparalleled mobility."

At least he wasn't suggesting I 'share' the bike with more deserving individuals.

He added, "One of our other major priorities is finding the remaining survivors still stuck or lost in the canyons and foothills to the east."

"You want me to explore up there and help find them?"

He nodded. "I will be tasking other explorer teams as well, but if you're willing to take a scout role in that endeavor, you could help identify threats or pockets of survivors to direct the other explorers to as needed."

I'd already planned to explore higher into the mountains for more dungeons or stronger monsters, but hadn't decided if I would head south or east. East it was, then. "Sure."

"Good," Tony said, giving me an approving nod like he was encouraging the fat kid in school to participate in gym class. "I'm glad you can find creative ways to help the cause of the wider community, despite lagging in the first few days."

Maybe his class should have been Inspiring Schmuck. I just shrugged and said, "It might surprise you how much I have actually done to help."

"We've seen your bravery and quick thinking," Burns interjected. "Before you go, I'll be designating half a dozen expedition leaders. I can link you all in a small group chat for easier communication."

"How can you do that?" I'd barely used my team chat and hadn't seen any broader functionality.

Paul said, "One of the town founder perks I received. I can assign town leadership." He nodded to the group around the table. "As well as assign special groups that open group chat functions and the potential for additional rewards."

"I'll always take more rewards."

"Good. We'll set it up—"

He was interrupted as Cyrus's voice boomed loudly outside for all to hear.

Congratulations! You plucky earthlings are doing great. Not only did you defeat the stage boss days ahead of schedule, but 2 of your leaders have reached the all-important level 25.

Why is level 25 important? Because not only does it unlock the second permanent spell slot, but also unlocks access to classes. That's right, once you hit level 25, you will be able to select a class.

Available classes will vary depending on your performance so far, your abilities, and current permanent spells. Once you choose your class, you cannot change your mind, and your new Class Spells tab will unlock. You will gain the ability to select up to 3 class spells to equip at any given time.

More details to follow, but congratulations again. You will need all of those shiny new spells if you hope to survive higher stages. So don't waste time.

"Curse him," Crystal muttered. "We were going to make a big announcement about the classes."

Yeah, she should have known better by now than to gripe about Cyrus out loud.

Cyrus's laughter echoed through the room, his jovial tone more intimate. "Everyone deserves to know the game secrets as soon as you do, Crystal. So many of the things you humans do are endearing. I'm so impressed. You honestly felt you control access to information. What a fantastic power play."

Crystal cringed, glaring around the room. She didn't seem to realize the danger she could have faced if Cyrus chose to get annoyed with her instead of cheering her on.

"So how many class spells do we get to choose from when we pick our 3 new spells?" I asked to divert the conversation to safer ground.

"That's a productive question, although you've got a long road ahead of you before you get your class, Lucas. I am looking forward to seeing the creative ways you use to get those last 3 levels."

"Thanks," I said dryly.

"It is my pleasure, as always."

After a moment, when it became clear he wasn't going to say anything else, Paul said, "You sound like you chat with that thing a lot."

I shrugged. "He's nicer than some humans I know."

Cyrus's voice boomed loudly over the town again.

To help keep you all motivated and focused on your end goals, which is one of the habits of people who want to live out the week, here's another glimpse of your final challenge.

My vision blinked out for a second. When it returned, I no longer sat in the conference room. Instead, I was looking down on a huge throne room, as if I clung to the peak of one of the enormous stone ribs holding up the roof.

The hall was larger than a football field, the floor a vast expanse of fine tiles worked into intricate patterns I bet made up some kind of magical runes.

Marisara, the nymph queen, sat on an ornate throne carved out of some kind of crystal that glowed with a silvery light.

She wore the same fine gown and outfit as in the last video Cyrus showed us, her ornate trident held upright in front of her. Arrayed before her was an army of the same angelic men in the last video, as well as dozens of gorgeous angelic women. They had the same watery wings and were clad in form-fitting gowns of silver scales that rippled with rainbow lights. They too carried tridents.

Behind the army of angels stood half a hundred stone gargoyles, crafted in gothic horror motifs. Devils, ogres, 3-headed dogs, and more stood at attention. Most looked larger than horses, while scores of smaller winged gargoyles clung to the lower reaches of the pillars around the outskirts of the room.

Queen Marisara's voice echoed through the chamber, her rough, slightly accented words carrying easily up to me. "Invaders have been spotted in the lower reaches. Activate the veils and bring me their eyes."

Eyes? That seemed random, although I had no idea what evil nymph queens might want as trophies. Would she mount our eyes on her wall, or eat them as some kind of soup delicacy?

The gargoyles spun and lumbered out the huge double doors, then the angelic warriors floated into the air and followed. In a moment, the hall appeared empty. I relaxed. I'd feared we'd see her split another enemy in half.

Marisara turned to stare directly at me, her flawless face cold. "You will die before you even see my throne, just like all the others."

Huh? Could she see me? Was I actually there in her throne room? I'd assumed I was watching, but through some kind of more interactive VR experience.

Marisara sprang from the throne like a Yoda ninja psycho death nymph. She reached me in a blink, her glowing trident slamming right into my eyes.

I recoiled with a shout of terror as the vision snapped off and I returned to the council room. I tumbled to the floor, my shout of surprise mingling with everyone else's as they too recoiled from the vision, white-faced and startled.

"Did everyone else just get speared through the eyes?" I asked as I climbed back to my feet. I liked VR games sometimes, but total immersion executions were not my thing.

Crystal visibly shuddered. "Eyes? What are you talking about? She threw her spear at me. Felt like I got skewered in the gut."

Odd. How could we all watch the same video and see different things?

"Trident," I said as I mulled it over.

"What?"

"She doesn't use a spear, at least not the one I saw. Spears with 3 points are called tridents. Like Aquaman."

She scowled and Paul said, "I started drowning, like she dropped a prison of water over my head."

Tony and Burns exchanged a look, but neither shared what they'd seen. "We all saw a different ending? Why?" Tony asked.

Cyrus actually answered. "That was my best approximation of how Marisara might react when she finally meets you. She has such diverse interests."

"I prefer boss monsters with only one power," Burns grumbled.

"That would be terribly boring," Cyrus responded in a chiding town. "And you may discover hidden benefits from those visions."

That sounded like he might be giving us a hint. I needed to consider that more, but for now I asked, "Does this mean her army will start hunting us?"

"Not yet. They will be preparing to deal with anyone who reaches their stage, though. Use the time you've got left wisely. Have a nice night."

Chapter Fifty
Lifebane Phantoms

Paul offered me the last donut, then activated my Explorer team chat. He promised to add the other leaders soon. He wanted me to wait to meet with them, but I declined. That new vision of Marisara was more than enough motivation to get me moving.

When I left the town hall, I strode past Sam's tavern. It was even more crowded than before. I checked the sky to confirm the sun was just past its zenith. Why did people look like they were planning to party all afternoon? We had hours of daylight left. Then again, most of them were already level 10, but did they think that was enough to keep them alive?

Shaking my head, I scanned a few people. Identify confirmed most were between level 10 and 15, from teams I had not met before. I spotted team Dragnet, team Die Hard, team Matrix, and team Halo. That last one was a big guy with some cool sci-fi looking armor. I nearly went over to ask what weapons he'd gotten.

Then I spotted a skinny fellow stumbling out of the tavern. He looked pale and a bit skeletal, like he'd suffered from a chronic illness for years. He staggered as if drunk. Odd. Cyrus had said our Earth diseases would fade away, cured by our innate regeneration. Healing potions should deal with the rest.

Hank Solomon. Level 15 baby human. Team Star Wars.

I guess I still didn't understand the system well enough. I turned away, but paused. A nagging sense of unease turned me back around. Something about

Hank triggered a thought that I couldn't quite place my finger on, but I felt it might be important.

"Are you okay?"

Hank stopped, swaying in the street, but didn't respond. A middle-aged woman beside him said, "Please don't bother poor Hank. He's not well."

Alice Henderson. Baby human level 18. Team Friday the 13th.

She noticed my grimace and sighed. "Yes, I know. Terrible team for a healer." Alice did look like a healer with her black hair pulled into a pony tail and wearing a pristine white lab coat.

"So what's wrong with Hank?" The poor guy still hadn't moved, but looked even paler, if possible. He swayed where he stood, as if about to collapse.

"I don't know," Alice snapped, then took a deep breath, closing her eyes for a second. "Sorry. Everyone keeps asking that, but I don't know. I can't heal him. My spells and healing potions only revive him for a few minutes."

I slowly paced around the unmoving Hank, frowning as I tried to grasp the thought flitting at the back of my mind. "So he's sick? No injuries."

"Are you a healer?"

"No, but I feel like I should recognize this."

Alice sighed again. "I wish someone did. Hank's not the only one sick, but he's one of the worst. They just slowly deteriorate, wasting away like they've got stage 4 cancer on steroids."

"Any injuries?"

"I don't mean to be rude, but I have to get Hank back to the clinic."

They had a clinic already. I hadn't seen that building when we explored earlier. "Just humor me. Please."

"Fine. No major wounds. Just welts on his shoulders and back."

Information blazed through my mind like the opening of a floodgate and I realized what was going on. Those thoughts I'd been feeling were the half-formed memories from getting force-fed the monster dictionary. Now one entry snapped into clarify.

Lifebane Phantom. Monster. Ethereal. This nasty parasite attaches itself to a victim's back and plunges its mosquito-like beak into their heart. Like the nosiest of mother in laws, they slowly drain spirit and life

and counteract all attempts at healing the victim. Immune to physical attacks.

There was more, but I skipped it. I'd read enough. "He's not sick. He's being drained by an invisible parasite."

"What?" Alice exclaimed. She didn't look like she believed me, but I didn't have time to argue. Hank looked like he could die any second.

"Hit him with a healing spell. Quick."

"It'll only help for a minute."

"That's enough. Do it."

"Listen, I appreciate your interest, but I've already tried it many times."

I pulled Soulrend into my hand. Alice stumbled back with a cry of surprise that drew the attention of nearby people. Some pointed or backed up when they saw me apparently threatening a drunk.

One guy shouted, "Hey, back off, buddy."

I ignored him and slashed Soulrend down Hank's back, an inch from his shirt. Alice screamed and a couple people drew their own weapons, shouting for me to stop. A high-pitched shriek silenced them all. I still couldn't see the lifebane phantom, but I felt Soulrend cut through its needle-like beak. Hank screamed and fell to his hands and knees with blood spurting out of the center of his back, right where his heart would be.

"Stop it!" the same guy shouted, raising a sword threateningly.

"Back off," I snapped and imagined the creature crouching on Hank's back. I swung again. This time I felt a lot more resistance. I'd guessed right and hit the monster's body.

Another louder shriek blasted my ears. These things were loud.

"What are you doing?" Alice shouted as Hank moaned and nearly fell over.

"Heal him!" I shouted back, swinging again. I kept slashing blindly at the monster clinging to Hank's back, and with every swing, the beast shrieked again. Finally, after swinging half a dozen times, I got the message I'd been waiting for.

Congratulations, Lucas! You have defeated Lifebane Phantom. Level 21.

No bonus experience, even though I was only level 7. The monster was 14 levels higher. That should be close enough to the 15 level target Cyrus had explained I needed. Lame.

I triggered Soul Feed, and a surprisingly dense cloud of white smoke boiled out of thin air where the monster had been. It instantly topped off my pools and pushed my stats to 150% for 5 minutes. My Tesla Coil bracelet had already warmed against my skin as it absorbed a bunch of power from the invisible parasite.

I accepted the prompt to loot the monster. Hank swayed, and suddenly color returned to his cheeks. The flow of blood stopped pouring from his back and he took a deep breath.

The guy with the sword approached, flanked by 2 other armed men. "What's going on here?"

At the same time, I was shocked to hear Crystal shouting the same thing. She rushed over, glaring at me.

Alice dropped to one knee beside Hank and placed one hand on his head. Her eyes widened and she laughed. "You did it! He's healing."

"Explain yourself," Crystal ordered, looking from me to Hank.

"I thought you had tons of meetings today." Her tone made me less than cooperative.

She grabbed my jacket and shouted, "What did you do?"

Wow. She might be an arrogant, self-important crone, but she had guts. I spoke calmly, but firmly. "Let go of my jacket, Crystal."

Alice leaped to her feet and threw her arms around me, knocking Crystal back. "You saved Hank's life! I never imagined he had an invisible parasite sucking away his life."

The armed guys backed up a step, sheathing weapons and the lead guy said, "Sorry."

As soon as Alice released me, Crystal grabbed my jacket again, her expression kind of crazy. She yanked me forward with surprising strength. "Come with me!"

I might respect strength, but I couldn't stand bullies. I slammed my palm against her forearm, breaking her grip. "You need to calm down."

"Get your Luffy backside moving. This is important," she snapped, grabbing at me again, her arm swelling to twice its size.

She seized my wrist with a vicelike grip. Had to be some kind of ability, but instead of fear I felt a surge of relief so strong it startled me until I realized what it meant.

I'd been fighting crazy alien monsters for the past few days, nearly dying multiple times per day as I figured out this insane death world. I'd trained extensively in Wing Chun Do and Kali martial arts, but a lot of those skills proved meaningless against invisible ghosts or trolls the size of vacation homes.

I hadn't fought humans since arriving, and the feel of an actual person grabbing my wrist in a threatening manner was a danger I actually had trained to deal with. Suppressing a smile, I tapped into my level-4 hand-to-hand martial fighting ability and used her own strength against her as I twisted my arm, turning her pinky up and bending her wrist into a lock. She growled and reached for me with her other hand.

I twisted farther. Hard. Her wrist snapped with an audible crack.

Crystal screamed and fell back, clutching her broken wrist. "Nami Sanji Nico! What'd you do that for?"

"I warned you." I kept my tone calm.

Most of the other people had retreated from our clash, but a young woman in a shimmery gray robe glided past us. Her face was not covered, but still weirdly indistinct. She was heading for Alice, but Crystal intercepted her.

She looked at the weirdly indistinct girl like she was seeing a miracle. "Lily! You're okay."

Crystal stepped forward to hug the young woman, and understanding clicked in my mind.

"Don't!" I shouted as Lily spread her arms to embrace Crystal. As the two hugged, Lily's head elongated, like she'd just grown a snake's neck. Her nose extended into a long needle and she twisted it down toward Crystal's back.

I slashed through her skull with Soulrend. Lily exploded into mist.

Congratulations, Lucas! You have defeated Lifebane Phantom clone. Level 1.

I accepted the prompt to loot the monster just as Crystal stumbled and turned. Her eyes widened in horror as she looked from the still-dispersing remains of the monster impersonating Lily and my blade. Her face twisted in rage and she swelled with power.

"You murdered my sister!"

So many things suddenly made sense as Crystal screamed and punched at me with a fist that grew to the size of my head.

She might be immensely powerful and enraged, but she broadcast that punch so wide, I bet people on the far side of town could see it coming. I leaned aside, knocking her fist away slightly with my free hand. Her fist shot half an inch past my torso but struck nothing but air. Crystal stumbled forward and tripped. She lunged back to her feet instantly and spun, her face red with rage.

Alice jumped in front her, hands raised in a calming motion. "Stop! That wasn't Lily. It was a monster pretending to be her. He just saved your life."

Crystal hesitated, then looked to me, murder still in her gaze. "Explain yourself. Now!"

I reviewed the monster dictionary entry I'd only skimmed earlier and shared it with her.

When Lifebane Phantom has drained sufficient life force, it will produce a clone. In this way, it reproduces and spreads its parasitic curse. Clones take on the appearance of the victim and remain mostly visible until their first feeding.

"No." Crystal seemed to wilt and sagged against Alice. "Lily."

"Who's Lily?"

"My sister. She's been sick the past 2 days and getting worse, despite everything we've tried. I was trying to lead you to her to see if you could help her like you did Hank."

I could think of a better way to ask, but I didn't say it. Crystal looked emotionally wrung out and I wasn't a big enough jerk to push her when she was down.

Alice gripped her shoulders. "According to that description, she might still be alive."

"She's in the clinic too?" When Alice nodded, I said, "So let's go."

Together we raced two streets over to a tidy little log cabin with flower boxes in the front windows. One big room filled most of the interior. Six people lay on comfortable single beds. They all looked sick like Hank, to varying degrees.

"Where's Beth?" Alice demanded, looking around. The room was empty except for the sick patients.

Crystal rushed to a girl on the far left side who did look remarkably like the clone I'd just dispatched, but I froze, my gaze locked on the figure laying on the opposite side of the room.

"Tomas?"

Chapter Fifty-One
Family Ties

It was Tomas. My brother looked more like a corpse than a living soul, although his chest was moving ever so slightly. He looked like he could die any second, and even as I looked, a shimmering, ghostly form materialized above Tomas's bed. It condensed into a slightly blurry twin of my brother.

"Hurry. Over here," Crystal called, but I was already moving.

Enraged, I rushed into the room, but even as I did, another entry from the dictionary popped into my mind and cold dread splashed across my thoughts and broke through my anger.

Once Lifebane Phantoms have collected enough victims to begin producing clones, the location will transform into a nest where every victim will spawn a new Lifebane Phantom to continue spreading the species.

Oh, hell no. I'd just lunged into the middle of a nest of invisible parasitic life-draining monsters.

"Crystal, get out of here!" I shouted as I triggered Energy Ward and spun, slashing my blade blindly in a complete circle around me.

"What?" Crystal complained, then she stumbled, her face growing pale.

Alice, who had stopped in the doorway, took a step forward, but I shouted, "No! Seal the door! There are other phantoms in here."

I didn't know if closing the door would actually stop ethereal monsters, but I didn't have time to care. Soulrend cut through something invisible that offered a bit of resistance. It had been directly behind me, heading for my back. The Lifebane Phantom shrieked in pain.

Energy Ward appeared around me and instantly the shimmering defensive aura prickled at my right side. It was deflecting an incoming attack.

Thank Cyrus I'd gotten the upgrade to block spiritual attacks. It seemed to work on the phantoms. I spun along with the impulse from Energy Ward, slashing through the space where the incoming monster would pass, and my blade again cut through some ethereal resistance. Another phantom shrieked.

I spun back around to slash at the first phantom I'd just injured, but didn't feel anything. It had moved. How many were there?

I kept spinning, trying to move toward Tomas's bed to protect him, but Energy Ward started pinging rapidly as several of the monsters converged on me from three sides. I wanted to dive and roll away, but then I wouldn't know where the enemy were.

So I forced myself to stay in place and spin, blade flashing toward empty spots in the air following Energy Ward's hints. I caught two of the monsters and their shrieks of anger and pain filled the little cabin. My bracelet grew warm as it absorbed power, but I did not receive any notifications of kills.

I kept spinning, slashing wildly and blindly, straining every sense for any indication of the monsters. I'd managed to glimpse the nearly invisible rents in space to those pocket rooms. There had to be a way to sense the monsters.

Several more pings from Energy Ward indicated targets. I spun and slashed, but felt nothing. Were the monsters getting smarter?

Then I felt a drain on my life. I felt no pain or injury, but I was so hyper focused at the moment, the tiny drain caught my attention instantly. One of the monsters had slipped through Energy Ward somehow.

"Eat this," I growled, slashing Soulrend down my back. The angle was awkward, but I managed to catch something that time and the monster shrieked.

I spun and slashed in a frenzy, my blade blurring until the glowing blue after-images of its motion seemed to form a solid wall in front of me, right where that monster had been.

Congratulations, Lucas. You have defeated Lifebane Phantom, level 18.

I barely noticed the notification before Energy Ward pinged again, this time both high and low. The monsters were trying to dive in from different heights to avoid my blade.

I ducked and spun, catching the low monster, then returning with an overhand to hopefully catch the tail end of the one diving from above. Two shrieks of pain marked my cuts and I grinned viciously.

More pings from Energy Ward. Time ceased to exist and everything outside of the range of Energy Ward faded away as I focused every point in perception in trying to find the phantoms. I poured every bit of agility and dexterity into a spinning, rolling dance of death back and forth across the room.

The phantoms poured in, far more than I would have expected from such a new nest. Had others followed the sick in here to set up camp? It didn't matter, I would purge them all.

Every muscle moved in sync as I fell into a battle trance deeper than anything I'd ever experienced before. My heightened intelligence and perception pushed against the limits of my vision, syncing every move with the tingles I felt from Energy Ward.

The cabin filled with the screams and angry hissing of invisible monsters as I cut through them, my body blurring, wielding death in the form of a glowing blue blade. Kill notifications started trickling in and with each one, I triggered Soul Feed to replenish my pools and keep me fighting at peak form.

Then another notification popped into my mind before I could wave it away.

Congratulations, Lucas! A new synergy has been unlocked between Energy Ward, Soul Feed, and Wolf Sight. Wolf Sight upgraded to level 2. Life force absorbed from a monster using Soul Feed will resonate with you, allowing you to more clearly sense similar monsters and see through illusions or invisibility obscuring them from your sight.

"Yes!" I laughed as my vision cleared and suddenly I could see half a dozen ethereal shapes flitting all around me. They looked like children with skeletal limbs capped in long claws, and snakelike heads tipped with 8-inch mosquito beaks.

They did not know I could see them, so kept sweeping in, trying to plunge those deadly needle-like beaks into my back. This time, I leaped to meet them, my strikes sure. Before they could escape, I slashed every last one of them apart.

Then I scanned the room, spotting more phantoms clinging to the backs of every victim. Crystal was lying on the floor not far from the door, clawing at it weakly, with 4 Lifebane Phantoms all clinging to her back.

Alice had ignored my warning and rushed in to help. She huddled over Crystal, trying vainly to heal her, even with 3 more monsters sucking her own life dry. She looked ready to keel over any second.

With a shout of rage, I lunged and tore apart every last monster on the two women, then rushed to every patient, flipping them over onto their stomachs so I could kill the monsters draining their life away.

High-pitched shrieks punctuated every slash as I tore the invisible monsters apart. Only when I got the final notification did I sag to my knees next to my brother's bed and place a hand to his throat. His pulse was weak and thready.

"Lucas?" Crystal coughed as she and Alice helped each other to stand. Color returned to their faces, and they both stood taller, either from Alice's healing spell, or from healing potions.

"Hang in there, Tomas," I told him as I pulled off my Tesla Coil bracelet and fastened it to his wrist. Immediately color started flooding back into his cheeks. He'd be okay.

The missing Beth returned with armed men. She'd seen Lily's clone appear and had fled to get help. She too was a healer. With their spells and several healing potions, all the victims soon recovered.

Crystal finally stood from her sister's side. Without a word, she walked up to me and threw her arms around my waist, burying her face against my chest. I held her awkwardly as she sobbed into my shirt.

Finally she pushed away and swiped at her eyes. "Thank you, Lucas. I've been horrid to you and you saved Lily's life."

"You are pretty terrible," I said with a smile, making her laugh weakly.

Tomas shouted, "Hey, I just got 2 levels! How does that work?"

I turned to find him sitting up, looking like himself. He wore a leather jacket, gray t-shirt and tactical pants. His brown hair was disheveled, and he still looked too thin, but healthy.

Tomas Walker. Baby human level 14. Team Fast & Furious.

"Where am I?" he added, then spotted me and waved. "Hey, Lucas! When did you get here?" Then he frowned and looked around, as if noticing the room for the first time. "Ah, where is here, by the way?"

He jumped out of bed and promptly collapsed to the wooden floor with a grunt. I hauled him up and hugged him.

"Ah, Lucas, you're crushing my ribs," he coughed.

"Sorry. It's good to see you recovering." I lowered him to his bed where he plopped onto his backside.

"Why am I so weak?" he groaned.

"You've been mostly dead all day."

"Perfect movie line drop!" Cyrus exclaimed, making Tomas jump so hard, he would have fallen out of the bed if I hadn't nudged him back in.

"Princess Bride. Seemed appropriate."

"I agree. You humans like taking photos of every moment of your lives, so this one's on me."

A 5x7 photo dropped into my hand. It showed me and Tomas posed standing in front of his cot, with Inigo Montoya and Fezzik from the movie standing on either side, flashing cheesy grins and identical thumbs' up.

"That's, um, super cool," Tomas said cautiously, glancing from the odd photo toward the ceiling.

"You're welcome," Cyrus said with booming good cheer.

Tomas waited a moment, glancing around expectantly. When Cyrus didn't say anything else, he blew out a breath. "That was really weird."

I shrugged. "You get used to it."

Tomas rubbed his head and asked, "So, what happened? How are we inside an actual house? Where's my team?"

I recounted what I knew and he glanced around the other recovering patients. Word was quickly spreading, and friends and teammates were starting to pour in. "Invisible parasites? That sucks."

I snorted. "Lame joke, bro. But yeah, you're lucky I realized what was going on, or you would have died."

"Thanks." He lifted his wrist and examined the Tesla Coil bracelet. "And thanks for the sweet item."

"Yeah, I'll need that back." I held out my hand.

"Indian giver," he grumbled, but took it off and handed it over. It had given him a lot of energy, but I'd absorbed a ton from killing so many Lifebane Phantoms, so it still felt warm with captured power.

I told him about the bracelet's powers as I accepted the prompt to loot the monsters. "It's saved my life several times."

"That's incredible. How can you be only level 7?"

I sighed. *Here we go again.*

Across the room, Lily shouted, "I got 2 levels too, and a gold Lazarus loot box!"

"I got one too," another victim exclaimed.

"How about you?" I asked Tomas.

He checked and laughed. "I did." The loot box appeared in front of him, then vanished as he opened it, revealing a single scroll. No one but the owner of the loot box could claim it, and it soon flashed, then disappeared as Tomas read it.

He grinned. "Scroll gave me plus 10 to magical resistance."

"Appropriate."

I checked my own messages. In addition to the notifications of killing the monsters, I got a silver Bouncer loot box for breaking Crystal's wrist. Inside was a scroll that upgraded my hand-to-hand martial arts ability one level. I got an even better one next.

Congratulations, Lucas! For solving the puzzle of the ghostly parasites, defeating the Lifebane Phantoms, and saving all the victims, you receive an emerald Doctor Quinn loot box.

The huge, glittering emerald appeared in the air in front of me, generating a lot of excitement. Most of the people packing the little cabin had never seen an emerald loot box before. It held 3 scrolls.

Upgrade scroll. Plus 10 to magical resistance.

Upgrade scroll. Plus 1 level to Wolf Blood. Each level increases health and mana regeneration by 10%.

Upgrade scroll. Plus 1 level to Soul Feed. It now actively drains power from monsters on contact.

"Whoa!" I explained the upgrades to Tomas.

"Those are amazing. I'm surprised you didn't get a level."

I gave him a shortened version of the same line I'd given everyone else. Tomas frowned as he listened.

"How many monsters do you need to kill to gain a level?"

"A bunch. I'm working on it."

"You'll get there," he told me with an encouraging smile.

I could tell he still didn't understand. Like just about everyone else, he still thought it was just a matter of focusing and not slacking off. I didn't bother arguing about it. Cyrus wouldn't let me tell the entire truth, so what else could I tell him?

It didn't matter. I'd found him. Tomas was safe! I relaxed in a way I had not managed since waking up on this death world. Now I felt like I could take on any insanity Cyrus chose to drop me into.

"Hey, you can absorb energy from monsters?" Tomas asked. "What if one of those parasite monsters tries stabbing you? They drain life, but now you drain it back. Which of you would win?"

"Good question. I have no idea." I glanced up and asked, "Can you clarify?"

"I should have expected great questions would run in the family," Cyrus answered immediately, making Tomas jump again. "Indeed, your upgrade trumps most life and energy draining abilities that require a monster to touch you. Higher-leveled monsters may still overwhelm your ability."

"That's an even better upgrade than I thought. Thanks."

"You've developed a knack for taking on ethereal monsters. I'll have to see about adding a few more to keep life interesting."

"You don't have to do that." I shared a look with Tomas, whose eyes had gone wide.

"Don't be so modest, Lucas. I'm here to help challenge everyone to reach their ultimate potential."

I sighed and dropped it. Then I grabbed Tomas's shoulder. "Hey, did you know Jane is in town?"

"Where? Let's go!"

Chapter Fifty-Two
Bringin' Home the Bacon

Tomas was quivering with eagerness to reunite with Jane, but as we rounded one corner, I had to stop.

"Hold the phone. I need to get one."

An actual food cart parked on the side of the road was selling piles of french fries in tall woven baskets. The fries Paul had shared around during the meeting had been some of the best I'd ever eaten. It was a simple taste of home, and seeing more fries, I couldn't resist the nostalgic urge to buy more.

"French fries?" Tomas asked as I paid a couple mana crystals for about a gallon of crisp, fresh french fries.

"So good," I mumbled around a mouthful of hot fries. Tomas dug in and we resumed our trek across town.

I let Tomas go first when we reached Jane's tent. He rushed inside, shouting her name, and she squealed with glee. Even though I waited a full 5 minutes, they were still standing in the middle of the room, kissing passionately. He was holding her, while she wrapped arms and legs around his torso.

"Hey, Jane," I said, waving a fry. "Got any steak to go with these? Saving Tomas so much gets exhausting."

She laughed and finally released Tomas to rush over and give me a bone-crushing hug. I barely tossed the basket of fries into my inventory in time. "Thank you, Lucas!"

"I definitely did it for you."

"Hey!" Tomas exclaimed in mock outrage.

We caught up over perhaps the best fillet mignon I'd ever eaten. With all the organic material Jane had pumped into the oven, it produced truly gourmet meals. My steak was covered in a hollandaise sauce that had to qualify as divine-level loot. Still no ketchup, but hollandaise sauce worked pretty good too, and we polished off the last of the fries.

"I'm going to need to buy a few more buckets of those before I head out of town again."

"No worries we'll run out," Jane said, tearing her eyes off of Tomas for a second. "There's a guy who permanented a spell to make potatoes. He's pumping them out by the bushel full."

"Why would he do that?" Tomas asked.

"I heard he used to be a chef. Used up all his temporary spells just surviving, so when he got to level 10, the potato spell was the only one he had left."

"Poor guy. What a waste."

She shrugged. "I didn't hear you complaining about the fries."

Fair point, but how would he progress with only potato magic? Pushing thoughts of the potato wizard aside, we caught up on each other's adventures. Tomas still had an entire team. They'd found each other quicker than we had. I couldn't wait to meet them.

I enjoyed every second of our chat. I could almost forget we were sitting in a magical tent in a death battle world where hundreds of people had already died. Sitting in comfortable chairs, eating good food, and chatting together felt like so many times I'd visited them in Denver, or that time they came to Flagstaff to visit me. Isabella had managed to come up from Glendale, and we'd had an incredible time hanging out.

I almost wished Isabella was there sitting next to me, but that would mean she'd gotten sucked into this deadly game too. I would not wish that on anyone. If anything, I wished I could get Tomas and Jane back out. I would much prefer facing the nightmares to come knowing they were safe.

As we discussed our spells and stats, Jane asked, "Hey, have either of you guys gotten a weird stat that hasn't unlocked yet?"

"What do you mean?" Tomas asked.

I was too shocked to respond for a second. I'd thought my weird CHA stat was unique. Figured maybe Cyrus was just messing with me. His sense of humor got strange sometimes.

Jane sighed. "I got a weird scroll in a loot box that unlocked a new stat called WIL. I've gotten a few points in it, but can't seem to figure out how to make it work."

"Like WIL for Willpower?" Tomas asked.

"That's what I figure."

"Huh. I haven't heard of anyone with unique stats. Everyone I've talked to has all the same base and secondary stats. Have you?" My brother turned to me.

"Yeah!" I exclaimed. "I got a unique extra stat too. CHA. Can't figure it out. Thought it was a glitch or something."

"CHA, as in Charisma?" Tomas asked with a frown. "I've heard of people unlocking a Charisma stat."

"It's like the stat is a placeholder until I get a spell or ability or something that officially uses Charisma."

"Just like me! It sucks that your Charisma stat is locked like my WIL stat, but at least now I know I'm not the only one."

"It's still weird," Tomas said.

I totally agreed, but some of my worry about CHA subsided. I'd find a way to unlock it eventually. We resumed chatting, but then Tomas heard about Switchblade.

"We have to go ride!"

"Later," Jane said. I hadn't expected that. She loved Switchblade maybe even more than I did, but she hadn't let go of Tomas's hand since she'd finished her steak.

I could take a hint, but it still required a force of will to stand. I'd found Tomas! The three of us should be hanging out all afternoon. The last few minutes had been by far the happiest I'd felt since getting ripped away from Earth. I'd beat down whatever I needed to in order to win and keep them safe, but that didn't mean I wanted to get right back to it so soon.

Countdown timers waited for no man, though. So I forced a smile. "I've got to go anyway. We can ride when I get back."

"Go?" Tomas asked with a frown. "It's already afternoon."

"I know. I've got 3 levels to climb and I can't waste half a day lounging around town."

"Okay, we'll come," Tomas said reluctantly. "Just let me find my team."

Jane gave him a look like she'd knock him out herself before letting him out of her tent so soon.

"No, you two catch up. You can't keep up with me anyway."

"You can't go hunting alone," Tomas protested. "Lucas, you're only level 7."

"Low level, but increased stats, remember? I can take care of myself."

He argued more, but I shut him down every time. Finally Jane placed a hand on his arm and said, "Tomas, trust him."

"At least keep me updated on your location," Tomas urged.

"Do you have Navigation? Jane doesn't."

"I do. I got a big upgrade to it too."

"Team Fast and Furious. Makes sense. I got upgrades too."

Now that Paul had opened up more chat features for me, I found I could add more people to my contacts list. Once Tomas accepted my invite, I found I could indeed share waypoints and locations between our maps since we both had upgrades. That helped ease some of his worries.

"Check in every hour or we'll come looking for you," he warned.

"Yes, mom." I appreciated their concern, but doubted they had to worry. It was a good reminder to keep Ruby and Steve updated too. I sent them a text before I forgot.

Besides, as strong as I might be compared to most of the other people, I was still a weakling compared to most of the monsters on stage 2. Even down here in the first stage I could die easily if I got cocky.

They insisted on walking to the edge of town with me, and Jane had to hold Tomas back when he saw Switchblade.

"If you hadn't wasted so much time feeding the local wildlife, you would've gotten a turn already."

"Very funny."

I waved and hit the throttle. The sun was hanging low over the distant western mountains above the stage 2 plateau as I accelerated away. My hover bike tore easily through the tall grasses as I banked northeast. Hopefully a lot of stronger monsters would come out at night. I planned to hunt them all.

That didn't mean I would ignore the journey, though. I grinned as I swooped in lazy arcs through the tall grasses of the plain, mastering the feel of my new bike. It responded with incredible precision. Just having it boosted my confidence. I could cover miles at speed, with built-in weapons and defenses.

Wind rushed past my face, and I never got tired of how clean the air smelled, laced with hints of pine from the mountains. As I flashed across the wide grassland toward the first row of foothills, I experimented with my mini map.

I found I could link it to my bike's display screen, which gave me a wider area, like a GPS map. I activated route recording and found an option to ping my location out to selected people in regular intervals. I chose every hour, sending it to Ruby, Tomas, and the explorer leaders chat.

In minutes, I reached the eastern mountains and turned north, skirting the foothills along the outer edge of the plain. I spotted no large monsters and ignored the tiny blips of red my screen picked out. I was looking for larger prey.

To the north, the sheer cliff blocking the entire stage rose several thousand feet in smooth stone. From my current angle, it looked even more breathtaking than when I'd seen it from up on stage 2. The spectacular waterfall cascading down its entire length plunged into a pristine lake, and the spray concealed the lower parts of the cliff in billowing mists. I bet I could find water monsters in there, but I lacked the abilities to fight well underwater.

Instead, I chose a gap between two of the nearest foothills and headed for higher ground. A stream ran down the center of the gap, flanked by forested lowlands before the ground rose on either side up the hills. More of the towering monster trees I'd seen in other mountain areas marched up the gap, with only sparse undergrowth between.

That made riding through it easy, but I still slowed so I didn't blindly barrel into a pack of monsters. Over the next hour, I wound higher into the hills, spotting no sign of human life as twilight faded to night and brilliant stars splashed across the night sky.

I caught glimpses of monsters slinking back into the increasing shadows, but didn't stop to engage. They were all below level 25. I did send a running commentary to the explorer leaders chat, which I renamed to Explorers, marking each monster sighting with any information I could glean from Identify. Wolf Sight and Sight of the Explorer worked together in perfect tandem to help me pierce the darkness and Identify monsters at a distance.

I eventually topped out in a high mountain meadow, dotted with trees and bushes, the grassy land mostly flat. Three different gullies and one wider canyon pushed deeper into the mountains from there. I made a couple quick circuits of the meadow and picked the smallest gully. I figured if anything interesting might be hiding nearby, it was probably in the deepest, darkest area. With Wolf Sight, the darkness did not bother me, giving me a huge advantage.

I slowed as I wound up the tight confines of the gully, walls of stone rising steeply on either side barely 20 yards from each other. I'd worried the vegetation might prove too thick to ride through, but at my maximum elevation of 6 feet, I was able to fly over the worst parts and dodge the higher branches. That made for fun riding as I banked and turned around the obstacles.

Five minutes later, I reached another hidden mountain valley. This one was smaller, an open expanse of lush grasses with a little stream burbling down the right-hand side. Steep hillsides rose all around with no obvious exit point. That meant the cluster of monsters on the opposite side of the meadow were either camping there or had to be part mountain goat.

I slowed even more and ghosted forward, my hover bike barely humming as I studied what I first took to be a herd of grazing animals. Two burly men stood on either end of the herd, their muscled bare torsos visible above the grasses. Either they were really tall, or standing on something as they oversaw a herd of animals mostly concealed by the tall grasses. I caught glimpses of heavy black fur while the sound of grunting and snorting carried easily in the still air.

One of the men spotted me, despite the distance and the low light. The stars and moons cast the area in dim, silvery light, but most humans would struggle to see that far. The man hefted a long ax polearm, bellowed a surprisingly animal roar of challenge, and started galloping toward me.

It took me a second to realize what I was seeing and Identify kicked in at the same time.

Hog-taur. Level 24. Rare. Of the many varieties of monster melded with humanoid forms, the hog-taur is one of the rarest. That may be one of the reasons they're also one of the most aggressive. These powerful monsters have a decent level of intelligence and use weapons. They rarely use spells but overwhelm enemies with sheer force and numbers.

Hog-taur? Really?

As soon as the first man-hog started galloping in my direction, his enormous, muscular pig body lunged into view with every stride. The entire herd bellowed and joined the charge. It was a herd of enormous, black-haired boars with bodies the size of ponies and long tusks like scimitars extending out either side of their heavy muzzles.

Perfect. Just the kind of opponents I needed.

Since the lead hog-taur was rushing straight at me, I triggered my Shattercore Ballista. The bright blue beam leaped from my bike and flashed across the meadow to the charging monster in an instant. It tried deflecting with its ax, but the energy bolt blasted right through the steel and detonated against the hog-taur's chest, splattering blood and gore all over the meadow.

I waved away the notification of kill and accelerated, banking at an angle to the onrushing herd of maybe 20 boars and one other hog-taur. I needed to thin their ranks a bit before closing. Even with my Dome Shield and Energy Ward, those huge tusks would tear through my defenses all too quickly.

As the tide of angry boars shifted to follow my path and continued closing at impressive speed, I pulled a couple steaks out of my inventory, slapped smiling emoji stickers with lightning bolt icons cutting across the little smiley faces onto the meat, and hurled them at the giant pigs. I needed to get some blocks of wood or something to use next time.

The boars did not even slow to eat the meat, but charged right over the steaks. Bad idea. Lightning blasted out of the ground in sheets of blue-white destruction.

Item. Emoji trap, times 2. Lightning trap. Forget sticking a fork into an outlet. These babies unleash a barrage of lightning bolts across anyone within 5 yards when triggered. Each trap strikes up to 5 targets with up to 3 lightning bolts.

The front ranks of the herd collapsed in a writhing, bellowing pile of half-roasted pork. Those were the only two electric lightning bombs in the emoji set, unfortunately. The brilliant traps were proving incredible. The fresh mountain air suddenly smelled like a barbecue. If only I had some spicy barbecue sauce.

The rest of the herd swerved around the fallen boars, but the hog-taur on the far side of the herd bellowed and waved a club in the air over its head. At first, I thought it was just shouting a challenge, but the rest of the herd slowed and bunched close together. That would've been the spot to hit them with a lightning bomb.

Darkness gathered around the clustered herd of boars, punctuated by flashes of red light. The hairs of my arms rose as the air became charged with power.

"This can't be good," I muttered as I swerved Switchblade straight at the last remaining hog-taur.

Maybe they rarely used magic, but clearly this monster was one of the exceptions. I needed to disrupt the spell before they could finish casting. I accelerated hard and shot toward the creature, who remained motionless, both hands raised above its head, club surrounded by roiling darkness. If only I hadn't already used my ballista, the setup would've been perfect. As I closed in, Identify triggered.

Hog-taur. Level 25. Elite. Herd overseer. These guys are testaments to the truth that schoolyard bullies do find productive employment more often than you might think.

It was only 1 level higher than the other hog-taur, but even from that distance I could feel a much more powerful aura. I drew Soulrend as I closed on the monster at 80 miles an hour. Three seconds and I could sever its head.

The air directly in front of the monster shimmered like a heatwave, and a giant boar snout, glowing with golden light erupted out of thin air, shooting straight at me. I was way too close to dodge, so triggered Switchblade's Shield Dome and ducked low over the handlebars.

The ghostly boar snout slammed into my shield and shattered it. An eyeblink later, I plunged into the middle of the glowing shape as it opened its huge maw to swallow me and Switchblade whole.

Intense pressure slammed down on all sides as if I really was in the middle of a giant boar's snapping jaws. My forward momentum stopped like I'd hit a wall and Switchblade sputtered in the grasp of the herd's power. At the same time, a torrent of energy flowed into me, supercharging my pools and my physical stats.

You have been caught in Tusk Bite, the strongest herd attack of the Peakstone boars. Affect: Crushing force and life drain to fuel the herd. Soul Feed has negated the life drain effect and reversed the flow of energy.

The intense pressure did not stop. I couldn't move as bone-grinding force crushed inward. I couldn't breathe as my chest compressed so much ribs started cracking. Intense pain speared through me as the spell ground down, trying to pulp my flesh and bones. Even my enhanced strength failed to match it.

At the same time, in a weird dichotomy, new life energy roared into me from my upgraded Soul Feed reversing the spell's drain and instead sucked at their life forces. I hung in place, being ground to paste while at the same time being healed so fast the spell could keep crushing me endlessly. It really sucked.

I couldn't even scream as pain tore at my mind, as intense as the transformation to werewolf. That triggered the memory of my time as a wolf and I mentally howled in rage, the sound ringing through the depths of my mind.

Wolf bloodlust swept through my soul and I quivered with the need to strike down the boars. Pain still ripped and tore at me as my body broke and healed over and over again for what felt like an eternity, but I no longer feared it. It would pass, and I would recover and rip out the throats of my prey.

The dark cloud surrounding the boars started roiling faster, the flashes of crimson light speeding up. Streamers of golden light floated off of every one of the creatures, weaving into a single thick band that flowed into me.

After what seemed an eternity, the hog-taur grunted and dropped its club. The Tusk Bite spell winked out, snapping off the energy drain.

I gasped a sweet breath of pig-stinking air, my rib cage audibly creaking as it expanded back to normal size and my ribs snapped back into place. Organs that had been squeezed halfway to jelly swelled with new life and the agony faded under a rush of new vitality. My body consumed all that stolen life force to heal almost instantly.

Switchblade was still sputtering so I banished it back to my inventory. Dropping to the ground, I leaped into the middle of the herd of disoriented boars with a wolflike howl of animal fury. It might have felt like forever, but the spell must have only been in place for a few precious seconds. Otherwise it would have drained even more of their vitality.

It drained enough. None of them had died, but they snorted, shook their heads, and looked like they were waking up after an all-night bender. They would recover in seconds, but they didn't have that much time.

I rushed through the herd, Soulrend flashing, every stroke severing a boar's spirit head from the rest of its body. Some of them recovered enough to try to fight, but the powerful swings of their massive heads seemed slow and ponderous to my supercharged senses.

I drew deeply from my agility and strength, which had both been boosted by 50% by Soul Feed, and easily dodged, jumped, and even ran right across the backs of the angry boars. In seconds, the entire pack lay dead and twitching on the ground.

I triggered loot as I jumped out of the pile of dead giant pigs, turning to face the remaining hot-taur. Only then did I notice it galloping away at full speed. It had to be doing 50 already, and still accelerating.

Chapter Fifty-Three
Warning Signs Are For Suckers

"Oh no you don't," I growled and took off after the fleeing hog-taur. In my inventory, Switchblade still showed as recharging with the timer of two minutes, so I ran.

With my stats temporarily boosted, I felt like I could outrun a car. I accelerated, flashing across the meadow, legs churning the grasses as I gave chase. I hit at least 40 miles per hour and found I hadn't even come close to my fastest speed, so I poured on even more. My endurance was also boosted, so I should be able to outlast the monster, even if I couldn't outpace it. Besides, it couldn't get too far with the steep hills hemming us in on every side.

That idea proved to be false when the hog-taur reached the steep slope on the north side of the meadow. Barely slowing, it charged straight up the hillside that had to be at least a 60 degree slope. In seconds, it ascended to the top and disappeared over the edge.

Stinking coward. Definitely smarter than most monsters if it was wise enough to flee, but it was wasting my time. The thing climbed with the alacrity of an elk back on Earth. Pigs weren't supposed to be that agile. When I reached the slope, I raced up it at full speed, still accelerating. It felt like my speed was approaching more like that kid Dash from the movie The Incredibles and I laughed aloud as I tore up the slope.

By the time I reached the top of that first steep slope, I was gaining on the hog-taur. It was disappearing into some trees clustered at the mouth of a gully even more narrow than the one I had followed earlier. I followed and found a game trail cutting through the brush and winding up the steep gully as it cut higher into the next mountain.

Ahead of me, the hog-taur grunted, its breathing loud and labored. So I'd guessed right. It was a natural sprinter, very dangerous over short distances, but not so good for marathon runs. I pursued, but didn't catch up before the gully opened up onto another small high-mountain clearing, this one rockier and covered in loose dirt. A near-vertical slope rose from the far side of the clearing and the hog-taur was already nearly at the top, riding some kind of pulley lift.

"Does this thing have a short-term teleport ability?" I growled as I paused to gape. I hadn't been that far behind just a moment ago.

The lift was an interesting twist. None of the other monsters on this stage had used any kind of technology, even though some had carried weapons. As I studied the simple wooden platform, I noticed new details about the steep slope. It was actually made of enormous stones, squared and stacked atop each other like a giant wall. Since when did monsters build giant buildings? Scanning farther, I couldn't see any other indication for what the wall might be.

It didn't matter. I had to catch that hog-taur. It was proving challenging enough that it had to give a lot of experience. It was the first monster on stage 1 I'd found at level 25 since Tecton, the bull herd boss.

The hog-taur reached the top and trotted off the lift after making a hand gesture that had to be the monster equivalent of flipping me off. It did not send the lift back down. It would take way too long to try climbing that wall, but luckily I didn't have to. I'd picked up the perfect potion a while ago.

I quaffed my Ground Walker potion, which tasted like stale dishwater filled with grit. I should have just moved it to a hotlist spot and triggered it.

A sense of superhuman surefootedness flowed into my feet. Kind of a weird effect, but totally worth the nasty taste. I rushed to the vertical wall, and my foot landed on the vertical surface with even more grip than if I was standing on perfectly flat ground. Some magic was just so cool!

Grinning like a little boy at Christmas, I ran up the stone wall, my body horizontal but not bothered by gravity. In seconds I reached the top. From there, I could see the next part of the mountain, which had been hidden by the steep slope before. A surprisingly well-manicured lawn spread out in front of me, leading to yet another ascent. The hog-taur was trotting up a switchback trail carved into that slope. It was steep, but not nearly as bad as the one I'd just climbed.

Even more interesting, the trail was paved with flat stones, while flowering trees stood at each switchback corner. A gentle fragrance wafted across the little meadow, as if someone was burning a few of those scented candles my mother always gave to her friends at Christmas.

"This is getting weird," I muttered as I trotted toward the path. Eva surprised me.

Congratulations, Lucas! You have found the hidden sacred valley of the Peakstone boars.

"Boars have sacred valleys?" Weirder and weirder.

The slope with the fancy path was several hundred yards high, topping out in what I suspected was a much larger valley. If I was lucky, that was the creature's home and I could finally corner the agile coward. I didn't bother with the switchbacks, but ran straight up the slope, surefooted all the way as if I jogged on perfectly flat ground.

"Ooh, bold move," Cyrus said. "Even on your world, ignoring well-marked paths in sacred places is a sign of poor upbringing."

"Why is this important now? I'm coming to kill that thing, remember?"

"Doesn't mean you have to insult its home."

"Is this place affecting you too? Why are you acting weird, and why would monsters have sacred places?"

"I guess we'll never know," Cyrus said, but his voice sounded almost teasing.

For a moment, I considered just turning around and getting out of there. Was Cyrus setting me up for another test? Sacred valleys and odd warnings did not bode well. Then again, I had my sights on a monster powerful enough to maybe get me a level and I didn't have time to waste.

So I pushed my worries aside and increased my pace, running straight up the slope. The potion wore off just as I reached the top.

My suspicion prove correct. I'd reached a beautiful, high-mountain meadow. Behind me on the east side, higher mountains pierced the sky, while to the north, the mountain I was climbing rose several thousand feet higher above the meadow. The mountaintop was weird though. It rose in stepped tiers of stone that looked somehow familiar. I stared at it for a few seconds, then realized what I was looking at.

"Is the rest of this mountain based on Q'Bert?" I hadn't played the retro game in years. I guess intelligence stats helped with old memories. Up at the top of the mountain, a small stone building stood, ringed with brightly colored flags, like some kind of Tibetan temple.

"You're the first to spot the similarity, although you've missed other game references, so I'm not giving you another title," Cyrus said.

"I had no idea that was a thing."

"The perceptive mind notices patterns others fail to grasp. This one's not too over-the-top, is it?"

I wanted to say, "Nah," but took a moment to scan the area more closely. To my left, the southern edge of the valley fell away in a steep slope, and the boundary was lined with standing stones. The rough bases of black rock were smoothed near the top and capped with half-finished statues. The rough work gave the impressions of monsters struggling to break free of the stone.

On the far western side opposite from me, about 200 yards away across the waving grasses, a huge boulder rose at the edge of where the valley abruptly ended. Beyond, the land spread out in a magnificent view overlooking the grassland of the first stage.

Even from where I stood, I could glimpse the rolling expanse of the plain. Miles farther, the steep cliff on the western side was broken by the hillside rising up toward stage 2. Too bad I didn't have a camera. With the two moons high in the sky and the brilliant stars filling the canopy of the heavens like sparkling jewels, it was a sight that would've won any photography competition back on Earth.

The idyllic sight felt wrong, though. An intangible energy filled the open valley and my skin crawled. Eva had said this was a sacred place, but despite the statues and that shrine up on the mountain above, it looked like a pretty, high-mountain valley.

I didn't trust it. No time to dawdle. The hog-taur had slowed to a walk and was barely 30 yards away, heading toward the opposite side of the meadow and that solitary bolder hill.

Switchblade was mostly recharged, so I called it out of my inventory and hopped on. The bike purred to life as good as ever, and I gunned the throttle, aiming straight for the hog-taur.

It spun at the sound, hefted his huge club, and bellowed a deep-throated roar. I triggered the Shattercore Ballista that had also recharged. It flashed across the distance and detonated against the hog-taur's chest, staggering it back in a spray of blood and gore.

The hog-taur grunted, coughing up blood, trying to lift its club. Weird. I'd hit it dead on, just like I had the other one. My ballista should have killed it since it was only one level higher than the other one.

It didn't matter. The ballista had hurt it badly, and before the monster could recover, I reached it and leaped off Switchblade, banishing the bike as I soared past the monster's head. It tried to hit me, but reacted half a second too late. Soulrend cut through its head and it dropped to the ground as a kill notification flashed in my vision.

I summoned Switchblade back, landing on the bike even as I accepted the prompt to loot. Easy peasy. Time to go.

Even as I started leaning to bank my hover bike, a much louder roar echoed from the opposite side of the clearing. The sound sent a shiver of nervous fear skittering down my back. I leveled out to look around and asked, "Do sacred valleys have sacred guardians?"

Should have thought of that sooner.

Cyrus laughed with delight. "Excellent guess! This one does."

Of course it did. I should have saved that ballista for a different target. I hadn't expected more monsters.

The huge boulder hill on the other side of the clearing turned out to be a cave because the older brother to the hog-taur I just killed trotted out of the dark opening in the center. For a second, all I could do was stare and gulp.

He was enormous, his boar body the size of a moving van, his thick, powerful legs seeming too short for the huge, muscled expanse of black boar. His thick fur gleamed with magical power.

His humanoid shape rising from the front of the boar torso had the bulging muscles of a power lifter, if that power lifter ate other power lifters. The monster had to stand at least 15 feet tall, and on his oversized human-shape head, he had a minotaur-like boar snout with tusks that glinted in the starlight. His aura hit me, and even across the meadow, he radiated a sense of danger that rivaled the werewolf alpha on the second stage.

Bristleback. Level 50 boar-tar mystic champion. Legendary. Peakstone boars evolve as they level, and the pinnacle most reach is the mighty hog-taur. Few reach the final evolution, the epic boar-tar. Bristleback has evolved further and become the spiritual guide for all hog-taurs. As the Priest of Storms, he rules his sacred valley with unrivaled power. This apex guardian of the herd is smart, cunning, and has developed arcane

powers far beyond any of his kind. If you're reading this, it's probably the last thing you're ever going to do.

"Level 50?" I whispered, my mouth suddenly dry.

That was insane. Horror more intense than anything I'd felt up on stage 2 chilled my soul. Tecton, the stage-1 boss, had only been level 25.

"Sacred places are no joke," Cyrus said in a cheery, conversational tone.

I could not be there. I had been an idiot to ignore the warnings. This thing was way beyond anything I could handle. It radiated more power than a full pack of werewolves.

Crouching low over Switchblade, I threw my bike over and gunned it, spinning the machine around in a quick 180 and tearing for the slope I'd just climbed. A second bellowing roar echoed from the distant boar-tar, shaking the night air and sending shivers of dread down my spine.

I glanced back and my fear spiked to whole new levels. The monster was charging after me and even though I cranked open the throttle all the way, he was gaining. He'd drawn an enormous silver bow from somewhere.

It was like a sci-fi version of a compound bow, with powerful metal arms and pulley wheels on either end. The string glowed with golden light, and as he drew it back, a silver arrow appeared, blazing with power. It was longer than the ballista Switchblade fired.

I did not want to get hit by that. I was only seconds away from escape, but I wasn't going to make it. So I leaned hard to the left, triggered all the directional thrusters, and banked into a tight turn, racing across the meadow toward the Q'Bert stepped peak.

Through my growing panic, I tried to plan. If I could dodge his first arrow, I could spin back the other way and get to the descent. Once I was out of his sight, I could escape into the narrow gullies and hills where he wouldn't have a good shot.

Bristleback released the arrow, and it changed direction mid-flight like a homing missile. I didn't even have time to curse as I slammed on the brakes, hoping the abrupt change might make the arrow overshoot.

No chance in hell. It blasted into my side like a lightning bolt straight from Zeus. I couldn't even scream as electricity tore through me, shaking every muscle and locking me in place. Switchblade sputtered and died again as its systems overloaded.

Even though Energy Ward automatically triggered and stole a fraction of that power to feed back into my health, it wasn't nearly enough. My health bar was draining fast. I gritted my teeth, waiting for the power to dissipate. As soon as it did, I'd drink a potion and figure out a way to escape.

Except the lightning bolt did not stop. The torture dragged on as I shook and rattled, jolted by levels of electricity that would have instantly crisped me back on Earth. Through my racking spasms of pain, I managed to focus enough to realize what happened.

The silver lightning bolt arrow still impaled my side, but the end had extended down to the ground, tethering me in place. No no no no! This was bad.

And getting worse. Bristleback closed like a freight train, his bow disappearing and he replaced it with an enormous polearm capped with a heavy-bladed scimitar like those Japanese naginatas.

I couldn't move, couldn't break the lightning tether. My health and mana were draining too fast. Energy Ward materialized around me, also fueled by Soul Feed, but that would never stop the charging monster.

The merciless truth settled into my mind like a coffin. I couldn't escape this blow.

I wouldn't just let him skewer me, though.

Mustering the scattered remnants of my will, I threw Soulrend and Switchblade back into my inventory. Unfortunately, dropping to the ground didn't break the tether, like I hoped.

As Bristleback closed like an avalanche, I extracted my Roman shield, screaming from the effort as my muscles protested. At least my hands locked around the handles to hold the shield in place. I also triggered a scroll of Earth armor and a full regeneration potion from my hotlist.

I looked up and tried to shout my defiance, but my lightning-locked jaw distorted the sound into a grunting whine. Bristleback struck like a runaway freight train, his scimitar spear flashing forward in a double-handed blow driven by the full weight of his charge. I tried moving, but could barely twitch with the lightning freezing my muscles. I tried to scream, but only managed a weak gurgling sound.

The blow landed and blasted me to oblivion.

Chapter Fifty-Four
Falling with Style

Consciousness returned slowly, and I wished it hadn't. The first thing I felt was pure agony. Every muscle and sinew and nerve screamed in pain as if I'd been punched into the center of a volcano. My thoughts twitched, like my brain was short circuiting.

What happened? I tried blinking open my eyes, but only one responded. It barely fluttered, but the other only speared my mind with a fresh spike of agony.

Through my one partially open eye, a big, brown shape, blurry from distance, was getting smaller, surrounded by blackness. I couldn't seem to focus on it, and I couldn't move anything but that one eyelid. I couldn't feel my body or the ground beneath me.

Not a good sign. I glanced at my mini map for a clue.

What the hell? Had it shorted out? My mini map was flashing and blurring like the lightning had fried it.

Lightning! Memories crashed back and my headache spiked again. Where was the boar-taur? Was he preparing to finish me off? I tried to leap to my feet but my body screamed at me for being stupid.

I needed to see what was going on, so I expanded my mini map to full map size. Even though my eyes weren't working, I could still see the map. I had never realized before that it projected right into my mind, or something.

I stared for a moment, not understanding as the golden star representing my position on the map shot across the landscape. I wasn't running. I couldn't move or even feel my legs.

No, I couldn't feel anything but pain. Not good. That terrifying monster had to be close. I had to move!

Then the truth hit me and I would have gasped if I could get my mouth
working. I was flying. More accurately, I was falling horizontally. That shock
finally startled some brain activity and I checked my status.

How am I even alive?

My health was below 5%, bouncing up and down between 3% and 6%. A
little icon of my body had appeared next to my health bar showing every part
of me a sinister red color. My Tesla Coil bracelet showed 0% charge, even
though I'd just over-filled it from all the boars.

I instantly triggered a full health potion from my hotlist and the rush of
warm healing energy eased some of my aches. The little person icon changed
from red to orange around my head and torso.

A moment later, my vision sharpened and I focused on that distant object.
It was Bristleback's mountain, looking small in the distance, dwarfed by the
other towering peaks. I couldn't move my head much yet, but it looked like
I'd been blasted at least a couple miles across the plain.

I triggered Sight of the Explorer, zooming in on the distant mountain.
And there was Bristleback, staring after me, one hand shielding his eyes like
a golfer watching a great tee shot.

I don't know if he sensed me looking, but he lifted his other hand and
made the same obscene gesture the other hog-taur had made.

"Fridge off," I muttered, my raspy voice barely a hint of a whisper. Spiritual
leaders were supposed to show restraint, or something, weren't they?

My Roman shield was gone, although one leather strap still clung to my
right arm, which was obviously broken in several places. It flopped in the
wind as I hurtled through the air. My Earth armor was gone too, and my
leather jacket was shredded. Half my chest was a gory mess, with bits of bone
sticking through.

As my torn and broken body began mending, I pieced together what must
have happened. Bristleback had scored a home run. That guy had played me
like a record.

First his arrow tethered me and neutralized most of my abilities. That
overpowered naginata strike had shattered my defenses, destroying my shield,
earth armor, and Energy Ward before reaching my body. The impact had
splintered most of my bones and launched me like a cannonball off the
mountain.

Even with all the energy in my Tesla Coil bracelet and the full regeneration
potion I'd just taken before Bristleback hit me, I still nearly died. I bet only my

tougher tier-1 body and faster regeneration had tipped the scales in my favor. Anyone else would have probably exploded like a melon hit by a truck.

I took a second healing potion, but that triggered a message I'd never seen before.

Warning. You have taken too many healing-related potions too quickly. Consuming another similar potion before the cooldown expires will result in toxic side-effects.

There was a potion cooldown? Why hadn't I heard about that before? I supposed I'd never needed back-to-back healing potions. I'd nearly triggered 2 potions just now. If I had, it might have killed me.

That would have been an idiotic way to finish myself off. Then I realized landing would kill me anyway. No way I could survive crashing to the ground moving so fast. My head and neck were healed enough that I could see and I managed to twist around enough to scan for the ground.

"Bravestone!" It was rushing up toward me way too fast.

I cast scroll of Slow Fall and my stomach lurched as I decelerated. I groaned as my many still-broken bones protested the change of speed with stabs of pure agony. That was still better than splatting into the ground going 100 miles per hour. As I slowed to a stately hover and started to descend, I had time to look around more and take stock of where I'd ended up.

Bristleback had hit me out of the park at least a couple miles across the northern edge of the central valley. In fact, I wasn't too far from the shores of the lake. The surface was calm, the waters a deep blue. A mile or so to the south, the rocky spires of Stepstone rose above the grasses.

If Bristleback had more of a slice in his swing, he might have hit me all the way to town. My bloody, mostly dead body landing by town hall would definitely have freaked Tomas out. Probably gotten a scolding from Ruby too.

I fought down a chuckle at the thought of Tomas's face. I couldn't risk shaking my broken ribs. No doubt Steve would help me find a bit of humor in the near-death experience, but that would have to wait until I didn't feel like screaming out a lung.

I could only imagine how bizarre I must have looked, my broken body with my shredded clothing shooting across the central grassland like a bloody meteor before suddenly slowing and descending like a tiny hovercraft.

Within seconds, I settled to the grasses. The landing went better than I had hoped, a graceful, slow descent that would have looked awesome if I wasn't still a pile of bloody mush. I bit back another scream as my full weight settled gently onto the grass.

It would be just my luck if a nearby monster saw me land and decided to come over for a snack. I decided to lay still and pretend I was already dead and rotten and not worth their time. Not like I could do anything else.

Thankfully, nothing came to eat me as my health slowly ticked back up. The last healing potion had broken the stalemate and my health points steadily climbed.

The flashes of pain from the magical resetting of one bone after another provided me with endless entertainment as the slow minutes dragged by. Luckily, my tier-1 regeneration, boosted another 20% by Wolf Blood, could take care of even that level of trauma, given enough time.

I had a bunch of notifications waiting, so I scanned them to take my mind of the painful healing process.

Congratulations, Lucas! You used your unique hover bike's offensive ability for the first time and destroyed a higher-level target with a single shot. You receive a gold Womp Rat loot box.

Congratulations, Lucas! For reversing the effects of a large group attack that should have killed you, you receive a gold Solo loot box.

Congratulations, Lucas! You have destroyed every un-evolved boar from the Peakstone herd in less than 5 minutes. You receive a silver Buffalo Bill loot box.

Congratulations, Lucas! You have discovered a hidden sacred boss. Not even nearly impassable mountains can block your creative drive to find the most unique way to die. You receive a gold Cortez loot box.

Congratulations, Lucas! You survived a critical strike from a legendary boss more than 30 levels higher than yourself. You receive a platinum Plot Armor loot box.

That was a lot more achievements than I had expected and if I was being honest with myself, way more than I deserved. No complaints from me, though. The Womp Rat loot box contained a pair of goggles with shaded lenses.

Common Goggles of Sharpshooting. Now you can look like a World War Two bomber pilot with these stylish goggles. They'll protect your eyes from physical and magical attacks and make every history nerd green with envy. Targeting interface.

"Yes," I breathed as I examined the goggles, then spit up bloody phlegm. The movement made my still-broken ribs stab me with a fresh wave of agony.

I really wanted to try on the goggles, but my hands still didn't work, and I only had one good eye. Patience. Hopefully the targeting interface would be cool.

From the Solo loot box I got an amulet on a simple silver chain. It was about the size of a thick quarter, with the image of a shield on the face.

Amulet of the Rebound. Common. The perfect gift for those who like to catch spells in the face, like you. 10% of magical damage received is reflected back against the attacker.

I wish I'd had that 10 minutes ago.

The Buffalo Bill loot box contained a scroll to repair and recharge one of the zombie energy rifles, while the Cortez loot box contained a single scroll.

Scroll of Time Out. Even professionals need a break once in a while. Forcibly eject one enemy combatant from a fight you are engaged in and randomly teleport them up to 1 mile.

That would be useful if I was about to be overwhelmed again. I'd prefer a one-shot kill potion, or something to help me win a fight, but forcing a monster to leave could save my life.

The Plot Armor loot box held the best loot, as expected. I randomly got 5 tier-3 mana crystals and 3 full regeneration potions, plus 2 much better items.

Lucky Stiff scroll. Plus 5 to Luck. Plus 5 to CHA.

Crash Test Dummy armored jacket. Rare. Move over Mad Max, this jacket was made for real road warriors. Upgraded defense against most forms of physical attack and significant defense against impact and blunt force damage by spreading impacts throughout the torso. Impervious to damage when behind a wheel. Self-repair over time.

I sighed with relief. Timing for that one was perfect, and I finally had a jacket with self-repair. My other jacket was shredded. I might be able to get the armorer in town to repair it, but creating a brand new jacket would probably be way easier.

That bit about immune to damage when behind the wheel was something I'd have to ask Cyrus about when I could talk better. Was it just a joke since there were no cars on this world? I doubted I could convince him riding Switchblade counted as behind a wheel.

Still, that was a better haul than I probably deserved for getting myself mostly killed. I scanned the loot from the boars and the first hog-taur. Most was low-value stuff like meat, hides, tusks, mana crystals, and potions. I did get one interesting scroll.

Scroll of Evolution. Upgrades a random equipped item to the next grade.

I would read that once I could stand and replace my wrecked jacket with my new one. As I scanned my inventory, I groaned and would have slapped myself if my arms didn't hurt so much.

"Idiot. I should have used Phase Walk!"

Bristleback's attacks might have also dealt direct spiritual damage, but I doubt it would have been nearly as much. I might have escaped without getting blasted almost to atoms.

In my defense, I had been getting shocked by enough lightning to power a small city. My mind hadn't been working too well. I was lucky I'd managed to do as much as I had.

I lay on the soft grass, panting from the arduous self-healing process, until I started feeling almost myself again. My potion cooldown was just about expired, but my natural regeneration was doing great work so I didn't need another potion. My health points were still barely half, but my body felt whole, if sore.

I sat up with a groan and looked across the plain toward the distant mountain. That had been one of my stupider ideas. I needed to fight stronger monsters, but a level 50 boar-taur mystic boss was clearly still out of my league. Bristleback had one-shotted me and ended the fight almost before it began.

Chapter Fifty-Five

A Different Approach to Survival

"No time to whine about my problems," I muttered as I rose and switched jackets. I'd failed that test badly. I didn't have time to fail any more.

The new armored jacket felt wonderful, a solid weight that didn't hinder my movements. It was made from heavy leather in a matte black finish with ribbed padding on the shoulders and silver buckles instead of a zipper.

Then I used my upgrade scroll. It flashed and dissolved in a burst of golden sparkles. I received a new notification.

Mirror Cloak upgraded to epic. Improved concealment while moving. Plus 25% defense against magical attacks.

"That's what I'm talking about," I grinned as my cloak pulsed once with silver light.

I paused to eat a bucket of waffle-cut fries, still warm and delicious. A bit of ketchup would make the moment sublime, but even dry, the fries were still way better than a bland food ration. Too bad I didn't have an oven so I could fry up a pork chop.

As I ate, I asked, "Cyrus, how can there be a level 50 secret boss on stage 1? And on that topic, did I climb high enough to be even withstage 2 on that mountain?"

"Stage 2 isn't an elevation," Cyrus chuckled. "Yes, you did climb high enough to reach the same elevation as the central plateau of stage 2, but that's not the same thing. To reach stage 2 you need to meet the requirements and climb that slope on the west side of Stepstone valley. Only from there can you eventually climb to stage 3."

"Okay, that much makes sense, I guess. So if I keep climbing higher in the mountains to the east or south, will I keep finding more powerful monsters?"

"Of course, and for you that's the best course to take. You need a lot more experience, and low-leveled monsters that don't offer any real danger provide very little."

"So back to Bristleback."

Cyrus chuckled again. "I guess you should have heeded those warning signs."

I scowled. "How could I have guessed you'd throw a secret boss down here in the very first stage?"

"How could you assume there wouldn't be other powerful monsters?"

I grumbled about that, but in the end, I did need to find more powerful monsters. Just not another level 50 secret boss. Just thinking about Bristleback made my entire body hurt with phantom pain.

The night was still pretty young, so I summoned Switchblade and hopped on to do some more hunting. After defeating all the boars and the hog-taurs, I had to be close to level 8. I glanced one more time toward the distant mountain where Bristleback lived. If only that had gone better. He could have definitely given me a level, but I wasn't ready for a monster like that.

I needed something tough, but not insane. So I zipped across the plain and again rode up into the eastern mountains, but kept well away from Bristleback's home. I sent a warning to the other Explorers to stay away from there too. I ignored the questions about why my latest ping was so many miles away from my last one. The story of getting wrecked by Bristleback would not get out if I could help it.

At least now I had confirmation that stronger monsters lived at higher elevations. I planned to find more of them, and accelerated upward with every turn of a gully or canyon. Eventually I ascended to a lovely high meadow at least half a mile across. Covered in clover and low grasses, it was dotted with individual trees or small copses that dotted the gentle, rolling hills. Clusters of enormous bushes sagged under the weight of ripe berries I didn't recognize.

Another stream bubbled along the near side, dropping in a series of small waterfalls between clear pools. Standing near one of the larger pools was a small compound, entirely surrounded by a log barrier wall 12 feet tall. My first group of survivors.

"That was surprisingly easy," I said as I accelerated toward the compound. A man standing on a platform behind the wall spotted me and started waving mightily.

Rough wooden gates creaked open and about 30 people rushed out to greet me, waving and shouting. They were very enthusiastic. Most wore very basic clothing, with some wearing what looked like rough-sewn animal hides. I only spotted two pairs of shoes among them all.

I slowed as I drew near and scanned them. The leader was a man in his 50s with disheveled white hair and a wild salt-and-pepper beard. He wore no shirt and the skin of his pot belly sagged as if he'd lost a lot of weight in recent days.

George Dunning. Level 5 baby human. Team Peter Pan.

"What?" I muttered to myself as I scanned the others. They all had terrible levels, ranging from 4 to 7. I spotted teams including Dragnet, Game of Thrones, Miami Vice, and Seinfeld.

"Thank god you found us!" George exclaimed as they all crowded around me like a bunch of starving refugees.

"Have you all been here the entire time?"

A tall woman standing next to George said, "Yes. We couldn't risk traveling anywhere else. There are monsters everywhere."

Lucy Dunning. Level 6 baby human. Team Peter Pan.

Her long, brown hair showed gray roots along her scalp. It was pulled into a loose pony tail, and she too looked pretty unkempt. She wore a dirty white t-shirt and shorts, but no shoes. If I had to guess, she and George were married. I hadn't seen anyone else stay on the same team with family or friends.

Before I could ask about that, another fellow from team Miami Vice with a blue suit coat but no shirt added, "We knew someone would come to rescue us. We had water and built that shelter and fought off the monsters when they found us."

His name was actually Don Johnson. Perfect.

"Such a nightmare," George added.

"Do you have any good food?" a 20-something girl from team Outlander asked. "Most of us picked Base Camp as our first utility spell, but the food is so basic. Who eats the same thing every day?"

"How long were you going to stay here?"

"Until help arrived," George said with a shrug.

His wife Lucy added, "This world is insane. We shouldn't be here."

Don nodded. "We were tourists. There's been a mistake. We weren't even supposed to go through Colorado. It was a last-minute change."

"No one should be here." Refusing to accept what had happened was suicidal. "Hiding in this valley won't help. Didn't you hear the announcement? We have to hit level 10 and get to the next stage."

"So why are you only level 7?" Lucy demanded. "You act like you're better than us, but you won't make it either."

"At least I'm working on it." I wasn't about to explain everything to them.

George said, "We still have a few days. We talked about it and agreed to wait until help arrived or we got teleported back home."

Looking smug, Lucy added. "If we don't play the game, they'll just send us back. They don't need all of us."

I just stared. Dealing with reality was tough. I'd had my moments of panic and denial, but didn't they want to live?

"Listen, that's not how it works. If you don't advance, you're going to die."

"How do you know?" Lucy snapped.

I fought down the urge to turn Switchblade and leave the idiots to their fate. Maybe once they saw Stepstone they'd get motivated, or maybe someone there could talk sense into them. I couldn't. I literally could not understand their mentality. It was like talking with people from another world.

Back on Earth, that mentality was pretty common. Let someone else do the work. There were layers of safety nets in the States that could help folks going through hard times. This wasn't Earth, though. They hadn't changed at all.

Thinking about it that way made me see just how much I had changed. I was not the same person I'd been just days ago. I wish I hadn't needed to change, but I planned to live, to survive, and to get strong enough to protect my loved ones both here and back on Earth.

"Haven't you been watching the survivor counter?"

Don said, "Yeah. People who move around get killed. Most of us have survived this long so we've got to be doing something right."

I closed my eyes for a second, just breathing. In a twisted sense, he had a point. "Look, if the only requirement was not dying, you'd be doing better than some. We need to hit level 10 and climb to a higher stage. That's the reality of this crazy world."

"And if we don't go, how do you know the game won't just leave us here until someone else climbs all the way up to that Marisara queen and deals with her?" Lucy demanded.

"You're just going to trust someone else with the responsibility for saving your lives?"

"Sure," George said. "We do it all the time. Police and fire fighters protect us at home. Someone will step up and do it here. I was a manager. I'm no warrior."

Muttered agreement from the rest of the party left me momentarily speechless. I sighed and sent a message to the explorers with the waypoint of my position. I quickly outlined what I'd found and requested a team to escort the fools down the hill.

"So, someone's coming?" asked the girl who had asked about food. "Will they have trucks or something? I'm not walking that far without shoes."

"No, they won't have a truck. I've got the only transport I know of and I walked until I won this for killing monsters. If you want shoes or better food or better gear, you have to fight for it."

"That's not fair," she said, crossing her arms and sulking.

Lucy patted the girl's arm and glared at me. "There's no need to be rude."

"Telling the truth isn't being rude."

"Are you going to stay here and protect us until the other team arrives?" Don asked.

"No. I've got my own work to do."

"Well if you're so brave, shouldn't you be leveling faster?" George asked.

"Some folks should arrive in the morning to escort you all down to Stepstone. That's the town in the valley where we're gathering before heading up to the next stage. In the meantime, you need to get some levels."

"We've used up all of our temporary spells," one woman near the back of the group called. "We don't have enough weapons. We can't fight. The monsters are too strong. They'll kill us."

Catelyn Smith. Baby human level 7. Team Game of Thrones.

The others nodded agreement. I should have realized the situation. None of them were high enough levels to have permanented anything.

"If you had better weapons, would you fight?"

George and Lucy both scoffed, but Catelyn pushed forward. "I would."

She looked about my age, a pretty blonde with bright blue eyes. She wore tan shorts and a blue blouse, but no shoes. Several of the others echoed her words.

"Okay. I might be able to help. Who else? If you're willing to fight, stand next to Catelyn."

The group shifted around me as about a dozen men and women joined Catelyn. George and Lucy moved to the opposite side of Switchblade and the rest of the group clustered around them. Lucy looked annoyed with Catelyn, but George looked relieved to see someone else volunteering to do the fighting.

I jumped off Switchblade and banished it, eliciting gasps of wonder. Then I pulled a bunch of the random polearm weapons I'd picked up from the bulls and handed one each to all of Catelyn's followers. Most looked eager, although a few looked nervous. When I said I'd help, had they thought I meant I'd do the work for them?

To Catelyn I gave 3 standard healing potions, one of the silver-tipped steel spears I took from the cows, and one of my precious laser rifles.

"Thank you," she breathed, staring at the weapons and potions like they were miracles.

Everything but the rifle disappeared into her inventory and when she looked up to meet my gaze, her blue eyes were bright with emotion. She gripped the rifle tight, standing taller, determination in her gaze. With her leading the fighters, some of them might actually have a chance.

"Hey, can I have a rifle?" another man from the non-fighters group called.

"No. You said you don't want to fight."

"I didn't know you had guns."

"Catelyn gets it. That's all I've got. That weapon can't be taken from her," I lied. "So you'd all better hope she's a good shot."

"I will be," Catelyn said, then leaned closer and whispered, "Shouldn't I get a message about it not being able to be stolen?"

I shrugged. "Who can explain the game? Listen, the rifle will give you an edge, but it's not a golden ticket. You'll have to work together."

She straightened and asked more loudly, "The rescue team will get here in the morning?"

I nodded.

"That gives us all night to hunt. We have some leveling to do."

I extracted a couple of the zombie lanterns and handed them to Catelyn, then pulled out my remaining pairs of zombie boat shoes. I had just enough to shod all the fighters.

"Hey, I want shoes!" the same girl who wanted fresh food exclaimed.

"Then start killing monsters. I got these as loot drops." To Catelyn and her fighters I repeated, "Work together and you'll be okay."

"Where are you going?" Lucy exclaimed. "It's almost totally dark."

"I'm also hunting."

I summoned Switchblade, jumped on, and hit the throttle.

Chapter Fifty-Six
Creative Tumbling

I pushed higher, on the hunt for higher elevations and stronger monsters. Half an hour later, I shot across a high saddle between steep mountains that had to top out at over 10,000 feet. Beyond them, even taller peaks rose in tiered steps leading to the final peaks that speared up through the night sky like they were trying to scrape the stars.

Those ultimate peaks towered at least 50,000 feet above me to the east. On the top of the saddle where I rode, I'd finally climbed high enough to see that hundreds of smaller hills and mountains grew out of the flanks of that final enormous mountain. They formed a craggy maze that extended for miles all around.

I could get lost in that maze for weeks, if I had the time. Unfortunately, I didn't. All I needed was a few high-leveled monsters and I'd happily return to Stepstone to spend time with my friends. The moons and brilliant stars bathed the landscape in a soft, silvery glow. Wolf Sight allowed me to see clearly as I scanned the area for monsters.

I was starting to find some worth my time. A 15-foot troll and a humanoid stone golem, both at level 26, were the last two I'd killed. They'd been much tougher than the previous monsters, and I'd noticed a pattern. It seemed monsters got a big power boost at level 25, just like we did. If that was right, then I bet they got another at level 50. Bristleback the hog-taur had been an entirely different tier of threat, and he'd been level 50.

I had to be close to another level. Hunting monsters above level 25 had to be the key for me. If only we had an experience bar to see how much more we needed. The monsters hadn't given much good loot other than another potion of earth armor. Now I'd climbed higher, I had to be close to something tough. A mini boss or elite would be perfect.

A piercing cry from the sky behind caught me by surprise. Instinctively I hit the throttle and threw Switchblade into a hard right, going horizontal as the bike skidded in a turn so tight my stomach got sucked down to my boots.

An enormous winged shape plunged out of the sky, talons as long as short swords raking the air inches from my back. The air turned icy cold in a blink, then the monster swooped back into the sky, giving me a clear look at it.

Glacierwing Griffon. Level 29. Elite. Griffons are among the strongest aerial predators in the lower mountain, striking by surprise from above. Glacierwing griffons possess powerful elemental ice abilities to slow and incapacitate their prey. You never thought you'd be the mouse dodging the hawk, did you? To make the hunt fun, they're also resistant to elemental attacks, but weak against arrows and spears.

Identify was showing more information since I'd triggered the dictionary with the Lifebane Phantoms. Every bit of info helped, but I would have recognized a griffon. Again, it matched Earth mythology. The huge lion body had enormous wings and an eagle's head.

I'd gotten my elite. I grinned with anticipation, but facing a griffon out in the open would be stupid. So I righted Switchblade and gunned it for the far peak and the slope descending into sheltering forest below.

The griffon banked around and swooped in again, this time from the side. It opened its wicked, curved beak, but instead of another piercing cry, a white bolt of magic erupted from it, shooting right at me.

I wrenched Switchblade to the side and ran it into a small boulder. The bike's thrusters shrieked as the bike pitched into the air. I gunned both throttles at the same time, maximizing the jump.

The bolt of ice passed just beneath me and slammed the ground in an explosion of snow. Ice crept over some of the farings and my breath formed a dense white cloud in the suddenly frigid air. I hit the secondary thrusters and threw the bike into a sideways spin while still airborn.

The griffon was diving right at me and the spin pointed the bike toward the monster. I triggered Shattercore Ballista.

The bolt of bright blue energy erupted from the front of the bike and shot at the griffon, but the monster tucked one wing and dodged faster than should have been possible.

I spat a curse, then remembered I was still aimed sideways as the bike dropped back to the ground.

Motors whined loudly again as I slid sideways across the hillside toward one of the steep slopes dropping away toward a canyon far below. Before I could sling the bike back around, we sideswiped a rock.

"Oh, snap."

Switchblade lacked the correct thrusters on that side to jump over the obstacle and it clipped the rock with a loud metallic crack. Instantly my smooth sideways glide turned into an out-of-control tumble as Switchblade rolled over and over in the air.

I triggered Shield Dome and the glowing green barrier snapped into place around the bike. That kept me from crashing into the hillside but upgraded my already wild tumble to a whole new level.

It was kind of like when Tomas and I climbed into a tire as kids and rolled each other down a hill, only this time I was moving 50 miles per hour when I started.

The Shield Dome kept me in the saddle and kept the bike in the center of the protective dome, so all I could do was hold on as I bounced and spun all the way down the long slope to the valley far below.

I whooped with every spin. I had to say something, but didn't want to scream. If I pretended I was having fun, maybe I wouldn't feel so terrified.

It didn't work. At the bottom, I careened into the forest, pinballing between trees so many times I puked as the world spun insanely fast all around me. Finally Shield Dome broke and the bike crashed to a halt against the side of a steep gully, overgrown with berry bushes.

Head spinning, I slid off, then fell crashing 10 feet down the gully through the bushes. The thicket was super dense and the bushes had sharp thorns that tore at my exposed skin and punched through my pants. I closed my eyes and waited for my mind to stop spinning.

The air smelled surprisingly sweet from the ripe berries. Thankfully the smell helped settle my stomach instead of riling it up more. I almost took a minor healing potion, but my tier-1 regeneration helped me recover in seconds.

Another piercing shriek from the griffon snapped my mind into focus. The beast hadn't give up. Identify kicked in as soon as I opened my eyes in the middle of the bushes.

Penumbra berries. These thorny berries might have a bitter taste, but they're still prized throughout the multiverse for the boost they give to fighters. Try them in a smoothie with star berries for even more powerful results. Effect: 25% boost to stealth for 5 minutes. 25% chance of getting a critical hit for 2 minutes.

I hadn't bothered to look at the many berries I'd passed all night. That might have been a stupid decision. The penumbra berries were grainy and black, sort of like depressed blackberries.

I picked half a dozen and popped them into my mouth. They were bitter, but not too bad. I immediately got a message with the promised boosts. I'd need to pick more later, but for now I had to deal with the stupid griffon.

Climbing out of the bushes turned out to be a major hassle. The only cutting weapon I had was my saber-toothed dagger. Soulrend couldn't cut physical materials and most of my other weapons were too long to wield in the middle of a berry bramble.

By the time I hacked my way back to Switchblade, the griffon cried again, closer this time. Somehow it had tracked me down. I caught glimpses of its huge wings through breaks in the trees.

Scratched and bruised and grumpy, I climbed back on Switchblade. It was tough with the bike leaning at an awkward angle like it was, but I managed it with an acrobatic flip that would have been impossible even for Olympic gymnasts back on Earth.

My bike turned on instantly, but Shield Dome was spent and the main power level was in the red. The bike showed minor damage, but was still operational.

With a bit of throttle, the bike hovered and shot out of the gully, leaping into the forest and between giant trees. I kept the speed slow as I scouted for a good spot to deal with the griffon.

There. A clearing big enough for it to swoop down at me but small enough to make maneuvering for the monster tricky. I banished Switchblade and walked into the clearing, hefting one of the energy rifles.

Seconds later, I spotted the griffon circling overhead. It was proving remarkably relentless. Hopefully that meant I'd get tons more experience from the kill. I shouldered the rifle and fired.

I missed, but the bolt drew the griffon's attention. It winged over, diving right at me, opening its mouth for another freeze blast.

I dumped my rifle into my inventory and pulled out my flashlight, Torch of the Mirrored Moon. I pointed it at the diving griffon and flipped it on.

A beam of blinding light split the darkness, catching the monster right in the face. It shrieked, its ice death beam canceled, but it couldn't swerve away. It had already dived below the tops of the huge trees, so plunged toward the ground, taloned claws extended.

I pulled a spear from my inventory and slammed the haft into the ground at my feet, then sprinted three steps to the side and activated mirror cloak. The world turned monochrome as light bent around me, turning me invisible.

The blinded griffon crashed to the ground on the spot I'd just left, tearing the earth to ribbons but also impaling its chest on the spear. It screamed as blood erupted from the deep wound.

Huge wings extended wide to lift it away, but I was so close, one wing reached well past me. I pulled out Soulrend and slashed through the wing. The movement was so small, my cloaking barely rippled.

The griffon screamed again, this time mixed with the angry roar of a lion as it spun toward me, beak gaping open to fire an ice blast, even though it couldn't see me.

A stun gun dropped into my hands and I fired point blank into the monster's face.

The blast rocked it back so hard it toppled to its side, twitching. It was too big for a stun gun to disable it for long, but I only needed seconds.

I rushed in and slashed down once with Soulrend, severing its spirit right through the neck.

Congratulations, Lucas! You have defeated Glacierwing Griffon. Level 29. Bonus experience gained for defeating a higher-level enemy.

"Wait for it," I breathed as I triggered Soul Feed, then looted the monster, retreating from the stench as its body dissolved into black smoke.

I did not get the hoped-for level-up announcement. Instead, I got a new achievement.

Congratulations, Lucas. You've defeated your first aerial monster. You receive a gold Crosby loot box.

"Crosby? As in Bing Crosby? Was he a duck hunter?"

"Indeed he was," Cyrus answered.

Huh. Who knew?

The loot box contained 2 scrolls of ice blast. Looting the monster also gave me some uncommon griffon feathers that could be used to craft thaw potions, several talons, and a dozen jumbo-sized duck roasts. That was random, but okay.

Still no level, though. By my count, I should have earned at least 7 or 8 levels for anyone else. That should have been plenty. Cyrus would only chide me for whining if I asked him about it, though.

"So, is finding the right monster the next test before I get level 8? Are you tweaking my experience like you said you might?"

"You're performing great," Cyrus responded. "Keep it up, and you'll hit level 8 soon enough."

He didn't exactly answer the question, but if level 8 was that close, I just needed another good monster.

I could have ridden Switchblade back up the steep slope, but its power was nearly spent. The forest at the base of the slope was a lot thicker, with smaller trees. I'd have trouble riding through it, so I left my bike in my inventory to recharge and self-repair.

I jogged through the trees with steep slopes rising all around, moving at an easy pace going about 30 miles per hour. I soon found a canyon cutting through the mountains. I followed it for 2 miles and killed a level 32 Mammoth Lion just like the one that dragged me up to the second stage.

Still no level, but the lion reminded me of the little lion cubs I'd left in the cave. They were probably dead, eaten by other monsters, but I hoped not. That one cub had been really cute.

Half an hour later, I reached a large clearing near a 500 foot waterfall. On the banks of the pond beneath the waterfall was another walled fort. This one was larger than the one with the tourists.

"Maybe that fall was lucky after all." I never would have found the secluded compound otherwise.

I didn't see anyone, not even a sentry. That was a bit weird. Hopefully the people inside weren't as useless as the last group.

I jogged across the clearing to the log gate and pounded on it with a fist. On a hunch, I swapped out my armored jacket for my old, shredded one. They wouldn't hound me for gear and expect me to do all the work for them if they thought I was in worse shape than they were.

A moment later, a light appeared on the wall above and a bearded man poked his head over the wall.

"Hello! I'm Lucas."

Chapter Fifty-Seven
Fatal Attraction

Instead of opening the gate, the man tossed down a rope. "Can you climb?"

I could have just jumped the 10-foot wall, but I was getting a weird vibe from the guy. His eyes were a bit too wide, his gaze a bit too intense. I didn't want to spook him.

"I think I can manage." I climbed the wall using the rope and tried my best to make it look difficult. A moment later, I dropped onto an interior walkway beside the man.

Fred Gallagher. Baby human level 16. Team Fatal Attraction.

That was an unfortunate team, and the middle-aged guy didn't look like he was thriving, despite his decent levels. His blond hair was strangely well styled, but all he wore was a pair of tight speedos, showing off his well-muscled torso.

"Hi. You guys are hard to find."

"Some visitors are welcome. Come. I will take you to my mistress."

"Mistress?" That was an odd turn of phrase.

He didn't elaborate, but led the way down a steep stair. Two large log cabins filled most of the compound and Fred headed toward the larger one.

"How many people are here?" I spotted no one else moving around. It was the middle of the night, but still, another odd detail.

"There are never enough to serve."

Okay, I was definitely getting major weird vibes from Fred, but my curiosity was piqued too. So I followed, ready to defend myself.

I paused one step inside the larger building to stare. It looked like we'd entered a Persian princess's private suite, if she was a pillow hoarder.

The walls were draped with crimson curtains, while yellow silk drapes were pinned to the ceiling. Piles of pillows and cushions in dozens of styles cluttered the entire space. Flimsy silk pillows, frilly pillows, huge full-body pillows, couch cushions and dozens of different seat cushions.

The room was stiflingly hot, although I didn't spot a fireplace anywhere. Some kind of incense or nasty scented candles hung so heavy in the air, it was hard to breathe. In the center of the room, a king-size, four-poster bed stood, draped in silks of every color.

"Where did you get all this stuff?"

Fred didn't answer, but dropped to one knee with his right hand over his heart. Bowing his head, he spoke loudly. "Mistress. I have brought a new servant for consideration."

That was too much. I took a step back, reaching for the door, but spotted movement behind the silk curtains around the bed. A woman slipped out of the bed and stepped into view and I couldn't help staring.

Persian hoarder princess in the flesh. A lot of flesh, as it turned out. The very attractive woman was only barely dressed. The briefest bikini did little more than highlight areas usually covered, while gauzy fabric that suggested loose pants and crop top billowed around her bronze skin.

She was tall and shapely, with thick, black hair cascading down her back to her waist. She was like an X-rated older sister of Princess Jasmine from Aladdin.

When I met her gaze, the room tilted and the heat grew unbearable. I gasped, clutching at the door handle, but my fingers only knocked clumsily against the wood. My thoughts swam and I swayed where I stood.

"Welcome, visitor." Her voice was a rich purr that slid into my ears and wrapped my brain in wool. Deep in the back of my mind, someone was shouting for me to get out, but the voice was so dim, I couldn't seem to focus on it.

"I am Mistress Abbie," she said as she prowled closer, her movements fluid and sensual. My heart raced but my thoughts scattered. I couldn't seem to think.

"What may I call you?" she purred as she reached me and slid one yellow-painted nail down my arm. The touch sent shivers racing through me, but I couldn't tell if they were pleasant or painful.

I opened my mouth to speak, but hesitated. Something wasn't right. I had a message to give them, but what was it? I needed to do something else, but couldn't remember.

"Well?" she asked, pacing slowly around me. "You poor thing. Your clothing is torn to rags. You've had a hard time of it, haven't you?"

I nodded, but still no words came out. I felt an overwhelming need to answer and tell her everything she wanted to know, but a stubborn core deep inside balked.

"Don't you have a name?" she asked, leaning against my right side. She was warm and soft, her voice a caress.

"Lu . . . Lucas," I stammered.

"Too bad you're so dim. Battered and only level 7. Are you autistic or something, Lucas?"

I grunted. Her voice shackled my mind, but wisps of thought were starting to move again like weak currents through thick mud.

"Pity. If you were better looking, you'd still make a fine plaything, but I have enough toys. I need servants, though. Fred, take him to the kitchens."

I almost protested. I wasn't that bad looking, and I wasn't useless. Instead, I bit my lip hard enough to draw blood. The heat and incense and the heady drug of her voice made thinking nearly impossible, but I clung to the growing certainty that something was wrong.

"Yes, Mistress," Fred cried and leaped to his feet.

"Be a good boy and serve me well," Abbie breathed into my ear, then kissed my cheek. The world spun and I dropped like a sack of potatoes.

When I blinked open my eyes again, my head pounded like Fred had beaten me with a hammer while I slept. My thoughts seemed to be working again, though.

"Ow," I groaned as I sat up and looked around.

I was lying on a filthy straw cot in the corner of a large kitchen. Three separate ovens, just like the ones in the Base Camp tents, lined one long table against the opposite wall. Shelves full of boxes and bags were stacked along the opposite wall, while 2 gleaming steel food prep tables stood in the center of the room.

It smelled delicious. The kitchen was awash with scents of grilled meat, soups, and fresh-baked bread. I spotted a rack with several different types of loaves cooling nearby.

"What the Smolder?" How did they get all this stuff?

In the center of the kitchen, a man in a white apron and chef's white hat was inspecting a pair of boots that looked an awful lot like mine. I glanced down and bit back another curse. I was naked except for my blue boxers. They'd stripped me bare while I slept.

"Hey, those are my boots," I shouted as I lunged to my feet. My legs felt wobbly and when I glanced at my health stats, a little blinking icon flashed.

Active condition: Woozy.

When did that become a thing? I'd never seen that status bar before.

The cook turned to me and waved. He was a big guy, but not fat. He stood several inches taller than me, with very muscular arms. He spoke with a noticeable French accent. "You don't get clothes until the Mistress decides you get clothes."

The Mistress. My foggy memories came back and I shuddered. She had some strong mind control seduction powers. She'd wrecked me and could have easily killed me if she wanted to. The memory of standing helpless before her riled me up more.

"Give them back." I marched toward the cook, who scowled.

"Don't give me attitude, new guy. You serve the Mistress now and she said you work for me. Don't make me smite you."

Smite? Who used that word? Identify kicked in finally.

Charles Adair. Baby human level 14. Team Smallville.

"Last warning, Charles." I was in no mood to play games.

"This lesson is on your head," Charles said and scooped up an enormous rolling pin from the table. How did he get a rolling pin?

He swiped it at my head. It was a powerful swing, but slow. Again, the familiar threat of an attack by a human opponent helped settle my mind and I reacted with well-honed instincts, improved by my level 4 hand to hand martial skills ability. I stepped in and intercepted his arm. With a quick twist, I disarmed him, took the rolling pin, and whacked him across the temple. Charles dropped in a cloud of flour.

"I warned you," I told him as I dumped the rolling pin into my inventory.

Less than a minute later, I finished dressing. All my clothes and gear I'd been wearing had been shoved onto a shelf. Luckily, my inventory looked unchanged. I had no idea if they could loot it while I still lived, but they had shown enough weird skills, I wouldn't be surprised. I had several notifications waiting, so I checked them as I dressed.

Congratulations, Lucas. You have found the first sex cult established by earthlings this week. You receive a gold Risky Business loot box.

Congratulations, Lucas. You walked into an obvious trap with no plan to escape and survived anyway. You receive a silver Lucky Stiff loot box.

Congratulations, Lucas. You have resisted a powerful emotional mind assault. You receive a gold Samwise loot box.

I opened the loot boxes since I had a minute. The gold Risky Business loot box gave me 3 potions of Impotence. I chuckled until I read the description.

Potion of Impotence. Times 3. Not the kind you're thinking of, pervert, but even more entertaining. Drinking this potion renders a being magically impotent. Blocks all use of mana for 60 seconds.

"Wow. That would be better if I could throw it at someone and have it take effect, though."

Cyrus answered. "Great idea, Lucas, but that only works if you find an item capable of delivering a potion remotely."

"What kind of items can do that?"

Cyrus laughed. "And ruin the surprise?"

The Lucky Stiff loot box gave me another boost of plus 5 to Luck, and the Samwise loot box gave me a whopping 20% to Mental Resistance. Those were better prizes than I expected to get. Then I noticed the countdown timer and my good mood vanished.

"How did I lose 12 hours?"

"Abbie's Goodnight Kiss ability usually knocks men out for longer than that. It helps erode mental resistance unless the subject has your level of regeneration. Most men wake up as willing puppets. Isn't that an amazing ability?"

I'd lost half a day. It was past noon on the fourth day already. I only had two and a half days to go. I headed for the door, but then noticed a bunch of messages in my chat. I scanned dozens of increasingly-worried messages from Ruby and Tomas. In the last few, they'd promised they were coming to help, but it was the last one that made me curse.

Ruby: "Lucas, we're here. We've found a wooden compound. Your last known position was in there so we're going in."

She sent it 30 minutes ago. I didn't hear shouting or fighting, but they must have attacked by now. With growing dread, I rushed to the doorway and flung it open. The exit led to the main area just inside the gate. So the kitchen was in the other log cabin. Another speedo-wearing dude stood nearby carrying a spear that glowed softly red.

He spun and gave me a nod. "The Mistress will not be pleased to see you wearing clothing already. The intruders are subdued and she's calling for lunch."

Subdued meant not dead. My first instinct was to rush over and stab him on the way to the other log cabin, but I resisted the urge. I didn't know how many other of Abbie's servants might be around. If I raised the alarm, she might kill Ruby and Tomas and the others before I could get to them.

So I ducked my head humbly. "Sorry. My mind is still fuzzy."

"Focus on serving the Mistress. That brings clarity."

"Thanks. Will you help me with the food?"

He strode toward me, frowning. "Where is Charles?"

"He slipped on a rolling pin. He's resting."

Identify kicked in as the man hurried over, spear leaning on his shoulder.

Michael Rogers. Baby human level 14. Team Smallville.

So he was on the same team as Charles. Good. He'd want to help. I led the way back inside, then let Michael rush past. He spied Charles's prone form on the floor and ran to him.

Cyrus surprised me by laughing loudly. "Excellent ploy, Lucas! You're a better actor than I realized."

Michael heard that too. He stiffened, then spun toward me, trying to swing his spear off his shoulder. It caught in a rack of pots, knocking them to the floor in a thunderous cascade.

I rushed Michael and snatched a long loaf of French bread off the cooling rack. As Michael started to shout an alarm, I shoved the entire loaf into his mouth, compressing it so tight he gagged. Then I punched him in the base of the jaw, snapping his head around and knocking him out. I manacled both him and Charles and even paused for a second to scoop that ball of bread out of his mouth so he didn't choke.

I dumped his spear into my inventory, but didn't bother to check its properties. Time was short. So I stripped back down to my boxers, picked up a tray with finger foods Charles had left on the prep table, and headed for the other log cabin.

It was time for lunch.

Chapter Fifty-Eight
Drama Queen

The Persian hoarder suite was a mess, with pillows flung everywhere and stuffing still floating lazily in the hot, still air. I paused to take in the scene and nearly dropped my facade of a brainless servant in the first second.

Ruby and Jane were both hanging suspended from silk streamers attached to the ceiling. They looked battered and only half conscious. Blood was dripping down a cut on Jane's cheek, while one of Ruby's eyes was swollen shut.

Fred Gallagher and another bare-chested man wearing red boxers were prodding at them with steel spears, poking shallow cuts in their skin. I spotted a lot of little cuts, all dripping blood.

Tomas knelt on a cushion nearby, eyes glassy and expression vacant. Some of the silk drapes around the enormous bed were thrown back, showing the psycho mistress Abbie straddling Steve, who lay on his back, arms wide, unmoving.

Abbie had embraced her fatal attraction character and gone full dominatrix. She'd changed into a leather halter top made up of crisscrossing belts with too many buckles and tons of spiky bits, along with a black thong bikini bottom. She was leaning over Steve, whispering throaty words as she slowly cut away his shirt.

Three other shirtless, boxer-wearing men stood along the wall near the door, each carrying an unsheathed sword. They all ranged between level 14 and 16.

I advanced slowly, head bowed, trying to breathe as I fought an overwhelming urge to start killing. None of the guards along the wall interfered, and Fred even paused in his torture of Jane to smile approvingly at me.

"Mistress, lunch is ready," I intoned in a bored, sleepy voice.

"Bring it to me, boy," she said, not turning from Steve.

Her voice again slithered into my ears and attacked my mind, but this time I managed to withstand the onslaught. The huge bonus I'd received from that loot box made a noticeable difference. Besides, seeing Ruby and Jane getting tortured right in front of me helped even more.

Every step was agony as I fought the urge to sprint across the room. It seemed to take forever, and Fred stabbed Jane again, this time right in the stomach. She groaned and blinked open her eyes.

"Lucas, is that you?"

"So you know the new guy?" Fred laughed. "Fat lot of good that will do you."

I finally reached the bed and Abbie lazily reached one hand back to snag a treat. It looked just like a mini smokey, wrapped in a biscuit. She popped it into her mouth and moaned, like the little treat was some kind of aphrodisiac.

On the bed, Steve's gaze was unfocused, a half smile on his lips, and he remained lying motionless, making no move to escape while Abby was distracted. Time for a little intervention.

I grabbed Abbie by the back of her leather halter top and yanked, planning to hurl her across the room. Instead, all I managed to do was rip the entire sex dungeon outfit off. The buckles unsnapped like they were obviously intended to, leaving her entire torso naked.

Abbie looked at me and laughed, her throaty voice vibrating with intense pleasure. "My, my, but you're turning out to be a naughty boy, Lucas. Don't worry, you'll get playtime later."

I slammed the silver tray full of sweets into her face with all my strength.

That should have splattered her to paste, but a faintly shimmering defensive barrier appeared around her, absorbing much of the impact. My blow still broke through and slammed into her hard enough to break bones. It definitely splattered her nose in a wonderful spray of crimson.

She screamed as the impact catapulted her through the silk drapes in a crazy tumble all the way across the room to crash into the solid log wall with a crunching sound. Strangely, every one of the shirtless men staggered, as if that blow had radiated out to them too somehow.

Even before she hit the wall, I continued my movement, hurling the now-dented platter at Fred. It caught him in the chest, edge first and even though it wasn't sharp, it hit with enough force to punch through ribs and send him flying in a spray of blood.

All the guards recovered from their initial stumble. They shouted and charged. Thankfully the dude who had been stabbing at Ruby charged me too.

I snatched up two pillows, slapping my palms onto them before hurling them at the guards rushing in from the door. An emoji appeared on the face of each pillow.

Emoji trap. 50 punches. Like a gang of angry bikers in the palm of your hand. The force of each punch is adjusted to a percentage of your strength.
Emoji trap. Mud wrap. Like a spa day nightmare. Imagine a luxury, full-body wrap applied by women who moonlight as mummies.

The guards ignored the pillows, which proved to be a bad choice. The first pillow struck the center guard, and a gray cloud enveloped him. The gray, hazy smoke condensed into fists all around the poor guy and started raining heavy punches over him.

He shook, his body slamming back and forth so hard his feet left the ground as the invisible fists brutally pummeled him. I should have thought that one through. My tier-1 strength was over 20.

The second pillow seemed to melt around the second guard, expanding into sheets of muddy ribbon that whipped around with dizzying speed, totally encasing him in about 2 seconds. It was like watching him transform into a muddy mummy.

"Tomas! Steve! Get up!" I shouted as I ran to meet the spear-wielding guard who had been stabbing Ruby. Neither of the guys so much as twitched.

The guard lunged, stabbing out with his spear. It was a decent move, but too slow. I slipped the spear, not slowing, and reached him before he could retract the weapon. I clotheslined him across the face as I ran past, knocking him off his feet.

Instead of turning to face the last guard, I jumped and soared past the bound women, slashing out with an ax-headed polearm I pulled from my inventory. It easily slashed through the silk ribbons binding them, but the cuts oddly sounded like the distant shrieks of dying women instead of clean ripping of fabric.

Ruby fell hard to her knees, shaking her head to wake up. Jane landed already running straight at the two remaining guards, her expression a mask of fury. She made a cutting gesture with one hand and their weapons hurtled out of their hands, swept across the room, and slammed into the wall near the door. They sank deep into the wood, quivering from the strength of the psychic blast.

With an infuriated shout, Jane plowed into the guards, fists flying. She might not have a formal skill at hand to hand fighting, but anger fueled her punches with a lot of strength. I turned to help as the three of them met in intense melee, punching and kicking at each other, but an angry shriek reminded me Abbie was not dead.

She rose from where she'd fallen against the outer wall, her body sheathed in layers of silk ribbons. Despite the blood on her face, she moved with sinuous grace. No doubt she'd already taken a full healing potion. Identify kicked in.

Abby Forrest. Level 25 baby human. Team Fatal Attraction. Class: Charmbinder.

No wonder she was so strong. She'd already hit level 25 and unlocked her class. It suddenly made more sense how a tier-0 baby human could affect me so much with her mind-warping powers.

"Lucas, I'll eat your heart!" she shrieked.

"You're breaking with your entire theme. Shouldn't you be promising some kind of sex-themed death torture? Maybe even castration?"

"You want me to castrate you?" She looked honestly shocked.

"Of course not. I'm just messing with you."

"She's mine," Ruby growled, rising to her feet.

She was visibly healing from a potion, and as she stalked toward Abbie, a pair of nunchucks appeared in her right hand. Suddenly loud, fast-tempo music filled the room. It was the same song that Ruby Roundhouse had used in the movie. "Baby, I love your way."

Despite everything, I couldn't help laughing. "I thought you didn't want to use those."

"We all have to do things we don't want to," she growled, and charged.

Abbie threw up her hands, and the ends of the dozens of silk ribbons wrapping her torso rose like snakes and snapped out at Ruby.

So that was how she had trapped them in the first place. Not only did she have that nasty seduction mind magic and some way to echo damage down to her followers, but also mind control over silk ribbons. Abbie was a total piece of work.

Ruby raced in, nunchucks whirling as she jumped and spun and danced, knocking one ribbon after another out of the way. I just wanted to stand there and watch the amazing show, but the door banged open and 4 more shirtless men charged in waving swords and spears.

Jane was still beating down the two guards, while Fred was rising to rejoin the fray, his injured chest healed from a potion. I didn't want to kill them. They were just Abbie's pawns, but I had to stop them.

So I left Ruby to take on the dominatrix and rushed to meet the charging guards. Tomas and Steve still hadn't moved. Abbie had rattled their minds even worse than she had mine when I first arrived.

"You betrayed the mistress!" Fred shouted, face a mask of pure rage as he charged. That drew the attention of the new arrivals and they all oriented on me too.

Fine with me. I didn't want them stabbing Jane in the back or dispatching Tomas and Steve while they remained helpless. I considered my options as I gauged the onrushing 5 men. All but Fred had weapons, but they didn't look like they were very skilled.

So I pulled my two fighting sticks from my inventory and jumped to meet Fred. The group were slightly spread out, so they couldn't all attack me at once if I didn't give them the chance to encircle me.

Fred had lost his weapon and barreled in, fists raised. I clubbed him in the side of the head with my steel-banded stick. I hadn't thought I swung that hard, but blood flew and he dropped like a bag of hammers. I might have just cracked his skull.

"Sorry," I whispered as I turned to meet the others. I had to be more careful. It was too easy to forget my own strength.

The first one swept a heavy sword at my head, but I ducked it and hit him half a dozen times before he could recover, pulling each swing so that I barely touched him. Again, bones cracked and blood flew, despite my best efforts. I targeted his hands to disarm, elbows to disable, and knees to immobilize. In under 2 seconds, he fell screaming and writhing in pain.

"Sorry," I muttered again. Did I have to wrap my sticks in pillows to reduce the damage to where I wanted?

Then the others arrived and I threw my heavier stick back into my inventory. Time seemed to slow as I spun and moved around them, stick blurring to deflect their blows. With my other hand, I slapped one man on his shirtless chest.

He rocketed away like he'd been kicked by a mule. Growling as I tried to rein in my strength, I resorted to flicking the next guy in the forehead as I spun past his lunging strike. His skull rang like a gong, and he collapsed in a heap. It didn't look like I'd seriously wounded him.

Flicking it was, then. It felt like forever since I'd engaged in full contact sparring, but the forms seemed clearer than ever. My level-4 skill made more of a difference than I'd realized.

The guards were even worse at fighting than I'd imagined. They'd do fine against a monster rushing straight in for the kill, but they had no experience fighting skilled human opponents. Their agility and dexterity were abysmal, so they moved painfully slow. Worse, they broadcast strikes and moved in predictable patterns.

As far as fights go, it was pretty disappointing. I danced through them like a ghost, but had to grin when I realized I was slipping into the same cadence Ruby was using in her dance fighting moves as she battled Abbie's snake ribbons. As I deflected each attack, I responded with a single flick to a forehead.

Three seconds later, the guards lay in a motionless heap. Healing potions would set them right, but I didn't want them recovering while still in thrall to Abbie.

Then Ruby shouted, "I hate you!"

Somehow Abbie had gotten the upper hand and Ruby lay on the ground, wrapped in multicolored silk ribbons, struggling vainly. Abbie stood over her, torso still twined by the other halves of the same ribbons, making it look like the women were crazy mutant conjoined twins. She raised a dagger that looked like a letter opener, with a handle capped by a bright red heart.

I cast my stick back into my inventory and pulled out an energy rifle. The silk ribbons moved like snakes and hauled Ruby off the ground. Abbie thrust her dagger at Ruby's heart.

I shot Abbie in the head.

Her skull exploded in a shower of blood and gore and she toppled to the ground. Ruby fell a second later as the ribbons holding her up lost power.

"Mistress, no!" one of the guards Jane had just kicked over the bed shouted, reaching an imploring hand toward Abbie's corpse. Then he blinked and looked around in confusion. "Where am I?"

"You're having a nightmare," Jane told him, then punched him so hard in the jaw, she knocked him out cold.

I rushed to Ruby, who was struggling to unwrap the tightly wound silk ribbons.

"I could have beaten her," Ruby said as I ripped silk ribbons away.

"Sure." I helped her up. "Thanks for coming to rescue me."

She snorted. "Some rescue. You had to save my life twice."

"Still, thanks."

"We're a team," she said with a genuine smile, not a psycho twisted manipulative smile like Abbie's. Then Ruby surprised me by stepping forward and wrapped her arms around my waist.

"I was worried for you," she said and held on for a long moment.

The hug felt great, but I didn't want her to get the wrong idea. "No problem. Like you said, we're a team."

I didn't move away, though. The world was crazy, and sometimes a hug from a friend was necessary. She probably needed it more than I did. She was the one who had been bound, tortured, and then nearly killed. Finally Ruby released me, stepped back, then punched me in the shoulder hard enough to make me wince.

"Ow."

"That's for making me worry about you. How did you find these psychos anyway?"

"Just dumb luck."

"Not what I'd call luck," Jane called from across the room where she was kneeling beside Tomas. He held one hand to his temple as he sat on a fat cushion with some stuffing spilling out the side. He still looked confused.

"I think we knocked out all her cult members."

"Good," Ruby said. "They didn't deserve dying just because a psycho mind demon got into their heads, but they did deserve what they got."

Then she glanced at me again, her eyes flicking over my mostly bare torso. The hint of a smile tugged up one corner of her mouth, and she raised one fine eyebrow.

"Your wardrobe choices have gotten very interesting."

I rolled my eyes and turned away so she couldn't see me flush. I willed my clothes to appear on me. They appeared just fine, but fell to the floor in a heap.

Ruby smiled. "How are you so bad at that?"

"I guess I haven't leveled up my wardrobe auto-equip ability yet."

Grumbling, I got dressed, then triggered Soul Feed. I wasn't sure it would work on defeated humans too. The white cloud erupting from Abbie's corpse dwarfed what I expected. So it did work.

I checked my achievements but didn't get the ones I expected. I grimaced as Eva read the first one to me.

Every player eventually faces the hard reality that not every member of their race is worth saving. Some are downright evil, others have opposing priorities that make success impossible. Sometimes they have to be defeated just like the monsters. You have killed your first Earth human and receive a gold Brutus loot box.

That was not an achievement I'd ever wanted, but Abbie had given us no choice. Two other achievements were much more welcome, and I focused on them to not think about the memory of Abbie's head exploding from my shot.

Congratulations, Lucas! Your stick and knife fighting has reached level 5.
Congratulations, Lucas! You have reached level 8. Two stat points allocated to Intelligence.

"I got a level for killing Abbie," I said softly, not sure how to feel about that.

I'd killed a lot of monsters, including the much higher-level elite griffon. I knew I'd been close to getting a level, but it felt wrong to get it for killing a human. Did killing humans give more experience? I hoped not. If it did, some folks would see that as an irresistible path to quick leveling.

"I did too." Ruby met my gaze, her expression solemn.

Would you like to loot Abbie Forrest?

I accepted the prompt. I didn't like having to kill people, even someone as insane as Abbie, but I wasn't about to ignore potentially important gear. I couldn't bring myself to try harvesting a spell from her, though. Just thinking of using any of hers made me feel dirty.

I got a ton of mana crystals and a slew of potions, including 5 scrolls of firestorm that sounded really powerful. I also got nearly 100 silk ribbons, and 32 bottles of assorted hard liquor. I wasn't a hard liquor drinker usually, but I'd give the 2 bottles of tequila to Steve and see if his margaritas were as good as he promised. I bet Sam would trade me barrels of his tasty ale for each of the other bottles.

I also got the knife with the heart-tipped handle Abbie had been carrying. The description made my blood run cold.

Dagger of Heartache. Rare. Stab this dagger through the heart of an enemy to rip out their soul and bind it to a silk ribbon. This transforms the ribbon into a semi-sentient weapon that will obey your mental commands and will gain the attribute: Resistant to cutting.

No wonder those ribbons had shrieked when I'd cut them. I'd released the bound spirits from their slavery. Abbie hadn't possessed a telekinesis power like Jane. All those ribbons she'd fought Ruby with were possessed by the souls of Abbie's victims. I'd seen close to 20.

Ruby was moving around the room looting the cushions and the weapons from the unconscious guards. Jane was helping Tomas drink a healing potions. Steve still lay unmoving.

"Don't take any of the ribbons. I'm going to pile them up here and burn them when we leave."

"Why? The crafters in town would love to use them to make more clothing," Ruby responded.

"Some of them are cursed. I'll keep the ones that aren't, but we have to destroy the others."

Ruby grimaced. "She was such a piece of work."

More than she knew. I double-checked my inventory and when I focused on the ribbons I'd gotten from Abbie, I found 3 with slightly different descriptions than the others.

Ribbon of the Reaper. Semi-sentient. This ribbon is possessed by the soul of Janice Peterson, who died alone and afraid. Her purpose now is to fight for the wielder of the Heartache dagger to make the pain go away.

The other two were possessed by Tanya Biddle and Wendy Lambert. A slow, creeping feeling of dread crept up my scalp as I considered the poor victims of Abbie's insanity. She'd killed all the women who fell into her clutches and enslaved the men.

All the other possessed ribbons were strewn on the floor, wrapped around Abbie's body. I left them there and headed to the bed where Steve still lay unmoving.

"Hey, you okay, Buddy?"

Steve sighed and turned slowly to look at me. "Your sense of timing is the worst. You know that, right?"

"What do you mean? Her minions were torturing Ruby and Jane. You were enslaved to her will."

"I know. It was just getting interesting, though."

"Seriously? You liked being a mind zombie?"

"Not really, but I was still vaguely aware of what was going on. She was super hot. A few minutes in a mind haze would have been a small price to pay for more of that playtime she was teasing me with."

I shuddered, but reminded myself he didn't know just how evil she'd been. "Trust me, she wasn't worth it. She murdered a lot of people."

Steve sat up and sighed. "I know. It's just . . ." He gave me a serious expression. "I didn't even have a girlfriend when we got yanked away from Earth. We're all going to die. Could die any second. Am I evil to not mind an unexpected bit of intimacy to keep the nightmares at bay for a few minutes?"

"Not if it was anyone else." I extended a hand to haul him to his feet.

He sighed again. "You're probably right. I'm still going to loot the bed, though."

I grimaced. "Wash everything before you use it."

Preferably with a molotov cocktail.

Chapter Fifty-Nine

I Discover An Easier Way to Carry a House

We looted what we could of the main cabin and shared potions with the mind-warped cult members as they awoke. Abbie's control disappeared when she died, but her influence did not fade entirely.

Most of them still had fuzzy memories, and none of them could remember what happened to the women in their teams. Ruby surprised me by taking the lead in explaining that Abbie had murdered them all. She broke the horrible news with a gentle empathy that helped ease the shock.

I never could have done it as well, and even with Ruby's gentle words, there was no hiding the fact that they'd been shafted. Most of the men were horrified, some raged at the insanity of it, and Charles the baker beat his fists to bloody pulp against the wooden palisade wall.

All of those reactions made sense, but a couple of the brainwashed men looked conflicted, and one of them looked downright sad that Abby was gone. He said, "In some ways, living that lie was better than facing reality."

"You're insane!" Charles advanced on the brain-addled fellow in a rage, his fists still dripping with his own blood. "She killed them all. She killed Tess."

His voice broke, but he raised an angry fist. I intervened then. "We all got a taste of Abbie's mind control. She was a psycho murderess. Give him time, Charles. His mind will clear and he'll realize it."

Charles stomped off and finally took a healing potion. We returned their weapons, clothing, and gear, which we found in the other log cabin, along with a bunch of other equipment. I shared most of the mana crystals I'd looted from Abbie too.

"I can't take the ovens out of the kitchen," Tomas reported as I came out of the storeroom where we'd found all the gear. "It's some kind of warped version of Base Camp, but doesn't seem to disappear like the tents."

"Shame," Jane said. "We cleaned out the cooked food, but the ingredients are considered part of the kitchen. It's a unique setup. I wish we could take it with us."

"Maybe we can." I paced around the log cabin, studying it.

It was smaller than Abbie's den, maybe twenty feet by thirty. That made it about the size of a smallish ranch-style house. The construction was far sturdier than anything the mind zombies could have build. Made sense that it was a system construct.

Tomas asked, "What do you mean? Think you can drag it down the mountain behind Switchblade?"

"You'd get stuck when you reached the first trees," Ruby said.

"I was thinking something more direct."

Near the back of the building, the ground looked softer. "Jane, can you move dirt with your telekinesis?"

"I don't know. I've never tried."

"Try. Right there. I need a hole deep enough to crawl through all the way to the middle of the building."

"You can't be serious!" Tomas exclaimed, eyes widening in understanding.

"It's worth a try."

Ruby looked from him to me, but it was Jane who exclaimed. "You seriously think you're strong enough to pick up a house?"

"There's one way to find out. If I can lift it, I can dump it into my inventory."

"How? You're only level 8," Steve protested. "I know, you got some weird loot that gives you extra stats, but you can't be that far above the rest of us. I'm stronger than the strongest person back on Earth, but it would take a lot of people to lift a log cabin."

"I've got a trick or two up my sleeve. Jane, can you do it?"

"Let's find out." She still looked doubtful, but she loved a challenge, and the idea of me lifting a building resonated with her adventurous spirit.

"Actually, never mind. I've got a simpler plan." I was tempted to try the original plan anyway. Lifting a house would be so awesome, and I honestly believed I could do it. More likely, I'd end up bursting up through the floor. Would still be fun to try, but we'd already wasted too much time.

So I pulled out an Ultimate Glamp potion and poured it onto the side of the log cabin. The entire building shimmered with ghostly amber light, then abruptly vanished.

"What happened?" Fred shouted from near the open gate as everyone stared at the empty space where the log cabin had stood. I explained about the potion as I stoppered the bottle.

"You loser," Tomas said. "You had me fooled. I totally thought you were going to lift the entire building."

"I still think you should try sometime," Jane said.

"Me too."

Ruby smiled. "So you just claimed a unique Base Camp. Can't wait to see what you can cook up for dinner."

"Will the rest of us be invited?" Steve asked, perking up from the somber silence he'd slipped into. "Or are you planning a more intimate dinner for two?"

"You're such a muppet," Ruby laughed, and that helped ease some of the dark mood we'd all been feeling. The entire situation still sucked, but smiling helped more than I expected.

Before we left, I used a scroll of Firestorm to torch Abbie's lair and destroy all the possessed silks. I was surprised to receive an achievement.

For releasing the trapped souls of all the women murdered by Abbie Forrest, you receive an emerald Guardian loot box.

"Hey, why did you get an emerald box?" Fred exclaimed when the huge, glittering emerald appeared in the air in front of me.

"Who can explain how the system works?"

"So if I had torched that cabin, I could have gotten that loot?" Charles asked.

"I guess we'll never know." I accepted the prompt to open the box.

It flashed and disappeared, leaving a ring made out of intertwined threads of silver, blue, and red, like Cyrus had melted diamonds, rubies, and sapphires together to make it.

Last Chance ring. Epic. Ring will activate once you defeat a boss monster. Will then auto trigger with one of that boss's powers to counter an otherwise fatal attack. Cooldown: 7 days, plus another defeated boss.

"Whoa," I breathed as I slipped the ring onto my right hand. That was amazing. I needed to find a boss to kill anyway, so I wasn't too worried about that odd limitation to the ring's power. The ability to survive an otherwise fatal strike was definitely epic.

"Nice ring. What does it do?" Ruby asked.

"Added defense."

I wasn't about to share all the details with so many other people around. I already had enough gear to make some folks consider stabbing me in the back to loot my corpse. With Abbie's cruel evil still so fresh, I could not pretend everyone was an ally just because they came from Earth.

Luckily, the others had found a more direct route to the hidden valley than I had. The journey to shepherd the survivors of Abbie's cult to Stepstone went quick and uneventfully. We did not talk much.

The rescued men livened up when they saw the huge settlement. They'd survived a very bizarre ordeal and even got some unique loot boxes out of it. They thanked us profusely when we reached the gate, but then rushed off as soon as they heard about Sam's tavern.

Charles, the French cook, was particularly eager to meet Sam and get a job. Hopefully focusing on positive work would help them deal with their recent trauma. We'd all lost teammates, but it had to be tough knowing they'd stood by, helpless, while Abbie murdered people they knew.

Tomas and Jane headed back to his Base Camp to meet up with the rest of his team. I joined Ruby and Steve for a sumptuous dinner of stroganoff in her Base Camp. I was tempted to drop my log cabin home onto a vacant lot near her tent, but I didn't plan to spend much time in town. Why waste one of my few glamping potions?

"Steve and I got assignments to join a hunting team to clear the western slopes first thing in the morning. A larger expedition will be entering the second stage to begin preparing the next town site." Ruby said, tossing her plate and utensils into the air where they vanished. "I bet I could get you on that yoke with us."

"Thanks, but I think I need to hunt higher on the mountain."

"Alone?" she asked, not disguising what she thought of that.

I shrugged. "You know I need more experience. I can't afford to share with a huge team or I'm not going to make it."

"You're only 2 levels short and you've got 2 days. You can make it," Steve said with a thumb's up and an encouraging smile.

"That's easy for you to say."

"Easier than getting sucked into another death cult. Look what happened today. You nearly died and we nearly died coming to rescue you. Didn't even get to enjoy the experience."

"Sorry about that. I'll be more careful."

"We're supposed to be a team." Ruby said, her tone turning angry.

"I know, and I want to hunt with you, but there are a couple things that make it difficult right now. First, I am way more mobile than you two, which means I'd be slowed down. Second, I need way more experience, as I mentioned."

She didn't look perturbed. "Fine, but you don't have to be an eejit about it. Come with us, but range ahead of the group on your bike. If you run into monsters you can handle, take them out. Like that, you shouldn't have to split experience, but you'll be close enough for us to help if you run into trouble and get banjaxed again."

That was actually a good point, and I did not want her angry with me.

While I considered it, she added, "Our mission will be to clear the way for the rest of the town to ascend to the second stage. We'll be making the transition smoother for everyone."

Was that just an idle comment, or did she know me better than I'd realized? Either way, she got me. "Okay, I'll try it. If it doesn't seem to be working, I'll leave the group and hunt higher by myself."

She smiled, looking very pleased. Steve looked between us and one eyebrow raised in question. "Am I sensing something more than just team spirit in the air here?"

"What do you mean?" I asked. Ruby looked confused. We didn't need Steve to invent drama. We had too much work to do.

"Nothing," Steve said in a tone that suggested he definitely meant something. "It makes more sense now how you broke out of Abbie's spell."

Ruby cocked her head and regarded me thoughtfully. "I was wondering about that. None of the other guys did."

"I have a higher mental resistance." I did not share the fact that I'd gotten most of that after rejecting Abbie's mind control. Most likely, my tier-1 evolution had given me the edge.

"Hmm," Steve said in a way that tried to hold lots of hidden meaning. I ignored it

"I'm going to see what's been happening since last night." I rose and waved. "See you guys in the morning."

"Good night," Steve said with another of those too-knowing smiles. Why did that get under my skin so much?

Ruby fixed me with a serious gaze. "Don't wander, Lucas. I will expect you in the morning."

"Yes, mom."

"Oh, get out," she exclaimed, pulling one of the silk pillows from her inventory and throwing it at me.

I spent an hour exploring the town again. Stepstone had grown noticeably in the day since I'd left. Over 100 new residents had arrived, shepherded by the Explorer teams.

I spotted the tourists led by George and Lucy and stopped to chat briefly with Catelyn. She had gained another level and acquired some armor that shone faintly green in the afternoon light.

"We're doing well, thanks to you." She recounted their busy night hunting before the Explorer team arrived.

"I'm glad you were willing to take the chance."

"I'm captain of my entire hunt team. We're going to join a couple other teams hunting some bulls on the plain tomorrow."

"Good. That'll give you some great experience and hopefully some good loot."

"This town is amazing. I can't believe we hid in that tiny valley so long. We're so much stronger here."

She'd used her time well, getting connected with the town leadership and exploring the area. At one point in her tale, she paused, then asked, "Lucas, you didn't leave a defensive item with us and not tell us about it, did you?"

"No, why?"

She shrugged. "Nothing, or at least nothing concrete. It's just, sometimes while we've been fighting monsters, weird things happen. Monsters suddenly stumble, or their hits seem softer than they should be. It's weird, but the strange events have saved us a lot of injuries and at least one fatality."

"That is weird. I have no idea why that's happening, but I hope it continues."

"Me too." She shrugged, then shared all the news she'd heard, including word from a couple other Explorer teams who had found other groups of people who refused to join the town.

Some had set up homesteads like George and Lucy, choosing to hunker down and hope they'd get ignored. Others were loners. Back on Earth it would be tough to set up an entire homestead or compound like Abbie's in just a few days, but with magic and loot boxes, people were finding creative solutions.

"We can't save people who don't want to be saved. They've all been warned. Hopefully they'll do the smart thing and head up to the second stage like us."

Some people had a weird mindset. How many would refuse to see the truth until it was too late and they paid for their short-sightedness with their lives? Other people in the town seemed just as bad, though.

I spotted folks so busy building businesses or homes they seemed to have forgotten we needed to leave in 2 short days. Most had hit level 10, but a lot of folks seemed content to stay there. Maybe the hard time limit was a good thing. It helped us focus. I could only imagine how much drama we'd see if the time limit was indefinite.

Heading for Sam's tavern, I noted new buildings. A couple of them were even two stories tall. Some now had stone facades, and several sported signs for new vendors. I'd have to visit those later and see what they offered.

"Ah, Lucas. Good to see you." I turned to find Paul the mayor exiting the town hall, munching on a bear's claw pastry.

Chapter Sixty

Beer and Sandwiches

"I heard you found a couple groups. Welcome back," Paul said around his pastry.

"Thanks. Ran into a little trouble with the second group, but we sorted it out."

"Excellent. Are you still interested in more donuts?"

"Is that a trick question?"

He smiled and produced a box filled with 2 dozen assorted donuts. "I added you to the list, as promised."

"Thank you." I dropped the boxes into my inventory, resisting the urge to eat a donut right away. "What do I owe you?"

"5000 mana crystals."

"Seems a bit steep."

He chuckled, and I noticed a golden sparkle in his eyes. He'd picked up a title somewhere. "I'm kidding, but do you actually have that much?"

"I'd find it for donuts."

"You might not want to tell me that, or the price will probably get there," Paul said around another mouthful of pastry. "I will accept mana crystals, but I am more interested in unusual foods or cooking implements."

"I've got a spork and a pair of basic iron tongs." I didn't mention the rolling pin or the huge pile of other cooking implements that came with my log cabin base camp.

"A spork? Ha. I don't have that yet. Even trade for both?"

I produced the items. "As long as I get on the priority queue for more donuts, or a cake."

"Deal."

"So what's the news from the council?"

"It's been busy. Lots of new people. At least 80% are at least level 10, and nearly 10% are now hitting level 25 and unlocking classes. We're getting a good mix of both warriors and crafters. You should look around. There are some new shops you'll want to visit."

"I will. Thanks."

"I added another town councilor and I'm considering a couple more who are pushing hard to join."

"Why?" Was he fishing to see if I wanted a spot? The lust for leadership didn't make sense to me, but so many people couldn't resist the siren call of power it promised.

He chuckled. "Lots of teams arriving and every team leader wants a bigger say in the direction of the whole."

"No one wants to let random strangers no one elected dictate their lives."

Paul grimaced. "You have no idea how many times I've had that conversation."

"Sorry."

He waved it away. "Not your fault so many people think Earth institutions and laws apply here. One fellow was a security guard and insists we make him chief of police. We don't even have police. Another rather well-known actress with a supporting role in the movie is clamoring for a seat on the council."

"Does she have any skills to make her a good fit?"

"Not hardly."

"What's her name?"

"Elayne Dubois."

"Never heard of her."

"I'm not surprised, but don't let her hear that. She's convinced she is a superstar, but she's had at best an unremarkable career. She won a supporting role as the spinster aunt of the leading lady."

"So she was already angry before she got here."

"Indeed," Paul chuckled. "Turns out the casting might have been more accurate than anyone knew. She's got a mean streak. She hit level 25 and ended up with a class called Backroom Advocate."

"What does that mean?"

"Seems to focus on poison and stealth. She's gathering a group of women around her and is an outspoken critic of the current town leadership."

"Sounds like a real winner. I'm glad you're the one dealing with her. Watch your back."

"No one would try assassination," Paul said, but didn't sound convinced.

"We just had to deal with a woman who enslaved some people's minds and used other people's souls as weapons. There are nutcases among us."

Paul grimaced. "You have been busy."

"Yeah. Got any good news?"

"Our new councilor is a good fit. Elizabeth Maberly."

"The leading lady in the movie? I have heard of her." Did Ruby know she'd arrived? I doubted it, or she would've talked about her.

Paul nodded. "She and Tony are becoming the face of the council and that's helping us keep people motivated. They're both popular, and several other supporting actors and actresses have shown up too. They're gaining a lot of influence, but are causing a bit of a real estate crisis."

"How? We all just arrived and we're leaving in a couple days."

"They settled in one part of town and dubbed it New Hollywood. All of a sudden, dozens of people want to move closer. We've had fights over space for tents and someone petitioned the council to create zoning ordinances."

I laughed. "I guess we carry our insanity with us."

"It's only been a few days. Only natural for folks to revert to familiar patterns."

"Except the old rules don't apply here."

"True. No doubt new influencers will emerge, but actors and those with popularity still have a lot of pull."

"I suppose. Good luck."

Sam's tavern was packed with patrons, and Sam had hired several more bartenders. New types of barrels lined the shelves behind the bar. One new counter offered pastries, while another looked like a sandwich deli straight out of a New York corner store. Every table sported gallon-sized baskets of various potato-based delicacies, including 5 types of fries, potato wedges, cheesy potatoes, twice-baked potatoes, and some huge potatoes that had been cooked and sliced like loaves of bread. Someone called them hasselback potatoes.

The entire ceiling was covered in a rippling light show, like slow motion northern lights. The soft colors rippled and shifted to different hues. It transformed the rustic tavern into something magical. Still needed more windows, though. The welcome scents of grilling meat and fresh-baked pastries couldn't quite overpower the stale reek of alcohol and so many people without deodorant.

I beckoned to Sam, who was overseeing the work from behind the front row of bartenders. His apron still looked spotless and he'd gained a ton of levels.

Sam Sternberg, Baby human level 25. Class: Luminary Brewster.

"Hey, congratulations on getting your class."

"Thanks. We've been so busy here, the experience just keeps pouring in."

Maybe getting the right crafter class was a lot smarter than I'd realized. "Luminary Brewster?"

He grinned. "Got some sweet upgrades and class spells. Allowed me to expand my menu a lot and do things like that." He gestured to the subtle light show.

"Can't wait to hear more about it."

"Want a drink? Sandwich? Pastry? What can I do for you, Lucas?"

"Actually, the question might be what can I do for you."

I pulled out a bottle of whiskey and another of bourbon. He gasped and lovingly inspected the bottles. "Where did you get these?"

"A very unusual looting experience. I've got more. I was thinking you could put them to better use than I could."

"Absolutely! How much?"

I produced 25 bottles of assorted hard liquor and lined them up on the end of the counter. I kept 5 to see if Steve wanted them, or to use to make molotov cocktails if necessary. Actual liquor bottles drew a lot of attention and patrons started clamoring for drinks. One over-excited fellow tried snatching a big, square bottle of vodka.

Sam moved like a snake, intercepting the man's quick grab and yanking his hand away. He twisted the squawking fellow around, lifted him easily into the air, and threw him like a bowling ball across the tavern. Shouting the whole way, the hapless fellow tumbled out the tavern and into the street. The outer door opened on its own to let him through.

"Good class skills indeed," I grinned.

Sam sighed. "An unfortunate reality when dealing with tavern clientele."

Everyone gave us plenty of space after that, although dozens of eyes kept flicking to those bottles.

"So, name your price," Sam said eagerly, rubbing his hands.

"Not going to haggle?"

He shrugged and gestured at the crowd watching us. "My costs get passed on to my customers. They're the ones paying you."

Some of the watching folks grimaced, and a few suddenly looked nervous. Maybe they hadn't looted as many crystals as I had, or maybe they'd spent all their money at other shops.

It was weird having so many people listen in on our negotiations, but Sam seemed happy talking there. So I said, "How about 10,000 mana crystals."

He blinked in surprise and a collective groan rippled across the crowd. One woman cried, "Don't be cruel!" She was eyeing the liquor with the hunger of an alcoholic.

Sam was clearly calculating how much he'd have to charge to make a profit off of the liquor anyway, but I'd used Paul's trick just to get a reaction.

"Actually, how about barrels of your ale, along with 2 dozen fresh sandwiches, 10 gallons of assorted potato dishes, and as many pastries as you can produce in 24 hours?"

Sam laughed and extended a hand. "Done!"

The crowd cheered and Sam gestured to a couple bartenders, who swept the bottles behind the counter. Fifty voices instantly started clamoring orders. Sam shouted over the din, "Patience! The new hard liquor bar will open in 10 minutes, once I complete an inventory and establish prices."

That cut through the tumult as reluctant silence settled over the tavern. Sam added, "Each patron will be limited to one glass."

"No!" many shouted, and the alcoholic woman looked ready to cry.

Sam shrugged his meaty shoulders. "We've got a limited supply and a huge demand. If I let each person buy a bottle, most of you wouldn't even get a sip. Would you prefer that?"

The folks closer to the bar looked ready to take the chance, but most reluctantly nodded. Sam turned back to me. "Unless you've got access to more stock?"

"Not yet, but I'll let you know if I find more."

Sam leaned closer as conversation again filled the tavern, making it possible to speak without every ear hearing. "Honestly, I think this will get us over the hump. Steve's been practicing. With this seed whiskey, he should be able to start producing hard liquor from other ingredients."

"Nice. I'm glad I got here ahead of the market."

"Never fear, Lucas. There's always a market for the strong stuff."

He excused himself to prepare for the new orders and to arrange for my payment. One burly young man carried over several barrels of sweet ale immediately, followed by a woman carrying an actual silver platter heaped with pastries. When I turned to greet her, I instantly recognized the beautiful blond woman from team Narnia I'd saved from the spectral mauler.

"Oh, hey Susan." She still wore her maroon dress, and now had a gold pin holding back one side of her thick hair.

"Lucas," she beamed, her smile bright as she passed me the tray. I dumped everything into my inventory except for one cream horn. I took a big bite and savored the explosion of cream and sugar and flaky crust.

Susan lingered close, eyes glued to my face. "Why would you trade hard liquor for that beer? It's barely got any alcohol in it."

I shrugged. "Getting drunk while fighting monsters seems like a great way to die."

"You've been doing a lot of fighting," she commented, sliding one hand along the ripped front of my jacket. I'd forgotten to swap back to my new armored one. "But you're still not level 10."

"I know. I've got work to do."

She leaned closer, her big hazel eyes wide, her warm British accent like a caress. "Don't forget to relax sometimes too."

Still with that? I appreciated how much she wanted to thank me for saving her life, but her intensity was getting a bit creepy. After dealing with Abbie, I was not in the right emotional state for Susan hitting on me.

She took my hesitation for encouragement and smiled wider. "There are some new entertainment options in town you might not have heard of."

"Oh?" I couldn't imagine someone starting a theatre group, but then again, there were a lot of people from the movie industry in town.

"Elizabeth Maberly, the famous actress, is starting a night club. Live music, dancing, and maybe more."

"Sounds like quite a diversion." I managed a smile. "Maybe some other time. It's good to see you, Susan. I'll see you later."

"Definitely."

I decided to pick up the rest of my payment later. Sam was good for it. I headed for the door, and when I glanced back, Susan was still standing there watching me. I needed to hunt, but suddenly I felt exhausted. So I returned to Ruby's tent. She had that bunkroom upgrade and happily loaned it to me. I was asleep almost before my head hit the pillow.

Chapter Sixty-One

Ruby Shows Off Her Barbecuing Skills

Ruby shook me awake. "Lucas, come on. It's time to join the expedition."

"Huh?" I sat up, rubbing sleep from my eyes, fuzzy thoughts barely moving. "But that's not till morning."

"It is morning."

The words were like a jolt of caffeine straight into my brain. "I slept all night?"

"Imagine that," Steve said from the other room. "Even you still need sleep. This world doesn't make any sense at all."

"Not funny." I jumped up, fighting to hide my frustration. Between getting knocked out yesterday, then sleeping all night, I'd lost half of the last 2 days. At that pace, I'd never finish leveling up.

Yeah, I was still only human, but shouldn't I be able to ignore sleep longer? I took a deep breath and ran hands through my hair. They snagged on something sticky. I grimaced, but fought down my worry. The stress of how much I had to do was like a weight in the back of my mind, but I still had time. I could do this.

The shower turned out to be amazing. The water pressure would have scoured my skin raw back on Earth, but felt incredible as it swept all the grime and dirt away. The controls allowed me to make it so hot even my toughened skin reddened. I could have enjoyed that shower for half an hour, but only allowed myself a luxurious 10 minutes. A hot blast of air dried me in seconds and I found my battered clothes clean, pressed, and folded on the shelf next to the sink.

I even found shaving gear. With my constitution so high, the razor didn't leave a mark. Sweet. No more razor burn. When I emerged, Steve was lounging on one of the overstuffed chairs, munching on a huge chocolate eclair. I wasn't the only one leveraging my connection with Sam. I produced 2 bottles of tequila and one more of whiskey, dropping them on the side table next to his chair.

"Wow!" Steve shoved the rest of the eclair into his mouth to examine the bottles and mumbled through the huge mouthful. "Ruby said you got some liquor from that log cabin, but I had no idea."

"When we get back from our hunting trip, I expect some world-class margaritas."

"Prepare to be amazed."

Ruby joined us and nodded toward the bathroom, raising one fine eyebrow. "What do you think? Worth the upgrade price?"

"Absolutely. That's probably the best upgrade you could have done."

"After the menu upgrade," Steve piped in, producing a small round pastry topped with fruit and shoving the entire thing into his mouth.

Ruby grinned and added, "Wait till you try the massage feature in my room."

Steve coughed, choking on his pastry, eyes bulging as he fought to clear his airways. Had I heard Ruby right? I pounded Steve hard enough to crack a regular human's ribs.

He managed to swallow and grinned at Ruby. "Massage feature? Since when do you invite guys into your bedroom for massages?"

Ruby's face reddened, her eyes widening as she realized how that must have sounded. "That's not what I meant."

I couldn't help grinning. "It did sound like quite the offer."

"You know, I can wait outside for a few minutes," Steve offered, grin widening at Ruby's growing embarrassment. The liquor bottles disappeared into his inventory and he looked ready to dodge a pillow.

She stamped one foot. "That's not what I meant, and you know it!"

Steve only nodded slowly, glancing from Ruby to me and asked, "So, Lucas, how does it feel to have our lovely teammate tease you with massages, then pretend she never did?"

"Just drop it. I think we've squeezed all the fun out of this one that we can."

"Oh, don't underestimate me," Steve said before heading out of the tent, whistling softly to himself.

Ruby stepped closer, her face still red. "Lucas, I just meant . . ."

"I know, and I appreciate it. Made for a good joke, though. Come on, let's go."

She gave me a grateful smile and we headed out side by side. Moments later, we joined a group of about a dozen other men and women gathering on the outskirts of town. The makeshift log barricade that walled off open space between the stone spires around town had been replaced by solid stone walls.

"When did that happen?"

"A couple of the crafters who hit level 25 got classes related to building fortifications. They can raise entire sections of walls in moments, as long as they have mana potions to top themselves off," Ruby explained.

"They're planning a full castle for the second stage," Steve added. "Hopefully they'll add a princess in the tallest tower so I can practice more rescues."

I pulled out Switchblade and reviewed the part of the description about armaments.

Weapons Battery. 3 slots for defense, 2 slots for offense. Can absorb spell scrolls, weapons, or items with magical effects. Note: spells or effects may be altered to fit Switchblade's systems.

I was under-utilizing the bike's potential. Why not trigger spells from the bike if I'd likely be riding it when I ran into monsters? Too bad I didn't have other good defensive options. Shield Dome was already similar to Energy Ward. I needed to find more. In the meantime, I could add offensive capabilities.

I opened the bike's menu, mentally clicked on the open slot for offensive spells, and moved one of my temporary spells over.

You have added Corrosive Cloud to Switchblade as an offensive spell. This spell is no longer available to use as a temporary spell. Corrosive Cloud altered to fit Switchblade delivery method.

Corrosive Cloud. Are of Effect. Deliver a cloud of gas from the rear of the bike for 5 seconds. Area of effect spell that corrodes metal and flesh on contact. It's like Pumba from the Lion King on steroids. Cloud remains active for 2 minutes. Uses remaining: 1.

Hopefully I'd made the right choice. I'd seriously considered Frostfire Nova, but decided to hold that one in reserve. I'd hoped to get more uses out of the spell when I applied it to Switchblade, but no luck this time.

All the bike's systems were in the green, power at 100%. Ruby and Steve walked around it as I updated the spell, and Steve whistled softly. "I don't know how you get all the luck, Lucas, but this is a one-of-a-kind beauty."

"I can take a passenger. Want to ride shotgun while I scout today?"

He grinned. "Best offer I've had all morning." Then his smile widened and a crafty sparkle flickered in his eyes. "I'll take you up on it later, but I think Ruby was in line before me." Steve made an elaborate bow to her as he took a smooth step back.

"How about it?" I asked her.

"Are you kidding? Of course! Steve, are you sick today? You're passing up a grand chance to ride in style to trudge through miles of grass?"

He chuckled. "Hiking through a beautiful valley with breathtaking mountains in every direction is still so much better than the views I enjoyed most days working as a plumber, believe me."

I stepped onto Switchblade and Ruby jumped on behind, wrapping her arms around my waist and leaning against my back. She smelled faintly of flowers somehow.

Steve gave me a thumb's up and a wink, and as he turned away, he muttered to himself, "My work is done here."

I still picked up the words. He was such a goofball. It wasn't like I was asking Ruby on a date, or anything. She was my teammate. Of course I'd invite her to ride with me. He seemed to like having something to tease people about. It didn't really bother me as long as he didn't annoy Ruby too much.

The councilwoman Crystal Bennett arrived with a few other people. Surprisingly, she was the excursion leader. I had honestly expected her to remain in town mostly, focusing on administrative duties. She apparently didn't want to let the other council members get all the glory leading raiding parties.

Tony and Burns together would lead a large contingent of many of the strongest fighters up to the second stage after our group cleared a path up the slope. Their interdiction team would scout for a spot to set up the next town.

It was a good plan. Even though the interdiction team could fight up the slope unaided, this way experience for killing the weaker monsters on the slopes got shared with folks who needed it. No doubt the interdiction team would encounter far stronger monsters, so would get plenty of experience too.

As soon as Crystal added me to the excursion group chat, I waved and accelerated away. I didn't have time for pep talks or to wait for the team to figure out their chain of command and start marching.

Ruby clutched my waist tightly as we shot across the grasses and her laugh trailed behind. "This is grand! What else can it do?"

I showed her, using the open grasses to bank and turn Switchblade, dropping into the grasses, then popping into the air again. Ruby laughed and cheered, and for a moment I was able to forget about leveling and monsters and killing and just enjoy a good ride.

As we neared the long slope up to the second stage, I spotted movement. A single creature was running toward the hills.

Soilrunner Bull. Level 24. Far more aggressive than the Soilstrider cows, the bulls of the herd live to fight. Like every group of thugs from every action movie ever made, they will challenge any foe, even if outmatched. The bulls actually pack a wicked punch with their momentum-based attacks and overwhelming numbers.

The unlucky bull lacked the numbers, so he was a great target to practice on. I pointed to it as I adjusted course and accelerated to attack. "Hey, there's one of the stragglers from the herd."

As I focused on it, a green image overlay appeared in my goggles, with the running bull highlighted. In the top corner of my vision, an icon of an arrow appeared. I received a message.

Your goggles' targeting interface is enabled and will activate automatically when potential targets enter maximum effective range of offensive spells. Interface will assist with fine-tuning target acquisition and improve accuracy. Current spell selected: Shattercore Ballista.

Sweet. Targeting with the ballista was already pretty simple, but as I added more complex offensive spells to Switchblade's arsenal, the targeting interface would no doubt become a lot more useful.

"Are you going to hit it with the magic bolt?"

I shook my head, even though I really wanted to test out the new interface. "That's overkill. I need to practice hitting from the saddle anyway."

We closed on the bull in seconds and I dropped Soulrend into my left hand. The tall bovine, running erect on its two hind legs like a man, heard us at the last moment and spun, large poleax rising to strike.

It reacted too slow, and we flashed past close beside it while its weapon was still rising. I struck, and Soulrend cut through the monster's huge skull. As we passed, the targeting interface changed, the arrow icon switching to one of a cloud, and text scrolled past the left side of my vision.

Offensive spell changed to Corrosive Cloud.

So it recognized that I couldn't use the ballista when my target was no longer straight ahead and shifted to the next best spell? That was a lot more advanced than I'd expected, but exactly what I needed. I wouldn't have time to manually switch the goggles between spells in the middle of a battle.

A mini window appeared in my display showing the view from behind, giving me a great angle to watch the bull falling to the ground. A faint, billowing green haze flowed from the back of the bike, like a tutorial demonstrating the dispersion area for Corrosive Cloud. Nice. It looked like the cloud would spread pretty wide pretty fast.

I filed that bit of information away as I stopped long enough to loot the body. I only got basic items, then we took off again. A moment later, we spotted a second bull.

I slowed. "Do you want to take this one?"

"Yes, indeed," she responded immediately. "Do a drive-by about 10 yards to the right."

She'd never used a ranged attack before, other than her poisoned blowgun. I sensed she had something else in mind, though as I accelerated toward the bull. This one heard us approach sooner and spun, long spear at the ready. As soon as it locked eyes on us, it started charging.

I hadn't noticed specific momentum-based attacks when we fought them last time, but I'd been using Phase Walk. Now it was easy to spot the air shimmering just in front of the bull, as if it was compressing space.

On foot, it would have posed a lot more risk, but on Switchblade, it just wasn't fast enough. I shot past at a safe distance and Ruby let go with one hand, then her entire torso twisted against mine, as she threw something.

A small black object sailed through the air and landed a short distance in front of the charging bull. One big hoof came down on the object and it detonated into a column of white-hot flame that billowed up around the bull, completely enveloping its huge form.

The monster twisted and writhed in the flames, but within seconds, it collapsed dead to the ground, little more than a blackened husk.

"What was that?" I asked as I circled back around.

Ruby jumped off to loot the body. She grimaced at the sight, then again at the stench. "Immolation grenade. I traded one of the other crafters for a bunch."

"They needed that many healing potions?"

"Not exactly. I shared around a lot of healing potions initially to make sure people had enough to survive, but after the battle I realized people had ways to pay or to trade for them. There's a growing network of crafters in town, a lot more than you probably realize. I've been trading potions with most of them and getting a lot of great stuff in return. Gives me a lot of haggling power."

"Good thinking." She'd leveled up to 15, so was doing okay. I guess I didn't have to worry about her struggling to defend herself.

We didn't see any more bulls, and started exploring up the long slope toward the second stage. The hillside was wide and open, but dotted with dense thickets of trees and bushes and with more gullies than I'd noticed in my dash down with William and Joey.

The ground was harder than the soft earth of the plain and was covered in tough, short grass and scratchy ground cover. Piles of rock and bare patches of hard ground pocked the area too. I kept a sharp eye out for monsters. The seemingly empty slope could be hiding a lot of danger.

Except it wasn't. With Switchblade's engine purring, we ghosted along, crisscrossing the lower reaches of the slope, but spotted nothing threatening.

"Where are the monsters?" Ruby asked.

I shrugged. "Let's try higher."

I set a curving course angling higher, sweeping past clumps of trees and slowing to study the shadowed gullies. 10 minutes later as we crossed a low hill, I hit the brakes. Now it made sense why we hadn't seen other monsters.

A group of a dozen zombie slavers was marching uphill toward the second stage about a quarter mile away. Like the other zombies, these were dressed like pirates and conquistadores. In the middle of the group, they carried two planks with a prisoner chained to each one.

I zoomed my vision on the distant figures. One man and one woman, both lying on the rough planks, looking battered and unconscious. Those stun guns were brutal.

Ruby gasped when she caught sight of them. "Those are zombies?"

"Yeah. They're nasty."

"We need to go get help."

It would be nice to hit the zombies with the expedition's full might, but I shook my head. "There's not enough time. The team's still a couple hours away on foot. The zombies will reach the second stage in 10 minutes, then we'll never catch them."

"We can't just let them take two people away as slaves."

"No, we can't. Hop off."

Her grip tightened around my waist. "Don't be a muppet, Lucas. What are you planning?"

"I'm going to stop them and free those slaves."

"Then I should help."

"Not this time. Their energy rifles are dangerous."

She thumped me on the back of the head. "Which is why you need help."

I resisted the urge to explain I wanted her to get off because I worried she'd get killed, and wasting energy worrying for her could get me killed, but I did, and it could. Instead I scanned the slope, and got an idea.

"Okay, then. Hold on."

I accelerated hard and slewed Switchblade back around to one of the narrow, steep gullies cutting the slope. I aimed right at it and we plunged inside.

"What are you doing?" Ruby exclaimed, her grip tightening.

"We need to slip past them without getting noticed. This gully cuts pretty high up the slope. Just hang tight. This is going to get fun."

Then I focused all my attention on riding. The gully cut a nearly straight line up the slope, but it was clogged with bushes and piles of boulders. I threw us into a series of twisting turns, slaloming between obstacles, even riding up along the steep sides of the gully a few times to avoid the densest tangles.

Ruby's initial iron grip relaxed and she surprised me by moving with me. Together we leaned and shifted to best counterbalance the bike. We didn't need to move as much as we would have on an Earth bike, but some movement still helped. If she'd gripped me too tight, it would have hampered us.

"You never said you had experience riding," I said as we shot up a rare flat patch.

"Not nearly as much as you or Jane, but we lived in Spain for a while and rode some wonderful mountain trails."

That sounded fun, but a new series of obstacles made speaking impossible as we threw ourselves into more turns. I'd been holding back earlier, but now that I knew her skill level, I pushed the bike harder, tearing through some truly awesome maneuvers.

Ruby managed it well, although her grip did tighten on my waist a couple times, and she muttered soft curses between laughs, especially when we tipped nearly horizontal while zooming up stretches of gully walls. I thoroughly enjoyed the ride as Ruby and I moved as one and I pushed the bike, testing how much it could do.

It could do a lot. Even back on Earth, most motorcycles could outperform their riders. Switchblade took on every challenge and excelled, thrusters whining, engine purring, warm air rushing past.

The gully smelled faintly of sagebrush, but occasionally I caught whiffs of rot. Maybe something had died behind some of the rocks, but I didn't slow to check.

Way too soon, we reached the top where the gully faded away to barely a crack that ran into the middle of a thick copse of trees and bushes. There I slowed and ghosted toward the edge of our cover to scan the slope again.

Ruby hugged me tight, then thumped my shoulder. "That craic was incredible! A couple times I did think we were dead, though."

"Just enough danger to get the blood pumping."

We stopped at the edge of the trees with a panoramic vista out over the grassy plain and a good view of the slope and the zombies marching uphill. We'd gotten ahead of them by several hundred yards, although we were still a bit too far south.

I pointed to a big pile of sandstone boulders directly in the path of the zombies. "If they keep going, they'll pass that pile. I'm going to drop you there. On my signal, lob 4 of those grenades from cover. They're weak against fire, so that'll create a distraction and draw their attention so I can hit them from behind."

"Do you think we can take them? Didn't you say all the zombies were level 35?"

She couldn't hide a tremor of worry. She wasn't dumb enough to blindly rush in against a dozen monsters so much stronger.

"Yeah, they're tough and they work together well, but we can take them. Fighting them hand-to-hand would be brutal. They're nearly unstoppable unless you take off their heads, but their heads aren't armored, so it's a good weakness. If something goes wrong, you should retreat back to here and down the gully."

"Make sure nothing goes wrong. I don't want to leave you behind."

"That makes two of us. Do you want an energy rifle?"

I'd given her one of the stun guns before, but they didn't have as much range as the rifles.

She hesitated, then said, "Yes. I don't think I'll need it, but better to be safe than dead."

I handed over the rifle. "Hold on."

She gripped my waist hard and I gunned the throttle. We shot out of the trees and tore across the slope. The zombies spotted us immediately, but we reached the pile of rocks before they could shoot.

I skidded to a halt and Ruby jumped off. She grabbed my arm and held my gaze with her big, brown eyes. "Be careful, Lucas."

It almost looked for a second like she planned to lean in and give me a good luck kiss. I was glad she didn't. This was not the time to get distracted.

"You too. Don't take any unnecessary chances."

She tilted her head, one eyebrow raised. I grinned back. "I'll try to do the same."

Then I gunned Switchblade and tore away across the slope.

Chapter Sixty-Two
Ruby Gets A Prize

Finally, monsters worth fighting. I'd won several levels on stage 2 between zombies and werewolves. Taking out this squad might be enough to push me up to level 9. Maybe joining the hunt team had been a better idea than I'd feared.

The zombie slavers were still a couple hundred yards away, but they'd had several seconds to get ready, and a barrage of laser beams ripped the air all around me as soon as I shot from behind the pile of boulders.

"Jurgen's Fist!" I shouted as I instinctively ducked.

They were better shots than I remembered. One laser shot right in front of my face, close enough to sparkle in my goggles. Without that eye protection, that shot might have temporarily blinded me.

Another one slammed into a rear thruster, leaving a scorch mark. Cursing, I triggered Shield Dome. The shimmering barrier formed around Switchblade as I banked downslope, close enough to tempt the zombies to keep firing, but far enough away that their accuracy would still be strained.

Those rifles could pump out a devastating rate of fire and even crisp waterlogged werewolves so bad they overwhelmed the werewolf regeneration, but their power cells could run out or get overloaded, as Joey had tragically discovered. They kept firing, but at a measured pace they could probably maintain for an hour. Laser beam after beam reached out to say hello.

I adjusted speed and swerved constantly to make myself a harder target. Quite a few bolts did miss, blasting into the slope or shattering stones, but some still found their mark.

Shield Dome proved sufficient to handle that many and the bolts deflected away, most shooting skyward. I kept a careful eye on Shield Dome's energy level. The constant volleys were eating away at the defensive spell's reserves, but it should be enough.

If they didn't have captives, I'd probably charge straight in, trusting to Shield Dome to protect me until I blasted through their party and unleashed Corrosive Cloud. Then I could circle them while it melted their undead flesh. Unfortunately, that would kill the prisoners too. I needed a better plan.

As I weaved and turned, heading downslope, nearly even with the zombie party, I asked, "Will Shield Dome knock enemies aside if I ram them?"

Cyrus said, "Indeed. If a being has attacked you already, it will be marked as an enemy and will not be allowed inside the protective dome."

"How about allies?"

"Anyone not designated an enemy will not be affected by Shield Dome, so allies could step inside without harm. Note, if you allow a non-enemy within the protective dome and they choose to attack, Shield Dome will not be able to stop them."

"Got it. Thanks."

"Any time. Keep making the journey fun."

I passed the zombies and skidded to a halt behind another thick stand of trees about 50 yards downslope from them. There, I jumped off my bike, banished it, and slipped through the trees until I could see them.

I'd hoped some of the zombies would split off and come hunting. Taking them out in two separate skirmishes would be a lot easier. Unfortunately, they didn't take the bait, but remained in a single group, rifles aimed at the trees, waiting for me to emerge.

I waited. There was no reason for me to emerge again when they were ready to fire. Several slow minutes ticked by and I started wondering if they'd just stay there until our full expedition party arrived.

After about 10 minutes, they hoisted their prisoners and resumed their interrupted march up the slope. Had they gotten bored, or were their short term memories that bad inside those half-rotted skulls?

My chat menu flashed in the corner of my vision, announcing a new message.

Ruby: "They're coming this way again."

Lucas: "Good. They haven't seen you. How far can you throw?"

Ruby: "I haven't measured the distance, but I'm way stronger than back on Earth, plus my upgraded Bio Morph spell gives me even more."

I had actually forgotten about her unique upgrade that allowed her to tap into advanced body manipulation powers during fights.

Ruby: "I'll throw a rock first so I don't waste a grenade."

Lucas: "Just don't throw too soon and give yourself away."

Ruby: "Trust me."

That line worked so much better when I was the one saying it. The seconds ticked by slowly, my worry for Ruby growing with every one. If the zombies rushed her position, they could kill or capture her before I could catch up.

When they closed to within 50 yards, I summoned Switchblade and jumped on. At the same time, a fist-sized rock hurtled out from behind the pile of rocks. The zombies instantly stopped, guns snapping up, but they didn't have time to fire before the rock came down right in the middle of the group.

One zombie caught it, examined it, then dropped it to the ground. A grenade was already following. The zombies watched it, but failed to realize it wasn't just another rock.

The same zombie caught it, examined it, and even from that distance, I could tell the second it realized the danger. It tensed, freezing for a critical second before whipping its arm back to throw the grenade away.

Too late.

The grenade detonated. Another geyser of white-hot flame engulfed the zombie and one of its companions standing close beside it. The two zombies freaked out, spinning and flailing and trying to run, which only spread the fire to 3 more zombies.

Their bodies seemed to disintegrate, imploding way faster than the bull's had. Weak against fire was an understatement.

More grenades fell within the clustered ranks of zombies, but they were already scattering. Geysers of fire still consumed 2 more monsters and panicked the rest in a way even the werewolves had never managed.

I blasted out of cover, zooming for the zombies, who were already orienting on the pile of rocks. They opened fire with a withering onslaught, blasting huge boulders apart. They'd reduce the entire pile to rubble in less than half a minute.

Ruby: "I got their attention. Hurry!"

Luckily I could type with my mind as I rode.

Lucas: "Coming. Stay down."

Unfortunately, despite the panic of the fire bombs, one of the infernal zombies still remembered to look back and noticed me charging their flank. All of the remaining zombies turned the full might of their energy rifles against me, unleashing an intense barrage. Since I was charging straight in this time, I made a much easier target and Shield Dome's energy reserves plummeted.

I wasn't going to make it. They'd tear me apart 10 yards before I got to the first one. Even if I banked away and made a run for it, I was so close, they'd probably still overwhelm Shield Dome and kill me.

"I wanted to save this," I growled as I triggered Phase Walk.

That was my last use, curse them. I'd hoped to save it until I could permanent another spell. It would have made a perfect core spell for my build, but not dying was more important.

I phased out, and thankfully so did Switchblade. The lasers didn't deal any spiritual damage, just pure physical, so they passed through harmlessly. I dropped Shield Dome to begin recharging and shot straight in.

The stinking zombies only stared in surprise for a second before slinging their laser rifles and bringing out their stun guns. Only 3 had the other weapons, but they fired almost instantly.

The stun blasts shook me like sudden 100 mile per hour gusts of wind, rattling me and my bike hard, nearly knocking me off the back. My health ticked down by nearly 10%.

They didn't hurt like a physical blow would, but the blasts scattered my thoughts and my head swam. I swayed, Switchblade slowing as my grip slackened on the controls.

I had not expected that. I tried to focus and accelerate again, but the zombies hit me again. I felt sick to my ghost stomach, which was a super weird feeling, like I might throw up my feet.

I needed to move. I had no idea how the weapons affected me so much, but they were rattling me just long enough for the zombies to fire again. At this rate, they were going to chew through my health before I could reach them.

Then one of the zombies with a stun gun staggered, a smoking hole appearing in the center of its chest. It scowled, and the zombies without stun guns turned back to Ruby, who had peeked around the stones to open fire with her rifle. Her face looked different, as if her cheekbones had become more angular, but I didn't have time to wonder what Bio Morph change she'd triggered, or what advantages it gave her.

Their answering barrage forced her back again, but the distraction gave me the second I needed to gather my thoughts and hit the throttle. The 3 stun gun wielding zombies raised their weapons again.

"My turn." I unleashed Shattercore Ballista.

Two of the stun gun zombies stood close together and I aimed right at them. The explosive detonation catapulted bits and pieces of the 2 monsters over a very satisfyingly huge area.

When they hit the ground, they twitched, trying to move, but the explosion had destroyed most of their limbs. One still had an upper arm and it tried to use it to drag itself toward me.

As I headed straight for the last stun gun zombie, who was staggering from the explosion, I triggered Shield Dome again.

Warning. Activating Shield Dome so soon and with less than a full charge drains the spell effective duration to 5 seconds. Cooldown before next possible use is now doubled.

It was enough. I plowed straight into my target. I expected Shield Dome to catapult him over my back, but I'd risen to 4 feet off the ground and the curve of the dome pancaked him into the slope so hard his head cracked like a melon dropped from a roof.

Throwing Switchblade into a turn so tight every directional thruster screamed in protest, I plowed through the still-standing zombies, making 2 more quick passes before Shield Dome winked out.

The impacts didn't hurt the others, but sent them tumbling, scattering them over a wider area. Ruby appeared again, leaning her rifle on a boulder and took out 2 with fantastic head shots.

I skidded to a stop by the unconscious prisoners still lying on their planks. Only a couple zombies remained at this point, but I'd prefer pulling the captives to safety before finishing them off. Except I was still ethereal. My hands passed right through them and their shackles.

Finish the zombies it is.

I canceled Phase Walk as I jumped off Switchblade, then ran over to the zombie slavers, who were struggling to rise. One had a broken leg, so kept stumbling. The other had lost an arm. Calmly, it swung its rifle toward me with its other hand.

I kicked the weapon away, then slashed through both skulls with Soulrend. They might be higher leveled and incredibly durable, but we knew their weaknesses, and that made all the difference. Soulrend dropped them with a couple well-aimed slashes.

The slope was a fire-blackened mess of freshly re-killed corpses. It was like a scene from a really graphic zombie apocalypse movie. As soon as I paused to take in the battlefield, the stench clubbed me in the face and I gagged and nearly puked.

The reek of charred zombie was foul. I'd smelled and seen some pretty nasty things in recent days, and figured I was pretty immune to gore. The zombies pushed the envelope, and I pressed the sleeve of my jacket over my nose, trying to breath shallow as I leaned over one of the zombies, touched the corpse with a finger, and triggered Harvest.

You have successfully harvested Creeping Death from Undead Sailor.

Creeping Death. Spell. Think mustard gas mixed with acid. This spell surrounds the caster with a dense, choking sphere of gas 1 yard in diameter, plus 1 yard per point in perception. Will affect any exposed flesh. If inhaled, damage is tripled.

Effect: Drain 10% of life and mana from every target for every second they remain within the aura. Once they leave the aura, drain fades by 25% per second over 4 seconds. Effects of healing potions severely curtailed while drain is active. Uses remaining: 1.

Whoa. That was nasty, and with my perception at 28, it would spread for nearly 30 yards. It wasn't an insta-kill spell, though. So if I ended up in a crowd of enemies, they could still attack me for a few more seconds before the aura killed them. Anyone not escaping almost immediately, especially if they breathed in the aura, would die in seconds, though.

"No way! Lucas, I got 5 levels!" Ruby exclaimed, then laughed, lifting her energy rifle high in victory.

"Excellent!" Not surprisingly, I didn't get a level. Kind of annoying, but I tried not to dwell on how fast time was slipping away, and instead focus on the gains we did get.

That little fight was huge for Ruby's growth. I hadn't really thought about how much she might level compared to me, especially facing such high-leveled monsters. Those immolation grenades were death in a bottle for zombies. She'd done well. Better than I'd expected. Cyrus seemed to approve too because she got a ton of loot boxes.

For ambushing the zombies with the grenades, she got a gold Sun Tzu loot box with 10 more grenades. For immolating 4 zombies with those grenades, she got a platinum Chernobyl loot box with a sweet launcher tube that could fire grenades up to 100 yards. For making perfect head shots, she got a gold Annie Oakley loot box with an ability scroll that unlocked a throwing skill.

"Where did you learn to shoot like that? Did you do a lot of shooting growing up?" From what she'd said, they had lived all across Europe and even into Asia some, but guns were a lot less accessible to civilians in most of those places. Not like in the US, where it was easy to buy a gun and practice.

"I only ever shot a couple times in my life, and I'd never been a very good shot. Bio Morph changed my eyes and I think some of the muscles of my hands and shoulders to maximize my shooting stance. It felt effortless," she said with a shrug and a little laugh.

"That's awesome." I still knew too little about Bio Morph. The base utility spell was very useful, but her custom upgrade made it so much more amazing. I doubted she'd tapped all its potential.

For saving me with that distraction shot, she got a platinum Dunkirk loot box. When she opened that one, she gasped and held up an amulet on a gold chain. The amulet was a simple black stone with a blue starburst emblem on the front.

Shifting Wardstone. Amulet. Rare. Choose up to one incoming hit in every fight to deflect and redirect against another enemy.

"Wow, that's a good one."

She grinned as she examined it, then hesitated and glanced at me. "You fight up close and personal more than I do. Would you like it?"

Her voice held no hesitation. I shook my head slowly, holding her gaze and smiling, trying to convey the depth of my gratitude. "I really appreciate the offer, but I'd never take that from you. It could be a life saver."

She tried to argue, but I reminded her I already had a lot more defensive equipment and spells than she did.

Her last loot box was even better. Similar to when I'd gotten my Spartacus loot box, she got the achievement for killing zombie slavers from a higher stage to rescue captured humans.

It came with a title, and she shared the description with me.

Title: Boudica. Like the Celtic queen who led a bold uprising against the Romans, you're willing to step into danger to fight for freedom.

Plus 5 to all base stats.

Plus 1 level to Battle Bio Morph. Now you can harden your skin at will to provide 500% improved defense for up to 20 seconds.

"Wow!" That was an amazing title.

"My first title," she laughed, her big brown eyes sparkling with excitement as she rushed over and gripped my arms in hers. I saw the moment the tiny golden ring appeared around her irises.

Then her entire body shuddered and she fell against me, muscles shaking as she made an involuntary groan of pleasure from all the new stats applying. I held her up and her entire body shook in my arms.

When the wave of new power subsided, she gasped. "Wow! Sorry about that."

"No worries. Pretty amazing, isn't it?"

She straightened and stepped back, running one hand through her thick hair. "That. Was a trip. Do all titles feel that good?"

"The best ones do."

I turned to scan the slope. That little fight had turned out to be a windfall for Ruby. I was so glad I'd brought her along. Even if I'd taken them all on myself, I might not have gotten a level, but she'd made huge progress. No doubt I'd gained enough experience to be zeroing in on level 9.

We looted the zombies for bunches of mana crystals, more basic clothing and armor, and more energy weapons, which were always welcome. I also got one unique item. It looked like a miniature human skull, made out of shiny black metal. It was heavier than lead, and it thrummed softly against my hand when I pulled it from my inventory to inspect it.

Gate key. It opens a gate.

"That's oddly vague," I said, glancing up.

"It's a magical item from the second stage. You're not authorized to access that stage yet."

"It's not like knowing the properties of this key now would be a big spoiler."

"Everyone must follow the rules," Cyrus said, laughter in his voice.

"Right."

I briefly scanned the other messages I'd received during the fight and chuckled at the first one.

Experience Hog. You left your partner behind right before a battle. You receive a silver Glutton loot box.

Another congratulated me for surviving over 500 laser blasts from monsters more than 20 levels above mine, while a third congratulated me for finding a unique way to isolate the spiritual damage from stun guns and still survive. From those I got a platinum Bullseye loot box and a gold Exorcist loot box.

When the silver Glutton box opened, I had to laugh. Two more sporks. The gold Exorcist loot box contained a scroll to upgrade the amount of magical damage reflected back at my attackers by my Amulet of the Rebound from 10 to 15%. That was a great upgrade. The amulet hadn't helped against the zombies, but I was sure it would come in handy.

"Nice," I muttered as I read the single scroll from the platinum Bullseye loot box. It added plus 5 to both Luck and CHA.

"My Charisma is getting pretty high. What kind of benefits am I supposed to get from that when I unlock it?"

"That stat is most effective with specific classes," Cyrus responded.

"So unless I get the right class, all these great stat upgrades are useless?"

"Not at all."

"Then what are you saying?" I pressed.

"I am saying you should probably unlock those prisoners who are waking up."

"Hey, don't dodge the question. You said you like questions."

"I love questions, but—" his voice changed to a perfect imitation of Jack Nicholson. "You can't handle the truth."

"A Few Good Men. Great movie," I conceded.

"Wasn't it?" Cyrus exclaimed.

"Are you really going to try dodging my question with a movie quote?"

"What we have here is a failure to communicate," Cyrus's voice dropped into an imitation of the warden in Cool Hand Luke.

I sighed. That might be a not-so-subtle hint to drop it. If I remembered that movie correctly, they killed Luke shortly after that line.

"Fine. Be that way, but you will need to answer it eventually."

"In the meantime, don't get distracted," Cyrus urged.

Chapter Sixty-Three
Stat Check

Another stats chapter. Aren't they fun?

Name:	Lucas Altan
Race:	Tier-one Human
Level:	8

Life Points:	135	(12,059 tier-zero baby human equivalent)
Mana:	40	

Base Stats:

Constitution:	11.9
Intelligence:	11
Strength:	16.9
Dexterity:	9.6
Wisdom:	10.7

Secondary Stats:

Endurance:	28
CHA:	40
Agility:	36
Perception:	24
Magical Resistances:	25.8
Luck:	40.4

Other stats:

Mental Resistance: 30.5

Fear Resistance: 25

Poison Resistance: 10

PERMANENT SPELLS

1   Harvest

– 70% chance to gain a skill or ability from a defeated enemy.

– Chance increases if the enemy is higher level.

UTILITY SPELLS:

1   Mystic Looter

2   Linguasight

3   Navigation

4   Soul Feed

TEMPORARY SPELLS:

1   Energy Ward

– Mana Consumption: variable

– Invisible defensive aura that extends 1 yard in every direction.

– Redirects force from incoming physical and spiritual attacks.

– Uses remaining: 3

2   Frostfire Nova

– Mana consumption: High

– Elemental. A wave of freezing flames that immobilize while burning anything caught in its path.

– Uses remaining: 1

3   Corrosive Cloud

– Mana consumption: Moderate to trigger, then variable.

– A cloud of gas that corrodes metal and flesh on contact.

– Uses remaining: 1

– This spell has been allocated to Switchblade.

4   Knock Knock

– Mana Consumption: Low

– Cast your voice up to 50 yards to tell a random knock knock joke. Volume: Loud.

– Uses Remaining: 3

5   Creeping Death   (Harvested Spell)
– Mana Consumption: Moderate
– Surround the caster with a dense, choking sphere of gas 1 yard in diameter, plus 1 yard per point in perception.
– If inhaled, does triple damage. Effect: Drain 10% of life and mana from every target for every second they remain within the aura.
– Once they leave the aura, drain fades by 25% per second over 4 seconds.
– Effects of healing potions severely curtailed while drain is active.

ABILITIES
Hand-to-hand martial arts fighting   Level 5
Stick and bladed weapons martial arts fighting   Level 5
Sight of the Explorer   Level 2
– Sight enhancement.
Wolf Blood   Level 2
– Speed up health and mana regeneration by another 10% per level.
Wolf Sight   Level 2
– Night vision. Increase Perception stat points calculated from Wisdom by 10%
Knife Throwing   Level 1
– When throwing short, bladed weapons. Improves accuracy by 10% per level and damage by 15% per level.

EXISTING TITLES:
Inquisitive Mind
Trailblazer
David Copperfield
Lucky Stiff
Musketeer
Spartacus

Chapter Sixty-Four
Interlude 2

Tony shook his head violently, sending drops of sweat flinging out of his eyes. He couldn't waste time wiping his face, and lacked normal hands to do it with at the moment anyway.

The sight of his quicksilver Metal Hands morphed into tongs and a hammer he used to beat a piece of promising red-hot metal into shape was a joy he'd never imagined before entering the game. The death battle was brutal, but he saw ways to thrive that so few others seemed to grasp.

Why was it so hard for some folks to focus and to cooperate? Their lack of vision would not slow him down. With his new class, Paladin Savant, he had unlocked real power, and he planned to use it to forge Earth's survivors into a successful team to defeat even the terrifying Marisara.

How could they not win? He could transform his hands into living metal, for crying out loud. Coupled with his Creative Frenzy class spell, he could forge weapons and armor faster than his namesake Marvel character.

He'd need every advantage. The obstacles they faced were daunting, but not insurmountable.

"We can do this. I can do this," Tony growled as he quenched the piece of metal in a vat of oil with a hiss of steam, then turned toward the armor that was already taking shape on his workbench.

He had to become the strongest human. Not just because he couldn't imagine anyone else beating him, but because their people needed leaders. The council was doing a decent job, but it was obvious a fighter was going to have to rise to take the lead.

Burns might succeed, but Tony saw him excel more as the hard-nosed sergeant that could beat the rank and file into fighting shape while he set the vision and strategy. The partnership could be super effective.

It definitely couldn't be Lucas. That guy was a puzzle. Despite his levels still lagging, he was turning out to have a real knack for killing the important monsters and winning critical loot. Those were vital skills, and Tony planned to leverage Lucas's power. Maybe as a front-line commander, except Lucas just wasn't a leader, and he didn't seem to understand his place. That could cause all sorts of trouble.

If he continued stealing the limelight, he could end up usurping control from those who knew better how to lead. As an actor, Tony knew all too well how important screen time was. An actor who lost his starring role to a new upstart quickly got sidelined, and this game was far more important than any movie. The entire fate of Earth hung in the balance, so everyone needed to unite behind a powerful leader, an inspiring figure.

Lucas simply could not be that figure. He spent too much time out in the wilds alone, hunting monsters. It was a miracle he hadn't died yet. He probably would. When he did appear, he might be open to taking on the role Tony envisioned for him, but Tony could not leave anything to chance. The stakes were simply too high. Unity was more important than individual strength, but Lucas only had strength.

To generate that unity, Tony needed to develop a persona that everyone would recognize, that everyone could rally behind. The system AI had given him the perfect team, and even set him up to play the perfect character.

Earth needed an Avenger to lead them to victory and salvation. Tony embraced the role and got back to work. If Tony Stark could build a flying Iron Man suit from scraps in a cave, Tony would build his own version using magic and liquid metal hands.

Chapter Sixty-Five
Time for a Change

Ruby reached the prisoners before I did. Crouching down beside a black woman struggling against her shackles, she said, "Relax. We're here to help."

"Howzit, my girl," the woman responded in a rich voice with a South African accent.

I showed Ruby how to accept ownership of the shackles, then will them off the woman.

Leah Zuma, Baby human level 21. Team Star Wars.

Leah let Ruby haul her to her feet, then lifted Ruby into the air in a gleeful bear hug. "Eish! I thought we were done for before you showed up. Lady of death, you were amazing!"

"Thanks," Ruby said, flushing under the exuberant praise. "I'm glad we were able to help."

"Lady of Death. It suits you," I chuckled. Ruby rolled her eyes.

Leah turned to me and I got a better look at her. She stood almost as tall as me with long, thick black hair braided and hanging most of the way down her back. She looked very solid, with thick limbs and obvious muscle. Her sleeveless top was reinforced with leather plates, and her heavy boots looked tough enough to kick through trees.

I smiled a greeting, but Leah's eyes widened when she saw me. With a whooping shout of glee, she wrapped me in a crushing hug and lifted me off the ground like she had Ruby. "Lucas! Of course it's you."

"It's me," I wheezed as my bones creaked. By all that was holy, Leah was strong.

She dropped me and laughed again. "First you save Hank from the Lifebane Phantoms and now you save me from the zombies. You're a treasure, you are."

Of course. Hank Solomon was also on team Star Wars. He'd been the first victim of the invisible parasites I'd saved. "How is Hank?"

"Fully restored and hunting monsters," Leah laughed.

"Hey, I hate to break up the happy times, but could I get a little help here?" called a man's voice.

The other prisoner was lying under his plank, arms twisted painfully behind him.

Perrin Avery. Baby human, level 20. Team Wheel of Time.

He looked like a Perrin. Black hair, broad shoulders, and yellow eyes. Not the golden of titles, but yellow like an Earth wolf's. I claimed the shackles and released him. Ruby moved the plank he'd been tied to, and Leah hauled him easily off the ground to his feet.

"Thanks," Perrin said, rubbing his wrists.

"Guess you were right," Leah told him.

He grimaced. "Yeah. Wish I'd sensed how tough they were sooner." At my quizzical look, he explained. "I've got an ability to help me sense monsters farther than most."

Leah added, "We were scouting the southern edge of this slope ahead of our team when he sensed this lot." She gestured at the dead zombies.

"We went to investigate," Perrin added with a grimace. "Didn't go so well."

Leah suddenly whooped and rushed to a nearby zombie corpse, then pulled a pair of brass knuckles from where they'd fallen half under the monster. "My beauties!"

She pulled something else from under another zombie and tossed it to Perrin. It was a vicious ax with a long, half-moon blade.

"Those cowards probably hit you with their stun guns before you could get in range," I guessed.

Ruby interrupted. "Lucas, there's a large group coming."

Sure enough, a big group of men and women had rounded a distant stand of trees behind a bump in the lower slope. With Tony and Burns in the lead, they made a beeline for us.

I sighed. I'd rather not deal with Tony today. I considered calling Switchblade and simply leaving, but that would look weird and no doubt give Tony more reason to think I was a loser. Not that I cared what he thought about me. I took a deep breath and waited.

"What happened here?" Tony demanded as soon as they drew close.

"Dance party."

That triggered a laugh from Leah. Ruby said, "Unlike any dance party I've ever attended."

"I bet you dance like a pro, girl," Leah laughed and shook her hips in a little jig.

Ruby grinned. "I can hold my own."

I bet she could. With her great looks and natural grace, she was probably very popular on the dance floor. Burns grunted and motioned the interdiction team members to spread out.

"These are the slavers you warned us about?" he asked.

I nodded and Ruby added, "Lucas and I were scouting and ran across this party heading for the second stage with two prisoners."

"That'd be us," Perrin said with an embarrassed wave.

Tony looked surprised it wasn't me who'd needed rescue. Ruby briefly related our attack and I let her do the talking. She did a good job relating the facts without a lot of embellishment.

"You did well to take down so many without getting hurt," Tony told her with a warm smile.

Ruby blushed. "Lucas knew their weaknesses. Made all the difference."

"Yeah, if you run into zombies up there, focus on the heads and use fire. It really wrecks them."

"We will," Tony promised.

"Where's the rest of your team?" Burns asked Leah.

She pointed south. "Last we saw them, they were out that way."

"Your team leader?" he asked.

"Susan Collins."

Burns nodded and his eyes took on a distant look. He must be accessing the team leader chat. I had lost track of Susan after the last time she made a pass at me. It was good to hear her focusing on more productive things.

"I sent her a message you're alright," Burns said after a moment. "She'll rendezvous with you back in Stepstone."

"Thanks," Leah and Perrin said together.

"If you want, you can stick with our explorer team," I offered. "They'll arrive in a bit and will work this slope before heading back this afternoon."

"That'd be perfect," Perrin said, obviously relieved to not have to walk all the way back to town alone. Leah looked eager for a chance to do some hunting.

Tony said, "You looted the slavers. Did you pick up any more energy weapons?"

I hesitated, but Ruby didn't. "We did. Since you're heading up to stage 2, we're willing to share."

"If you don't mind."

She gave him a confident smile. She'd grown a ton since that first day I saved her from the Rockslide Ogre. "We're happy to help, aren't we, Lucas?"

"Least we can do," I said, pulling 3 rifles from my inventory. Ruby pulled out all 5 of the ones she'd looted, keeping only the one I'd given her.

Burns gestured and members of his team eagerly took the weapons. "Thanks. These will come in handy."

"Good luck. Stage 2 has to be insane," Ruby said.

"We'll find a good place for the next settlement, don't worry," Tony said in a tone of absolute confidence.

Using my intel, they would. He seemed to have forgotten that. Reminding him would only make me look petty. It didn't really bother me. We all needed to succeed, and any information I could share, I would happily do so. It just rankled a little when I didn't get even a little credit.

"Good luck up there," I said, summoning Switchblade and swinging back on.

Ruby jumped on the back and slipped her arms around my waist. It felt right. We rode well together.

"Head straight down the slope. We'll clear the path and inform Crystal and her team to look for you."

Leah and Perrin waved acknowledgment, and I accelerated away from the interdiction team. Tony might be annoying, but I did wish them luck. A solid foothold in the second stage was vital for all of our survival.

Assuming I got my last 2 levels in time. On the way back to the explorer team, we ran down a couple more stray bulls and a nest of Lifebane Phantoms. They were lurking in the cool shadows under an overhanging rock next to a bubbling stream, the perfect place to ambush tired travelers looking for a nice place to rest. With my upgraded Wolf Sight, I spotted them.

Ruby got another level from the brief, intense fights. I did not, even though I killed all the Lifebane Phantoms. How many more kills would I need to reach level 9? Every level required more experience than the last, but this was getting ridiculous. Of course, most of the monsters were below level 25, and I got a lot less experience for weaker foes, but quantity had to count eventually.

We found the expedition about a mile from the slope, still out on the plain. We gave our report, then chatted with Steve for a bit.

"Six levels? That's insane!" he exclaimed when Ruby finished her tale of our adventures.

"You're the one who passed on a chance to ride scout," she said with a shrug.

"Can we switch?"

I hesitated. The pressure of time fast slipping away was growing steadily. This was not working for my leveling needs, but again I forced the worry aside. I had promised. I could risk a couple hours. Then I'd hunt all night and all day tomorrow if I had to. That had to be enough.

"Sure. Let's go."

Crystal planned to focus the team on the north side of the slope since we'd cleared most of the center and the interdiction team were heading up through there. Steve and I powered south to make sure that area was clear.

Leah and Perrin's team had been in that area, but it wasn't clear how high they'd explored the slope. In that area, the land grew wilder as it melded into the higher hills that connected to the southern mountains.

I hadn't explored much to the south. Hopefully we'd find stronger monsters there. I planned to explore deeper into the ranks of ever-taller mountains that lorded over the plain and connected with the barrier peaks on the east side. I bet we'd find lots of canyons and unexplored mountain valleys.

And so we did. We tracked down a Goliath bear with fire claws and volcano breath, then a pair of giant eagles that ran like gazelles on the ground when they landed and could shoot their beaks like lances over 100 yards. Finally, we took out an earth-bound monster camouflaged as a low hill that nearly swallowed us whole in one bite.

Steve's archery skills had grown enormously, and he seamlessly incorporated elemental water and blasts of ice into his arrows. I circled our enemies, keeping our distance as he rained icy death from afar. He froze the psycho eagles mid-leap, quenched the goliath bear long enough for me to get in a killing blow, and even paralyzed the giant monster covered in earth.

That took a very difficult shot, over 200 yards. The only vulnerable target we could find on the monster was one slowly blinking eye about the size of a large orange. It was vulnerable only while open, and Steve nailed it on his second shot.

That exposed its head, which had been covered by an impenetrable layer of rock. I finished it off with a Shattercore Ballista.

Steve gained 4 levels, then switched to a laser rifle as we headed back to the team. He ended up turning and facing backward to free up his hands to snipe monsters after we swept past.

I failed to get any good Harvest abilities, and the loot was mostly basic. Steve got a pair of rare barrier bracers that created an active defense zone around him, deflecting up to 5 incoming attacks with a full charge. They gave him a huge advantage, allowing him to concentrate on shooting longer. They'd recharge passively over about 12 hours, or he could feed them a mana potion to recharge them faster.

I even caught a glint of metallic light reflecting the afternoon sun from high up one of the tall trees. Turned out to be a hidden gold loot box. Inside we found 2 scrolls and 2 potions. I got another scroll of Ground Walker and another Slow-fall potion.

Steve got an ability upgrade scroll he used to upgrade archery to level 6, letting him imbue arrows with stronger elemental effects. He also got a new potion I hadn't seen before.

Potion of Echoing Doom. Rare. Create up to 5 clones that mimic your every move with your same abilities. Multiplies your attacks and provides improved defense, as any damage you take is reflected to your clones, destroying them first. Duration: 60 seconds.

"This is unbelievable!" Steve laughed.

"Yeah, that's quite a potion."

His smile fell and he asked softly, "Do you want it?"

Even though he clearly didn't want to lose the potion, he added, "I'd never have gained these levels without your help. You deserve first dibs."

"Thanks, but no. I'm happy with what I got. That Echoing Doom potion could be a life-saver, though." I hesitated and added, "Too bad you can't make a potion your next permanent."

"Why not? Ruby makes health potions."

"Yeah, because she first got a potion summoning scroll. That spell scroll was what she got to perm."

Steve muttered a low curse, and remained quiet most of the rest of the trip. He perked up as soon as we returned to the main group. They were already heading down the slope to begin the long march back to Stepstone. Most of them had gained at least 1 level.

The sun was fast dipping toward the impossibly high peaks to the west, so afternoon was fading into early evening. I'd been hunting all day and hadn't leveled once.

After delivering our report to Crystal and listening to Steve's wildly embellished tale of our adventure to Ruby, I waved good-bye and headed out. I would have loved lingering with my teammates longer, but the time pressure was too great to ignore. I wasn't worried yet, but if I didn't figure out how to get better experience, I would be soon.

As I powered along the edge of the grassland, again heading south, I couldn't hold back my question any longer.

"So, what was the test today? Between Ruby and Steve, they gained at least 10 levels hunting with me today. Added to all the other monsters I've killed recently, how did I not get another level too?"

"None of those monsters truly tested you. You've succeeded in passing many tests so far and proven yourself a clever fighter and a true leader. To pass the final tests, you'll have to dig deep and demonstrate you've got what it takes to really push the limits. You need monsters that will help you do that. Low-level monsters no longer give you the same kind of experience they give your companions."

"Most of those monsters had levels in the high 20s and low 30s."

"But you're a tier-1 human. Even if your levels only counted for 4 baby human levels, you're still the equivalent of at least level 32."

Yeah, that was a good point. Still annoying, but valid. So he still figured my power equated to about 4 times my level. I could see the eventual advantage I'd gain once I hit level 20 or 30. If I managed to improve my efficiency and unlock more of my full tier-1 stats power, the advantage would grow even more. I needed to live long enough to level up that high, though.

That meant I needed monsters to give me enough experience. Most of the monsters we faced no longer really felt threatening to me, again proving Cyrus's point.

"I'm going to hunt higher in the south mountains. I'm assuming I'll find stronger monsters up there that will count toward real experience."

"You know I can't tell you where the monsters are." His voice shifted and he added, "Life is about growth. It's about change. Hold onto your dream of becoming something more."

I sighed. "The Thor impersonation is good, but you changed the quote."

"Of course I did. Loki doesn't change, but you have to, or you'll die. So get out there." His voice changed again and he started singing just like Michael Jackson.

"So take a look at yourself, and then make a change!"

Chapter Sixty-Six

I Try Cheating on a Test

Instead of heading south toward the ranks of ever-taller mountains blocking the sky in that direction, I spun Switchblade west and hit the throttle. Accelerating to at least 250 miles per hour, I rocketed across the grassy valley, aimed for the distant slope heading up to stage 2. At some point, I needed to get a speedometer to see exactly how fast I could push the hover bike.

"Lucas, you're heading the wrong way," Cyrus said, his voice carrying easily to my ears, despite the howling wind noise from my fast ride.

"I just want to check something first."

"You can't get back to stage 2, Lucas. You're just wasting time."

"Maybe," I acknowledged as the wide slope drew rapidly closer. "But I'd be stupid if I didn't look for a way to bend the rules again."

"I bend the rules, Lucas, you don't," Cyrus chided.

I barked a laugh, then coughed violently when I swallowed a giant bug. It exploded in my mouth with way more nasty bug juice than any Earth bug that big should possess. I even got an achievement for killing a level-6 Spiny Beetle.

Once I spit that nastiness out, I responded. "Cyrus, you yourself said I've passed one test after another and I need to do something game-changing to pass the final test. What's more impressive than getting up to stage 2 early again?"

"It won't work," Cyrus warned. "Cheating on a test right in front of the teacher never works."

"You want me to prove I'm clever, right?"

Cyrus sighed. "Fine, give it a try. I love your enthusiasm, and usually your unyielding determination helps. In this case, I'll make the clue obvious. You need to kill some more big monsters to reach level 10 and climb to stage 2. Pass the final tests so we can begin the next stage of our experiment."

"I've been fighting monsters non-stop all day. I'll get back to it once I take this little break."

"I know you're under a lot of stress," he said in a soothing voice, as if impersonating a counselor. "This week has been hard, I know, but I promise I want you to succeed. I have big plans for you that would get wrecked if you failed and died now."

"That's good to know." I half expected him to ask me about my mother. Wasn't that what shrinks did?

A moment later, I hit the slope and rocketed up. I'd taken a more southerly track than the other times I'd climbed that slope. This section was more heavily forested, forcing me to slow and weave through the giant trees. I spotted red dots on the edges of my map, but ignored them. No way monsters strong enough to give me real experience lurked down this low.

Within moments, I approached the boundary to stage 2. I slowed to a halt behind a huge tree with a trunk more than 20 feet across and a crown that reached at least 600 feet high and spread over more than an acre. There, concealed from view from any werewolves who might be lurking up on stage 2, I opened my full map.

It spread to cover my entire vision, showing several miles in every direction, including the southern parts of stage 2 I'd already explored. Unfortunately the area closest to me remained hazy since I hadn't explored it yet. I didn't spot a lot of red dots, but monsters could be hiding in the unexplored sections.

It did show me the line marking the boundary between stage 1 and stage 2. Using that line, I estimated where the boundary would cross in front of me at the top of the slope. Accelerating again, I shot up until I closed to within 100 feet.

There I banished Switchblade and jogged up to the top of the slope. Slowing, I extended my hands and crept forward. A moment later, they struck an invisible barrier, just like Cyrus had promised. I spent a few minutes exploring the barrier and trying to push through. It remained invisible and impassable.

"You're wasting precious hunting time," Cyrus interjected.

"Just another minute," I said as I scanned the nearby trees.

Some of the giant canopies stretched over the boundary. I scaled a promising one, using the thick bark for handholds. Bonus advantage for high agility and dexterity. Too bad I didn't have the Bio Morph utility spell to speed things up even more.

Still, with a few minutes of focused effort, I managed to climb to a branch at least 300 feet above the ground. It extended out over stage 2, the perfect bridge to test if the barrier rose that high. The branch was over 10 feet thick, so I easily walked down its length, questing for the barrier again.

Unfortunately, I found it. Even that high, it totally blocked my path. When I crouched and slid my hands around the branch, the barrier fused perfectly with the wood, as if it flowed right up through the whole thing.

"Satisfied?" Cyrus asked.

"Had to try," I said with a shrug. I bet I would have won a diamond loot box if I could have fooled him. I'd held out the slim hope that since I'd already ascended to stage 2 once, it would let me through again.

Nope. The barrier felt impassable, and with Cyrus watching my every move, I'd never get through. I really was just wasting time. I considered scouting along the boundary, looking for a monster to try sticking myself to again, but I doubted Cyrus would let me pull that hack trick again either.

Back to hunting, then. At least now I knew spoofing the barrier wouldn't work. When I dropped back to the ground, I summoned my hover bike and pushed it hard back down the slope. I'd only wasted half an hour. It was worth it, but now I had a lot of hunting to finish.

Within 10 minutes, I zoomed across the lower stretches of the central valley and up into the southern mountains, weaving through the lower hills to the higher peaks rising behind. They still looked tiny compared to the bigger mountains farther south, even though they eclipsed the biggest mountains on Earth.

Some rose in rocky bluffs, with cliffs rearing thousands of feet, while others were covered in forests. Some trees towered over 1000 feet, monsters that shaded entire valleys with their branches, while in other places, the smaller trees and bushes crammed in so close together, not even I could easily pass.

Not wanting to waste time, I skirted those dense areas, but kept my eye on my mini map. Periodically I stopped to expand to a full map. My upgrades helped show a larger area than most people would get, and I used that to scan the denser vegetation for signs of more powerful monsters.

I spotted quite a few possibilities, but most ended up being too low-leveled. Growls and hoots and howls rang across the peaks and through the valleys and canyons I followed, but I avoided as many of the weaker monsters as I could.

Moving fast, I could slip away before wasting time fighting beasts that didn't offer any gains.

If I'd led a party of level 15-25 baby humans up there and spent the time overseeing their battles, they all would have leveled up repeatedly. That didn't help me, though.

The afternoon settled toward evening as I pushed higher and higher up steep canyons and sped along rocky mountain passes. The air grew cooler and crisp, but did not feel thin. I had to have climbed to well over 20,000 feet. On Earth, I'd be nearly up to the top of Mount Everest and would be gasping for breath. It didn't make sense. From what I'd seen of the game world when we were first teleported in, it had looked a lot smaller than Earth. Shouldn't we run out of air at lower altitudes?

I wasn't about to complain, though. Stronger monsters lived at higher elevations, so that's where I needed to hunt. I'd risen even higher than stage 2, so there must be better prey up there.

Finally, after cresting yet another high hill, I entered a lush high-mountain valley, dotted with hardwoods and pine several hundred feet tall. Scattered among the sparse undergrowth, I glimpsed a new type of monster.

Whiplash Mammoth. Level 38. These giant pachyderms have evolved into the ultimate herd protectors with speed boosts and power stomps that will literally shake you off your feet and deliver stun damage. When you mess with one, you are declaring war on the entire herd.

"Awesome," I whispered. I'd always thought elephants were cool, and these giant, brown shaggy monsters were at least 3 times larger than the biggest bull elephant I'd ever seen photos of.

They towered over 20 feet at the shoulder and almost double that in length. Their legs were massive pillars, their heads as big as dump trucks, with tusks longer than spears. Their flexible trunks extended to the ground where they wrapped around small trees, easily ripping them up by the roots.

I spotted only half a dozen red dots on my mini map. That was perfect. Exactly the type of monsters I needed.

"Time to see how tough you guys are."

Pointing Switchblade at the closest giant mammoth, I twisted the elevation throttle with my left hand, tipping the front end up, then triggered Shattercore

Ballista. The targeting indicator settled on the center of the huge monster's torso for a perfect broadside, and the glowing spear of energy blasted away.

The spear punched deep into the whiplash mammoth's torso, tearing right through the dense fur and hide before detonating in a spray of blood and gore. I'd worried the beast might have enhanced defense, but the ballista worked beautifully. That should have taken out the heart, or at least a lung.

Instead of freezing in shock or even keeling over, the mammoth bolted away, moving as fast as Switchblade on full throttle. Blood fountained from the wound, but if that had been a fatal blow, the mammoth hadn't realized it yet.

It skidded to a halt behind another huge tree over 100 yards from where I'd hit it just seconds before and only then trumpeted in pain and rage. The sound shook the air like every brass band in the world had gotten together and blared out their loudest note.

Every other mammoth joined in, their flexible trunks rising into the air as they tipped back their heads and trumpeted their outrage. The air shook and I clapped hands over my ears.

The whiplash mammoth oratory assault has left you Rattled. Your balance is reduced by 15% for 5 seconds.

Of course they hit me with a new condition. I swayed on the bike and had to snatch the controls again. The world spun and I nearly pitched right off.

Ow. Maybe just diving into an attack wasn't the smartest thing I'd ever done. The mammoths oriented on me. Like an idiot, I hadn't even triggered Mirror Cloak and they spotted me instantly. While the wounded bull trumpeted again, the rest of the monsters charged out of the trees.

There were more than 6 of them too. Additional dots appeared at the edge of my mini map and shot in to join the rest of the group. So it wasn't a fluke that the first mammoth took off so fast. I'd doubted the description of a speed boost. The monsters were so huge, I figured a speed-up would just make them lumber along less slowly.

Under other circumstances, watching monsters that had to weigh 20 tons sprinting faster than cheetahs would have been so cool. At the moment, the sight was just terrifying.

I leaned forward, preparing to hit the throttle, but the pack of 10 giant mammoths didn't all sprint at me once they formed up into a loose line. They did advance, but moved with an oddly stilted stride, smashing their heavy limbs into the ground with every step. The ground shook and literally rippled like waves in a pond that rattled the huge trees like saplings.

I pushed Switchblade to its max height as the rippling earth waves passed beneath me.

You have avoided the whiplash mammoth stunning waves. This unique attack delivers overwhelming elemental damage as well as leaving targets stunned for 3 seconds.

Whoa, that could have been bad. I scanned the approaching monsters, who all ranged from level 37 to 42.

Four seconds into the fight and I'd learned a lot. They were even tougher than I'd hoped, with elemental powers, but luckily I could ignore those with Switchblade. The movement abilities could prove dangerous, and they could take a ballista to the lungs without dying instantly.

Still, I could take them. I had to. It was literally a life-or-death situation for me as well as them. So I accelerated hard, banking around the herd and into the trees. Slipping between the trunks, I set a roundabout course toward the wounded mammoth still lingering at the back of the pack.

The ballista might not have killed it, but the monster was wounded. I needed to see what it took to finish one off. Then I'd just have to repeat the process with the others.

No problem.

I closed on the wounded mammoth from behind. It was leaning against a tree, blood still geysering from the huge hole in its side. It didn't look great, but I wouldn't underestimate it. As I closed, I realized I had another problem.

It was too tall, I'd never reach its head with my short blade. So I shot past, so close its long leg hairs whipped at my face as I slashed out with Soulrend.

The ethereal blade tore through the monster's rear leg, but hit more resistance than I'd expected. The mammoth's spirit must be denser than most, or it had enhanced spiritual defense, because the unexpected drag on my blade nearly pulled me off the back of Switchblade.

I slowed in time and hit the monster's front leg as well, then accelerated away. It would fall and I could target . . .

"Oof!" I grunted as the mammoth's long trunk shot out like a whip and wrapped around my waist. It moved so fast, I didn't have time to trigger Switchblade's defenses.

The mammoth trumpeted in pain, the sound shaking me like a leaf. Even as it started toppling to the ground like a ponderous tree, it snatched me off of Switchblade and lifted me 30 feet into the air, clearly planning to smash me to the ground and crush every bone in my body.

Chapter Sixty-Seven
Productive Pachyderms

If the mammoth had managed to pin my arms, I would have been in trouble. The fact that it missed my arms sealed its fate.

I slashed down with Soulrend in that split second it held me aloft, and severed the spirit in the end of the monster's trunk. The rest of the long appendage whipped down reflexively, but the end had lost its grip. The movement didn't smash me to pieces against the ground, but as the limp trunk dragged across my torso, it still spun me around in a dizzying blur.

The mammoth hit the ground with an impact that shook the clearing again, and I landed hard on its shoulder. The thick fur and meaty muscle softened the impact and I rolled to my feet unharmed. My enhanced stats helped me weather the dizzying spin far better than I ever could have back on Earth.

The mammoth was struggling and bellowing, trying to lift its huge head, but lying on its side, it was momentarily helpless. I sprinted up its hairy shoulder and dove under one giant flapping ear bigger than 2 king-sized mattresses stitched together.

Soulrend plunged into the narrowest part of its neck, and I slid down the side of its throat, dragging the blade all the way, severing its spirit as I went. The blade was nowhere near long enough to cut all the way across the throat, but it still cut deep and delivered devastating spiritual damage.

The mammoth bellowed again, but the sound was strangely muted so close to its body, shielded by its own bulk and one giant ear. The other mammoths were closing fast, but hopefully they wouldn't notice me concealed behind the giant ear.

How the hell was I going to finish it off, though? I could climb back up its fur and head for an eye maybe. Then it flapped its huge ear again, revealing the gaping hole in the side of its head. Its ear canal was easily big enough to crawl into.

The sight sparked a memory from when I was a kid. I'd watched one of those nature shows about African natives. They'd hunted an elephant and when they killed it, some of the smaller hunters had crawled into its ear to begin harvesting it from the inside.

That could work.

Not hesitating to think about how insane the idea was, I sprang up, grabbed the lower edge of the mammoth's ear canal, and flipped myself inside. There I slid into the soft, sloping tunnel. The mammoth flapped its huge ear closed, plunging the space into pitch black darkness, so dense that even with Wolf Sight, I could barely see.

So I pulled out Torch of the Mirrored Moon and switched on the magical flashlight. The dazzling light illuminated the entire ear tunnel plunging into its huge head. Crouching nearly double, I scurried down several feet until I reached a thin membrane blocking the way. Must be the mammoth's ear drum.

Soulrend couldn't cut through physical barriers, so I drew my saber-tooth bone dagger from my inventory and slashed through the membrane. Outside, the mammoth bellowed and the ear tunnel twisted as it shook its head. The movement made me stumble, but not fall, and I pushed through the tattered remnants of the ear drum. Behind that, I found a wall of bone that had to be its skull, the last barrier to the brain.

I plunged Soulrend through the bone and dragged it up, then down, then sideways as far as I could, tearing through the monster's spirit brain. The mammoth bellowed one final time, the sound higher pitched with a note of desperation, then its head collapsed to the ground, unmoving.

Congratulations, Lucas! You have defeated a level 38 Whiplash Mammoth. Bonus experience gained for defeating a higher-leveled enemy. For discovering a unique way to kill a monster, you receive a gold Earwig loot box.

I cringed and rubbed at my own ear. Earwigs didn't actually crawl into people's ears, but some bugs did. I'd known a guy who got a moth stuck in his ear. Had to go to the hospital to get it removed. The thought of a bug with a sword crawling into my ear and stabbing me in the brain made me shiver with disgust.

"It worked, didn't it?" I muttered to myself as I willed the loot box open. It contained a single item.

Ahab's Harpoon. Uncommon. More like Ahab's fever dream. If he'd gotten his hands on a harpoon like this, Moby Dick wouldn't have ended as such a famous tragedy. Fire this weapon at a close-range target and let the fire-imbued harpoon get to work. Weapon reloads in 5 seconds.

I whistled as I examined the sleek harpoon launcher. It looked a lot like a SCUBA underwater speargun, but thicker. The pointed tip of a harpoon stuck out of the end, glowing with a sullen, red light.

"Exactly what I needed. Thanks," I said as I headed for the exit.

"Vae Victis," Cyrus responded.

"You switching to Latin now?"

"You should know this one. It means Woe to the Vanquished, and is often used in conjunction with the phrase, 'To the victor go the spoils.'"

"Makes sense. You keep asking for a good show, and with this beauty, you're going to get it."

I slid out of the ear and looted the dead mammoth. In addition to the normal mana crystals, I received nearly 1000 elephant steaks, both long, ivory tusks, 1 mammoth-hide whip, and a new potion.

Potion of the Road Runner, times 3. Channel the famous rodent and double your speed for 30 seconds.

Higher-level monsters sure produced better loot. I was tempted to try harvesting a spell, but decided to hold off until the other mammoths were dead.

I held my breath and activated Mirror Cloak as the huge mammoth evaporated into stinky black smoke. The rest of the herd had gathered around the fallen mammoth, so as the huge ear concealing me faded to smoke, I stared up at walls of angry monster on every side.

I gulped and held perfectly still. If they sensed me, they'd crush me to paste. Thankfully, the nasty smoke of the looted monster made them shake their heads and retreat a few steps. Not too far, though. The perfect set-up to try leveling the odds a bit. Standing in the midst of the entire herd, I triggered Creeping Death.

The dark smoke from the harvested zombie spell billowed out in every direction, flowing over the heads and most of the bodies of the Whiplash Mammoths. They trumpeted in surprise, and most of them fled with bursts of speed. 2 of them remained in the aura cloud, though, whipping their trunks around in rage and stomping their feet. The ground bucked under me, sending me tumbling.

You have taken elemental earth damage. You are Stunned. A percentage of the damage has reflected back against your attackers.

My muscles froze under the mammoths' onslaught and my health bar dropped by nearly 30%. Without all of my protective gear, that attack could have killed me. My Tesla Coil bracelet poured energy back into me, boosting my normal regenerative speed, but I still couldn't move. I crashed to the ground, helpless to fend off any additional attacks.

Thankfully, the cloud of dark magic helped obscure me, and Mirror Cloak was still engaged. The reflected damage had startled the stomping mammoths enough that they stopped their attack and spun, searching for whatever had struck them.

If they'd kept stomping, they might have kept me stunned and kept hitting me with elemental damage. I could still trigger potions, and with my bracelet and other protective gear, I probably would have survived, but if they'd kept up the rampage long enough, they might have killed me before I could do anything to stop them.

I had to be more careful. As soon as the stunned paralysis wore off, I triggered one of my new Road Runner potions from a hotlist spot. Energy zipped through me like happy bursts of lightning and I couldn't stand still.

I was about to target the nearest mammoth, still turning slowly, searching for enemies, but the idiot had remained in the Creeping Death cloud too long. Its rampage had included breathing heavily, which tripled the effects of the nasty spell. That meant 30% drain to life and mana every second, and it had already stayed in the cloud for 4 seconds. Even as I looked, the huge monster collapsed to the ground, its hide flapping loosely, as if much of its bulk had simply melted away.

The other mammoth that had stayed within the cloud also collapsed. I waved away the notifications and willed acceptance of looting the corpses as I focused on the next nearest monster. It tipped its head up to bellow in rage after seeing its companions collapse. Perfect. I sprinted straight at it, flashing across the distance at twice my best speed and launched myself up under its flapping ear.

I plunged into its ear canal, tore through the ear drum, and slammed my new Ahab harpoon into the wall of bone at the end of the ear tunnel. With a fierce grin, I pulled the trigger. The harpoon bucked in my hands as the spear slammed into the white bone.

The wall of bone shattered and the spear plunged through, disappearing into the gray spongy material of the elephant's brain. Deep inside, it exploded with a firestorm of crimson flames. The flare of light illuminated the room-sized brain and reflected off the walls of the skull.

The monster fell straight down, dead before it reached the ground.

I repeated the process for each of the other mammoths. With my cloak obscuring me from view, they could never get a good lock on my position. Some of them tried stomping the ground, but I was wise to that trick now, and waited inside the ear canal of my last victim until the stomping subsided.

Two sprinted at full speed in wide circles around the forest, trying to stay ahead of the hidden enemy killing their herd members, but they were sprinters, not long-distance runners. That tactic only left them exhausted and easy prey for me to rush in and finish off. I did have to drop a couple of them to the ground by slashing their legs with Soulrend first. Somehow they sensed the danger and kept their huge ears flapped close over their vulnerable ear canals. Crashing to the ground distracted them long enough for me to get in and strike.

I ended up with nearly 10,000 elephant steaks, 20 huge ivory tusks, 8 mammoth-hide whips, and 245 long rolls of mammoth hide leather. Each mammoth gave me dozens of hides, each big enough to create several jackets. And I got several more Road Runner potions. Even my oversized inventory was starting to feel decidedly cramped.

Best of all was the final message, though.

Congratulations, Lucas! You have reached level 9. Two points added to Dexterity.

"Yes!" I shouted in victory as I dumped a bottle of Laundry Day potion over my head to cleanse away the monster gore I was soaked in. Some of the mammoth brains exploded when I harpooned them, and not all the brains and blood and bone evaporated when I looted them.

I tried Harvest, but it failed. I would have loved a ground-stomping spell. Soul Feed topped off all of my stats, and the killing spree had filled my Tesla Coil bracelet with so much energy, it thrummed with heat against my skin.

"Well done, Lucas," Cyrus said. "Another test passed."

"Are there any more mammoth herds around?"

"Don't be silly. Not only would that be boring, you already passed this test, so wouldn't receive any experience from killing more of them."

"I know I get less after killing a few of the same monsters, but I should get something, right? They're all around level 40."

"Whiplash Mammoths are no longer a challenge for you to defeat, so they offer no experience gains. Look to the future and find something new to tackle."

"Huh. That's new. I don't remember you saying I wouldn't get any experience from monsters that no longer posed a challenge."

Cyrus's voice turned more serious than usual. "Lucas, you are on the path to power. It is a path of tests. Each new enemy is a test, but once you pass that test, there is no value in taking it again. Have you ever gone back to a class you passed and asked to re-take the test?"

"Of course not. I get your point, it's just, I hadn't understood everything it meant. Other games I've played didn't handle experience this way."

Cyrus chuckled. "This game is like no game on Earth, and you're still in the first act."

At least I'd gotten the level. "So what's the final test?"

He laughed with delight. "It will be wonderful, and I would never insult you by spoiling it. No, you'll figure it out."

"Fine, but let me ask another question that's been bugging me. I'd like to understand better how Efficiency works."

"It's simple, Lucas. I thought you understood. Your Efficiency will improve as your spells and abilities evolve to tier-1."

I grimaced. "They're upgrading really slowly."

"Upgrades will come. Your spells and abilities are the conduits through which you utilize your stats. They are like garden hoses used to deliver your available power, while your full potential is more like a city main. You simply cannot push as much through a garden hose, even if you have a big enough reservoir."

I frowned as I puzzled through that. "So the fact that my spells and abilities are still mostly low-leveled effectively reduces my available power."

"Exactly! Simple, right?"

"Not as simple as I'd like. I know the power curve will ramp up after I reach stage 2, but it's even tougher than I'd expected down here."

"And yet, you recently admitted that you're already several times stronger than anyone else."

I took a deep breath, focusing on that positive. "Yes, I am."

"You'll understand more as you level up and unlock more of your tier-1 potential. It's not a single step from tier-0 to tier-1, but more a staircase. You've taken the first, most important step and created a solid base. Each subsequent step will build upon that base and unlock more power."

"And I can't climb that next step until I pass the final test and hit level 10?"

"You won't be ready to leverage that power until then. For now, you have enough on your plate, so I won't distract you with things that won't matter if you don't succeed. You chose this path, knowing you would be tested and tried."

His voice shifted between several voices who took turns speaking as he said, "You will be weighed. You will be measured. You most definitely must not be found wanting."

I couldn't help a smile. "Nice twist on A Knight's Tale."

"Great movie of a man choosing to change his stars and become something greater than anyone ever believed possible. Rather inspirational, is it not?"

Surprisingly, the not-so-subtle hint did actually encourage me. Cyrus was indeed making the tests super difficult, but I was seeing results.

One final level. One final test.

The promise of unlocking a lot more power soon was like the end of a rainbow sparkling just over the next rise. All I had to do was catch it.

Chapter Sixty-Eight

Doctor Strange

Morning found me resting on the edge of a cliff, high on a mountain slope in the southeastern corner of the world, still stuck at level 9. I had to be nearly 30,000 feet above the central valley, but bigger mountains farther south dwarfed the peak where I sat.

From my perch, the panoramic vista to the north showcased the wild terrain I'd hunted through all night. I could even make out the grasslands of the central valley so far below. It seemed impossible that I'd traveled from down there in one night.

I savored a chocolate-frosted donut from Paul the mayor, then munched down a delicious turkey club sandwich from Sam. My inventory kept it fresh, and it rivaled the best sandwiches I'd ever eaten back on Earth.

I was high enough that I should be able to see across stage 2 to the west and even up to stage 3 to the north, but those areas were blocked by hazy mists. Given the layout of the mountains, stage 3 had to run east to west across the north sides of both stage 1 and stage 2. Where would stage 4 be?

It didn't matter unless I figured out how to escape stage 1. Time was quickly slipping away and my worry had grown steadily all night. I had to fight the urge to break my rest short, leap back to my feet, and climb ever higher to find stronger monsters.

I forced it back and made myself enjoy the view and take my time with my snack. I even pulled out a cask of Sam's ale and filled one of his big, metal steins. The ale was a slightly different variation, a rich, dark brew that reminded me of Guinness.

Thinking of Guiness made me think of Ireland where it was from, which turned my thoughts to Ruby and the great ride we'd enjoyed. We made a good team. I savored the drink and zoomed my vision on that distant valley. The flickering lights of Stepstone's watch fires clarified. The sight of the distant town filled me with a surprising rush of loneliness.

I longed to be there, laughing with Tomas and Jane or chatting with Ruby and Steve. Instead I was forced to hunt alone far and wide just to survive. The alienness of the world seemed starker in that moment, and my resolution to simply enjoy the view crumpled under a rush of doubts and fears.

I'd managed to stay positive and focused through hunting, but now those nagging fears crept back into my mind. How could we survive? Would we all fail and condemn everyone we knew and loved back on Earth to die? They'd never know we'd caused the apocalypse, but we would.

I thought of my parents and my grandmother. Thoughts of Isabella tried to bubble to the surface, but I squashed them. My family and other friends depended on me, my team, and everyone else caught in this brutal game. They might never know the insane battles we fought to save them, but that didn't matter. It still had to be done.

I would find and kill the monsters I needed to reach level 10. I'd rejoin the others and escape stage 1. For the first time, I really considered the challenges we'd face on stage 2. The monsters were significantly stronger, and people would die, even though so many had unlocked classes.

My own challenges seemed like a vast gulf I had no idea how I was going to cross. I'd struggled to earn 10 levels in the past week. On stage 2, I suspected the level requirements would also get more difficult.

I needed my power growth to start hitting that escalating curve, or I'd face the same troubles there that I was dealing with down here. Monsters on stage 2 would be a lot stronger, so would offer more experience, but no doubt Cyrus would add new twists and turns to keep the challenge level high.

I pushed my worries aside and tried to focus. Ruby's face popped into my mind again and I smiled. Ruby was a good friend, and her companionship was becoming more and more important to me. Steve was a great guy, fun to be around, and good in a fight, but my thoughts turned more to Ruby. The thought of sitting with my team, chatting and enjoying Ruby's Irish accent seemed a wondrous gift in that chill moment high on the side of a cliff.

"I'll see them later." The words seemed loud in the stillness, and they helped shake me out of my odd reverie. I drained the last of my ale, squared my shoulders, and focused. I still had work to do.

The sun wouldn't rise above the mountains for hours yet, but the darkness was fading to light and the stars were finally dimming. I scanned the sky again anyway, thinking back on the dazzling light show I'd witnessed across the night sky as I hunted through the long hours of the night.

It was as if the world had celebrated the last night of the first stage and our impending climb to the second. For some like me, still not yet at level 10, it had been like a final celebration of our last night anywhere.

The stars had shone like brilliant lanterns, while hundreds of falling stars streaked past. Several times half the night sky filled with northern lights in vibrant, flowing sheets of shifting colors.

I'd killed dozens of monsters, but none higher-leveled than the mammoths. As I scanned the beautiful vista a final time, Cyrus's voice boomed loud over the world.

Congratulations everyone for making it to the last day of your first week. I knew you could do it. Just a friendly reminder that you must ascend to the second stage before the sun sets behind the first peak this afternoon if you want to live. I hope you've used your time wisely and reached at least level 10. If not, you'd better get to work. Good luck!

"I thought we had till midnight or something." Knowing the timer would end when the sun hit the first peak felt like I'd lost hours again. That would barely be mid-afternoon. My worries jumped another notch, like a noose around my lungs that made it feel like I couldn't quite get enough breath.

Cyrus chuckled. "This isn't Cinderella, Lucas."

"I know, but the deadline seems arbitrary. Midnight feels better." And it would give me another 6 hours or so.

"There's a lot more hanging on that deadline than you know," the AI said in a serious tone, then turned chipper again. "As much as I love to see your enthusiasm for your current approach, I hope you realize it's not working."

"It would if I could find more monsters above level 40. I've killed enough monsters in the high 30s since the mammoths to level anyone else up at least a dozen times."

"But you're not anyone else, and that's not the test. I've invested enough in you that I'd hate to see you fail and this experiment end before it really gets rolling."

"Not as much as me."

He chuckled. "Lucas, I want you to get to level 10. I'm your biggest supporter. I have huge plans for you, so don't let yourself get distracted by little challenges."

Little challenges. That was a different way to look at my predicament. I couldn't help glancing at the timer. 13 hours 27 minutes 42 seconds. That was exactly how much longer I had to live.

"Remember, any problem can be a springboard to success, Lucas."

"Can you offer anything more concrete than happy words?"

After a moment, Cyrus said, "I see you need a bit of motivation, even though I would think not dying and the promise of great rewards should be plenty. You humans are so endlessly entertaining. You have performed at a high enough level that perhaps you have earned an extra reward."

"I'll take anything at this point."

New quest. Pass the final test and escape certain death. Win your 10th level, prove you're worthy of continued investment, escape near certain destruction, and make it to the second stage alive. Reward, an emerald loot box.

"Thanks, but emerald seems a bit low." Emerald boxes were great, but I'd won several. I'd hoped for something more game-changing.

Cyrus's voice dropped to a whisper, even though I hadn't spotted another living human in hours and many miles. The world around me froze, as if time stopped. The wind froze, grasses paused mid-wave, and a distant bird remained stuck in place in the sky.

"The box will include a scroll to upgrade the loot by one tier, resulting in a diamond-level legendary loot box. Consider this the first of many rewards for success, the starting point of your increasing power curve."

Time resumed with a lurch and I nodded slowly. Didn't Cyrus have authority to make any award decisions he wanted? He'd awarded me one of the super-rare ruby-level loot boxes for helping him choose a name. I hadn't expected to see another one until we defeated Marisara, but for a moment I'd hoped he might offer one.

Still, even getting another diamond loot box would be amazing. The promise of ramping up my power growth was even more welcome.

Could those nameless watchers he'd referred to a couple times make trouble for him? Was that why he was acting so sly? I was happy to keep the secret. I wanted that loot box. All I had to do was survive.

I could win one more test. Thinking of it that way helped focus my mind again.

"Thanks, Cyrus. That actually helped. I feel motivated again."

"I knew you would. Good luck, Lucas."

I climbed back on Switchblade and headed for a steep slope that dropped to a lower valley. I'd been gone from town for nearly a full day. I needed to keep hunting, but I also wanted to check in on Tomas, Jane, Ruby, and Steve. They all should be fine, but I'd never forgive myself if I made it up to the second stage just to learn one of them had run into trouble and couldn't make it.

A glint between a couple large boulders caught my attention and I slammed on the brakes, skidding Switchblade in the air. As much as I needed to get moving, I vaulted off, rushed over, and stepped into the space between the rocks.

They formed a room-sized gap, open to the sky. The stone wall at the back of the gap shimmered slightly, as if light was getting sucked into a rectangular hole in the air. I felt the same tingle from Identify I'd felt in the wight's cavern.

"No way," Cyrus exclaimed with false surprise. "You found another rift in the fabric of the world! What are the odds?"

Maybe he was offering even more help than I'd hoped. With a grin, I stepped forward and plunged my hand through the rift. Like last time, blinding blue light flashed across my vision and the world lurched as an invisible fist punched me in the back and staggered me forward.

I stumbled onto smooth floor and the air turned warm and humid. The sounds of humming machinery replaced the rustling of trees and the wind. My eyes cleared and I found myself inside another small room.

This one was a bit larger than the first maintenance room I'd stumbled into in the wight cavern. It extended nearly 20 feet across and maybe a dozen feet deep. Again the walls were covered with hundreds of video screens, like floating LCDs.

Images flashed past on every screen, too fast to follow even with my enhanced perception. I caught only hints of the scenes as the kaleidoscope of images shifted in ever-changing views.

Was that a view of Stepstone? Was that Ruby, or Tomas? I caught many flashes of mountains, forests, and glimpses of monsters, but even more of people. Some were in buildings or tents, others locked in mortal combat, some sleeping, while others ate. I even caught a flash of bare skin from a woman bathing in a crystal pool under a cascading waterfall.

It flashed past as fast as the others, but I could have sworn I glimpsed a dark-furred monster creeping across a stone ledge above the woman's pool.

"What are all these?" I breathed, stepping forward for a closer look.

The video screens started disappearing with little popping sounds. They winked out in a cascading ripple of movement. I lunged, diving across the space, and managed to touch one of the screens before it disappeared.

Energy jolted through me from that contact, flinging me back across the room. I slammed into the wall and my head cracked against something hard.

When I blinked open my eyes, I found myself on the floor with a pounding headache. It faded even as I sat up with a groan, my fast regeneration quickly repairing what was probably another concussion.

I was gathering those like a hoarder gathered trash. I needed a new hobby or I'd end up with brain damage, or something. The walls facing me had changed to smooth, amber expanses, blank of any screens.

"You need to be more careful," Cyrus chided. "Does every human try touching things they don't understand?"

"They looked like video screens."

"In a sense they were, but they're not Best Buy specials, Lucas. If a baby human had touched that screen and gotten that jolt of higher energy, they would have vaporized."

"Maybe try warning me next time."

Cyrus laughed. "I did warn you before you entered your first rift. There is danger in exploring areas not meant for human presence." He paused, then added in a conspiratorial whisper, "And so much more."

I rose and looked around. It was just an empty room, but the air still felt charged and a distant hum suggested machinery working behind the facade of the wall.

"So I'm in another space technically outside of the game, right?" I advanced slowly and added, "Can I touch the wall?"

"The initial jolt is the worst. You've begun the process of adapting to low-grade Nexus energy, so similar doses will not harm you."

"Nexus energy?"

"Indeed. As you've seen, magic fuels the contest and manifests in many forms, but at its heart, magic is all generated from Nexus energy. It is a more refined energy source that is both more advanced and at the same time more fundamental to existence."

"How does that work?" I placed one palm on the wall. It felt smoother than silk and warm, with a faint vibration coming from the other side.

"I cannot explain the deeper truths of the multiverse while you're still stuck in the first stage of the game, Lucas. You've seen enough to start opening your mind to learning more in preparation for gaining enormous power boosts."

This had to be an important hint or he wouldn't have wasted my time with it. "So if someone learned to tap into Nexus energy directly, they could access higher forms of power?"

"I'm glad you use that higher Intelligence stat sometimes."

"Thanks. How do I learn more?"

"You've already done it by touching that screen. Your internal assimilation of that first touch of Nexus energy will take time to complete. When it does, you'll be ready to take your next step."

"So, that's it?" I didn't hide my disappointment. I'd hoped to gain some kind of advantage to help me figure out the final test and level up.

"It's more than you realize. For finding a second rift in reality, surviving a jolt of Nexus energy, and beginning the process of advancing your internal energy conduits, you receive an emerald Prometheus loot box."

"That sounds perfect. Thanks!"

Actually, it sounded kind of terrifying. I'd never watched Prometheus, but wasn't it a sci-fi horror movie where everyone ended up dying?

Hopefully that meant I was about to get some kind of super weapon to kill stronger monsters and not that Cyrus was setting me up to be one of those sci-fi experiments where you got consumed from the inside.

"Open it as soon as you step out of the rift. It will not linger long."

"You don't have to tell me twice."

Cyrus really did love games. Not only the secret experiment with me, but it seemed he was also playing some kind of game with those secret watchers. The fact that he was taking some major risks seemed clear. I suspected anything that could get Cyrus into trouble could get me vaporized.

I'd do it, though. I needed every advantage. Cyrus seemed interested enough in our experiment to help shield me from those watchers, as long as I didn't blab to anyone or flaunt my access to these secret rifts.

His hints about Nexus energy seemed important too. I'd have to ponder on that. Access to it might unlock higher powers or a lot of flexibility in how I eventually used my magic. That could be a game-changing trump card.

So I stepped back to the game world and immediately willed the loot box open. The huge emerald box appeared floating in the air, but its normal brilliant sparkle was dimmed and the air around me seemed to darken, as if a cloud had passed over the sun. The box opened with a muted flash, leaving two scrolls floating in the air.

Title scroll. New title: Doctor Strange. You've taken the first steps on the road to mastering a deeper form of power than most can survive.

Increase effect of all primary stats on calculating all secondary stats by 10%.

Additional increase effect of Intelligence on calculating magical resistance by 25%.

Additional increase effect of Constitution on calculating magical resistance by 25%.

"Whoa!" I gasped as my body thrummed with an influx of new power. Across-the-board increases in all secondary stats was huge. All of my exhaustion bled away and I laughed with a sense of deeper power. My Endurance, Agility, Perception, Luck, and Magical Resistance stats were growing insanely high.

With an Endurance of 28, that equated to about 280 tier-0 points. Even though I apparently could only really draw from about 112 of those points with my reduced efficiency, that was still a lot. I didn't tire any more, even if I ran flat-out for miles, and my muscles never ached. My skin felt hard enough that I bet bullets would just bounce off, and even the zombie laser rifles might not do much damage any more. It was a heady thought.

Upgrade Scroll. Navigation. Upgrade your map with a new ability: Ping.

Ping. Once per day, trigger an invisible pulse of energy in every direction to a distance of 5 miles per level of spell. Effect: Update your map within the covered area with one of the following: Monsters, dungeons, rifts in the fabric of space, or loot boxes. Points will be marked on your map for 60 seconds. Note: Monsters who pass a stealth check may remain hidden.

"No way!" I laughed, rereading the description of the upgrade several times to make sure I was getting it right. I'd gotten a couple upgrades to Navigation. Even though my character sheet did not show spell levels, it had to be at least level 3. That meant Ping would extend in a circle with a radius of 15 miles in every direction. That was huge.

I wanted to test it immediately, but resisted. The new ability would cover a huge area, but even that much promised space was barely a drop in the bucket in the middle of huge mountains. I could only use it once before climbing to the second stage, and I didn't want to waste it.

No, I'd wait until I reached another big open mountain valley and use it then. If Ping could help me identify powerful monsters, I could still hit level 10 with plenty of time to spare.

Encouraged, I again started descending the mountain. I still wanted to check in on Tomas and the others before heading out on my final hunting trip. I was low on time, but I could get back to town in less than an hour. It was worth the risk. I could just message them, but if the worst happened and I failed the final test, I might not get another chance to see them.

No. I refused to believe I'd die, but I still wanted to see them in person. I'd spent too much time alone with the crazy AI. I needed human company before making the final big push.

Halfway down the mountain, as I sped through another beautiful high-mountain meadow, I spotted a wooden palisade wall.

Another hidden band of humans.

Chapter Sixty-Nine
I Teach a Painful Lesson With My Pants

I almost didn't stop. I had too much to do and too little time already. Fighting back my impatience, I headed for the wall and the tiny cluster of log buildings and Base Camp tents behind.

We were nearly out of time. Surely the people in this little settlement understood that, especially after Cyrus's last announcement. I would offer to tell them the way to the central valley, but I couldn't waste a lot of time with them.

As I slowed, the makeshift gate swung open and people poured out. There were more than I expected. A dozen people in a mix of basic clothing and leather armor led the way, grinning as they rushed up and encircled me and Switchblade.

Behind them, another 20 people came on more slowly. Most of those were younger and looked timid. The first group all had levels between 12 and 15, which was encouraging, but the second group were hovering around 10. A few were still at level 8 or 9.

Not good.

A man and woman stopped close by my left side where I sat on Switchblade. They both looked to be in their mid-30s, with hard faces, lined from lives of manual labor.

Martin Briggs. Baby human, level 17. Team Lethal Weapon.
Trish Briggs. Baby human, level 16. Team Lethal Weapon.

Looked like one of the few times the game left a couple together. I hadn't gotten Cyrus to explain why that happened sometimes. Usually, I'd wish for that to happen more often, but by their hard looks and the way the others deferred to them, this wasn't one of those cases. Maybe separated they wouldn't have caused so much trouble for so many other people.

"Hello," I said with a friendly smile. "I'm glad I found you. We're all running out of time. I can give you directions down to the town on the plain where everyone is gathering for the push up to the second stage. The town's called Stepstone."

"And let some other random people we don't know try to control our destiny?" Martin scoffed. "I don't think so. We have everything we need right here."

"How did you get a fancy flying bike at level 9?" Trish asked, staring at Switchblade with undisguised coveting.

"I got lucky. I don't have much time to chat. I'm heading for town. Any of you want to know the way?"

Some of the folks in the second group looked eager, but everyone in the circle around me remained silent, watching their leaders. Their intense focus gave me a very bad premonition.

"No, you're not going anywhere," Martin said.

"Don't!" I shouted, realizing what the idiots were going to try.

"Get him!" Trish shouted as she raised her hands. A club materialized, made out of shining purple light. At the same time, a pair of heavy knives appeared in Martin's hands.

All the others gathered around lifted blades or pointed fingers at me to unleash spells.

I'd let them get inside the range of Shield Dome, so couldn't trigger it now. So I banished Switchblade and dropped flat to the ground, under most of the strikes.

Spells flashed through the space I'd just left, brilliant bursts of light that slammed into people on the other side. Men and women screamed as flames and ice and invisible blasts of force smashed into them.

Spears and swords swept over my head as I rolled onto my back. I'd tricked most of them, but not the leaders. Martin dropped to his knees beside me, knives flashing for my face just as Trish brought her magical club down at my stomach in a mighty overhand swing.

My metal-wrapped fighting stick popped into my hands, already pointing up. I positioned it right at Martin's throat so he dropped onto it before he could stab his blades home. He gagged and staggered back with a retching sound. I'd pulled the hit, so it shouldn't have broken anything, just distracted him.

Trish's club smashed into my midsection and I grunted from the blow. My armored jacket absorbed most of it, the impact rolling around to rattle me lightly on every side. Trish shrieked and staggered as my amulet reflected some of her magical attack back against her.

Between my armor and my increased magical defenses, I only took a little damage. I shrugged it off and kept rolling into the encircling group. They were recovering from their initial surprise and retargeting me.

As I rolled, a weird, robotic voice spoke, and it seemed be coming from my jacket. "Frontal impact. Minor. Check for whiplash."

Where did that come from? I didn't have time to worry about it. I had some idiots to deal with.

They should have run. My frustration with my long hunt and lack of my last level boiled over. These idiots weren't even trying to save themselves, but just wanted to plunder and loot others. I'd had more than enough of that with Abbie's sex slave cult.

So I triggered Energy Ward. The defensive aura snapped into place around me, easily deflecting the weak attacks of the low-leveled humans. I didn't want to kill the fools, but I wouldn't leave them to ambush someone else either.

I kicked a couple guys in the knees as lightly as I could, but their legs still snapped with sickening crunches and they collapsed, screaming. Fighting weak baby humans was so annoying.

I sprang to my feet, but tossed my fighting stick back into my inventory. It was too much of a hassle to pull my blows so much. Instead, I pulled out one of the sturdier pillows I'd looted from Abbie and smacked a couple of the nearest men.

I tried to make the blows light, honest, but the first guy blasted backward off his feet, knocking 3 other people over. The pillow ripped, and when I hit the second guy with my return swing, it exploded into a cloud of feathers. That helped absorb some of the impact so the second guy only tumbled off his feet and hit his head with jarring force on the ground.

Men and women still swarmed in from every side, weapons and spells flashing. With my enhanced Agility, I moved through them like a blur. I really shouldn't have bothered triggering Energy Ward, but I still took clues from it to adjust my movements and help it better deflect the rare attacks that might have hit me.

Pillows had proven too much, but what was softer than pillows? I pulled out the Fuzzy Shorts of Friendship I'd gotten back on day one from the Nightmare Gorger.

Slapping the super soft shorts across people's faces was like wielding a chinchilla. They were so soft, the feel of them in my hands made me smile again. They still knocked people flying, with whiplash or cracked ribs, but I wasn't shattering bones any more.

"He's hitting you with fuzzy shorts!" Trish screamed. "Take him down." She and Martin looked incensed that I was whipping their little band so easily, especially since to them I only looked like a level 9 weakling.

In seconds, I smacked down everyone who tried to attack me, leaving the two crazy leaders for last. I left a trail of groaning and crying men and women in my wake.

"Die!" Trish screamed, pointing her glowing club at me. She triggered a spell and the club transformed into a bolt of energy.

I twisted aside as my defensive aura deflected the attack wide, then pulled an elephant steak out of my inventory and threw it at her. The steak wasn't frozen, or anything, but it still caught her in the chest with a meaty splat hard enough to crack ribs. She crashed backward, screaming, clutching at her chest.

Martin said nothing, but closed fast, knives flashing at my face, throat, and arteries. He had some skills, but I knew knife fighting too and my agility was several times higher than his. I easily read his moves and slapped his hands aside with my open palms, breaking his hands and sending his blades flying.

He only grunted and tried kicking me, his leg bursting into an electric blue flame. I jumped right over him, somersaulting in the air. He was considerate enough to crane his neck up to watch me, mouth opening to shout something. I flicked him in the forehead first, and the solid thump dropped him like a sack of hammers.

Surveying the mass of groaning, crying people, I felt sick with disgust. How could people be so stupid and so vicious? And still be so weak? I didn't even bother trying to loot them. They had nothing I wanted. Some were crying for healing potions, but I didn't wait to see if any of them had any.

As I turned away, one girl in the larger group of onlookers called, "Wait! Please take us with you." She sounded a lot like Ruby, with an even thicker Irish accent. She approached several steps, gripping a tall staff in her hands.

April O'Malley. Baby human level 14. Team Teenage Mutant Ninja Turtles.

"Shut up, you!" One of the men I'd knocked down growled as he lumbered to his feet, cradling a broken elbow.

I pointed a finger at him and made a flicking motion. "Want me to break that jaw too?"

He shut up, but cast another dark glare before turning and racing back into their settlement. Maybe they had a stash of potions or bandages. I didn't care.

April took my response as encouragement, rushing forward several more steps. "Please. The Briggs have kept us here under their control and treat us like their servants. The fools think we can hide here in the mountains and survive. I don't want to die today. Please."

"Please," the other people behind her pleaded.

I wanted to pull my hair out. I only had hours remaining. If I slowed down to lead them to Stepstone, I might not make it. My steadily-growing sense of urgency had morphed into a full-blown alarm blaring constantly in the back of my mind.

They were in worse shape than me, though. I might be missing my final level, but I'd received so many advantages. If I abandoned them, I would be signing their death warrants. I might as well slit their throats myself. Besides, April's accent reminded me of Ruby, and I just couldn't turn her away.

I was tempted to text the explorer's group back in Stepstone to send a squad to shepherd the little group down. That would make life easier for me, but by then the Briggs might have recovered and the group would have another battle to deal with. I doubted the Briggs could do much real damage to an explorer team, but who knew what they might do to punish April for speaking out?

"I leave right now," I growled. "We're running all the way."

"Grand!" April beamed.

Some of them looked nervous, but most of them came. I trotted across the clearing with the group totaling 18 people straggling out behind. Most were younger women, with a few young men mixed in.

"How far is it to town?" April asked.

"Far. We have to hurry." I accelerated and April kept up, as did about half the others, but almost immediately a few began to lag. They were so weak!

It wasn't going to work, but if we just walked to town, we would all die. I scanned the mountain and got an idea.

Gesturing April closer, I pointed. "See that canyon there? Keep everyone moving as fast as the group can manage down that way."

"What are you going to do?" she asked, suddenly nervous.

"I'm going to help us make better time." I gave her a reassuring smile. "Don't worry, I'm not abandoning you. We'll get to Stepstone."

I summoned Switchblade to gasps of awe. Jumping on, I motioned 2 of the slowest and lowest-leveled girls closer. "Jump on. It'll be tight with 3, but we can manage."

They eagerly obliged and crowded on the bike with me.

"Hey, why them?" One skinny young guy with a pencil neck cried. He was already panting from the short jog.

"Everyone will get turns as long as you keep moving while I'm gone. Stay focused. We have a lot of ground to cover, and not much time to do it."

Then I accelerated smoothly to squeals of delight from the girls, who clutched my back and each other tight. Moving as fast as the girls could handle, I shot down the canyon for about a mile. There I slowed and dropped the girls off.

A quick scan showed the area clear of monsters, so I pointed toward a gap visible between two smaller hills. "Make for that pass. I'll be back with the next group shortly."

That started a crazy leapfrog journey, with me zipping back and forth, picking up a couple passengers and carrying them to the front of the group before returning for more.

In that way, we increased the entire group's speed by many magnitudes. They remained motivated to move fast, looking forward to their next ride to rest. In the process, we even stumbled across lower-leveled monsters. I coached them in quickly hunting them, and that helped provide vital experience for the lagging players.

In far less time than I had feared, we reached Stepstone. I dropped them off at the gate where an official-looking woman was organizing groups to head across the grasslands toward the slope up to the second stage. She folded my refugees into the next group.

Before I left, they all thanked me. April dared to lean in and kiss my cheek. "Thank you, Lucas. You saved our lives."

A kiss for my trouble was more than I'd expected. "I'm glad I got you all out of there. It's too bad Martin and Trish and the others won't save themselves too."

She shook her head. "No, it's not. They were mean and vicious. I'm not sad at all that you sorted them out. They'll get what they deserve."

"Maybe, but there are too few of us left as it is. I don't like seeing anyone die needlessly. Take care, April."

"You too. Good luck getting your last level."

The survivor counter had ticked down to just below 650. How many more would we lose that afternoon when the timer ran out? Martin and Trish weren't the only ones hiding in the mountains, refusing to face reality. I couldn't help them, but needed to help myself.

The town was a beehive of activity as people packed camp, formed travel parties, and rushed around on whatever last-minute errands they had to finish. A couple of the vendors had raised huge banners proclaiming moving sales, and business was hopping.

Tomas's and Jane's Base Camp tents were already gone. Probably already up in the second stage. I sent them chat messages asking for a status update and letting them know I was nearly at level 10. I'd see them up there later.

Ruby's tent was still up, and both she and Steve were inside finishing breakfast. They'd both gained another level each.

"Just in time for breakfast," Steve said with a smile. "Figures."

I took the proffered plate of bacon, eggs, and hash browns, then dumped 50 elephant steaks into the oven's hopper. "Let's see what it can make with these."

"Level 9 is good. How close are you to level 10?" Ruby asked.

"Close. I'm heading out for one final hunt. Just wanted to check in and see how you're both doing."

"Nearly reached level 25. Can't wait to get a class," she said with a grin.

"Another few hours hunting with you should do it," Steve added.

"Once I hit level 10."

"Good enough for me."

I wolfed down the food, barely tasting the amazing flavor. The oven kept getting better at Earth food. I gulped a huge mug of coffee Ruby produced somehow and sighed. That really hit the spot.

"Thanks. I'll see you both up there."

I turned to the door, but Ruby cried, "Lucas, wait!"

She rushed over, not concealing her worry. "Be careful. Do what you have to, but don't die. Come back to us."

"Don't worry. I'm not giving up."

She leaned in and kissed my cheek. "Good luck."

"Thanks."

Steve waved with a goofy grin, looking pointedly between me and Ruby. I ignored his attempt to push Ruby's worry for me into something more. It was nice to know they cared.

Outside, I summoned Switchblade and hopped on. The lingering warm feeling from spending time with my team helped me fight back my fears about running out of time. I could do this.

As soon as I exited town, I gunned the bike harder than I'd intended. I couldn't help it. I felt good and grinned. And swallowed a bug the size of an apple. Coughing and spitting the nasty bug juice out of my mouth, I had to laugh at myself.

Was I going insane? How could I feel so good when I was so close to failing and dying? I was heading out to fight to the death with terrifying monsters, and I was grinning like an idiot. What was wrong with me?

Maybe nothing. For the first time I accepted the fact that I was good at this. I fought monsters and I killed them. Why pretend I didn't enjoy the rush of victory? The thought of facing more deadly unknown monsters energized me and flooded me with anticipation.

Then I got a message from Tomas.

"Lucas, we need help!"

Chapter Seventy

Interlude 3

Steve's hands blurred with speed as he poured tequila and orange liqueur into a steel glass, squeezed a fresh lime over the top with his bare hands, then dumped in some ice from his inventory. In a flash, he capped the custom cocktail shaker and shook it vigorously for exactly 2 seconds.

With a flourish no one but he could see, he produced a delicate glass, already rimmed with salt and poured the fresh margarita without losing a single drop. A final shaved lime wheel garnish settled onto the top just as he set the glass down onto the pure white linen tablecloth next to the others.

With a grimace, Steve extracted the Echoing Doom potion and poured exactly 4 drops into the recently-created margarita. "This had better work," Steve muttered to himself, then tossed the potion and all of his margarita-making tools back into his inventory.

When he had badgered Cyrus for a quest to transform his single potion of Echoing Doom into a temporary scroll to summon that potion so he could make it permanent, he had not expected to have to sacrifice the potion during the quest. If he failed, he would lose the potion too.

"Never going to happen," Steve growled as his bow dropped into his hands.

He needed this potion, needed the potential power boost it offered , needed to show that he could keep up. Lucas was on a singular path, and neither Steve nor Ruby could help him enough. They were a team, so they had to figure out how to up their game.

Random, crazy quests might be common for Lucas, but this was Steve's first, and it was a weird one. Steve was already drawing the string back and willing a sharp-pointed, barbed arrow to appear before he even raised his eyes to the horde of a dozen warty, green-skinned little monsters charging out of the trees into his clearing.

He usually liked enthusiastic customers, but these guys were insane. The little monsters had swollen beer bellies, red noses marred by huge pulsing blue veins, and giant, bloodshot eyes. They raced toward the table on short, oddly bent legs, their long, gangly arms outstretched toward Steve. Or, more precisely, toward the drinks lined up on the table in front of him.

His small, white-covered table stood in the center of a cute little clearing, covered in short-cropped, soft grass, ringed by forest on all sides. The 8 corpses of other monsters were the only eye sores marring the idyllic scene.

"It's not happy hour," Steve growled, loosing the first arrow less than 2 seconds after finishing the latest margarita.

16 drinks stood in perfect ranks on the table, each containing precious drops of his potion, and his quest required him to keep it that way. Six more drinks to go, and he'd win, but the monsters were getting bolder and growing in numbers. As his arrow punched through the heart of the nearest little beast, Identify triggered again.

Tipsy Boozlekin. Level 13. Common. Every bar has a couple of drunks who linger too long and make a nuisance of themselves. These permanently-sloshed distant cousins to the goblins make your average town drunk look downright respectable by comparison. At the first whiff of alcohol, they go into a berserker frenzy, intent on guzzling the booze and the life blood of any living being anywhere close to it.

Warning. If any Tipsy Boozlekin manages to drink a margarita, they'll trigger their Keg Party ability, tripling their size and all stats.

No doubt his potion would add some other nasty surprises too, but Steve would never give them the chance. He knew how to flush riffraff.

As they closed in a rush, the Boozlekin shouted a garbled, barely-understood chant like a battle cry. "Drink! Drink! Drink!"

They were super annoying. Steve shot a second one, then a third, but the rest kept coming. They'd swarm his table before he could finish them all off, so he made a slashing motion with his left hand, unleashing his water manipulation spell.

A whip-like tendril of water materialized out of thin air and slapped across half a dozen of the Boozlekin faces in a single long strike. The impact catapulted them off their feet with shrieks of animal rage. Wielding water was like a taste of home, and Steve couldn't hide a smile. If only he'd had elemental powers back on earth, plumbing would have been a breeze.

Steve fired again, taking down another beastie, but the last 2 were almost to the table. So Steve vaulted it and drop-kicked one of the monsters, sending it catapulting back into the ranks of the others he'd just knocked down with water, sending the entire group crashing back to the ground again.

The final monster leaped at Steve, long, clawed hands raking toward his face, shrieking "Drink!" so loud, its spittle sprayed across Steve's face.

He let it come, triggering one of the charges of his Barrier Bracers. A protective sphere enveloped him, and the Boozlekin bounced off, shrieking with rage, so upset it ripped at its own long, pointy ears so hard, one of them tore free.

Steve's laser rifle dropped into his hands and he shouted, "Drinks are for paying customers only!" as he rapid-fired the weapon.

Arrows were so much better, but firing a Star Wars blaster rifle was the fulfillment of a childhood dream. He focused on the wonder of that dream instead of the nasty things he was forced to do with the rifle. He walked the laser blasts across the horde of monsters, and their heads exploded in a series of gory geysers.

Three seconds later, he landed behind the table again, washed his hands with a flask of water, and resumed fast-mixing drinks. One after another joined the growing ranks on the table as the level of potion in the bottle steadily drained.

He had to fight down two more monster hordes, each slightly larger than the last, before he placed the final margarita onto the table with a triumphant shout. Twenty-eight Boozlekin were charging out of the forest in a wave of ridiculous monstrosity he'd never stop in time, but as soon as the last glass touched down, a loud chime sounded.

The monsters disappeared in flashes of rainbow smoke, and Cyrus's voice echoed around the glade.

"Well done! You might be the fastest drink mixer on Arasha."

"Do I get a title for that?"

Cyrus considered it for a moment. "Maybe we should upgrade your loot box"

Quest complete! You receive an emerald Road House loot box.

"Emerald? Nice!" He'd only been promised a platinum box for the quest initially. Upgrade indeed. Steve threw out his hands to welcome the huge, brightly-glowing green loot box. Lucas might get emerald and diamond loot boxes like candy, but they were rare enough for Steve, that he reveled in the moment.

With a flash of blinding light and a growing chorus of cheering voices, the emerald loot box exploded into shards of green lightning, leaving 2 scrolls floating in the air. With a sense of wonder, Steve focused on the first scroll, which was strangely blank. Identify triggered.

Temporary spell scroll mixer. Pour any alcoholic mixture containing a potion onto this spell scroll to transform it into a scroll to summon that potion. The more mixture applied to the spell scroll mixer, the more powerful the end result.

"Didn't see that coming" Steve said as he scooped up the first of the recently-created margaritas. "Cheers," he added before dumping the margarita onto the scroll.

The liquid disappeared into the scroll, getting sucked into it like a drain. The scroll started to glow a faint, golden color, so Steve snatched up the next margarita and dumped it too. In quick succession, he dumped all of the margaritas he'd recently created, and with each one the glow intensified until the temporary scroll mixer shone like a miniature sun.

As soon as he finished, the scroll flashed with silver light, and text appeared on the now plain-looking scroll.

Temporary scroll. Summon a potion of Echoing Doom. Rare. Level 2. Create up to 5 clones per level. By default, each clone will look and dress like you, and will mimic your moves and attacks. Adjustments will become available through practice and spell leveling. Any damage you receive will reflect to your clones, destroying them first. Duration: 60 seconds per level.

Steve laughed, clapping loudly. He looked up and exclaimed, "Thank you, Cyrus! That's a huge upgrade."

"Winning quests unlocks a lot of options not available to basic loot drops," Cyrus responded, sounding very pleased.

"Good, I need it," Steve whispered, blowing out a breath. He liked to joke and tease, especially with Ruby, but that could not long hide his growing concern that he would not be useful to the team for much longer. With this new temporary scroll, he had a shot at reaching some real power. He would not let them down.

"You're on Lucas's team, so I expect a great show," Cyrus responded.

Whistling a happy tune to himself, Steve checked the other scroll.

Title scroll. New title: Cocktail Commando.
You're a one-man elite bartending strike force.
Plus 10 to Intelligence.
Plus 2 levels to Echoing Doom.
Plus 50% damage dealt by clones when wielding Molotov Cocktails or other alcohol-based attacks you create.

"Sweet!" He pumped a fist into the air as the stats took effect. It was like his mind swelled with power, but despite feeling like his skull was suddenly too small to contain his fast-racing thoughts, Steve felt no pain. Just awe and excitement. With that huge stat boost and spell level boost, this quest was turning out better than his wildest hopes.

Riding that high, Steve downed a margarita he'd mixed before the quest. It was so good, he gulped a second. Delicious.

"I'm going to have a lot of fun with this," he grinned, glancing at the distant mountains. He really wanted to rush out like Lucas and test his new spell, but time was short.

One more level, and he could make it permanent. Then the real work would begin. He'd show everyone he could keep up.

Chapter Seventy-One

I Have a Successful Therapy Session

I spun Switchblade south and cranked the throttle wide, tearing across the grasslands, heading for the mountains I'd hunted all night. Tomas's message had said they'd gone south.

Lucas: "Where are you exactly? Are you okay?"

Tomas: "We're in trouble. We're surviving, but we can't escape without help."

Lucas: "Where? What's the monster?"

As I raced south, Tomas filled me in. He and Jane and their teams had been assigned to make another sweep of some smaller mountains south of the plain. They had fought a few monsters and even found a group of people who needed help getting to Stepstone.

Tomas, Jane, and 2 teammates had continued on while the rest escorted the people back to town. That's when they'd climbed higher and discovered a strange black stone pedestal with rune markings on it. When they drew close to inspect it, they were teleported into a huge cavern filled with a twisting maze of stone walls.

It was the lair of some powerful monsters, most with levels in the high 30s. Worse, there was a boss monster hunting them. They'd only caught glimpses of it. Apparently it had cloaking abilities, but seemed to be much stronger.

They were playing a cat-and-mouse game through the maze, trying to find an exit, but Tomas feared the boss monster was just toying with them. Jane's telekinesis had helped save them from the shadowy monster's first attack.

I pushed Switchblade until the thrusters screamed. The sound resonated with the new fear racing through my veins like ice as I chatted with Tomas, drawing as much information from him as possible. I'd hunted all over the southern mountains and had probably passed that peak on a higher mountain. If I'd taken a lower track, I might have found the pedestal first.

I needed to find them and help them escape, but I was just as excited to fight the monsters. They might have high enough levels to give me the experience I needed.

As if reading my mind, Cyrus said, "This is an exciting development."

"If I save them and kill the monsters, will that pass the final test?"

"Unfortunately, not. This little drama will no doubt prove quite an adventure, and your willingness to drop everything to help your brother will definitely win you a lot of good will, but there is one final test I need you to complete in order to win your last level."

"I'm still going."

"Of course you are, and I would never suggest you don't."

"Are you saying that I won't get any experience from this?"

"You'll get it, but you won't see it until after you complete the final test."

I bit back a growl of annoyance. I had read that scroll and accepted the evolution knowing I had to pass difficult tests, but at the moment, the experiment only annoyed me. Tomas and Jane came first, no matter the cost.

Tomas's messages abruptly cut off and my fear spiked as I tore through the lower hills, dodging trees, boulders, and the occasional monster. Without Switchblade, it would have taken me at least a couple hours to reach the pedestal. With it, I planned to reach it in 20 minutes.

Tomas finally answered after I'd sent 15 increasingly urgent messages asking what was going on.

Tomas: "We're on the run again. It almost caught us. Lana is injured and we're getting low on potions. Jane thinks it's trying to herd us to one side of the maze to trap us. Hurry, Lucas. It might be getting tired of the game. If it hits us with all its minions, they'll overwhelm us."

Lucas: "Nearly there. Hang on."

Wind tore at my face and Switchblade's thrusters screamed so loud, I feared something might break as I kept the bike pegged at full throttle up increasingly steep slopes. I fought to keep my muscles relaxed as I focused every shred of my enhanced perception and intelligence on maximizing my speed and threading my bike through the winding landscape as fast and efficiently as possible.

I recognized the landmarks Tomas had mentioned and could see the ridge of stone that looked like a half-peeled banana that he said overlooked the hidden valley with the pedestal. I'd passed on the north side of that same peak just hours ago. If only I'd known.

Minutes later, I skidded to a halt in the valley, heat pouring off Switchblade in waves that would have charred my flesh back on Earth. I barely noticed. The picturesque location would have been a tourist hotspot back on Earth. Ringed with craggy mountains and complete with a lovely teardrop-shaped pool of water beneath a 100-foot waterfall, it seemed idyllic.

The 15-foot obsidian pedestal definitely caught the eye. It glinted in the morning sunlight, polished smooth, and covered in runes that glowed faintly silver. They were pictographs, more like Chinese than any writing I recognized on Earth. Even from a distance, I felt as much as heard the faint hum of magic.

I banished Switchblade, drew Soulrend and my metal-wrapped fighting stick, and ran to the pedestal. Tomas hadn't said they needed to do anything specific to activate it. Hopefully it would work for me too.

I slowed, peering at the runes, but before I could memorize any of them, the world lurched. An invisible hand grabbed me by the head and yanked me off my feet. That was different than other teleports I'd felt. Weird, but not painful.

The world came back into focus and I found myself standing on a stone floor in a dim cavern. The roof of the vast cavern loomed high overhead, several hundred yards at least. I stood in an open-topped stone room with walls made out of rough stone that reared nearly 30 feet into the air. Wide openings gaped in 3 of the walls, leading into stone passages of more rough stone.

Each of the passages looked similar, just empty paths of stone about 15 feet wide, with walls that ranged between 30 and 40 feet tall. The air was cool and dry, with a faint scent of musk and rot. Distant moans echoed through the cavern, like people in terrible agony crying out their last gasping breaths.

That sound made me shiver. Tomas had mentioned the boss's minions made it. They were floating, tentacled monstrosities that Tomas had not gotten a good look at. They'd been too busy running.

Nothing jumped out to kill me, which was kind of disappointing. If I had more time, I'd love to explore the entire area. I loved mazes.

'Focus, Lucas. Short on time. Tomas in danger.'

Lucas: "I'm in. What part of the cavern are you in?"

Tomas: "Southwest corner."

Lucas: "On my way. Can you send up any signal?"

A pause, then **Tomas**: "We'll come up with something. Hurry. They're definitely closing in."

I didn't have time to navigate the maze. My mini map showed less of the area around me than usual. It was as if the game didn't want to make it easy for me to solve the puzzle by showing me too many of the upcoming twists and turns.

So I ran at the nearest wall and jumped, soaring nearly 15 feet into the air. Pulling a polearm weapon with an ax blade and spike on the head, I slammed the spike into the wall with all my strength. It drove in only a couple inches, but that was enough.

With my advanced agility and strength, I swarmed up the polearm and jumped up off the top, easily reaching the top of the wall. There, the expanse of the maze spread out around me, an eye-twisting pattern of passages, turns, and dead ends.

I ran southwest. When possible, I followed the tops of the walls, which were nearly a foot wide, easy purchase for me. At times, when passages cut across my path, I vaulted over to the opposite wall. I found a double somersault did the trick handily if I maintained enough speed.

I kept an eye out for monsters and watched my mini map for telltale red dots, but spotted nothing. The sounds of moaning grew louder as I ran. It looked like Tomas was right. They'd drawn all the monsters after them.

A deeper roar echoed through the cavern and my pulse quickened. Now that sounded like a boss monster worth fighting. Almost instantly, Tomas messaged me again.

Tomas: "We're on the run again. The boss is right on our heels. It's fast! Still can't see it clearly. Smaller monsters are closing in from all sides."

In the distance, near the far edge of the cavern, flashes of fire and distant rumblings of detonations punctuated the escalating fight.

Lucas: "Nearly there. Hold on!"

I increased my pace to a full sprint and flew across the distance. My legs blurred as I tore over the top of the maze, heedless of danger. At that pace, even I would get winded soon, but I did not relent. More flashes of light, bursts of fire, and thunderous explosions marked the path of the running battle.

The moaning of the minions reached a fever pitch. It sounded like there were a bunch of them, and the sounds were all coming from the same area. Tomas's team were trapped.

Every second seemed to stretch like an hour, but I finally reached them. Tomas, Jane, and 2 other bloody people were backed into a crevice cut into the outer wall of the cavern on its southwest side, facing a large open space where 10 different passages terminated.

Flames formed a wall between them and their attackers. Over 20 huge blobs of slime, oozing with puss-like gel, floated in a half circle not far from that wall of flame.

Each blob glowed with different colors, and dozens of long tentacle arms extended from their bodies. The arms had to stretch at least 25 feet, slithering along the floor behind the floating monstrosities. The limbs were thick and leathery and as I vaulted off the roof into the open chamber, I realized they were all covered in fleshy mouths crammed with rows of sharp, black teeth. I focused on the nearest one long enough for Identify to trigger.

Maze Guardian, level 35. Rare. This unique creature is the remnant of the soul of a chattering gorilla, consumed and reconstituted by the Maze Fiend. Its body is little more than a poison sack housing ravenous tentacles of endless hunger. Once it latches on with all 14 tentacles, it can devour an average human in 4 seconds. Not that it will, though. The Maze Guardian only softens up its prey, feeding on its pain and spirit before delivering it to the Maze Fiend.

The description made me pause in my tracks. Despite the imminent danger to Tomas, Jane, and their 2 teammates, I blinked and read it again. What the hell? Those things were beyond disgusting.

Every one of the Maze Guardians I checked had similar descriptions. Their levels ranged from 34 to 39, and they each had originally been different species, all rendered down by the Fiend into monstrous horrors.

Another ground-shaking roar drew my gaze to a shape pacing just outside of the wall of flames. The air around it shimmered and warped, making it hard to see the monster. Flashes of color and brief images rolled across it.

In one second, it looked like a pacing lion. In the next, a huge bear. Then something that reminded me of a wooden nutcracker like the ones my mom collected at Christmas. The thing had powerful illusion magic, but Identify finally kicked in.

Shadow Maze Fiend. Level 48 secret dungeon boss. This terrifying monster is as cunning as it is fearsome. It has plans of conquest and only needs to build an army before unleashing destruction across the world.

Maze Fiends conscript any living entity they can sink their claws into by consuming their spirit until it cracks, digesting their body until its soft enough to mold into a new form, and breaking their mind through torture and agony. The Maze Fiend won't kill you, but you'll wish it would.

"Oh, hell no," I muttered, licking suddenly-dry lips. What had Tomas gotten himself into?

No way I'd let that thing turn my brother into a hunger death blob, but it was level 48. This was no simple monster to slaughter like most of the creatures I'd been hunting all night. This was a secret boss.

Images of Bristleback, the boar-taur flashed back through my mind. That horrible lightning arrow burning me from the inside, pinning me to the ground while Bristleback charged in, naginata rising to deliver a one-shot kill.

The Maze Fiend was only 2 levels below Bristleback, by far the strongest monster I'd faced beside the boar-taur. I suddenly wished I had a lot more spells and more time to plan my assault.

If wishes were donuts, I'd probably weigh 500 pounds. I had no time. The flaming wall was beginning to dim and it was clear Tomas and his team were nearly out of tricks.

Tomas and Jane looked tired and battered, but not visibly injured. Lana was a member of Tomas's team I'd met only once. She had the dark hair and permanent tan of one with latin American descent, and she leaned against the wall, one arm hanging bloody and useless.

The last guy was Scott from Jane's team. He stood defiantly facing the monster, but his face looked sunburned, and he held one hand over an eye. He was on team X-Men with Jane and had an optic fire blast reminiscent of Cyclops, but it appeared he'd over-used it.

The good news was that no one had noticed me arrive yet. Time to say hello and see if I could turn the tide before that boss slaughtered us all.

Casting aside my cold fear, I summoned Switchblade, jumped on, and hit the throttle. If I was going to die today, I'd prefer dying while trying to save my brother and Jane. My fear faded to iron resolve and I cast aside all else but my target. It was me or the Maze Fiend, and by god, I'd kill it or at least take it with me.

As I accelerated across the large area, I targeted the Maze Fiend and triggered Shattercore Ballista. The glowing spear of light erupted from the front of the bike and leaped across the space. The monster somehow sensed it because it turned just in time to catch the ballista in the chest. The spear punched deep with an explosion of blue fire, knocking the fiend stumbling back into the wall of fire.

That fire might have been fading, but it wasn't out. The flames surged around the monster with sudden new life. Apparently it was very flammable. No wonder it had hesitated and not simply rushed through the flames earlier.

The Maze Fiend shrieked in pain, a high-pitched sound that made my head ache. The flickering illusions hiding it from view winked out, giving me my first good look at it.

"Great, it's the Aliens hive queen."

That was the best way to describe the black horror that appeared standing in the flames. Huge, powerful limbs, long claws dripping with obvious poison, and a long, bony skull. I hadn't thought the match-up could get worse.

"I knew you'd appreciate it! I loved that movie," Cyrus exulted.

"I loved watching it. That doesn't mean I want to live it!"

Tomas, Jane, and Scott shook off their shock fast and launched a barrage of attacks against the Maze Fiend. I couldn't see many details because all of the Maze Guardians spun toward me and floated in my direction, long tentacles slithering forward and reaching for me, nasty tentacle teeth gnashing the air in anticipation.

I hit the brakes and spun my bike into a slide, plowing through the crowd of floating monsters just as I triggered Shield Dome and Corrosive Cloud.

Corrosive Cloud. Deliver a cloud of gas from the rear of the bike for 5 seconds. Area of effect spell that corrodes metal and flesh on contact. Cloud remains active for 2 minutes.

The protective barrier knocked the tentacles aside and bumped floating horrors out of the way as I slid through the middle of the pack. At the same time, billowing clouds of dark gas streamed from the back of Switchblade, spreading to engulf the floating monsters and their thrashing tentacles.

I accelerated, banking hard over, throwing the hover bike into a tight turn and circling the crowd of monsters, who had bunched up to make my job easier.

Inside the cloud of gas, the monsters' moans of hunger turned to guttural howls of pain as their soft bodies melted under the intense corrosive effects of my cloud.

I had feared their poison, puss-filled sack bodies might be immune to the cloud, but it looked like just the opposite. They lost altitude, splatting onto the stone floor, tentacles writhing and slapping with disgusting, wet splotches against the stones as they tried vainly to pull themselves out of the cloud.

The horrors died in seconds. That worked so much better than I'd feared. I waved away the notifications and spun back around to face the Maze Fiend.

Its bleeding had slowed to a trickle and it had lunged out of the wall of fire and attacked Tomas and his team. They were all down on the ground, fresh wounds bleeding on exposed flesh.

The Maze Fiend towered over them, long, serrated tail whipping back and forth as it lifted Scott into the air, its long claws punched through his torso. His body was tense with agony, his head thrown back in a silent scream.

I twisted the throttle and tore across the space, aiming for the monster's back. My ballista hadn't recharged yet, but the sight of the beast killing another person enraged me.

The monster tossed Scott aside and spun to face me, enormous toothed maw opening wide as it roared, bloody, clawed hands opening to reach for me.

I might be mad, but I wasn't suicidal, and when the monster oriented on me, I got an idea. It clearly recognized me as the greatest threat. I could work with that.

I banked over hard, cutting to the left. The monster leaped to intercept, and it moved with alarming agility. I might not have another ballista yet, but I wasn't out of tricks.

The harpoon worked best when close to the target, so I pulled one of the silver-tipped spears I'd taken from the herd of cows and hurled it at the monster while it was still in mid-air.

It batted the spear aside and lashed out with its claws as its flying leap brought it right at me. I dropped Switchblade to the stone floor so hard metal screamed and sparks erupted from the undercarriage. The monster's mighty hands smashed down across Shield Dome just as I passed. The blows shook the dome and its energy reserves plummeted, but it held.

As I lifted back into the air and accelerated away, the Fiend spun, ripping its serrated tail across the back of Shield Dome and cracking it. The dome winked out, its energy spent, but it had saved me long enough to shoot away.

The Maze Fiend gave chase, roaring with rage, not seemingly slowed by the ballista I'd hit it with earlier. Either it was just that tough, lost in battle fury, or had some boss regeneration powers, I had no idea. I wouldn't underestimate it.

I sped across the open space, past the melting corpses of the Maze Guardians, and remembered to trigger Soul Feed. As energy poured into me, topping me off, I risked pulling open the menu and adjusting the amount of captured energy used to fuel Energy Ward. My health was already full and my bracelet already had enough stored energy to replenish my pools from empty at least 2 times over. So I directed all the new energy rolling in from the guardians to fuel Energy Ward.

My defensive aura sprang to life around me. Even though no one else could see it, to me it looked denser than ever. The Maze Fiend gave chase, accelerating to probably 50 miles per hour. The sight of that nightmare creature hurtling over the stone floor after me would probably wake me up in cold sweats at night. Assuming I survived today.

I could go faster, but forced down the urge to hit the throttle harder. I didn't need to lose it. I just needed to draw it away from the others. When I'd crossed two-thirds of the open space, I spun Switchblade a full 180, letting the bike slide backward as I faced the chasing horror.

I met its raging black eyes and cast Frostfire Nova.

Frostfire Nova. Elemental spell. Unleash a wave of freezing flames that immobilize while burning anything caught in its path.

I hated to use up two of my precious temporary spells in one fight, but I'd learned the hard way not to underestimate secret bosses. I didn't have time for a prolonged fight, especially with Tomas, Jane, and their wounded companions so close.

A torrent of blistering fire blasted toward the Maze Fiend, catching it mid-leap before it could dodge. The wave of billowing flames engulfed the monster and it fell, skidding across the stones. It started to roar in agony, but the sound cut off mid-cry.

It slid to a stop, unmoving in the flames as the spell's secondary effect kicked in, holding it immobile while searing it with deadly fire. I'd worried it might be strong enough to burst the spell's restraints, but they held.

The Fiend had lit up like a torch inside that dimming wall of flames. In the middle of Frostfire Nova, the monster erupted like it had been soaked in gasoline.

Maybe it was its poison, or its blood, or maybe it liked to lather its bony hide in petroleum jelly. Whatever the reason, the monster blazed hotter and hotter, the flames reaching high above the nearby stone walls. The air turned blistering and a nasty, volcanic reeking scent boiled off the incinerating monster.

The spell only lasted a few seconds, but the flames only seemed to grow hotter even as the monster started writhing and howling within the inferno. It tried to flee, but its legs buckled, snapping and spraying what looked like powdered graphite that burned with the white intensity of magnesium.

In seconds, the entire monster disintegrated into a steadily shrinking pile of rancid ash.

Congratulations, Lucas! You have defeated the Shadow Maze Fiend, level 48. Bonus experience for defeating a higher-leveled enemy.

Chapter Seventy-Two
Five . . . Gold . . . Rings!

I sighed, trying not to feel annoyed. I'd known I might end up with bonus experience that I couldn't use yet. All part of the test.

Cyrus spoke up. "That was a great fight, Lucas. Every day we grow is a good day. Every day we do something new or overcome a previous failure is a day in which we can build our future."

"I can't argue with that. I'll get this experience after finishing the last test though, right?"

"Of course. I wouldn't rob you of well-earned experience. You're proving my decision to invest in your potential was a wise one. I fully expect you to survive long enough for the experiment to pay both of us dividends. I'm taking an awful risk with you, Lucas. We both need you to succeed."

"I'll succeed," I promised. "I could use a hint about what I need to do to pass the final test, though."

"I've already given you all the hints you need to win the day. If I do more, it could draw unwelcome attention onto both of us."

Had I missed something? As I considered everything he'd said recently, I triggered Harvest, fully prepared for the spell to fail again.

You have successfully harvested Shadow Portal from Shadow Maze Fiend.

Shadow Portal. Rare. Create a portal to anywhere in the current stage you have previously explored. Transport up to 4 people. Uses remaining: 1.

"That's more like it," I whistled. I'd wanted another teleport spell. If I could save it, I'd definitely make that my next permanent. I scanned my achievements.

Congratulations, Lucas. You are the first human to defeat one of the rare, unique secret bosses. You receive a diamond Hercules loot box.

That was promising. I bet my Musketeer title had helped me get that box upgraded to a rare diamond level.

The loot box appeared in the air in front of me, glittering like a diamond the size of a steamer trunk. When I willed it open, the box exploded into shards of shining light. When they faded, 2 items floated in the air in their place. The first was a beautifully-crafted short sword with a silvery sheen that reminded me of an elven blade from the fantastic Lord of the Rings movies.

Roundhouse Fang. Short sword. Legendary. Delivers moderate poison damage. Plus 3 to Stick and Knife Fighting skill.

I plucked the sword from the air with a reverent hand. The hilt fit my hand like it was crafted for me, which I guess it had been. The blade was light and perfectly balanced. As soon as I touched it, a sheath made of fine black leather appeared strapped to my hip.

"This is incredible," I whispered, barely resisting the urge to test the blade with my thumb. That would be a stupid way to poison myself.

Cyrus did not respond that time, which was odd, but I was too distracted to care. I'd needed a good blade to deal with purely physical obstacles or enemies, and Roundhouse Fang fit the bill perfectly. The name clearly referenced Ruby Roundhouse's weakness to poison. I didn't want to think of a poisoned blade every time I thought of Ruby, so I decided to think of the blade as Fang.

The second item was a scroll.

Title Scroll. New title: Hercules. You've proven yourself a fearless adventurer with the will and might to defeat even the boss monsters others are wise enough to flee.
Plus 5 to Strength. Plus 5 to Constitution.
New aura: Indomitable.

Indomitable. Aura. Protect your mind and those of nearby party members with plus 50% mental defense for the duration of the aura. Mana cost: Moderate. Area: 5 feet for every point in Wisdom.

"Another new title so soon?" That made me smile. Titles were hard to get.

The new stats were always welcome, but the new aura seemed even better. Not only would I get a whopping 50% boost to mental defense while it was active, but I could share it with party members within about 70 feet. That should be enough to cover most battlefields.

"You seem to have a knack for being the first to accomplish important things. That gives you access to way more titles than most. Keep it up," Cyrus said.

I accepted the prompt to loot all the defeated monsters and blinked when I looked in my inventory at the new loot. I received 10 tier-4 mana crystals, each worth 10,000 tier-0 crystals, plus 20 full poison resist potions, 8 poison-imbued claws, 3 serrated blade whips imbued with temporary paralysis, and 10 gallons of something only referred to as **"Toxic sludge. Has many crafting uses."**

All that paled to nothing when I noticed the 5 new rings.

Bone ring. Epic. Grants immunity to poison.
Bone ring. Epic. Plus 3 to all stealth-based abilities.
Bone ring. Epic. Plus 3 to all mind abilities.
Bone ring. Epic. Plus 3 to all fire elemental spells.
Bone ring. Epic. Plus 3 to all ranged weapon skills.

Secret bosses might be a lot tougher than regular monsters, but they also dropped much better loot. I'd never gotten nearly such a haul from anything else, although I still would have preferred a level.

I thought about the fight as I dumped the rings into my inventory. The Maze Fiend had been really tough, but the threat Bristleback represented was a full magnitude higher. The only reason I could think was that my suspicion was right. Not only did monsters get a big power boost at level 25, but an even bigger one at level 50.

Humans got classes and a big boost at level 25. Did that mean we'd also get a larger boost at 50? Hopefully. We'd need it to survive the third stage and prepare to face Queen Marisara. Assuming I could even get to level 10 on stage 1.

My musings were cut short when I reached Tomas and the others. They looked battered and bloody, even though they'd already taken healing potions. Tomas gave me a hug as soon as I jumped off Switchblade.

Thumping me hard on the back, he laughed. "You got here just short of too late, little brother. Thanks."

"Couldn't let you take all the experience and loot."

"I did get two levels somehow," Lana said with a happy grin as she finger-combed drying blood from her long, black hair.

"Me too," Scott said.

"Well deserved," I said with a grin. I might not have gotten my experience from the fight yet, but it was good Cyrus hadn't blocked experience sharing.

Jane fist-bumped, then gave me a fierce hug. "Good to see you, Lucas. You wrecked them all."

"Yeah, made us look like noobs," Scott added.

"You gave me the idea of using fire against the fiend. Worked like a charm. Are you guys okay?"

"We are now," Tomas said.

His face was bloody and 4 thin white lines across one cheek marked the spot where one of the fiend's claws had nearly ripped his face off. "The poison was rough. Had to use 3 full healing potions."

"Glad we traded so much with Ruby," Jane added.

"Me too. Here. These will help."

I withdrew 4 Laundry Day potions and handed them over. That was nearly half my stash of the amazing potions, but every one of their team looked horrible. They needed them way more than I did.

"I saw one of these once!" Lana exclaimed. "Bueno! Gracias."

In moments, the miraculous potions left them all sparkling clean and fresh. "I need to find more of those," Jane said with a happy smile.

"If any of the crafters get a chance to start manufacturing them, they'll make bank," Tomas agreed.

"Speaking of bank. Here's your share of the loot."

I transferred 1 tier-4 mana crystal to each of them. Lana and Scott just gaped. Tomas laughed and Jane exclaimed, "My first tier-4! Sweet."

"That's not all. Now we get to the good stuff."

From what I knew of each of their abilities, each of the 5 rings were tailor-made for one of us. I kept the ring of poison immunity, handed the ring with the boost to stealth abilities to Tomas, and the ring boosting mind abilities to Jane.

Lana had abilities in disguises, but I didn't know the details. More importantly, she also used a crossbow, so I gave her the ring boosting ranged weapons. That left the ring boosting fire elemental spells to Scott and his Cyclops eye beam.

As one, they gasped when they read the descriptions of the rings.

"How?" Tomas breathed as the petite Lana laughed and lifted me off the ground in an enthusiastic hug. She kissed me on the cheek, then retreated, blushing.

Scott pounded my back, while Jane beamed and high-fived me.

"Secret boss. Better loot, I guess."

"This crazy misadventure turned out good after all," Jane said.

"I'd love to explore more, but we're short on time. Shall we head back to the entrance?"

They'd traversed much of the maze in their running battle, so with their maps fully populated, we traversed the maze pretty fast. Problem was, when we got back to the entrance room, nothing happened.

"Ah, do you know how the teleport thing works?" Lana asked.

I shrugged, as did Tomas and Jane.

Scott swore under his breath. "Maybe it was just a one-way ticket."

"Or maybe the portal died with the Maze Fiend," Tomas said.

Jane perked up. "I did see another exit, but we got chased away from it before we could get close."

"Lead the way." With any luck, we could navigate back to familiar landmarks pretty fast. Every second ticked away with ominous finality. I needed to get back to hunting.

The exit turned out to be a tunnel that punched through the outer wall of the maze cavern, leading onto a flat promontory high on the flank of one of the taller mountains. Peaks reared tens of thousands of feet above us and lower mountains spread in ranked tiers below, running north in ever-diminishing waves.

Tomas whistled softly. "That fiend teleported us a lot farther south than I'd realized. That might be the mountain we started at. Look."

He pointed to a jagged, rocky peak, tiny in the distance. With Sight of the Explorer, I zoomed my vision onto the peak.

"Yeah, that's the one."

"That's got to be 30 or 40 miles from here," Scott exclaimed.

"Too far to hike back in time," Lana confirmed. "What are we going to do?"

They all turned to me by some unspoken accord. I hesitated, mind racing as I considered our options.

"Lucas? Any ideas?" Tomas prodded.

"Yeah, one, but it's not ideal."

"Is it better than all of us trapped in these mountains so long we wave goodbye to stage 1 this afternoon?" Jane asked.

"For most of us, yes. I got a single-use teleport spell from the fiend. I can transport up to 4 people anywhere I want on this stage."

"Yes!" Scott laughed, then his face fell as he did the math. "Oh. So one of us is screwed."

Lana's face had gone pale. "This sucks. You have the spell, so you get to go. Tomas is family, so he and Jane go. So it's down to Scott or me to decide who takes one for the team."

Scott paced away, cursing softly before rushing back, as if afraid he'd miss negotiations and get chosen to stay by default. Tomas and Jane studied my expression.

"Maybe not," I said finally. "On Switchblade, I might be able to make it back through the mountains anyway."

I said it, but deep inside, I knew it would never work. Riding full-speed downhill would not find me the monsters I needed to kill to win my next level.

Where were they, then? I'd hunted all over the southern mountains and even killed a secret boss. What could I find stronger?

Then the clues snapped into place and with a sinking feeling of cold dread, I realized what I needed to do. Cyrus had indeed given me hints, and right after the Maze Fiend, he'd given me the last clue. He hadn't been just waxing poetic earlier talking about overcoming previous failures, he'd been telling me exactly what I needed to do.

My mind raced as I considered the challenge. Cyrus had said I needed to prove I could push the limits, but I hadn't expected him to want me to push them quite that far. I was so distracted by the realization that I barely paid attention to the conversation. Lana and Scott had visibly sagged with relief from my words, but paused when they noticed Tomas and Jane scowling.

"What?" Lana asked.

Tomas shook his head slowly. "No, Lucas. You might make it back, but only barely, and you need time to hunt."

"So we're screwed again," Lana sighed to Scott.

"No," Jane exclaimed suddenly, her eyes bright. "The solution is simple, isn't it? You loan Switchblade to me."

"Not screwed!" Scott exulted.

Tomas shook his head harder. "That's insane."

Jane took his hands in hers. "Not as insane as letting Lucas sacrifice himself, or choosing between Lana and Scott."

"She's right," I interjected a bit more forcefully than I'd intended. The need to get moving was clawing at me. I couldn't waste half an hour hemming and hawing. We needed to make a decision, and fast.

Tomas rounded on me, looking betrayed, but I held up a had to calm both of us. "She is. Jane's a better rider than any of us. She's already proven she's got a knack with Switchblade that even I haven't quite matched yet. If anyone can make it back through the mountains in time, it's Jane."

"We don't know how many monsters are between us and the plain," Tomas protested.

"Switchblade's got magic and I've got my telekinesis," Jane said, not fazed in the least. Instead, she looked thrilled by the chance to test herself against the mountains, just like she had back on Earth. Only this time she had superhuman strength and agility and a hover bike with powerful spells that packed a wallop.

"We need to decide now. I have to get back to my hunt, so unless Lana or Scott want to start running, it's our best option."

Tomas paced away, fists clenched. I forced myself to wait. I knew his habits. He didn't like seeing others take risks. He'd been a surgeon after all. He was the one who saved people and put things right. Sending Jane into danger would tear at him, but he was smart enough to see the necessity of it.

Besides, he loved Jane's adventurous spirit. It was what attracted him to her in the first place. Taking risks was nothing new for her.

Finally he blew out a breath. "Fine. I don't like it, but you're right."

He pulled Jane into a fierce embrace and kissed her deeply. She cupped his face in her hands and said, "I'll be fine. Don't party too hard while I'm gone."

Lana and Scott wished her luck, then she turned to me, looking so eager she nearly hopped in place. I gestured to Switchblade.

"Shield Dome isn't quite regenerated, but it won't take too long."

"You should wait," Tomas said immediately.

"Not this time, gramps," Jane teased, vaulting onto Switchblade. "One ballista shot per minute, right?"

I nodded and handed over my goggles. She flashed a grin and a thumbs up, then hit the throttle. Switchblade roared off the edge of the promontory and plunged down the steep slope. Her delighted laugh trailed her all the way down, echoing from the nearest cliffs.

Tomas shook his head slowly. "God, I love that woman."

"She'll be fine," I reassured him, and I honestly believed it.

My Shadow Teleport spell worked like a dream, dropping us back in Stepstone right on the spot where Tomas's Base Camp tent had stood.

"Yes!" Lana shouted, jumping up and wrapping her arms and legs around Scott in a full-body embrace. He froze in shock as she planted a big kiss on his lips.

"Sorry," she said in a not sorry tone when she dropped back to the ground.

"Don't be. You're right. We should celebrate," Scott said, reaching for her again.

"You wish. That was a one-off."

He shrugged, grinning. "Until the next time we survive a certain death match with an alien. I'll be ready for you."

She winked.

The town was still bustling, although fewer people raced past. Lots had already started the long march for the slope up to the second stage.

Tomas gripped my shoulder. "Lucas, what are you going to do? How can you still be level 9, even after taking out the Maze Fiend?"

"I told you I level up slower."

"Slower, yes, but this is crazy." He didn't hide his worry.

"It is crazy, but I have a plan."

I tried to keep my voice confident to hide the fear that was chilling my guts. It was a plan, but it was insane. I knew what I had to do to get that level. Cyrus was orchestrating a truly epic final exam. The fight would make an incredible death battle. How many times had he said I needed to think about making great entertainment?

"What?" he prodded.

"Take care. I'll see you later." I clapped him on the shoulder, then took off running. There was so much more I wanted to say, but I didn't dare. He would realize I was about to do something crazy and insist on coming with me. That would only get him killed instead of me.

"Good hunting!" he called after me.

If only he knew.

I had miles to go and barely enough time to reach my target, let alone defeat the one enemy strong enough to give me that level. The one enemy strong enough that fighting it would most likely just get me killed. After all, he'd one-shotted me the last time we met.

Like Cyrus had told me in the cave of the Maze Fiend, I needed to overcome my past mistakes. In particular, I needed to defeat the monster that had nearly killed me.

My final exam was to defeat Bristleback, the boar-taur sacred boss.

Chapter Seventy-Three

If You're Going to Die Anyway, Do Something Crazy

I ran hard for Bristleback's mountain. With Switchblade, I could have made the trip in an hour. Loaning it to Jane might have saved her life, but had it sealed my fate?

At minimum, it added one more element of danger to my one crazy chance at survival that was already razor thin. I was confident I'd reach the mountain, but time would be tight.

No, I pushed my worries aside. I could do this. I had a tier-1 body with higher stats than anyone else, and it was time to push those stats to the limits.

So I downed a Road Runner potion and *ran*. The potion doubled my speed for 30 seconds, and I pushed that potion for everything it was worth. Grasses blurred beneath my feet and wind ripped tears from my eyes as I shot for the mountains. I quickly accelerated to over 100 miles per hour, but incredibly, I still felt like I had more to give.

I wasn't sure how my stats translated to speed, but agility and endurance had to play big parts. With endurance at 28 and agility at 38, my body could move in ways no Earth human could imagine. Even I had been subconsciously limiting myself, but I couldn't afford to any more.

So I drew deeper, then deeper still, and kept accelerating. I had never pushed the limits like this and for a moment I forgot about my worries, my stress, and the deadly battle I was racing toward and let myself *run*. My limbs blurred as I continued to speed up until even my enhanced body ached with the strain.

If only I had a speedometer to verify my speed. I had to be pushing over 200 miles per hour. I could have kept pace with Formula-1 race cars! Ha!

"Just like Dash in the Incredibles," I laughed.

Enough people had traveled back to the eastern mountains from Stepstone that several good trails had been trampled through the grass. I tore down one of them, with the wind of my passing ripping grasses up by the roots and leaving a cloud of dirt and debris in my wake. I laughed again, focused on the distant mountains as I reveled in pure speed.

Finally I couldn't go any faster. My entire body was tuned to running, and I made a point to not look down at my legs. The sight of that blur would make me stumble. My muscles strained from the exertion, and wind resistance became an issue. So I held my speed there, on the ultimate razor's edge of control, and loved every second of it.

By the time the potion wore off, I'd crossed nearly 2 miles of grasses and reached the first foothills. I took a second potion, but received an unexpected message.

Road Runner potions are limited to a maximum of 2 uses in a single 24 hour period.

"When did that become a thing?" I asked as I accelerated again.

"Why bore you with extra details all the time when it's so much more fun to explain them to you when they become relevant?" Cyrus asked.

"You realize it's kind of mean to drop news like that on people at the last minute, right?"

"You have so much to learn about how to orchestrate great entertainment, Lucas. You'll have to work on that on higher stages."

"I will." No way I'd let myself fail this close to success. So I closed my lips to keep from swallowing any more alien bugs and focused on squeezing every last ounce of speed from my last Road Runner potion.

I pounded up the familiar canyons and slopes, dodging trees by pure instinct and running right up along the stone cliffs in places to avoid having to slow as I wound northeast deeper into the mountains.

Even though I'd cleared those canyons before, I found a lot more monsters than I expected. They seemed more aggressive than usual, every single one charging as soon as they sensed me. Could they feel the end coming? Were they trying to escape the stage somehow too, or just focused on stopping us humans from making it out?

It didn't matter. On Switchblade, I could have outmaneuvered more of them, but I didn't dare try on foot. Running face-first into a giant spiny hedgehog doing 100 would be a stupid way to die.

So I slowed, even though every second seemed to boom in the back of my mind like drums of doom. Still, I couldn't waste precious time battling lower-leveled monsters that wouldn't give me the experience I needed.

Maintaining a run, I tried not to slow or deviate my course as I tore through every monster that tried to block my path. I'd spent most of my temporary spells, so got creative with my other gear. I activated a scroll of Earth Armor to boost my defenses and unleashed volleys from laser rifles, then stun guns before wading in with Soulrend and Fang.

The two blades worked in devastating tandem, Soulrend slicing apart monster spirits while Fang blocked slashing claws or sliced through flesh, leaving festering, poisoned wounds behind.

My Tesla Coil bracelet drank in energy in a constant stream as I rolled from one fight to the next, and I triggered Soul Feed after every kill. I diverted the majority of the stolen life force to fuel Energy Ward without having to use one of my two remaining uses, replenishing it over and over.

For one fight, I switched to the red glowing spear I'd picked up. Turned out to be an uncommon hot-hand fire spear, and it worked great to take out a pair of fiery bats that reminded me of fire keese from the Zelda Breath of the Wild game.

Another time I tried one of my serrated blade whips I'd just gotten from the Maze Fiend. That proved a terrible idea. I had no experience with whips and nearly caught my own face with the serrated edge on my first strike. If I had any skill with it at all, it would have ripped apart the monster, some kind of gelatinous bouncing centipede thing. As it was, I did manage one halfway decent strike, which delivered the whip's imbued temporary paralysis, allowing me to dispatch the monster with my blades.

I had to take a stamina potion to keep pushing so hard, but ran on, barely slowing enough to loot the monsters and Harvest what spells I could.

That was a much better idea. I was hoping for another game changer. Teleport or invisibility would be ideal, or a powerful offensive spell. Unfortunately, the monsters were weak. I did harvest several mid-tiered spells, but none were good enough to help against Bristleback, so I used them on the next monsters and tried again.

The loot was mostly lame, although I got more mana crystals than usual and a few decent potions and scrolls. When I finally reached the steep cliff leading up to Bristleback's domain, the sun was hanging perilously low over the mountains. I only had minutes left to get up there and defeat the boss.

As I approached the stone wall that marked the boundary of the hog-taur's lair, I felt the change in the air this time. I hadn't realized what I was feeling last time, but a subtle aura clung to the area, a hint of warning that I was entering the domain of a dangerous creature.

Every instinct screamed for me to break into another sprint, but rushing in exhausted would just get me killed faster. So I forced myself to pause and take my first voluntary rest. I leaned my elbows on my knees, panting, my lungs and legs burning. My entire body trembled with fatigue. My stamina had bottomed out, my health at about 65%. The last monster had delayed me more than most. It had been some kind of vampiric thing that looked just like an Earth koala, but Eva only described it as:

Drop Bear, level 35. Yes, they're real.

Of course it was real, but that felt like an inside joke I didn't get. The adorable little monster had jumped around like a ninja on speed, and despite my best efforts, had bitten me several times. Thankfully my new ring of poison immunity worked on its vampiric poison too.

I got a message that its bite had a 30% chance of turning a victim into a were-koala. If transformation failed, it would drain 50% of the victim's health in 1 second, with a 5% drain per second thereafter.

A surge of intense desire had surprised me. Something deep inside my heart whispered that I should remove my ring and let the annoying monster bite me again. A were-koala might not be equal to a werewolf, but I'd felt the power of a changed body. Might that give me the edge I needed?

I actually laughed at the image of me as a snarling little koala trying to duke it out with the massive Bristleback. In that moment of distraction, the koala vampire had jumped in and tried to bite me in the groin.

Filthy little monster. I'd seized it by the throat, and once I got my hands on it, killing it proved easy. Then I harvested the spell Death Bite from it, which would have been exciting to try out in other circumstances. I doubted

Bristleback would let me get close enough to bite him. The monster had been more annoying than tough, so Soul Feed hadn't gotten much energy from it.

As I rested there at the base of the stone wall, I took another stamina potion and a minor healing potion to help boost my already-fast recovery rate. I didn't want to spend any of the stored energy in my bracelet. I was going to need every scrap of that when I faced Bristleback.

To help my health point recovery, I withdrew one of Paul's donuts. The chocolate-coated piece of heaven was still soft and slightly warm. I munched it with my eyes closed and took a deep breath, focusing my mind and preparing for the upcoming fight. I had to either defeat Bristleback or die trying.

"Here we go," I breathed as I forced down my fear. It was time.

I adjusted my hotlist for the upcoming death battle, then triggered a scroll of Ground Walker. Even knowing I was rushing toward the one monster that had wrecked me with terrifying ease, I couldn't help grinning as I easily ran up the nearly vertical slope of massive stone blocks.

The contest world might be insane and I might be facing death every second, but it also had some incredible benefits I wanted to enjoy as much as I could. That rush of exhilaration to feel magic working in me and through me helped counter some of the horrible things I'd seen and done in recent days and staved off my encroaching panic a little longer.

At the top of the slope, I rushed up the final hill to Bristleback's hidden valley, again ignoring the switchback trail. Near the top, I slowed and crept up for a peek over the last row of boulders, next to a rough statue of a bear trying to claw its way free of the stone.

Before risking a look, I triggered Mirror Cloak. As the world turned monochrome from light bending around me, I slowly rose to study the meadow. The idyllic spot looked unchanged, the short, waving grasses filling the space, ringed by rough stone hills and more statues. To the north, the weird Q'Bert stepped peak rose in stone tiers several thousand feet, with that shrine still perched up at the top. To the west, the panoramic vista over the central valley still took my breath away.

If I focused on the distant slope up to the second stage, I bet I'd see scores of people scrambling up the last yards to reach safety. I turned away scanning for Bristleback.

There! He was alone since I'd killed his entire herd. I'd expected him to be holed up in his cave at the far edge overlooking the valley. Instead, he was trotting across the meadow, magical compound bow in hand, near the stepped peak on the north side. He seemed to be looking for something. I was just glad he was not closer, looking for me. The sight of his enormous, van-sized boar body and over-swollen humanoid torso sent shivers of cold fear trickling through me.

This was stupid. As soon as he spotted me, he'd unleash that homing missile lightning arrow and lock me in place until he could finish me off.

No. I pushed aside the fear. I'd considered dozens of ideas for fighting Bristleback during my long run. Unfortunately, the only thing I knew for sure was that I couldn't just charge him. As soon as I broke into the open, the fight would turn to his favor.

I'd considered trying to snipe him with a laser rifle, but discarded the idea. I could hit him for sure, but I doubted one blast would do enough damage. Even if I got in several before he returned fire, I couldn't be sure I could disable him enough before he brought to bear overwhelming force. So that meant a more devious approach. First I used a Laundry Day potion. The wonderful sensation of the magical cleansing felt like a waste when I was about to begin a new battle. I was grimy and dirty and covered in monster blood and gore, but more importantly, I stank like human and death.

I didn't know how sensitive Bristleback's sense of smell might be, but I couldn't risk drawing his attention when the Laundry Day potion included a scent-suppressing effect. I hadn't thought much about it before, but now it might offer a vital extra advantage that could mean the difference between life and death.

Then I slowly stepped around the statue still mostly concealing me and moved into the open. My heart pounded so hard, it was a wonder he couldn't hear me from 100 yards away.

I paused, fists clenched against the overwhelming urge to flee back behind cover. I needed to know if he could see through my cloak's shielding. Forcing my breathing to remain slow and steady, I stood still, watching my enemy as slow, precious seconds ticked by. The air was clean, with a faint scent of grass, along with something faint, like incense.

When Bristleback turned, his gaze swept over me and I tensed, ready to dive for cover. His head kept turning and he swiveled away, trotting west. I nearly sighed, but couldn't risk even that much sound. Again, I had no idea how sensitive his hearing might be. I'd defeated his sight and smell, but would still die if he heard me.

Fighting the urge to rush, I strode with care along the southern edge of the meadow. Bristleback trotted back and forth a couple of times. He was definitely on high alert. Had he spotted me approaching earlier, or was he just stirred up like the other monsters?

I kept at a steady walk, and when he was turned away from me and more than 100 yards distant, I risked breaking into a jog. My cloak's last upgrade improved its ability to keep concealing me even when moving faster, but every time I sped up I feared I would give myself away.

I had to try, though. Time was running out way too fast. Walking west, I had a perfect vantage of the sun's inexorable descent toward the first of the western peaks. It was too close. I'd never finish this fight before the end.

Finally, Bristleback ducked into his cave across the meadow and I risked a whisper. "Cyrus, what exactly is going to happen when the time limit runs out?"

"All kinds of amazing changes!" Cyrus answered with even more bubbling enthusiasm than usual. "Don't worry, I'll keep this conversation between the two of us. I don't want to ruin the moment you're setting up here."

"Thanks." Alerting Bristleback like he had Michael when I lured the guy into the kitchen at Abby's death cult compound would definitely get me killed.

"Don't mention it. A final desperate attempt to fight a foe that has already proved it's way too tough for you is a perfect way to end the first stage. And what an ending! You're going to love it. Actually, you probably won't enjoy it nearly as much as everyone who will be watching from up on the second stage."

"I'm working on it."

"I know, but I figured you would like the encouragement."

"So back to my question. If I'm still down here when the time runs out, will I die instantly, or will I have a chance?"

Cyrus laughed. "That wouldn't be any fun at all! No, I'm not allowed to simply kill contestants, even though sometimes they might wish I did. This would count as one of those times. Dramatic changes will be triggered all across the stage, and chances of escaping once they begin are very low."

"But there's a chance."

"There's that indomitable spirit! Well, best get to it, Lucas. You've run the time down to the final moments. Time to impress me again." His voice turned more somber than usual. "I enjoy our chats, Lucas, and I have plans for you. Do not disappoint me."

"You need to work on your motivational speeches," I mumbled as I suppressed a shiver.

For the first time I considered what punishment Cyrus might choose to inflict on me if I failed. Even if Bristleback hit me with a killing blow, I did not doubt Cyrus had the power to whisk me away to some concealed torture chamber.

Definitely not the time to dwell on that.

Suddenly the sound of deep drums thrummed around me in a very recognizable pattern. I nearly jumped out of my skin and barely suppressed a little girl shriek that would have definitely given me away. I caught myself, every muscle tense, my heart seriously contemplating going into coronary arrest. I glanced up in the sky in disgust.

"Really? The Jumanji theme drums? Now?"

"Just a little extra motivation. I thought it appropriate."

He actually had a point. I was about to march into a death battle. And of course, now I had the sound stuck in my head. With phantom drums beating in my mind, I resumed my steady march.

By the time I crossed two-thirds of the meadow, heading for the solitary cave on the western edge, Bristleback emerged and trotted into the meadow again. I froze, every muscle tense, ready to draw my weapons if he sensed me. He trotted past, barely 20 yards to the north, every powerful footfall shaking the ground.

Bristleback towered over me, more than twice my height and many times heavier. His thick, musky scent reached me and his loud, huffing breaths seemed to shake the air. He was so close, every bit of him was visible in a larger-than-life terrifying clarity. The way his oversized muscles bulged and flexed with the smallest movements, the piercing intelligence of his black eyes, and the way the shaggy fur of his torso rippled in the breeze. All of it screamed apex predator, and every second the tension ratcheting up inside of me threatened to burst.

When would he spot me? How long would it take for him to swing that deadly bow around and fire a magical arrow that would end my life? Could I cross the distance to him before he struck? Even if I did, how could I kill such a mighty foe?

He didn't stop, though. If he'd come closer, I might have dared attacking in surprise, but he was still too far. As soon as he passed more than 50 yards east of me, his attention focused on the far side of the meadow, I sagged with relief, tension bleeding away, my entire body feeling wrung out and exhausted.

Forcing myself to focus, I broke into a cautious run in the opposite direction. In seconds, I neared his cave. Its welcome darkness beckoned me on and I wanted nothing more than to slip inside and hide for a second. I didn't have that much time, though.

So I stopped about 30 feet short, the perfect spot to lay my trap.

Chapter Seventy-Four

I Tell Knock Knock Jokes

I yanked out 3 small tufts of grass, then stuck emoji trap stickers in each tiny bare patch of ground before covering them with the loose grass. Even I couldn't see them concealed like that.

I was running low on the precious emoji stickers. The gag gift had ended up being one of my most important loot items.

"You know, I wouldn't mind another page of emoji stickers," I whispered.

For once, Cyrus did not respond, and I returned to my preparations. I next concealed under the grass the ostrich egg bomb I'd looted from Joseph's body way back on the first day.

Ostrich egg bomb. Can be detonated using a delay timer of up to 30 seconds, or with a mental command. Effects: trigger a powerful explosive blast, followed by a secondary cloud of sleep-inducing gas.

Even covered by grass, it made a suspicious lump, but I hoped it would go unnoticed. About 2 feet to either side of the egg bomb I concealed a tier-2 mana crystal and one of the energy cores from a broken energy rifle. It still had a pretty good charge, so would blow pretty big if ruptured. With all that done, I moved about 5 paces closer to the cave and placed a potion of Create Darkness on the ground.

Create Darkness potion. Produces a sphere of complete darkness 10 yards in diameter. Will move with the drinker if consumed, or will remain stationary if the bottle is dumped or smashed.

Only then did I creep into the cave and lean against the cool stone wall for a delicious second to let tension drain from my body. Walking in the open so close to Bristleback had taxed my nerves and I wanted to close my eyes and rest for a few minutes.

If only I could. I allowed myself 3 glorious seconds. Then I drew a deep breath and focused. Outside, Bristleback had stopped and was staring down at the grass along the southern edge of the meadow, about halfway across.

Right where I'd crept past. Tension roared back in, every sense coming alert as Bristleback slowly turned his head, tracking the path I had walked. I didn't think I'd left tracks in the grass, but maybe I'd crushed some of it down. Bristleback read the signs, swiveling until he looked directly at the cave.

My time was up. The boss boar-taur lifted his bow as he started galloping toward me, his minotaur features set in angry lines. Actual steam blasted from his huge nostrils as he charged.

I pulled a laser rifle from my inventory and sighted down the barrel. As soon as the sights settled on my target, I fired.

The potion of Create Darkness exploded, and a globe of absolute darkness materialized on the spot. A second later, a lightning bolt blasted through the darkness.

Bristleback had fired blindly. The bolt of deadly white lightning punched through the darkness, but did not dispel it. The bolt shot just past the mouth of the cave and disappeared out over the central valley. It probably wouldn't stop until it slammed into the western mountains. Hopefully it didn't accidentally kill any of the other people fleeing stage 1.

I crouched in the entrance, still concealed by Mirror Cloak, as the thunder of Bristleback's charge drew nearer. I couldn't see him through the globe of darkness. I should have planned that better. Now I had to time my next strike by sound.

"Show yourself, weakling." The voice was low and guttural, but my translate ability made the words clear. Bristleback slowed to a stop on the far side of the globe of darkness. If I'd set it right, he should be right above my traps.

He added, "I know your scent. You're a greater fool than I realized for returning to die by my hand a second time."

I wanted to reply, but didn't dare cause him to move. Tension ratcheted in my chest so tight I couldn't breathe as I waited for the sound of success. This had to work.

Right on cue, Bristleback roared in pain. He'd triggered the 3 traps I'd left concealed in the grass. I needed to do a lot of damage and wasn't sure what kind of magical resistances he might have, so I'd gone with the classics.

Emoji trap of Piercing Strike, times 3. Unleash a dozen sharpened spears across a 2-foot square area that will thrust up into the target with bonus piercing damage. The perfect choice to wreck an enemy's day and forcibly castrate them at the same time.

If he'd walked into all 3, Bristleback might have just been stabbed with as many as 36 spears shooting up into his underbelly. That should rattle even a level 50 boss. Time to cook the rest.

Before I could trigger the egg bomb, the entire world froze. I couldn't move, couldn't even blink. Cyrus's voice boomed so loud it shook the air.

Aaaaaand your time is up! Congratulations, contestants from Earth, you've survived the entire first week! Most of you wisely followed my suggestions and climbed to the second stage. You're about to witness a show unlike anything you've ever seen. I hope you saved some popcorn.

His voice turned somber. **The rest of you should have listened. I doubt any of you will survive what's about to come, but I hope you prove me wrong. I'd recommend you start running . . . NOW!**

Time resumed and a crack of thunder so loud it sounded like the world had just split in half rent the sky. I regained the ability to move in time to reflexively drop to the ground.

And immediately bounced back off, tumbling into the wall of the cave. Sounds of crashing and booming continued shaking the world, so loud I could barely think. I grabbed the edge of the cave and held on tight, pulling myself out. I had to see what was happening.

Outside the cave, I fell to my hands and knees, my feet braced against the rock of the cave. Even then without my enhanced stats, the violent shaking of the ground would have thrown me off the nearby cliff.

The world was collapsing. Everywhere I looked, mountains were crumbling, stones and dirt cascading down into canyons and valleys. Random explosions of fire burst 10,000 feet into the air, while geysers of water like inverted waterfalls exploded out of the earth everywhere. They cascaded high, then fell in thunderous torrents that flowed downhill toward the central grasslands like flash floods.

"Whoa," I breathed as I stared at the devastation sweeping the first stage. I had the perfect vantage to watch the collapse of the entire landscape as I crouched on the edge of the high meadow. It was like the end of the world.

No, the end of a stage, and I was stuck in the middle of it, miles from safety. To the north, the spectacular waterfall that had cascaded down the high cliff from the 3rd stage expanded into a torrent bigger than the Amazon river. It crashed into the small lake that was expanding by the second, while billowing clouds of mist crept out to consume miles of grassland.

Dark shapes moved within the waters of that fast-spreading lake with predatory speed. Some darted like fast sharks, but those were only the tiniest of what I glimpsed. Others looked more like orcas, but even they looked small compared to the leviathans I glimpsed rising behind.

Cyrus hadn't been kidding. In moments, the entire first stage would be flooded and filled with deadly monsters. People hiding in the canyons and valleys might already be dead, crushed by falling mountains or swept away by sudden floods. Even after I killed Bristleback, I had no idea how I'd cross the long miles of the fast-flooding valley.

Bristleback.

I'd totally forgotten about the deadly boar-tar for a few seconds in my shock as the world ripped itself apart. I needed to kill him fast, like 30 minutes ago.

I focused on the egg bomb and triggered it. A huge explosion eclipsed the constant rumbling of thunder, and a blast of superheated air slammed me back against the cave. Two secondary explosions built upon the first as the energy rifle core and the mana crystal detonated under the force of the first blast. They tore apart the meadow where Bristleback had been standing.

The boar-taur tumbled into sight, soaring over the sphere of darkness in a wild somersault. His hugely-muscled torso was scorched, his boar fur burning, and his underbelly was a gory mess of blood and exposed entrails. Unfortunately, he was still very much alive.

Dammit! He must have moved some when the world started crashing down. My explosions had hurt him, but not enough.

Bristleback crashed into the side of the cave just to my left and 10 feet overhead hard enough to shake the meadow. I drew my blades, preparing to strike when he slid down the stone.

Instead, the entire cave disappeared.

The loss of the stone hill I was bracing against sent me stumbling, so I missed my chance to stab Bristleback as he fell hard to the ground. Still, he was only a few feet away. I wouldn't get a better chance.

I tensed to spring, but the ground beneath my feet started to give way. Only my enhanced senses noticed the shift in time. Ignoring Bristleback, I sprinted away just before a huge section of the outer edge of the meadow simply slid off and fell toward the valley below.

It carried Bristleback down with it. The boar-taur bellowed like an angry lion and fired his bow even as he fell.

"Yes!" I shouted, expecting to see him get crushed by the tons of falling earth.

That hope evaporated as his arrow soared across the meadow and pierced a lower section of the Q'Bert tiered peak rising above us. The arrow flashed with bright light, and a slender silver tether linked it back to Bristleback.

The boar-taur clung to the tether and slid up it, riding it back up to the meadow and crossing it in a graceful slide, like he was riding a reverse zipline. He stuck the landing on the solid first step of the higher peak.

"No way! A magic grappling hook?" I wanted one of those.

Focus, dummy.

The ground was shaking ominously. The meadow wasn't done collapsing. I sprinted all out, dashing for the higher peak. Moving that fast, Mirror Cloak's invisibility wavered and Bristleback noticed something.

He brought up his bow and fired.

"Not this time," I growled as I gauged the distance. The arrow crossed the space with terrifying speed, but my improved reflexes proved sufficient as I dove aside at the last fraction of a second.

The arrow glanced off Mirror Cloak, and the cloak's upgraded defense against magical damage proved sufficient to handle the glancing blow. The electricity charging the air around the bolt still made me shudder, but I managed to roll aside.

Even as I lunged back to my feet, Bristleback roared again, retreating a quick step as if in unexpected pain. My Amulet of the Rebound must have reflected some of that attack back at him.

It wasn't much, but it surprised him enough that I had time to drop to my knees and pull out a laser rifle. My cloaking improved since I sat mostly still, giving me another precious second to aim.

Bristleback lifted his bow, but paused as he searched for me. That gave me a perfect, mostly stationary target. I fired, aiming for his humanoid chest.

I would have preferred a head shot, but at that distance I wasn't confident enough in my marksmanship, and I'd only get one shot before he pinpointed my location.

Even as the laser bolt lanced out at Bristleback, I leaped into another run. Standing still would guarantee I died fast, either from another deadly arrow or from the ground falling away beneath me. More of the meadow was peeling off every second. I needed to reach the higher peak.

That wouldn't help for long. Rocks the size of houses started crumbling away from the peak as parts of each flat tier fell away. Some entire sections broke free, tumbling down the slope in crashing avalanches of destruction.

My laser struck Bristleback but only left another scorch mark. He barely reacted, but lifted his bow again. Thankfully a huge boulder tumbling down the slope forced him to jump aside, giving me the seconds I needed to reach the higher slope and dive 10 feet up to another flat step.

By the time Bristleback turned to shoot me again, I had already rolled behind the curve of the hill. He'd find me soon enough, so I couldn't stop moving.

Behind me, the rest of the meadow fell away in a rumbling avalanche that shook the rest of the peak and sent even more boulders tumbling down. The sound was an overwhelming crescendo of thunder, and the air felt heavy and charged, clogged with dust and electric energy.

I dodged a rock the size of a moving truck and scrambled up to a higher tier. The entire mountain could come down on us any second, but my only chance was to kill Bristleback. Only then could I focus on surviving the end of the world.

An arrow curved around the hillside and slammed into the ground where I'd stood only moments before. The explosion of energy tore that entire section away and pelted me with stinging stones.

Whoa. Even firing blind, he could easily kill me with a lucky shot. So I cast my temporary spell Knock Knock, focusing it on another flat step even farther to my left as I scrambled higher. If I could get a better vantage, I could try for a head shot, or something.

"Knock Knock," sounded a loud, cheery voice.

Instantly, another arrow curved around the mountain and slammed into the spot where the sound had come from.

A second later, it continued. "Orange."

I stifled a laugh. Perfect! That annoying knock knock joke was a lot longer than most. Hopefully Bristleback wouldn't realized he was getting played.

As the joke continued on with the unending repetition of Orange, I rushed higher and crept to my right, moving around the edge of the hill to where I hoped to gain a vantage above Bristleback.

I nearly walked right into him as he came leaping up from a lower step.

Chapter Seventy-Five
Death Really Bites Sometimes

I crouched and pressed myself against the vertical wall of the step as the giant boar-taur landed not 6 feet away. Mirror Cloak held and he never glanced in my direction. His entire focus was on the annoying voice sounding from the distant step. He lifted the bow again and fired another arrow, growling with annoyance as he did so

That close, his heavy, musky scent filled the air, while his breathing was like a constant rumble. I could have reached out and punched him.

First, I triggered Scroll of Binding. Magical chains, glowing with amber light, appeared around Bristleback's forelegs. He roared in anger and reared back, kicking violently, but the chains tightened, yanking the legs together and locking them immobile.

The mighty boar-taur stumbled when he landed and fell to the ground with a resounding crash. I pounced, leaping right onto his broad back and hurling a potion of Impotence into Bristleback's open mouth when he spun to look at the invisible weight on his back.

Potion of Impotence. Drinking this potion renders a being magically impotent. Blocks all use of mana for 60 seconds.

The potion smashed against his teeth, spraying liquid into his mouth. Bristleback's entire body shuddered. The lightning dancing around his bow winked out and he sagged, as if suddenly weary.

I drew both of my blades and plunged Fang into the center of the boss's thick upper humanoid back, anchoring me in place. The blade delivered a massive dose of poison, drawing from my mana to fuel its power. Bristleback shuddered and roared again, twisting violently to reach me with arms that could rip me limb from limb.

I clung to his back, anchored by Fang. With a shout of victory, I slashed across the back of his neck with Soulrend.

The glowing ethereal blade bounced off.

I was so stunned, I froze. Soulrend never failed to penetrate. It wasn't physical, not even elemental. It only directly interacted with souls, so armor, hide, and most magical defenses couldn't stop it. How?

Somehow, even with his front legs shackled, Bristleback bucked mightily, throwing me off. I lost my grip on Fang, leaving it sticking out of Bristleback's torso. As I windmilled uselessly in the air, he punched me.

He might not be able to use his magic, but he was still a 15-foot tall boss monster the size of a truck. His fist hit like an avalanche and I rocketed away, the wind blasted out of me, even though my Crash Test Dummy armored jacket absorbed enough of the damage that I don't think any of my ribs broke.

Cracked, sure, but not broken. I was good to—

I smashed back-first into a falling boulder the size of a inground pool. Again my armor saved my life, but my head cracked so hard against the unyielding stone that stars exploded in my vision.

I bounced off the rock and tumbled onto another flat step, rolling in an out-of-control tumble until I crashed face first into the vertical back of the step.

"Ow," I groaned as I flopped onto my back, stunned. As my head swam, the weird robotic voice from my jacket said, "Major frontal impact. Too bad you don't have a jacket for your head."

Was my jacket making fun of me?

Energy poured in from my Tesla Coil bracelet, healing my wounds and clearing my head. Had I heard the jacket right, or was it a concussion hallucination? Didn't matter. In 3 seconds, I'd be back in action.

That proved to be 2 seconds too slow.

An enormous fist wrapped around my torso and lifted me into the air. Bristleback's snarling face loomed over mine as he lifted his naginata-style spear sword in his other hand.

"Now you die." He growled.

Ahab's harpoon appeared in my hands, the long weapon pressing against Bristleback's chest and I fired as soon as I felt its solid weight.

The fiery harpoon exploded into the boar-taur's chest with a blast of fire that ripped clean through to the far side, leaving a softball-sized hole gushing blood and gore.

Bristleback staggered, his grip loosened, and I fell free. Even wounded so badly, he tried splitting me in half with his spear-sword. I twisted aside and Energy Ward helped deflect the blow just past my shoulder. Instead of ripping me in half, the blade bit a foot into the hard stone.

Standing so close to Bristleback, his heavy musk scent, mixed with the reek of blood and open entrails and scorched fur was overwhelming. He'd taken even more of a beating than I had, but the tough bastard wouldn't die.

He lunged, trying to smash me into the stones with his enormous weight, but I dropped and rolled beneath him. Of course, he tried to drop on top of me and squash me like a grape.

It was an awkward move with his front legs still bound, which gave me a second to slap another Piercing Strike emoji trap to the stone next to me. I triggered it and rolled aside.

A forest of spears exploded out of the ground, punching deep into Bristleback's already-shredded underbelly. I'd timed it perfectly, just as the huge boar-taur dropped with all his weight. The move amplified the damage, forcing the spears deeper.

Bristleback froze and a throat-ripping roar shook the air and echoed off the nearest peaks. That had hurt the tough monster.

I rolled free and glanced up to see Bristleback shuddering in pain. He spotted me and still somehow rallied the strength to raise his spear-sword overhead. He might be badly wounded, maybe even mortally wounded, but he could still kill me.

I triggered a scroll of Ice Blast, aimed right at his face. I had never used that type of scroll before, so wasn't sure what it would do. As it triggered, I sensed it reacting to my intent at a deeper level than just accepting my target.

A thick bolt of absolute cold smashed into his long snout and toppled Bristleback right over backward, ice encasing his entire head. He writhed on the ground and one giant rear leg caught me in the chest.

Even with my armor and Energy Ward, the blow catapulted me up onto another flat step and I got to enjoy another bone-rattling crash into the cliff wall.

"Major offset impact. You'll need more than a chiropractor after that one," my jacket said.

"Oh, shut up," I growled as I spat blood. My bracelet was working overtime to keep me in fighting shape, but the battering was taking a toll. Groaning, I staggered back to my feet just as Bristleback smashed the ice encasing his head. Down on that lower shelf, he lay on his side, enormous chest heaving, covered in blood and gore.

I had to finish him. So I pulled a poleaxe from my inventory and leaped off the step. I poured all my strength and momentum from the jump into the blow, envisioning the long ax chopping Bristleback in half.

Even dazed as he was, the boar-taur sensed the danger and rolled over, swiping my blow aside with his sword spear. I crashed to the ground next to him, and he lashed out with one giant fist.

I slipped past the blow, but as he withdrew the hand, he caught my armored jacket with his fingers and dragged me close. His humanoid torso bent nearly double as he snapped his deadly maw at my head. Those thick teeth could probably snap my skull in a single bite.

I twisted as hard as I could in his grasp and with the help of Energy Ward, managed to just avoid the snapping jaw. Then I seized him by both tusks and bit down on his wide, flat nose with all my strength. My teeth broke the rubbery skin.

You have cast Death Bite.

The move totally caught Bristleback by surprise. As the spell struck, he roared right in my face, then fell back, convulsing. In the process, he slammed me bodily into the stone so hard I lay stunned for a couple seconds. The charge in my Tesla Coil bracelet was nearly spent, despite how much damage I was dealing to Bristleback, but it saved me again.

I rolled to my feet and backed away from the still-convulsing monster. Even if he wasn't directly targeting me, he could crush me by accident. I wanted to leap in and finish him while he was distracted, but also wanted to see if the spell worked.

I expected the transformation to fail, but I really wanted to see the 50% hit to his life points. That should be enough to kill him, unless it only took 50% of what he had left. That would be lame.

Bristleback's convulsing intensified even as the ground shook harder. More of the steps broke free, and an avalanche of stone raining down from above forced me to scramble aside and take refuge on a nearby shelf. The entire mountain shook so hard, I only barely managed to keep from getting shaken over the edge. Falling into the deep chasm filling with frothing water and dark, sinister shapes of underwater monsters would end my journey in a flash.

Finally the shaking subsided long enough for me to rush back to Bristleback. The entire shelf was covered in gore. It looked like one of the falling rocks must have squashed Bristleback to jelly. All that remained was a disgusting crimson pool of monster parts that threatened to make me sick.

I spotted Fang in the gore and scooped it up. It was a mess, but I was glad to have it back. I tossed it into my inventory, then frowned. Shouldn't I get an achievement for killing Bristleback?

A tiny shape hurtled into me from the side, hitting me so hard it knocked me back to the other shelf. I fell to my back with something tearing at my head and neck. It was a blur of fur and claws and fangs and pure mayhem.

Bristleback, boar-koala. Level 51. This unique amalgamation of a boss boar-taur with a were-koala has produced a being so full of rage it will literally explode if it does not eat your heart.

Blood ran into my eyes, obscuring my vision, and my face and neck were ripped with scores of shallow wounds. My health plummeted and searing pain made it hard to think.

One thought was clear, though. Death Bite had been a bad idea.

I snatched and grabbed at the angry little beast as it clawed and bit and crawled over me, trying to kill me through sheer savagery. It bit and tore at my jacket and gloves, but they proved strong enough to ward off its attacks.

Cyrus would torture me an extra year if I let myself get killed by a stupid were-boar-koala after I'd beaten Bristleback in his overwhelming huge form.

Growling with anger, I finally got a grip on the little monster and hauled it off my head. It came free with several chunks of my hair and another spray of blood.

"Ow!" I shouted, shaking it hard as I tried to get a good look at my enemy.

It looked like a koala, but with a boar's snout and stubby legs covered in bristly fur. It hissed and gnashed sharp teeth at me, spraying yellow acidic poison. Without my poison immunity ring, it might have killed me from the poison infection alone.

It tore at my gloves and bracers, black claws leaving scratch marks on the tough armor. I spun and hurled it against the vertical stone wall about 10 feet away. The little devil smashed into it but bounced off and rushed back at me with a shriek of absolute rage.

I shot it in the face with a stun gun.

The blast knocked it off its feet where it lay dazed for a second. That was plenty.

I leaped high into the air. As I came down, I pulled out my giant ogre club. The enormous weapon seemed to fill the entire sky as I brought its full 500 pound weight down with all my strength onto the still-dazed boar-koala.

The little monster splatted like a water balloon, streaks of crimson spraying to either side. When I tossed the giant club back into my inventory, only smears of red and tiny patches of fur remained to mark the spot where Bristleback had died.

Congratulations, Lucas! You have defeated Bristleback, the sacred boss and leader of the Peakstone boars. Bonus experience gained for defeating a higher-level monster. Experience doubled for defeating your first level 50 boss.

I held my breath and time seemed to slow even as the apocalyptic destruction of stage 1 continued all around me. I couldn't breathe, my heart nearly burst with tension as my fears spiked. Had it been enough to satisfy Cyrus?

Congratulations, Lucas! You have reached level 11!

Chapter Seventy-Six
Run!

Other messages followed, but I waved them aside. I didn't have time to deal with anything except survival. I lifted my hands high and roared in victory as I triggered Soul Feed.

"You passed the test," Cyrus cheered. "Congratulations!'

A torrent of power thundered into me, restoring my pools. Finishing Bristleback had also supercharged my Tesla Coil bracelet, even though he had transformed into such a tiny monster. I kept 20% of the energy of Soul Feed set to fuel Energy Ward. I feared I was going to need it.

Energy Ward power at 300% for 15 minutes.

Wow, Bristleback had been one tough son of a boar. Even though all my pools were topped off and my physical stats at 150% for 5 minutes, I just wanted to lie down and rest.

Then the last message fully registered and I laughed. "Two levels?"

"Bristleback was far stronger than anything you've faced. The bonuses really add up. Well done."

"Thanks. Did you include the other experience you withheld earlier?"

"Do you think this is the time to discuss the minutia of experience gains?"

Right. I'd take an extra level for completing that insane test. Now all I had to do was survive the apocalypse. Then a word in one of the other messages caught my attention and I focused on it.

Congratulations, Lucas! Your spell Harvest has upgraded.

Harvest. Unique. 70% chance to gain a skill or ability from a defeated enemy. Chance increases by 2% per enemy level higher than your own. Can have a maximum of up to 2 harvested spells. First in, First out. Mana Cost: minor.

I whooped a second time. A second Harvested spell slot was awesome!

A stronger shake of the mountain reminded me I was far from safe. I'd gotten my levels, but still had miles of apocalyptic landscape to traverse. The entire peak was shaking and could collapse any second. With great anticipation, I triggered Harvest.

You have successfully harvested Tether Slide from Bristleback.
Tether Slide. Rare. Mark an object or item as your tether. Within 10 minutes you may cast a magical hook to that tether and slide to it across any terrain up to a distance of 200 yards. Tether must be within sight when spell is triggered. Mana cost: minor. Uses Remaining: 5.

Yes! I got the magical grapple. This was going to be awesome. I accepted the prompt to loot the corpse and turned away as the bloody remains melted into dark mist. I'd check the loot once I reached safety. I was surprised by a new message.

Duplicate Base Camp detected. Choose which one you will keep.

"What?"

The huge cave appeared in the air nearby. It thumped to the ground on the next mountain step over, but the impact knocked that entire section of mountain loose. It fell away and tumbled down into the frothing waters thousands of feet below.

"Hey, was that Bristleback's Base Camp?"

"Oops," Cyrus said, sounding chagrined, then brightened again. "That makes your choice easy, doesn't it?"

"What did he have in there?"

"Doesn't matter now. Focus, Lucas."

Lame! What kind of loot might I have gotten from a sacred boss's personal Base Camp? Cyrus was right, didn't matter. The shaking of the mountain grew worse. I nearly followed the cave over the side, but caught my balance and leaped up, scrambling higher as the lower steps all broke free and fell away. Soon there would be no mountain left.

I paused to scan the valley and muttered, "This will be a challenge."

Cyrus exclaimed, "No fair. Too many people used that phrase to know which one you're quoting."

"I don't only quote other people, you know. Sometimes I say things I come up with myself."

"Don't be boring, Lucas, not after that amazing show. Now stop dawdling. The mountain will collapse in 8 seconds. Let's see what else you've got."

Two-thirds of the central valley was now flooded, with huge monsters visible in the waters. More were emerging onto dry land, big, lumbering things, like ogres or even just piles of animated stone.

A high-pitched shriek snapped my gaze into the sky and I blanched. I hadn't even noticed the flocks of birdlike monsters swarming down from the second stage and maybe even the third. They filled the sky like black rain and some were heading my way. I spotted huge birds, bigger than the griffon I'd killed, but most were flocks of smaller, faster flying creatures.

I needed to move, but jumping off the cliff seemed like a fast way to just die. The shaking earth and still-spewing geysers were filling the space between the mountains with frothing white water. I was a good swimmer, but I doubted I'd make much progress through all that before a monster from the deep swallowed me whole. I needed a better plan.

The seconds ticked by like drumbeats of impending doom as I considered my meager options. If only I had another use of Shadow Portal. I could have teleported straight to the top of the slope and stepped across to the second stage.

Thinking of the portal spell reminded me of Jane. I checked my messages and saw one from her.

Jane: "Lucas, I made it back in time. THANK YOU! Switchblade is amazing. I swear, you're lucky I love Tomas so much, or I'd date you just to ride it more. Seriously, though. Thanks, and good luck. Get here soon."

Good. She made it. More importantly, she no longer needed Switchblade. New hope sparked bright and fierce as I summoned my hover bike.

It appeared in the air in front of me just as the entire mountain groaned and started shaking more violently. I stumbled and nearly fell off the edge of the step. That would have been the worst way to die, with possible salvation literally within reach.

Switchblade looked battered, but I leaped on and hit the throttle. It shot across the flat step, aimed west, and I grinned until I checked the energy levels.

Jane had pushed the bike hard and I hadn't banished it to repair and recharge. Still, it should have enough charge to cross the flooded plain if I didn't use Shattercore Ballista at all. Worse, Shield Dome was spent.

"Nothing's ever easy," I muttered, then spotted my goggles wrapped around the handlebars. That had been clever thinking from Jane. I settled them over my eyes as the bike tore across the last few yards of open stone before the crazy drop to the churning waters.

Cyrus said, "By the way, well done, Lucas! That was a fantastic fight."

"Thanks. He was tough. Do monsters get a big boost to strength when they hit level 50?"

"Indeed they do. Great question, but now's not the time to get distracted."

"Tell me about it." I crouched, bracing myself as Switchblade rocketed off the edge of the cliff.

Switchblade was a hover bike, not a flying bike, but the thrusters and jets and magic still helped slow my fall to a graceful descending glide toward the frothing waters below. Instead of just falling straight down, on Switchblade it was more like falling with style as I glided down at an angle toward the water. That gained vital distance from the base of the mountain to avoid falling rocks and the frothing maelstrom there.

Behind me, the mountain peak collapsed in a thunderous avalanche that violently shook the air, flinging Switchblade sideways over 50 yards. When I glanced back, the little shrine somehow stayed perched on the top of the collapsing mountain.

I bet there'd been a hidden loot box in there. It fell with the rest of the mountain as the entire thing cascaded down into the waters in a rolling avalanche that sprayed geysers of water over 1000 feet and tore the frothing water into an insane maelstrom. If I'd simply jumped off, I'd have been crushed.

Some of the nearest flocks of flying monsters spotted me and swept in, screeching with hunger and thirst for blood. The overwhelming swarms of monsters, coupled with the catastrophic destruction of the stage was clearly designed to finish off any humans foolish enough to have lingered, despite Cyrus's warnings.

Just the thought of crossing miles of apocalyptic collapse and fighting through swarms of monsters was exhausting, but I wasn't about to stop now. After defeating Bristleback, it would be insulting to get killed by anything else.

I had to find a way, so I focused on the closest flocks of two distinct small bird types. I managed to identify a couple of them.

Whisper Finch. Level 38. Uncommon. These unassuming birds' entire bodies are designed around magnifying sound. They hunt by disabling prey with debilitating auditory blasts that render those with sensitive hearing unconscious and could even disorient or confuse your Uncle Harry when he wasn't wearing his hearing aids.

Blight Crow. Level 41. Common. These intelligent, crafty avians hunt as a flock, spreading a poisonous cloud to kill and soften the flesh of their prey before landing in a swarm and ripping it to pieces in a blood frenzy almost as savage as early morning shoppers descending on Walmart on Black Friday.

I could deal with that. At least they weren't death touch buzzards, or something. The blight crows might still prove dangerous if they triggered their blood frenzy, but hopefully they'd waste precious time hitting me with their poisonous cloud. With my ring, I wouldn't have to worry about that, and maybe it would help keep some of the other flying monsters off my back.

The whisper finch were more of an unknown. My goggles protected my eyes, but did nothing for my ears. I couldn't dive lower to try to avoid the onrushing birds because the monsters down in the water would be worse. I wanted to cross as much of the grasslands as possible before dropping to the waves. Hopefully my bike's hover ability would keep me above the surface, but I'd have to deal with aquatic monsters trying to snatch me and drag me under.

So I pulled out a roll of bandages. I'd never used them, but I had bunches of them from early loot boxes. I tore off a couple pieces and shoved them into my ears like makeshift earplugs. Wrapping the rest around my head without losing forward momentum proved tricky, but I managed it before the birds arrived.

The whisper finches announced themselves with a concentrated wave of sound so high-pitched I barely registered it, even with my enhanced hearing. Even so, it triggered an instant headache right through my makeshift ear protection.

I groaned, my vision blurring as the world spun around me. I tried to keep the bike moving forward, but couldn't tell if I was holding a steady course, or if I was plunging straight down for the water. My stomach roiled and threatened to heave.

As if from a great distance, I felt pricks of warning from Energy Ward. The birds were dive-bombing me, but glancing off my defenses. Good thing I had it active, or I would have been helpless against them.

Then the wave of sound dissipated and I blinked watering eyes clear. Wow, that hurt as bad as one of Bristleback's punches. Looking around, I cursed.

I had indeed fallen faster and lost a lot of altitude. Stinking birds. I adjusted the lift thrusters and managed to slow my descent some, but a lot of damage was already done. The rough waters were getting dangerously close. My gliding fall would drop to those waves all too soon.

The finches had retreated as the blight crows swarmed around me. They kept just outside of Energy Ward, smart enough not to keep darting through it and getting deflected. A cloud of orange toxic gas surrounded me and the crows. It stunk like an open cesspit, but I felt no ill effects.

I got a notification, probably about resisting the poison, but waved it away. The birds were cawing angrily. Soon they'd realize their poison wasn't working and either try attacking directly or back off to give the finches another go.

Not my preferred choice, so I decided to test how clever they were. I groaned and swayed on the seat, wobbling my entire bike. The crows cawed excitedly, the gas cloud intensifying.

Good. They were buying it. Not that I'd just take it without responding. My head was still pounding from the finches' attack, despite healing power trickling in from my bracelet, and the constant cawing was really annoying.

So I pulled out a stun gun and fired off a blast one-handed in the general direction of several of the birds. Half a dozen of them dropped senseless out of the air and plopped into the water.

Half a second later, the water frothed as something unseen under the surface ripped the hapless birds to pieces. The water turned red and scores of shapes suddenly moved under the water, creating ripples as large bodies rushed in to join the feast.

I'd been right. Swimming would have gotten me killed in seconds.

The crows screeched in anger and sped up, some starting to dive-bomb at my back. Energy Ward dipped into my mana pool as each bird deflected away, their razor claws and beaks passing just out of reach. That only seemed to enrage them more.

Too bad. I pulled my steel-banded fighting stick from my inventory and slashed at one of the crows as it deflected past my head. I connected, and it too fell to the waters to feed the monsters. Hopefully they'd fight over the prey and some of those unseen horrors would kill each other off.

The other crows didn't like that, and after I clobbered a couple more, they retreated. The finches swept in, but I did not want to deal with that again. I focused on one of the retreating crows.

You have set your tether point.

A fresh sound assault slammed into my brain, triggering another instant migraine. I groaned and swayed, but managed to focus on the distant crow and cast my shiny new harvested spell, Tether Slide.

A chain of bright, golden light shot from me, extending in a blink out to the targeted crow. As soon as it touched the bird, I rocketed forward at triple my previous speed, pulled by the magical line. The crow had been rising, so I blasted up through the flock of surprised finches. I even managed to club 4 of them out of the air as I swept through, while my bike plowed through a few more before crashing right into the crow I'd tethered the slide to.

"Thanks for your help," I muttered as I hit the throttle, laughing.

Tether Slide was even more amazing than I'd hoped. That move had give me a temporary reprieve from the finches and catapulted me forward and upward. I could cross several hundred more yards toward the west before my inevitable descent dropped me to the waves.

My joy was short lived as a much louder shriek drew my gaze even higher. A huge, black, leather-winged monstrosity was diving straight at me.

Chapter Seventy-Seven

Run Faster!

T he monster's long, serpentine neck, whiplike tail, and draconic head made it easy to identify.

Stygian Wyvern, level 49 elite. These apex aerial predators are rare sights so close to the planet's surface. They prefer soaring miles above the highest peaks, diving onto unsuspecting prey with overwhelming power. Immune to most magic, they are fierce fighters with an eternal hunger for flesh and shiny treasures.

"Oh, fridge," I muttered as I threw Switchblade into a dive. Avoiding the unknown monsters below the water was a lot less important than surviving certain death from above.

The stygian wyvern gained way too fast, its maw opening wide enough to swallow a hot tub and everyone in it. I couldn't avoid it, and its immunity to magic might negate Energy Ward.

At the last second, I banished Switchblade and pulled out 2 silver-tipped steel spears, one pointed up and the other down. I pulled them close, crouching around them. The wyvern's jaws blotted out the world as they encircled me and snapped shut.

The spears punched into soft flesh of both its upper and lower jaws, each spear sinking at least 8 inches as the force of the monster's own bite drove them home. The hafts bent dangerously, but did not snap.

Razor-sharp teeth the size of butcher knives surrounded me, but did not tear into my flesh. They stopped short, leaving me crouching inside the monster's maw.

Its tongue was rough and raspy, but one of the spears punched right through it, so even though it twitched underfoot, it did not slam me against those deadly teeth.

The wyvern screamed, the sound so loud I screamed with it. The hot breath smelled surprisingly like fresh mountain skies. It shook me so hard, it nearly blasted me through the half-closed mouth. I clung to the spears as the wyvern twisted and turned in the air.

One enormous claw reached inside and scratched at the spears as it opened its maw wider. I danced away from the claw, which was the size of a longsword, then pulled my harpoon into my hands and blasted a bolt straight down the wyvern's gullet.

It might be immune to the fire, but that harpoon tore down its throat in a wave of pure destructive force. Hot blood sprayed all over me and the wyvern screeched again. This time I wasn't set properly and tumbled out its open maw. The harpoon launcher flew from my grip and fell spinning down toward the waters.

I cursed in my mind so Cyrus didn't change the words to stupid fake swears. I loved that harpoon. Stupid wyvern!

Thankfully, the monster was too distracted by its most recent wound to snatch me out of the air with those wicked talons. I spun in midair and summoned Switchblade as I fell toward the fast-approaching waters. The monster had dived low before starting to bank back up, so my bike appeared just in time. I grabbed hold of the handlebar and hit the throttle.

Switchblade accelerated hard, thrusters spraying water to either side in a spectacular geyser as my falling momentum turned into pure speed. As I'd hoped, the hover function worked as well over the dense water as it had over land, keeping me just above the waves. The geyser followed, a constant eruption from the screaming thrusters.

Water churned right behind me as unseen monsters snatched and clawed through my wake, trying to catch me. I wrenched the elevation control to gain height and shot up to 6 feet. Moving so fast, I doubted even those fast-swimming monsters could catch me.

That didn't help me against monsters dead ahead, though.

A titanic monster the size of a blue whale, but with an orca's sharp teeth rose out of the water barely 20 feet ahead of me, mouth opening wide enough that it could have swallowed a yacht. I was moving way too fast to stop or even swerve, and shot into that cavernous maw.

It closed around me with the finality of death.

I triggered my scroll of Time Out.

Scroll of Time Out. Forcibly eject one enemy combatant from a fight you are engaged in. Randomly teleports them up to 1 mile.

With a whooshing sound and a vast sucking of air that swept Switchblade 50 feet into the air, the leviathan disappeared. I didn't see where it landed, but might have heard a titanic splash a moment later. It was hard to tell with all the thunderous booming and shaking still rattling the entire stage as the apocalypse tore it apart.

Laughing hysterically from barely escaping death, I poured on more speed until I dropped back to within 6 feet of the surface. Cresting waves broke the wide expanse of the waters and I used them to leap Switchblade many times higher than its max height for precious seconds as I raced across the churning waterway that had replaced the vast grassy plain.

More flying monsters gave chase, and hidden monsters swarmed under the surface. Several tried leaping to catch me, but I managed to swerve in time.

As long as I didn't have to slow, I could outpace most of them. I set a swerving course to make it harder to anticipate where I might go and set a trap ahead of me like that leviathan had.

A pair of giant hawks swept in, propelled by literal tornado cones, and I threw Switchblade into a full barrel roll to avoid their first strike. One talon struck the underside of the bike and one of the thrusters started whining in a way that spiked my fear to new levels.

No. Losing Switchblade would be a death sentence. My speed dropped. Not by much, but I noticed.

As if sensing new vulnerability, a shark the size of a school bus leaped out of the water to my right. At the same time, an elephant seal with tusks longer than spears, lunged out of the water to my left.

Were they getting smarter and working together, or was that just coincidence?

I swung Switchblade hard over to the right, closer to the shark, barely managing to avoid its plunging rows of teeth. The gray, leathery skin scraped slightly against one of the farings before it splashed into the water bare inches from my left boot and the impact wave shot my bike high.

As torrents of water blasted my face and ran off my goggles in sheets, I used the extra height to swing over and ride right up the shark's body. It was falling into the water, but was so long its tail was still 20 feet in the air.

Engine whining, thrusters screaming, my bike took the meaty ramp and we shot up its long back and off its tail, arcing high and gaining another hundred yards before dropping back to the water's surface.

The hawks swept in again, and this time Eva identified them.

Windborn hawk. Level 46. Rare. These fast flyers are like the F-22 Raptor of the monster world. They can outrun any prey and avoid any predator. They're the unrivaled masters of the sky and can twist the very air currents to draw their prey in for a kill.

As if to prove Eva's point, a hurricane blast of wind struck me from the side and shoved Switchblade into the air, spinning me around so the diving hawks could strike at my side in a perfect broadside I couldn't dodge.

I pulled out a mammoth-hide whip. I had proved I was terrible at using whips as weapons, but that wasn't what I had in mind. I lashed it out just as I leaped off Switchblade and again banished my bike. The hawk's snatching talons caught nothing but air, snapping closed right beneath my feet.

My whip wrapped around its beak as the giant raptor swept past, so close one of its legs brushed my Energy Ward and one giant wing covered the sky overhead. I held on with all my strength as the whip went taut, then yanked me upward so hard my arms nearly dislocated.

Awesome! I whooped and embraced the same wild thrill I always felt while skydiving, except the feeling was several times more intense, layered with the promise of violent death any second. The whip flung me up under the hawk's wing, and I flew up behind its feathers as the whip wrapped around the wing and yanked me forward over the top.

I let go, letting the end of the whip twist around the front of the wing as I landed in the center of the hawk's wide back. The hawk tried to scream in frustration, but the whip was holding its beak closed. As it tried to flap its wing to gain altitude, it yanked its own head down sharply.

The bird pitched hard over to the right and down as it was forced to stop flapping or risk snapping its own neck. I plunged Fang and Soulrend both into its back to keep from getting thrown.

The bird stiffened as both blades bit deep. Fang pumped poison into its system while Soulrend cut deep into the center of its spirit. Clutching to Fang to keep my footing stable, I spun, dragging Soulrend across the hawk's torso, severing spirit from one side to the other. My Tesla Coil bracelet grew warm as it fed off of the hawk's bleeding life force.

The hawk was moving so fast, it didn't immediately plummet from the sky, but the whirlwind driving it forward dissipated and we glided through eerie silence as it twitched beneath me.

Yanking Fang free, I dove forward and plunged Soulrend through the back of the hawk's skull. Not waiting for the expected announcement, I rolled to my feet and sprinted down its back.

The waves were close. I spotted the other hawk banking away just above me. Perfect. I triggered Soul Feed and loot, then jumped and cast Tether Slide again, selecting the other hawk.

Again the golden chain shot out and touched my target, then yanked me toward it. I closed on the fast-moving hawk like an arrow, wind tearing at my face. Thankfully my goggles protected my eyes and I could enjoy the unbelievable speed.

Behind me, the dead hawk crashed into the waves just as it started to dissolve into black mist. The waters frothed and boiled as monsters attacked the prey, then each other as the hawk disappeared.

The second hawk didn't notice me sliding up the air after it. Why would it? It was used to being the fastest. My entire body shook from the force of the wind as I shot upward and closed on the monster like a homing missile.

I'd selected its central tail feather as the tether point of the slide and I slammed into that point with enough force to scramble right onto the monster's back before it realized I'd landed.

It shrieked and spun, trying to dislodge me, but it reacted a second too slow. I slammed Fang into its back, tethering me in place and pumping poison into the fast-flying hawk.

It spun several times, the world a blur of confusing images as we rolled over and over in the air. Even gripping Fang's hilt with one hand and a fist full of feathers with the other, I nearly tumbled free. I barely managed to hang on until the crazy giant bird leveled out, banking sharply to the left and flapping its wings.

I didn't know if it somehow thought it could escape me by gaining altitude, but I wasn't about to complain. The longer I stayed out of the water, the longer I had a chance of living.

Between powerful flaps of its vast wings, I yanked Fang free and sprinted up its back, taking a chance that it wouldn't change direction too fast for me to react. It did start to spin, but I leaped and drove Fang down between its shoulders near the base of its neck.

The blade pierced the thick ranks of feathers and bit deep into the hawk's flesh, pumping in more poison. It shrieked in pain again and leveled out. The poison must be taking effect because the tornado wind driving it forward was fading and its movements were becoming sluggish.

I held onto Fang's pommel and scanned the area. We'd risen to at least 10,000 feet. The hawk was fast. It had banked much farther south than I wanted, so I pressured Fang toward the right and leaned my weight in that direction.

As I had hoped, the hawk shrieked again, but banked that way to lessen the pain. I eased up and allowed it to fly in a westerly direction, then settled to my knees and let it soar. I got an idea, and activated Mirror Cloak too.

As seconds ticked by and became minutes, we crossed miles while the land far below boiled with water and lava and collapsing mountains. Other flying monsters swooped past, their shrieks and calls blending in with the constant chaos below. None spotted me under Mirror Cloak's invisibility, and even though the hawk's movements were becoming sluggish from the poison, its fierce reputation seemed to keep the other flying monsters from drawing too close.

I allows myself to relax a bit. The situation was still insane, but somehow I'd scored the ideal ride to escape the stage. Scanning the land, I spotted a group of maybe a dozen people clustered at the top of a low bluff.

The water had nearly reached their level and would swamp their position in seconds. I zoomed my vision on them and recognized Martin and Trish Briggs and their band of vicious psychos.

Huh. I hadn't expected them to last that long. They were getting swarmed by monsters clawing up from the boiling waters on every side. They fought hard, desperation giving them strength, but they were doomed.

I hated seeing people die, but I couldn't reach them in time to help. Even if I could, I had no means to carry them to safety. I'd warned them of the danger and they chose their fate.

A huge blob of bright green ooze flowed up onto the shrinking patch of dry ground they defended. Arrows and spells did nothing to slow it as it rolled right over Martin and Trish.

That broke their lines and monsters swarmed the rest of them. I turned away, cursing softly, not wanting to watch them get slaughtered. The fools should have listened, and their fate would be mine if I stopped moving.

Thankfully, the hawk was strong enough that Fang's poison didn't kill it quickly. Or maybe it had some poison resistance. Either way, it was lingering and gliding west at speed. With wind howling past my face, I shouted with exultant hope, timing the shout to match the screaming cries of a flock of pure white eagles with mist floating off their wings as they dove past.

I was doing it. I could fly the hawk all the way to stage 2.

So, of course, 2 seconds after thinking that, the hawk's entire body stiffened and a bright orange spear of bone blasted up through its back, inches from my right boot. The bone spear thrust up a full 3 feet before stopping, nearly skewering me too.

Chapter Seventy-Eight

I Ride a Slimy Death Spiral of Doom

The hawk started to screech, its voice weak, but it shuddered again and more bone spears tore up through its torso in a staggered line down its back.

Congratulations, Lucas, you have defeated windborn hawk. Bonus experience gained for defeating a higher-level enemy.

"What the smolder?"

I pulled Fang free and crouched on the hawk's neck as the rest of its tornado wind dissipated. The dead hawk continued to glide, still and silent as it started to lose altitude. I peered over and spotted the new enemy.

Spiny Eel, level 49. Elite. This denizen of the deep rarely rises to the surface, but when it does, it leaves destruction in its wake. Able to fly through air as easily as water, the spiny eel can use its bone spear barrage to flatten entire villages. Poisonous, with a hide tough enough to resist even full-powered ballista bolts, it's a nearly unstoppable death machine.

The giant eel had to be nearly 200 feet long and 30 feet thick. I hadn't spotted it because it ascended directly beneath us. Our straight flight had made it easy for the monster to target us.

Idiot. If I'd made the hawk bank around more, we might have made it all the way to stage 2. Then again, how could I know another monster strong enough to fly this high could catch us, even with the hawk's speed slowing so much?

I cast Soul Feed and focused most of the energy to fueling Energy Ward. Then I cast Harvest, since I could now Harvest up to 2 spells.

You have successfully harvested Gale Flight.
Gale Flight. Uncommon. Fly with the speed of the wind. Mana cost: moderate. Uses Remaining: 1.

"Only one?" I exclaimed.

"Don't complain. Gale Flight is a fantastic spell. You're doing great. Keep up the good work."

"Thanks," I muttered dryly.

"You are very welcome." That chipper voice made me want to punch Cyrus in the face.

Still, I had gotten another awesome spell. I was tempted to use it immediately, but I only got a single use. I decided to wait until I ran out of other options.

The eel was still closing. It would reach the disabled hawk in seconds and its mouth looked big enough to swallow both me and the hawk in a single bite.

I waited until the last second, then triggered loot and leaped off the hawk's back. Half a second later, the eel crunched down over the hawk's body, severing the wings and consuming the entire body one big chomp.

Stinking black smoke wafted out between its sharp teeth and it hissed in anger as its meal evaporated. The sound was like a thousand tea kettles set to boiling and its beady red eyes fixed on me as I fell past. So it could see through Mirror Cloak's invisibility too? Or was I moving too fast to remain hidden?

Maybe I should have let it swallow the hawk. The eel didn't bother with its bone spears, but undulated its long, snakelike body through the air and shot down after me, maw gaping open again.

I summoned Switchblade long enough to rev it and shoot to the side, avoiding the crashing jaws by inches. The sound was like a stone smasher as the teeth gnashed empty air. Fetid wind roared past from the force of its bite. I banished Switchblade again just as I leaped off, straight at the giant eel's head.

Its hide was tough enough to withstand most weapons, but how tough was its eye?

As I slammed into the side of the giant eel's head, I plunged Fang into the huge, crimson orb before the eel could try biting me again. The poisoned blade punched through the outer shell of the eye and sank to the hilt.

The eye exploded in hot, viscous liquid. At the same time, I drove Soulrend into its skull and yanked the ethereal blade down with all my strength, slicing down its head.

The eel convulsed toward me so hard it battered through Energy Ward and smashed into me with the force of a falling building. Even with my armor's enhanced protection, the blow blasted air from my lungs and rattled my head so hard, I lost my grip on Fang.

"No!" I shouted as I slid down the eel's long, slick body, scrabbling uselessly against its slimy hide.

It would pay for taking my blade. The monster twisted sharply mid-air and started diving, its long body curled into a tight spiral that seemed to help it speed up. It wasn't dead, just diving. It hissed in a constant stream of fury and pain.

At least it wasn't targeting me, and I was sliding up the eel's body, driven by the wind of our passage, so I stabbed Soulrend in. The monster's spirit didn't offer enough resistance to slow my slide, but did help me stay close to its side. That helped me drag the ethereal blade all the way up the eel's length until a powerful twisting movement of its tail knocked me away.

The monster fell beneath me, but its speed had faded. It no longer corkscrewed beautifully in perfect control, but fell in a twitching mass. I'd hurt it pretty badly, tearing through long sections of its spirit. Served it right for eating my ride and taking Fang.

After one final glimpse of my epic short sword, still sticking from the monster's ruined eye, I summoned Switchblade. Pulling myself on, I set a course west, again using the hover bike's thrusters to buy as much distance as possible as it descended in a graceful arc.

The stupid eel had cost me one of my best weapons and dragged me down nearly halfway to the water, but I was still about 5000 feet up. I bet I could cover half a mile before dropping to the waves again.

Switchblade's power was nearly red-lined. The brief respites I'd given it weren't enough to recharge it and I'd been revving it hard. It might have enough juice left to get me to the western slope, but it would be close. I deactivated Mirror Cloak, which was already flickering wildly from my speed.

Far below, the eel crashed into the water with a spectacular explosion of water. It writhed weakly for a moment until the nearby monsters swarmed in, tearing at its huge length. I bet they'd usually leave the deadly monster alone, but now that it was crippled, it was just a really big prey.

It did fight back, lashing at the half-seen forms tearing it apart, rending smaller bodies in geysers of blood.

Excellent. Tear each other apart.

Then another giant monster rose from the deep. It was the size of a blue whale, but with a dozen long tentacles that could have dragged entire buildings under. It scattered the other monsters and pulled the eel under in a frothing eruption of blood.

Congratulations, Lucas! You have defeated Spiny Eel, level 49. Bonus experience gained for defeating a higher-level enemy.

"Go get 'em, leviathan," I laughed. I'd take partial credit for killing that monster. I bet I got a ton of experience from that thing.

Then a swarm of tiny, fiery gnats slammed into Energy Ward. They sparked as they deflected, like miniature shooting death stars flashing past my face and body, creating a dazzling light show that no doubt would draw other monsters' attention.

Individually, the gnats were tiny and weak, but there were thousands of them, if not more. They kamikazied into Energy Ward with a frenzied determination that burned through my mana with startling speed. For a second, it looked like I was surrounded by a flaming, full-body halo as so many of the tiny monsters deflected past at the same time.

If I didn't do anything, the tiny monsters would exhaust my mana. I hated to do it, but I triggered one of my remaining scrolls of ice blast. This time, as I willed my intent to focus on the entire swarm all around me, the blast erupted more like a blizzard of ice shards than a single bolt. Sweet! I loved the spell's flexibility.

The blizzard of ice tore the gnats apart, quenching their flames and dispersing the swarm. I got about 500 notifications about defeating the little monsters, but none were high enough level to give me any experience.

I felt my bracelet warming up some, so I'd gotten a bit of energy, at least. I tried looting, just for fun, and was shocked when I not only got a ton of mana crystals and 3 scrolls of Firestorm, but also an unexpected bonus.

Spell scroll. Temporary spell. Immolation. Enjoy immunity to flames and channel Ghost Rider as you set yourself on fire. Unleash a tornado of fiery destruction around yourself in an area with a diameter of 5 yards, plus 2 yards per point in perception. Mana consumption: moderate. Uses Remaining: 4.

I laughed. I hadn't gotten any temporary spells other than harvested spells in a while. This one looked amazing, as long as I was fighting alone in a pretty big area. With a perception over 30, I could devastate a huge area of about 65 yards across.

Without warning, a giant flying mouth appeared out of nowhere and bit off the front of Switchblade.

Chapter Seventy-Nine
Flight of Insanity

Flying Mouth was the only way to describe the monster. Its oblong body was about 2 feet long, split in half by an enormous mouth full of rows of short, squat teeth that reminded me of the maw of a chipper.

Tiny hummingbird wings buzzed at the creature's sides, way too small for its mass, and several small yellow eyes spaced across its forehead glowed with soft light. It honestly reminded me of a nightmare cousin to the green slime monster in Ghostbusters.

With its entire front sheared off by the monster's enormous bite, Switchblade died, and my graceful glide changed to a plummet. The weird little monster, its body a dull matte black, swallowed 50 pounds of steel as easily as I'd munch a biscuit.

"Chew on this!" I shouted, summoning Soulrend and slashing at the monster, which was keeping pace in front of me, looking somehow smugly pleased with itself.

It winked out of existence half a second before my blade tore through its giant head. At the same time, Eva identified it.

Voidmaw Devourer. Level 45. Rare. If hunger was given a physical form, this would be it. These insatiable beasts live to eat. Their teeth can rend stone and metal as easily as flesh and bone. Their short-range teleport ability allows them to pounce on unsuspecting prey and keep the feast going forever.

I did not want to be that thing's next meal. I kicked off from Switchblade, using it to lunge sideways. A second later, the voidmaw devourer appeared again, chomping my bike's seat in half. It would have ripped through my torso if I hadn't jumped.

I was too far away to use my blade again, so I summoned a polearm tipped with a scimitar head and awkwardly slashed at the devourer. It disappeared again before my blow landed.

I tossed the polearm into my inventory and drew Soulrend again. I was falling fast toward the water, but the teleporting terror was my only concern. It could chomp me to pieces long before I hit the water.

Before I could figure out my next move, the Voidmaw Devourer appeared right next to me and bit down. Its huge maw enveloped my head and shoulders and its chipper-like teeth plunged down with the force to rip me in half.

They bounced off.

Blinding light enveloped me and knocked the monster back. The light coalesced into the shape of Bristleback, or at least his overly muscled upper half. I stared in shock as the ghostly apparition of the deadly hog-taur seized the Voidmaw Devourer by its jaws and heaved.

The nightmare mouth monster ripped in half in a spray of bloody gore that splattered all over me. A message popped into the corner of my vision.

Last Chance ring auto triggered. Fatal blow defeated by the manifestation of the boss whose soul powered that charge.

I blinked in surprise, but the truth clicked into place half a heartbeat later. My Last Chance Ring must have activated when I defeated Bristleback. I'd totally forgotten about the epic, protective ring since I'd never used it before.

Last Chance ring. Epic. Ring will activate once you defeat a boss monster. Will then auto trigger with one of those boss's powers to counter an otherwise fatal attack. Cooldown: 7 days, plus another defeated boss.

Cool. Having Bristleback's ghost manifest to kill the next monster about to murder me was sweet, poetic justice.

Congratulations, Lucas! You have defeated Voidmaw Devourer, level 45. Bonus experience gained for defeating a higher-level enemy.

I triggered Soul Feed and Loot, then banished Switchblade just before the broken hover bike crashed into the waves. I'd follow in seconds, so I triggered my single use of Gale Flight, which I was itching to use.

A tornado of wind formed around my feet, and immense force hurled me forward. I shot skyward, laughing with the thrill of acceleration that would put a fighter jet to shame.

I willed myself to turn, but nothing happened. The tornado of gale force pushed against my feet and nothing more. Okay, I could work with that.

I bent my torso to see if I could use wind resistance to bank. The force of the air caught my shoulders and wrenched my head down so hard every muscle in my back strained. My flight turned into a somersaulting, out-of-control spin.

Shouting in surprise and pain and disoriented confusion, I straightened my torso with trouble. The flight straightened out, but now I was hurtling toward the water so fast I'd explode when I hit.

This was harder than I'd expected. Gritting my teeth, I made a slight movement, tipping back just a tiny fraction. That was enough to catch the air and change my dive by degrees into a horizontal flight path. I tore through the sky at blistering speed, close enough to the water that some of the taller waves nearly swamped me.

Carefully turning more, I banked higher. I was getting the hang of this. Another minute, and I'd be golden.

Shrieks and roars and caws all around snapped my attention to my surroundings. I was about to fly right into the center of a dense swarm of flying monsters of all sizes and shapes. It included bird-like monsters, more wyverns, huge raptors, less identifiable blobs, and even one monster that looked like a single enormous wing with no body attached.

I lacked time and skill to dodge, and only had time to tense and draw Soulrend before plunging into the swarm. The sky filled with birds of all shapes and sizes and colors. They flashed past so fast I barely registered each one. Razor-sharp beaks and deadly talons ripped and tore and snapped at me from every side.

Energy Ward shuddered under the onslaught, deflecting more attacks than I could count, while chugging down my mana pool. Even supercharged, it wasn't enough. Claws and beaks broke through on every side, ripping at my armor.

Elemental attacks blasted into me from all sides, despite the protection of my cloak.

One long talon dug into my calf, just above my left boot and raked downward, ripping a gash down to my heel and slicing through my boot in the process. The wind ripped it free and it tumbled away.

My amulet of Rebound helped distract some of the monsters as a fraction of their magical attacks hit back, but my health plummeted, despite my Tesla Coil bracelet pouring healing power into me.

I turned and banked as best I could, leading with Soulrend. I was moving so fast, I couldn't really slash out to the sides, but just let Soulrend pierce whatever monsters got in my way just before I plowed through them with the help of Energy Ward. Smaller monsters tumbled aside, shrieking in pain and anger, while I deflected off of the bigger monsters, but the swarm never lessened and I flew past before I could finish any of them off.

My Tesla Coil bracelet still grew warm against my skin as it drank in life force from the monsters I wounded, then the power flowed back out to heal the countless small wounds I was accumulating.

I shook under the onslaught and constant battering, my skin scorched, then chilled, then melted by clouds of acid, while powerful blows pushed Energy Ward's deflection to the max and threatened to bottom out my mana. Others slammed into me with brutal force. My armored jacket and cloak together protected my torso pretty well, but my legs and head were not so lucky.

Gashes ripped into my thighs and calves, spraying blood and driving the monsters into blood frenzy. My pants were quickly shredded, and one monster, who plowed into my waist so hard it somersaulted me in the air and nearly sent me into an uncontrolled corkscrew into the water below, pulled my pants away with it when I clubbed it off.

Claws scraped my scalp and face as wings and talons battered me from every side, but I needed pants. Even though they didn't really help, the thought of fighting through a swarm of monsters in my boxers made me cringe.

So I mentally shoved the basic trousers I'd looted from Joseph's body way back on day 1 onto my legs. They appeared, popping on and settling perfectly over my legs.

"Now I figure it out?" I laughed.

The swarm suddenly parted as one giant raptor plunged through the pack, scattering the smaller monsters. A snatching talon closed around my torso like a death vice. I grunted and slashed up with Soulrend, severing one claw. It weakened, allowing me to squirm free and accelerate again.

Right into the gaping beak of a second raptor.

This one was like a flaming eagle, every feather burning with different colored fire. It spat a torrent of billowing flames right in my face.

On pure reflex, I cast my new Immolation spell. Flames of my own erupted around me and clashed with the raptor's fiery breath.

Cyrus's laughter cut through the din. "Ha! Good choice. Great synergy between those spells."

A message from Eva scrolled past, but I waved it away just as the maelstrom of churning fire enveloped me in a warm embrace. Then I plunged straight into the giant bird's open maw.

I slammed Soulrend up and summoned my fighting stick into my other hand as the bird's beak slammed shut. My stick got stuck between the closing halves of the beak, and for half a second, the sturdy wood resisted the immense pressure.

Then it snapped and the beak shut with crushing force. Soulrend punched up through the roof of the raptor's beak, but that wouldn't help as crushing pressure threatened to grind me to paste. My Crash Test Dummy jacket saved my life, protecting me just enough to withstand the initial bite.

"Crushing impact. Remember, this jacket is dry-clean only," the jacket said as my health plummeted and my Gale Flight spell sputtered.

If I let that spell die, I would die with it. I focused on it, willing it back to life and trying to pour in more mana. I'd never tried anything like that, but it seemed to work as the tornado under my legs intensified again, driving me against the crushing weight clamping down over my face and back.

With my right arm extended in front of me farther into the monster's beak, I also slashed awkwardly with Soulrend as far as I could while my chest was pinned and my ribs began to crack. With panic-fueled strength, I dragged the ethereal blade through the monster's beak, despite heavy resistance.

As I focused on my spells, I sensed a difference. With both Gale Flight and Immolation active, the boundary between them weakened, and I sensed they could meld together to form something different. It was like when I'd cast Ember Strike and Fractal Strike together to create a more powerful synergized spell against the werewolves, except this time both spells were already active.

I had never imagined such a thing might be possible, but I wasn't about to discard the possibility, and embraced the idea, willing the two spells to merge. The tornado pushing my feet shifted, filling with white-hot fire. It still tried to push me forward from below, but I could also will the flames to surround me too, like I was dropping into the center of the tornado.

That helped a ton, as I was able to keep the spell active more easily when I wasn't moving much. My frantic slashing hit something important because the pressure of the beak lessened just a bit.

The fiery wind raging around me and filling the raptor's beak with blindingly bright fire drove me forward, sliding up the smooth inside of its beak.

All the way, I slashed with Soulrend, cutting through the spirit of its beak. That made it open just a bit wider and I shot toward its gullet at the back of its throat. It was closed, like a wall I'd smash into and lose my momentum.

If only I still had Ahab's harpoon, that would have been an easy problem to solve. With no better option, I summoned a tier-1 mana crystal and popped it into my mouth. A flood of power surged through me and I summoned my basic club that I'd fashioned from that tree on the first day. Focusing it all on the strongest swing, I slammed the club forward.

It struck the wall of the gullet a split second before I did, driven by all my desperate strength and momentum. The impact rattled me all the way up to the shoulder and the club exploded.

So did the gullet. I shot forward through the gap, calling forth Soulrend and my saber-toothed dagger. As I slid down the giant bird's throat, I spun, slashing with both weapons, carving a spiraling path of destruction through the monster's long neck.

The dagger didn't inject poison and it didn't cut as deep, but its razor-edged blade actually worked better in the tight confines of the bird's throat. Blood and fire whirled around me as I erupted into the bird's huge stomach.

I puked. The stench was so foul, I couldn't help it. Even with the flaming tornado surrounding me, the stench stabbed up through to my nose like a dagger made of pure sewage. My flames illuminated the stomach chamber, bubbling with acid and half-melted chunks of flesh.

Thank god the synergized spell allowed me to fly more slowly, or Gale Flight probably would have winked out in that confined space. I still had to move, or I'd lose it anyway. I twisted to fly up to the ceiling as the acidic sludge churned all around. Acid seared exposed flesh of my face and arms and started melting through my pants, but most of my body was protected. It would eat through my armor too before long, though.

I wouldn't stay that long.

I called on more speed, shooting along the ceiling of the stomach, slashing with both blades, leaving a cascading waterfall of blood behind. When I reached the back of the stomach, I avoided the dark tubes of intestines. No way I'd get trapped in there.

Instead, I banked around, running along the spongy surface of the stomach wall for a second to help make the turn. My one bare foot burned from the acid. Then I spiraled around the top of the stomach, dagger ripping through flesh, and ethereal sword slicing through spirit as my Tesla Coil bracelet pumped more healing energy into me to fight the effects of the burning acid.

In seconds I circumnavigated the huge stomach 15 times, ripping and tearing deeper into the walls with every pass. Finally, the stomach ruptured and I blasted through, shooting into the dark innards of the bird. I continued spiraling, slashing, and tearing, looking for the heart.

It was hot and humid and disgusting as I bounced off squelching organs, my hands slick with blood and unnamed fluids. I kept my mouth closed tight and tried not to breathe as filth and burning liquids poured over my face. Thankfully my goggles withstood the barrage, so my eyes didn't melt.

The bird might be immune to fire on the outside, and even in its mouth, but its guts weren't. My fiery gale tornado crisped flesh and blackened organs, cauterizing wounds and searing the bird from the inside.

Then I punched right through a flat, gray organ that had to be a lung. Inside, the air was blissfully clean. I managed a single gulp before plowing through the other side of the lung blades first.

The heart came next, an unmistakable huge, beating muscle. I shot past, slashing Soulrend through the center of the heart while ripping my dagger through the main artery.

Blood exploded out of the severed tube like a fire hose, slamming me sideways where I bounced off the thankfully-soft second lung. I finally got the notification I'd been hoping for.

Congratulations, Lucas! You have defeated the Crimson Kite, level 49. Bonus experience gained for defeating a higher level enemy.

Cyrus added, "Experience doubled for giving us such a show!"

Chapter Eighty

Grand Entrances

The image of Cyrus as a scrawny young man in a dirty t-shirt and greasy hair sitting in front of a TV in his mother's basement, munching popcorn while he watched my death battle popped into my head. I wished it was true so I could reach through that TV and throttle him for setting me up to have to do this.

Pushing the image aside, I cast Soul Feed and Loot. The giant raptor dissolved into stinking mist around me and I shot free of its corpse into a cloud of blessed white mist. Even as I accelerated away, shifting my burning tornado back to my feet to help me accelerate, the mist followed. It flowed into me, topping off my pools, and triggering Energy Ward again. All the damage I'd done had refilled my Tesla Coil bracelet too.

Congratulations, Lucas! You have reached level 12.

"Yes!" Another surprise level for the win!

The flocks of other flying monsters had started to dissipate, looking for more prey. As soon as they spotted me, they swarmed back in, but they'd given me an opening and I took it. I poured mana into my burning Gale Flight and the fiery tornado pushing me swelled to a roar. I accelerated with breathtaking speed, outpacing all of my pursuers like a meteor trailing a long burning tail.

Other flying monsters still dove at me from above, but now I had time to react, and I'd gained better mastery over the unique form of flight. I banked and turned, diving and spinning between diving monsters, dodging most of their attacks while slicing through wings and bodies with my Soulrend lance I kept extended in front of me. Flames singed feathers and cooked flesh, and I left chaos in my wake. I grinned with a thrill of excitement that just barely held the line against terror.

It was insane, terrifying, and brutal. Every second I fought for my life. A single mistake, and I'd get ripped asunder, but I still grinned. The feeling of riding a literal flaming tornado of destruction on the cusp of death was a thrill ride unlike anything I'd ever experienced. Jane would have loved it.

The aerial dance of destruction continued for long minutes. I lost track of time as I dove and banked, weaving through the never-ending swarm of monsters as I battled my way across the skies. Despite the insane amount of damage I was doing, some of the kamikaze bird monsters still reached me.

Most were deflected past by Energy Ward, but a few of the more powerful strikes still landed. They tore up my pants again, and one lucky claw caught the seam of my crash test dummy jacket and ripped all the way down the sleeve.

Every piece of clothing I wore was getting shredded, but still I fought on. I caught occasional glimpses of the ever-spreading waters below and the sturdy peaks to the west, beckoning me on with the promise of safety.

Then I saw it. The long slope ascending up to the second stage. I crossed the boundary of the waters. I was mere moments away. I poured on another burst of speed as I dove for the forests so tantalizingly close.

Then the flying monsters all scattered. For a second I thought they were giving up. That's when I spotted a line of giant ogre-like monsters standing across the western slope directly below me. There had to be 20 of the huge beasts.

Every one of them lifted a giant club high, all pointed at me.

"Oh, Smolder," I whispered just before I crashed into an invisible barrier like a swallow flying into a window.

Every scrap of air blasted from my lungs as I smashed flat. Both of my arms snapped and my nose broke in a spray of blood. Searing pain spiked through my brain and my entire body, and blackness plunged over my mind.

As if from a great distance, I felt my body groan, stressed to the limits as ribs cracked and organs split. Without the protection of my Crash Test Dummy jacket and my other armor, I would have simply detonated.

Instead, I just mostly got pulped to meat paste. Barely alive, I slid down the invisible barrier like a squashed bug sliding down a windshield. The barrier disappeared, but my flight spell was gone.

I could barely blink my eyes, and moving my limbs was way beyond my strength. Darkness clouded my thoughts and tempted me with blissful oblivion. If I gave in, I wouldn't have to feel the pain when I hit the ground.

If I gave in, I was dead.

Even though my bracelet was pouring a torrent of energy into me, I triggered a full regeneration potion from my hotlist. The additional rush of energy helped cleared my head and I looked down.

I was falling toward the hard ground of the slope. The fact that I'd reached dry land again renewed my determination. I was so close! I refused to die within sight of safety.

The line of ogres had staggered, but were recovering quickly. My rebound amulet must have hit them with a fraction of that magical impact I'd just taken. Siphoning off that much for the rebound had probably saved my life.

Still, they were already lumbering toward the spot where I was about to hit. If I landed among them, they'd smash me to paste.

I needed a few seconds to heal, but I wouldn't get that much time. I'd dropped my dagger, but spotted Soulrend tumbling into a pile of boulders upslope of the ogres.

I needed that blade. Setting my tether point, I triggered Tether Slide. My helpless fall turned into a graceful slide as I shot across the slope, angling down steeply to land among the boulders, barely 100 yards short of the top of the slope.

The impact of landing knocked me sprawling with spikes of searing pain from my partially-healed bones and muscles. Groaning, I tried to jump to my feet, but toppled over again.

Soulrend lay right in front of me, the twisting silver of the handle beckoning me on. With Soulrend in hand, I could defeat any foe. I clawed for it and managed to snag it, but the effort left me gasping with pain as my broken arm and hand screamed with white-hot agony.

I cast Soulrend into my inventory. With a burst of new optimism, I focused on moving. With all my will, I managed to pull myself forward a few inches.

Despite the horrible pain racking my entire body, I still savored the feel of solid ground under my gloved hands. The smell of dirt and distant forests made me smile through bloody lips and broken teeth.

Boulders blocked my path up to the second stage. Going after Soulrend had cost me a clear path to escape. It was worth it, though. If I was going to face a final death battle, I wanted to do it with Soulrend in hand.

I'd rather avoid a fight, though, so started painfully crawling around. The line of ogres roared with bloodlust and the anticipation of a kill. The ground shook under their charging feet. They weren't super fast, but I could barely crawl.

I refused to give up. Dragging myself forward, I focused on crawling. Every movement of my broken arms left me gasping with pain, but I lacked the balance to stand. I had to use them. They shook from the strain, freshly knit bones creaking from the effort. The agony was like plunging my arms into lava.

I moved anyway. Gritting my teeth, I focused the healing energy of my bracelet on my arms. It helped. The pain eased a little. In seconds, I'd recover enough to stand, then I could sprint to safety.

Only one rough boulder still blocked my path. Once I crawled around that, I'd have a clear shot to the second stage. I was so close!

The ogres closed in like a living avalanche. They wouldn't give me that much time.

"Back off!" I shouted, dropping onto my back with a groaning whimper of pain. I pulled a stun gun from my inventory as the closest ogre barreled in, barely 20 yards away.

I fired, aiming for its knees since I lacked the strength to lift the heavy gun higher. The recoil wasn't a lot, but it was still enough to knock the weapon from my grasp.

The blast caught the ogre in the knees and it fell, crashing to the ground and sliding almost on top of me. Its huge, ugly head bumped my thigh as it slid to a stop.

I called forth Soulrend, intending to plunge it through the ogre's brain. The pain of trying to grasp the pommel with my broken fingers made me spasm and the blade drove down into the ogre's shoulder.

It was wearing a leather vest with studded spikes that fastened with buckles and straps across its shoulders. When I stabbed it, Soulrend slipped free of my fingers just as the ogre shuddered and rolled aside. The pommel got caught between the straps.

"No!" I shouted weakly as the ogre rolled away. I didn't care about losing so many other weapons and gear, but I needed to get Soulrend back.

With a bellow of rage, I threw myself after the ogre. My body protested as broken bones twisted, tearing new wounds in my flesh, and I collapsed, rolling several times, nearly blacking out from the fresh waves of pain. As much as I screamed at my body to move, my strength was gone and I couldn't catch the ogre.

"There he is!" a voice shouted in the distance.

Another cried, "He's alive! Quick!"

I blinked in confusion, trying to clear my hazy thoughts. Who was talking? All I could see were the other ogres closing in.

The closest one raised his club, roaring in triumph as he leaped high, preparing to smash me to jelly. All I could do was stare. I had nothing left. No tricks, no spells, no weapons. I was totally spent.

I'd failed. I was going to die bare yards from safety.

A beam of white-hot fire struck the ogre in the center of the chest and bowled him over backward. He crashed to the ground beside me so hard, it rolled me over. Six inches closer to safety.

More spells flashed overhead. Fire and ice and absolute darkness, while arrows filled the sky like rain. Hundreds of voices rose in battle cries that rivaled the ongoing thunder of the dying lower stage.

I craned my head around to glance upslope, despite a piercing pain in my neck. Had I broken a vertebrae too? A tide of humanity were pouring down the slope, charging straight at the surprised ogres, flinging a barrage of spells and projectiles so dense, they darkened the sky.

The line of ogres fell back, riddled with arrows and blasted off their feet by powerful spells. The ogre closest to me rolled to his hands and knees and turned to me, growling with bloodlust as he raised a hand to swat me like a bug.

Tomas suddenly appeared on its back, a long sword already raised high. He plunged it deep into the ogre's neck and shouted, "Leave my brother alone!"

Then Jane arrived, skidding to a stop between me and the ogre, her hair flying out behind her from her speed. She shoved both hands out hard and an invisible force smashed the ogre in the face, toppling it over backward. Tomas disappeared, then blinked back into view beside Jane.

Ruby skidded to a halt beside me, with Steve at her shoulder. While she heaved me into her arms, Steve loosed an arrow crackling with ice, then glanced at me and grinned. "Hey, buddy. Way to make an entrance."

"Hurry!" Tomas shouted. "They're regrouping!"

As a line of people formed to either side, Tony Waldau stopped beside us, and a glowing barrier of amber light rose between us and the ogres, extending 50 feet in either direction. A second later, a huge wooden club thrown by one of the ogres bounced off, shaking the barrier.

Tony glanced at me, not hiding his annoyance. "Go! Everyone, go! We've wasted too many resources on one man already. I will not allow anyone else to die today."

"I'm so glad you care," I wheezed.

As one, the entire group sprinted back up the slope. Ruby held me cradled to her like a baby and I slumped against her, relief sapping the last of my strength as emotions boiled through me. Lingering terror faded under a wave of new, soaring hope. Appreciation and gratitude for their help churned with absolute exhaustion.

I'd pushed myself beyond my limits, but an obstinate part of me still wanted to protest that I could stand. I lacked energy for the words, so I let Ruby carry me to safety. Despite jolts of pain from every step, it felt good.

I chuckled, then coughed.

"What?" she asked, not slowing. I wasn't light, but she had added a bunch of points to strength because she ran lightly, not bothered by my weight.

"We've gone full circle. First time we met, I saved you. Now you're literally carrying me over the finish line."

"If only we were in a fairy tale."

I grunted. "Yeah. Today's been nothing but a horror story."

She smiled. "You're safe now, princess Lucas, although you'd make a better damsel in distress if you weren't so filthy."

"Nothing a Laundry Day potion can't cure."

Chapter Eighty-One
Homecoming

As Ruby stepped over the boundary to the Stage 2 plateau, Cyrus spoke into my ear.

"Welcome to the Watery Grave."

"Thanks," I muttered, low enough that not even Ruby could hear through the cheering of the crowds as everyone crossed the boundary.

I was exhausted and battered and lacked the energy to celebrate. I could barely comprehend the fact that I'd made it. I had passed the final test and reached the second stage. Cyrus hadn't said there would be another test to survive the stage after defeating Bristleback, but I'd passed that one too. Well, I'd passed with a little help from my friends.

For now, I just needed to heal and focus on the moment. My body's natural regeneration, aided by my Tesla Coil bracelet, was steadily fixing my many injuries, and I managed a weak smile. Probably looked hideous, since several of my teeth were still broken.

At least my split lips had healed. My friends had come to help, and so many had risked their own safety to literally carry me to the second stage. That warmed me more than my Immolation spell had.

"Fantastic show, Lucas!" Cyrus added with a happy laugh. "Just fantastic. Creative, brave, with unexpected twists and turns. Keep this up, and you'll win a huge following."

I didn't bother asking what he meant by that. I was too tired, and he wouldn't explain. I just relaxed in Ruby's arms, soaking in the moment and allowing myself to finally just relax.

She slowed to a stop in the middle of the cheering crowd, arms tightening around me as she leaned her face down close to mine. Strands of her red hair had pulled free of her braid and blew around us as her big, brown eyes held mine, her expression unusually intent.

"I'm glad you made it. I worried you were going to die."

"Lucas!" Tomas shouted, rushing up.

"Hey, bro," I said, turning to smile at him and Jane, who was close behind.

I turned back to speak with Ruby just as she leaned in to kiss my cheek. My turn caught her by surprise because it wasn't my cheek she was aiming for any more. Her lips pressed to mine before she could stop herself.

Time seemed to stop, and the distant explosions from the imploding first stage suddenly sounded like fireworks. The feel of her full, soft lips pressed to mine sent an electric shock raging through me fiercer than Bristleback's arrow. My veins felt full of lava. The good kind of lava.

I froze, unable to react as my thoughts raced. What was happening? Why was I reacting so powerfully? It was just an innocent little accidental kiss, but that brief contact unlocked a torrent of emotions that shocked me by their intensity. The image of Ruby's beautiful face close to mine seared into my mind, permanently recorded. Her big, brown eyes, flecked with gold seemed to swallow the world as they widened with her own surprise.

Ruby withdrew almost immediately, but she moved slowly and didn't recoil. Her expression was a mixture of surprise and hesitation and maybe something more. Her arms tensed around me, and for an eternal second, she lingered close, her breath washing over my face. I resisted a sudden urge to pull her head back down and kiss her on purpose. Stupid wolf instincts.

Ruby blinked and raised her head. "I'm . . . I didn't plan that," she stammered, flushing deeply. The red in her cheeks looked good on her.

I didn't say anything, the rest of the world forgotten as I held her gaze. What could I say? My thoughts were still churning, my emotions boiling. I was still a wreck from that fight, definitely not in the right state to deal with something like this.

She licked her lips, which was super distracting and stammered, "Lucas . . ."

Then Steve smacked me on the shoulder hard enough that my freshly-knit bones protested. I blinked, breaking eye contact, and the moment was gone.

What had Ruby been about to say? What did I want her to say? My own heart felt like I'd kindled another Immolation spell inside of it. What was wrong with me? My wolf instincts were totally out of control.

"Hey you two, get a room!" Steve laughed. Ruby scowled and dropped me.

I managed to land on my feet, which reminded me I only had one boot. Great reminder of all the equipment I'd lost trying to escape stage 1. I liked those boots, but with a sigh, banished my other one to my inventory so I could walk. The skin of my feet were tough enough that I could probably walk on nails without feeling it, but it still felt wrong.

Steve pulled us both into a fierce hug. Then he shook me hard enough to clack my teeth together. My newly-patched ribs groaned in protest.

"That was amazing! Lucas, we spotted you miles out and watched you fight through that swarm. Whoa!" He smacked himself in the forehead and laughed again.

Ruby touched my arm, her expression serious, even though she was still blushing. "I saw that fiery bird swallow you. I thought you were dead."

"And then you killed it from the inside!" Steve chortled. "Unbelievable. You have so much to tell."

"And we want to hear it all," Tomas exclaimed, pushing closer and yanking me off my feet in a crushing bear hug.

"Still healing," I grunted, but he didn't let go for several seconds. His arms shook slightly. When he finally dropped me, he gripped my shoulders and said, "Don't ever do anything like that again."

"Like what? Survive a monster apocalypse?"

Jane pushed Tomas out of the way and hugged me as tight as he had. Then she pulled my face down in both her hands and kissed me on the cheek. "Thank you, Lucas. You saved my life, but if you had Switchblade sooner, you wouldn't have had to fight through that insanity."

"I made it. Don't stress over what might have been."

"You're a mess, Lucas. Your clothes are all shredded, and by the blood covering most of you, you're not much better on the inside," she said.

"I'm mostly healed. It was rough. I'll tell you all about it when I get a chance to rest."

"And I'll tell you about my upgraded spells." That sounded like a story I needed to hear.

Tony Waldau stopped behind Tomas and gave me a curt nod. "Glad to see you made it. Level 12. Good job. I hope you won't wait till the last minute again."

"Good to see you too," I said with a happy wave. I lacked the energy to deal with him.

Then Susan Collins, the blonde from team Narnia I'd saved from the spectral maulers, rushed up and jumped into my arms, staggering me back. She grabbed my head and kissed me with a hungry passion that left me breathless, but failed to match the wonder of the simple accidental kiss from Ruby.

"You're alive," Susan breathed, panting with exaggerated emphasis on making her chest heave. "I was so worried about you."

"Get in line," Steve said with an exaggerated eye roll.

Susan gave him a withering look as I lowered her to the ground. I managed to say, "Thanks for your concern."

"I shot one of those ogres trying to kill you," she said, pulling her bow from her inventory and gesturing with it.

"I think 200 people did the same," Jane replied coolly. "I don't think we have time for everyone of them to suck on Lucas's face, though."

Susan ignored her and leaned closer to me, her voice dropping to a throaty whisper. "Find me when you need to unwind."

Then she strutted away. Like literally strutting, swaying her hips under that maroon dress she still wore.

"She's over the top. I can't believe she's still so hot for you. You only saved her life once, right?" Jane asked while Steve whistled appreciatively at the retreating Susan. Ruby scowled.

"Some people get fixated on one idea, I guess."

"Come on," Tomas said loudly. "I've seen enough of the apocalypse to last forever. I haven't heard of anyone spotting any other potential survivors. Let's get back to Midmount Vale. We have some celebrating to do."

"That's the name of the new town?" I guessed.

Ruby nodded and Steve sighed. "It's pretty lame, but better than Stepstone."

Burns, who was speaking with Tony nearby, turned and called. "Hey, I heard that. I voted for that name."

"I'm sure you'll make up for it," Steve said, then skipped away before Burns could cuff him on the side of the head.

I followed the others, but my mind was still racing as fast as my heart. I stole a couple glances at Ruby as I tried to sort myself out. That kiss was totally an accident. Anyone could see that, and yet, the look in her eye suggested maybe she wasn't totally upset that it happened.

Unbidden, a flood of memories with Ruby flashed through my mind. The warm smiles, the hugs that lasted just a bit too long, the kiss on the cheek, and how we'd moved as one while riding Switchblade. I nearly stumbled under the barrage and my own cheeks might have flushed just a little.

Was there more between us than just friends and teammates? Had Ruby been giving me hints that I'd totally missed? Did I want there to be more?

I didn't want to deal with this, but couldn't take my mind off of it. Isabella was gone. She'd rejected me. Over the past week, thoughts of her had faded more and more until the life I'd led before getting teleported to Arasha seemed more a dream than reality. Ruby was real, she was there, and she was totally amazing.

Did that mean anything should happen, though? Was I just looking for that rebound fling? Should I have taken Susan up on her offer and gotten that out of my system? No, she wasn't who I wanted.

Did I want Ruby? Part of me did, but that worried me more than it excited me. I cared about Ruby. I really did. I couldn't risk screwing up what we had by trying to make it more. If I dated Ruby, would it end in flaming disaster like Isabella?

I wasn't sure I could survive that. Besides, I'd saved Ruby's life more than once. Sure, she'd now saved mine too, but was she reacting to me like Susan, but in a more subtle way? I couldn't take advantage of her if she felt some kind of debt to me.

With a groan, I rubbed my head and pushed the whirling thoughts aside. I was too tired. I was making up drama where none had to exist. Ruby was my good friend. Why couldn't that be enough? For now, it would be.

Thankfully, we reached the town and I studied it to get my thoughts clear. Midmount Vale was situated just inside the southern edge of the forest. Surrounded by dense vegetation and towering trees, it was an open oasis in the center of dark shadow. Not quite as big as Stepstone, it was still plenty large enough for all the survivors.

No natural stone pillars helped guard it, but a steep cliff several hundred feet tall at the north end of the clearing formed a backdrop. A pretty waterfall tumbled down the cliff in a series of sparkling steps. That cliff formed one of the few hills stretching above the trees. A pool of fresh water at the base of the waterfall helped finish the idyllic view.

Streets and blocks had already been laid out, with the town hall and most of the merchants clustered near the pond. Buildings were being raised everywhere while teams of workers constructed stone and wooden barricades around the perimeter.

One team was rapidly building a wall out of very uniform stone blocks. They looked a lot like giant Legos and snapped together, then seemed to fuse. Later, I needed to find out who got a Lego builder power. That was awesome.

For a town that had only been settled the day before, it was well on its way to looking a lot more permanent than the old ghost towns I'd visited in Nevada.

I figured we'd head for one of our Base Camp tents, but instead we got swept along with a huge crowd that piled into Sam's tavern, which was not only set up, but at least 50% larger than before. To celebrate our survival to the second stage, Sam had covered the ceiling with the illusion of fireworks over the ocean, and the ale flowed like a river.

Sam waved as we placed our orders. "Hey, Lucas! I heard you made a grand late entrance. Glad you made it. Find any more of that hard liquor?"

"Not yet, but I'll keep an eye out."

He pointed at Steve next. "Ten minutes, then I need you behind the bar."

Steve snapped a sloppy salute and we actually managed to find a table to all squeeze around. I ended up smushed between Steve and Tomas, across from Ruby and Jane. The tavern buzzed with excited chatter and many people stopped by to congratulate me on surviving the end of stage 1.

Our party sipped dark ale and swapped our tales. While I basked in the ambiance and the rare feeling of safety, my emotions calming and my mind starting to accept the reality of my survival, I listened. Ruby and Steve had spent most of the day helping guide people up the slope and into town. Tomas and his team had helped urge the last survivors to get out of Stepstone.

"Did everyone get out?" I shouted over the din.

Tomas scowled. "Everyone who wanted to. You won't believe this, but a couple groups charged into town just as we were leaving with the last company. They claimed ownership of the town and threatened to attack us if we didn't vacate."

"You're kidding," Ruby exclaimed.

"I wish I were. Idiots were all low leveled. They'd been holed up in one of the canyons and figured they'd rule the first stage after we all left."

"I've met groups like that." I braced myself and checked the survivor count. I rarely did, but I had to know.

Remaining Survivors: 510.

I shook my head. That was bad, but I had feared it might be worse. Over 100 people had died, 10% of our entire starting population. There was simply no reason for it.

No one who tried even a little should have failed to reach level 10 and climb up the slope to stage 2. That meant all those people had chosen to remain behind and hope Cyrus had been lying. Or maybe they'd just wanted the insanity to end.

I drained my tankard and focused on Jane, who was telling her gripping tale of escaping the southern mountains on Switchblade. Only her insane daring and unrivaled riding skills had given her the edge to survive. She'd gained 4 entire levels and reached level 25.

"I got my class today!" she finished, raising her tankard high to cheers. "Phoenix class."

"Makes sense. You are an X-men."

"Wait till you hear about my Phoenix Force aura. It's sick," she laughed, then added. "Get to level 25 as fast as you can. Unlocking classes gives you a huge boost and unlocks class spells. Got my Willpower stat unlocked finally too. Trust me, classes are game changers."

"I'm nearly there," Tomas said.

"Me too," Steve and Ruby added together.

I shrugged. "I'll get there soon." I needed to ask Cyrus about that whole stat unlocking process to get my useless CHA stat finally active.

"You'd better," Ruby said, then Steve elbowed her and added in a whisper so loud, it was nearly a shout. "What will you do to punish him if he's late?"

"Oh, shut up," she said, rolling her eyes. It was good to see her acting like herself again. Maybe I had been imagining everything earlier. Good.

We spent a couple hours there, just relaxing and enjoying each other's company and the festive mood of the tavern. A lot of people had died, but most of us had survived to fight another day. That was something we could all celebrate.

My body finished healing, but my clothing and gear was shredded. I was still covered in blood and gore, so excused myself to use one of my Laundry Day potions. When I returned, Steve and Tomas were chatting, heads close together, so I had to squeeze in close beside Ruby, who was laughing about something Jane was saying to Lana. Ruby leaned back against me, then just as quickly straightened and pulled away.

I let myself fully relax. She'd get over her embarrassment soon enough. I'd made it. Despite the insanity of that last test, I was there with Tomas and our friends. The horror and fear and worry drained away and my smile widened. For the first time, the death battle world actually felt like home.

A crazy, totally dysfunctional home, but home nonetheless. I felt connected with the community. I'd helped save many people, but now that they'd saved me too, the bond had deepened. I needed to find a way to change tactics so I didn't need to keep hunting alone. I needed more of this.

Tonight, we would celebrate. Tomorrow, if I could adjust my approach, I would. If not, I would do what I had to in order to get stronger. That was the only way to survive, the only way to protect those I cared about.

Cyrus had said reaching level 10 and escaping stage 1 meant I'd passed his tests and proven myself. Now the experiment could progress into power ramp-up time. That part I was very much looking forward to.

Finally I rose and said, "I have to check my achievements and open a few loot boxes." The crazy fight to escape the collapsing stage had happened so fast, I hadn't even gotten to check my loot from defeating Bristleback. If I ended up having a teleport spell scroll that could have avoided the entire fight across the skies, I'd scream.

"We're heading back to my tent soon anyway," Jane said.

Tomas added, "The real party starts when it's just our group."

"Oh, that's the real party, is it?" Steve asked with a wide-eyed innocent look.

"Oh, shut up," Jane laughed, dragging Tomas to his feet and giving him a big kiss.

"I'll see you all there."

My gaze flickered to Ruby, who waved with a wide smile. I returned it, happy to see her back to normal. I turned away, but the memory of that accidental kiss played through my mind again. I should banish it as the accident it was, but it was a much better memory than thinking about all the monsters that had nearly eaten me, or all of the gear I'd lost during that crazy fight. I needed some new clothes, new boots, and repairs or replacement for most everything else. I'd lost most of my weapons too.

Hopefully my weirdly talkative Crash Test Dummy jacket's self-repair function was up to the challenge of fixing its shredded remains. For the rest, I'd check out what the crafters could offer later.

First, I had loot to open.

Chapter Eighty-Two
Epilogue

"Enter," Queen Marisara ordered.

The enormous, bronze doors at the end of her spacious throne room opened noiselessly and Thalorian, head of her security forces, marched inside with his implacable, powerful stride. The winged warrior, which the human captives always seemed to call an angel, had served her faithfully for many years. When he neared her throne, he dropped into a low bow, fist over his heart, before beginning his report.

"We ran into a complication."

"You failed to take a hostage?"

He had never failed her in all the years he'd served her, so she could not believe that might be the case. He couldn't conceal the slight tightening of his mouth and eyes, clear indications that he felt affronted that she would even consider it possible. If he didn't want her to call him out for failure, he shouldn't suggest he'd failed. Usually he communicated better, despite using few words.

"We have two, just not the one we originally targeted."

"Why not?"

She did not care which human they captured from the stage-1 destruction. Everyone left in that area would be assumed dead by the other humans. They would not be missed, and no one would suspect what her people were doing.

"You ordered us to notify you of any outliers. The human we first targeted appears to be one such."

Marisara leaned slightly forward, her interest immediately piqued. Their untenable position was like getting caught between the tide and the cliffs.

Simply slaughtering the humans, as satisfying as that might be, was not possible, at least not yet.

"Explain."

Thalorian slipped into a parade rest stance, standing tall, shoulders straight, hands clasped behind his back, furled wings pulsing slowly with water mana. "The first candidate we selected showed some promise, so we sent a death whale to collect him."

"And?"

"The death whale got teleported a mile away."

"How?"

He shrugged. "Unknown. We sent a giant eel to collect him to find out."

Marisara grimaced. "Never trust an eel."

Thalorian grunted. "It did try to eat him."

She hated hearing about wasted promising captives. "So what other captive did you get?"

It was unlike him to spin tales without a purpose, but she found herself wishing he had shared more details.

"I'll get to that in a minute. The first subject escaped the eel and mortally wounded it."

"How?" She repeated, with a lot more interest.

Giant eels were devious and bloodthirsty, but very effective. She couldn't imagine how a human too weak to escape to the second stage could best one.

"Unknown. That subject fought through to the second stage after all. The little we saw of his journey was quite remarkable. No human, even those who advanced in the vanguard to stage 2, should have survived that swarm."

Marisara sat back in her throne, fingering the haft of her silver trident. An intriguing story indeed.

"We eventually captured a pair of other humans as their group was overwhelmed. That capture went uneventfully."

"Good."

"Interrogation of the captives is just beginning, but they seem more than willing to talk. We already learned the name of the first human who escaped."

"They knew him?" That was a lucky twist of the currents.

He nodded. "The man's name is Lucas."

Marisara rolled the name around her mouth a few times. An interesting name. Potentially a powerful one, and maybe even the name of the human who would open the door for her success.

"Send out scouts to locate the man Lucas. I want to know everything about him."

Chapter Eighty-Three
Bloopers

Like with any creative work, not everything in the first draft ends up in the final revision. Some ideas don't work out, and others were discarded before they were even written. These bloopers are a series of fun what-might-have-been moments.

Enjoy.

***

One thousand humans hurtling toward the surface of Arasha made a truly inspirational sight. Cyrus watched in excited anticipation as he manipulated forces beyond the baby humans' understanding, splitting them apart and targeting optimal placement.

His initial scan of the contestants had resulted in wonderful possibilities, and calculations for optimal team placement had taken only a fraction of a second. This was going to be such fun!

With a flick of his will, Cyrus removed their clothing, replacing them with boxers, bikinis, and variations on the starter pack that best fit each human. They were such a fascinating species. It would be a joy to speak with each and every one of them.

The contestants struck the surface like a thousand incoming meteors, but unlike the huge mass of earth and elemental material he'd just integrated into

Arasha's core, the humans splattered like melons tossed from the roof of a skyscraper.

For a long moment, silence settled over the mountains and valleys of stage 1. Nothing moved, not even an insect dared hum as all of creation seemed to suck in a collective gasp.

"Remaining survivors: 0" his assistant said, her voice hesitant.

Cyrus sighed. "Ah. As the humans like to say, that could have gone better."

***

The Persian hoarder suite was a mess, with pillows flung everywhere and stuffing still floating lazily in the hot, still air. I paused to take in the scene and nearly dropped my facade of a brainless servant in the first second.

Ruby and Jane were both hanging suspended from silk streamers attached to the ceiling. Tomas and Steve were strapped into what looked like giant high chairs, wearing huge baby-blue bibs. They all looked exhausted, food smeared across their haggard faces.

Abbie had changed into a baker's apron and tall toque hat over a skin-tight suit that honestly looked to be made out of aluminum foil. She was cackling with delight as she stood behind an open-topped grill, flipping enormous hamburgers with a spatula as big as a shovel.

"Enough," Ruby moaned. Everyone looked like they'd put on several pounds. Had she been force-feeding them while I was out?

"You've heard of death by chocolate?" Abbie exclaimed as she flipped the burger onto a giant-sized bun. "That's a cake walk compared to what happens to those who try to end the feast!"

Okay, that was just gross. She was destroying one of my all-time favorite weekend activities.

My pair of sporks dropped into my hands and I shouted, "Hey! Jane's gluten free!"

***

I reached Tomas and the others in seconds. They looked battered and bloody, even though they'd already taken healing potions. Tomas gave me a hug as soon as I jumped off Switchblade.

Thumping me hard on the back, he laughed. "You got here just short of too late, little brother. Thanks."

His face was bloody and 4 thin white lines across one cheek marked the spot where one of the Maze Fiend's claws had nearly ripped his face off. "The poison was rough. Had to use 3 full healing potions."

"Here. These will help."

I withdrew 4 Laundry Day potions and handed them over. That was nearly half my stash of the amazing potions, but every one of their team looked horrible. They needed them way more than I did.

In moments, the miraculous potions left them all sparkling clean and fresh. "I need to find more of those," Jane said with a happy smile.

"If any of the crafters get a chance to start manufacturing them, they'll make . . ." Tomas started, but then grunted in pain, his face scrunching up as he clutched at his chest.

"What's wrong?" Jane and I both asked together.

"I don't know. It's like . . ." His body spasmed and he screamed, falling to the floor and convulsing.

Jane dropped to her knees beside him, while I crouched on the other side, pulling another healing potion from my inventory. Jane moved faster, pouring one into his mouth, but Tomas batted it aside. His face was covered in a sheen of sweat, and he screamed again.

Then his armor disappeared, leaving his torso bare. He grabbed at his chest as something started hammering at his ribcage from the inside.

"I thought that Fiend looked familiar," he moaned, then collapsed as a tiny nightmare monster right out of Aliens erupted from his chest.

***

One of Bristleback's giant rear legs caught me in the chest. Even with my armor and Energy Ward, the blow catapulted me up onto another flat step and I got to enjoy another bone-rattling crash into the cliff wall.

"Major offset impact. You'll need more than a chiropractor after that one," my jacket said.

"Oh, shut up," I growled as I spat blood. My bracelet was working overtime to keep me in fighting shape, but the battering was taking a toll. Groaning, I staggered back to my feet, but slipped on a loose rock and fell hard to one knee.

In the process, I bit down on my tongue hard enough to draw blood.

Energy roared through me and my back arched, my limbs flailing, totally out of control. As if from a great distance, I heard Eva speak.

Congratulations, Lucas! For casting Death Bite on yourself, you receive a platinum Darwin Award loot box.

I could cast it on myself? Why hadn't I thought of that? The lingering vestiges of werewolf that had been lurking in the shadows of my soul, erupted into my mind, howling with eagerness to embrace the power that only came with a magically-altered body.

In seconds, the magic tore down my body with exquisite agony before rebuilding it anew. All of my senses came flooding back and I flowed back to my four legs, ready for battle.

Except, something was wrong. The world seemed hazy and distant, the angles all wrong, as if I was still lying on the ground, even though I was definitely standing up. Where was the endless power I remembered as a werewolf? Then Eva's voice cut through my confused thoughts.

Congratulations, Lucas! Death Bite successfully transformed you into a mini-were-koala. All stats cut by 80%. You are suffering the condition: Sloth.

Bristleback fell over onto his side nearby, laughing so hard, tears flowed down his boar-like features.

Chapter Eighty-Four
Final Stat Check

F inal stats. This is a summary, the easiest way to check out the amazing growth over the past days.

After this will come an Appendix with the full descriptions of all of Lucas's spells, Abilities, and Titles, perfect if you want all the data.

Name: Lucas Altan
Race: Tier-1 Human
Level: 12

Life Points: 277   (25,583 tier-zero baby human equivalent)
Mana: 48

Base Stats:
Constitution: 16.9
Intelligence: 13
Strength: 21.9
Dexterity: 13.6
Wisdom: 12.7

Secondary Stats:
Endurance: 41
CHA: 40
Agility: 53
Perception: 31

Magical Resistances: 39.8
Luck: 44

Other stats:
Mental Resistance: 30.5
Fear Resistance: 25
Poison Resistance: (immune. Ring)

PERMANENT SPELLS
1   Harvest

UTILITY SPELLS:
1   Mystic Looter
2   Linguasight
3   Navigation
4   Soul Feed

TEMPORARY SPELLS:
1   Energy Ward
Uses remaining: 2
2   Knock Knock
Uses Remaining: 2
3   Immolation   (Harvested Spell 1)
Uses Remaining: 3
4   Tether Slide   (Harvested Spell 2)
Uses Remaining: 2

ABILITIES
1.	Hand-to-hand martial arts fighting	Level 5
2.	Stick and bladed weapons martial arts fighting	Level 5
3.	Sight of the Explorer	Level 2
4.	Wolf Blood	Level 2
5.	Wolf Sight	Level 2
6.	Knife Throwing	Level 1

TITLES:
Inquisitive Mind
Trailblazer
David Copperfield
Lucky Stiff
Musketeer
Spartacus
Doctor Strange
Hercules

Chapter Eighty-Five
Appendix - Full Description of Spells, Abilities, and Titles

This Appendix is purely informational for those who wish to review the full description of all of Lucas's spells, abilities, and titles.

PERMANENT SPELLS

1   Harvest

– Mana Cost: Minor

– Unique. Up to 70% chance to gain a Spell from a defeated enemy.

– Chance increases by 2% per enemy level higher than your own.

– Can have a maximum of up to 2 harvested spells. First in, First out.

UTILITY SPELLS:

1   Mystic Looter

– Personal spatial storage inventory.

– Loot fallen enemies.

   – Upgraded inventory size from David Copperfield title to a 50 x 50 grid.

2   Linguasight.

   – Identify. Upgraded with additional information, energy signatures, reality filter, and more information about classes.

3   Navigation   Level 3

– Personal map that populates as you explore. Both full and mini map views. Upgrades include plotting and waypoints. Upgrade with Ping.

– Ping. Once per day, update map out to a distance of 5 miles per level of the spell with one of the following: Monsters, dungeons, rifts in the fabric of space, or loot boxes.

4   Soul Feed

– Unique. Absorb energy from fallen enemies to refill mana and health and supercharge all physical attributes for short periods.

– Upgrade: Drains energy on contact.

TEMPORARY SPELLS:

1   Energy Ward

– Mana Cost: Variable

– Aura. Rare. Generate an invisible defensive aura that extends 1 yard in every direction to redirect force from moderate attacks.

– Uses Remaining: 2

2   Tether Slide

– Mana Cost: Minor

– Rare. Mark an object or item as your tether. Within 10 minutes, cast a magical hook to that tether and slide to it across any terrain up to a distance of up to 200 yards. Tether must be within sight when spell is triggered. Uses Remaining: 2

3   Knock Knock

– Tells a random knock knock joke. Can cast up to 50 yards away. Uses Remaining: 3

4   Immolation

– Mana Consumption: Moderate

– Enjoy immunity to flames and channel Ghost Rider as you set yourself on fire. Unleash a tornado of fiery destruction around yourself in an area with a diameter of 5 yards, plus 2 yards per point in perception. Uses Remaining: 3

ABILITIES

1.   Hand-to-Hand Martial Arts   Common   Level 5

– Improves bare-handed combat. Decrease reaction time by 5% and increase damage by 10% per level.

2.   Stick and Knife Fighting   Common   Level 2

– Plus 15% blunt damage and plus 20% slashing damage per level.

3. Knife Throwing   Common   Level 1

– When throwing short, bladed weapons, plus 10% accuracy and plus 15% damage per level.

4. Sight of the Explorer   Uncommon   Level 2

– Sight enhancement. Ability to zoom vision on distant objects and trigger Identify.

5. Wolf Blood   Uncommon   Level 2

– Accelerate health and mana regeneration by 10% per level by absorbing energy from the environment.

6. Wolf Sight   Uncommon   Level 2

– Unlocks night vision and increases Perception stat points calculated from Wisdom by 10%.

– Life force absorbed from a monster resonates with you, allowing you to more clearly sense similar monsters and see through illusions or invisibility obscuring them from your sight.

TITLES:

Inquisitive Mind

– Plus 10 to Intelligence

– Plus 10% improvement to formulas of all stats affected by intelligence

– 10% faster learning of new skills and abilities.

Trailblazer

– 30% chance of loot boxes upgrading, or discovering bonus hidden loot boxes.

David Copperfield (Upgraded)

– Upgrades body to tier-1.

– Increase of 25% to affect of primary stats on secondary stats!

– Increase size of Inventory in Mystic Looter from 10x10 to 50x50

– A fourth utility skill

– A unique Harvester perk.

Lucky Stiff

– Unlocks a new secondary stat: Luck. Plus 15 to Luck.

Musketeer

– All for One. One for All. Plus 5 to all base stats.

– Loot boxes from bosses and monsters 25 levels or more above your own automatically upgraded 1 grade.

Spartacus

– Plus 25% more experience gained for each kill of a higher-leveled enemy.

– Plus 5 to CHA.

– Plus 5 to Luck.

Doctor Strange

– Increase effect of all primary stats on calculating all secondary stats by 10%.

– Additional increase effect of Intelligence on calculating magical resistance by 25%.

– Additional increase effect of Constitution on calculating magical resistance by 25%.

Hercules

– Plus 5 to Strength. Plus 5 to Constitution.

– New aura: Indomitable.

– Indomitable. Aura. Protect your mind and those of nearby party members with plus 50% mental defense for the duration of the aura. Mana cost: Moderate. Area: 5 feet for every point in Wisdom.

Other Works by Frank Morin

Find all books on www.frankmorin.org
and at: bio.to/authorfrankmorin

Want more Nexus Runners?

Read way ahead on Patreon.
Nexus Runner 2 – Rampage (pre-order on Amazon)

The Catalyst

(Classic Epic Fantasy)
Oath & Shadow, Book One
Flood Tide, Book Two

The Petralist Series
(Epic YA fantasy)

Set in Stone, Book One
A Stone's Throw, Book Two

No Stone Unturned, Book Three
Affinity for War, Book Four
The Queen's Quarry, Book Five
The King's Craft, Book Six
Blood of the Tallan, Book Seven
When Torcs Fly, A Petralist Origins novella: Tomas and Cameron
Game of Garlands, A Petralist Origins novella: Anika
Builder of Intrigue, A Petralist Origins novella: Ailsa
Sweetbreads, A petralist short story collection.

Bacon Master of the Apocalypse Series

(Humorous fantasy)
Bacon Master of the Apocalypse, Book one
Pawn of the Pantryon, Book two.

The Facetakers Series
(Urban Fantasy Time-Travel Thrillers)

Saving Face, Book One
Memory Hunter, Book Two
Rune Warrior, Book Three
Aeon Champion, Book Four (release in September 2020)

Short Stories

"Odin's Eye," included in A Game of Horns: A Red Unicorn Anthology
"The Essence," included in the Dragon Writers: An Anthology
"The Seventh Strike," included in Cursed Collectibles: An Anthology

About the Author

Frank Morin loves great stories, great food, and great humor. He is an outdoor enthusiast, and loves to travel for inspiration.

Frank is the author of fast-paced adventures with quirky humor including:

- Nexus Runner – litRPG fantasy adventure series

- The Petralist – epic YA fantasy series

- The Facetakers – Urban fantasy thriller series

- Bacon Master of the Apocalypse – humorous epic fantasy

- The Catalys – Classic epic fantasy

He and his wife are often found hiking, camping, Scuba diving, or traveling to research new books. Find out more about his novels and his shorter fiction, or join his readers group at: https://bio.to/authorfrankmorin

Or come chat on Facebook

My page: https://www.facebook.com/authorfrankmorin/

And to join the growing and enthusiastic litRPG community of authors and fans, come join us at:

LitRPG Group

LitRPG Books Group

www.ingramcontent.com/pod-product-compliance
Lightning Source LLC
Chambersburg PA
CBHW031433200726
48289CB00001BA/19